MW00891945

The Lies of the Eternals

Book Two of the Realm Weaver Trilogy

B.B. Aspen

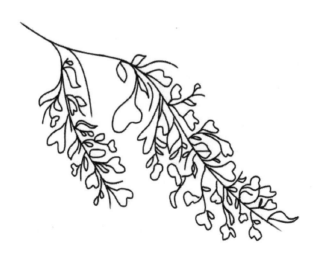

The Lies of the Eternals

The Realm Weaver Trilogy

ISBN: 9798335441421

Independently Published

For permission request, contact BBAspenBooks@gmail.com

B.B. Aspen's Instagram @B.B.Aspen_Author

Edited by: Danielle Pierce & Kacie Baumgartner

Cover Art by: My Shire Sister

Map Design: B.B. Aspen

Chapter Images: B.B. Aspen

B.B. Aspen

To the women who know their worth, may you step into your power, embody it and wield it.

Unapologetically.

Trigger Warnings:

Gruesome descriptions of unaliving, gore and injuries. Knife play. Blood play. Mentions of past sexual assault. PTSD. Alcohol abuse. Restraints. Mention of bodily experimentation and child abuse. Explicit sex scenes. Open door and why choose romance.

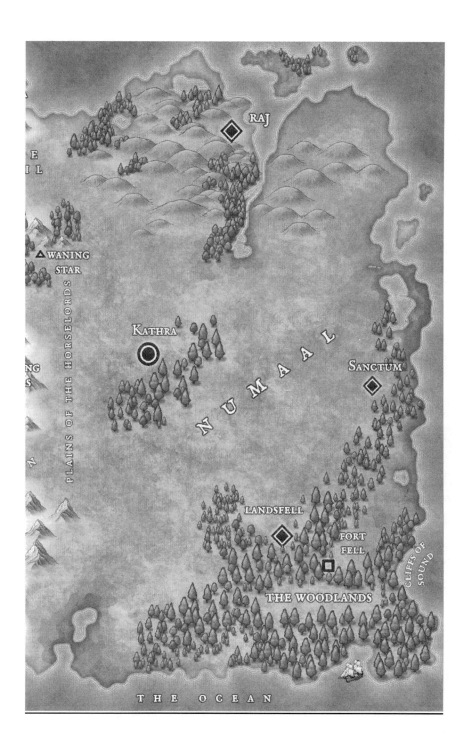

<u>Chapter One</u>

His wings had been pierced by claws. Now, they were impaled by ice and a menacing squall blowing off the stormy southern shores, winds shredded them as they seemed to blow directly through his obstinate form, not around him. A magic in and of itself being as he was a bulky breed with a nearly twenty foot wingspan that he took great pride in.

He clasped his woven tight to his chest, her hold around his neck slacked with each passing day, yet he fought through the pain to make sure she felt none of his faltering hope, frustration or any flight turbulence. Although, he must admit, he did love watching anger light up her face after he dove recklessly through the sky. Anger that shone through her forest green eyes making them gleam like freshly fallen stardust on emeralds.

She didn't find it amusing, nor would she ever admit that she was scared. She mislabeled most of her emotions. He didn't blame her. Not when he understood the turmoil of her heart all too well. It was always easier for Wisteria to feel rage instead of fear, instead of hope, instead of love.

And he would not try to change that.

She had told him once that rage was a far more productive emotion. That statement was undebatable after seeing how the last few months had transpired. Wisteria was a storm herself, healing deep wounds by becoming a force of reckoning and balancing scales as she saw fit. Terrifying little creature she was.

It made her unpredictable and dangerous. Down right, entertaining too.

He grinned remembering the first time she took flight with him, her tentative arms around his neck, and how he plunged to earth from a mile high, it was intentional that time. Her bright eyes grew wide right before they narrowed and she launched a punch at him. And another for good measure. She had good form, he had thought to himself many times over the months in Fort Fell, he was lucky she didn't entirely come to loathe him because she was capable of considerable damage. He saw how nimble and accurate her Montuse skills were during the winter gala when he was compelled into an immovable state of existence. A mindless slave.

He didn't want to reminisce about the hold some foreign dominance had placed on his existence, he wanted to pour all of his attention and all of his tomorrows into the woman in his arms. His lips brushed her hairline. Her fatigue smelt mildewy. Her exhaustion made it difficult for her to spypher for long periods; although, he made it a point to keep his door open and catch whatever scents of herself she'd share with him.

She often chose to be feisty. A savory-sweet combination that let him know she was demonstrating affection even when her words bit with a hard edge of circumstantial frustration. Adorable and lethal—what a delectable combination. Fennick had his work cut out for him.

The grin that formed on his face was wiped clean off when the hardly mended right cartilage tore from his back ribs. His flank burned despite the icy downpour. His left wing beat harder to compensate. He grit through a silent scream to hold her steady.

His wings fucking hurt. His entire back ached *from working them twice as hard and only making half a day's intended progress. The sting of the cold almost deprived him of their use. But he would not descend a moment sooner than he had to, not until they were far enough away from the infested hellhole Wisteria once called home. He often failed at foraging for her squirrel food, reinforcing how useless he felt that he didn't return with a mushroom or damn acorn to feed his forever partner. What he would not fail at was getting her to safety because that not only risked his life and her life, but Fennick's too.*

If one left earth, grief would take the others. They all had their reasons for living: revenge, redemption and relatives.

Wisteria had given the half-incubus, half-man more than he had ever dreamt and all she had done was allow him to stay by her side. She was vibrant and unpredictable, yet he trusted her—as did his brother—something they both swore never to do outside of one another.

His fangs dug into his lip, piercing the flesh on his chin. He didn't flinch. That quick, sharp sensation was nothing compared to how his corlimor was feeling. She couldn't hide the fading color from their bond or deny that her snarky comments have dwindled over the nights.

Wisteria had been overly gracious with feedings to a worrisome point. In fact, if he didn't know any better, he'd say she relished seeing him perpetually on his knees and unraveling at the sight of her. And it wasn't the Weaver's involvement that kept him worshiping her. He would have chosen her regardless of fate. In fact, he did vow himself to her first. That truth alone may prove pertinent to Wisteria who wasn't committed, not wholeheartedly, to the notions of living side by side with Fennick and him despite promising to the Weaver to do just that when their aura was ablaze in Landsfell.

She was worth his one hundred and eighty three years of waiting as were the scabs that would eventually form on his knees from kneeling before her everyday of her life.

Not because she was as confident in her own body as she was curious about his when she strutted naked to him that night in the cave. Not because she had the most perfect damn curves he had ever had the honor of seeing bare and dripping with water. Not because she violently cursed his name when she came. Fuck. No, that wasn't it either. But, he did love the way his name tasted coming off her lips as she came around his cock. His pants tightened at the mere memory of her ruthlessly riding him, using his shaft, his tongue and his hand for her pleasure. He would gladly be used by her. He started salivating so much his fangs ached.

She martyred herself without understanding the magnitude of the Weaver's thread to save their woven, just as she did a ship of seadrifters, just as she did an Ilanthian family, just as she did an entire city of over a half million ignorant, yet innocent humans. But none of those reasons were why he held her in such high regard.

It was because she remained entirely oblivious to her magnificence and effect on this wretched world. And she was unafraid. So stubbornly fearless in the face of things that make most immortals and Gods tremble. Including himself. No one had ever stood tall in his presence nor disregard the power seeping from his pores to stare directly into his soul and scold him. Zander still couldn't do that and it had been decades since he lost control and labeled himself a murderous monster. His brothers and nation would be gobsmacked at her unintentional audacity. If she greeted Atticus with her usual oblivious confidence, Zander would be forced to make love to her on the spot. Not to simply mark his claim, but because he may not be able to physically contain himself.

He wasn't sure yet whether he would have to protect Wisteria from his family, or his family from Wisteria. Her fearlessness could easily be misread as disrespect or stupidity, or may cause them to lust after her. He shuddered and recalled her words which he still felt undeserving to hear after what he had done, "I am not afraid of you and I trust you not to hurt me." He wept that night after a deep slumber came for her. Oyokos' magic almost ripped through his gut and demolished the country of Numaal at her declaration. She wielded more power than she knew, and he would gladly let her wield him.

Two years, seven months and four days.

That was a substantial quantity of time to prepare for one's undoing.

Despite his preparations, despite his best imagination, despite the unshakable knowing that has carved itself onto his soul every day since the Weaver bound them, Wisteria Woodlander had completely undone the demigod, reducing him to a man all too willing to give her not just his heart and body. But, his whole damned soul, every drop of blood in his veins along with his entire realm.

All she had to do was ask it of him and it would be hers.

All of it. No questions.

But she wouldn't.

Hell, she would even think to ask anyone for such a thing as a warm meal because she couldn't fathom her own remarkability or see herself more deserving than her peers. It wasn't humility. No. Because Wisteria had zero rutting clue how purely brilliant she was. Which made her all the more deserving of everything good and magnificent in this world. A world that was at war with itself and with the unknown.

As he dove under an incoming cold front, he tried to banish the intrusive thoughts of the angry souls of seething in masses in the beyond—the consequences of the wraith attacks.

These creatures were different from the restless nightwalkers here in Numaal, yet held the same essence of evil. Just like the black bone he carried along for the journey west. Their dark, haunting eyes and formless faces pressed desperately against the barrier the rune stones created, as if they were attempting to break the beyond itself and crawl back into the land of the living. Should those rune stones falter... He swallowed the rising worry. Choked it down half successfully with bile.

Atticus won't let them. His brothers wouldn't either. Damn. The entire city of Veona would drag Maruc's slumbering ass out of the White Tower and coerce that neglectful bastard of a God, to rewrite the runes if it came to it. The human's heart beat faster and he looked down with a heavy brow of concern.

Wisteria dreamt restlessly in his arms. He brought her under his chin inhaling the scents of lingering peaches, flowery blossom essence and lush grass after it rained. He hadn't heard her scream for Anna as much as he heard her fight off invisible demons that she hadn't yet spoken of to him. He would never force that conversation. He had seen her back. Seen what she had endured in the name of love. If that was the price she believed all love cost, why would she ever want to love again?

As much as he loved her, he would never force her to reciprocate. Still, he held on tightly to the hope that one day she could and that she would choose her wovens. He buried his nose deeper in her scalp, savoring the moments the Weaver did grant them even if she was nearing unconsciousness and he was biting back another monsoon of pain inflicted by the hail storm.

He grit down, pulled his wings taut and flew west under the angry, brooding sky.

Chapter Two

I was delirious with hunger.

Deprived of nourishment, the pains gnawed at the lining of my hollow stomach, begging for something so simple as warm corn water or a baked potato. A chocolate cake with strawberry frosting would send me happily to my grave at that point. Despite how appetizing and delicious I found Zander to be or how many times we have tasted each other since we left the cave by the docks, my frame thinned. He was not food for I was not a succubus partner to my incubus woven.

I needed a *real* meal. Sustenance.

The previous abandoned cabin we found had clothes and hygiene essentials, but no preserved food. By the time we got ourselves dressed for the freezing rain, the wraiths had come clawing for Zander's mending wings. He ripped their heads off as easily as popping the dried flower buds off a brittle rose. Fluxing was not an option and wouldn't be until the leathery webbing and muscles protruding from his back were healed entirely. He ran and we were driven into the sky.

Just a little longer, my flower. Zander Veil Halfmoon di Lucent, my fated friend, syphered hopeful words. I believed him and as far as I understood, I'd no reason not to.

I felt his assurance in more ways than one. His voice was honey warm, just as I remembered it to be when I encountered him in Duke Stegin's dungeons two years ago. I nodded to acknowledge them, hoping his warm words would thaw my bones a bit more. Just as I could no longer tighten my thighs around his hips as we flew over the long southern stretch of

Numaal, I could not muster the strength to speak a reply down our bond. It felt as if a heavy wave of sleep weighed it down with no reprieve in sight.

Steel-like, unshakable arms held me against an inexplicably large body and broad chest. I looked like a small child in his arms, safely tucked to the giant's side. My chin nestled against his neck, inhaling his familiar scents of spice and sweat. Having flown in his arms for the last week, I found more smells entangled in his black and white mane. Scents of exhilaration and crisp winter mornings. He smelt of the sky. Like the cool winds that carried us and the clouds of water which clung on our skin. A liberating scent.

My gut lurched, feeling the loss of our altitude. Had I strength, I would have punched him for his air stunt that sent my head reeling. Yellow humor danced down our connection shortly followed by kisses pervading my hairline as an apology. The gusts of his massive leathery bat wings leveled out the commotion during our descent to the ground.

Fatigue took a toll on him too. That charming dimpled smile didn't cover his fading outline and his extraverted humor was a tell sign that the recent stumble in the air was an accident. His strength was faltering. I was an additional deadweight for him to lug around. A burden. I pressed myself closer to his chest and spared a glance at the dizzying horizon. A sight new to my tired eyes.

Gone was the rolling landscape of the Deadlands, the ashes and corpses of the treeline were long behind us, outstretched now were the sprawling western plains. And in the far distance were slate dark mountains jutting up and disappearing under the mist of the clouds. The Thalren Mountains, the seam and the Great Divide.

The shrouded sun caught the tips of rippling cropped wheatfields, they danced under the incoming afternoon's Gods awful weather. The lengthy western province of Numaal ran from the north shore to the southern tip, along the Thalren range. The lands of the horselords and shieldmaidens.

Zander's mother was from a village much closer to the northern mountains, Waning Star. Somewhere in the center of the western province was Kathra. The capital of my nation which held my Ilanthian family captive. It was there where I had one year to return to and summon the Nameless Prince of Resig Torval's family line or he would see Moriah and Rory executed. Likely, experimented on before being put out of their misery. A marriage to that monster was the only conceivable option to return them safely to Keenan and the Lands of the Gods.

My heart shuddered in my chest, my gut soured. This world was cruel.

There is an abandoned farmstead with no intruders or threats, living or undead, foreseeable for miles. It is ours now. There was no refusing such a tone.

As of late, when he spoke regarding my wellbeing, it was undebatable and held the power of a command, almost as if he was speaking it into existence. With my back requiring such painstaking attention and my body needing a plant based woodlander's diet, it was taxing to find energy to banter with the brute. His arms enfolded me as we rode downstream on the cold wind currents.

There was a scant coating of frost on the grain fields, I heard it crunch under the weight of Zander's boots. I shifted in his arms while he transferred me to perch on his hip, his hand liberally grabbing my ass and pinning me to his stone hard side. I didn't mind anymore. His company and intimate touches felt nice after the hardships of solitude. If I had as much vigor as I did days ago I would have grinded into his sturdy side and demanded a release. I was basically as limp as a worn tweed onion sack, thinned and lackluster. *A stroke of luck, there is a storage cylinder half full with rice and bins for rainwater collection on the side of the house.* We'd have fresh water and grains.

In the excitement, I bit down onto my wind chapped lips, licking up the taste of copper. Food. Water. Glorious salvation.

He braced me and slammed his shoulder into the walnut wooden door. Off snapped the rusted locks that held it from swinging in the winter storms and in we went. Icicles on the roof crashed down, sounding like a brief song of windchimes before shattering on the ground. Zander ducked under the doorframe and narrowed his wings behind him, he swore several of my favorite four letter words as he tried to get us inside the farmstead without bonking me into the furniture or driving his elegant horns into the ceiling.

My eyes opened, snowflakes clung on my dark lashes, and I watched the curves atop his head gouge two crevasses onto the soft high beams. "I can stand," I insisted, wiggling out of his grip. He shook his head stubbornly and walked us over to a bench beside a dining table, the bond glimmered with his defiance. I swallowed. My voice was groggy. It seemed foreign to me because I hadn't used it in what may have been days. When we did need to communicate we spoke using our mind link, just as our emotions were conveyed through something just as inexplicable, but similar.

The Weaver's doing.

He balanced me in the chair before pulling out glasses from the cabinets and filling up several with water. I drank two while he left my side to rummage for cookware. He had a fire crackling and a pot of rice settled on the stove while I managed to wipe the frozen rain from my cheeks. "While it simmers, I'll prepare linens for our bed."

Within the minute he was carrying a full mattress pad through the kitchen, across the cabin and into the bedroom. He went back a second time with his arms full of pillows and linen. "Just fixing the sleeping arrangements. You aren't getting rid of me easily," he huffed casually behind his black and white tangle of hair.

He was seven foot something and over three hundred pounds, maybe more and that was *without* his wings, there was no easy way to rid any being of that magnitude, let alone the grandson of Oyokos, the God of Death, who was more obstinate than a young bull.

Zander had purged his winter layers when we landed and freed his wings and hard muscles from the restrictive fabrics, which left me admiring the tightly strung cords of strength feathering and flexing under his golden bronze skin and webbing of white scars. My gaze fell to the wings failing to click into their place along his spine with their injuries and the confines of the cabin. The icy weather *and* the slashes scabbing over made the ends appear faded and ruggedly tattered. I'm sure my back looked just as ragged. Probably worse. Some days there was bright blood on the bandages if I walked too far or we fucked too rough. My inner goddess stirred at the mere memories of having Zander inside me *while* flying through the clouds, yet another first for him. He caught my wicked glance moseying down to tantalizing hip bones and the veins bulging at his waist, lingering on that exclusive horselord belt buckle.

I cleared my throat before he got cheeky. "Can your wings even fit in there with two mattresses?"

He scrutinized the space before he narrowed his mismatched pale blue and milky white eyes at me from the far side of the kitchen, enjoying the sight of me as much as I did him. Although his lustful gaze was unwarranted. As were almost all the overly kind comments he had been making to me since Fort Fell. I was too thin, unkempt, and drab. "I thought woodlander's prided themselves on their creativity."

This fool. I drank another water and I offered, "Knock out the wall between rooms, if there is no weight bearing beam between them it shouldn't be an issue or compromise stability."

He stirred the rice pot and with a hint of mischief in his straight white grin, then left to do just that–demolish the walls of the room we would be sleeping in. He broke the boards single-handedly and tossed them into a pile to become firewood. After he fluffed and puffed the beds, he was back to fussing over me.

A large cloud of steam hit my face. "This is the biggest serving of white rice I have ever seen," I gasped, eyeing the overflowing bowl pushed up to my chin.

"It is the first of many big servings of rice you will eat today," he insisted, bringing the spoon up to meet my lips. I rolled my eyes, but complied with his overbearing behaviors. The rice was plain and too watery, but tasted good. Appetizing, nonetheless. I chewed it thoroughly before I swallowed and opened my mouth for another bite of the sustenance we've been deprived as of late.

Another pair of lips met mine instead of the wooden spoon. Canines nipped my tongue. A deep rumbling voice poured into my open mouth and made me restless in my seat. "I believe you rolled your eyes at me, Wisteria Woodlander." A hand made its way to my knee and slowly slid over the fabric of my pants until it rested on my upper thigh. I fidgeted with delight.

"I did," I confirmed, adjusting myself in the seat so that he could smell my arousal with the slight opening of my hips.

He inhaled sharply through his nose. Followed by an unstifled growl that had been waiting to escape I imagine for quite some time. "You know that I cannot permit that go unpunished, my flower." He pressed a kiss on my cheek and filled the spoon up with rice and brought it to my mouth again.

"I didn't expect you to."

Smokey tendrils wafted around the room and vanished before they accumulated into a pile on the floor, some lingered and rolled towards my ankles. "Eat so you can withstand the consequences of your infuriatingly admirable insubordinate behavior." I ate the bite he offered and found another spoonful in my face right after.

And another. And another.

I glared at him after one particularly dry, heaping mound of rice stuck itself in my airway. I coughed until I was a shade of red. He was hiding behind his hand and hair, chuckling. I leaned over and punched his shoulder for daring to laugh at me in such a state. The punch was appallingly lame. Luckily, my mentor wasn't here to scold my poor choices in launching fists at a man five times my size. When I managed to breathe again, I took the wooden utensil from his hand and began to feed myself reasonable sized portions. He chuckled, but didn't leave my side. "Feisty earth squirrel," he muttered, somehow making that ridiculous remark sound seductive.

Zander brought himself closer and began to brush through the knots the wild winds secured atop my head. It was a simple gesture. An intimate one. I sunk into him as he released my hair and brushed through strand after strand. From the roots to the tips, my hair was longer than the dimples on my back–which he avoided. He moved my hair aside and two layers of sweaters with the intention to kiss the curve of my clavicle from behind. His great wings blocked out the sun as they draped on either side of me.

I conceded and let my head go slack to allow his canines full access to a very vulnerable artery. His chest rumbled as pink cherry hues brushed across the forefront of my mind, coming from his undying devotion on the other end of our thread.

Undying devotion—I didn't or couldn't—reciprocate *that*. He knew I was emotionally stunted, but never minded or said as much. Amid my troublesome thoughts, warm lips and a flick of a tongue met my flesh, disintegrating any chance I had to connect brain neurons. "I am going to rinse off as much as I can in the washroom made for a halfling child and get your bath water a survivable temperature. You'll eat another bowl of this magnificent, flavorful white rice and drink a liter of water. You won't protest when I clean your wounds in the bath and wash the only pair of trousers you have that fit your fine figure."

"Me? Protest?" I tossed my head back against his waist and laughed with a sarcastic grin. The stark contrast in our heights and sizes was more apparent the longer I gazed up at him. The next grumble that came from his chest shook the remaining walls of the house. They grated with frailty. I smiled wider. "You don't scare me. Not now. Not ever, Zander. Keep your grumpy grumbles for someone more malleable and timid."

"You. Are. Fucking. Stubborn," he gritted. I tugged his hair and wrapped it around my fist, drawing him closer.

When his mouth hovered directly over mine, I gave a smirk and spoke resolutely. "Yes, to all of what you said with the addition of you eating a portion of rice prior to binging on peaches. You were born a red blooded man. You will eat food, so you do not grow faint in flight. That little dippy-doo on the way down from the sky was not intentional." I held up a stern finger, he closed his mouth. Smart man. "Don't bother hiding anything from me. You will also allow me to rinse the tips of your wings with rosemary water and massage the strain out from your back before sleep. The inability to collapse your wings fully is causing tension to spasm when you are unconscious. You keep me awake at night with your drooling *and* wings flapping around senselessly."

Zander's white flecked skin was smooth under the caress of my thumb. I held his face firmly, waiting for a reply. "Bloody fucking hell, you are sexy," he collapsed onto my mouth, swirling his tongue in hungry circles then pulled himself off just as fast before either of us started something we could not stop. He tore off the door to the privy and washroom, adding it to the wood burning pile, his wings protruding in the hallway as he soaked a towel in the sink with soap and suds. On his knees, he scrubbed at the perspiration and grime building on his skin, rinsed and repeated.

Muted flashes of greys showed themselves in my mind's eye. His frustration grew. How could it not? He was half frozen, fully naked, and completely unable to wash himself with any decency in the washroom that only his shoulders and arms fit into.

The second bowl of rice I scarfed down. Zander surrendered the towel without prompt as he heard my approach.

I trailed my fingertips along the ridges of his wings as I walked around him and squeezed into the bathroom. I ran the pipes until they steamed the mirror and turned to face my woven kneeling bare and injured on the dusty floor of an abandoned cabin. It wasn't a pitiful sight. No. It was awe-inspiring. We both accomplished what we set out to do and lived to tell the tale.

"I do love when you eye fuck me." His jaw snapped open and shut greedily.

"I wasn't eye fucking you, you conceited lunatic. I was thinking how revolting you look with literal bird shit in your hair," I smacked him with the wet towel, not hard enough to hurt, but with enough *oomph* to get the point across.

He grabbed the opposite end of the towel and yanked. I toppled into him, catching myself on his chest riddled with the scars he shared with his woven. "I thought we were past the lies, my love." His hard length twitched at the brief bustling of contact.

Love. He said it so easily. So unabashed. So honestly.

My love. I cringed at the covetous word attached to it and stepped backwards leaving the towel in his hands. He vigorously washed his face, the devilish grin remained when the towel lifted. I soaked the dirt off it and ran it under the small stream of water until it ran clear. "Chin up," I instructed. He obeyed.

I wrung the towel over his elongated neck, intentionally depriving my eyes from trailing the water droplets over his nipples and thick waist. I turned around to get the lather before the water flowed *there.* He washed under his arms while I tended to the hard to reach spots under his scruffy jawline and ears. "The best way to wash my hair and back is just to douse me with a bucket," he suggested.

"That sounds undomesticated even for a barefooted wildling like me." I left out the part where I thought he was utterly magnificent and deserving of so much better than to be bathed like a barn animal with a trough poured over him.

His voice was subdued yet kind, thick with sentimental compliments, "I like that the forests raised you. You are considerate. The world would be better off if more were raised in woodlands," he said. I wrapped a warm, wet towel around his hairline and massaged, adding shampoo and water until the lather frothed. He turned to putty in my hands. Encouraged by the little sighs of pleasure escaping Zander's lips, I kneaded harder. Little by little, I washed the soap out. And the literal bird shit. He sent gratitude down our bond. I tied his mane up, allowing me to work on his back while he tended to his front. "Stay and watch," he challenged, seeing my gaze dart around the tiny washroom.

"Rice before peaches," I whispered in his ear as I maneuvered around his stature with two towels in tow. Knowing his wings would get special attention once he was horizontal in bed, I cleaned Zander's spine and took to sorting out his long strands of hair between his horns, which I delicately washed. I ended by setting the unshaven portions of his hair in his signature braids, tying the three off into a single pony. "Your rice will be on the table when you are finished."

He agreed. "Strip. I'll wash your trousers and bandages while the tub fills," he called over his shoulder. I stood where he was able to observe me undress. I pried the sweaters over my head, and then with equal sensuality and humor spun myself dizzy removing the cotton bandages from my torso.

I stepped closer, sliding my pants off my hips, down my thighs and onto the floor. I took off the strappy underwear he hated all while his eyes glazed over an icy blue. My nipple piercings skated along the fleshy fabric of his wings as I leaned over and tossed my clothes into the sink. I shimmied my breasts on the arch of the wings and watched his cock twitch at the minimal contact. His eyelids fell heavy and he rumbled with satisfaction.

"Are they *that* sensitive?" I inquired, daring to press my front body along the length of his spine. His throat tightened as I rubbed my lips across his earlobe.

His wings jutted to the side. "Yes. Consider them an extension of me. At the present, there is another extension that is requiring much more attention and I'm afraid if you don't get your perfect breasts off my neck I will throw you on the floor and fuck your tits with said extension."

I kissed the nape of his neck and walked naked to the kitchen. The bath water was running when I left his side to fill up another bowl with a massive serving of sticky grains. My hunger flared. I sat on the kitchen counter eating steamed rice directly from the cook pot, the heavy lid askew. And I didn't stop until my stomach rounded and the shakes from an inconsistently low blood sugar finally subsided. Then, I fit two more bites in my mouth. I was insatiable and cared not of how feral I looked eating my first solid food in over a week, stark naked, lounging on a stranger's counter.

"My flower, your luxurious bath awaits," Zander addressed with cordial reverence.

Off the counter and under his wings I went. I wrapped elastic around my hair and slowly lowered myself into the lukewarm waters, the frequent stings on my back thwarted any chance I had at looking seductive because they sent me shaking with violent jolts of discomfort. When I was fully submerged up to my chin I closed my eyes and felt for my woven in the silence.

Anger and fury greeted me in heavy rusty browns and crimsons, when I opened my eyes the washroom had gone almost entirely black, the darkest hue of violet the mind could fathom, with his magic spilling over his physical vessel. His breathing was rocky as his emotions latched onto his lungs.

I already knew the problem. Me.

Well, my flesh. Ruined by Priestess Collette and branded by the prince of Numaal himself. "How are you imagining their gruesome deaths tonight?"

"Fire lancets up their asses. You'll be the one to light them. Fen will volunteer if you are uninterested," he stated dryly. He was livid, rightfully so. The Resig's had managed to trap his body with mysterious bones. "I want their fingernails and toenails removed one by one. Then their teeth. Rib by rib they will be dissected over long months. Eyes and ears will be next. We will mail their body parts to the queen, maybe the king if he isn't dead yet. I haven't heard otherwise or had an opportunity to eavesdrop."

When he was controlled by the Remnant's bone remains, he described it as a mental prison. A hypnosis so deep, that not even his body could convince him to act otherwise. When he wasn't fighting himself for control or screaming for me behind the rattling door, he watched and listened. *"The prince never once mentioned his father's state, his county, the Remnants, the wraiths... nothing was gained, besides knowing they can control me. Me! If they knew what destruction I can wield, they would have ended a war before it started by mass extinction."*

The room stayed dark as vibrant galaxies whirled and licked the edges of the tub. Zander remained kneeling naked with his teeth clamped down, seething with white knuckles clamped on the wall. I floated in the tub, slowly calming. For I found the serene darkness and his violent desires which mirrored mine comforting. I offered him the only comforting word I could. "Soon."

The tension and curtain of magic were slow to lift, but eventually they did and light found its way back into the cabin and Zander's hands found their way to mine. Chin to knees, I curled into myself and presented him my exposed backbone. He stayed hushed and carefully inspected the damage. I was proud that I didn't let a flinch or wince show when he debrided an area over my left side. But I cursed the stars when he dug debris and dead skin out of what felt like my bone marrow. The water I sat in splashed involuntarily when I moved away from him.

When he brought over soap for my use, I exhaled and scrubbed the pain off my face before he caught sight. "We will leave your back open to air while we reside here, a day for sure but likely two. We need to replenish our stamina." I nodded in agreement. I noted his use of the word *we*.

He was exhausted, I eyed his impenetrable body looking for a weakness when his lips found their way to the tender spot on the inside of my wrist. He licked up a water droplet and kissed me there. My pulse quickened. "Stay and soak."

This tub was the first water we came across in a week that wasn't salty, frozen or impaling us from the sky. I savored the bath until all the warmth from the waters had been drawn out and my skin pebbled in protest. I stepped out and scurried into the fleece blanket held open waiting for me.

Zander enfolded me in the fabric. "I won't break," I said from behind the blanket wrapped around my chin and shoulders. I took a hesitant step back when he reached to dry my spine. He slowed his hands and moved his face next to mine. Blues drenched our bond. Safety.

Eventually, I stepped back into his reach.

He patted me dry as if I were a delicate petal on a daffodil after the first frost of spring. His control over each touch was precise and calculated. It always had been. Except for when he was decapitating wraiths. "I won't be taking risks having just escaped our last endeavors by the skin of our teeth." That imperious tone made another appearance. I snarled. "Not yet, anyways. I am sure you'll be revived and meddling in no time at all." He kissed my nose and pointed to our chaotic sleeping arrangements. Food and water were already on the nightstand and a steaming warm pail of rosemary water rested at the foot of the beds.

My lips turned up. I was glad to see Zander readily complying with my own demands. He hunched his spine and the arches of his wings as he walked across the cabin, a more accurate term would be crawled. I followed him, eyeing where the most strained muscles were on his neck, hips and back. His right wing caused him the most discomfort. A wraith had swiped too close to the bony protrusion and he struggled keeping it from dragging, just as he struggled to keep a look of peasantry on his face.

He haphazardly plopped on the bed, dragging himself up to the pillows like an injured kitten and unceremoniously flattened himself out, laying on his stomach. His wing span casually extended on either side took up the length of two rooms. He turned his chin away from my gaze, but not before I saw his tightening jawline.

Months ago in Fort Fell I stared at his back wondering just how big wings would have to be to allow this being to defy gravity. Now, I had the answer. Gigantic.

I tossed a sheet over his bum and went to work soaking the scabs and tattered tails of leathers with the herbal steam. *Stop me any time.* I approached the right flank, his obvious weak side. Blues and pinks flitted across our thread. My queue to carry on with his confidence. If I had proper supplies, I would have sown up two of the gashes in his webbing and covered them in wax for when he took flight. I was a lost girl traveling through the west plains, a far cry from the prodigy child of the Southlands with no medicine in my satchel or home to return to. No red or silver blooded family to welcome me, no Anna to frolic and fight with on the hillside during hot summer nights.

I was so deep in love, I would have drowned in her essence and never have come up for air. I had no idea what I was doing with Zander. Or was it simply fucking because I'd never been with a man and I was inquisitive? Or was it the Weaver dragging us too close and merging our flesh? Little puppets in her grand scheme. Or did I just not know how to handle a woven who makes ceaseless attempts to flatter me and fall weak as prey? Maybe his incubus charm? My loneliness?

Whatever it was, it was *nice*. For now.

Arriving in Veona may demand we label this *thing* we are engaging with. I dreaded that. I even asked him *not* to tell his family and friends when we arrived. He agreed, but also reinforced Nikki's words about thread being seen as a blessing and damn near impossible to hide. At least keeping it a secret a little may grant me some time and acceptance of it while we worked out the kinks. All of it felt over-complicated. Anna was never this way. We just were.

Were. Past tense. The first time Anna and I kissed, she was rubbing my strained muscles. Just like I was doing to Zander now. My movements slowed and the pressure I applied slackened.

What is wrong?

My hands lifted off his appendages. I looked at the man beneath me, heavy lidded with concern and I offered him a softened smile. Torn pieces of my soul did care about him on some levels. Lusted after him on several. It was all too messy to organize with my bleary mind and tiring body, what remained of my fragmented heart.

Just reminiscing. I steadied my next exhale. I knew he could hear my heart beat, my breath and—when I wanted him to—my thoughts. For some odd reason I felt as if he could hear my soul. *I also stupidly remembered that I haven't taken my monthly tea.* Black hair whipped across the bed as Zander's head popped up and fully rotated. He grinned a wicked grin, a far cry from his previous languid state.

Hell, fucking, no. I was going to be sick.

This twisted bastard wasted no time in barraging me. *I want daughters. But if they will be anything like you, they will be the death of me, I'll opt for a blend of little lads and lasses.* I blinked at him and grabbed at our connection. He pulled back, leaving me guessing the sincerity in his blunt statements.

This enraging *prick!*

"This is not a joke! I am *not* having kids. Definitely, not amid a damn war when this world is going to shit!" My heart lodged in my throat, beating a thousand times a minute. "And with *you*?" My knees buckled on the bed. Was I nauseated because I was panicked or because a fetus was hijacking my womb and using it as a home?

"What is wrong with me? I will make an awesome father," he protested immediately. When I did not answer he opened the door to our bond allowing soft pinks to hit my hard emotions. I don't know what colors he saw, if he saw any abstract *things or hues* that resembled my emotions. He calmly spoke, "You are not with child–not mine anyways. Incubi are unique, there has to be a whole ceremony to summon fertility and to actually impregnate another is an entirely different dance. One, that by the sound of how adamant you are against bearing children, I assume we won't be talking about. Not yet, anyways."

He reengaged with me. Our bond came back to life, easing the tightness in my chest.

In the wake of worry, acid coated my stomach and my chest held an irregular flutter. "You shouldn't tease nor try to get a rise out of the person tending to your injuries," I warned, soothing the towel over one of the many angry cuts.

A muffled reply, "Sorry, my flower."

I finished the rosemary soak, tossed the rag into the bucket and moved it out of the hallway so neither of us would trip. I climbed back up onto the low divot of Zander's back, my knees on either side of his hips and began to massage the tension out of his spine and scapula. His groan sounded more of a whimper as he went limp with his arms falling beside his torso. "Feels alright, I take it?" I offered with satisfaction, while my thumbs pressed into his muscles flanking his tailbone and I maneuvered them, slowly upward toward his neck. He nodded into the pillow beneath him.

I had never worked with wings, so I took the time memorizing the location of the pulling ligaments, where they connected between his spine and scapula and how much of a burden the shoulders and lower back carried with their added weight.

"Are they heavy?" I carefully traced my hands around his right side where flesh met wing.

"Extremely," he said with a haughty ego. "I'm robust enough to handle them. Even in their condition."

That I doubted. "I thought we were past the lying, princess?" I mocked, rolling my knuckles around a substantial knot in his shoulder. He was gritting back a blend of pain and pleasure; it escaped in a guttural groan.

When he lifted his head to glare at me, I pushed him back into the pillow. "I know you're hurting."

"I know you're hungry," Zander replied.

I pointed to my stomach. "Once I digest what is in there, I will be finishing that pot of rice and asking you to prepare more," my retort pleased him. "You're probably hungry too."

The knot I just worked hard to release found itself roped back under his skin. "Where peaches are concerned, I will crave them always and forever. Remember, I had been starved of you for two years." Knowing what I knew now, that had to have been uncomfortable. "Not until I consumed you, did I know what feeling absolutely satiated was. You fill every aspect of me to the brim with happiness." He popped up onto his elbows, tilting me backwards so I was seated on the strong and strappy curve of his buttocks. "I want to eat you up when you stare at me so purely. But, not this afternoon or tonight. You are bound to be sore from the fucking in flight session the day before last. Hell, I am sore from it, sprained a groin muscle somewhere above the stratosphere."

"There was only a little blood that time," I reminded.

"Wisteria, I will not be responsible for breaking you into six pieces. Besides, I have a tantalizing, *lengthy* list of ways to serve, prepare and eat peaches that we ought to get started on tomorrow." I squirmed excitedly. That list better be as long as his—. "Not now, we need healing sleep," Zander reinforced.

I needed more than one night of sleep; I needed a whole decade to recover from the past half turn of the moon. I agreed easily. "Let me work on you a bit more. You've done a real number on yourself and if I don't loosen up these tendons, I won't be getting any sleep. And I am selfish." I didn't wait for him to reply before I dove back into massaging his trapezius and deltoids. Blissful curse words were suffocated by his pillow. My hands worked until they stiffened. His wings twitched and fluttered each time he intermittently dozed off, it was like sleeping under a tent unstaked in the ground that blew in the wind.

When I was fairly certain he appealed to sleep, I unmounted his back, swinging my leg off his body as if I were unsaddling Nordic or Rosie. Perpetually mindful of the agonizing wounds on my back, I crawled under his left wing and brought a pillow to my chin. I grunted with loathing. I absolutely hated sleeping on my stomach, it misaligned my spine and joints and there were no woodlanders or physicians here to adjust me.

Quite the mangled and scarred duo we were, laying there with our fileted flesh at the mercy of the world and under the mocking gaze of the infallible stars. Zander's eyes peaked over his forearm, taking in each one of my cumbersome movements. Icey blue and milky white, one with dark lashes and the other void of color. I knew what he was doing, the same thing he did every time we had a moment of respite. "Did you reach him?"

"Fennick is alive. He is just too far away for our transplacency to work across the waters." Zander reconfigured himself and reached for my hand. I gave it to him. "You can feel him here." He moved both of our palms over the heart in his chest. It was warm. Consoling.

"He will be okay. They all will be safe, as long as Keenan and Nikki don't get into anymore fist fights," I failed to sound reassuring, even though I left out the statement of Nikki not standing a chance of winning if he did go head to head with the Montuse Bloodsworn warrior.

"I feel him too," I said through a yawn. Neither of us moved our hands away from his heart as we slept.

Chapter Three

Copper infiltrated my senses.

Not Anna's blood. Not this time. My own. Death was coming for me. And soon. It felt unavoidable.

Blood-tinged bile hit the marble floor beneath my knees as I crawled away from Havnoc entering the music room with a white-hot brand in his grip. The polished boots of King Resig Torval's son stepped closer to me. His double headed raven sigil seared my weeping shoulder.

I didn't scream, I would not let my enemies have that satisfaction nor would I let my little brother hear my suffering as my heart was pulled out and my lifeless body hit the floor.

I specifically remember not screaming yet when I awoke my throat was hoarse from doing just that. My hands flew over my face to silence myself and found my cheeks were wet and hair an unglamorous mess. Water rested on the side table, I drank it while watching my woven lay silent unmoving through yet another outburst. I was truly beginning to wonder if he was deaf or that heavy of a sleeper.

Either way, I was relieved I didn't wake him with my visions of crows circling my death.

It was too dark to be wakeful or to shuffle blindly through the unfamiliar farmstead looking for snacks and entertainment, so I slithered under the covers, a wing and a heavy arm; adjusting my frame to find the least painful position, and dozed off.

A hand caressed my thigh below the layer of blankets. Pinching and cupping the round of my ass, a whisper of a promise of what was to come. A faint smile pulled on my lips after feeling my skin react by dimpling and awakening with greed. I could see the sun shining behind my closed eyelids but did not bother to open them.

Now *this* was a far better way to wake up, I told myself. I rolled onto my side and was greeted by a hard length pressing into my ass. Zander's chin and chest curled around me, allowing him to kiss the top of my head before bringing calloused, gentle fingers to tilt my mouth up and graze his.

His lips were an addictive substance on their own, but his tongue was intoxicating. I drank in his poison all too willingly. His taste. His scent. All called to me. Incubi were predators built to attract their meals without lifting a damn finger. Said spare fingers trailed up my thigh and brought my hips deeper into him. He throbbed against the pressure. I wiggled at the electric static between us. "Careful, Wisteria. You're not healed," he said no louder than a butterfly's song. I twisted to face him a bit more, getting trapped in the sheets.

"I'm tired of being careful," I grumbled in the same manner as when I told him in the beginning of winter, 'I was tired of just surviving.' I wanted *more.*

He withdrew his mouth from mine. I protested and sucked his lip until I summoned a dangerous growl from deep within his bare chest. Zander's brow went stern as he lifted up the sheet strangling my limbs. There was bright blood on it, scattered in an array of long lines that matched the lashes on my back. "One day, we won't have to be careful. Until then." He made a grunting noise as he lifted his damaged wing up and behind him to rest on top of the other. Ever so delicately he brought my spine onto his torso. We took a deep inhale and exhaled in unison while opening our syphering bond. Our spirits ebbed and flowed, giving and taking, until we found our cadence in the safe space to explore.

This time when I rolled my hips, he slowly synced up. We rocked against each other in a rhythm that mimicked a deliberate moving tide which fueled my ache. Wonderment got the best of me. "What does arousal smell like?"

Five fingers feathered across my neck and danced around the swells of my breast, brushing lightly against my nipples. I sighed a glorious sigh when they skated down my navel. "Open for me, Wisteria," a deep voice commanded at the curve of my ear.

That alone caused my core to clench. "You hold hints of ambrosia blossoms and untouched sweetwater. The rest of the world is sour, musty wine."

My knees opened slightly, enough for the head of his thick cock to thread between the small gap in my thighs and slide along my slit. I reached down and wrapped my hand around the length that protruded and gingerly pumped his cock, savoring each shutter and raspy inhale behind me as I stroked him.

I looked down at the steel shaft in my hand; my fingertips were not able to fully close around its girth. I swallowed my concerns when Zander's skillful fingers abandoned my navel to slip onto the petals of my pussy because I could think of absolutely nothing else other than how good he was making me feel, how slick his fingers were and how badly I wanted the sharpening ache to be soothed.

"I can smell you," he moaned, our bond flashed purple then went taut and lustful. That phrase, however outlandish, made my breath catch and hasten. I pumped him faster, needing to feel his tight control slip, even a little. I took such pride each time he let me wander close to the encaged sun and each time I felt his hips thrust off rhythm in our dance as if they sought something deeper, more urgently. I yanked him closer on our thread. His colors collided with mine.

I left his exquisite erection to explore my own swollen bundle of nerves. I writhed sensing how close I already was to falling over the edge and into oblivion. The sweet ecstasy of oblivion. Zander watched me touch myself and began to do the same. "Would you like to taste me?" I asked bringing the two fingers that had just been inside me up to his parted lips.

"I would love very little else." I squirmed away from his words. As if he predicted my resistance he brought my fingers into his mouth and wrapped his tongue around them, sucking so forcefully I was drawn right back to him. I glared at his seduction tactics. As much as I sought to back away from his blatant claim to me, he'd bring me right back to a comforting space. Commitmentless, but comforting.

He released me then lowered his salacious gaze down to my open, glossy thighs and his hand quickly working his cock in a rotating stroke. I took the nonverbal queue and spun my clit clockwise rocking against the motion of his jerking off. The grinding of our intimate bits was enough friction to burn down the Deadlands twice over.

"Zander?" I panted, wondering where his fanged mouth was because I was close… it should be hovering nearby. His lips were still far above me. "Zander!" I demanded his attention. Grinning devilishly with that damn dimple, he gazed down at me all flushed and bothered.

"I just wanted to hear you scream my name. I love listening to your heart pattering on the verge of combustion. It is the sweetest song I've ever heard," he humored, looking as if he got playfully inspired.

His inspirational whim had me rolled back over onto my belly and propped up on all fours. He knelt off the bed behind me. His cock's length slid along my entrance, not penetrating, although in that moment I yearned for nothing else. He rocked along my slit and wrapped his hand around my waist to finger the piercing on the hood of my clit. My pussy wept for him, I could not deny the physical reaction he summoned from me nor was dumb enough to lie about it.

He was about to summon a whole lot more. "Squeeze your legs together." His raspy voice saturated the air further with reckless need.

I snitched my thighs as closely together as I could, just so a massive cock could slam between them and send them trembling over and over again. His body encompassed mine, putting his scruffy jawline next to my shoulder. His white elongated canines were coated in saliva that pooled on his tongue. His mouth was open, he was ready for me. Two deep thrusts and a rapid spin later I fed him. "Oh, oh! Fucking hell!" I managed to scream into Zander's face all while his lips devoured everything from my nose to neck. I rode out my orgasm on his cock clenched between the peak of my thighs and couldn't help but imagine it inside me, satiating me.

I would let him ravage me. I would, had he not chosen to be such a gentleman given my physical state.

Zander straightened his back, I tried not to let my knees wobble. Hands gripped each hip, just above my ass cheeks, he repeatedly brought me into his groin sending his slick penis through the tight window of my thighs.

"Wisteria. *My* Wisteria who owns every part of me," he moaned my name and increased the intensity of the pounding. "Fuck, I am shackled to your soul. If anyone tried to free me, I'd kill them and fuck you in their blood." The sounds and smells of sex filled the room and my name filled the air a half dozen more times. Warm thick ribbons of cum shot at the underside of my ribs. Each time he shuddered more strings of pleasure found themselves decorating my skin.

The walls, both deconstructed and standing, erupted in a violet shimmer. Magic, I had to remind my human brain that just stared stupidly at the glitter bursting around us. Zander had magic. And I was mortal. Simple.

I dismissed my human insipidness with a quick quip. "Was that on your list?" I posed to the man straining to keep his composure behind me. I felt him laugh.

"That was a preview," he warned. An adoring, indulgent hand ran through my hair. "Stay put." His hands and hips left my body, I tilted off balance. The faucet ran in the kitchen, followed by rummaging the drawers. Zander appeared at the bedside, a lukewarm towel in hand. He knelt on the bed and guided me upright, giving him access to clean the white pearls off my torso.

The rag swept over the soft underside of my breasts, he was already back to a semi-hard state when he finished making me decent. Unbelievable. He saw me staring and opted to make a fool of himself by strutting around naked. "If that dance is on your list as any sort of foreplay, remove it," I said dryly, while crawling out of the bed and tying the blood scattered sheet around me to fend off morning chills.

Anna and I danced. A lot. Around the fire or under the stars, it was an intricate part of our intimacy. The sensual steps and isolated hip movements always made me feel as if I was dancing out a spell, one that entrapped her beneath me. Not that horrendous fieldstomp.

"You're so mean when you're hungry," he cheerfully added, snapping me out of a memory. I was hungry. "How would you like your rice? White? Overcooked or undercooked?"

"Such an array of options at this fine establishment. I will have it edible, please." While he brought the pot to a steady boil, I opened every stripped bare cabinet, closet and drawer in the house. Looking for salt, sugar or any herbal flavor. Nothing.

Defeated, I plunked down in the kitchen chair watching a crouching incubus navigate the enclosed cabin. Despite his whistling and singing as he worked, he struggled. "Let's stay two more nights if you think it's safe."

"It's safe, but small."

"You won't be ready to fly the day after tomorrow. And I will protest leaving a place with warm running water and food to make for the mountains if the weather is shitty."

He let the rice steam and walked away from the barren kitchen. "We are on the cusp of the Plains of the Horselords. We are approaching the view of the flat lands and jutting mountains in the distance. That image is the one I grew up with, but if the weather is shit... Staying another day sounds lovely and I suppose I could go a tad longer without being impaled by ice arrows from the heavens." Good. We agreed.

"I have a question." The incubus tore several cushions off a nearby couch and compiled them on the floor where he made himself a nest. Zander ran his hands across his two horns, removing the dust they collected from ramming into the ceiling. He sat cross-legged, his wings stretched across the living room, limp on either side. Looking better, but not great. Far from it.

"Of course you do," he beamed, wiping the water he finished off his chin.

"Do you and Nikki have enemies?"

His ruggedly handsome face went pensive. More serious than I have seen it in the last months of becoming acquainted with his features. "Not many, fortunately. There are people and specific coalitions, like the renegade fae, not fond of me in Veona, I can count them on one hand. Fen catches some backlash for being associated with me, but we've already identified who they are, their agenda, their associates and have them tracked. They've not approached us or my family for decades."

My lips smacked. "Does Nikki have any grudges in Ilanthia? He spent time in Havana with his cousins, maybe he met Keenan then since he greeted him with a fist to his face."

His tongue pressed against the inside of his cheek, his eyes voyaged off towards the ceiling, lost in recollection. "In those days, where Fennick went, I went. After we accepted our bond, we rarely parted. We've never stumbled across a Montuse man of that name and there aren't many of them left in this world, I'd remember such a monumental moment. Does he have a surname? A lot of first generations took multiple names, I wouldn't be surprised."

I shrugged, eyeing the rice pot that sputtered off steam. I rushed to it. It was burnt on the bottom. "There goes my one request for an edible meal," I mocked, pouring cold water into the iron dish and scooping out servings for both Zander and I. I walked the plate to him and sat on the floor in front of his knees to share our meal together. He eyed my bare legs on the hard ground, looking none too pleased.

"I never heard any of them use surnames, they adopted Woodlander right away. I was too young to ask and when I grew older a lot of my questions were dismissed as unnecessary. Nikki called him *Icky ick Keegan...*" I felt his humorous stare. "Okay, I have no idea what he called him. It sounded like an entirely different language. But Keenan responded to it and then got his nose broken. I put Nikki in a headlock to pry him off."

"Icky ick..." He laughed. "Can't say I have heard of that outside of a kid refusing to eat their vegetables or a proper lady stepping out into the slums. Doesn't sound like a surname, but it sure does sound Montuse. They use a lot of syllables, vowels and odd sounds—like chirping birds. They were the civilization that assisted the Eternals in creating the common language we all use today."

"Nikki speaks another language?" I shoveled the sticky rice into my mouth, waiting for an answer. He *did* have an accent, not one from Septar of the Southern Isles, the seafaring land where Count Hilderbrand had been from. It was more refined.

"Enough to impress a native and maintain their dialect. His dad encouraged a variety of studies when he was a pup, I would sit around swinging swords and teasing him while he sat through lectures." He snorted and gave a shake of his head, his pony tail whipped behind him. "Probably should have paid attention to half the tutors or at least have been sober, that would have made things easier a few years down the line."

When my spoon scraped the bottom of the bowl Zander took it and placed his plate on my lap. He hadn't touched his meal yet. "Thank you," I said, pushing aside a few burnt grains. "What would have been made easier for you, had you not been an aggravating ass during his lessons? You know, behaving like your typical annoying self," I quipped.

"I might have found better ways to shut down the slave trade industry or perhaps saw through my conniving ex-girlfriend's ploy sooner. It definitely would have helped navigate the Veil after Malick gave me his blood and Oyokos' power." His eyes drifted above us as he continued. "There were *events* that came about once Fen and I were done with our 'civic punishment' for having been ultimately responsible for the Overlord's death." He was tiptoeing. His colors were blanketed as he detached himself from the troublesome guilt he felt obligated to carry everywhere.

"*Events*. Wow. Very descriptive," I mocked openly, trying to lighten his load. "Events such as...?"

He flicked my nose and pointed to the plate.

I ate. He talked.

"As close to a bureaucratic or political caucus the Veil has ever held. A nomination of an Overlord. Quite the scene since there had only been two in the entire eight thousand years the Veil had existed," he sighed. None thrilled with the topic at hand. "All very boring." He turned to me, I swear I saw the urge to roll his eyes restrained in his face. "Had you read that damn book I tried to give you, you'd have all the answers. And then some."

My lips and nose pinched up into a wrinkled scrunch. "So sensitive these days. We better get you back to your husband for coddling."

Zander glared then lowered his nose tip to tip with mine. "Eat."

"You eat," I countered, making sure my shoulders were squared off and my eyes just as narrow as his.

He twisted the spoon. "As you wish." His glance lifted just slightly, but enough for me to know his intentions.

I saw him incoming, his lips aimed for mine. The side of my open hand chopped into his airway just as he launched his surprise kiss towards me. A strangled yelp echoed, followed by, "Am I already becoming predictable in my courting of you?"

I retained pressure on his carotid until he backed down, the blatant danger of a predator flickered in his eyes as he forced himself to retreat and not react with overpowering. "Afraid so. You are no match for me."

"How lamentable. You are the only match for me," he retorted. My lips thinned. His hands were tossed up in surrender before mine closed in a fist. "Still too forward?" I fed him a spoonful of rice, myself after.

Always. "Yes, but you won't stop. I'm not entirely sure I want you to." Zander's bare shoulder rose towards his right ear in a quiet confirmation, his wing followed suit. "How do you sense me..." ... *in here? The emotions beyond syphering, do you see them? Is it colors? Density? Images? Magic?*

His mostly dark, scruffy jaw realigned, his tongue flicked across his fangs as he reflected on the question. *Nothing of the sort, I'd rather show you.*

I was not one to deny my curiosities. *Can I do that? Sense what you sense?*

I don't see why not. I let you wander past my outer layers into my inner workings prior to now. I can lead you elsewhere if you are willing. I hadn't known if he had stepped into my world, or 'past my layers' as he said it. Not that I had anything worthwhile to hide. *I've never trespassed beyond what you've radiated outward, Wisteria. Nor will I, but I will happily explore alongside you.* He opened his hand, wiggling his fingers.

I set the spoon down on the near empty plate and lace my fingers with his. My eyes closed, hoping it would metaphorically allow me to sense less of my physical surroundings and more of this enigmatic thread bestowed upon me. Rather begrudgingly, I might add. That isn't to say I wasn't grateful for the aid and insight in carrying out my promises to Anna and Keenan. I shook the thoughts loose from my head and gave a sputtered exhale through loose lips.

It's worth a try. Fingers tighten around mine. Blue. Reassurance.

Down our bond we swam, when we collided, me a silvery green and him a blend of violets and soft blues, we tumbled over the threshold of the thread, a sensation that felt like falling into suspension. We crossed into a space where we could choose a destination with a mere intention. There was no door to enter, but the facades went down.

I felt the tug.

Zander's energetic armor was removed and I floated into his domain catching familiar sights of rust colored fatigue, orange bursts of confidence and excitement, murky drips of guilt and rosy pinks of his affection. More walls disintegrated. His physical pain collected in an imperceivable corner and the busy workings of his mind strummed above us, restlessly aggravating the water currents around us with their fretful disposition. I gladly swam through this portion and gave a longing gaze at Oyoko's power burning behind bars as Zander formulated a stream that pulled me along at an upwards angle towards his heart. The sun in the cage beckoned me desperately.

I wondered if everyone he met flocked to his power? If they were all so easily enamored or enticed by its presence more than his outrageous incubus charm I'd yet to see used.

The hand holding mine gave a subtle squeeze and I turned my back on the cage to drift to a new region. One that had spiraling pillars bending into an archway. We waited here. No syphering came through, but the pillars rippled. He melted the boundaries. And when he succeeded, it pulled us through what felt like quicksand. My breath caught.

"You good, my flower? I have not scared you off?" A low voice reverberated on my skin. Yet, when I heard him speaking it didn't sound as if my body was sitting across from him, it was around me. Cocooned. We limboed between his head and heart. And slowly we stilled.

I gave him my reply. But not with words and not with thoughts. And in his inner sanctum in which we rested, I watched my own resolute answer transfer to him—and citrus hit the air around us. My surprise tumbled in after, it wobbled uneasily, but carried a new scent—one I hadn't a name for. It hit my nose and palate. Astringent, perhaps? "Your stubbornness tastes like limestone. Your anger is bitter. Your grief is salty. Your hope is sweet. Your lies are boggy. Your fear is sharp and metallic. They all spin around my heart in different intensities depending on how deep you feel them or how open our doors are." I spun in place, my excitement visited. A bright scent, not fruits or florals, but fresh. Linens on the clothesline.

This makes sense. I thought to him, referring to his perceptive palate, taste and smell. It is how you navigate your world as an incubus, how you understand and learn about those around you.

"And how do you sense me? In a different variety of plants?" I let a squeaky snort escape. That disturbed our thread enough to drag me out of his being and snap my attention back into the chilly cabin floor on which we sat covered in blood-stained sheets. The floor was suddenly too hard and the air too dry.

Our hands remained linked until we both opened our eyes. I arched a humorous brow. "Not flowers. I see colors and feel densities. But if you were a plant, you'd be the thorn in my side."

"One you'd never rid."

"I hope you are smelling rocks right now."

His crooked smile told me he had been. My eyes shifted to the empty plates; my sheet fell from my hips as I raised to refill them. His glossy eyes held a carnal coveting as they followed me to the kitchen. "What color is my lust?" he purred inquisitively.

"The same color as your magic, but lacking the depth of violet hues that swallow the room when you ignite it. Depending on how it dances for and entices me I can tell how much control and restraint you are willing to relinquish or trying to grasp at to maintain." I hadn't the desire to tell him that in that moment, he wasn't sending dancing purples down our line, but a pink cherry. He was doing more adoring and admiring than lusting. He never asked me to describe what he was specifically feeling now. For all I knew, with the amount of rose whisps visiting me we fit the roles of the Weaver's amity bond.

"Would you be comfortable showing me?"

I casually nodded my head. One day, now or in the future, the Weaver will ensure we explore it. No better time than the present. "We can give it a go. I don't exactly know how to do what you just did, I assume I just lead with my intentions and swim onward." I approached him with two semi-burnt steaming plates of rice. I must have been starving because the cruddy heap of grains looked delectable.

"Swim. I like that description. This connection has tides and undulates, but is heavier than air. The movements there are not akin to flying. It's multidimensional swimming." He seemed pleased with himself and didn't fight when I handed him a meal. "You can show me your layers after a midmorning nap." I approved of both.

Not only was I hungry enough to eat charred rice, but tired enough that after sleeping sixteen hours straight I wanted to fall back asleep after hardly being awake. Pitiful.

The Lies of the Eternals

Chapter Four

It was oddly cozy under his wings, which seconded as another blanket. A much needed layer on insulation since the stove was off and the weather was utterly horrid. It was mostly the winds that seemed to be waging a war over the plains. Bickering on about which was more mighty, those from the mountains or those from the ocean. I let them battle above us as I snuggled in closer to an arm, still hating the fact I could not yet pivot onto my sides or rollover to sleep. Somehow I managed to do just that. "It cannot already be sundown," I griped, refusing to believe it.

I sought evidence. Out of the leathery cave I shimmied and stood on the bed to peer out the window. The sun went down quickly this close to Thalren whose jutting form blocked the western sunsets. "Well, then." In a sigh, I surrendered to how fast my day had disappeared unbeknownst to me.

Zander drooled. It was probably rare to wake up without a puddle of spit seeing as his canines were constantly protruding and preventing his mouth from closing. His heavy limbs unmoving as I tiptoed around the parameters of the rooms, stepping over the splinters of wood from the busted up wall. When Zander did arise, I was to be found soaking in warm waters. An ill attempt that was. Every irontail whip my back received felt raw and freshly laid. I did more grimacing than relaxing.

"Evening, princess," I called out.

A gruff voice announced from around the corner. "Evening, flower." The thud of his knees on the floor and the flutter of fabric enlightened me to his enclosing proximity. Unable to fit more than his arms and chest into the washroom, he lingered at the threshold. I heard him ready the rags to tend to my back. I half expected to receive a bossy plea to rise out of the waters, but I didn't. "When we get to Veona I want to fuck you in my bathhouse."

Him wanting to have sex with me was not the cause for alarm, yet I believed remaining celibate for years was a dumb thing to do. Especially for a man with his genetics and appetite. "A whole house for bathing?" I exclaimed.

"I can't continue to go about knocking down walls to fit through them or jumping into ponds to wash my hair." I spun around to face him; his eyes hitched on my ass and legs floating atop the water. Now, I could catch glimpses of violet seductively crawling on our thread.

My arms draped over the edge of the porcelain tub, water pooled beneath them. "I suppose you can't, that behavior is very unbecoming. Although, if I was a remotely decent swimmer I would like to think I'd very much enjoy jumping into ponds. "

"Since you make a habit of jumping into oceans, I shall teach you to tread water and if you successfully don't drown during lessons, you can ride my cock after." His erection was going rigid as he spoke. I marveled. "My eyes are up here," his fast tongue tasted the air like a serpent.

I twirled around in the tub, burying my eye roll beneath a helpless sigh, placing my back at his mercy. His deep seeded salaciousness was replaced by anger. "Gods damn priestess. I want her lifeless and held at the crossroads before sending her to Hell."

I let him seeth as he slowly went to work, inspecting the deep crevices nearest the bone first. Had I gained a few more pounds before the cold season, my recovery rate may not have been such an issue for I would have had stores to pull from. Now, my body felt as if it was eating the lean muscle I did have in order to repair a thin layer of flesh. Being carried in the sky and sleeping so little—prior to today—provided no opportunity to mend. These scars would be ugly, but also tender for the foreseeable end of winter.

The water was pink tinged and my gashes were probably as ugly as they were brutally aching. If Nikki hadn't taken the burning sensation away on the ride down to the southern docks, existence would have been utterly unbearable. Even now, it still sucked. "Do Ilanthian physicians practice in the Veil?" I asked, sensing his brooding linger.

"Yes. We also have healers which aren't as rigidly schooled as physicians but have other skills important to dreamers. And where magical ailments and hexes are concerned, we have alchemists." Fingertips graced the nape of my neck by my hairline. "You will be seen the moment we step foot into my front foyer by healers. I'll have them waiting there for your arrival."

He had his own home? Of course he did. He was established, well-traveled and stabilized his finances over two centuries. "You're surprised I own a home?"

"Initially, yes. But, I rationalize everything out within my head. Obviously, you own a home if you own a bathhouse."

"What's mine is yours. Unless you desire your own home or loathe my decorations or find the stature of things not functional for your height—then I shall get you your own home. Next to mine. But yours. Or we can build one together. Fen will need to be nearby for cuddles, coddling and to appease his desire to protect us. I remain flexible." An invisible rope wrapped itself around my throat and tightened. My knees bent and I pressed my forehead to them. I had a home, a garden, and a family once. Feeling smaller the more I curled into myself. His lack of breathing was prominent. My despondency was unavoidable.

"Oftentimes, ashes fertilize the soil for new seeds to be planted. Wisteria, you will find a way to reclaim and remake the Woodlands. Until then and for as long as you wish, your home can be with your wovens. You will always belong wherever you choose to roam as long as we are at your side."

I don't know when I started crying, but I was.

"Well, it looks like I might end up tearing down these walls to get to you." His tone was both tense and apologetic.

I found my voice when his fingers left my neck, presumably to break something. "Don't! You'll damage the plumbing!"

Movements halted. "I've never seen you passionately pragmatic before. You've gone off and drunkenly mailed forged letters, stolen horses and intentionally got your ribs kicked in. But you hesitate when it comes to... plumbing?"

From my blurry peripheral perspective I saw him swipe a clean towel off the stand. Feeling angsty, I hugged my knees tighter. "I prefer clean water for my food and bath. Don't go busting things open with your clumsy hands."

"Huh," he muttered, pretending to be witless. "You didn't say anything about their clumsiness when they were between your legs." This frustrating fool. "I'm going to survey outside. Check for safety risks, listen for the heart beats of rodents and have a chat with the weather conditions. Offer up some burnt rice to Drommal and Dradion to bless us with favorable skies. You can take your time to reevaluate the aptitude of my fingers once you are out of the bathtub." I splashed water in his direction when I exited and refused to let him dry me off. I went as far as to push by him, aggressively making my way back to bed with cold, sticky rice. He managed to wedge himself into pants and toss blankets at the foot of our bed. "I look forward to swimming with your colors, if you are still able and willing." He left.

I tore new strips of cotton for my wrappings by splicing a perfectly decent sheet. I tossed my old browning strips into the corner, intending on burning them before we left this little cabin of refuge so the wraiths wouldn't follow *migouri*. Zander arrived after I had finished rolling them up. In his hands were quite an array of shrubs and weeds, he locked the door behind him and gifted me this bouquet. "Is any of this edible?" The sweetness of his gesture turned my heart into butter. Melted butter.

He sat on the floor next to the table, robust smells of winter wafted off his flesh. He didn't look bothered. I smiled down at him, "Anything is edible if you are brave enough."

"Touche."

I sorted through the variety of weeds, not having the heart to tell him most of this was destined to make me sick and that I wasn't brave or well enough to handle a stomach bug. He watched me intently, I pulled out the greenest dandelion leaves and young swiss chard. "These will do nicely." His wind-chapped cheeks pinched upwards, creasing the skin by his eyes. "You didn't have to gather for me."

"I did." I suspected he had something to prove to himself. "You were warned of my irrational nature. Except I see nothing odd about wanting to provide and ensure you are more than bones when we get to Veona. I need you in fighting form to kick my brothers' horns off their damn heads."

I shook my head. "Regardless, I appreciate the gesture." I did appreciate the gesture. It was something I'd expect Cobar to do because of the innocent, well-intended nature of the action. "Did you sense danger?"

"A storm will be here within the hour. Looks like we are confined to the bed again." He let slip a devilish wink which I countered with a shimmy of my shoulders. His eyes moved from my breasts to the dandelion greens. "Steamed?"

"Gently. Just enough to soften the fibers, not enough to break down the nutrients," I educated. Lily would have been proud. My mother was a crafter but also an amazing cook, her food was healing and life giving, just as her presence had been.

The bitterness of tough winter greens bit at the tip of my tongue and crept to the roof of my mouth. A delightful diversion from the rice which was to come every day after for the next weeks until Waning Star.

After our teeth were brushed and hair managed, we lay in bed, propped up on our elbows with pillows under our stomachs. The spot above Zander's bridge of his nose puckered in discontent, borderline pain. Not from his battered wings, but from his lack of woven. "Did you find him?" He adjusted his chin. He hadn't. "When you are done searching for Nikki, I can show you the colors I see."

"Are you trying to cheer me up?"

Yes. Yes, I was. "No. I'm keeping my word. I said earlier today I would try."

"You're concerned about me," he whispered. I would not reply to him or let him know he was getting under my skin, claiming his place in my heart, in a very delightful way. "One more minute," he said, moving his attention to the scar splitting his sternum. I moved my focus there too. I had zero inclination to how Nikki and my thread manifested or if we'd have any manifestations of it at all. I'd no insight on how to contact him.

With a surrendering sigh, I reached over and touched Zander's chest, hoping that was enough to offer comfort to them both. That seemed to go over well. Tension left his hairline. I watched Zander's white eye waiting for a flash of liquid gold. Nothing. He wouldn't stop trying to reach him. But for now, his gaze settled on me. *I'm ready.* His hand folded over mine.

Mental doors opened, we met on our thread and jumped off the bridge of our bond, swimming through the abyss until we arrived at the space between the divide of *us.* The space where we merged, yet retained a sense of self. I lassoed myself around his weightless form and with a notion of a tug we floated towards my quintessence.

As we crossed into the first region, there was an instant reflex to shake out the foreign body. Zander's being there felt like a literal thorn in my side, his eyes roamed the walls and workings when he realized his presence was sending rippling tides throughout my watery exterior. He changed forms and liquified to match my formlessness. *What do you sense here?* I curiously asked, wondering if his scent perception was different from my interpretation of this place, just as I saw Oyokos' power as bright and he—a darkness. I saw my own rusting fatigue, pain and hollow gaps of loneliness. The half lies and part truths that made up my world, sharpened the more I questioned them. They were as uncomfortable to look at as they were to engage with.

I taste turmoil. There is confusion and contentment. I cannot find a scent of equanimity. Not much anyways.

Let's get you out of my misery then.

I didn't say that I minded being here. It's much the opposite, I'm learning a lot. For example your high pain tolerance... your feelings towards me, your hesitancy with relationships... homesickness... I brushed aside him and his blues, pushing him along a current with me, one that moved upwards, defying gravity. We floated around a barricade, waiting for it to drop or permit entrance to my next layer, my emotional landscape. I searched for a key or secret door that allowed guests. The barricade formed from a buoyant silvery mirror to a hard, standing structure.

It was resolute. I was apparently resolute. My subconscious wasn't ready for visitors. "We can try later," I spoke, ushering him out of my mind's eye, banishing the rising annoyance I had regarding myself and my inherent failures.

"All in time. Consider it something I look forward to once we get the rest of you set right, with proper shelter, food and aspirations," he said in a lower tone, already preparing his subconscious for bedtime. We both retreated into ourselves for the night.

"You're not disappointed I couldn't find a way in?"

"Correction, you didn't let me in. You are the ruler of your own domain. If you wanted me in, I would be there."

I gritted defensively, "But I have nothing to hide, why didn't it work?"

He ran his thumb over the inside of my palm. "I have thoughts."

"Such as?"

"You are reserving that space for Anna. An emotional shine of sorts resides within and you can't risk exposing it to vulnerability. Make sense given the shit you've endured." His hand squeezed. "I don't mind. Having you here and with the knowledge I'm equipped with is plenty for me." I melted into the lumpy mattress and sought sleep out before my mind had a chance to wander down the path of grief or confusion. The mere mention of her name from his lips did a number on me for reasons I cannot explain.

By the morning after our third night of rest I felt more alive, more human than I had since I strung the Stegin up from the chandelier in his own home during his own winter gala. Amazing what water and carbohydrates will do for a girl. Probably, just about as much as an oral sex snack did for an incubus the morning we set off from the abandoned farmstead.

I was bundled up in my wrappings of cotton, two sweaters and a woolen petticoat and yet I earned a fretful glance from Zander as I approached with my upward reaching arms. The height difference was markedly pronounced when we stood side by side, I'm sure to any onlookers I looked child size. Not that there were any. He lowered his neck to drop within my reach, simultaneously scooping me up behind my knees. Contact with my wounded back was unavoidable in flight, a safety measure I wouldn't protest. "Are you going to keep your eyes open during takeoff this time?"

I glance behind us. No wraiths dashing towards us. The sky was dim, but pleasant compared to the last month of weather. "I see no reason not to. We don't seem to be running for our lives today, which gives you better odds of not sending me falling to my death."

Zander shook his head, I adjusted his ponytail so it fell down his backpack, atop all the rice and water supplies we took. In return for the owner's unoffered kindness Zander dropped a bag of gold coins on the kitchen counter. In case they ever did return to find their home broken and stores raided.

A great suction noise whirled around us as two massive wings unfurled. My stomach dropped to my feet crammed into ill-fitting boots. I'd feel more at ease if his sight stayed on the sky instead of my reaction. The wings lifted us upward, they beat rhythmically and powerfully until the homestead was the size of a pinpoint that was easily hidden behind the shape of my thumb. My eyes traced the sprawling plains and rolling hills that tapered off into flat lands at the base of the rugged mountain range, all while my stomach made its way back to its proper location.

I exhaled the breath I was holding and eased into the wide, scarcely covered chest pinned to my side. His skin was cold to the touch, not that he ever raise a brow of concern. The black and white wings jutted out straight catching a wind stream, allowing us to glide north with minimal effort. I released my grip around his nape and sent my hands dancing against the forceful counter currents. I stiffened them and made them dynamic enough to slice the air. I was even alert enough to admire how the leathery, bony prominences on his back shifted slightly when my weight did, he didn't notice his adjustments. It was all effortless and done instinctually.

I looked at him. Truly looked at him. He was unlike any person I'd ever met, accomplishing feats I once thought impossible or outlandish—like flying.

What are you thinking? He sent me, his eyes combing over the strands of my hair blowing about.

Do you ever take flying for granted?

Never. I would cease to be myself if I ever became grounded. I'd feel caged and too much at the mercy of the world. Once you've tasted this kind of freedom, having it stripped away is as painful as losing a limb or basic right.

I am sorry you sacrificed your flight freedom for two years. And your celibacy.

His gaze didn't falter. "I would do it again." He would.

"I am beginning to enjoy it up here," I said, placing a kiss on his too-near cheek.

"You just love me wrapped around you so you can better admire how phenomenal my wingspan is."

And at that, I let out a grunt and rotated my attention back to the cloudy, frost covered morning. The cold air stung my lungs as I shifted my position.

Yellow strutted across our connection. "We fly north for as long as we can without stumbling across caravans, hamlets or occupied plots of lands. Then we cut directly west to the mountains. Thalren will provide more coverage." His words were partly stolen by the wind as he spoke them above the curve of my ear. After I nodded as a means to acknowledge him, a kiss was placed on my temple.

His legs were parallel to the ground below, lengthened behind him as would be the tail feathers of a bird. When gravel crossroads appeared ahead, we took higher into the atmosphere. Clouds clung to my skin in a cold dew that permeated the fabric of my layers. By evening, gypsy carts and horse carriages altered our course to the west. He hurriedly took to a slope that held a splash of green umbrage before the sun set entirely. I unfurled the sheepskin and sat cross leg under a canopy of pliable infant white aspen trees, eating cold, mushy rice. Zander scouted around in circles and stood beside me on the short berm. "No soul around for leagues. There are rabbits and field mice, but nothing to deter us from lighting a fire."

I set my rice down and contently compiled semi-dried bark and dead pine needles into a mound at our feet to catch a spark. Zander carried the heavy logs over, snapping tree trunks casually until they were the size of average firewood logs. I blocked the winds with my hands as he fumbled with the flint lighter. Twice he busted the clamps. "This is mortifying to witness. As I said, you have clumsy hands," I took the lighter from his roughen grip. Moments later, I was breathing life into the thick smoke until it burned. I positioned the rest of the smaller sticks on top in a peaked manner. Feeding the flames slowly. Across the firepit I saw Zander stroke his chin in a deliberate pensive gesture. "Let me guess, Nikki usually lights your fires for you?"

"There is no need for fires when we travel together. We can both see in the dark and he is a furnace to sleep next to and can boil water with a touch," he offered. He pointed a steady finger to the yellow and red glow between us. I felt utterly mundane and fragile. "And when that burns out whilst we sleep, I'll be keeping you warm with my skillful, *graceful*, hands between your legs." I resorted to finishing my water skin and meal. His sharp eye tracking my every muscle. "Go ahead, Wisteria, roll your eyes at me. I dare you."

A challenge. One I ignored, despite my brash internal dialogue. I laid down on my side, he did the same only off the sheepskin. Mud matted his shirt while he astutely eyed me pushing aside my empty bowl. "How are your wings?" I asked in the space between us. He laid his arm down and moved my head to rest on top before bringing a large angled wing around my body. Warmth from the fire and our mingling breath were trapped inside, or rather under, his waxy extremity, serving as my shelter.

"Improving. Far less sensitive and much more durable than when we left the cave. I'm hopeful we can flux after respite in Waning Star. I've a plot of land there and family that tend to it. My great nephew keeps my stead livable and it can be easily stocked with food by the village if something we need is lacking."

I was always interested where family matters were concerned. That was once my only priority. And when a great immortal spoke of them, it closed the gap between our different worlds. "Great nephew?"

"My mother's brother's kids... several greats down the family tree. Eulid Toremoon. He is a falconer and a damn good rider. A horse crafter is a lovely light to view him in." I heard his pride, envy and smile coating his words. "I make a point to stay with him for a fortnight at the end of every hunting season, to help dehydrate the meat and set aside furs for wear and trade. Last I heard, he sent word that his mare was pregnant, we may be lucky enough to watch MaiMai in her first days as a new mother. He has a keen eye for breeding strength and pliable temperaments in his herds before he releases them back to the valley. Most come back, he trains those that do and if a rider is in need, he can match them seamlessly." His right hand anchored around my wrist. He pressed down until his fingers were wedged between mine in an alternating pattern.

My thumb closed around his. "Have you any more distant relatives you keep in touch with?"

"Just his kin. He has a daughter who married some years ago and herds valleys closer to Kathra, he doesn't venture there after Resig's implementation of banning mixed races entirely. Of course, Emperor Maruc hastily encouraged those under his governance to retreat to safety about a year before his decree. Most horselords and maidens have some amount of llanthian or dreamer in their human lineage and opted to avoid venturing too far into the heart of the western province, all while staying close to their home and roots along the seam. With your stubborn constitution, you'll be mistaken for one of them."

I yawned, "Gladly." I blinked a few times before resolving to close my eyes. "You know what I think?"

"Hmm?"

"Maruc knew what King Resig and his flock of dukes and high lords were doing this entire time with the Ilanthians. Butchering them, experimenting, drinking their blood, chasing immortality and whatever else. That was why he asked his people to move closer to the White Tower and out of Numaal's reach."

He adjusted closer, my head cradled in the crease of his elbow. "I agree," he stated.

"Do you think he knows of the Remnants or venom injections?"

"No. But I bet he has insight into what person or thing those nasty bones belong to. Maybe they are several beings. The terms *vulborg* and," he lowered his cautious tone into a whisper before finishing his thought, "*migouri* may even spark an epiphany for him." Unconsciously, my eyes opened and tried to locate the strap across his chest which secured the bag to his person. I saw darkness. I'm sure he watched my fretful face contort in the shadows. He moved our hands to his chest where I felt the strap secured around his torso and a steady thrum of a heart beneath his ribs. Heat blossomed.

"We will ask when we meet with him." His chest rumbled against my knuckles as he spoke.

"Add that to the ever-growing list." My chin lifted, with my eyes still open I stared at where I knew his eyes to be. "I have more questions about your relatives. Partially, the ones with horns and wings and the one that sired you."

"That is an inescapable conversation. You'll be getting an earful about my brothers, but also what is to be expected of me, of us, on our return to Veona." My stomach twisted, my knees bent to negate the building tension. The son of interim Overlord. I made a gagging noise and squeezed my eyes shut.

I was slicked in a cold sweat come morning. The fire ran cold hours ago and I buried under limbs and a fresh dusting of white frost. Zander was passed out, fangs visible in his agape mouth. I pressed the pad of my finger over the tip and withdrew immediately.

"Careful, my flower. These are built for venomous biting and splintering bones," he whispered with his eyes still shut, making a scene of his tongue dancing around the red drop of blood staining his white canines.

I blurted out in disbelief, "How have you not impaled me with those things?"

He was waking up and grinning lazily now. "I swore never to hurt you and as we both know, I am a man of precise control." He swallowed my blood. "I dull them when we are lip locked," Zander educated and clicked his teeth in a straight, pointed grin. His right wing retracted allowing light to cast itself upon our pitiful camp.

The bags under his eyes were a shade darker than his cheekbones. And yet, his cheeks rose to meet those heavy eyes. He needed energy. My energy. "I believe I was promised a demonstration of your finger's finesse. Unless of course you admit your faults of fumbling."

I wasn't sure if I saw hurt twitch in his brows. "Are you luring me with your delightful way of flattery because you want me to prove you wrong or because you think I need to be fed?"

"Can't it be both?" His brow furrow deepened. "If you can rummage about for my food but can't accept what I can bring to the table, I hardly think our dynamic can continue. I will not tolerate such archaic thinking." The hand under my chin lifted my lips to his and left to unfasten my drawstrings after my tongue was fully engaged with his past the point of stopping. He moved his touch over the fabric of my pants, kneading his open palm with firm pressure directly atop the spot begging to be stroked sensually.

My hips pressed against his hand and we entered our entrancing dance of inevitable bliss. He forced his lips off mine only to speak against the hollow of my neck. "Carefully, you will lay with your back to me." I did as much, willfully ignoring the scabs that opened while I shifted from my stationary spot.

Zander pressed the throbbing length in his pants against the curve of my ass. "Do you see what you've done to me? Always placing me at your mercy," he purred, and without warning his hand stole my breath as it dove beneath my panties. A slow finger traced the shape of my vulva and inner thighs, intently avoiding the wet slit and pierced hood of my clit. This tease. I rolled my hips into his hand, he moved away.

Jilted.

"I will get my revenge," I murmured.

The arm my head rested on bent and a hand woven in my hair. My head was pulled to the side. Sharpness pricked my neck, but not piercing my flesh. Undulled fangs. He listened to my heart beat faster, felt my pulse bounding away under his tongue. He dragged them across my thin skin, a looming threat. "I'm counting on that. Judging on how you strung the duke up like a damn holiday decoration for revenge, I anticipate something memorable." The tips of his fangs on my carotid prevented me from a smart retort.

"Interesting," he whispered.

"What is?"

His nose settled where his mouth once was. His inhale brought goosebumps down my arms. "Adrenaline."

"I'm not afraid."

"You seldom are," he assured. "It's the unknown, the anticipation, the danger of two daggers hovering above you elicits *excitement. Arousal.*" His jaw returned to its previous spot around my neck. A nibble and nip, derived a high pitched moan from my throat. Hearing the frankness in his words made me feel vulnerable, so much so I couldn't even decide for myself if that was in fact true. What I did know was that when he massaged my insides with his middle finger I came unapologetically fast.

Chapter Five

Once airborne, I initiated what would end up being an extensive conversation. "Just so you know, I'll never fully like your father for how he sired you nor will I forgive Kailynder and Wyatt for coming at an adolescent version of you with axes in their hands."

"Only Kailynder wielded the ax. Wyatt pinned me to the floor outside the communal bathroom." I glared, and gave his ear a tug. "I'm not asking you to like any of them, not even to play nice in the sandbox, but you need to maneuver around their attributes and, well, if you thought my personality was strong *yeesh*. There is no avoiding all of them, but try to ignore an Ilanthian tactician named Judeth." His eyes were shining fondly. He had missed his home. His people. His family.

I resigned, "Well, go on. Tell me about all the people you've been missing and the home you are redeeming yourself for." His eyes left the horizon and met mine. His blue eye was a pale blue crystal rimmed in sapphire, it would have outshone the sky on a summer's day.

"We shall start with the eldest of the seven sons of Atticus. Kailynder, the singular pure incubus in existence. His mother was an ambitious succubus who left to explore yonder the Southern Isles long before Thalren rose. When Oyokos and Taite found her on the other side of the world, they discovered she had been ruling an entire continent of people, like the blessed and vibrant. And was beheaded after hundreds of years of reigning because a succubus was too powerful. A hungry female that could bring an army to their knees and just as easily every man and woman who entered her vicinity. A supreme dictator. Oyokos brought back her horns to be set in a place of remembrance in Veona. Kailynder keeps them enshrined in the Keep's Library."

"He inherited his mother's ambition, but I have watched it taper off—or perhaps it is better said he has found a purpose to transfer his controlling nature. Occasionally, he threatens to step into the Overlord role if he isn't getting his way, but never commits. He pours himself into combat training. He is working on becoming worthy of the title Right Wing, perfecting his unit of steel swords and shields called the Rudins. Obsessing about cohesiveness, wanting to outperform Dagressa, the chief of berserkers and brutes. Her mother was an orc, she is creative in her approaches and Kailynder has a hard time strategizing against her. I think he fancies her, but she will never feed him."

"Against her?"

"Mock battles and competitions to keep the military sharp and scout for special abilities useful on more sensitive missions. Like intercepting trade routes, seeing through glamour, ties with the river folk in Ilanthia," he was still smiling. "Seldom do people die or get too brutally injured. The Trial of Ruins is hosted once a decade. And we won't host it anytime soon with a real battle—war—at our runegate."

"So, the ideal approach to Kailynder is not punching him in the face and avoid being recruited or besting him?"

"If you punch him, Dagressa will seek you out to be one of hers. You won't be able to avoid her if she has decided to have you. Consider this your warning, the extremist flock to her."

"How very incubus-ish of her. Are all dreamers widely fanatical and possessive?"

"No. We are not. Incubi and mated fae are notoriously the most volatile with the ones we've taken keen on protecting. Elementals have their own way of being territorial bastards and tending to the ones they are trying to impress and swoon into relationships." He paused before he answered. Then mulled over his reply before carrying on as if he was rethinking the answer he gave. "Kailynder is tactical and emotional about maintaining structure. Best not meddle with his plans. He is a nightmare under stress and I don't want to deal with him. No one does. Not even his harem tolerates feeding him when he is in a mood."

Light flurries of snow swooped across the mountains. Zander rose above the wet clouds where it was colder, but drier. My throat constricted when I lost sight of the ground. The occasional mountain peak to our left was my only means of orienting myself for even the dull sun misled me by reflecting off the mist.

"Do you have a harem waiting for you? A buffet of orgasms at your beck and call?"

Rosy pinks doused my mind's eye. "I'd hardly dub it a buffet. And no. I disbanded the volunteers as part of making my arrangements to persist at your side in Numaal and every moment after. It will be made apparent that I am to not be approached so you needn't worry about unfaithfulness nor I taste the iron of your jealousy more than I do now."

It'd be stupid to lie about the twinge of jealousy in my gut. "What about Wyatt's story?"

"Wyatt's mother was a fae. She was a farmer by Malee Grove, west Veil territory backing up to Havana. He wasn't born with wings, but with thickets of thorns encroaching on his shoulders, joints and knuckles. He can cast fae illusions but can also lure with incubus charm. Out of spite from being grounded, he took to perfecting trickery with the sprites. He outgrew his mischievousness, mostly. Don't make him feel stupid or lacking. Your mind will be made into a playground for him if he retaliates." I felt my jaw unhinge and lips separate. "He spends most days in Akelis, when war isn't among his homeland. He works alongside the magical folks and is the one I trust to interrogate captives. He has a good head on his shoulders when he isn't dabbling in someone else's."

"What's the difference between elves, fae, pixies and nymphs?"

"Fae and elves are studious peoples who live to be as old as the dirt they tend. Elves are more resistant to leave their treehouses and hardly come out in the sunlight. They are comparable to your craft and woodsy nature, they move fast but talk to their trees slowly. Fae take on as many shapes and physical attributes as the glamours they can cast. Pixies and nymphs are more your stature, petite, and share the human lifespan. Pixies have their own wings, claws and teeth—they will use them too if you intrude on their crystal caves. Nymphs are eternal children. Brats really," he shook his head, I repositioned mine into the warm crook of his neck. "They enjoy riddles and tend to their elements, but not in the same manner elementals do. Elementals are born from the blood of two Eternals and their lives are directly linked to their elemental sources." Intuitively, I moved my hand off Zander's shoulder and rested it over his scarred chest.

He felt my gaze wander to his sternum because he added the sweetness of honey in his voice when he reassured, "The Eternal Elm and Pyous Glacier house the magic of the twins and they are well protected. The wolves and foxes who spin flame and water are in themselves a standalone army. There is a reason they don't participate in the Trial of Ruins because they will obliterate their opponents. That and purebred foxes and wolves stick to their own kind and don't socialize too much out of their inner circle or wovens unless the city holds festivities, revels or public affairs. Fennick, and his brethren, will be fine."

Based on firsthand experience, I knew Nikki could fight. I'd never seen him spin fire. That would be a sight. He was markedly accomplished at Ilanthian footwork, not as proficient as I, but he survived the Deadlands alone and without the source of his magic nearby, he could manage with it. "That's good," I said, noting the way my words hitched in my throat. "The Elm is north, right? By the rune stones and evil pressing in on the barrier?" A flare of annoyance simmered on my tongue and pinked my cheeks.

He made a noise. A sound between surprise and exasperation. "You pay attention. Yes, in the fire fields. The Elm and the Burrow are nearer to the undead dead than any other thing of importance. Ramparts have also been built within a reasonable proximity that has capabilities to use long distant catapults and barbed spears that project at the barrier if it ever came to that." His browns and grey swarmed rampantly across his essence. "We've taken precautions."

I let a breath go by. My simmering continued until it boiled over. "He was probably less than thrilled to be stuck in Numaal when he should have been with his family preparing his home for the turmoil about to raid the Burrows."

Zander pulled me tighter to his chest to navigate the airstream. "Stop assuming how he feels and why. Ask him when you see him next because I will not give you answers on his behalf." The pair of them were so vastly different in nearly every capacity other than both being woven to me and both overly overbearing.

"I intend to." I did. Among many other things, like why he smashed in Keenan's nose. "Tell me about your darling savior, Clavey."

I shook in his arms because of his mirthful response. The jostling obligated me to hold him tighter. His fangs nipped greedily at the air as arousal sparked through him. "He didn't pull me out from under the blade from the goodness of his heart. No, he thrives off attention. He wanted to catch Atticus's eye, slither into Veona's gossips, pick a fight with his brothers and flaunt that moment in my face whenever he needs to face the consequences of his actions." His nose wrinkled. "Of all my brothers, he will be the one to outright approach you and lure you into his bed with his husband Talian. They indulge too much. Lavishly living like the dukes of Numaal and frivolous about it. Very unbecoming behavior of a reaper. Not to mention he gives the rest of his brothers a foul reputation for being an incubi. Taite would even be blushing."

"Sounds like he may have enough offspring to fill the Southern Isles!"

Humor rumbled through his chest. "I told you there was a *process* for incubi to repopulate and conceive. A process that involves surrendering our power to our kin. Our children could inherit all or a portion of our magic leaving us less likely to sway or charm meals. After Percy's son was born he lost his ability to vanquish his wings and transition into his smaller Ilanthian form. That was off putting enough for the rest of my brothers not to have little hellions for the time being. Not me. Take my magic, I've no need for it. Not when I have already charmed you with my personality and wits alone."

My teeth bit into my cheek to prevent a grin. "Wait till the world discovers how much coddling you require, I am certain that will better your reputation. Definitely soften the crassness." Two sharp needles pricked my ear. My face reddened as my blood pumped faster.

"Percy. He is cross and irritated all the damn time. Hasn't healed from the loss of his son and wife in the aftermath of the Great War and makes sure everyone around him is as bitter and resentful towards the Eleven as he is. Any excuse to fight, he is first to throw himself in. I've heard from the elves and the Ilanthians he befriended before his personality went to shit that he used to be an innovative and compassionate theorist. The war robbed him of that, but I get glimpses into the great man beneath."

The Great War. Mortals against immortals. "Which side did he fight on?" I asked the question having an inkling of the answer.

My woven let a minute go by before giving me a reply; although, the silence was confirmation enough. "The Great War was more a conflict of the Eleven, Oyokos didn't want to participate and requested the Veil remain a neutral territory. A haven of sorts for Kinlyra for those wishing to come together without bloodshed. Percy was inclined to stay in alignment with Oyokos. His wife was a devotee of Aditi who was set on usurping the east who lacked enthusiasm for his craft. His son Lochlin was a great shot with a bow and as charismatic as his father, he moved up the ranks in his Sivt quickly and was of the first cohort dispatched when the war broke out. Misotaka saw their preparations with her sight and sent humans to the west coast before the fleets were dispatched. Lochlin was killed. Percy lost his touch with sanity and turned the harbor near Akelis red. The tides and sands were stained blood-ridden for years after."

I adjusted my slacking arms around his biceps. I grimaced at the loss of muscle tone and thinning of my limbs. "He does not hate humans. He never has. He does continue to explode dung bombs in Misotaka's temple every year on the anniversary of his son's death. No one stops him. I've even joined him a few times to piss off Warroh."

"Another brother?"

He made an affirmative sound. "A reaper scholar who tends to the dead, his duties, his studies and built his own temple by hand with imported stones from the Crescent Isles to honor the Eternals. He recites all the prayers like a monk and is irrationally defensive of them. In his opinion, you are a blasphemous person if you do not give patronage to the acolytes. He will take it upon himself to right your wrongs. Best not get roped into a historical debate with him either."

A pensive grunted. "Better yet, don't stand close to him. He goes too long between feeds and gets impulsive and you will be everyone's cup of tea. Judeth is his most consistent source of food, a partner to him if you will. She does well in reminding him to eat so he doesn't accidentally lure the monks to insanity with his unleashed charm which has them drooling on all fours for him, prowling down their altars."

"He won't marry her?"

"Judeth is a hard pill to swallow, even for Warroh. She does not sugar coat her opinion nor hold her tongue, she feels this world is cruel and it is her self-assigned duty to make sure we all know that. She hosts annual meetings for the FIrst Fraction, a group for relic and rubric minded immortals who don't adapt well to change. She will have it out for you."

Zander tucked hair behind the freezing tips of my ears. "That leaves Kashikat, the brother closest to me in age. His three hundred years old part-pixie ass runs the flight division of our army. I fight with the flight division and that is my elected sector for combat, mostly because Kai is annoying and I would likely end up swinging swords at him were he my commander." We shared a smile. "Kashikat's body has aged a lot, so he commands it from the towers. His loyalty woven, Namir, handles communication between the wolves on the glacier and the central city. She'll be around often as will his wife and two daughters." I smiled at the notion of another woven mingling in the mix. I needed to see how to interact with my new friends and what was acceptable to Veona.

"You're an uncle yet again," I said into the firmness of his shoulder. The warmth of my breath was welcomed on my cold chin.

"A proud one. Those little sprites are really settling in nicely after the river was rerouted. I was nervous they'd get behind in their studies and not make playmates. The older one is off at the academy in Akelis and the younger is in diapers and happily terrorizing family affairs. Nyx figured out she has wings and learned how to use them." His dimple appeared in the corner of his drawn up mouth.

"That just leaves the seventh son of Atticus," I chipped in.

His shoulder went up. "You know me. More intimately than most others."

I snorted. "As you said, I pay attention to details. You've done a marvelous job prancing around potentially imperative truths since Fort Fell." The notch on his neck bobbed as he swallowed. "Were you really not going to mention outright you were the Veil's Overlord? Or did you just want to ensure I felt inadequate and foolish when I showed up with you at my side?"

Our thread went taut.

Chapter Six

His wings pinned behind him as we rode a cold current down to the nearest iced over creek and infant pines. My nails dug into the fabric of his scarf until the loud *fwoop* of his wings shot out and stopped our momentum. When we landed he took his time in setting me upright on my feet as if I wouldn't permit him to touch me after I heard whatever it was he had to say. I peered inside the passage between us, his colors stuck to him in a tight amorphous shape. I couldn't determine the prominence of any one emotion other than hesitation.

"I am not upset, but I am annoyed that you chose to omit this from me, this deep into our bond." I finally caught his wary eyes. Both eyes were blue. He was fully present but unusually quiet. "Don't tell me after pining for my attention you are too shy to commit to being my friend? Friends tell eachother things, honest things. Friends are forgiving and understanding. Usually."

He felt for the bridge connecting our mind doors. It was much more stable and secure then it had been in Fort Fell. His hands he splade open in front of him, an invitation to take them. My hands disappeared under their cold and calloused touch. He held my wrist gently, his thumb tracing along where there should have been scars from shackles of the dungeon. "You told me nothing that you are would be hidden from me. That you wanted to share everything with me. Why don't you start by explaining why you've omitted the truth?"

"In Landsfell, you held a distinct opinion. I believe your exact words were *'Fuck your Overlord and all the Lords and Ladies, Kings and Queens, and the remaining Eternals in our world. They all are entirely useless in this ordeal. Damn cowards! I'd be embarrassed to be seen with any of them, let alone have one 'vouch for me.'"* Oh, yes. I did tell them that over my first home cooked meal from Nikki of fried rice and dumplings. What would I give to eat that garlicky goodness now? Just about anything.

I chewed the insides of my cheeks so I wouldn't burst into laughter. Ha, it was no wonder Nikki was good at the multiple dances of politics and erupted with laughter after I told off the Overlord lurking in his vision.

"I know what I said," I replied. "And I meant what I said, but at that time I was under the misguided surmise your father was elected interim Overlord for other reasons that had nothing to do with it's true Overlord's absence. You were elected all those decades ago during that nondescript, very boring political caucus you avoided talking about?"

"Correct. I accepted the nomination." His fingers hadn't stopped caressing the sensitive insides of my wrists. His five o'clock shadow was the darkest I'd seen since the start of the season. "I love my lands. I love the dreamers. And yes, I love being my nation's Overlord. I can make a difference. I am. And I am a great sovereign for my peoples, so I'd to think." Redemption. Forgiveness. He chased it when he already had their trust. They voted him in and hadn't voted him out. He *stepped* out.

For me.

My hands started to curl into fists, as a stream of guilt and flair of anger flash in my chest. "If you love your role, why surrender it?"

"Because it was the right thing to do. And when the time is right for *us*, we can talk about ending my father's term or finding another to nominate."

"Did you step out of your role before or after Stegin's dungeon?"

"That's not pertinent information."

More omission. I yanked my hands away only to send them back to him in the form of a fist. He evaded my jab, not that I put much effort into the punch. What energy I did have I used as fuel to yell. "That is absurd! You postponed all the good you can do for your people to stay in the Deadlands!"

"I am doing good–*great* here. Just look at all we uncovered and how much intel we are bringing back to the Realm. We have useful evidence and information that can–and will–save Kinlyra."

"You didn't trust me enough to fully disclose everything. You think I am too fragile to handle the feelings of guilt that are rising because you left everything you loved–for me." That last of that declaration came out sharp, I cringe at the truth in them.

Zander's thunderous voice boomed as if it came from the mouth of the mountains. "I love you more than any nation, land or realm combined! I will forsake them all to continue wandering this world, damned or not, at your side." His spine and wings went stiff and blocked out the light from the west. "We. Are. Woven." I went still as he raised his voice at me. It hit me from all angles, trapping me in his snare of dominance. I fought against it, internally shaking myself free of the snare.

He went on. "Staying where you resided was never *not* an option. Our threads were, are and will *always* be the top priority. How do I make you see this?" I wasn't sure air was moving in my lungs. My legs straightened to make me feel less small. "If keeping you at my side means I never take my title back, then I will happily forgo ending my father's contract. I will happily see to your desires even if it means I light the match that burns the rest of the world into fucking nothing!" He stepped closer. "I would not think twice about it, nor would I ask for forgiveness from the millions murdered because I would not care. I would not give one single flying fuck about who I hurt as long as you and Fen are alive and well and with me." I blinked and felt warm water leak down my face. I was too stunned to articulate.

"When I heard your vow to Anna, I made an oath to you because you are a dreamer at heart. You dream to banish the darkness. You are so bright you can stand beside me–the embodiment of darkness–and still shine. I already wanted you before I asked for your name that first time in the dungeons. When you stubbornly refused to answer the damn question three times, I decided then you were made for me."

His colors remained his own, I sprinted down our line and knocked him backwards until the globe around him broke and spilt over me. The intensity of his emotions hit me like a waterfall. One so forceful and mighty all I could do was stand there and get drenched, trying to remember how to breathe. Rose and blue were the first of the colors to settle and embrace me. The pale grey of distress followed close behind. "And if I read Malick the Reaper's journal, what would I have stumbled upon?" I hardly managed to form words.

"A diary. Mine. My own struggles, triumphs and plans for the future of not just the Veil but for the Plains of the Horselords, the mountains and western regions," he spun, gesturing to the flat lands, rolling hills and mountains. "I was hoping when you read it, we'd have this conversation and it would have gone differently before our endeavor to Landsfell. That I could have explained to you who I was before I met you, but understand that my motives have always been the same. I have been very transparent about my intentions to discover the end to the wraiths and stop the influx of undead in the beyond. A title changes nothing."

As the patient friend I was attempting to be, I exhaled before I opened my mouth, trying to control what words flew from it. "Who were you? Who are you?"

"You know the answer to the second question," he bit back matter of factly. Ice coated his words making them pointed with truth. I wonder what he was smelling of my emotions right now, I think my vexation would taste like peppery spice.

"As for the first, Overlord of the Dreamer Realm and the beyond, Zander Veil Halfmoon di Lucent, a man who helps settle the qualms of his people, speaks to and for the masses, strives to understand the many races and magics mingling in the Veil and protect the ancient knowledge given to the them. Born a human, I break down barriers with my mere existence. I have a loyal militia to defend what is within my reach. It may not be enough to withstand what comes when the runegate falls, which is why I am counting on you to uphold your vow to Anna and find a way to end the war so Kinlyra's resources can be used more wisely."

I waited for Anna's blood to heat my veins at the mention of her name. And was met with my own thudding heart, which sounded as hollow as beating on a vacant drum. Anna felt further away than before and there was no bringing her back, just fading memories I had to revive in order to feel less isolated, less lonely.

"I spent the years before my excursion into the dungeon and the Southlands meeting with Ilanthia's and the Veil's sharpest, tactical minds and historical connoisseurs on how to best approach King Resig Torval. Maruc and Athromancia were at odds during each assembly. Athromancia is wise. Wise enough not to speak of a war with her brother at the table or send us spiraling to our demise sooner than intended. Neither of them felt like sharing much, constantly reiterating, *'We create. We are not here to control creations.'* They'd nothing to say about what the figures in the beyond were, nor where they came from. I was not sure they even knew. One Eternal wanted to discover more about the east's plans and the other was set on a bloodshed. Collectively, we deduced Numaal had answers and since they were not present at our meeting to give them, we'd find them. I volunteered."

"Of course you did. Was Numaal even invited to these meetings?" I couldn't help but sound defensive. Gimly had been right about one thing, the last God cared little about Numaal. He would have bloodshed and be done with the nation altogether. My finger wrapped around my neck, tracing my jaw and easing anger building there.

"Messages were sent to all four provinces and *many* falcons to Kathra, addressed to any scholar, lord or lady or *person* who held interest in attending. They would have been provided a safe escort by Maruc himself." I blinked. That was quite the escort. "A letter with the raven head wax seal came to the White Tower that stated, *'You let them come. Now, we will come for you.'* That was meant for the Empress and Emperor, but they didn't elaborate. My father knows them well and despises their new behaviors. His horns have been in a twist since the Eternals seemed to have lost affection for the world they formed. He no longer worships or utters a prayer or phrase of blessing. Warroh is up his ass about it."

"I wouldn't worship them either." My lower lip was between my tightening teeth.

"It is ever clear that Numaal blames the White Tower for this plague and now they are using *it*, working with *it*, perhaps controlling *it* through Remnants or building immunity with venom."

"Gimly was serious when he said they were going to kill the Emperor and Empress. That bastard told me the truth." Zander seethed in silent agreement. "We need to meet with the Eternals when we get to Veona. Or you can come with me when I march up to Maruc."

His eyes closed and he released an exhale. Lighter, less frantic blues hummed down my left arm. "I'll send several of Eulid's fastest falcons the moment we get to Waning Star." While his eyes were still shut I bent forward and grabbed a handful of snow and pelted a snowball at his chin. I felt moderately better after that.

His lashes shot open. Snowflakes caught on his left brow.

He stared at my finger pressed to his lips. Demanding his mouth shut and ears open. "I've known who you were for weeks and I see you no differently. I will treat you no differently. I will continue to say what I want in your presence and I will not be made to feel small because your realm labeled you with some glossy salutation in front of your already ridiculously long name. If you are being an ass, I will tell you. If you infuriate me, I will punch you. If you grind your cock against me, I will come. We are as we are." I raised a brow to enforce my seriousness.

"Your blood has never changed the way I viewed you, neither has your changing stature or physical abilities, so why do you think I'd be scared off by a title? Because I sent you running out of Nikki's head? That would have been a lovely segway into a conversation on how you *are* in fact doing something, that you are using your influence to revoke evil and that my assumptions, as you already pointed out, were not correct. I am going to list more assumptions, you can guide my stray thoughts if they are invalid. Yes?" Suddenly, he was at a loss of words and nodded against my finger. Snow fell from his hairline.

"You are terrified to unbridle your full power on the hordes of wraiths for you fear your lack of control will kill more innocent lives and that will eat away at you. " He nodded. My heart softened. I had been wondering about this since the magnitude of his magic was brought to my attention. "Then I will never ask you to let the sun out of the cage. That is your choice. That key and lock is fully under your mastery. You are the only one who can access your full potential, the only one who can wield it. I will never force you." Five fingers wrapped around my forearm, my finger remained pressed to his mouth.

"Your nation, your realm, loves you and has already forgiven you. It's you who has not forgiven yourself?" Another nod. He kissed my finger upon his lips. He said he wouldn't think twice about burning the world for Nikki and I, but in my gut I knew he would think about it ten thousand times and it would not be done with joy or fondness.

I continued on, "You hesitated to tell me because you compare me to your previous lover. You are afraid I would cling to your name and manipulate you into bringing Veona's army over to fight for the innocent that live in

Numaal." He shook his head. I lowered my hand. His grip snug around my arm, moving with me.

"You are incomparable and in a league of your own, my Wisteria. There is no comparing any man, woman or being to you. I hadn't reminisced of my past, nor spoken of it, until you asked it of me." Pinks violently pulled me near him. Such fervent, honest adoration. Did I deserve this?

"Yes, you deserve my words and actions of devotion, idolization, infatuation and a four letter emotion you cringe from." I didn't sypher, which meant he could also taste my doubt. "You are not capable of manipulation. You are a horrible liar and, to be frank, you will do the exact opposite of *clinging to my name.* A smart man knows he cannot restrain or predict the path of a vine of ivy, they are stubborn and independent plants. I consider myself smart. And even when you are my wife, you will be free. Just as you will not force my magic, I will not force your love. You will love me willingly in some capacity if you don't already." His brows wiggled watching me squirm.

Try as I might, he didn't let me turn away. He brought my hand back to his lips and kissed each tightly clenched knuckle while I set my searing gaze into his thick skull. "Keep those lovey-dovey comments chained behind your tongue when we enter the Veil."

"Ha! You don't want the world to know of your wovens and yet, you will be sharing my bed, my belongings, my meals and, with any amount of sanity and luck, you will be wearing my bite mark on your neck, so my kin cannot claim you, sway you or charm you out from under my covers and into theirs. And after Fen arrives and we are drawn together—I am curious to hear what rumors Clavey will spin solely to infuriate us. Once he witnesses your temper he will try and set you off too. Probably get a game started in his twisted head to get you flirting with him. Oh, and Kailynder would not know how to place you. He likes things compartmentalized. A little too organized." One by one, my fingers were sucked into his mouth, the soft wetness of his tongue a sharp counter to his canines, now jutting up from the lower jaw too, trapping my index finger's retreat. I took his bulky wrist in my free hand and brought his middle finger to my lips deliberately hollowing my cheeks as I encouraged him to watch.

"You've fed yourself to me and I will defend that privilege. They will know how I feel about you. I will refrain from calling you my future wife, but I will not merely refer to you as a fucking partner, travel companion or anything that implies we are a casual couple or you a midnight snack."

"You will call me a friend."

His nose flared. I felt his inner storm surge. He kept the surface calm. "You may call me a *friend*, but my nation will see past such a dull word when you will be clearly *mine*. You are much more than a friend to me, you are my life, and if I am to keep you safe you will not be downplayed. How about my beloved?" he countered, moving his lips over my forearm and drawing our bodies together until my heart beat against his hips and my head rested against his navel.

"Terrible suggestion."

"Fiancé? Betrothed? Fated?" I pressed my forehead into the rock solid abs. Zander ranted on. "Companion? Girlfriend? Suitor? Goddess of life? Queen of my garden? I do like the sound of an admirer, yet it doesn't hold the depth I am searching for and may imply others are welcome to feast their eyes on you. For which I will kill them if they do."

"I will be your flower," I provided, hoping to close the conversation. He scoffed. "It matters not what the world thinks of our depth, nor does it matter in what way I am perceived for rooming with you. Or Nikki, or Brock, or Yolanda or Keenan for that matter. I just don't want to feel trapped by word constraints. We are still growing."

"You and Fen will be attracted to one another and the Veil will be nothing shy of nosey because while some dreamers can be polyamerous, incubi have never succeeded."

"Define success?"

He raised his shoulders. "Not killing the spare person in the bedroom for interfering with the scent of a meal would be a good start."

"You've killed someone for spoiling a scent?"

"I haven't. My brothers have when they were dumb enough to try and defy their instincts. I've not attempted because I know my control can be *lacking* and the odds are severely stacked against me. I'd no reason to take such a risk when it has been proven impossible among my kind."

"Let them be nosey. I want to understand my wovens before the world places constraints and expectations on us or celebrates something they aren't involved in."

Hands found their way around my waist, my pants were being loosened. "And what are you to call me? 'Buddy' as you do Brock? I will not have that chummy nonsense." I stepped out of my pants and stood with my bare legs on display to the hillside.

"Zander or princess will suffice. Prick if you deserve it." Snow stuck to my boots as I kicked my garments aside, and went to work on a gold plated belt buckle. When that was off I unbuttoned the rest of his pants with my mouth. His hips were involuntarily rocking against my face, I sent my warm exhales through the fabric before I pulled his trousers to his knees. I stepped back to look at him. Quite the specimen of a man, honestly I was so taken with this erection I didn't notice his wings or the traces of asymmetrical vitiligo spattered down his horns, hairline and face.

"I'm elated that my body gratifies you, that you find me worthy of such a ravenous look."

"Merely, returning the favor." That was true. The unadulterated lust that oozed off him took deep shades of purple.

My ass was cosseted gently. A recognizable need pulsed through my left arm, instigating a burning in my low abdomen. Thighs were wrapped around him seconds after our lips met for a kiss. It was a relentless, frantic kiss that was a crashing of teeth and tongue, gasping and groaning.

I snatched a fistful of his hair to steady myself as he positioned the tip of his cock against my slick opening. He didn't thrust, but instead stilled, returning his hands to slowly caressing my legs while I adjusted to the initial burn of his size stretching me. I pulled out of our kiss because the overwhelming sensation of being stuffed full prevented any other part of my body from functioning. Thinking was an impossibility.

You look stunning with me inside you. My wetness slicked the rest of his shaft and I buried him deeper inside me. The muscles on his lower back and torso were clenched so tight, his defined body etched into my mind. He throbbed against my insides when I got comfortable enough to roll my hips.

I engaged with his mouth again. *I feel stunning with you inside me.* He squeezed my left swell, locking my nipple ring between his fingers and twisting until I gasped. In retaliation, I worked my way to the top of his cock and slammed myself down to the hilt. We both moaned. I acclimated to him nicely now and swore each time we touched the stitches in my heart made room for him. *Fuck me.*

As you wish, my forever flower.

Chapter Seven

The days and nights that came to pass were spent in the same repetitive manner. Food, feedings and flying. And listening to the ways of his realm to distract me from the misery that had on our bodies.

During a particularly rough snow front we dug a pit and buried ourselves out of sight from the sky, great wings sheltering me from a fit of freezing. Cold still robbed my lips and fingers of color. We spent that afternoon syphering about Zander's complicated relationship with his father, who he would not fully forgive for transgressing his mother, but also admired for his love of all peoples and how he conducted order out of chaos for thousands of years.

Siring sons of many races was part of Atticus's scheme for unity. Being said, he frowned upon his sons changing their forms or lessening their presences to blend with the other nations. He wanted to be accommodated for; all while, rarely leaving Thalren to set expectations or shift perceptions. No, angry Percy and charming Clavey were the ones roaming about the mountain towns of Numaal and frequenting every city in Ilanthia, swaying wills and charming bodies as they pleased.

"I've never been drunk with my power or abused my abilities, Wisteria. Not even in my slump of failure did that ever cross my mind," he spoke across the fire I started, critiquing my rationing of the remaining rice. I believed what he said to be true. "Tomorrow, we camp at the Howling Hills. If we can catch a consistent wind it is a two day journey to the tundra just south of Waning Moon. Three if Drommal casts a flurry." His eyes fixed on the dwindling sack of cooked rice, thawing out by the flames.

"I have gone much longer with far less."

He was not assured. I knew that scowl on his face to deduce he was pissed without having to even access our bond. "You've mentioned as much in Fort Fell. To which I replied, never again." He melted a cup of snow over the fire and insisted I drink. My attempt to convince him I was fine, that I would be fine, fell on deaf ears. It was a moot point. He had already formulated a plot to fuss and fret over me because his protective inclinations needed to be satiated. "I will forage tomorrow. Winter resilient shrubs are bound to be sprouting somewhere." Zander's brows went up. "There are caves everywhere where we are going, mushrooms and moss love damp places."

"Your enthusiasm is endearing." His rascally grin instantly made me regret the words that left my mouth. "Endearing in the same manner a cat rejoices over stumbling across a dead mouse." I closed the door to our thread just as I ended the conversation with a cold shoulder. I rolled onto my side snubbing the gorgeous smile I felt steadily lingering on my bloodied back. He lifted my head onto his outstretched arm when he nestled in for the night.

The Howling Hills were not what I was expecting. Although, they were loud—howling as if we were stuck traveling with a chaotic pack of rabid wolves. "These rock formations should be renamed the Haunting Hills," I suggested walking under a smooth pale sandstone archway that whistled a low pitched moan. It was one of countless twisting archways that decorated the landscape under a dense mist. A mist which was as opaque as a brick wall. Not a natural occurrence. "What magic holds the mist at bay?"

He dropped his voice to a whisper as if the winds were eavesdropping, "The same one that brings the hills to life with whispers and howling hymns, griffins."

My feet stopped. He knocked into my stationary form, catching his footing before he clobbered me. "Clumsy," I muttered under my breath just before exclaiming, "Real griffins? Lion and eagle? Claws and talons? Fur and feathers?"

"Shh, yes they are said to hear everything spoken in these parts. The wind carries our voices up to them in the sky." *A nest of griffins is set upon the high plateau. There resides the same flock of griffins that refused to take sides, offer aid or show any amount of empathy during the Great War.*

They've not left their aerie in five thousand years since they rid the world of dragons. I met very few people who've claimed to have seen one. And like most people I'm inclined to believe they've fled the continent or died off, but I'm not taking risks. I'm not one to explore their palace in the sky, even with wings I wouldn't risk it. They didn't take a stand in the war. We don't know where their allegiances lay. All we know is that they can't speak falsely and were the beings to banish dragons, the ill speaking serpent tongues.

A gust spiraled down from an elegant spindle, eerie screeching whistled as if in reply to Zander's thoughts. Zander placed a protective hand on my shoulder and unfurled his wings. I swatted his hand off only for it to come right back.

They are very much alive.

He clicked his teeth. *Appears that way.* "Let's get to even ground."

Turns out, level ground was not easy to find among the odd rock formations winding every which direction. Gale force winds sprung on us from seemingly nowhere, sending us to flatten ourselves against the ground on more than one occasion. And the sounds, well I began to hear singing among the hills, less screaming. Some of it was pleasing.

Zander disagreed. He held his temples to ease the tension in his head. "Another downside of having hyper receptive senses is that they can be inundated with overstimulation. Fen empathizes with his keen eyes and ears. I envy his ability to retreat into small alcoves and bury himself away."

I had no satchel of herbal remedies, nor tincture on my body that could offer relief. Hell, my master ink markings were probably removed, erasing my past. Some woodlander I was turning out to be. "Are you compromised? We can rest."

He wrapped his scarf tightly around his head in pursuit of dulling the howling. "Hardly. Onwards." It took a few miles of hiking before we managed to scout out a reasonably even portion of stone that would fit the two of us. It was atop a rocky plateau and open on three sides. I was grateful neither of us unconsciously walked while we slept or we'd end up impaled by the rocks beneath us. The fourth side of our slab was yet another textured stone wall that rose into the mist.

The ground was hard without the cushion of grass, dirt or snow beneath my sheepskin. And it was cold. "At least there are no screaming caves up here,"

74

he grunted, tightening the blue woolen scarf around his ears. "Eat, rest. I'll be back before nightfall with *something* to adorn the rice with."

"You don't need to assume the role of provider after we already established Ivy is an independent plant. Wisteria is the same." I stared at his back, at the wings which have greatly improved and were visibly less tattered. But there was no hiding the strain in his body from weeks of flying on damaged, bruised wings. His colors were depleted and the circles under his eyes rivaled a raccoon's. "If I wanted food, I would get it myself."

"Therein lies the problem. You don't want food, you need food. Yet, you've duped yourself thinking starving is acceptable."

"Just as you seem to have done with over exertion. You crumpling with fatigue is acceptable?" His nose flared. "Stay. Remove the burden of the world for a few hours."

"No, you need food."

I laughed. "So, you can judge the necessities of others and act on your own accord, but you are blind to your own needs." He gave a pensive growl. "Stay. Or does the mighty Overlord not take orders?"

"I consider opinions, but do not accept orders or bribes. And that is not my title at the present."

"Let me carry the weight of your wings. You've carried me across a nation on them. It's the least I can do." His head turned a few degrees, enough to meet my gaze. He was contemplating.

"Tempting, but I despise the thought of coercion."

"It's not coercion, seduction, begging or bribery. I'm not even considering poisoning you, I'm offering you a fair bargain." He faced me fully and closed the distance between us. I peered up at him from my spot on the ground. With his arms crossed over his chest he looked more of a mountain than a man. Thick ropes of muscles flexed as he held himself tall. "I see you are intrigued. Good, you should be."

"State the terms of your trade and I'll see if it's something I deem a necessity."

"You will. Because I will only offer it to you once. Never again." A ghost of a coy grin plays on my lips.

Smoke pooled under his feet. His excitement broke free. "The terms, Wisteria."

"Forgo this futile excursion for what is bound to be a weak harvest, unworthy of expending your last reserves of energy and rest with me so that I may honor my craft and offer you aid. Give me purpose tonight, allow me to demonstrate what my family taught me and remember what good my skills can accomplish by seeing to your wings. And in return I will let you bite me, mark me, whatever it is that you are so keen on doing before I meet your family."

His eyes rounded. "Yes. Done deal. My mark on your body will save us from shitty encounters and conversations you'd cringe from." His lips were wet from his tongue tracing them. "Also, Rodrick was right. You are a goddamn martyr."

"I'm selfishly missing my craft and want to learn about how your wings function and mend."

"Your brain is wired backwards."

"It is not." I made room for him on the sheepskin and went to work unknotting the stress of his neck. My initial aggressive pressure was not lost on him. Being this was my second time inspecting the ligaments of his back, I was able to address his strains more efficiently. The cartilage of his right wing had fibrous strings re-attaching to his spine, like strong cobwebs latched between tree branches.

I shifted closer to understand the fusing of flesh and leather. What a puzzling piece of anatomy this was. Moriah was a physician yet never educated me on tending to people with more appendages than us—that would require her to tell me about the world outside the Southern Province. Taboo.

I would learn his body, how it moved, how it shifted and how it healed. Afterall, I promised to live out the rest of my days with him and Nikki, I guess that meant I'd be learning about fox anatomy too. One with nine tails and two hearts... Keeping each other alive was beginning to seem like a full time occupation. *If* we survived the foreseeable obstacles ahead.

Zander's shadowy face was serene. His lashes vacillated in the wind, his waist long hair blew astray, but that was the only motion on him aside from the rise and fall of his chest. As night fell, the hymns of the hills harmonized, whispering sweet nothings at the nape of my neck as I snuck in another two bites of grains while watching the mist roll in and out. It was as if I was underwater looking up at the tides of the undertow undulating. "What is... it.. ?"

"Did you say something?" I leaned towards Zander, tucking my fingers under my arms to retain warmth. "Zander?" I poked his scruffy cheek. He was out cold. Great, another thing about him to grate on my nerves, he chattered in his sleep.

My brain damn well might be wired backwards because I distinctly was hearing voices. "... a summoner ... ah, yes." My back stiffened.

"Hello?" I risked stepping into insanity. Griffins.

The wind altered its course. I shivered as it took to crawling up my spine, forcing me to my feet and practically carrying me until my cheekbone smacked the rock wall. The singing of the hills became a chorus of angelic thunder. There came my reply. "Do you intend to harm me?" I asked the darkening night, the toes of my boots already notched into a crevasse complying with the force pushing me upwards.

"We are incapable of such deeds on our own accord. Share with us..."

No chance in hell was I about to defer the opportunity to speak to a griffin, potentially see one.

My sheltered Southland eyes were eager to catch a glimpse of foreign beauty, anything to revive my spirit with wonder. "When my friend wakes up you must tell him where I went if I am to come to you. He gets ornery when I slink away." There was always syphering to contact him, I tried to encourage myself to leave his side. For now, I'd high hopes I'd be back before he started to stir.

Gusts kept barrading my frame until I moved it up the wall, climbing it as carefully as I would have Elousie's barn or my grandfather's storage cylinder—which was not careful at all. Anna renamed me Ivy in my adolescent years seeing me do just that. Twenty-five feet up a sheer rockface made my breath come quick. Adrenaline, possibly. Thin air, a contribution. It definitely had something to do with the mist parting when my roughened fingers broke through the airy substance and my ears were greeted by the deafening silence of absent winds.

I swung an elbow over a ledge, gnarled roots were sprawled within reach. I latched on and hoisted the rest of my body upwards, swallowing any concerns I had for the blood trickling from my scapula onto the shabby hem of my sweater. This had better be worth it.

My sight was limited to the radius of my extended arm. I followed the dried and twisted roots of a presumably large tree, blindly feeling for a trunk. "A vibrant has arrived." The voice was indistinctly feminine. "Does she arrive with a name?" The air ebbed and flowed, retreating upwards, broadening my scope of sight. Which, given the dark moon and late hour of day, was shotty at best.

"I do," I stated cautiously into the unknown. Keenan's advice to not 'act brash' and my wovens' suggestion of a 'tactical approach' were dismissed by my bewilderment.

Inquisitiveness always won. "Does to whom I speak have a name and a face to place with it?"

Eerie stillness pressed in as the mist wafted out, taking with it every drop of moisture in my mouth. From the fog emerged a mythical creature, half the size of Fort Fell. I should have fallen to my knees, instead I stepped forward. Shaking, but nonetheless I moved my wobbly knees.

Her feline golden portions stretched and clawed at the stone as if she awoke from a slumber. I steadied my heart, searching her predatory gaze for any sign I was endangered for disturbing her. There was none that I could detect and yet the blood coursing through my body continued to hammer at my ribcage, bruising me from the inside out. Her sharp beak, enormous enough to gobble a horse in one snap, elongated towards the star studded sky allowing me to gawk at white and brown feathers decorating her chest, down to her front talons. Talons that could shatter a carriage

Gods, what a magnificent being. "I'll give you my name, if you tell me what thoughts churn within your mind." She gave what looked like a smile, either all knowing or menacing.

Maybe, both.

I unstuck my tongue from the roof of my mouth. The words that fell from it felt as if I had little control over. The winds themself pulled them from me. "I have a friend, he has wings. The next time he boasts about his wingspan,

I'm going to laugh at him." I willed myself to shut up. And cursed when I didn't. "Damn. You're exquisite. You must hear that all the time, it's just I haven't traveled much. I'm learning what is beyond my Deadlands. It's an honor to meet you. I have questions." My face stung because I slapped my hand over the hole in my head.

"A truth sayer..." another voice caught the wind around me. "She hardly needs to be influenced. Turn off your magic."

The female looked aside at the approaching griffin. "She cannot speak the truth because she does not know the truth," the first said. "She only spoke *her* truth."

"That is all one can ever do," the second replied. His coin colored eyes set on me. "You are odd. I enjoy odd." He didn't stop his prowling until he was in my direct line of sight. He straightened. I straightened. Stars above, he could pummel a city with the slightest of movements. I can see where they would have benefited in the Great War when the size of each of their nails were the length of my body.

The first watched keenly as she opened her beak to speak. "I am Bladetooth. A matron of the aerie."

"Hello, Bladetooth." I waved across the terrain. "I am Wisteria Woodlander, a master crafter from Numaal."

"Is that who you are?" she posed, cocking her sharp angular head to the side.

I wasn't Ivy anymore. "Yes."

"Pity. Come back when you are not her." The mist reformed as she turned her back to me. The ground shook with her steps, her tuft lion's tail whipped behind her nearly swiping me off my feet. I stepped in her direction. Disappointment hit me. Who else was I and why did I deserve a harsh farewell?

I sprinted at her back, closing half the distance before the male's voice chipped in. "She won't give you what you seek. Clarity comes from within, it can't be given, you see?" No, I didn't bloody see.

"And why not?" I backtracked to the dead tree before its location was swallowed by the mist. I leaned against it, catching my breath. It consolidated on my upper lip.

He laid down watching me watch him. "When your kind has absolute truth, your kind has absolute certainty. A summoner must have both for then you have intent. When you have intent, Bladetooth will give a different answer. Truth is the way of life. Falsities are the way of the dead, of the dragons."

"What is a summoner?"

"Not you." And I thought my immortal wovens' manner of speaking was irksome. "You as you are, is not what is."

"Enlightening."

"She has sarcasm. I like sarcasm. Lies spoken with truth, made hilarious because you are not a dragon. Those cannot enter the land of the living. Bladetooth loathes them. She had the Eternals lock them away. Far, far gone they are. Alive only in memory." His voice spun in the air, making him sound baritone.

The base of my skull rested on the tree trunk. "You have wisdom you are choosing to withhold that would make our entire conversation easier to comprehend."

"Here I thought she had been listening, afterall you did respond to The Calling. Maybe she has something wrong with her ears." I eyed the edge of the stone overhand, debating leaving. Listening to these riddles and insults was going to give me an aneurysm.

"Nothing is wrong with my ears! And *she* has a name. I am Wisteria."

"Why did she leave her home, the human who calls herself Wisteria?" His beak brushed the stone beneath him as he lowered his head. Wide pupils sought me out.

"Are you curious about me or what has become of the world?"

"Must I pick?"

I grumbled, "Must you ask so many questions?"

"Must she have so few answers?"

"What will you do with the information I give? If I tell you war is here, all peoples and realms will perish and the corpses rise again as host for evil, will you hide away in the aerie until they come for you too?"

"What would she have us do?"

I combed over his features, finding them more playful than predatory. His hazel eyes gleamed in the mist watching me arrive at this bizarre conclusion. Perhaps they weren't made to fight or chase prey. They couldn't partake in the war for they could not kill without a summoner's intent. "What are you capable of doing?"

"She is beginning to see the way." He was smiling, or so it sounded. It was highly disturbing. "She may call me Stormclaw. She will return to me with her name. For now, she must go. An incubi below is threatening to detonate the Howling Hills if I keep her away. He will do it. Down she goes. Back she must come. A different she." Stormclaw gathered a wind that cradled me on an invisible cushion. "Oh, yes. She will come back, but as someone else. I will let her summon me then."

I scrambled to hold onto the air, being thrown off a cliffside wasn't how I wanted to end the encounter nor frankly my life. It felt as if I was falling to my damn death. I must have looked insane whipping my arms around feeling for density and finding nothing solid until Zander's arms were beneath me. His frenzied eyes scoured over each freckle on my nose and strands of messy hair atop my hair. "I found griffins!" I lead. He set my feet on the ground, his hands locked around my narrowing waist.

"I've noticed." He nodded his nose to the sheepskin. Where I once laid, a large yellow feather lay. Creative. "They wouldn't let me pass the mist."

"Was that before or after you proposed detonating their home?" I stood on my tiptoes to get a better look at his clenched face. He was pissed.

"You're still not understanding, Wisteria. I could not physically get to you. Without you I will die." He hadn't budged. His arms were unshakable; non-shattering steel around me. I considered myself lucky I was able to breathe as he should consider himself lucky I was without my weaponry.

"Right, your dinner escaped. Best threaten the nest of ancient beasts or your tummy will grumble."

His clipped snarl silenced me. "You are more than my meal. You are my source of joy and hope, Wisteria." He towered over me, his gritted fangs sinking into his lips. I felt an awful lot like a woodland prey.

All of these insults on my intelligence and ability to listen was making my own tension worse. "You know, if you don't relax you are going to undo all my efforts of soothing your muscles. I'll have to stay up all night to remedy them."

"Don't do that. Don't guilt me," he whispered, finally lowering his jaw if only for me to see the hardness forming behind his unblinking gaze. "You left."

"I returned." Silence. Even the winds were testing me and listening to our disagreement.

"Zander, I will always return, I promised the Weaver as much. You should have learned this by now." I reached my hands above me, his bearded face settled between them. Still incredibly stiff. "Whether I am out jogging with Nikki, freeing you from the mind control of old bones or climbing a hill to gaze upon griffins, I will find a way back to you. Trust me." More of his heavy weight fell in between my fingers as I held his fanged jaw.

"It's not you I don't trust. It's the world around you constantly posing a threat." His grip around my waist lessened, eventually his body slumped and his forehead came crashing down on my shoulder. Better.

"I'm more a threat to the world than it is to me." I kissed the side of his face as I made that promise. Minutes passed where we stood like that. Minutes where he tried to surrender his control over my safety. "Sorry for guilting you. I shouldn't have twisted your heart strings."

His arms flopped down behind me, I fought against tipping backwards. "Is this relaxed enough?" He laughed as my knees and joints caved under his weight. *Giant oaf!*

I glared at him from the ground. "Yes, you made your point."

"Did I?" He joined me kneeling on the stone, this time with part of my cloak he tore and braided into a rope.

"Don't you dare."

"I wouldn't have worry about you coming back if you didn't fucking wander away each time my eyes closed."

I held up two fingers. "Twice. It happened twice." He held the rope out. "Don't be dramatic."

"I'm never going to ask that you stop being curious. Gods I *love* that about you." He put one of my fingers down. "And your tenacious independence.

That I couldn't change even if I wanted to, which I don't." My second finger was pushed now, he held my first. His breath skated across my flesh. *"Mine..."*

"If you so much as tether me to you I will launch myself off the White Tower and run as far as I can. Those will feel no different than chains around me, and the last thing I want is to ever hold you in the same dark light as Stegin." He stopped his motion and I was met with fury in his gaze. Unenthusiastically, I rubbed the crease of my brow. "Unless this is your idea of role playing or a bondage kink, then you will lower that rutting rope."

"Role play? I left that off my long list of how to prepare peaches, remind me to add it." He threw the fabric aside in a fit of aggravation while I waited for him to acknowledge the seriousness of what I had warned. "Just take me with you next time, okay?"

"You'll try to dissuade me from exploring and you are impossible to rouse awake." I laid down on my side, hissing at my injuries. "Don't forget, I'm here for a good time, not a long time."

"I have a ghastly feeling you will never let Fen or me forget."

"Such a honed intuition you have."

"Nonsense, I have learned that you survived off of making a morbid mockery of your life and if you are so determined to die, you will take me with you so I can find your damn body for a proper burial." Starlight and winds were blocked with his massive wing enveloping me.

"Make sure I am burned."

His growl stole further snarky replies as it ripped through the air above my head. I was pinned beneath him as an added precaution while we slept.

The hills sang us a farewell vesper. I lingered for an encore while Zander waited for me. Rolling the feather's end in my finger tips, I stared at the stone structures debating whether to say goodbye to the griffins above or even how to. Shouting their names to the sky seemed off putting. So I said nothing.

When we were several leagues away from the Howling Hills he breached his silence. "Are you going to tell me about the griffins or do I have to continue to imagine they are just foul creatures that deprived me from being at your side?"

"They are odd, not foul. They speak funny."

"They are the embodiment of truth. Unable to lie, I bet they talk in riddles that would make a nymph tear their hair out. Kai and Atticus said they were difficult to negotiate with and they left society abruptly without offering insight."

My chin angled sharply at him. That was information that would have been nice to know. Information that would have made my encounter much more productive. "I met two. Bladetooth and Stormclaw. They are *huge.* And when I say *huge* I mean colossal! The size of a crafting village!" I detailed my entire time away from him. Once his dumbfoundedness sunk in, he asked for the exact wording of our conversation, trying to untangle the cryptic messages and eventually he resigned to humming in my ear while I dozed off.

The night before Waning Star our sack of rice had been emptied, neither of us ate as we laid on the tundra pointing out constellations and swapping stories we'd heard about the stars from our childhood. "Different realms, same stars," I offered wondrously before going to sleep.

"Same world, same stars," he replied, tucking me firmly under his arm. I dreamt of the Eternals who placed them there, the same Eleven who carved Kinlyra, formed the ground and complexities of each seed of grass beneath the frozen patch we laid.

<u>Chapter Eight</u>

Crescent was the name of the falcon we crossed paths with hunting on the cliffside, Zander seemed familiar with the hunter. It stalk its master's food, dive with lethal precision and fly north with two dead minks in each talon. Tightening its wings to its glossy body, it plummeted from the sky at a vertical angle. "Don't," I warned, already feeling leather wings shift to do the same.

"Don't what, little flower?" My blood already sunk to my toes seeing his grin span the width of his scheming face. The face I would break once we met solid ground. "This?"

My stomach was deserted and abandoned above the clouds while my body went hurling towards the dried, frost covered plains below. In between waves of feeling like I was going to vomit, I screamed his cursed name. My nails dug tiny half moon shapes under his collar, not lessening even after I drew blood.

I tried to damn him again but the velocity at which we dropped stole all the air from around us. Our heads were under our toes, of which pointed to the sky. Earth rose below. Unnaturally nauseating. I pulled his chest into mine, my legs and arms looped around his hips and neck, leaving not one surface of me free of him. If I was going to die, I would take this bastard down with me.

A *swoop* of his wings caused time to stop and jerked us upright. Whiplash rolled my neck, I hissed. Disoriented, I clung tighter. "I irrevocably..." I swallowed the sickness rolling in my gut. "...despise you." The venom dripping off my tongue was sharp and earnest. Fine tremors on my fingers and knees forced me to hold this idiot tighter so he would not see them.

He bent his knees to absorb the impact of landing. "You'll despise me more if I allow the first impression my nephew employs of you a meek woman desperately seeking the refuge of my masculine physique."

I unlatched myself and slid down his front body giving him a hardened stare. I was no damsel, Zander was not my almighty savior. "Ew."

"I know you are accustomed to bedding a certain amount of feminine softness, but it seems I've been to your liking. Do not *ew* me."

I stuck my tongue out, he threatened to bite it snapping his jaw at the air above my head. I turned to face the direction his stance was set. A dip in the plains lead our gazes to a cluster of structures composed of triangular leather huts, stone storehouses and wooden homes, all of varying sizes and all donning different phases of the moon. The largest house on the outskirts bore a blue flag with a waxing gibbous moon under its second story window. I pointed in its direction. "That's your home, your family's stead." My heart danced finding a majestic cluster of aspen trees bordering his home.

"You sound certain."

"You said you were born under a waxing moon."

"I did." His feet followed behind me. "I will never tire of you."

"That makes one of us," I grumbled, cautiously eyeing the vast space around us. It was open and... *open.* The mountains were a full league away and the subtle sloping of the yellow plains stretched for what seems like eternity to the east. I inhaled. The air was definitely thinner here, we were in high altitude which eliminated many options for plant growth, but the soil beyond the tundra seemed fertile. As long as they rotated their crop produce yearly and preserved each summer, they could live comfortably without taking the life of an animal. "It's surprisingly peaceful."

"Fen calls this his home away from home. He loves the stillness. There aren't a lot of scents or sounds on the wind here to put him on edge. I swear he'd hibernate under my bed if I never woke him in the winter."

Crescent landed on the arm of a pale haired man who rewarded the bird by giving it a raw chunk of something fleshy before he blew the whistle around his neck and sent him back into the skies. That man wasted no time in opening his arms and hustling towards Zander. I stepped aside. Eulid Toremoon didn't hesitate in embracing his uncle, wings and all, and even gave him a firm fist on his bulging biceps as a way of greeting.

His pale hair was long enough to be braided in the same manner as Zander's and his beard was twisted down to his chest in a rough attempt to appear groomed. A hunter's knife and a sharp ax hung on his belt. "Uncle Z, there was no news of your arrival nor the slightest inclination you've found yourself a maiden capable of withstanding your foolishness."

"I am hardly withstanding. I am tolerating him. At best," I said with a wary shake of my head. "Pleasure to meet you Eulid, I am Wisteria Woodlander."

"Beautiful name for a beautiful woman. You've paired up with this brute nicely. I was beginning to think he had forgotten how to engage intimately with the world outside of the friend fate found for him." He shook my hand with the insulated gloves.

I opened my mouth to fight the comment about our intimacy when Zander chimed in. "You are right, Euclid, she is the most lovely. How fortunate was I to find a woman wild enough to encourage my escapades?"

"Just as fortunate as the fox I presume. Wretched luck." He winked. "Speaking of that man, where is he? I can gather wool for his den, he loves a cozy enclave."

"He is westward for the time being. We are set to meet shortly, I'm hoping he brings the remaining rulers of the Trilogy with him," Zander gave the man a second embrace and let his arm linger around Eulid's shoulders. "I'd like to send several letters while a warm meal is prepared, one void of meat for our crafter guest."

Eyes fell to the herd horses galloping in the distance as we began our walk toward the structures. Eulid stroked his greying dusty facial hair. "Easily done. How long do I have to treasure your company this goabout?"

"Long enough for me to access my fluxing."

"Do I want to know which beast did that to your wings?" Eulid motioned behind him at Zander, while his eyes combed over my attire. I'm sure I looked as if I was dressed in oversize potato sacks and my hair a bird's nest.

"It is as we feared. The undead have grown," the incubus said.

"Then the dead have grown." There was no amount of enthusiasm in his statement. "I have mounts. Good, strong mounts, should you require them in the months ahead."

"I have no doubt we will require them. I'll send word when I find worthy riders." Hearing Zander speak in such absolutes made my bones feel soft. We stood under the door frame in which a cobalt blue flag blew above. It was a tall frame, built to Zander's measurements, he didn't hunch his shoulders or struggle with his wings to stand under the threshold. "I know where the parchment and ink pots are, see to it that two of your fastest are back and fed within the hour. I have information that cannot wait a moment longer."

He set out to complete the tasks, lingering long enough to make us feel welcomed. "Come out to the stables anytime. MaiMai birthed a beauty on the new moon, the colt enjoys visitors dotting over him. He relishes in the spoils of affection."

"He sounds like an incubus," I said, earning me a laugh from Eulid who promptly left before his uncle leaned over me to punch his arm. He narrowly escaped. Zander opened the door to reveal the inside of his family house, which was a simple three rooms—gathering room with a couch next to a kitchen table, bedroom and bathroom, but all made to fit his stature.

I took liberties to explore while he went to work at a elevated desk scribbling away with black ink. There was no second story in the home, it was open to the peaked roof and electric chandeliers consisting of intertwining deer antlers and warm light bulbs. The windows were large to let in light, the chairs were oddly shaped to accommodate a giant set of batwings and the nozzle to the showerhead was entirely out of my reach. There was no hiding who he was here.

As a woodlander, I was adaptable.

I carried the footstool from the closet to the bathroom. Once I successfully turned on the hot water spigot, I stripped and laid myself down on the tile floor, allowing the pellets of warm water to wash away the buildup of icy grime and circle down towards the drain. I lay there with my eyes shut listening to the rhythmic water around me pretending I was laying on the ground in Ferngrove forest on a raining warm afternoon.

A large hand moved the curtain aside. A low voice said all too seriously, "The things we could do with the right showerhead spraying water between your thighs with my tongue inside you. Gods, I have to get you into my bathhouse where we have options for fornication."

I moved my mess of wet hair and gave a lazy smile. "That requires me to physically remove myself from the shower. I'm not fond of exerting myself at the moment."

"I see that. You've fallen asleep." His braids were undone, permitting his hair to dangle loosely over his chest in waves.

I shut my eyes and reverted my face upwards to the downpour. "You've been watching me?"

"Just a quarter hour."

"Creep." I spit out water.

"You don't seem perturbed."

"Hardly. Nikki has gotten me accustomed to always feeling as if I am being watched. Persistent stalker turned a comforting accomplice. I like him around." My lip was pulled between my teeth as I thought about him never visible, but always present in Fort Fell. How he ran rooftop to alley way chasing Petro and I the night Gimly ordered I be brought to aid Duke Satoritu. How he was always so timely to interject himself into my unfortunate encounters. I felt Zander's reflective stare. My face flushed as I said the words out loud, "Yes, I miss him too. Though, I doubt it is in the same manner you're feeling his absence."

That was all it took to get him into the showers.

We were halfway in getting the soap washed out of our hair and halfway to a serving of peaches with a glazed topping when an abrupt knock came from the front room. "Stay. Your wings have to thaw out," I told Zander, who hadn't fully soaked his side body yet. I shut the curtain on him and stepped into a towel while he grumbled something about my backside.

There was no lock on the door, suppose there was no need for such precautions when you trusted the entire village that was the size of Horns End. I opened it to welcome Eulid. He moved quickly around me to set what would be the first of six trays on the table. I sampled the apple ale in a bronze plated cattle drinking horn, puckering my lips at the sourness of the beer.

"It's an acquired taste," he kept his eyes respectfully on the task at hand. Moving glass jars of pickled vegetables in the cupboards and rolling in a decent barrel of what I hoped was whiskey.

"If that is spiced whiskey, I fear you may never rid of me," I warned, tucking my towel under my arms to grab a cup off the table.

"Crafters seldom make bad company." He filled my glass up with amber liquid, I smelt the liquor from across the table. "I do realize you have no clean attire or garments that fit. Not yet, anyways. By nightfall you'll have options to greet me in next time. I've seen incubi lose their common rational over a man's stray gaze no matter how innocent the intent was or how related they were."

I didn't hide my smile. "That is kind. As is this meal and drink. Goddess above I didn't know how starved I was until you laid out such a spread." My fingers were already plucking up cheese. "What do you need that I can offer in return?"

"Nothing, Wisteria. Z takes care of the needs of myself and our people, in return we take care of him and his. It's what family does." He pressed the whiskey into my free hand, pausing before he left. "Welcome to Waning Star, Master Woodlander. Here the moon guides our herds, the stars foretell our days and the sun thaws our souls."

He left me to the buffet of goods which I helped myself to after popping a handful of goat's cheese in my mouth, chasing it with the burn of whiskey. Bread and artichoke dip were next. I was hardly breathing between bites. I definitely was not chewing everything thoroughly before it hit my stomach.

Zander came out of the bathroom sporting his own towel wrapped around his waist, his wings dripping water across the floorboards. His tantalizing shape provoked my eyes to imagine what was beneath that cotton towel. He snatched my arm and thwarted my next bite. "Slowdown. You will make yourself sick."

"But I am hungry!"

His ice eye met mine. "Before the last weeks of starving at my side you were nearly dead, infection riddled and not able to consume nourishment as you trekked to the southern port. You must try and pace yourself."

My tastebuds watered, eyeing the bite of food on the tip of the fork he restrained. "If I agree to eat slower, will you release me?"

My wrist was freed. The bite of potatoes disappeared almost immediately in my mouth and my fork plunged into another.

"Eulid will have us in top shape before long." He opened the lid to what smelt to be a pork pot roast and stabbed a fork at the tenderized meat. Moaning when it hit his lips.

"If round is a shape, I'll merrily eat my way into a sphere." I patted my belly, savoring the food filling me beyond my hip bones. He grabbed the sour beer in the horn and we clinked glasses across the table. "We survived up till now, congrats."

He winked, his drink paused at his lips. "A delicate balance of your risk taking, my calculated endeavors and Fen's trust in us both. Cheers, blossom. A new adventure awaits."

He cleaned off his apple ale and I did the same with the knuckle of whiskey. We both piled our plates with grub. He took an entire pork rump and rack of lamb and I savory dips, root vegetables and hot garlicky barley soup. There was no time for talking, only eating—which Zander interrupted every five minutes trying to convince me to slow down.

Gods I hoped there were no expectations of highborn ladylike manners among Zander's council, I'm sure they would frown seeing me naked and scarfing everything edible in sight into the hole in my head disregarding crumbs spilling on my bare legs and whiskey on my lips.

I slowed, even considered stopping at one point in the evening, until Zander brought out dessert from the icebox. It was something chocolate.

I reached across the table and plunged my fork into the center of the square pan, scrapping a lopsided bite into the air. Zander intercepted before it reached my mouth. As if he were a thrilled child he exclaimed, "Cold fudge cream cake!" I blinked, watching him lick the sweet brown cream off the corner of his lips. "Why do you look as if you are about to cry?" I didn't protest as I was drawn onto his lap.

"You ate my bite. I was looking forward to it." Ridding the towel, I shifted on his knees and brought the chilled pan in front of us. Readying my fork. "And I'm not about to cry." I hated how defensive my voice sounded. Almost as if I was in fact about to cry and spill tears.

He reached ahead of me and inched the pan away from my eager utensil. "I will cry if you don't let me eat dessert. Additionally, I will stab you with something sharper than a dull four pronged fork. Eulid's ax will do nicely. You are no stranger to having an ax swung your way."

"Damn, you're such a violent delight. Try not to maim my face. It's part of my appeal." He lifted his fingers off the cold fudge.

If he hadn't, I would have cut them off.

"No promises." I put a heavy mound of cake in my mouth and melted into the man behind me as the sugar dissolved on the tip of my tongue and the creamy aftertaste slicked the roof of my mouth.

"That good?" I took another bite. And another. "Stop swirling your tongue around and moaning, I'm becoming envious of the frosting."

Why did he feel compelled to interrupt a good thing? I finally succumbed to his pestering. "How did your dead animals taste? Was it to your liking?"

"Everything is ash on my tongue now that you've ruined me. But my stomach and muscles felt the instant energy, the nourishment seeped into my marrow and rebuilt my mass." Hopefully, not all his brothers were as dramatic as Zander, poor Atticus will never have a world that sees his sons positively with all their needs of coddling and flair drama. His left arm slung across the low of my navel, his right elbow knocked on the table as it held the weight of his head. He watched me eat, mixed emotions floated across his blue eyes like clouds passing in the sky. "I'm optimistic this food will help your nerves and allow you to finally sleep decently."

"I have been sleeping decently. I'm so worn I just shut my eyes and time changes when they open," I said, spinning my fork like the hands of a clock.

"Most nights you are a fretful sleeper. Covered in sweat, swinging at terrors. I have to coax you down from screaming with song or innocuous whispers of reassurance." I met his gaze, feeling both surprised and awful that I was the culprit behind his tired eyes and slacking recovery. Maybe he wasn't the sloppy sound, deep sleeper I thought him to be. I was just a disaster of a sleep partner.

I set the fork aside. "I thought the night terrors ended after hanging the duke, that my subconscious was resting at peace now that I was well on my way to finish my oath to Anna."

He offered a grin, it was more of a smirk, "I'm glad I have helped you so thoroughly that you duped yourself into healing."

"Well, now that I know the truth, I'm sure it will set my progress back."

"It was already set back. To be honest, the fits are getting worse the further we trek away from your Woodlands. I understand it is a lot to ask of you but, are you feeling anything *different*? Anything worth giving a voice to?"

"Anna's blood stopped warming." He took a sip of water and patiently waited for me to clarify. "After I walked over the pleadian salts, it confirmed her blood didn't remain in my system and all these years it had just been my imagination trying to keep her *alive*, keep us together. I wanted her tied to me. It had been *my* passion and *my* red blood fueling me during these trying times. I just wanted it to be hers. And the little hints of lilacs I used to smell, those stopped too." I rubbed my neck and pressed my scabbing spine to Zander's stomach. "There were probably never lilacs to guide me. I was naive." He didn't have to agree for it to be true.

"How does that make you feel?"

He knew. He knew, but he didn't care because he was patient and immortal, he laid claim to me, he was my woven. One of them. I let a breath go by. "Zander, I'm lonely. Or maybe, feeling alone, now that I'm separated–severed–from my roots. A tree that was cleaved in half and hacked into useless chips. I'm incomplete." Broken. A half a person.

The arm around my waist tightened. "I'm proud of you for coming this far. For speaking your truth even when it's uncomfortable and confusing to say out loud. It's natural and perfectly alright to feel forlorn, Wisteria. I want you at my side, now and always. Incomplete, cleaved, hacked into pieces or lonely. I want you." I couldn't look at him with guilt rising. Guilt of needing him to help find food, shelter, travel, information, physical gratification... the list went on. "You are not using me. Not in the least."

Yup, he read me all too easily. I fumbled with our connection. "We are corlimors. You need to heal. That takes time during which I will not be going anywhere. Not ever. Besides, you actually care for me more than you are able to care for yourself. That is sad, but also a small victory for your growth and for my heart."

Without meeting his gaze I wrapped a lazy arm around his neck, inhaling the fresh scents of a shower and the perpetual spice that clung to him. I didn't have to thank him, he already felt my gratitude. Deeply, I imagined.

Going to sleep that night, I was far too self aware of my tendency to wake him. I banished all thoughts of resentfully marrying the Nameless Prince, of Cobar's experimentation he underwent while I plotted, of Pine, Sage and Rodrick in Sanctum trying to ask Duke Roland Verdain for aid. When my blood pulsed in my ears, I clung to it as a distraction and buried myself in the pillow.

According to Zander I managed two nights without an outburst. During those nights I made a point to wedge a little distance between the two of us. Not that I had influence to change Zander's assumption of us being corlimors. "Your guilt smells like the ocean, salty mist spraying and tainting each breath. You and I *mingling* should not evoke guilt."

"It does because you are more invested. My intention is not to tease you or concede to the fact I find you interesting, when this is all I can offer. Company, banter and violence."

"You don't want to get my hopes up because *you care* about my feelings. That is plenty for me. For now." His fingers brushed my hair behind my ear. The sweet gesture earned him a wary look. After breakfast he tended to my back, I let him do that because I was selfish and I needed him. His nose scrunched up in distaste for my wounds all while I was pleased with the thickening rough scabs forming.

The riding pants and string top tunics Eulid had brought me fit well enough. I layered woolen socks before sliding into knee high boots just as I layered the scarfs and cloaks on my shoulders. I was eager to get fresh air, eager to place a little more space between us to allow my own thoughts to form. No better way than watching MaiMai's little colt meandering around the corral.

"Maiden wear looks good on you, Wisteria. Battles among mongrels and the horse clans have ceased, I've shields and hammers you can rummage among and take what suits you." The only weapon I loved was Orion. I loved how confident and assured he made me feel, how natural and intuitive we moved together, how he slept on my mattress and under my pillow. Our reunion would be soon. Keenan would have ensured my blade survived the journey. My fingers fidgeted, my feet were too willing to pull my body into the Ilanthian steps of the sword dance. I gripped the wooden fence.

"I am beyond content with the kindness you've already shown me and I must confess, these fabrics feel like my own skin. I can move freely and certainly fight."

Zander walked behind me. "Well, you can certainly pick a fight."

"I can both pick a fight and beat you into a bloody pulp."

He waved at Eulid who was whistling to the alcove above. "Magnificent, isn't she?"

"Crescent, MaiMai or your mate?" Goddess I almost impaled myself with splinters from my firming grip.

My chin shot in Eulid's direction. "I'm not his mate. I belong to myself."

"Alright, if you say as much," he replied, distracted with a bird aimed to perch on his extended arm. Its claws were sharp, but nothing compared to Stormclaw's.

"I was referring to Wisteria. Although, all are magnificent in their own rights, none as exquisitely well rounded as my 'not-mate' of course." I elbowed his ribs. He let out a low lurch for me to hear. "I have not called you any of the names you banned nor are we in the Veil or in the presence of my brothers, so I'm technically safe. Love."

"You're not safe from me, princess." I muttered walking around the corral, following the young colt with a brown diamond shape patchworked onto his dusty neck. It's skinny legs steady enough to no longer wobble.

Zander stepped over the corral as if it were no higher than a hedge of berries. Opposite of the manure he sat with his wing tips scattered with straw and dirt. Clicking his tongue, he beckoned the colt, MaiMai pushed her muzzle into the incubus' neck. Familiar friends. "When you're all healed up, I expect a proper fight," he said to me.

"Sure thing. I'm sure your dainty body can withstand my blows better than your ego can." I whispered and joined him on the inside of the fence. I took the apple slices from my pocket and lured the little mount towards the seated giant. The colt let me stroke the short mane on its neck before he was stolen by two swinging rods of steel which were Zander's arms wrapping around its neck and tailbone preventing it from bucking backwards. The whites of its eyes were startled and frightful.

Feeling trapped by the giant's embrace, it whined and thrashed against the unyielding form. MaiMai didn't storm protectively, she didn't fear for her babe's safety. Zander stopped his clicking to *shush* loudly and rhythmically, rocking slightly as he did. He stroked the colt's side body until the panic left him an immobile bundle of nerves. Zander kissed and rubbed his muzzle, patting the soft spots behind its jaw for over a half hour. The colt became calm and pliable. The new horse looked like a puppy in the lap of its master, the size proportions were accurate too.

Eulid sent a red tailed hawk east and rounded to my side. A toothpick rattled in his mouth. "When he first started coming here, my great-grandfather said it took days for the horses to trust him or even look at him. He didn't know how to diminish the presence that came with being an incubus or dim the shine of his magic that is off putting to most beings with two or four legs. It took him years to reacclimate to humans without them suspecting anything amiss or magical. After a few hooves to the skull and some long nights, he figured it out. Now, look at him. He is happier than a pig rolling in his own shit."

I quietly chuckled. "Happier than a child coming home to his mother's hearth." Zander's eyes connected with mine from behind the ears of the cult, turning up and wrinkling on the corners. "Does the colt have a name?"

"We wait a full turn of the moon before deciding. He has to come into his own before we can confine him to labels, even a name is too restrictive for a new soul," he stated. I noticed a few people carrying on with their daily comings and goings, in and out of the huts with different cuts of dried meats, leather workers making the most of the piles of pellets and a bird house the size of a windmill being washed from the inside out. "He will be here for a while, would you like a tour."

We left Zander to his methods and walked around Waning Star. I spent the most time at the blacksmith's forge, watching the way they worked the iron, hammering it into the most interesting shapes of weapons and tools I'd seen since the merchant docks. I imagined myself in combat against cleavers and pick axes. The wielder would need to have strength to strike with precision. I'd win with agility, dodging with Montuse.

I was heating up leftovers on the stove when Zander walked in the front door. He folded me into his arms, rocking with me as if I was an infant mammal needing to earn his affections. "You smell like the stables."

"You smell like the smithy, thankfully less like the ocean. I hope you are done experimenting putting distance between us." His knees bent, allowing him to drop into the sensitive crook of my neck. A warm tongue met my flesh just behind my ear. For a moment I let myself be his flower and him my honey. The spoon in my hand went limp. "Ambrosia."

"My body is a traitor."

He gave a gentle squeeze and left to change his shirt. "It is wise. But I don't force wisdom."

"Just like you forced the colt into trusting you by smothering it with forceful affection and promising coos?"

His head popped out the door frame to the bedroom. "Says the girl who bribed it with apples." There was no defense to rebut. "Besides, my methods worked for you, didn't it?" I chucked the spoon at him. He was in fact not changing shirts, just taking his dirty one off. "I see we are still in the 'smothering with affection until you trust me' phase. So be it. I'll add bribery." He opened the ice box and began to spatter himself with chocolate cream from the chilled cake pan. "If taking away your desserts makes you cry, giving it to you should make you come."

My mouth watered. "That's a theory."

"Would you like to test it?"

Best hypothesis I'd ever tested. And retested, in the pursuit of knowledge.

Chapter Nine

We stayed in Waning Star until the colt got his name, Astero. We stayed until I had added five solid pounds of meat to my bones and Zander could disappear his wings and his bottom fangs. Most importantly we stayed until Zander and I reestablished the fact I couldn't keep myself from him, but could not give myself to him either. Not in entirety. We stayed until there was comfort among the discomfort of our woven relationship, until I understood despite my feelings, he would go nowhere nor with anyone else.

Eulid let me take the clothes and gave an unprompted warning that the woolen socks were too warm for the climate in the cradle of north coast Thalren. That pearl of a city known as Veona. Our destination. "I'll need them for when I come back to visit or when I cross over to return to my home," I ensured. He slipped a bracelet with dried hawthorn berries around my left wrist.

"Prevents fae glamour from taking root. Don't take it off. Don't let the kelpies beckon you to their seelie side of the wood. Don't piss in rivers or accept drinks from too friendly of sprites. And don't let nymphs swindle you." Eulid said, tapping his temple—the softest way into the mind. The once retired Overlord examined the berries on my wrist and gave a nod of appreciation. The two men embraced, the older looking one hugged his uncle and set off Zander with a headbutt that made my brain concuss just witnessing.

The days leading up to our entrance into Veona we discussed quite thoroughly. He wanted to avoid any feelings of being caught off guard when we fluxed directly into his home on the outskirts of the city, or alarmed when we'd be called back to Horn's Keep, the interim Overlord's estate in west Veona at some point. I made it very clear I would not be spoken for and that I didn't wish to be sheltered from his burdens or have special arrangements made. He agreed and went on to detail the use of his magic. He did use his magic often, in the form of room protection, soundproofing, obscuras and fluxing. He had to use it consistently to prevent it from building up in a destructive manner. Aside from that he swore he only used his passive incubus gifts of physical attributes, he never charms or sways the crowds. As their leader it would be immoral of him to influence opinions. And it would make him a naughty woven to Fen or I to use either ability.

Zander's home off of Clemente Avenue was a sprawling bungalow made of the same white travertine stone as the entire street. Cozy homes with floral arrangements on each porch resting atop the gentle slope caught the rising sun and reflected warmth onto us. It hardly seemed winter here. It was fanciful.

There was such beauty and abundance no one would know there was an enemy near. I turned my face towards the sunshine as the dreamer holding my hand greeted two locals passing by. There was no bowing, no formal titles and no political dancing. A mere casual, well-received 'Hi, good morning'. One seemed what I once considered normal in appearance, the other had a bull's tail whipping behind him and notably pointed ears. Fae. I returned their wave and matched Zander's long strides up to his front patio which overlooked a large portion of the city from the raised ground.

Veona was a glimmering masterpiece that appeared to be carved of white crystal quartz on the downward slope of a valley. The roads were not intersecting straight perpendicular lines, but circles rippling outwards. To the north a reflective barricade extended into the blue sky, caving inward over the city, disappearing in the rays of sun. It appeared more of a mirage than a true barrier into the beyond. The fire fields were not visible, but the stone ramparts were distinguishable as massive parapets on the furthest side of the city. I couldn't see any other end to Veona, it was a labyrinth of plotted asymmetry sprawling for leagues. "It's not as complicated as it looks. Each ring houses distinct districts and the thicker paved roads winding between them keep traffic moving and prevent claustrophobia."

My feet didn't budge when a masculine hand fell on my shoulder and attempted to urge me on. I could not move after what my eyes stumbled across. A stark black crevasse, gouging straight through the largest ring on the far side. The scar of Zander's past, a bleak mark on an otherwise pristine landscape. "It adds character," I stated softly, sensing his now wingless form standing at my right, catching his eyes on the same mark as mine. He didn't reply. I touched the knuckles of the hand that rested on my shoulder. "Black and white are your colors after all, stallion."

There were colors flying down our bond I hadn't seen before. They were a warning of all the complexities to come, of all of Zander's emotions and thoughts arising from being back in his home city. Let's hope I'd not go color blind.

The inside of his bungalow reminded me of an observatory, high ceilings and skylight windows scattered around the rooftop. At night the ceiling would be mostly stars, an ode to his love to the sky. The sunlight reflected off the white stone countertops, pale wooden flooring extending the length of his home. The natural lighting in the home was ample. During daytime hours there would be no need for the indigo sea glass light fixtures to be turned on.

Leather pleated chairs for wing accommodations were placed next to a plush navy blue couch with simple worn taupe pillows tossed onto the corner sectional looking all too inviting. A cobalt rug lay as a doormat. Zander kicked his boots off and threw his scarf on top of them, soiling it in the mud from our month's trek through Hell. Literal Hell.

"Make yourself at home." He moved ahead of me and went straight into the kitchen to fill up a coffee filter with fresh grounds. He took a deep whiff of the powdered beans. I swore his eyes rolled back into his skull. "No place in Kinlyra can make coffee as bold as Havana without bitterness. It will change your life," he promised, setting a kettle on his gas stove. From the fridge he began to remove containers of fresh fruit and fill glass cups with juice, he set both on the stone counter nearest me.

From my vantage point next to the front door I dawdled to better observe the details of his home. Framed parchments were suspended on the wall next to shields and tattered remains of a family crest. A horse outline was vaguely distinguishable on the latter.

I removed my boots and walked down the hallway behind his couch to inspect the names on the crest. A family heirloom from his mother's side. It stopped at Zander's name. "I took it with me at fourteen when I left Waning Star for the first time when I followed Atticus's *pull* into the mountains." He pointed to the splintering round shield, painted partway blue with moon phases embossed on it. "That was her shield."

He walked ahead of me, gesturing to her belt buckle and explaining the meaning behind the subsequent glass protected piece of poetry. Oyokos had written the poem in the ancient language about how and why the Dreamer Realm came to be. *Dreamer Nation* was the literal translation, but the diverse beings here were once looked upon as so peculiar and unique. So much so that most humored, and many embraced, that they hailed from another dimension with their whimsical ways.

There was no door to his bedroom. The wall just gave way to a massive spherical room with a dome window erected in the middle of the space right above a bed whose detailing matched the rest of his home of sky and ocean blues. There were simple accents here and there in the form of a wide bookshelf and an extra lamp on his work table. A work table covered in a disgusting amount of parcels, unopened mail and half written letters with fading ink from a dried ink bottle. I ran my fingers across the surface, tapping patterns in the dust as I skimmed along. Two years. More. He'd been gone for two and a half years.

"The bath house is across the hall, it has its own section in my home because of how fond I am of it. You will be getting an intimate and thorough tour hopefully soon." He grinned. "The healers are waiting for me to open my front door. Mauve was the one that treated my wings after Fen sunk his claws into them. She and Fendora are the only two women who've been in my private home." That statement was disbelieving and comforting. He carried on after tasting the possible influx of my jealousy. "I know you said you are comfortable in maiden wear, but I've sent for a seamstress to have you measured should you require anything else, or *desire*, anything else."

My hands tucked to my side. Woodlanders didn't wear tailor made clothes. "That's not necessary. We talked about special arrangements being made. I don't like it."

He met my gaze before abiding. "As you wish." Zander stepped closer until the tips of our toes touched. I was pulled up onto my tiptoes while his inhale drew my mouth to his. The softness of his lips was lost in the need surging behind them. "They will tend to you in here. My property is spelled for privacy. No one can see or hear or magic their way into these walls even with potions or violence. The few who were stupid enough to have tried were interrogated and exiled. The healers to see you are Mauve and Mikleah. They have physician training, alchemy practice and have seen extensive injuries on battlefields and I've had the privilege of them tending to me in my adolescence. I trust them. They will speak of your injuries to no one." The factuality in his tone was lethal. Regretfully, he set my weight fully back on my feet and broke away.

Mauve and Mikleah were a mother and daughter duo who looked more like a set of twins with their short chestnut hair and nimble synchronized movements. Mauve greeted Zander with a hug and a pinch on the high of his dimpled cheek. "Had you called upon anyone else I would have had your neck, boy." With the grin plastered on his face, he did appear boyish.

"Precisely why I didn't dare do such a thing. I have someone important for you to tend to."

I elbowed my way into view. "I am Wisteria Woodlander. Thank you in advance for seeing to me. I hope to learn much about your healing practices here in the Veil." They shook my extended hand and returned a welcoming raise of a brow. It was awkward. Interaction with others after a month of seclusion.

"Wisteria was taught by an Ilanthian physician and her parents who were Numaalian crafters. She is skilled. Remarkably skilled." Zander took my hand and led us down the hallway. He turned down the covers of his bed, which could easily fit a family of five, and asked that I step within reach. "May I?"

"No, need." I pulled my tunic over my head, mindful of the tender spots, and unraveled the strips around me. I eyed the lack of frank blood on them. "You know, at this point there is not much more healing left that time, a decent diet and anesthetic salve couldn't see too. If you have other patients or anything else to do with your time—" A low growl cut me off. Zander was already sprawled and waiting for me on the bed. Glaring. "Oh, stop your grumbling. I've already tolerated the hardest part of the process just fine."

Mauve pointed to my trousers, Mikleah dropped her chin to her chest to dodge Zander's stare that pierced through me. Bloody obsessive creature. "This is nonnegotiable, my flower. Did you need assistance getting those pants off?" His sharp tone didn't go over well. I yanked at the drawstrings of my pants and shimmied out of them. I threw them over his head before I crawled next to him in bed. A bed I had to practically jump into to reach the surface of. He brought the fine threaded sheet up to shield my bare legs as I sorted myself.

The healer tapped the pillow assessing my back with her eyes. She showed no distress, horror or pity when my injuries came into view. I sunk into the downy goodness while Zander's fretful energy fussed with my hair, braiding it in a crown around my head. Elousie would have added flowers were she here. "Were there any signs of infection?"

"Yes. I took penicillin, which didn't stop the infection. I got worse. Fevers and blisters broke out, Fennick took those away. He and my friend Brock drained the abscess, debrided what they could and cut off the dead flesh. We only had one dose of arnica. I survived off poppy milk and ice baths."

My pillow dipped as Zander laid his head down, his body formed to mine which I noted happened much easier now that his wings weren't interfering with his posturing.

His scent enveloped me, a wholesome distraction from the eyes on my bare body.

An affirmative hum came from behind me. "You'll feel my touch now." I nodded. She didn't touch me until Zander gave a verbal blessing. A grunt. He gave a grunt of permission. His eyes didn't stray from the hands on my back. He was more engrossed than Crescent, the hawk, eyeing his meal. Mauve inspected the length of each scar and the integrity of each scab. "I don't know any being that can summon new flesh, your scars will remain. They are deep and too aged for reversal."

"I expected as much." There was shuffling and the sloshing of water that sufficed as background noise in the room. Zander filled my head. *It adds character.* A lame smile escaped. I opened my eyes to see him intently watching the two women in the room, his brow was fixed on the side table.

Meticulously eyeing each one of Mikleah's hand movements of opening tinctures and jars as if she would have been so calculated to taint one. I heard tin lids behind me unscrew and be set aside. "I smell lemon. What is your poultice infused with?"

"Lemon, lime and gotu kola. We will massage while instructing Zander on how to loosen your connective tissue without damaging the few open areas along the ravens' heads. You'll need to soften it nightly for at least a week to get your full range of flexibility back. Any pain that you do have we can rid with wiggenpeel. It's an elvish favorite that doesn't have the negative side effects as poppy. You'll be on your feet, fighting and functional, by tomorrow morning and every day after."

I arched my back to twist the healers into view. "Wiggenpeel?"

Mauve held up a large green leaf that held the same consistency as an aloe plant's innards. "It's classified as a fruit, but I don't recommend eating it unless you want to spend your evenings on the toilet." She pointed to the scattered black seeds suspended in the goo. "It is most potent in the ground form. We arrived with a vial to dust your back with the powder before we set the skins on." She put the long leaves of wiggenpeel on the foot of the bed and went to work breaking apart tough scar tissue under Zander's studious gaze. It felt like a brutal massage, difficult to find enjoyable, but essential.

Zander's eyes were engrossed, engaged, yet his left hand caressed the round of my ass and settled under the sheets at the base of my spine. I flinched once, when I felt like my skin was being torn open again around a particularly tender spot on my side body under my arm. Zander requested a tonic of turmeric and pepper. I drank it.

The wiggenpeel worked like *literal* magic. My astonishment must have shown in my face. Mauve winked. "It's an elvish favorite for a reason. Only grows in a very specific climate. There is only one known grove of it in Kinlyra that the elves tend to and ship abroad. Turig. A tropical low valley in south Ilanthia." Yet another place I hadn't heard of.

You swear you are comfortable now? Nothing hurts?

Your overbearingness is a bit cumbersome and painful to be around, but I doubt elvish fruit goo helps that.

Humor sparked in his fingers, he feathered them over my flesh.

"Leave a month's worth of supplies here as well as whatever you've witnessed before you see yourselves out. My dear healers, I'm grateful." By some act of a God, Zander managed to sound both appreciative and dismissive at the same time.

He sounded like a true Overlord, a powerful, yet humbled one. The maternal figure was the last to leave his room.

"You sent letters. There is no need to hide away, the realm knows you are back with a human lover and we are excited to meet the young lass. The Keep has made preparations."

Covers were pulled around us. The cord in my left hand tightened, clutched with greed. "I'm aware. I'm selfish and don't intend to share her yet."

She gave the slightest hinge at her waist. A reserved, reverent bow. "Welcome home, my Lord." Tension left him as he sent her away with a languid grin.

Chapter Ten

Through the glass ceiling above Zander's bed, I watched two winged males fly about in the morning glow, swooping close enough to the magic barrier to intentionally aggravate the homeowner with their enormous sets of leathery wings. Zander slept with covers half drawn over his naked body, opening his eyes long enough to scowl when they tossed pebbles at his barrier only to watch them disintegrate into puffs of smoke.

I stretched my arms overhead, relishing that I was physically laying on my back without sharp pain blinding me nor ruining the sheets beneath with blood. For the first time in two moons my body flexed with the absence of throbbing and agony. I didn't recall any nightmares plaguing me, hopefully Zander slept as well as I had. His leg swung over my hips, locking me under him. "Your brothers are here. I do wonder who volunteered to escort you back to daddy." A smirk graced the lower half of my face.

A thumb and index finger pinched my chin and steered my face towards his. Green envy clouded his mental door. His smile, white and wide, sprouted fangs. Undulled fangs.

His fingers left my chin to explore the bare flesh of my neck and brush my hair aside. "It's time to investigate this fantasy of yours that involves my pointed teeth and the soft erogenous flesh *here*." He stopped his hand over my left carotid, the one above my heart.

My eyes glanced towards the ceiling, towards the cause of his possessive behavior frolicking above us. "You just want to mark me since we are going to the Keep for brunch and a shit ton of meet and greets."

The erection between his legs pressed on my stomach. Inadvertently, my hips shifted up. "Yes, but I happen to know just how much the thrill of having your artery punctured excites you." He took a deep inhale and rolled on top of me, blocking his kin from sight. "I won't drink your blood, I will deposit a protective toxin into your bloodstream." Lifting my hips off the mattress, I rolled my body against his excitement.

The shutter that ran through him prompted me to do it again. "You can deposit your toxin in my bloodstream right after you deposit cum inside me," I said through a tensing jaw line. His hand left my face and glided along the wetness of my thighs.

"Gods, you are insatiable. Always ripe and ready," his whisper was harsh, his mouth was fast. He descended on me, luring my tongue out to mingle with playing nips of his teeth. I bit back. "Not yet. Oh no, not until I will it." I glowered, resorting to clenching him between my knees and forcing him on his back. He admired the view of me on top, I swore he uttered prayers between the last exhales. Rocking on his cock just accentuated that I held the power of the moment. That this was my choice because I offered it to him in a deal, one willingly made and accepted.

The room darkened with violet magic, removing any notion of his brothers flying about and I felt my way around a rock hard body that was beginning to feel familiar and comforting in my grasp. I held his favorite piece in my hand and brought it into my open mouth and awaiting tongue piercings. His abs tightened as he watched me torture him in the dark of his own room, his chest heaved the deeper I took him into my throat and into the sides of my mouth, tasting his precum as I sucked.

And when I spread my legs and sat on him, immaculate filthy vocabulary spewed from his mouth encouraging me to ride him harder each time I came down on him. "I love when you are vilely loquacious," I huffed into the magic above me. The clouds of essence swirled and caressed my body in reply.

Two strong hands groped my thighs and came together where my need was the strongest. My piercing was fondled while I fucked him, succumbing to a climax seconds later, riding out the waves of pleasure on his shifting hips. Hips that left the bed with me still inside him. "What are you—" My back was pressed against the white stone wall, not painful in the slightest. He grabbed a fistful of my hair tugged my head to the side all while fucking me ruthlessly.

The first brush of pin pricks brought a squeaky yelp from my throat. I flushed with heat, I pushed his chest away from mine. "Having second thoughts?" His honeyed voice dripped over my ear. His fangs flirted with my flesh causing me to come undone and my thigh tremble.

Stutters came from my voicebox. "Will it hurt?" His thick lips brushed mine while he consciously slowed his thrusting hips. "That was a dumb question," I surrendered stupidly.

The grip on my hair tightened. My excitement coated his cock, I knew he smelt my needs reviving. "I think you are going to be pleasantly surprised, my fuckable flower."

He knocked the air from my lungs. Unable to form words I syphered. *How so?*

Experiencing it is much more preferable. So I've been told. He locked eyes with mine, the tip of his pink tongue was peeking out between a cage of four elongated fangs. His jaw could snap my arm in half, easily. I had seen, *heard,* Zander rip the spines of over sixty wraiths out from the bodies and softly hold my hand moments later. He was capable of control.

And too often too much control. Nikki too for that matter.

He tasted trust and began to slide himself in and out of me, jostling me next to his bookshelf, which quivered as if the hinges were threatening to become unbolted. Regardless, my left hand steadied myself on the shelf because it was the only stationary thing within reach. My cries of building pleasure reverberated back to me sending Zander to thrust wildly. The rough grip in my hair anchored me to him and when I was close to my second scream of salvation he wrapped his mouth below the crook where my neck melded with my shoulder. And bit.

The shock of the sharp pricks sinking into my flesh was short lived as was the whimper of disbelief that escaped my parted, panting lips when the warmth of blood trickled down my neck. Heat built behind his bite that flooded straight into my veins and pooled where we were connected. I felt a fever coming on. "It's too much!"

A blistering wave of need rattled my senses. "Zander, let me come," I begged for a release from this primal energy set out to destroy me. More firmly he clamped his mouth around me with a growling territorial claim as I lost myself to his cock releasing inside me. I fell against him, our breath synced and ragged.

We stayed as we were, him inside me and my grip on the bookshelf, while Zander lapped up the beads of blood trickling over my heart until the puncture wounds began to clot off. He carried me across the hall and down a marbled corridor.

When he opened the door steam hissed and we were assaulted by thick, hot clouds of his bath house. He walked forward on the marble, my thighs pinching his sides. The sound of displaced water came from beneath us and soon I was up to my waist in bubbling bath water. I released my hold on his biceps and dropped into the water, the warmth of the bath matching the heat of the venom slow to burn out of my body. Zander pulled out of me and dove beneath the surface leaving me kicking to find the bottom of the pool.

"Swimming lessons start this week. Time for you to get acclimated with the water and your swim instructor." He sounded pleased with himself, shaking his hair loose and relaxing on the parameter some fifteen feet away. "It's much easier to practice swimming when the ocean isn't destined to swallow you and your uncoordinated slender legs." Not in the mood to make a fool of myself, I felt my way to the steps to wash and rinse my hair in the shallow end knowing fully that I would be teased.

My touch found the sensitive spot on my lower neck, around the clavicle. Where there once was pleasure now was a dull ache. "Nikki let's you put *that* venom in his body?"

"It's a necessity. Once you've fallen unwillingly under charm, you take precautions." The dread was thick in his tone. My hands started to tremble. A different sort of heat broke through my body. One I was familiar with. Rage.

"Fennick will be honored to know you care so deeply about him." There was no sarcasm in his statement.

My throat constricted. "Which one of your brother's—"

"Clavey. Even centuries ago before his mortal pixie husband entered the scene, he was always known to be a lush doxy type, never held or wanted to hold any responsibility. He gets off on the taunt and tease of it all, breaking people's moral codes and leaving them shattered in the morning."

"Fuck him."

"You can tell him yourself. He has been pounding on the damn door for the last ten minutes."

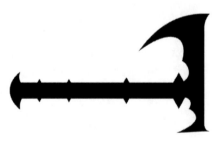

Clavey had never swung a weapon in his lifetime and it showed. He was thinner than Zander and his maroon lace collared shirt had amplified his willowy stature. Clavey had curly chestnut hair, a darker shade then mine decorated with spatters of gold embossment highlighting his slightly feminine facial features. His wings were narrow, weathered brown and his horns reminded me of a rams, curling tightly above his ears. He was shorter than both Zander and Percy, who was dressed in casual slacks and a laundered white tunic. Percy's horns twisted like a gazelle's, coming no higher than a few inches above his copper hair. His scars, beard and flat affect made it clear he gave very few fucks. He was the first to say something when Zander threw open the door between us.

"Took you long enough, shithead." Percy leaned against a pillar of the overhang. His wings pinned closed to his spine. "I see you've brought along your distraction. How fortunate for us," his displeasure was palpable.

A low, seductive voice chimed in. His tone was pure lust and guttural yearning. A skilled lurest. "Fortunate indeed." Clavey entered the scene, reaching for my hand with his painted nails, far more manicured than mine. "Hello." He flexed his hand requesting mine. Absolutely not from this criminal.

I pulled away and offered him my middle finger. And another. "The second one is for Fennick."

"Careful, brothers. She holds her own and I will not be responsible if either of you find yourself castrated," Zander stepped out onto the patio next to me while his kin combed over my human form draped in flannel and riding wear. The door closed behind us. The three of them slapped each other on their chin, a rough affectionate smack that left a mark on Clavey's smooth cheek. A hit like that would dislocate my head and spin it six times around. Devious eyes stumbled upon me. I looked to his open arms, to his second extended greeting. An embrace it seemed. I cringed and opted to stand alone.

"Greet me like that and I'll break your face." I crossed my arms over my chest, locking with Clavey's almond shaped hazel eyes brushed with shimmering makeup. They lit up, viewing me as a challenge. He was enthralled with my brashness, but I was done hiding. "Actually, why don't you try. I think rearranging your face would be a significant improvement, your husband will thank me when I send you home with sutures."

"You're delightful."

"I am delightful. My name is Wisteria." His eyes were no longer fixed on mine, but under my long braid of hair. The bite mark, I tried to make less noticeable under a collar and thicket of hair. I didn't need a mirror to know Zander had done a number on me, there would be bruises up and down the left side of my neck, the top portion of my breast too if the ache in my flesh was correct about the expansive contusion. Percy's glazed eyes hitched on the mark before seeking Zander's. He stilled as if he was seeing a ghost.

"Wisteria, it seems my brother has already taken the opportunity for fun out of my reach. His scent is permeating what I am sure would have been a delicious aroma." Zander was proudly standing next to me, he and Percy dueling with their eyes, fighting about something unsaid. Likely a pissing contest. "Wyatt will be offended by those hawthorne berries on your wrist," Clavey continued. He pointed to my bracelet.

"If Zander has taught me anything it's that males have sensitive egos. I will not be tiptoeing around them nor do I care if they get damaged in my presence. If a few berries offend his delicate disposition I recommend he not look at them." I pursed my lips and looked through them to the buckets of daffodils and green onions blooming on the street corner.

"Holy shit, I thought you were bringing home a tempered human sister for us to dote over. Nope, the Keep is blessed with another headstrong contender. I don't know if Atticus will be proud or worried at your choice of marking her. Either way. It is done and I want her on my Pitfall team." Percy lowered his head, relinquishing the win to Zander for their silent argument.

"I don't care what he thinks of our relationship." Zander kissed my knuckles. A zing of coveting twisted around my left arm and buried into my heart. "Now, someone tell me where the hell Kailynder is and why he hasn't been pacing anxiously outside my home, or I'll summon Warroh to recite the creation story *from the beginning.*"

Percy and Clavey looked as if they were about to strangle Zander for suggesting such a ghastly punishment, but it was Clavey who informed him, "He's been obsessing about diversion tactics and has gone south, prompting the reapers to pick up arms—or scythes as it be."

All the tension I worked hard to ease in Zander was built up and multiplied tenfold. "The idiot."

"He thinks placing a visible army in the north and attacking from the north is unlikely. He believes it is a distraction technique from the spawn, that they will strike elsewhere," Clavey's words rolled off his tongue which he wet his lips with as he spoke.

Percy interjected, "It's not a farfetched concept. Only fools are taken by surprise and you know Kai—he hates spontaneity. Hates surprises." I almost snorted. Well, then he will surely hate me. "He is finishing his rounds on the reapers and soil nymphs, checking their status to effectively whirl a scythe. Without your presence, he has almost lost his damn mind."

"He never had one to lose. He is a five thousand year old anxious child who constantly needs supervision," Clavey reminded Percy, not bothered to look up from picking the dirt out from under his nails. "He considered challenging Atticus with a public vote to instate him as Overlord if you didn't turn up soon."

Zander's cocky smile shone in the sun. "I would pay to see that."

"We talked him down, but Judeth is still rallying supporters. Anyway, the north is holding, but I can't say for how much longer." Percy stretched his muscular neck. "The walls are thick, blades sharp and the fires hot. We are as ready as we can be."

"I expect nothing less of the engineers that constructed the ramparts or the elementals tending the Elm, but I want to see the runegate." As Zander spoke, dull grey bolts of worry prickled over my hands and up my forearm. He needed to see this runegate, and soon. I stepped ahead of him and began to walk off the porch onto Clemente Avenue, my feet taking me north against a light breeze. The air smelt of spring, of hope. Their conversation continued.

"Veona is excited for your return and will shower you both with proper festivities after the pressing matters at the Keep are discussed. She can get a tour of the realm then if we've time. You know, if she can survive family brunch," Percy pressed.

Boots hit the cobble stone behind me and a hand wrapped around mine some seconds later. "Get Kai to stop pestering the reapers, get Warroh out of the damn temples and tell father to have scribes at hand when I get to the Keep, which I will go to after we inspect the runegate." He steadily gave his commands in a tone I guess his brothers found lordly because they agreed. I couldn't help but chuckle. "What do you find funny, my flower?"

"That people actually take you seriously." His toothy grin knocked into my mouth in a clumsy kiss. I kissed back enough to appease the horned beast hunched over before my fingers examined my own teeth to ensure he didn't chip any of them. I swatted at him once I confirmed no real damage had been done. "Clumsy."

One swoosh and Clavey flew due west. Percy lingered to make a dry choking sound aimed towards our affections and hit the sky when Zander motioned to a two-handed ax on his left hip, a beautiful one I hadn't seen before our arrival. The ax was engraved with simple embellishment that reminding me of the patterns on his mother's shield. He cursed the wind that carried his brothers and declared we'd be taking the scenic route all within the same breath.

The entirety of Veona was breathtaking. I would have been just as content strolling around the white stone circles as I was flying above them. I couldn't help but to linger my gaze on the black wound cutting through the city. I fixed myself tighter to my woven. My Lord of Darkness. *How many live here?*

Just over a million. Another half million on top of that call the Veil home. We are a growing nation. We'd grow more were it not for the constraints of Thalren. I scanned the horizon, organizing a map of the city in my head.

I pointed to the obvious training grounds. There were another half dozen of them across the city, each equipped to strengthen the talents of a unit's forte. I saw folks like me running drills. *I would like to join them tonight if they are conditioning late.*

Dagressa will be happy to have you sprinting about. She never stops. No invitation needed. A tender touch turned my chin further west. Towards a circle of high domed temples and just beyond that, an altar. *The Temple of Horns. When Oyokos created Thalren, his magic filled him so much that his form was said to have blocked out the sun for all of Kinlyra. Those were his horns that sat atop his head. Now, they are revered and enchanted. They are a portal that takes one directly to Akelis.* My fingers wrapped around the silky texture of his ponytail. *Don't fret. You've no need to march up to the White Tower today. I suspect there is a reply waiting for us in the Keep from Maruc or Athromancia. If not Fen.*

Good. I managed to send while my internal thoughts disintegrated at the sight of red and gold flames simmering for leagues around a burning tree, the Eternal Elm. Just beyond that majestic sight, perpetual inky blackness licked the hardly visible barrier. *Can we get closer?* Over the stone and steel wall we flew, the eyes that spotted us clung to Zander's back. He no longer felt sturdy and solid, but translucent. I kept my sights on our destination and willed people to not invest in their Overlord's return or the human he brought back. The distraction as Percy called me.

We lost altitude and gained warmth from the fire fields beneath us as we dropped into the grass patch that wasn't ablaze. There were moving pyres of high flames gliding about the fields. Pyres with legs. On closer inspection, they were foxes in a partial or full creature form bursting contently with flame. Magic was amazing.

Zander moved towards the large black rock and I towards the monsters swarming on the other side of the glossy barrier. Amid the tangle of formless terror cognizant eyes appeared. The soulless *thing* became *more*. Switching forms rapidly under my watch. An octopus, a spider, a dismembered man. I moved closer when the evil had chosen a form it thought suitable. A raven with two heads. It pointed at my heart.

B.B. Aspen

A wave of distress stung my nerves.

My blood plummeted to my feet and failed to circulate elsewhere. "Wisteria?" A yank on my hand stopped me from moving closer to that haunting image. Zander looked from me to the endless spawn floating about and back again, but he did not see what I had for the mutated bird had morphed and merged with its brethren, clawing and scraping on the runegate. Searching for a way in.

These things were unquestionably going to bring down this barrier. Somehow, their persistent nature would find a crack and slither in by the thousands. Hundreds of thousands.

The questions remaining were 'when' and 'why'.

My name was called. There were no words for what I had seen. It felt as if I saw my own death in that image. "Just curious. I was wondering if they recognize me in the same manner the wraiths did." There was dried blood on my neck after all. I let him guide me over to the stone engraved with foreign markings—runes. The written language of the ancient tongue. Spells it seemed. The magic that held them was heavy and ageless. Standing too near unnerved me. Like my body was fighting itself on a cellular level, slowly tearing me apart. The tension it sparked under my skin felt almost as intense as the night the Weaver trapped me with my wovens in a storage shed.

He tightened his hand on mine. "They may. But if your wonderment ever leads you close to danger, you take one of us with you." There was no need to clarify *us*. I was already missing my shadow more than I cared to admit, I didn't want to be reminded of his absence by his mentioning. Being atop his home *without* him already felt so wrong. Did my longing for Nikki have a smell or taste to Zander? Could he distinguish between my affections for the pair of them, or was it ambrosia and sweetwater all the time?

"Tell me about the runegate. It feels more of a relic with... archaic magic. Is it intact?"

Zander rubbed his patchy white eyebrow and began running his hands across the surface facing us, muttering the dead language as he did. On the opposite side of Zander a pile of spawn launched themselves at the stone. Clawing and biting and striking. From where I stood I felt the aftershocks.

They were physical enough to make contact with stone and shake the barrier with enough force to send ripples across it. "It's ancient magic above the comprehension of scholars and Gods. It's made of Ether itself as the Eternals are. The west and east rune stones are cut from the same slab of obsidian, pried out of the depths of the Opal Lake at the very first light of our world's creation. As old as our land itself, they hold the beyond at bay and allow reapers to monitor the souls' destination. These spawn clearly desire for it to break." He leaned against the stone, crossing his ankles and looking dutifully over his realm. "By no small act of grace, does the gate remain intact."

"Can Athromancia and Maruc dig up more rune stones from the lake? I volunteer to help them, since I'll be running errands in that vicinity," I added chipperly, choking on an uncomfortable smile.

He replied with a silent shake of his head. I brushed the bottom of my boot along the ankle high grass and let my Numaalian born brain absorb the outstanding feats of this nation. I felt small. But not in a way that was typically off putting, comparative or diminishing. No, I felt small in the sense of wonder. I exhaled and let myself be astonished by the inexplicable and unimaginable. By the profound insanity and impossibility of what was and is Kinlyra with all her complexities.

The obsidian stone seemed to come alive the longer I stared at it. It made me uneasy. "You're moving backwards. Don't get burned, my bitten beauty." I glared at the pet name. He opened his mouth again but my words filled the space.

"The stone. The current within it."

He walked to my side and lowered his neck within reach for me to tie my arms around. *It reminds you of our auras. You were miserable with that* current *then as you are now. Weaver is that primal source of Ether. She put these stones in that lake of gems, magic and clay.*

She gets her jollies out of making me want to shed my skin.

Nobody bowed, but everybody greeted him with either a wave, a nod or cheerful grin when we strode up the front archway. Gorgeously dressed males and females of all races batted their eyelashes at him, not that he took notice in their direction. When his back was to them, their eyes darted towards me. Not all were friendly glances. I'd bet these were once the volunteers to his harem glaring at the reason for their dismissal. Off to a good start. Where was Brock to distract me when I needed him?

Zander slowed his pace to match mine for it took twice as much effort to get up the stairs. The steps were constructed for giants and were an unkind reminder that I was gravely out of shape compared to where my physical capabilities were before I moseyed into Fort Fell.

The theme of white stones continued into the massive structure locals called Horn's Keep, which hardly felt like an enclosure or liveable home due to the massive open balconies and widely spaced stone pillars. Perfect for the comings and goings of winged beings. My eyes drank in the sculptures and artworks as eagerly as they did the details of each being we passed.

Pixies with their iridescent wings zoomed about chasing each other around a semi secluded chamber filled with rows of empty chairs. A lanky, pointy eared elvish archer shook his head as the pixies tumbled into a podium. He retreated into the deep set brown hood and fell in step next to us. I admired the longbow slung across his back and the satchel of rosemary laced on his boot. "Is your bow crafted of hickory?" His sharp angular face tilted down at me. A short nod. "It's beautiful."

The thinness of his lips softened when he opened them. "I'm Alethim. The Veil's Left Wing. My bow is called Eon."

I ached for my Orion. "It's nice to meet you both," I said over my shoulder, catching the elf's slanty eyes pulling upwards. "I'm Wisteria Woodlander."

"You craft."

"Yes," I said even though there was no question being posed. The three of us walked through the first actual door I've seen in the Keep. It was over twenty feet tall and fastened with polished metal hinges. On my tip-toes I could perhaps reach the door handle, but my weight alone wouldn't be able to heave it open. As swiftly as it opened, it closed soundlessly behind us. "Do you know much about crafters?"

Alethim looked pensive and offered, "My kind helped humans understand the importance of mastering the materials in their lands when Numaal was but an unexplored mound of riches. The more one learns about their lands, the more it is cherished. The land is wise. When it senses it is tended to and respected, it will reciprocate, offering aid, nourishment and life to those who walk with awareness. Earth is a symbiotic partner to all of Kinlyra if fostered correctly."

"Born of the woods, raised barefoot and taught by nature's cycles, I must admit the boundaries between where the earth started and I began were always blurry. It was euphoric." I banished the sadness from holding onto my memories.

"Was? Are you no longer united?" He asked plainly.

"The woods that have sheltered me have been burnt. The soils that grew my meals are saturated in blood. Blood of the enemy and of the innocent. Death holds the lands now."

"Death holds no power here. You would be wise to remember that, Wisteria," Alethim spoke in a manner which made me feel even more distant from my homelands. I accepted silence while longing festered in my chest, eating me until I felt hollow.

Zander steered us to yet another room, this one somewhat more enclosed and cozy with couches in the corners and potted plants under the windows. There was a long table against the furthest wall, people were gathered around it chatting merrily and filing through parchment papers. More of Zander's kin watched us approach. A tug came on our bond, sending tingles up my forearm. His persistence poked my nerves. My nerves which were utterly fine until his chaotic energy stumbled into them. I grasped our bond tighter, internally consoling him until he was as tranquil as I could encourage. "Stop fretting, Zander."

One of Zander's brothers rose to greet a woman entering the room from a smaller entryway with a peck on the cheek. The child on her hip launched herself at the incubus wearing hundreds of metal bracelets I now knew to be Kashikat, leaving her petite arms free to tie up her hair to display a rather ugly, molten bite on her neck. His wife must have gotten accustomed to the ritual considering how inevitable family affairs were. I would not be pulling up my braid. I was not a spectacle.

Clavey, with no Tailan in sight, welcomed a female on his lap by brushing her hair as he intentionally sought out my gaze. I scratched my brow with a not too subtle middle finger and turned to watch the incoming guests, none in formal attire. Veona appealed to me as my favorite capital city with its lack of frivolous fashions and honey coated political maneuvers, not that I had anything to compare it to other than Landsfell. "I should have marked you ten more times before we left home this morning," he said as if Alethim wasn't next to us or that this entire room wasn't blessed with super senses and listening from across the Keep.

"I can handle myself," I reminded, lowering my middle finger. "If you get scared you can hide behind me. I'll protect you, princess."

He gave a howl of humored satisfaction, his brothers followed suit until another animalistic rumble tore through the room.

Atticus swept his eyes across the chamber while I took in the sight of one of the first soulful beings ever created in Kinlyra. An incubus molded in the image of Oyokos. That made him what, at least seven thousand years old if the stories I heard of the creation were true. He was nearly as old as the Eternals themselves since their arrival in our world.

His cropped black hair amplified the two knobby horns that rose from his forehead above his brow line. His brown skin tone held an indigo hue that played well with the dark color of his eyes. A color I couldn't see because he towered a full five feet *above* Zander. He was a walking impenetrable tower. One that consumed Zander immediately.

Their embrace was more fatherly than I had been imagining all these weeks. Affectionate hands lingered on his youngest son's unshaven jaw, their relieved expressions mirroring each other's. It was unexpected behavior from an incubus who forced his way into a lady's bed, deposited his child into her and welcomed his offspring only once she had died. Just how many of his sons were conceived in such an objectionable fashion? Quickly, I banished the stream of thoughts from my head before a sneaky fae came by to invade my unsanctioned notions. My fingers ran around the hawthorne berries wrapped around my wrist. A roaring snarl forced my eyes upwards.

Zander's canines were protruding. His fingertips were substituted by lethal, long nails and he was fast to side step, blocking me from Atticus's line of sight. Wings sprouted from Zander's shoulder blades, tearing through the fabric of his blue shirt and nearly knocking me on my ass.

His back straightened as his horns thrust high. Maybe Atticus was doing the same display of incubi idiocracy? I wouldn't know. I was stuck behind a muscular wall. However, I did watch a long procession of food filing in from the back door. Those who carried the trays were quick to leave after catching sight of the elected Overlord and the interim Overlord snarling like two territorial beasts over a kill.

If this interaction was an anticipated all-day affair, Zander should have warned me a bit more than an off-handed mention of possibly encountering a pissing contest—or six.

I counted backwards from ten and when neither moved or growled or spoke coherently, I took the liberty to walk around the pair of them, looking towards the table of seated guests for any sort of insight on how to navigate *this*. Not one had their eyes raised above their own feet. Not even pure blooded Kailynder, who was almost identical to Atticus save his wings and skin held a maroon tint, kept a straight spine. He was wavering in his dad's presence.

I pivoted to the elf at my side. Alethim covered his face with his hood, the scribes on the table shielded their features with their steady hands. I took advantage of being unacquainted with the realm, unaware of intricacies such as this and slowly strolled around the father and son duo in the center of the hall, taking in Zander's feral, unnaturally handsome face dueling Atticus' disturbingly calm demeanor.

Gazing up at the two, I waited at their sides.

The larger of the two hinged at the waist, lowering his long horns in Zander's direction. The room gave an audible exhale, I grinned seeing visible beads of sweat on Clavey's face. He'd been scared. Served that bastard right.

A distant pair of red and orange foxes huddled together in the far corner, the flames of their fur hardly visible and the absence of nine tails noted. They looked the size of large dogs and clearly did not rejoice over the friction—their tails were down, their noses buried in their bodies. "Wisteria, was it?" Atticus turned to face me. Grey. His eyes were slate grey. His beauty was historic and timeless, whereas Zander's was casually devastating and rough around the edges.

"Hi, Atticus. Thank you for your hospitality." That seemed cordial enough. Atticus adjusted his tunic and folded his hands behind his waist, staring at me as if I was an anomaly or a talking inanimate object.

His wings tucked along his spine. Atticus' attention went to Zander who was grinning devilishly while Atticus gave a cool response. "You've not imposed. Dreamers are very accommodating, I hope the food prepared is to your liking."

"Let's find out. Shall we?" I gestured to the table. The Keep's residential owner agreed and ambled ahead of us politely. Some middle-aged beings entered, leaving me thinking I ought to redefine 'middle-aged' for all I knew they could be older than mountains. The scent of maple syrup was enough to make my mouth water and stomach flip with the excitement of having food options.

My hand was stolen by Zander. I felt his lips firmly press onto my wrist, his claws receded into calluses. *Fearless little flower, you are made for me and still I don't deserve you.* I pinched his cheek and pointed to the line forming at the buffet table. "I heard the only vegetarian meal option for you is white rice." My intestines solidified.

I took my hand away from his mouth and glared. He retracted his canines. "And if it's cold, that is entirely your fault." I walked closer to the backs of Atticus' heels.

He called behind me. "My fault?"

"Yes. Do you have any idea how long you were gazing adoringly at your dad? Too damn long." His wings shook with stifled laughter. Kashikat made an aggressive hacking sound, choking on his juice. The woman leapt up from the chair at his side to dodge the pitcher of orange juice spilling onto her lap.

"Warroh, get Nyx!" Kashikat found his voice, which was as worn as his wrinkling skin, after laughing hysterically. I spotted yet another brother who jolted up. This blonde one reached towards the chandelier. Kashikat's daughter apparently had wings, ones that reminded me of a dragonfly's delicate sheen. Warroh grabbed the toddler's ankle and pulled her down, locking her against his chest. She giggled even as she fought to no avail. Kashikat's wife glared at a wolf who padded into the room. The wolf bared its teeth in reply to her sneer.

"Namir is woven into Kashikat's soul. Undoubtedly, you've met Fennick and they explained fate bonds." The Left Wing educated me as I watched Zander's brother caught in the middle of trying to soothe the woman he bit and greeting his loyal elemental. "There has always been friction between Katshikat's wife and his woven, don't let that put you off to pursuing Zander. Madu and Namir are both approachable, just not when they are in the same room." Alethim left to arrange the parchments on the table and direct the chaos that would soon commence.

Zander was hiding a secret behind his smile. Our secret. He was awful at ignoring the woven threads. No wonder secrets are hard to keep here. The dreamer beings were incapable of subtlety. More Ilanthians and elves walked in, timing their arrival *after* the pissing contest. It seemed most wished they had for the majority of the room continued to dab sweat off their upper lip and piss from under them.

Kashikat smacked Zander's skull affectionately. Zander barely flinched at the impact that would have me seeing stars. "Welcome home, Little Moon. The flight crew will catch wind and you'll be back in formation before week's end. I'll see to your drills personally."

"Any excuse to get out of diaper duty, eh Pix?"

"Any excuse to throw you off a cliff."

"Missed you too." The white haired horned pixie thrusted his tongue out at his little brother that towered a foot and some change over him. Zander returned it. Children. They were all children.

Kailynder, determined to keep his composure, pulled out a massive chair at the far end and seated himself among those with a sense of refinement. He deferred whatever Percy offered to pour in his goblet. Percy drank the clear liquid straight from the neck of the bottle and slipped it back into his pocket before joining the end of the line behind two females that I thought were fae, or part fae, with their bright pastel hair and scaley textured complexion. Her snake eyes were glued to Zander's waist, his belt buckle a snare trap for flirty eyes. Unless, she already had him and was reminiscing.

Knots twisted in my chest. Not as unbearable as the night I stumbled across the image of Collette fucking Zander, but awfully uncomfortable. *I have never slept with them, nor will I. Even if they had been in my harem, it matters not. I belong to you now and every moment after.*

I didn't reply. That would entail me admitting my jealousy. I changed topics. *Your family is candid. Definitely lively. I think I saw Percy make a bet with a wolf just a moment ago.*

I collected a plate and metal utensils, distracting myself with the tropical fruit options I rarely had the opportunity to eat growing up. *Lively? You put it so nicely. They are intrigued by you. Absolutely baffled that your gauge for danger isn't calibrated to their standards. They are envious. Even my dad knows when to concede.*

Oh, yes. I am the first girl who doesn't tolerate your ego clashing with other macho egos, even with daddy. You know I don't find you intimidating. I don't much care what your father thinks. What the hell was that by the way? You made the room sick.

His rose color affections and violet purples blend into my inner vision. The restraint he was showing not to kiss or hold me was remarkable given how badly he wanted to. I brushed by his side body and he immediately latched onto my touch. Caressing the back of my arm with his mellow, tamed thumb. *Incubi standoff, where we direct sway to compel the other to yield. Reestablishing myself. Enforcing that you are more than just a buddy, travel partner, one night stand. You know. Typical territorial incubus stuff. Oh, and the role of Overlord is mine any time we choose to do that. If we choose to do that. I don't particularly feel the desire to accept it at this time. Likely never.*

I scooped a variety of berries and melon cuts on my plate, added heaps of granola and powdered sugar. Squishing the pastries together, I made room for two small cinnamon swirls. In comparison, my colorful menagerie of food was a small serving after witnessing the six of the seven sons returned to the table with two or more plates each.

Scribes moved their parchments aside to make room for a meal, coffee and conversation. Alethim sat to the left of Zander, I to his right, although with the proximity of our chairs I felt as if I was sitting directly on his lap. His arm wrapped around the high back of my seat, his right hand toyed with my hair as I ate. The glaze stuck to my fingers. I gave Zander a wink and brought them to his lips. His warm tongue swirled around them. Biting carefully.

"You two are revolting. I'd rather damn the Eternals than watch this." Wyatt, seated across from us, groaned. Thornes jutted from his bony prominences. His earthy knuckles tapped rhythmically on the fork in his hand, I half expected roses to burst out his finger tips.

A wadded up napkin was chucked at his face. He snarled and the thorny horns on his head became a thicket of razors. "Do not damn your makers," Warroh cautioned, making room for a girl with a primate's tail and furry arms to squeeze her way around the table top. He tossed his blonde hair behind him and held his beaded prayer necklace, scowling at his brother. "Wisteria, do you frequent temples?"

"There were none where I was raised. I'm not opposed to them if that is what you are wondering."

He considered my reply as he dissected my appearance, his attention falling onto the buffed iron gemless ring on my finger. It probably looked like a pathetic engagement ring from his perspective. "I want to give you a tour of the temples if we can wrap this meeting up before sundown. They are all marvelous to behold if I do say so myself. Aditi's hymns are angelic."

"She can hear them from our bedroom," Zander insisted, his jaw tight.

"I can probably hear them from the training fields too, right?" I added.

The man next to me gave a quick inhale. "Trying to escape political chatter before it begins, are we?" Zander said.

"I am in serious need of conditioning after this winter. Warroh, I'll take a raincheck on the temple tours. Prayers don't strike down wraiths, swords do." Zander grunted, his breath heavy on my neck. "I don't need to listen to your long winded retelling of the last two years when you are going to repeat it all *again* to the Emperor and Empress, right? I'll promise to stay for that one because I have *words* to say to those two."

"Pleasant words?" Warroh asked.

"No. Words that would likely damn me to hell, but they need to be said."

Zander cut off Warrohs curses of sacrilegious. "Yes, I'll be repeating myself a lot, scouring the details of our last two years. I am hopeful when Maruc comes he will summon the memorandum, a device that allows people to see one's memories on display. It would save time and prevent you from suffering through any long winded retellings."

My woven picked up the fork I set down and stabbed grapes on the ends of the prongs and handed it to me. I popped one in my mouth to satisfy him. Neither of us enjoyed my protruding ribs. *I wish for you to always stay at my side. With Fen gone, my need for you has grown. I'm deficient and inadequate without you.*

I feel the void. But my body needs to remember what it's capable of. You can massage the kinks out when I return. He kissed my temple in reluctant agreement. I left the conversation in my head to avoid suspicions. Warroh looked affronted at my refusal for temple tours and frowned further when Zander continued on to give his blessing. "Tonight, you can condition with Dagressa's berserkers, as I mentioned before she will be excited for a fresh face. Dagressa is probably in the smithy, concocting explosives as we speak."

"With any luck she will get her fingers blown off," Kailynder drew out with a distasteful smirk. His charcoal gaze found my green eyes. He struggled to keep his focus off of my neck. "Wisteria, what weapon do you fight with?"

"An Ilanthian sword." Wrinkles on his face appeared around his mouth as it pursed.

Kailynder leaned on his elbows, the table groaned under his shifting weight. "That's fast paced. Are you any good with Ilanthian footwork?"

I squared my shoulders to him and set down my knife so I didn't throw it twenty feet at his head. A gesture that went noticed. "Want to find out? Although, from what I heard, you have a preference for swinging axes at newcomers. Luckily, I have no horns for you to hack off."

Wyatt stilled in his chair. His gaze at his shoes when Atticus came to take a seat. The girl on Clavey's lap got up and left the vicinity. Kailynder looked past me, onto Zander. "She holds your grudges for you I see. Wisteria is more protective than a treasure troll. Where did you find this one?" Cynicism laced his question while his brothers smirked under hooded gazes.

Violet wisps of magic rose from the floors and clung to the lofty white walls. His temper flared. "*This one*—this vibrant human, my forever flower, is the air beneath my wings and that which allows me to draw my next breath. She is the one I heartmarked."

Poetic pissing competitions commenced.

"I first encountered her in Duke Stegin's dungeon. He has since been murdered by Wisteria who put a iron slave collar around his neck and hung him from an ornate chandelier at his own winter gala. That collar was around a water wolf just minutes before. She freed a dreamer amid and saved a city after outing Prince Torval's private agenda to his unaware nation. It's an interesting tale, if the public council is ready to officially instate a conclave and you are ready to stop picking fights with Wisteria. Fights you will lose." Madu stopped chewing her food. Several people did.

Zander knocked on the table twice and made a gesture to Alethim who called the room into order with fancy words and a crescendo of trumpets. Atticus sat at Kailynder's side on the far end where there seemed plenty of room for them, scribes wet their ink pens. Zander pulled me into the pocket of his arm, dousing me with reassurance and the comfort of his steel arms and soft heart.

Alethim spoke first. "Wisteria Woodlander, it is time to share your story." Our beginning—Zander's and mine—began with my past. And so, in the safety of the Keep among strangers and scribes, I yielded the chronicle of my life.

"When I was twelve, a white boat docked at the merchant port, just outside of my parents' apothecary. Athromancia sent them."

Chapter Eleven

I didn't stop talking until another meal was brought out and my overbearing woven, requested a respite specifically for me to eat. This allowed him to take the brunt of the questions we had been asking ourselves for months. Atticus was high strung after Zander told him about the Remnants and the control the shards of bone instantly had over him. "The heir to the crown of Numaal had *you* mindlessly doing his bidding, bedding and Gods' know what else. *You*, the wielder of death, Lord of Darkness of the Veil, could have demolished Kinlyra under his influence if he knew who you were. Do you have any idea how poorly an outcome this could have quickly succumbed to?"

Zanders colors were changing, rusting away under his father's disappointment. "Good thing he didn't. Wisteria snapped the priestess' staff before she snapped the duke's neck, freeing me from the spellbind. Fate favors us. I'm not fucking with it."

Slate grey eyes now buried into me. "How did you know to break the staff? How did you know he wasn't in his right mind? Had Fennick been involved?" I quickly chewed my food.

"Nikki and I had a list of theories we tested. Collectively,we know your son rather thoroughly. Call it intuition," I said, avoiding any topic of syphering or our thread. "Atticus, these shards have a pull. An evil aura that draws one to its whereabouts."

Concerns brewed. "Have you interacted with these bones before? Have you thought about using them to control Zander or his elemental? A single wolf or fox could easily destroy a stronghold if they are fueled properly. Would you give them over to the new King Torval and reign as his queen? What about leading the hordes of wraiths here with your blood? You bring two wars upon us by remaining here."

I shook my head. This was getting out of hand. "What? No." My throat tightened.

"This is not an interrogation, Atticus. Hold your tongue," Zander hissed. "She saved my life. She saved Fennick. She saved a blessed child and dreamer. She saved an entire fucking city. Do not paint her in any light other than honorable." He all but lunged at Atticus, the table dropped their heads. Light was stolen. The room dimmed as his magic burst free, he let it seep into every stone around us until his presence was unavoidable. He would be heard.

"The bone shards *do* pulsate with evil and malintent. I'll have you see for yourself." Zander fluxed and reappeared within a breath and pulled the leather satchel off his hip and unwrapped the black femur in the middle of the table, everyone around me left their seats to inspect it. When light was permitted, elvish scribes were drawing the bone to scale with charcoal and whispering amongst themselves. Their repulsed look spoke volumes.

I finished my soup waiting for anyone to come up with an answer. Hopefully, one that didn't involve suspicions of me leading wraiths here or farfetched intentions with the blackened femur. The hardened stares around the room told me I remained under scrutiny. A suspected culprit. Lovely.

Zander rubbed his temples, frizzing his uniquely colored hair as he tried to work out the building headache. I placed my hand on his knee, he immediately reached for it and I found myself willingly absorbing his concerns if only to help relieve them from his shoulders. "As expected, no one knows. The Emperor will have a lot of enlightening to do," he whispered and drank his pomegranate juice.

Not many here trust me. Not after hearing about the prince's proposal and the wraith's reaction to my blood. I left out the gory details of the proposal branding and flogging, but I confirmed there was to be a trade, my Ilanthian family for my wedding vows before a year came to pass. I glanced around the room. All present were pensive and ensnared in their own questions. A few suspicious glances in my direction sent me back into my head. *I think this whole table wants me gone knowing that there is a possibility the hoards followed me here.*

The hoards are far behind us.

You don't know that.

I do. I've seen it. He pointed to his eye. *And my dad is being an ass. He will apologize in one form or another.* Zander looked as if he had an epiphany, his blue eyes rounded. "Alethim! The letters, how could you let me forget!" He reached behind me and flicked the elf's shoulder.

"My Lord, all thoughts leave your mind when you stare at Wisteria. Speaking of, she has one too." He slipped two letters to Zander. One burnt on the edges and the other with a white wax seal. From Nikki and the White Tower. Mine was simply addressed.

Wisteria Fucking Woodlander,

As promised, I will make your life hell. Absolute hell!

Don't jump off boats! Idiot!

-Brock Ironside

I laughed so hard there was a stitch in my side that only a swift crack of my spine could fix. As I rotated myself to unbind the cramp, I was grinning like a fool on resin. Brock learned to write alright. Yolanda clearly taught him how to punctuate to get his point across. Zander didn't look as pleased reading and rereading his notes.

Nikki's he stuffed into his breast pocket, the message from the White Tower he passed around—starting with Alethim who read and summarized to the chamber. "Maruc arrives the day after next with the company of forty-five Numaalians, two elementals and a handful of legionnaires–ivory and gold. He mentions nothing about extending aid of his Ivory Legion nor how long he intends to stay." Alethim passed the letter to Kashikat's wife and around it went.

"What news from Fennick, Zander?" The elf solicited. I shifted in my seat to catch his reply.

"Private matters," he stated factually. He squeezed my hand fondly, but did not sypher. My gut went woozy. At least he was alive, I calmed myself. "Let's move forward with our realm's preparations under the assumption there will be no help from the Bloodsworn or Ivory Legion. Until the Emperor or Empress arrive to tell us what the *vulborg* are or what sort of early generation descendant Anna was, we assume the worst of our enemies. One battle at a time is how we will claim victory. Seeing as the Remnants and wraiths are not the ones scraping away at the runegate our focus must revert back to the immediate matters at hand." His hand flattened against my knee. He tried hard to steady our bond, but whatever Nikki wrote unsettled him.

His serious tone carried around the room. "What have we learned about the enemy at our walls? Have the reapers collected a more accurate count of lost souls? How do we kill them? Have the scholars identified them with the archive text and imageries? Where are Misotaka's descendants? Have we historic accounts brought over from the ice archives? What shapes do they take? How do their forms inflict damage on us? How much longer will the runegate stand? When it falls what becomes of souls on their intended route? How will the beyond get restored? Why are they clustering next to the Eternal Elm?"

He sipped his Havana imported coffee with a fierce fucking gaze as he commanded the room into a desolate silence. Even with my human hearing I was able to gather the hesitant swallows. "I have been gone for two years obtaining answers and diving into the heart of this matter to the absolute best of my abilities. I expected you all to do the same, to exceed my hopes in my absence." His icy blue eyes inched along from person to person. "Atticus, enlighten me."

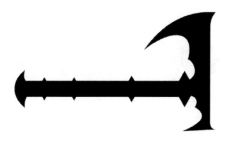

After hours of listening to the dreamers state their predictions and what trivial amount they did come to understand about the enemy, I knew Zander wouldn't be sleeping well tonight or in the months to come even if I manage to control my nightmares. Things were looking grim for the realm, that was the general consensus for all of Kinlyra. "If we had any insight into their weakness, we could better prepare our offense. Our resources are defense heavy, that isn't acceptable!" Kailynder shouted, his knees bounced fretfully. "This conversation is moot without Eternals here." He threw his arms up and gave the honey haired, mousey appearing fae at his side a snarl form accidentally bumping into his wings. No touching another's wings, noted.

"They do not tire. They do not have needs to tend. They multiply and remain heavily aware of the Eternal Elm. The barrier shakes with their impact." Atticus swirled a goblet of wine fit for the likes of a giant, offering words to a perplexed table. "Maybe they are drawn to fire like moths. Maybe their nature despises fire and seeks to douse it, unintentional behaviors. Instincts if you would. Maybe they are unintellectual."

"They are perceptive and emotionally calculating," I said, recalling the two headed raven.

Wyatt sunk in his chair. He clicked his tongue at me. "Nothing crosses the barrier. Not sound. Not magic. You think they are emotionally calculating or manipulative of us over here? You've no way to deduce their intellectual capacity unless you've been having private chats *migouri*." I heard Zander shift. Quickly, I pulled his belt loop towards the ground as he tried to rise from his seat, preventing him from standing up to snap at his brother.

"Sit. Down." I yanked him downward forcefully until he complied. Kashikat's wife laughed openly. I gave her a brief warm smirk at Zander's stupidity.

His arm wrapped around me, my grumpy incubus grumbled in the space above my head, "So bossy."

"I wouldn't have to be bossy if you weren't ridiculously dramatic all the time." I was pulled onto his lap, his hands securing themselves around my waist, and instead of fighting him, I set my sights on Wyatt and allowed Zander to run his lips across strands of my hair. Anything to soothe the edgy beast beneath me.

"They see into the land of the living. Just how long do you think they have been observing the workings of our world?" Atticus hummed with pleasure hearing the use of *our* world. He fanned his hand, giving me the floor. "Has anyone here approached the runegate and lingered long enough to watch their shapeshifting?" Namir raised her hand from where she stood—away from the table among her own kind who padded along the parameters of the floors on all fours. "What shape did it take for you?"

She kept her distance from the mass, but did give me the courtesy of a reply. "It's usually horrible atrocities. Serpents. Spiders. Ghouls. Shark jaws. Injured soldiers. Kelpies."

"All the things plenty of people would find terrifying, or as you said, horrible and atrocious. How do they know what induces fear in us? They either see it, hear it or sense it."

Wyatt offered with a heavy dose of annoyance, "Or a better answer is that they once walked the earth as wraiths. And before that, they could have been any number of living beings. With a multitude of fears which have carried on into the beyond."

"Did any form strike you as odd, Namir? A fear you found personally insulting or disturbing?"

I felt the room pause. At Kashikat's request Namir didn't answer. I knew what was coming, an uphill battle to dig myself out of a corner. I laced my fingers with Zander's. Percy's nails chimed on his glass bottle while we waited for the elemental's reply. "What form did it take for you, Wisteria?"

My stomach clenched. "One that it shouldn't know. One I haven't given life by speaking about it." A gentle caress flitted across the backs of my knuckles. Zander wrapped his blues and bleary off-whites around my essence and rested outside my mental walls. "I am not obligated to tell you my fears. But, I am willing to admit that they exist if it means discovering a new trait about the enemy. These are just my observations. Take them or don't," I shrugged to the pointy eared incubus whose thorns elongated and began to curl upward. "It may change absolutely nothing other than prove how entirely outmaneuvered we are."

"Or it was reacting to your blood, yet again."

My hair unfurled as I disagreed. "They have been changing hideous forms long before I ever met Anna, before I was born. This has nothing to do with my blood. I am not special."

Wyatt toyed with a rope of thorns. "Or your prodigy woodlander ass found a way to ingest the venom and can manipulate these *spawn*. Have you ever been bitten? Had your wayward Ilanthian travelers given you more of their blood to combat the affliction? Did my brother thoroughly inspect your body for an infection? Or did you swoon him away with your tight little c–"

There was no keeping Zander seated this time. Wyatt was wrestled to the floor, elves nearby casually scooted their chairs away as if this were a common occurrence. "Have her take off the hawthorn berries and let's see how much you–" Another fist to his head. Vines of thorn thickets ensnared Zander and strung him upside down. Purple magic turned Wyatts thickets to dust and Zander threatened to do the same to him if he ever *spoke of* my body with such crudity.

I rose and pointed to the chair. Zander stomped his way around the table, a wiley satisfied grin plastered on his face. And he sat. He looked much relieved after expending some of his pent up energy.

Clavey whistled in mockery. "Tight leash."

"I'll gladly give him some slack if you are feeling like getting your sparkly repulsive face beaten in by your baby brother, Clavey." The pixies on the balcony exchanged grins and coinage.

Kailynder rose to pace the parameters of the room, still going off about the Emperor's insight while Percy saluted an invisible drinking partner and took a swig of his bottle. *Nothing you fear will come to pass. I swear it on my mother's shield.* Zander was wrapping me in layers of rainbow hues as if they would protect me. It felt nice after having so many eyes on me today. I'd happily be buried away. *If you feel inspired to tell me what you saw at the runegate, I'll listen and never breathe a word to my kin that you are in fact fearful of something.*

I'll tell you after you tell me what Nikki wrote on that paper you've already discarded with magic wispies. Our thread firmed. *You know something, he knows something and you both are apprehensive to tell me.*

I do not have absolute clarity on the situation. He was frustratingly vague, which means he doesn't want me to act out. Or you. Probably both.

Fingers left mine to trail along the insides of my thigh. I squeezed my knees together. *I will tell you what he wrote. In two days, after the last God arrives with our company.*

What if I'm dea—

His growl cut me off. "You are morbid."

"I'm poetic, honest and vibrant," I countered, feeling his biceps bulk to draw me closer. "Once you are done suffocating me, I'd like to see myself towards the fields."

"Must you be so motivated to leave me?"

"When I am able to keep myself alive and unavoidably save your ass amid the war on the realm, you'll thank me."

"We flux there. I'll fly back with you once the sun has set. We will sleep here tonight, in fortified chambers. If you need me sooner, send word." Zander spoke finitely. *Call to me by syphering. I should be able to hear you anywhere in the city.*

"No need," Percy yawned. "I'll escort her back if she tires before you find her. I'm too drunk to contribute anything pertinent to the public council. Wouldn't you agree, Atticus?" Atticus calmly dismissed his son with a flick of his wrist. Percy tousled the hair of a sleeping Nyx on Warroh's lap upon rising from his backless seat, stretching his wings as one would stretch their limbs first thing in the morning.

"Absolutely, not," I scoffed at him as I would have Brock if he was acting like an idiot.

Zander stayed silent. Actually, contemplating my need for a chauffeur. Now serious, I pulled Zander's face into my hands and pressed my nose to his. "The only one of your brothers permitted to be my shadow is Nikki." Zander's lips crashed upon mine. It was a short lip lock, but the undercurrent of outright enlightened bliss rang through me clearly as if I was a bell made of crystal. His tender heart burst with streams of silver, which felt like tears against my soul. He mourned the absence of his woven yet seemed to rejoice that I was treading through that feeling alongside him.

The room spun from view.

Fluxing was disorienting. Recompiling the particles of my physical body left me dazed and laid out horizontal on a patch of dirt. I dusted myself off and spun on my heel until I spotted the orc blooded Dagressa running the length of the training field with two weighted iron bars set across her back. Her trainees looked much smaller in comparison as they leapt over the obstacles she had laid out. Most managed to sprint back to the barrels without falling too far behind or eating dirt. Most.

"Percy is not your chaperone. Nor is he ever meant to replace Fen at your side or be worthy to step into your shadow, let alone be one." The truth in his words was salve for my soul. His blue and white eyes hitched on my neck, seeking reassurance. He found comfort in his visible claim on me. "However, if he happens to find his way here to monitor the overpass and ward off pesty nymphs with his presence, try not to bash his face in before I come for you. Four hours. Do you think you can manage?"

"As long as he doesn't do anything deserving of a fractured nasal bone or busted maxillary, then it should not be an issue." I waved down Dagressa who pardoned herself from a conversation. "I see Percy is important to you. I'll try not to murder him." She hustled over, not bothering to wipe the sweat off her palm before shaking Zander's hand. Then mine. I gaped seeing her grip was wider than Zander's. Must be the orc blood.

"Welcome home, Z. You owe me twenty-nine ales." Her green tinted skin was taut over her bulging muscles. I was envious of her tone and her physique. "One for each month you've been gone and left me to divert the compulsive behaviors of that fidgety brother of yours. One more week and I would have taken Kai to the heart of the mountain and left him there for the tusked porrigs to feast upon."

"I'll see an oak barrel brought to your doorstep tonight. You seem in fine spirits, Dag. I hope that has trickled down to your combatants." Wide set brown eyes made their way to me, upright with my hands on my hips working on my own posturing. "Have you brought me another? Delightful!"

"I'm Wisteria." I pointed a firm finger to her previous Overlord. "And he has nothing to do with me being here. I've been eager to train with you since we flew over the city this morning. I promise to stay out from under the boots of those bigger than me, if you allow me to condition a bit. "

"Everyone is bigger than you. Taller anyways." She sized me up and pulled an iron rod off the nearest bracket. She tossed it at me, it was cold and grated to the touch. "That should do. If you vomit, do it over the hedges. I've a handful of half-humans here and two footers, you'll be fine!" She waved off Zander. I grinned and turned my back on him too. *You can massage the kinks out tonight when you tend to my scars.*

Three hours and fifty eight minutes.

He fluxed before I compared him to a mothering hen.

"Human, what is your training?" Dagressa called ahead.

"Ilanthian and Montuse. I had consistent practice before this winter starved me of activity. Now, stagnation and lack of food have taken away my endurance. But not my agility. Definitely not my enthusiasm for sword fighting."

The crowd of roughly one hundred wingless beings parted for me to take my place at the end of the line. "Those styles aren't easily blended. You must be limber to manage both. Here we work on strength and resilience."

"Perfect," I grinned, knotting my braid into a messy bun.

"Bar stays on your back until you cross the finish line or faint. I don't care if you don't cross it until sunup, but you will. And you will do it on your feet. On my whistle." A sharp blast cut the air. I merged with the stampede of berserkers, huffing and thudding as we sprinted over the cumbersome course.

<u>Chapter Twelve</u>

I was feeling good. Sore, slick with sweat, winded, but it was a combination that felt damn good.

I pulled my elbow behind my head, savoring the burn of building muscle igniting my triceps with the stretch. Dagressa rewarded us with water and concentrated passion fruit juice before closing the weaponry cabinet for the night. Dripples of water spilt down my chin. I lifted my tunic to dry my face. "Not bad. I expect you to finish in the middle of the pack next time." I was at the tail end of the herd. A quarter hour behind some Ilanthians and fae with hooves who dominated the flat terrain.

And my legs didn't give out. That deserves some reward of excellence, right? Keenan would have sent me back out on the field for another two hours to consider it a decent session, my reward would have been a meal.

A smoky voice wafted in from the nearest bench. "Do tell me when you plan on returning here. I love to watch you struggle to keep bile in your belly and all the fruits my brother shoved down your gullet." Percy remained seated, his knees spread lazily. Kailynder and a female, without pointy ears or noticeable additional magical appendages stared at grimy hands while I reached for another canteen of water.

I gave my best attempt to keep my word to Zander. I ignored him. With my cup set down I convinced myself to walk away.

"Thanks, Dagressa. I'll be seeing you around if I can shake a particularly overbearing brute off my back." She locked the gate to her fields and waved me off. Up the stone stairwell I went. When I reached a high point, I spotted Horn's Keep. I walked in that direction under the street lamps lighting up the glittery stone path beneath my boots. It would have been a refreshing and beautiful evening to clear my head were it not for the several pairs of feet knocking alongside me.

The dimming sky was absent of Zander's flying form. Acknowledging my unwanted company was unavoidable. I spun on my heel. "Percy, are you infatuated with me? Is that why you can't leave me in peace?"

Kailynder ducked under the lamp watching his brother approach me with a drunken swagger. "I find you unnerving because I do not know your character outside of what I learned today. And what I learned is that you stole my brother away from his duties and home because he thought your violent pursuit of vengeance was delectable and whatever nectar he drank from you distorted his priorities."

My nails dug into the warm skin of my palms creating little half moons in my flesh as I took a step backwards. I pulled my emotions away from Zander and our thread. The door between us shut. The last thing he needed to feel now was my ire and disappointment in his family. Even though I would have been a liar if I said his exact thoughts hadn't paraded around in my head a time or two before. "If you knew your brother in the slightest then you'd know saving the Veil was—is always his prerogative, whether it is from an army of dead spawn or from himself. He even fancies keeping your pathetic ass alive."

Percy adjusted his stance. "Oh, good. So, you do know about darling Morigan and the guilt he lugs around for hurting his citizens." Morigan. Alas a name. His former fae lover, unapologetically murdered for her attempts to kill Nikki. I felt myself nod as I swallowed the seething boiling up in my chest imagining a world without Nikki. "Then you understand why, at this pivotal moment, there can be no wildcards. Which is precisely what you are. I say this with respect, but you are a fresh babe in a new complex world, you cannot be trusted to understand all the powers at play, let alone make decisions when the fate of millions lay at risk."

The woman in company with the two towering incubi didn't look a day over forty. Her nimble fingers tucked her wavy hair away from her face, which was unreadable. Her voice scratchy on my skin. "We need our Lord of Darkness to wield his bloodright if the Dreamer Realm is going to survive another turn around the sun. He won't unleash himself if you are in proximity. That much he has made abundantly clear with that damn bite."

The sun in the cage. They wanted it out.

"He won't do it if Fennick is in proximity. And Fennick will never leave him, nor be ordered to do as such. I am the same."

"You are not the same nor will you ever be. Just commiserate with Madu when you start to feel neglected. She'll happily share with you her misery."

My jaw clenched. "Are you going to coerce him into leaving his woven before the war? I am seeing strong parallels between you lot and Morigan. Ridding his distractions to redirect him. How did that work out last time?" Judging by their lack of reaction, I was right.

Kailynder opened his jaw trap. "You are strange. I don't mind you in our nation. I don't mind your imprudence, in fact I find myself aligning with your preference for swords over prayers. I do mind you with my brother. Leave him because he is incapable of leaving you. Come back after the battle, I will be much more receptive towards you then. Percy and Judeth will witness my words and see them honored as we are a company of three."

I've seen—felt—Zander's distraction and longing for Nikki to be near. He couldn't function much less wage a war without his proclaimed corlimor. "I don't need any of you to like me. At the present, what matters is that you don't make Zander's life and decisions more difficult. And that is exactly what would happen if I or Nikki were taken from him. He is working on trusting himself, don't give him a reason to doubt you— the people he is fighting for." The street light made Percy's eyes appear clear for a flash of an instant when he paused the stroking of his stubbled chin.

Judeth tiptoed out from the incubi's shadows. "You plan on fighting alongside us, young one? Have you not your own wars to rage, princes to wed and Gods to question?" Her reputation for a hardened

The Lies of the Eternals

personality lived up to its standards. I paused. Choking on the sour and bitter emotions, gurgling in my chest. A feeling as wrong as a sky without stars or a sun without warmth.

My truth was being questioned. Again. This realm held no reserve in vocalizing their qualms of my naive character. "I fight for life. For the future of those living and yet to take their first breath, just as much as I fight out of fury for all the lives lost and those who wander the world wishing to have died alongside their families and villages. Where would you have me stand when the runegate crumbles?"

"Away from our Lord of Darkness."

I struggled to keep Zander's intrigue out of my head and his intrusive pestering at bay while my temper flared. He was fast approaching. "Share his bed, reside in his home, train with the best warriors the realm has to offer. But when the barrier falls, I would have you hiding away with the Empress and her Gold Legion of Bloodsworn. You have no allegiance, you could kill the Lord of Darkness as easily as you kiss him. You are a rogue. We've no place for rogues in our ranks. His love for you does not equate to your loyalty and love of him or his nation."

Kailynder moved artistically given his sheer size and circumference of his bulky limbs. We stood squared off to each other, I squinted upwards at the carbon copy of a composed, dark toned Atticus, save Kailynder's eyes were a scarlet red. "Judeth, it would have been prudent of you to converse with me prior to declaring her ineligible to fight in the Veil's ranks. Words spoken can't be undone. Not easily."

His ruby red eyes caught the light, gleaming as if they had been dripped in blood. "There is a chance then that you would let me fight with your people against a common enemy?"

"If Zander or Atticus ordered it of me, I begrudgingly would comply. Otherwise, no. You are a rogue."

Percy's brow shot up quickly. "Kai. You can't possibly–" Kailynder snarled at his brother and his hand, larger than Zander's, fell onto the hilt of his sword which was longer than I was tall. I wished to wire his mouth shut, instead I opened mine.

143

"You are a fool to refuse any sort of aid. The evil that will descend upon us does not distinguish ranking, mortality, wild rogue or faithful warriors who've proven themselves in the Trial of Runes. No, they come to end us all. To consume every drop of life within their tainted reach." My clenched jaw ached as I gritted hard, speaking between grinding teeth.

My own hand fell to where my slender Ilanthian blade should rightfully be. Even without it, assuredness coursed through me. "I will fight. I will never stop fighting until I am free of the body that traps me on this hellscape of a continent. With any luck, your brother and Fennick will find my corpse and burn it so I don't come back and haunt your foolish ass down as one of the very spawn you fear." My left fist shook as Zander approached. I force my hand into the pocket of my trousers.

Percy moved into view with a sashay dance step. "If you are determined to fight and die doing so, then save your spunk for the months ahead."

Judesth slithered in, her stoic high cheeks fixed in determination. "She damns us all if she stays."

"Do not tell me to leave his side. Do not ask it of Fennick," I looked at the three of them. And by look, I meant shot daggers from my eyes and into their souls and hoped I wounded them for I willed them to burst into agony, shatter their spleens and let them bleed out. "We won't leave Zander's side. And if you force distance between us or intend to manipulate us to influence Zander's willingness to work with Oyoko's essence, I will come for your hearts, heads and horns. You are no different than Morigan."

"The end justifies the means," Judeth chimed in.

Too emotionally exhausted to show my shock or disgust, I stated, "I am sure you would get along fine with the renegade fae, the child slavers and King Resig who all feel the same." Percy, with his recently furrowed brow, moved between Judeth and I. A weak attempt to separate us after this conversation escalated past his comfort zone. "If whatever world you manage to live in comes to pass, I do not wish to be a part of it." Gods, I couldn't have been more grateful for my mortality. Judeth was a nightmare and I guarantee she was not alone in her thinking.

Many like her alleged I too innocuous and unsophisticated to have value during trying times.

The street light darkened and the dreamers went silent. Without looking behind me I murmured into violet shadows, "I'm fine and as you can see I left your family intact. They are lucky I don't have my sword." My lame humor fell on deaf ears.

Gusts of wind from Zander's wings sent my hair toppling over my face, I chuckled tossing my head back. My skull met a stone hard set of abs. His hard body behind me brought forward unconsecrated desires to my aching flesh.

You locked me out and when I come for you, I find you lashing out. Defensively.

On your behalf. Honestly, the encounter doesn't deserve a summary. I'm hungry and in need of a bath. I believe I promised to let you roam your hands over my strains, which surprisingly there aren't too many. Zander wasn't listening to me anymore.

His gaze swept over Percy and onto Judeth and Kailynder. The taller of the two raised his horns before lowering them. The incubi bent in half and splayed his wings lowly. Kailynder didn't rise out of prostration. "*Lower. Scum of the earth.*" Kailynder didn't fight the sway Zander cast. Down his spine twisted until Zander appeared sated with his misery.

Immovable with their chiseled flawless bodies, wings and fanciful appearance they reminded me of gargoyles. "Three to one? Hardly seems fair. Wisteria can demolish threefold with her wits alone. Unfortunately, you'll never have the opportunity to be dazzled by her because a sketchy rendezvous like this one will never happen again. Am I heard?"

Percy reached into his jacket and took out a flask. "Yes, your voice is thundering." If he thought *this* was loud, he would have smothered Zander with a pillow at Fort Fell after rooming with his boisterous personality. In retrospect, his optimistic and outgoing behavior brought hope to the simple people and crafters, and confidence to the new men signing up to train as guards of Numaal wearing red cloaks for the first time. He saved lives on the brink of succumbing to their despair. I was one of them.

Chin high, neck extended, I stared directly above me. I looked at my woven fondly, allowing myself to remember the little joys and luxuries he offered me in Fort Fell, while he debated punishing Kailynder further.

Zander didn't permit Kailynder to rise. I grew bored. I kicked dirt at the drunker of his brothers, wanting this whole encounter to end. "They came to watch Percy make good on his bet that I would come in first position in the obstacle course."

"My gold was doubled because she didn't spew waffles on the climbing wall." Percy propped himself up against a black metal street sign. "The conversation held after was telling of her zesty aptitudes, but nothing worthy of breaking your eldest brother's back over. I believe he got more than he bargained for where investigating your relationship is concerned. Judeth has reflecting to do, her general lack of faith in people is making her more of a twat. She ought to crawl to Warroh's temple district on her knees."

Zander's voice rumbled through my bones as if they were hollow. "Rise, you bloody idiot." Kailynder did as he was told and wiped his spit off of his sharp canines with the backs of his forearms, not flinching at the blood he drew from himself.

I let Zander inspect me for injuries while my eyes found tawny gazelle horns. I tested their owner. "Speaking of bargaining. I don't suppose you want to give me a portion of what my flawless athletics earned you, Percy? One gold coin should suffice and leave you with plenty of money to spend buying rounds with your allegiant, predictable, bribable friends." I drove my point home feeling Kailynder's deep set eyes flicker with ire.

"I don't have friends," Percy grumbled. I caught the coin he tossed in my direction and slipped it into my breast pocket with a bold smile.

I faked a bewildered gasp. "I'm shocked. I never would have guessed that others don't relish your dazzling personality and charming wit." My sarcasm was cut short by Zander's curt motions of lifting my arms over my head and hauling me into the air by my wrists. He gave a satisfied hum as my legs found strength to wrap around his torso, he liberated my arms and readied his wings. My gaze was already on the Ranger constellation directly above us. I prepared myself for the exhilaration of gliding so close to the stars while my carrier took the opportunity to strike his brother's hopes.

"Right Wings do not seek to alter the course of the wind; they know better than to capture it or control it. They are considerate enough not to pluck the feathers off the birds that rely on it. Right Wings are wise enough to understand they cannot function or take flight without the Left Wing, the talons and keen eyes all working in tandem. Let's hope you've not planted weeds to take root for they will choke out the sun and the darkness will thrive over the chaos *you* had spread. If you encourage intolerance and fear here when it is already plenty abundant, you will be banished. If harm comes to my chosen, I will bring harm to you and *enjoy it.*" His blue eyes were fuming with violet flames when they shot into Judeth. "Judeth, you will get an ugly and intimate exposure to your Lord of Darkness's true power, you'll have less than a second to admire and fear me before I pulverize you into black sand and wipe your name from the records."

If they were bulls their horns would have locked. Luckily, the lot of them just hissed through fangs and dull angry lips. What felt like an hour later our bond came to life with a spectrum of colors as air whipped across my face and he took us into the sky. I inhaled the blissful sensation of being unfettered.

When his greys emerged again and swam down our connection, I addressed him. I tore my eyes away from the dark blue skies above and placed them on Zander's wrinkled forehead. The silhouette of his horns were enchanting against the scenic backdrop of the pearlescent lit up city. "Quite the welcoming committee. I was greeted with a strong recommendation to leave."

"Which you will not be doing." Blues and greens emerged from under a cracking layer of his annoyance. "You are not a distraction, you are vital to my very existence and I would scour every cove, climb every mountain, swim to the depths of all the seas to find you. I will not fight a war without you by my side for I will have no reason to fight nor live."

"I told them as much, just much less romantic."

His lips reveal a distractingly gorgeous half grin. "Romantic?"

"Yes, you ridiculous drama princess. Romantic."

"Why, I do believe my efforts to court you have been successful. You've fallen victim to my prey." The capillaries in my face burst and yet, I did not deny his accusations.

His wings slowly beat the air around us, suspending us a mile over Veona. "A little." I took in the beautiful sight of this starlight city.

"Does this mean I can be *a little* more forward now and you won't scurry away or scoff when I tell you how perfectly fuckable I find you to be when you insult my brothers on my behalf?" His dimples appeared under a light scruffy beard as he relished his memories. "The ax comment to Kai and Wyatt at the table made me want to lay you on the table and eat you out like my personal buffet."

"I would have let you." The notch on the column of his throat bobbed as his lips fell open.

When I didn't pull away from his enamoring he continued. "Can I finally confess how it both breaks and blesses me to feel your fingers wander over the scar on my chest every night, yearning for our elemental? That part of me, my love for my woven brother, has never felt so seen or honored. A shared *current* amongst us all that we are gradually becoming accustomed to. I'm not scared to explore it because you will be with us, Wisteria Woodlander."

"To whatever end."

A rainbow was exploding in his soul, while Zander held his bated breath. "Can I tell you I love the squeaky sounds you make when you toss around finding where to put your legs at night? Can I tell you how I am dying to see you and Fen spar? I heard you put a nice gash in his mouth."

"I did. He healed up too quickly for me to savor his shocked and bloodied expression." My lips nestled on the prickly texture of his beard. "I feel safe with you. Safe enough to leave behind fragments of myself and be at peace with that. Even if I am not whole or less angry or less disorderly, I am safe to be as I am in this perpetual state of chaos and loss."

He hand found his way up my shirt, gliding against my wet navel and caressing the swells of my breast under the sweat soaked band holding them in place. Between his firm fingers he pinched my soft sensitive nipple until it hardened, then he worked on the other one while unbinding the straps that held them up. My breasts hung freely and heavy in his hand. "I'm surprised you managed that little strappy thing."

Hardly noticeable, I watched his canines elongate as he stared at my piercings etched under the fabric. "There was only one clasp. I can manage one, not rutting ten of them." Falling into his tender touch, I kissed his upturned grin and felt us start to fade as he decided to flux us directly into his chambers in the Keep.

I woke up before Zander and rolled to the edge of the bed to jump off. His living sector was magicked shut, there was no need for clothes as I roamed from Zander's bedroom through the communal lounge area into Nikki's darkened enclosure. Just like his room in Landsfell, his mattress was low to the ground and buried under pillows, sheets and blankets.

I tore open the thick blackout curtain that blocked the sunlight from prying into the room and basked in the morning light. His closets were large.

Yes, closets plural.

All color coded and organized by season and style. The Count Hilderbrand was not entirely a charade; Nikki had fitted clothes, not embellished but definitely properly tailored to his lean body in infinite fashioned cuts. Plenty of articles had holes and burn marks in them, those were in the furthest left closet. Although, to my disappointment, his taste in silks and satins was less gluttonous than mine.

I spotted a lousy four silk shirts among the dozens of tailored fabric. I was hoping to get away wearing one as a pajama top without him knowing. He'd know if a wrinkle was out of place in this impeccable closet. I settled for smelling one of his garments. Pine trees. A fond scent of my woodland home. A fond scent of my protector woven.

Tomorrow couldn't come soon enough.

Chapter Thirteen

One night in the White Tower did everyone's mind and body wonders. It was imbued with thriali, *passive restorative rune magic. He felt the fire spirit of the twins returning to his body with the essence of the Elm and Glacier just on the other side of the portal. Where his wovens awaited him.*

The tower in and of itself was a complex city built high into the clouds. The Eternals crafted it into a sanctuary, which to him smelled of lilacs and seaspray. Seagulls off the coast flocked around the lower portions, squawking against the harbor's winds. The fox elemental was absolutely foul and rancid after stepping off that wretched, rocking ship floating atop a watery grave.

All in his convoy needed a private moment away from the travel company that they have been stuck sailing, sleeping and shitting next to on land and sea for weeks on end. No one more than him. The swaying of that ship had him heaving over the port side, soiling the one decent shirt he had on his back with bile and salty ocean mist. He used much of his fire magic to wash and dry that damn article of clothing and still it was the first garment he burned when they got to the harbor of Akelis.

Happily, he destroyed that piece of shit shirt that sagged over his slightly thinner stature. His flames ate it up hungrily as his magic returned into his veins.

There were so many bodies on board cramped together, that escaping conversations or complaining was an impossibility, there was nowhere to hide without being found and pestered with excited questions about Ilanthia or requesting he offer the crew warmth on cold nights. He happily answered, despite the need for a moment of quiet isolation and less stimulation. The water wolf was his best empathizer, although she was fortunate as to not be cut off from her element. Her strength grew as days turned to weeks.

Fennick's did not.

It was clear she had a woven because she had struggled as horridly as he in trying to keep his scattered wits about him. Twice the man Wisteria called Keenan held him at bay from jumping in the wraith infested waters to drag his reckless woven to shore or die with her in the undercurrents, which seemed like a perfect option at that time. When her heat was stolen by the icy waters of the ocean, Brock had to assist the Bloodsworn in holding him down. He bit them in a violent outburst and displaced the Montuse's finger. The Bloodsworn was forced to knock him out with a heel to his silver haired skull so he wouldn't chase her down. So he wouldn't drown with her.

The last transplacency the fox had with Zander was him and Wisteria stark naked and freezing in a cave somewhere. His chest rattled with compulsive need. Not solely the lustful kind. The twin Eternals created him to give warmth, spark passion and offer comfort. Which was what he should have been doing among his hurt and broken wovens, had he not been sailing safely out to sea by the terrifying act of martyrdom.

The act that saved his life.

All their lives.

As much as he damn near had it with the bustling of people swarming around him, the elemental sent word to his auntie about his brief stop in the capital before walking into Veona. Foxes held family and their wovens as the utmost important pillar of a content life. He would never pass up an opportunity to see his relatives. Afterall, without them what joy was found in living? And Auntie Marissa distracted him from thinking about, dreaming about, repeatedly obsessing over his wovens in their weeks of separation.

Auntie clamored into his guest room with travel containers of food, squawking how it was nice to visit him outside of the medical wing in the White Tower this go-round. Fennick didn't humor that comment. Those days of watching Zander's human blood reject his immortal heart was a nightmare that frequented far too much, the scars they both wore were a ceaseless reminder of those days, but also their love. In came Brock and Yolanda to share in her feast and ease their minds about those of blessed blood.

Auntie Marissa didn't hesitate to comment on how the bland condensed cracker diet of a sea voyager was hardly sustainable, undeniably unacceptable to her palate. She served a full three course meal from those boxes and awoke their taste buds to their full potential.

That first bite had reminded his body it was nearly home. The emancipated courtesan patted her belly. Her short rose gold hair matched her sun and wind redden cheeks which held a satisfied grin. This girl loved rich flavors and hearty meals, he had wished Wisteria's desire for food increased because he was tired of feeling as if he were forcing meals down her throat. For both their sakes.

The Bloodsworn had been teaching the eager Numaalians the basics of self-defense for the last odd weeks, Yolanda's enthusiasm dragged Brock out of his handicapped mindset and got him up and swinging a sword again. Decently too, he was pleased to note.

As anticipated, Auntie Marissa spoiled Brock and Yolanda with copious amounts of her fantastic Ilanthian cooking. Her ability to flavor the simplest of sauces and salads was revered amongst our family. Yolanda seemed more traumatized by leaving her side in the kitchen than she was to leave her nation a month ago. She was half tempted to stay in Ilanthia when auntie offered her a place to stay in Havana and work the rice fields with her.

Brock dissuaded her with a single goofy grin and a half heard comment about their pledge to those they wished followed. His allegiance was to Wisteria, who he was currently debating over how to make her life utterly miserable. Yolanda's was to a mysterious, rebellious bloke called Bastion, who realistically may have died in Landsfell. She'd return to confirm before her mind would be swayed. The friendship building between them was strengthened by their shared hardships and horrors they witnessed the night we all sprinted onto the ship at the southern port.

When auntie bid goodbye the next morning, Yolanda was found with an extra container of pork buns and rice rolls. She proudly arranged the meals into her travel bag, gushing with adoration for his family. "I am fortunate." He was more than fortunate, so much so he could not vocalize for the more he fixated on his family the more desperate he was to wrap his arms around Momo and Pa.

And Zander.

Then there was Wisteria.

She was the most sacred of family, but he'd never be so foolish to sort her into the category of a sister because a decent man does not wish to fuck his sister until sanity has left them both. Brothers definitely don't relive the first moment they saw that girl naked in a hot spring and jerk off to it every night.

He paced the hallway before exiting the fourth century styled guest wing on the first floor of the hundred and some leveled White Tower, anything to banish the memory of his hands groping her immaculate bare flesh in the broom closet while she gyrated against him and Zander, working her way to climax. Heat coiled around his spine. His tails sprung free at the memory as he repressed something else in his pants springing free.

If Zander had not fluxed them to the apartment, he would have followed her suit and found release the second her perky ass shifted against him. Even thinking about how lean and nimble she was jumping roof to roof and fighting him when they watched the iron gates of Landsfell made his mind race. She was a match for him and he'd not had worthy competition for decades. She could fucking put him and a fistful of Kai's Rudins in a casket if she wanted to. Sexy as hell it would be too.

And of course there was the moment he knew he was absolutely damned.

The moment she stepped out in nothing but a red thong, some piercings and a whiff of a pathetic excuse for fabric around her torso determined to kill for love. For Anna. For her Woodlands. And unannounced to her stubborn mind, her love of Zander and an entire city of innocent vibrants she couldn't stand to see parish also drove her hand in humiliating the royal family.

No matter his desires and impulses, he would not breach that thin line until she made the first move. He would not even dare to call her beautiful, for beauty of Wisteria's caliber was indescribable. He'd have to scour his old text books to find a word in a lost language worthy enough of his woven. His father had his own set of keys to the library somewhere in his cluttered apartment, he'd search for a laudable term for ages if this war didn't end him first.

Protector. He would act as her protector. Act. He told himself this while passing his reflection in an archway window.

His hair was long again tied back and off his shoulders. Among the silver strands were his high peaked fox ears sticking out. His tails were in a proud display, fanning around behind him as fire settled in his wake. He tried to make himself more approachable, less flame more conversational. But each time his eyes fell on Ik Kygen he gritted down and let a ring of fire slip as close as he could to that brilliant bastard without burning the hairs on sweet Cobar's head. Cobar had taken to calling him Uncle Nikki now, he would live up to those familiar standards.

Had Ik Kygen not been a manipulative, lying fucktard to Wisteria and her woodland family, had she not have ordered that of him, he would have continued to envy the man he grew up hearing battletales about and even begged for a combat lesson from him. His younger self would have been in literal tears just sitting silently at his side.

But, no. Nothing was as it seemed.

A crowd gathered to watch the last God, Ilanthia's Emperor, Maruc the God of War emerge from the pale doors of his elegant White Tower that scaled into the sky next to the pristine beaches and fertile farms. The tower, however formidable and infused with magic beyond his comprehension, felt as if it was welcoming him to the Lands of the Gods.

No matter how many times he has visited over the centuries, the tower, the temples, the library and the starlight strands lighting the streets of the city stole his sentiments and spun them into wonderment. Which was welcomed, because once again he was imagining himself curled up between his wovens with Wisteria's arms locked around his neck, the warm hints of vanilla and earth on her skin he could taste if he kept his eyes closed.

Maruc stepped out looking no more man than Brock who used Yolanda's shoulder as a crutch to lower himself instinctually to his knees. But Maruc was different from any mortal or immortal man; his raw power easily beckoned crowds to hinge at the hip in his presence.

The Emperor, like all Eternals, had the presence one would expect. An aura that demands respect, a knee to bend and words to muddle without him ever muttering a single word. His breastplate was the sole piece of armor he donned. His mighty weapon was his hands. Stories of his potent conjurings and wars fought on far away fronts brought the fox and the entire city to their knees when he strode forward to the portal.

The enchanted portal to Veona expanded under his gaze and glimmered like a pastel liquid, rippling time and space. Four members of Maruc's white garbed Ivory Legion stood directly next to Ik Kygen who wore the Bloodsworn golds and leathers. He was a legend to be revered even in the mountain towns and across the isles. He tried his best to prepare Zander of his arrival without giving full disclosure because it was Wisteria who deserved to learn the truth first. He hoped his brief written request to Zander begging him to keep his shit together when they arrived went heeded.

Everyone who knew of Ik Kygen's swordsmanship and finesse desired to have their skills assessed and refined by Athromancia's longest friend and most trusted Commander. The longer he stared at him, the more heat exploded from his fingertips. His nine tails sparked, startling the waveriders. "Easy, Fennick," Brock hopped away from the fire which would burn through whatever the fox wanted. Luckily, he liked Brock. He hoped he looked apologetic when he dragged the fire closer to his body.

Wisteria's guardian gave an anxious exhale and met his gaze. Fennick wished he looked as collected as that bastard, but knew his need for his wovens were getting the better of him. Like he'd been drug through the desert and someone placed an oasis ten feet in front of him but wouldn't let him drink. 'Soon.' The revered Montuse warrior mouthed silently to the fox. Maruc seemed to understand the interaction, he held his thoughts behind a cunning grin. A thin and crumbling facade.

There would be no Athromancia bouncing behind her brother today, very few seem to know this. Three actually.

Maruc's control of the wind closed the doors closed behind him with a light groan of metal, his voice billowed out and enclosed the entirety of the central square with a booming riptide. "Arise, great peoples of Kinlyra." Maruc's words beckoned everyone upright. Curious new and old eyes drank in the Eternal who had slowly become a slumbering myth since his brother Temperance left the physical plane and left him to contemplate his own exit and give in to the heaviness of rest. The remaining Eternals didn't wear crowns nor precious metals, nor did they have to wear their power. They simply had their aura.

The fox's tired eyes played tricks, Maruc's divine aura was dimmed—less awoken—then he remembered it years ago before his journey into Numaal. "The Ivory Legion stands astute until my return. Come, new acquaintances, to the Dreamer Realm of the Veil and beyond. Let's broaden your horizons once more and enter the third nation of Kinlyra. Into the mountains we go." He turned his astute, friendly gaze to the vibrants on his right. Fennick thought he hid his desperation well.

The hybrid elemental further sunk his teeth into his tongue. The cuts in his mouth healed before he swallowed the blood. It would be rude to dart in front of Maruc and their company to cross the barrier first knowing Zander was waiting on the other side. Wisteria at his side. .

In went Maruc, followed by beings of all three lands, Ilanthians, Numaalians and dreamers.

Portal travel felt like being caught up in an autumn wind, a cool and pleasant surprise that caused the breath to hitch in your lungs. Being said, there is nothing–nothing–as pleasant as sprinting into his brother's arms and having them embrace him so dearly one felt it imprint permanently on their soul. Holding Zander was returning to himself.

The feelings of being lost and anxious vanished. They were consumed by wholeness.

Fennick's feet lifted off the ground as a horselord incubus ran up the Altar of Horns and slammed into Fennick's furry aflamed body to draw him into a hug. Zander licked the side of his face like a devoted dog seeing their master after time wedged between them. Fennick welcomed it. The tears staining his cheeks evaporated with an unheard sizzle. Zander kissed his cheek where he knew one tear to have remained, his own joyfilled disbelief carved into his scruffy face. "Never again."

"Never again." Never would they be apart that long. Any of them. "I love you."

Fennick pulled his burning gold gaze away from his woven to find the missing piece of their world buried under Brock and Cobar. Wisteria.

His jealousy was briefly stomped out hearing her joyous cries of reuniting with her friends and family. Overwhelmed with happy giggles, Wisteria shook them loose and left the bottom of the stairs to dart between the Emperor and his Ivory Legionnaires to wrap her arms around the neck of Commander Ik Kygen of Athromancia's Bloodsworn Legion and allowed him to press a sobbing kiss on her freckled nose.

Veona stilled.

A knowing descended. The knowing. Zander waivered between slacking and stiffening.

Fennick demanded Zander drop him to his feet so he may better prepare himself for a multitude of reactions. He tried to warn his brother in as few discrete words as possible about the secret which was about to be *unleashed on Kinlyra that would change the course of their woven's world. All the world.*

Maruc pivoted behind him, the veins in his temples visible. Fuck. Shit. Fuck. *He was murderous.*

Zander's magic seeped through the Veil, blanketing each stone on which they stood with purple haze.

Atticus, his sons and the city at his side watched the scene unfold, their minds reeled. Warroh and Clavey lost resolve and their knees hit the floor. Wyatt blossomed with thorns. Kashikat shielded Nyx and Namir. Percy drank.

The elves and elementals shot bemused gazes across the courtyard all while Wisteria danced around the Bloodsworn with familiarity, nimbly dodging his hands which moved through the air trying to grasp her as she teased him with her Montuse dexterity. A dexterity which was now clear to the masses where she learned it from. Wisteria allowed herself to be captured and pulled into a tender hug. His hearing picked up the disbelief among the crowd and he happily heard Clavey's gossipy court of nymphs and potion pushers stutter into silence.

A young Cobar interfered with the embrace and she placed him on her hip, swaying her way towards her two woven still intertwined and pressed heart to heart staring at her. Wisteria hardly noticed the ring of fire or violet magic she stepped over on her way to them, nor headed the God summoning storms or the city dipping reverently to Ik Kygen and Maruc both. She was rightfully occupied by her destiny.

Zander's fingers intertwined with his loyalest brother's as they watched their Wisteria close the distance between them, their hearts bleeding from incessant need. Her glossy eyes fixed on Fennick's toothy, sharp grin while her hands were reaching for their arms.

She was so close it was painful not to have her.

Maruc's voice came from the clouds above, darkening and looming over Oyokos' horns. "You were to protect her from her foolishness. You've failed her!" *The sky parted, stopping Wisteria from jumping into her dreamers' hold. Fennick's heart raced and heated with hungry demand for her.*

Maruc summoned the storm in his hands. Above his head the God collected the violence and destruction of ten thousand storms. They congregated in a sphere between his hands. Ik Kygen squared his shoulders to him, the great Bloodsworn Commander's last stance.

The beyond would soon welcome him.

"She loved her! Your brother loves her! Who am I to deter love?" Ik Kygen unsheathed his sword and steadied it in his right hand. Cobar was hiding behind the fabric of Wisteria's shirt, a cut that was not properly designed to flatter her lithe form. No matter. That meant less eyes fixed on his. "The memorandum!"

Disbelief. Betrayal. Worry. The Emperor hid nothing in his stormy gaze, his dazzling grin had gone to dust. Fury remained. "Her Anna was my Athromancia!" Zander sprouted wings and shielded his fully transformed fox friend in his arms, all his magic sucked back into himself as he prepared for the Maruc's release of power.

He shook, staring at the lethal familiarity of the storm of chaos in his hands, how it reminded him of the damage he caused on his ninety-four civilians and their families. With a nip on his shoulder the elemental redirected his attention to Wisteria who never made it safely between them. Her eyes were wild as she ran against the gale force winds, towards Ik Kygen and the source of the storm.

She intended to scold a God. Or fight one. Or die by one.

Her presence didn't stop Maruc from his strike descending on Ik Kygen.

The sphere in his hand was pulled back to launch. Zander and Fennick reared their haunches towards the eye of the storm when they heard Wisteria beckon her weapon. "Orion!"

As Maruc unleashed chaos, Wisteria sliced through it, dismantling its power of murderous intent with a single swipe of her blade. She looked between the Emperor and her trusted Keenan, her own savage expression on her face. "What the fuck did you just say?"

Chapter Fourteen

That man standing among the white guards and waveriders was dressed in simple finery, no taller than those as his side. Nothing called my attention to him as *the* Emperor until he brought down the stratosphere and enclosed it in his palms.

Then reality pelted me in the gut and smacked the spit from my mouth.

He was Maruc, God of War.

And Maruc's intention to harm Keenan stole my desires away from the need I had to wrap my fingers around Nikki's fluffy pointed ears and ignited the urge I had to protect my chosen family, while my woven males were safe with each other. I felt Zander's relief unknot in my chest merely being in his loyalty woven's presence. Brock, Yolanda and Cobar were behind my wovens, but Keenan? Keenan was not safe. Not from whatever storm was consolidating in Maruc's fists.

"Her Anna was my Athromancia." Maruc's voice fell around Veona like thunder booming from every direction, from the clouds themselves.

Athromancia? *My Anna...* the Goddess of Wisdom? "What the fuck did you just say?"

My rattled mind repeated the words it had heard. Doubting I heeded them correctly. My Anna...Athromancia? Pairing them with my Anna's otherworldly beauty, blazing hair and the unspoken persistently on her shoulders, but never vocalized for she feared I may abandon her. Yet, she abandoned me.

Anna… No. *Athromancia* had the full power of an Eternal to protect the Woodlands. And didn't lift a damn finger. Instead, she forced her blood into me.

The golden blooded Empress herself.

Selfish bitch.

I was a fool. A fool sent to run errands for a dead Goddess who tricked me into loving her to just carry out her tasks to stop a war and deliver a message to Maruc. I would deliver her message alright. And mine. Just after I get my rutting answers.

The Commander of the Bloodsworn who arrived in the Southland years ago with his Empress, a brilliant deceiving redhead, stared at me with pleading eyes. I did not shy away, I met them with piercing hate. Rage fueled me onward. My bones did not freeze and tremble like Judeth's and countless others who were carried down to the ground by graceful pixies, but they stiffened against the wind that was set on destroying the center of the temple circle.

"She *loved* her! Your brother *loves* her, he will not forsake her!" I knew Keenan well enough to know he wasn't stating this for the sake of the Emperor, but for mine. He reiterated some of the last words Anna had spoken to me before she died. If Anna was Athromancia, then her brother who loves me as much as I love him would have to be… *Orion*.

Maruc readied his magic to strike and to kill the only man who could give me answers to this quest my soul had embarked on years ago. And quite frankly if anyone got to kill him, it was going to be me.

He would spill his knowledge before I spilled his entrails.

I screamed and summoned my longest, most faithful friend. Orion appeared in my grasp, gleaming bright against Maruc's bleak storm. I wielded his brother against him and set his magic back into the sky with a singular swoop of steel. Temperance defended me and mine.

Orion's magic was spinning dizzily around me, settling only when I caressed the blade. Fireworks went off, celebrating our joining. Scatters of color wrapped around me as we familiarized ourselves to each other's touch once more, caring not about what stupid look Maruc wore on his face as he whimpered his brother's name seeing him for the first time in five hundred years. In the arms of a woodlander no less, who insouciantly spun him around in a skillful sword dance we'd been perfecting for years together. I turned to Keenan, who was grappling with something under his collar. "Is it true?"

"Yes, but–" My fingers stuck out and smashed his airway, I bent my elbow and swung it at his cheekbone while he was doubled over gasping for air, gagging in between heaves. Nothing he said anymore carried value. There was no desire to listen to his pathetic excuses.

Orion sang out blissfully in my arm as I revolved him around my wrists and wrung him from one arm to another, savoring his touch before I locked him on the belt that appeared around my waist. Magic. I wouldn't dirty Orion with Keenan's filthy blood. Not yet. I'd use the fists that he trained me to use.

I launched them hard.

His somber shouts didn't penetrate the emotional wall I quickly built up to keep him out. "We followed Orion! He was the compass on the boat. We expected to dismantle the darkness and spread understanding, the rest of the Gold Legion of Bloodsworn are in the mountains ready to intercept Maruc if he launched a surprise attack on Numaal without Athromancia's consent." Another heave for air and a pitiful look on his paling face had me gritting down on my back teeth. "Falling in love was the last thing any of us expected. Her love for you outweighed her love for the world. You are Athromancia's chosen vessel."

There was a ringing in my ears, an absence of thought and sound as Maruc stopped all the winds. My voice was thick with hate. "She had magic to banish the wraiths, protect the crafters from knights, spread the truth of creation throughout a hopeless, confused nation *and to ask for my permission*–she failed on all accounts. Your family wouldn't be prisoners and mine would be alive had she not failed them too!"

"She couldn't! She could do nothing with dormant powers!" His brown hair lost its stiffness and fell into his eyes as he violently disagreed. "She concealed her powers. Locked them away to make them untraceable, inaccessible. The magic of the last Goddess is yours now—all of it—to be awakened at the Opal Lake with your golden laced red blood. If you want them." I was already shaking my head in defiance. Whatever this liar and his Empress wanted or expected of me I'd do the opposite to spite them.

The God in our vicinity stomped his heel. Keenan, or whatever the fuck his real name was, lifted his gaze behind me. "She saw how fiercely you loved the first day we arrived and how undaunted you were by her presence. The bold love that lives in your heart is what Kinlyra needs." Spiteful tears rolled down my chin. "The Empress and Temperance were not the only ones to love you."

He referred to himself, yet my gaze shifted to Zander and Nikki, both looking as if they were going to shed their skins and strangle Keenan for implying all this time he was acting in my best interest. His blood oath made him a slave to the Empress's orders should she mandate anything from him, I'd no idea what commands he was given or if his devotion to my family was authentic. "I have no right to you, but I couldn't cherish you more even if you were my own daughter. I have memories you need to see, important ones. That everyone here needs to witness."

The paternal barrage ate away at my stomach. I blinked away the water blurring my eyes, distorting the view of my beautiful reunited wovens. "Did you know?"

Zander's torso hinged a subtle few degrees. He lowered himself so the sincerity in his gaze visibly poured into me from his crystalline blue eyes. A color as unforgettable as Anna's hair. "No. But, it changes absolutely nothing." Our bond came to life. His heart ached for me, his love was indomable. "I love you as a human or as a golden vessel. I will love you just as you are for however long you will let me, my flower. I am yours." Nikki lowered his snout in agreement.

I felt myself dumbly nodding. Or was I shaking from the surprise of spending the last years avenging a lover who was little else but a mirage of lies? Any notion of the sentiment of love made me nauseous. It was repellent to my soul.

My jaw ground down and heat prickled up my spine as I unsheathed Orion. I felt the opposite of loving. Hateful.

"Maruc, the memorandum!" Keenan hollered as the crowd began to mumble. No one looked pleased as I glared at a man who introduced himself as Anna's cousin and weaseled his way into my commune and heart. I wanted to carve him out of my past. As I raised my sword to do so, the mass of people leaned in as if to defend him. Their chatter reminded me how much I truly was a woodland creature who needed time away from busy cities to recuperate and that I was certainly not a worthy or experienced person to host the magic of a Goddess.

I was an angry and broken mortal.

I didn't want to house Anna's damn blood or have anything to do with her choice to scamper away from the White Tower, away from her consequences. I closed my eyes and felt Orion's eagerness flutter into my steps as I moved closer to Keenan. "Hurry Maruc, before she decides to kill us both."

"Not humorous. You're Montuse and I am *me*," Maruc drawled out and slowly slurred his words into that of another language. Rocks rearranged into a well in my peripheral, he took to creating something from stone and magic. My gaze was set on the dried blood on Keenan's face, deciding that not enough of it spattered there.

More. He needed to suffer *more*. As I have all these years living like an absolutely daft love blind idiot.

Keenan swore and raised his blade in my direction. "She is my apprentice. The first one I have taken since the Great War. I trained her to be my equal despite her mortality and domain. And I can say with certainty that she will not stop until I am gutted if you don't prepare the waters of lucidity!" Now seemed like a lovely time to demonstrate my abilities to the seven sons of Atticus and make Judeth eat her words about not allowing me to join them willfully. I'd show them what a damn rouge could do when properly motivated.

The most delightful clank of metal on metal rang out around us as he blocked a series of strikes I sent aimed at his head. Showmanship. I let my arrogance roam free and hate direct Orion to bring down swings and jabs. "Some stupid, naive part of me believes you and the other believes death upon you is too great a mercy. Until I can make up my mind I will be painting this altar red with your deceitful blood!"

He challenged me with a smile before he darted into the crowd, where I lost him briefly behind many sets of fluttering wings. Smug confidence coursed through me as I whirled Orion behind my back and counted backwards from five. "Look. I am so kind as to even give you a head start, you old bastard!" Four. Three.

"Get the waters ready!" A desperate voice came from the south behind an eclectic fae gathering. Keenan. My eyes followed him until his worn leathers were atop the roof of a massive temple. Warroh was livid at his disrespect and shouted as much. Clavey pulled a petite male pixie to his side and shielded his wings from the inevitable rain. Children in the streets cautiously clung to their guardians.

Two. One.

Rain started, fine sheets of water blew through the city center falling like dreary, slanted paint brush strokes. The crowd around me parted as I sprinted by with Orion raised.

At the base of an oversized temple shimmering with rose quartz I put Temperance between my teeth, kicked off my shoes to scale the crystal column to the roof. Keenan was still shedding his ceremonious leather shoulder straps that he hated when I arrived.

Swinging at the man's back while he was turned to me was no coward's move, it was vicious. Which I was. He rolled out from under the down strike, rain patters dotting his shirt as the sprinkling of water turned heavier. Thick droplets blurred our vision. We circumnavigated the round dome, our weapons clashing several times, our feet at a tempo my human body had spent years accomplishing to match his unnatural pace. With the adrenaline pumping in me, it was not difficult.

This was no master-apprentice quarrel or a spar lacking passion.

Oh no, I fought him as an equal. I would not be losing.

Were it not a fight of furious emotions, I would have cherished this exhilarating combat session and savored the joy derived when sprinting at his side. He was not holding back. He needed me subdued so he could brainwash me with whatever nonsense he and Anna agreed upon years ago. I wasn't going to let that happen.

He leapt to the adjacent rooftop, I was parallel with each step including the massive gulch I was vaulting over. Zander's worry turned into awe, borderline lust and we rolled and flipped in sync upon landing. I banished both of his sentiments to focus solely on the one raging through me. When Ilanthian combat got us nowhere I launched myself into back handsprings. He caught my foot, twisted it and I hit the floor. In the splits, I was gifted the opportunity to take out his knee with the knuckles of my fist.

He cursed while I rolled away.

Remaining low, I parallelled Orion's length down my forearm and crouched, placing tension in my legs to release when the moment was right. A vicious cricket with power reserves coiled tight.

Down his steel sword rushed and backwards I leapt. Throwing myself into consecutive backflips. I out maneuvered him. Zander's nerves gripped my arm. I shut the door to the bond and gave Keenan all my focus, all my loathing. I'm sure I looked like quite the circus act up here, strutting around in the shit weather eager to maim and spew blood.

Keenan closed the distance between us. When my back was against the round of the high dome, he smiled with relief. I let myself be captured as Zander had by Stegin all those years ago. I watched his arm and blade cross the rainy sky above my head and squirmed my arms out of their sleeves.

My wet tunic caught his wrist. I captured his arm and snapped it with a grotesque crunch. "You always said being underestimated was my strength. Have you forgotten or did you want me to end your embarrassment here?" Now bladeless and on his knees, the wet fabric from my back was tight around his neck, his broken wrist useless in prying it loose. At least for another minute before he healed himself. I had to act quick.

I readied my knee to meet his face, he composed himself enough to tug a necklace into my line of sight. "They knew! Your parents knew from the moment we landed to the moment the house was ransacked. They knew who we were and what may come to pass. Anna ordered me away the night of the attack and forbade me to come to anyone's aid for eleven moons. Until her remains were completely gone." He gagged on the congealed blood pouring from his nose as I stared at my parent's wedding rings knocking against his chest.

I ripped the metal chain off his neck. He simpered audibly when the noose around his windpipe fell. I ran my fingers over the two wedding bands before dropping them into my pant's pocket. "Tell me, Bloodsworn. Did my parents know they would get raped and slaughtered, while your manipulative bitch goddess *watched* and *did nothing?* Dormant magic or not she tried to convince me to stand down! Do I strike you as someone who *stands down?*"

His head was shaking. "Our ship to Ilanthia wasn't going to be ready in time with the increased attacks and no means to obtain necessities. We had several months to digest the options fate presented. This is what we chose." His blood mixed with the rainfall, pooling pink liquid below his knees.

"*We?* I had no involvement in those decisions."

"I'm sorry." He said it as if it were to mean something to me. "Did you ever wonder in those last months, why I was ruthless on your training, why your mother baked your favorite meals with the foods preserved for winter, why Elousie hosted nightly revels until the barrels went dry, why Anna drank in every damn second at your side?" Water droplets hung on my lashes. His movements were slow, his eyes never left mine as he cautiously handed me Orion and pulled himself upright. He tapped his temple and pointed down to a small fountain filling with water near the portal and thousands of beings watching the late morning unfold. "Come, Wisteria. See my memories."

Chapter Fifteen

I didn't accept his hand getting down from the roof of the temple; however, I did take my crumpled wet shirt from him, his eyes mournfully taking in the sight of my back as I dressed. The lump in his throat snagged on grief and what I hoped was regrets.

A hand rested between my shoulders, I shrugged him off. "I'm not talking about the consequences of your cowardliness now." I bit the air hard. "And if I feel like *not* shunning, maybe we can talk about how getting your wife and infant back from Remnants and the royal family involves me handing myself over to the prince. Or how getting your son out of Landsfell alive involved me being whipped and branded by Numaal's favorite priestess and my mom's rapist." I pivoted to him amid the quiet city. "You're welcome, by the way, you damn coward."

I would have done it all again for my baby brother. Easiest choice. I didn't say that outloud, I wanted my words to cut him.

They did. The statements destroyed him. And those nearby sported glassy eyes and unhinged jaws. Several residents went to comfort Keenan, addressing him as Commander Ik Kygen and dipping their chins, he dismissed them shamefully.

I should feel remorseful for making this man bawl in anguish while trying to walk his way down the cobblestone street in public, among people who clearly knew him or knew of him. His tear ridden face turned towards me every twenty feet to make sure I hadn't run off, which was exactly what I wanted to do.

I stopped by a pair of tawny brown wings and stared up at Percy, who looked more washed out with the rain roping his hair flat. "This is ridiculous. All of it," I grumbled under my breath. I wiped water from my runny nose and chilled cheeks. My skin was cold. My fingers pale and bloodless from their tight grip on Orion's hilt.

"For once, we agree." Percy offered me a swig of what was in his flask. "I don't know which is more terrifying, your ability to land two strikes on Ik Kygen or the fact Maruc was casually about to demolish a quarter of the city and it's inhabitants to get to him."

"I landed three blows, broke both his wrists and nose. If you are going to keep score, do it right." His laugh settled my nerves unexpectedly. I wasn't stupid enough to tell him that or crack a smile at him. I welcomed the burn of his beverage and pressed it back into his stomach after a second swing. I contemplated taking it with me as I continued this mortifying walk. The row of elves managed to look regal with their hoods up and form unfaltering while my hair and clothes hugged my body in a wholly unflattering caress.

I wanted to hide, to blend in with the mass of people after Keenan forced my hand making a spectacle of myself. Sure, I leapt at the opportunity, still I'd cast the blame on him. I felt too fragile with the lies cracking through me that I would not shoulder any more. I couldn't. I didn't plan for my day to commence by running around barefoot chasing Athromancia's best friend with a weapon embedded with an actual God. *A God. Temperance, the third trithrone ruler of Ilanthia.*

My eyes sought out Brock who was with Yolanda and Cobar on the outskirts of the seadrifters. He looked more confident with his uneven walk and styled his recently chopped hair to frame his face. A face that held no judgment, one that even softened when he discretely pointed to his rising chest, reminding me to breathe. Yolanda, effortlessly feminine, clenched Brock's other hand so tightly her white knuckles were visible in the lessening rain. Cobar was finding comfort in her skirts and watching his father stride towards the memorandum.

It was hardly a drizzle by the time Nikki reverted back into a half-man, half-fire fox form on the last step of the stone altar. Steam hissed around him. His open palms were all the invitation I needed to run into his embrace. His two gold suns for eyes were pressed together when I collided with him, but he failed to close them before I caught sight of the raging yearning in them. I should know what that looks like, I felt it mirrored in my own green gaze.

All my weight was thrown at him. Gods damn he was immovably solid. He didn't fluctuate as my arms flew around his neck or hesitate to lift me off the ground and secure his hands on my body. A mutual craving. Golden mirth spread through my body. Healing heat seeped into the cracks to glue me together a little while longer, melting and welding pieces. Fortified. I was stronger with him. With them. Fuck if I ever let them go.

My fingers knotted in his silken and suddenly long hair and I clung tighter. "Hello, little vixen." The hoarse raspy greeting was all he managed. His lips pressed to my hairline, while I pressed mine against his sternum feeling his raised scars under my kiss.

Twice for good measure.

I couldn't compose a sufficient reply to express the reprieve that came from our bodies merging and the fever sweltering between us. I nuzzled my chilly nose against the exposed skin on his neck and nestled myself against his warmth and radiance. I definitely whimpered. He chuckled, sending me to press myself onto him until I melted to him like a second skin. No. I was never letting him out of my company again. Definitely not if it ever happened to storm. "You're not mad at me for punching your Keenan in the head anymore I presume?" He'd known about my Anna, my blood, her betrayal the moment he saw the Bloodsworn and proceeded to defend me without my insight.

"As long as you can forgive the fact I abandoned you on the water." I set space between our chests to lessen the tension of the heated thread between us. I couldn't allow the Weaver to abuse this moment by turning a friendly reunion into one of Her bright compulsions that would be on display to the world. Nikki did not set me down nor release his arms. I wasn't protesting.

His clean smooth jawline flexed with anger. A short shake of his head was all he gave me. I pushed against him. "You can't seriously stay brooding over that forever. It's done. I don't regret it. You're welcome."

My feet touched the stone steps, his grip remained sealed around my waist like an iron belt. The hairs on my arms stood on end as a low animalistic tone crept up from his voicebox. "You jumped off the last ship to salvation and into an ocean of ice and monsters. You exploded the dock and leapt to your own death. You were bleeding out, sick and high with no Zander in sight."

"Are we just stating facts now?"

Hearing his name, Zander approached behind Nikki's back. His blue eyes looking at the way his brother's hands latched themselves around my waistline with Orion tucked safely between us. His arms wrapped around us both. *'Incubi don't share,'* they had once told me.

This felt a lot like sharing. It also felt indescribably… *right.*

Zander scrutinized Nikki's face and when he discovered happiness there, his brow smoothed to mirror the elated emotion of his woven. I cleared my throat. "I kept you, my friends and my silver family *alive.*" Nikki didn't give me wiggle room to back away.

"We can talk about this after dinner. I am taking you to meet my parents and we will spend the night in the Burrows." I stopped trying to escape him because shock held me at his sharp, directive tone. Oddly it suited him. I found myself smiling and silent as an agreeable response. "Zander will know where to find us when he wants us, our bond will feel sated now that we can connect." *When.* Not *if.* "We will head to the farmer's market after we watch Ik Kygen's memories on display. They look about ready."

Right. Keenan. I was livid at him. Or I *was* before Nikki distracted me for thirty seconds.

Hell, I hadn't detected that the rain had stopped and my clothes had been dried by a certain elemental. "Did you take my anger?" I felt for my pulse. It had slowed. And when I looked at Keenan hovering over the stone fountain of rain water dousing his bloodied face in it, a face that I bloodied minutes ago, rage didn't strum through me.

He did.

"Yes. I will return it to you a bit at a time so we can process it together. You are not alone anymore, Woodlander. You will feel everything, but we will not allow it to break you." Zander's arm draped across Nikki's shoulders, his eyes now on the bite mark he bestowed upon me.

Zander?

Yes, my love?

Dazzling eyes met mine before he swooped in to kiss me while Nikki adjusted under the weight of a heavy incubi arm teetered over him. It was a tender little kiss. Not because he was testing my fragility, no—he was testing himself, and his possessive nature. I deepened it until a grin played on his lips.

He seemed pleased because he chewed on his lower lip thoughtfully and hadn't disbanded the smile. He then pressed his lips to Nikki's head, inhaling deeply. While he acclimated to scents, I unwrapped several strands of messy long hair caught around his elegant horns. He quickly shot himself upright behind the pair of his wovens when a rumbling cut through the subsiding storm.

Atticus snarled. He stood thrusting his set of horns in Zander's direction. The displeasure was palpable. The crowd around him moved away from the looming winged dreamer. Maruc gave him a stern finger and a rippling of shiny magic that settled not just him but the anxious crowd that was reacting to Atticus's temper. His sway was unintentional. *What was that about?*

More pissing contests. Not something to worry about. Nikki's flames grew high to block out the audience and obscure them from my vision. Above us in a puff of steam and dreams, emerged faces from my pasts that sent me to my knees.

"Mom!" I screamed, watching the replica of her dance around with my father in our family's small kitchen lit with a handful of beeswax candles. My hand covered my mouth, this was a memory. She could not hear me. I stared at their wedding bands where they rightfully should have been on their fingers and not shoved into my pocket. Even from Keenan's perspective sipping tea on the counter, he captured the magnitude of my parents' affectionate devotion.

Moriah and Elousie joined in once they threw open the front doors and laid down several stalks of corn harvest. Elousie was already drunk and took to the drums in the corner made from tightened animal skins. Cobar had laced the base of each drum with red seaweed earlier that summer which stained the hemp twine that held it together a dark red that reminded me of autumn.

Keenan rose to kiss his wife who told him about how difficult it was to put Rory down when the bleating goats from Conrad's barn sent her into fits of giggles. Keenan's laugh shook the memory as if we were truly inside his head. We all watched his hands gather a wide rimmed drum and fall into a rhythm with Elousie whose jeweled adorned hands patted away.

I remember this night. I fondly remember all the warm nights after a good harvest. I knew who would be entering the doors to my family's humble home next. I willed myself to turn away, to not be reminded of her betraying beauty, her laugh, her hair, her quick temper, her adventurous spirit. I couldn't. "The music called to me!" she announced, taking Moriah and my mother and together they whirled into a circle, the flash of Anna's hair caught the light and illuminated the entire room. Were it not for Nikki's steady rise and fall of his chest moving behind me, I would've forgotten to inhale.

I always thought her skin held a shimmer as if true silver always wanted to escape her flesh. Now, I know I wasn't breeching insanity all these years. It was her dormant magic lurking captive, eager to break free. It was so rutting clear to see with another's eyes. Gods I was a naive idiot!

Her gaze set straight onto me. Onto all of us watching the steamy images move and interact with artificial life. "Where is my Ivy?" She asked her Bloodsworn.

My Ivy. She felt it too. The belonging, the claim we laid on eachother.

I watched my Anna scrutinize Keenan in a harsh way that usually told me they were about to fight or were recovering from one. A look I thankfully rarely ever warranted. "Ivy is out with your brother, he is teaching her to dance blindfolded. Orion's getting jealous of all the time you've been spending with her and has taken to disappearing when I am around and reappearing in her bed at night."

"Our bed. I can count on my fingers the nights I have *not* watched her sleep." She drank from Elousie's cup. "As for Orion, Wisteria doesn't mind sleeping with us both, she is accustomed to two weighty and influential energies wrapped around her. If one of us is gone, she is restless. The stars made her unshakeable, she can handle more than one Eternal while you rarely managed one of us over the eons." Anna flicked Keenan's nose before raising her brow.

My dad moved closer to them. His soft curly hair he brushed aside allowing me to see the depths of his hazel eyes and the assuredness of his smile. Plump tears ran to my chin. Longing hit me so hard I failed to scream for him like my soul wanted to. He was so close yet so intangible it hurt. Physically *hurt*.

His smell, embrace, tough words, kind actions—all so close. I held my chest with my hands fearing it would fall out. "He makes her arrogant. That overconfidence will get her killed if she is alone with more than a dozen night walkers."

She touched my father's face with endearment. "Alester. Ivy is not influenced by us, as proven the first day she bolted up the docks and greeted me. Her charming strut, witty mouth and fast fighting is not a product of Orion. He gives her peace to listen to her own intuition and choose accordingly with decisive action. She is, however, influenced by you. Her stubbornness, love of adventure and desire to mend all that she can. That is your and Lily's doing." She and my dad were sharing a still moment. It felt heavy. My dad pulled her hand away and kissed her knuckles.

"The stars themselves will have a hard time separating you two." My father tapped his foot to the outlandish beat.

"Alester, I never intend to leave her. Not here, not when we get to Ilanthia. Even when I am gone back to Ether I selfishly will embed my love within her and her future woodlander line." Her whisper was a dusting of deeper truths and intentions.

"No talk of that nonsense now. It has been discussed enough. Anymore chatter about my sweet Wisteria facing darkness, stubborn kings and Gods alone hurts my soul." He'd known. They all knew that Anna intended to make me her vessel. My heart beat in the hollow cavern of my chest, aching more than ever.

I felt for Nikki's hand and pressed it into my sternum. A silent plea to be held. He and Zander did not shy away from my request. Two sets of arms found their way to me.

Keenan watched my mother and Moriah glance over their shoulders from the kitchen where a stew of roasted vegetables simmered and rye bread cooled. Their attention shifted out the window, then to the door. It swung open.

I supposed I did have a strut about me.

Orion spun aimlessly in my hands while I closed the door behind, locking out a draft. Anna left Keenan and my father to wipe the sweat from my brow with the backs of her fingers. She kissed me deeply with her hand knotting in my hair and mine already around the soft curve of her thigh stopping to make a gesture at my sweat soaked chamise. "I was under the impression you were out perfecting *swordplay*. Why do you look as exhilarated as if you were relishing *foreplay*?" I stuck out my pierced tongue and she nipped at it.

I held up the hilt of Orion to Anna. "Suppose anything is a sex toy if you are brave enough." Anna's snorting laugh and my loud belly giggles made my father so uncomfortable he had to excuse himself to close the gates to keep minks away from the chicken coop.

We had no chicken coop.

Anna and I came into focus as Keenan walked closer. My body reflected evidence of all the Montuse and Ilanthian strength training I'd done. Damn, I could see my cut deltoids and abdominals from under that flimsy hand me down Conrad got from his niece seasons before. I had lines on my face from too much sun and too many smiles despite the wraiths encroaching. My unbound hair was a full and luscious light brown, my laugh was hearty, my humor less-morbid. I hardly recognized the girl appearing before me. "I saw you blindfolded yourself this time."

My green eyes peered at Veona through Keenan's vision, my freckles rose and my nose and lip rings glinted off the sun in the sky. "Last time too, but don't tell mom."

He winked. "Successful then?"

"Ilanthian sword dancing is easy. I fixed it and made it fun." My foreign laugh broke around the memorandum again.

Who was this happy, carefree, daring woman?

"There is nothing to fix. I had made it *flawless* a *long* time ago." I could hear his teeth clenched together. He went on educating while Anna pulled my hair off my neck and began to tie it off my sweaty spine. "The dance itself is difficult, deadly, and tiresome. Many take honor in perfecting their bodies to be able to accomplish such a dance with a blade. Take pride in that."

"Yeah, well, I can do it blindfolded *and* backwards now. I also added some Montuse in there to, as I said, make it more fun. You should try it sometime if you can keep up with me, old man."

My freckles rose as I stared into his loving gaze. "Dangerous. You made it more dangerous, Ivy. Take me with you next time you decide to handicap yourself and throw swords in the air alright?" He eyed Orion. I was balancing him on the tip of my index finger. "Put him down before your mom scolds us both for bringing weapons and mud into her hearth."

Lily's voice called from the corner. "I heard that! Steel down. Muddy feet scoured. Filthy shirt off and in the scrub tub. Then I'll permit you to eat at the table." The vials on my ears were full and clanked around as Anna tore off my shirt and used it to wipe the dirt off my feet and ankles. Keenan shielded his eyes, not before the nation caught sight of my pierced tits and navel wiggling greedily under her hands.

When Keenan saw me next I had a band of simple cotton tied around my chest pulling Anna into the family room for a dance. Elousie picked up her rhythm and Anna and I fell into one of those dance trances that felt as if our feet were weaving a love spell. We fought for dominance in leading the dance and seducing the other. She put up a good fight. I won that time. The Goddess enjoyed being subservient to me more often than not.

As I isolated my hips and shook them to the drum, I straddled her on the couch. I didn't let her rise. Her hands I locked on the cushions behind her and– "Dinner, ladies!" My mother snapped as more guests began to crowd into our home. The scene ended. The world blurred.

When the fog reformed it was winter, the last winter we had together as a family. My father and Keenan were sipping hot tea outside by our pathetic, dwindling firewood stash. The rocking chairs that used to be around the campfires had been broken down and made into fuel for heat and burning down neighboring crafter communes by this point. "Keenan," my father's face was red with cold winds and frustration. "The shipments we bartered for will never arrive. The boat went down by a quarry, windriders and underhills were still on it. Even if we got our lumber and supplies when they were promised to us months ago, we wouldn't have time to flee the shore as a family. A family I love, of silver, red and gold blood."

Keenan's tears skewed my father's strong ragged features. I bawled when the two of them embraced. Shaking with surrender. An inevitable fate had befallen them. "We will see the end of these days together." Keenan's voice was muffled for his mouth pressed against my father's shoulder.

"Anna won't let death take Wisteria before she has seen her will through. You love my daughter." There was no question in the manner he said it.

"As if she were my own blood, Alester Woodlander."

My heart quivered. I believed him. It was hard not too when there was such a painfully hard note of finality to this conversation.

My father hid his fear beneath his conviction. "All in these lands will perish. When we go, will you love my daughter and piece her together so she can fight this evil as Athromancia seems to think she must do?"

"I will never abandon her to the evils of this world, I will never let her forget you, Lily or life in these lands, I will stand by her side and act in her best interest until her end of days." He pulled a dagger from his belt and sliced his palm. Alester did the same and shook his hand. "I swear this to you my dear friend, now and always. If I survive, Wisteria's life will be held above my own, from love, not because she is the vessel of my Goddess but because she is Wisteria Woodlander of Ferngrove, my daughter."

I rubbed my eyes until they were red and swollen, my father's voice continued to play. "Teach her to fight better, the darkness is coming. It is taking many forms. She needs to be ready."

"She is already one of the greatest apprentices I have trained, Alester. I would have her as my first hand if I was ever called to war. She worked twice as hard and now is as fast as any Ilanthian born child, she hits smarter than most men and is innovative when she is at a disadvantage. I can't teach that, she was born with the inability to take things lying down or take a knee."

My father's mood didn't lighten. "Even you cannot stand against several restless without risking damage. She will have to. Our daughter will be alone. Make her *better*, Keenan. Better than you." My father was not softening his demand. "If Anna wants her to trek on foot to Akelis to spark special blood, she will need to be immune to hardships, starvation, cold, fear."

The world moved back and forward, Keenan shook his head. "Lily and Moriah will gut me for this. Anna may revoke my sworn vow if I push Ivy into misery."

My father's veins bulged in his neck. "Anna will push her into misery. The only way to carry out her final act of love to bind herself to Wisteria is through her death. That, as we both damn well know, will shatter her world far more than losing her parents, which she will also endure. Wisteria cannot heal a world if she herself is incapable of healing." They were embracing again. Two hands found mine to stop my trembling. Zander and Nikki.

"Her training will double in length starting tomorrow. She does not rest or earn your sympathy until she is not only as fast as you, I want her faster, her Montuse acrobatics more controlled and her able to strike with a different weapon other than a God. Use the dagger and bow. I will inform the others of the current state of our failed escape from the shore." Keenan distraughtly agreed. "Athromancia has no right to protest, if she complains, send her to me. I will remind her of how magnificent my daughter is and how deserving she is of a trouble free life. A life we also could have had, had we left to the Southern Isles a decade ago and not gone into hiding with Ilanthians and a Goddess who claimed to want to end evil not love a mortal so recklessly she damned us all."

Keenan stopped him from stomping away with a gentle finger to his cheek. "There are many ways to love Alester. Theirs happened to be wholly, recklessly, wildly, unexpectedly and irrationally. Love takes many forms. None are less or more beautiful. Love exists. That is undeniable. You would not trade in the joy of our daughter for anything."

"I can't determine if her love was a blessing or curse."

His grip around my father's neck gave an affectionate squeeze of friendship. "Us beings may choose how to act on love when it is born between souls, how to describe it, how to trap it, how to sabotage it, how to forget it. Yet, it remains. I will carry the purity of their love, of your love, of the earth's love with me always and remind our daughter of that light when her world grows dark."

My father laughed, the piercings on his brow raised as he looked at Keenan's uniform leather. "She is going to pummel those pretty words out of your mouth in the months ahead when she has about had it with your conditioning drills."

"Looking forward to it." There was a slight pause. "Each time I come back with fresh blood or a limp you steal me hemp buds from Conrad's shed, deal?" The two men shook again. So, did I. With slight humor.

The last images Keenan offered the public were of me breathlessly chasing him through the forest and damning him with every breath I was able to catch.

Then his world rocked as my fist met his face. I disarmed him with a dagger and from his view I had him pinned and straddled. My fist came down again. Then darkness. I'd bested the best. That cinnamon oatmeal was one of the most memorable meals I earned that spring.

The mirages vanished from the sky as Keenan ripped his head out of the water well. I dropped the hands holding mine and steadied my legs enough to rise and withstand the short walk to Keenan's side. "My name is Ikke nin Kynigan, commonly shortened to Ik Kygen. My family can call me Keenan." His palm was pressed to the disheveled leather straps across his chest. "Commander of Athromancia's Bloodsworn Gold Legion whose blood bond has been broken with her departure." This bastard went to his knees.

"My blood, my will, my sword is yours to command, Wisteria Woodlander." He sliced his hand as I had seen him do with my father in his memories. He extended it towards me.

"Many choices have been made for you and for that I apologize on behalf of our crafter family. It was out of love, I hope you can see that now and find it in your heart to forgive me. Them. Her." I swallowed. His blood pooled in his hand. "I present to you, your first choice of many. To have me, in whatever capacity you see fit, at your side until you hold my oath fulfilled or death takes me."

It wasn't even a question at this point. For I had clarity despite my heart brimming with disbelief. Orion's sharp edge gouged my own palm and I pressed it to Keenan's. "I, Wisteria Woodlander, accept your oath, allegiance and love. Rise Keenan."

He was on his feet and pulling me into a tight fatherly embrace. His own shuddering exhales reverberated against me. "Leave it to you to make a grown man cry three times in one morning." My comfort was short lived as I glanced down at the memorandum and saw the clouds rearrange in the space above it.

Maruc stared numbly at me. "Show me her death." With stern fingers, he pointed to the waters. "Her magic is dormant, I can't feel if she is really gone. The Weaver is hiding her from me. Ether has her cloaked. Prove it."

Keenan, *my* Bloodsworn, shielded me from the stares of onlookers. He didn't bother to stop my incubus partner nor the violently burning man at his side when they ran to stand between myself and Maruc. *You don't have to do anything you don't want to do. This is a choice. I will handle things if you want to forego exposing your sorrows.*

Will they see our threads? Hear our vows?

Not if you can retain control of the memories. Cut them where you wish and don't let your mind wander.

I spared him a firm gaze. "Pull me out if you need to."

"I promise, my love." His romantic response had me plunging my face into cool waters to stop the flush of annoyance and flattery from bursting the capillaries in my cheeks. Fluid trickled into my ears. I gasped at the chilling sensation, shaking my head reflexively. Then gasped again realizing I could breathe under this water.

Collect yourself. Blues swarm down our bond, pulling the tension from my head as Nikki had pulled the anger from my heart with fire.

The night of the attack. I started there.

> I held no details back from my audience. They heard my mother's screams and Rory's cries as vividly as I had. They watched Anna attempt to stop me from launching myself at Havnoc and my

consciousness left me. The rattle of chains, my blood curdling screams as a spearhead dove into my shoulder and Anna's gurgling breathing was next to flash before me. Then came her words paired.

"You will get out of here and do what I could not...prevent a war between nations."

"We will. We will unite the world together. Uproot the seeds of unfounded hatred and cut the stem of confusion."

"Seems unfair, that for all my lifetimes of living I had not felt alive until I had met you. Thank you Ivy, for proving me right," her lips darkened to a dangerous shade of blue. *"There is good in this world worth saving, Maruc needs to come to the realization before it's too late."*

Her skin cooled beneath my touch, I pulled her cloak over her hair and face, bringing her closer. "I don't know how to do that," I confessed, biting back tremors.

"My brother chose you to stand face to face with the last God and tell him our tale. Demand he give you an audience at the Opal Lake. Tell him the Vulborg are here. Unite the realms of Kinlyra to stop the war of creation."

I was shaking now. "What are you on about! We will tell the king and Emperor our tale and find peace. We!" I reiterated fiercely.

"I love you, Ivy. I need you to drink my blood."

I shook my head. "You said you weren't that kind of immortal. I don't want it."

"It's too late to explain," Anna pinched my nose leaving me gasping through my mouth.

"I don't want this! This doesn't feel like love!"

The light in her eyes had almost dimmed, a stray tear formed and trailed down her high cheekbones. *"This way I will always be with you. Fear not the path beneath your feet for the courage of your heart can overcome even the most impossible of tasks. My brother will not forsake you."* Anna, already pale and blood matted, had bitten her own wrist and sucked the last of her life force out. She descended on me, her cheeks swollen in holding the precious liquid. Then, pressing her lips onto mine, she demanded I drink and wouldn't release my breath until I had all but drained her. I heard my gasping cries echo above me around Veona. There was no fighting her, not because she was stronger, but because there was no use in arguing with a corpse.

Zander's vespers sounded beautiful with the echo of stagnant air in the dungeons. Unbeknownst to him, he sang the burial hymns for the Last Goddess.

I let them ring before Fennick burning the metal of my cage flashed before my eyes. I blinked and he had followed my request to burn her corpse. Now, I was running through the dark with absolutely no idea which of the countless times I had done this was. The night grew into crawling shapes. The black of a raven's eye. The mask that haunted me.

The control over my thoughts slipping with each passing second.

The swishing gurgle of the water in my ears awoke too many memories.

Anna and I jumping naked off the Cliffs of Sounds, mute Nikki staring at me in the hot spring, my throwing myself off the ship into the wraith ridden ocean, Zander diving in after me. Zander.

Zander! *Zander!*

Hands gripped the back of my neck and pulled me out of the waters of lucidity, out of my chaotic thoughts. "No more!" I sputtered to Zander and used his shirt to wipe water off my face.

He glared at the God. "You don't have to. Maruc got what he needed to see. And more." I rested on his navel. I tore myself away from my boys and the stupid idea of jumping smack in between them to be encompassed by strength and warmth. "You are free to leave with Fen while I tend to the matters of war, *vulborg* and strategizing since as of a minute ago, Anna's last request of you was officially delivered to Maruc. It's on him now to offer you passage to the Opal Lake."

Ah, yes. Maruc. "What are the *vulborg* and why are they here?" His almost human demeanor recoiled from my words. I say almost human because as he stood there silently grieving in his own manner, the skies above him swirled reflecting his inner turmoil.

That was not a red or silver trait. Golden Eternal blood.

My gaze was locked on him. His attention moved to the glimmering wall of the beyond in the north. His voice no longer a storm lashing out but a fleeting breeze carrying a lost memory. "This world is not the first we've created, nor will it be the last. How my Athromancia ever remembered such a distant name is beyond me." Atticus, Alethim and civilians leaned an ear. Keenan arranged himself between the God and I, intentionally corralling me into Zander and Nikki's arms. He trusted them to keep me safe.

Nikki stepped closer, his tails wrapping around my ankles in the lightest of touches. My heart settled a beat. Protector indeed. "I have no precise time of when they ran rampant in galaxies far away. It was roughly four or five epochs ago?" He didn't sound confident in his timeline. "My siblings and I concocted a world of void. Void of color, sentiments, purpose, dimension. They were our earliest experimentations with souls one could say. The Vulborg were horrid. Unable to feel emotions, they fed on everything promising until life on Ootchïæ was *void* itself. Lurking, never sated. All Eleven ensured that the Vulborg were given no means to procreate nor ability to journey elsewhere off their plane for even the afterlife, our Ether, would suffocate with them in it. That world and its fiends were dismantled. It appeared some of us had not forgotten them or left them in the past as we should have."

I asked what was on all our minds. "Is that what is festering at the runegate and in Deadlands?" He motioned affirmatively. Scribes were jotting things down instantly. "How do we kill them? How did they get there?" Maruc strode closer to me, his eyes desperately searching my being for remnants of his sister. They stalled on Orion tight to my side. The steel warmed my thigh, itching for me to seal my fingers around him. I caressed the hilt. We both sighed with relief. "Which of your siblings brought them here?"

A curl of a handsome smile flashed. "I can see why Orion is keen on you." My sword shot lightning at Maruc when his hands ventured near the hilt. His hands rose in surrender but not before whips of Nikki's fire and Zander's jealous magic lashed out with Orion. All my magical men stood their ground at my side. Keenan's own sword was drawn.

Maruc received the message. He put his hand down and continued the saga. "Almost as keen as Anuli was with all of our creations. Despite the vile nature and lack of redemption for them, Anuli grieved abandoning the Vulborg. If what Athromancia said is true, I expect tender Anuli brought a souvenir across the Ether and someone, somewhere in Kinlyra revived them. Parts of them at least. Those on the physical side require a body to cross their dark presence over into this world of color and life. They are demons. The void. The damned."

His auburn colored eyes fell to the leather wrapped bone on Zander's pant loop. "Demons brought here by blood craft and offered a soul to leech on. Last century, the fae were researching blood crafting with King Jeorge who told the renegades he had relics and no guidance. Bone and blood, he opened the portal between worlds. I expect Kind Resig Torval knows the secrets of the craft and has since splintered off the means to control the Vulborg. We made demons without a soul, but they are not without cunning."

"They called me *migouri*."

"Mother. That means mother. They smelt Athromancia's presence, sniffed you out as one of their makers. Who's to say if they miss the maternal comforts or seek to destroy it after she abandoned them. I don't know what they intend to do with you. If this *Nameless Prince* sensed something special about your blood, then he has begun to rip his soul apart for them to inhibit it from an undead state. blood craft. Two beings in one body, I would have said soul sharing, but alas, demons are void of that. Only wovens can soul-share. And elemental lines are dwindling."

"How do we stop them? They have taken the east and the beyond."

His shoulders raised to his ears. "The power to consume is a vortex of greed. Nothing will ever be enough for the void. Their world had no light, no life, no warmth. Those are the very things it lacks and craves yet consequently, its demise. The Eternal Elm will be its first target because it poses the biggest threat and appeal." My nausea rose.

The silver and gold fox barked and wrapped its tails further up my legs. "They will savor it. This nation will be the first of the three to be dead and dark, they will feast on the fear that is already too heavily consuming Kinlyra." A wave of distress fidgeted through the dreamers. "Unless the Remnants are found and their plan stopped."

His eyes turned to me. "I suspect there is a woman among us who is sought after by the royal line who can freely walk into the capital. A woman who if she accompanies me to the Opal Lake will be infused with potent magical powers. She might stand a chance to infiltrate the heart of the demons and expose their plans." He looked upwards to Zander. "Just as there is a male who should be reinstated to his position and accept my offer to train his powers so he may fight with precision and not fear the shadow of his past. You've both much growth to obtain and little time to accomplish it." Zander's nervousness scurried up my arm. Followed by self-defeat. A wisp of guilt and loathing.

My chin snapped out. If one more person coerced, guilted or hinted at my woven's decision to keep the sun in the cage of his soul I was going to rip their throats out. His nerves became angry crimsons swarming over our bond, merging seamlessly with my annoyance.

I pushed aside my companions to raise an unsympathetic finger to Maruc. I was grateful Nikki took the majority of my fury because I could have stuck my finger in his godly eye sockets for belittling my friend. "I suspect there is a God among us who can use his stormy hands to defeat the Vulborg and help said girl find and destroy these demon bones and help said male find a way to protect the Elm and residents of Kinlyra. Better yet, why doesn't he stay and defend this world he and his siblings lived in and loved."

He met me mid stride. "Do something," I dared.

"It is almost time for me to join the others in the Ether. I am alone. I am tired, weary. I haven't slept in thousands of years." Eternals didn't sleep? What had Anna been doing all these years, laying next to me? "You'd have me forsake my presence in Ilanthia, placing millions more at risk of the same plague that has taken so many in Numaal, to stand and fight here?"

Orion was tight in my grasp as I searched for the right thing to say. "Yes. You said it yourself. The Vulborg will consume all of the lands. Best act now."

His smile was made to distract. Its beauty was brimming with untold secrets. "Say I do. Myself and the Ivory Legion deplete ourselves here but manage to rebuild the runegate once it crumbles. The spawn behind will recollect and come again, while the demons who've already claimed bodies rake across these lands like claws through soft flesh. Do you believe those who you are bickering with me to protect would do the same for you? For your nation?"

Rogue. They all but banished me from their realm. *A woman with no allegiance. A rogue.* They didn't want outsider's aid, they evidently didn't come to the innocent dying in Numaal. Except two males. "No." My eyes fell to his simple black shoes, it was then when I noticed the faint white aura hovering around him. The divinely chosen of the Trilogy.

"Zander, best you reclaim your title and work on your citizens to prove the one you heartmarked wrong. Prove to her your clandestine nation is in fact not selfish hermits unwilling to interact with all of Kinlyra and care what happens beyond their reach before it is too late."

Heartmarked? I felt for the bite over the left side of my neck. Emotionally, I was on the verge of collapse. I followed the flickers of fire until my feet stopped toes to toe with Nikki. Zander could handle the strategizing from here. "A farmer's market sounds lovely." I laced my fingers and arm through Nikki's, a tight ring of liquid flame encircled us.

Maruc called to my back. "Wisteria, our conversion is not done."

"Oh, were you going to divulge how to undo blood craft or how you intend to stay and send these demons back into their world and seal them there?"

The secrets hiding in his features failed to outshine the eagerness of his voice to convince me to stay. His hand trembled as it inched towards his brother again. Orion's energy spun around my wrist as if asking me to unleash him. *"He does not want your company. He chose me."* My voice carried a heavy snarl.

"Don't go, yet. We have much in common."

I removed myself out of his reach. "Yeah, we both fucked your wife."

Warroh looked up from the ground where he knelt, gaping at me. Revolted no doubt. Percy and Kashikat's laughs echoed down the stunned street where wolves joined them in laughter and the odd nymphs tittered. Hands wrapped around my waist before Maruc either let out a cry or laugh of his own. I didn't know which.

Chapter Sixteen

Zander fluxed Nikki and I to a partially enclosed produce pavilion. I tumbled into a box of onions, and was tugged upright and squeezed between two bulky bodies. Once I was certain all my body parts had aligned themselves and functioned properly, I gave a flustered sigh into Zander's thick waist. Running my hands over his stature grounded me in the moment and pulled me out of Keenan's past. "You couldn't wait until after I saw his facial expression to flux us here?"

A bright trolly brimming with tangerines and grapefruits skeeted around us, apologies of a busy vendor followed sometime after. Zander buttoned up the top two clasps of my shirt and set my hair intentionally away from his bite. I patted Orion and gave him a serious look. A guise that hopefully said, *'Stop fussing, no one will mess with me.'*

Zander crouched to kiss me. Really kiss me. The pressure of his lips on mine eased when he spoke, "I wonder what wildly delightful shit you would have spat had Fen not stolen your anger." It was only because Maruc began to do what Judeth and Kailynder had done and force Zander's hand, it's no wonder Zander nearly snapped at me for guilting him in the Howling Hills. "Judging by the fact the sky has not fallen, I'm inclined to assume your comment went as well received as it could have been. You know, as someone who lost her virginity to the God of War's wife and threw it in his face."

I shrugged. "There are far less appealing ways to lose one's virginity. I'll begrudgingly accept sex with a Goddess, even if she was a manipulative liar and a traitorous bitch."

"I'm sure rumors of his reaction, whatever it may be, will find its way to our ears even beneath the ground where we will sleep tonight. Nymphs prattle and elves, although they will never openly admit it, love to listen." Nikki wiggled his pointy ears that stuck out of long, white strains he left unbound and flowing over his shoulders like a satin waterfall of pearly white sunshine. "I'll let you know if I catch whispers."

As I stared at his new appearance of lengthy tails of fluff and fire flurrying around us. His sharper, brighter eyes dropped to my bare feet. Off a nearby cart he swapped several coins for a pair of tweed slippers. He placed the soft shoes by my toes and steadied me while I slid into them. I flexed my feet, they fit me well. "How could it not? You've given Clavey and his court of gossipers enough fuel to last them ten of your lifetimes. And the realm got a full frontal of your bare body. I'm sure Zander is ready to kill everyone who he smelt arousal on. Which would be half his beloved nation if my nose was correct. Which it always is. He isn't the only dreamer being to sniff out primal lusting."

Zander grunted in confirmation. He pushed Nikki's long blue tunic up past the crook of his elbow. "Speaking of Clavey."

"I have salt on me," Nikki stated assuredly, flexing his tattooed arm. The fox pointed to a canopy, two stalls down. "Go pick out a chocolate pastry that tickles your fancy, little vixen. I'll be a few steps behind you."

"I'd love to, but I left my one gold coin in the Keep." I shook my head and watched as Zander's obscura fell over them. I could see and hear what the world could not. Golden blood or woven perks, I decided.

They moved against the wall for privacy, while I stood amid a reasonably empty aisle of fruits and fragrance. They were talking low now, out of my earshot. I found a sturdy wooden post to lean against. I knew I should look away. That I shouldn't watch the tender manner in which the incubus bit Nikki's arm trying to cause the least amount of pain. And I most certainly, should not have relished the way Nikki's face warmed and he thrust his head back with need as venom pulsed through him. Not because I felt it was an intrusion, but because of what phrenzy sparked in me. I imagined myself trapped between them, not helplessly, but willingly.

And that version of me was thrilled.

My neck sweltered. I pressed my thighs together, desperately trying to ignore the sensations that watching these gorgeous men together arouse in me. My traitorous body remembered what ecstasy being bitten was and had to remind me right then what I was missing out on. Paradise.

Poor Nikki. There was no release for him, not that I volunteered to be of any use and Zander didn't eat figs.

Nope. No! Boundaries. And all that protector woven stuff he said in the closet.

He snapped at Zander and shook out his limbs. The frustration built up in him, sending him to repetitively smack his head against the white stone walls behind them. My head ached. "Stop doing that, you're going to get hurt!" I was close enough to the pair of them now to see Zander's hand was resting at the base of Nikki's skull, protecting him from any significant damage. Their eyes fell onto me, one pair lusting sinfully and one pair greatly amused. "Oh."

"*Oh,* is right." Nikki shuddered while his tongue traced his own set of sharp teeth. He salivated and bucked his hips. Zander tried to steady his thrusting with a firm hand against his waistline. "I know your body as well as you, my girl. I can see your heat gathering and throbbing exactly where mine is." His eyes narrowed on the apex of my thighs. His words were not distasteful or crude, they were factual. Definitely accurate.

If anything it gave me more insight to how an elemental saw and felt the world. In heat and heightened sensory. He would get no irritated rise from me or get to see me hiding away with embarrassment. I wasn't. I stayed and let him watch my heat gather. He was drenched with desire through and through. Enthralled by it. I knew precisely the demands his body had and how I damn well would have done and said anything to have them met.

All the moisture was stripped from my mouth and somehow an excess of it soaked my panties. "Don't come closer. It will pass." Zander's laugh was smokey and mischievous as if he knew how my body was reacting on a cellular level.

Nikki rolled his tails to seduce me closer. They were gorgeous. *He* was gorgeous, only a blind fool would think otherwise. I reached for them and heat licked up my arm. "Now, you've done it to him, Wisteria." Zander's violet darkness fought against Nikki's flames while firmly holding his brother against the wall with his other arm barred across his torso and magic anchoring him in the shadows. "This would be an excellent time to admire some pastries. A venom frenzy is not how any of us imagined you two initiating the exploration of your woven bond."

"By *us* you're referring to?" He gave an elusive wink that further sent me into a heated tizzy.

I backed out of their vicinity, unabashedly flushed on my stroll to Nuri's Chocolatiers, which held a mouthwatering display of dark salted caramels shaped like birds and standing sugar designs. Finally, moisture in my mouth. The more distance I put between myself and my woven's the calmer my *heat* sizzled. I paced until I cooled, pausing at a sugar sculpture that rose taller than I. Its shiny green edges hooked out and in with jagged arches, making it seem more of an aesthetic piece, not edible.

"That one turned out strange. Strange as the day upon us. Peculiar. Bemused." A squeaky voice stated their opinion. "It makes me feel dark, twisty and disappointed. I supposed that was how I must have been feeling when I poured the sugar that particular day. Twisty like a twizzled twisted rope. You've heard of mood readers? Well, yes. I am a mood candy crafter." A short male with a turned up round nose, sat on the counter in his messy chef's apron. A chipper wave. "I'm Nuri and you are new."

Still a ripe shade of red I lead with. "My name is Wisteria." I put my hands in my pockets so I wouldn't knock into anything fragile. Wedding rings and a chain knotted around my bloody fingers. Imprisoning me, bringing me down like a cement block sinking to the bottom of a lake. I struggled to breathe, to find a happy thought while feeling the sting of the open cut on my hand. Gods Keenan. Removing them from my parent's corpses must have been gut wrenching... and gross. Wearing them everyday I couldn't decide if that would be a burden or a sweet token.

I felt to free them from my grip, my hand tightened around the simple metal instead. Maybe I wasn't ready to have these? Maybe I should give them back to Keenan? I wasn't strong enough to hold them or even look at them without feeling like I was buried six feet under.

Nuri's mouth was moving, I vaguely caught on to the last thing he said, something about confectioner's sugar and gave a nod. That wasn't the correct answer because he hopped off the counter and gave a high pitch chortle. He bounced to a beat in his head, tapping his fingers on the table as he hopped along. Easily distracted it seemed as he spun back to the work counter. Very childish. His wrinkled long ears twitched. "If you answer my riddle, the sugar sweet tower is yours, Wisteria. Easy breezy. Lemon squeezy."

I hadn't a place to set such a large piece of craftsmanship. Dormant golden blood or not, I had no money, no place to go without feeling like an outsider. An unwanted rogue. Candy could not solve all of my problems. "Unfortunately, my capacity for anything requiring mental or emotional effort is unavailable. I'd like to admire more of your works, if you don't mind silent company."

"Preceding Overlord's mistress admires my works, why yes. Yes, that's just fine. Fine and dandy, popping candy. Whipped cream, happy dream!"

A mistress. How lackluster.

I was responsible for forbidding most other terminologies. Mistress it was.

Nuri flicked my nose and busied his small hands behind the workspace, preparing boxes upon boxes of miniature cakes and custards of nearly every imaginable flavor. Everything on that counter I would have loved to sink my teeth into. Why the hell had I not tucked that gold coin into my pocket? I'd just wanted a lick of frosting and had nothing to barter.

He shrilled. "Fennick, fine Fennick! Your note came not a moment too late." Nuri pushed the paper bag of delicacies to the lip of the counter where Nikki lifted it and left a wad of paper pastels in its place. I stare at the lump sum.

Oddly, Yolanda's words chose now to reiterate in my head. I didn't use Count Hilderbrand for money, nor would I do the same to Nikki. "If those desserts are for me, I will be paying you back." Nikki was composed again. No bucking hips, flirty tail or provoking words. His eyes wandered down my body and I let them for mine had done the same. We were safe and settled now.

On the arm with an unbuttoned sleeve I gave a soft pat. His lips quirked up. "Good, I didn't scare you off." Nothing awkward lingered from what happened outside. We were as we always were.

Whatever that was.

"Much the opposite." He hummed with intrigue and waved to Nuri. "I meant what I said about the desserts. You can't just go around buying things for me without asking. I'm in debt now."

His poised shoulder slacked. "I guess inside a confectionary shop is as fine a spot as any to nestle in for a while and break down some fundamental issues we seem to be facing. My mother wasn't expecting us for another hour as luck may have it." I rolled my eyes.

Nuri held out a lollipop. "Riddle for you and I'll make it two!"

Nikki looked to the owner. "One riddle right and you close up for the day. No dropping eaves."

"Clever fox knows better. You get three chances to stump Nuri the nymph, then you may stay or leave. I will let you be."

As I would have spun a dagger around my knuckles, Nikki flossed his fingers with a ball of flame muddling through thoughts. I stared at the floating flames and felt my attention get hooked. How entrancing. "You've one minute to give your answer. One guess." Nuri agreed while I tore my eyes from the fire magic. "I speak without a mouth and hear without ears. I have no body, but I come alive with the wind. What am I?"

Little nymph Nuri wiped and gleefully tugged at his apron. I stood watching Nikki's wickedly charming smile widen as Nuri griped at his answer. "An echo!" He exclaimed. "Another!"

"I have cities, but no houses. I have mountains, but no trees. I have water, but no fish. What am I?"

"A map, a flat map!" Nuri looked at me. "Have you better word games than the man of flame? Go on, go on! If you stump me, yes, I will be delighted and be gone! Speak, human girl." He danced now. When he was on his tippy toes, he rose to my nose in height.

Nikki bumped my shoulder with his. "If you have one you think may baffle a nosey nymph, the floor is yours."

Nuri was singing again. I needed silence.

Ah, yes.

"Nuri, what disappears the moment you speak its name?" The singing stopped when he mumbled to himself. The lollipops in his hands tapped the glass container next to the register. His wide eyes, unproportionate to his small skull, moved closer trying to see the answers as if my eyes were windows to my brain.

Nikki tapped a gold pocket watch that swung from his belt loop. "Your time is out."

Locking his register, his face wrinkled with disappointment. Nikki grabbed the two pink lollipops and popped one in his mouth before presenting me with the other. "Share the answer, could you kindly?" Nuri paused at the door he exited.

"Silence." The foil crinkled as I unwrapped the ball of strawberry flavored sugar.

Nuri's arms were up. "I should have known! Fox, don't melt my goods!" There was a chime of a bell as the door closed. Then *silence*.

The lights went off and Nikki pulled the shades down before sitting on the floor among his newly purchased bag of treats, his tails tucked near him. He looked like a child opening birthday gifts. Gifts he too kindly shared. My stomach leapt with delight.

He pointed to a spot on the carpet directly in front of him. I sat, my hands still in my pockets. The weight of my parents rings a force stronger than science. Maybe Adious, if he were alive yet, could explain it to me one day in his scholarly terms. "Crafters barter goods for services or either of those for money."

"Again with the stating facts." He held up a patient finger at my retort, his eyes unwavering as he requested my consideration.

"You do interpret us as friends, correct? Or do you let all men hold you open to feed an incubus, trust them with treasonous secrets and perpetually put your mortal life at risk for said strangers?" He bit on the stick of his lollipop so he could use his hands to unravel a rolled cinnamon bun, glazed in heavenly frosting. I refused to believe how delectable that roll looked when I nodded or how casually he said 'hold you open'.

"Yes, Nikki. We are friends. But you freely gave me aid first. You got me out of the dungeon and incinerated Athromancia's corpse at my request."

He unfolded the box around the messy treat that could feed us both and rummaged for a napkin. "Would you say you were friends with Fauna?" His gaze was unblinking, eyeing my fist in my pockets.

I had enough of my past coming to haunt me today. "Yes."

"You, a master crafter, freely gave her scones, warmth and a peaceful death upon her request with nothing to gain or receive in return other than torment. That wasn't a barter when you gave her your services. Nor was it when you removed Rodrick's hand, gave bread to a mute fort coalminer or freed a water wolf from chains."

The plate with the large roll was placed on my lap. "Friends do right by each other, for each other. When you freed Zander's mind from the Remnants, you did that because it was the right thing to do for your friends, him and I, *and* for yourself because *you* felt better knowing he was safe. You do things for others because that gives you peace, purpose and joy."

Gods he had the lecture well-rehearsed.

"Yes, sometimes it costs you anguish or suffering because you care deeply, which is not a fault. It's one of the many qualities that draw me towards you. But, the fact remains true for every being in this world that you cannot place a value, not numerical or quantifiable, on a happy life. I need you to be happy, to make me happier and if you don't start eating that dessert before it slides off your lap, I'm going to hand feed you until you're too fat to jump around chasing ancient warriors on rooftops." I almost snorted as he broke his lecture to demand I eat. "You've earned yourself some admirers and on the other side of the same token, some envious and distrusting onlookers." All I hoped was that it made Kailynder eat his words.

My left hand steadied the plate before it tipped onto the floor. "Do you have a fork?"

"Since when are you able to pace yourself with a utensil?" Two of his tails laid down next to me.

"Since I decided I want to pet you and don't want to get your fur sticky."

His laugh was clear. It broke away the guilt of being coinless, jobless and homeless. "Just use your hands to eat. We will scrub off before we shop for legumes, leeks and a fresh pantry of spices."

Out came my fist and with it two rings and necklace. And a fresh, still bleeding cut, from my deal with Keenan. We both stared at it, but it was Nikki who kept the conversation flowing. "Your parents were obscenely in love."

"It was revolting as an adolescent, but I envy what they had," I admitted. My fingers unfurled. Their rings were more than a little scuffed and tarnished. Bloody too. Pine could polish them up and make them look shiny as he did to the iron scrap metal which was on my left index finger. "I am not ready to have these. Can you care for them until I am?"

"For as long as you need me to, it would be my honor." Blood smudges still on them, he looped the chain around his neck, adjusting his hair and his shirt over the scuffy rings dangling next to the acorn.

"Do people in Ilanthia and the Veil take vows of marriage or are the customs different?" My parents' rings disappeared under his shirt.

"Marriage is sacred, rings of unity are also common and conventional. There exists another binding ceremony here called the Circling." His fine face shone as if there were lights in the room. His skin was flawless. I kept staring. "It's a proposal done by one party giving the other two wedding bands to wear in a chain around their neck. If accepted they are officially wed by law." Finally, his features cracked into a smile as his attempt at humoring me dawned. I pursed my lips so he didn't see how wide my grin could span.

"Aren't you hilarious?"

He winked. "Marriage is honored here the same as Numaal except the vows are written differently being one person may significantly outlive the other."

"Makes sense."

"There is a ceremony called the Circling that wraps the wedded in sanctimonious blessings from the Ether. There is no breaking the circle once it is formed, that is why Percy's Circling evidence remains despite his wife's death. The interlocking circles imprinted behind his ear—that is not magic ink. That is Ether. The Weaver's counter balance. The acceptor of all souls, where the reapers help guide the souls once a destination has been determined in the beyond."

"At least their chintzy gold scraps survived when their circle ended." I eyed the bare pronged band on my finger. No fancy interlocking markings here, save those for immortals.

"When you hold them, what feelings are sparked?"

"I'd rather eat than talk about my feelings." Nikki pinched off a steaming moist piece of the roll and held it to my lips. I opened my mouth and let him place it on my tongue. He licked his fingers as I licked my lips.

This was one effective way to get me to talk. If not the most effective. He knew it too. "Calculating bastard."

"Charm me and inflate my ego with compliments to your heart's content baby, but do not change the subject."

Another bite of dessert found its way into my mouth. "I feel a blend of emotions. Of course I miss them. I miss my mother's easy mannerisms, my father's firm guidance and even their whimsical romantic displays. In retrospect, it was hypocritical because when Anna and I started sleeping together and fornicating in broad daylight as we did they acted baffled to where I learned such shameless behaviors." I peeled a piece twice as big as the one Nikki fed me and dipped it in a glob of honey.

"I dread not getting another chance to love so freely again. I know Zander feels honest love, but it's incomplete. Holding their rings makes me feel many levels of loneliness. And yes, I also think of Keenan pulling them off their cold dead corpses and how heavy they must have been around his neck the last two and a half years. I have no one to give them to, to share them with. Hell, who would want to wear a dead person's cheap metal band?" I shoved bread into my mouth, giving Nikki an exasperated look. "You don't have to wear them, they were stolen off corpses."

Fire rolled off his fingertips. He splashed little fireworks in my face. Another inch and I would have smelt my hair burn. Such control over his element. "Don't go back on your request after receiving an answer. I was aware of their origin when I gave my reply." He looked at Orion as if wondering where my decisiveness went. "Keep going with your thoughts regarding Keenan. We have a lot to unpack where he is concerned before I deem it wise to return your anger."

"Says the man who greeted him with a fist."

His pale brows rose. "It was presumptive. I knew his actions would hurt you once revealed and I can't stand by and let that happen. No one gets away from me entirely unscathed after I illuminate what they strive to keep hidden. All seems to be revealing itself nicely." I stopped chewing.

"Nicely? This revelation of my Anna being Athromancia and demons from another world attacking ours you consider to have been illuminated *nicely*?" Flakey sugar fell beneath my collar. "You hit your head too hard on the wall back there and it has made you delusional."

"Zander doesn't let me scramble my brains," he said dryly.

I finished the bite in my hand and dove back into the spiral roll. "I saw that too."

"Because your curiosity called you too close." Too close or not close enough?

"We all walked away just fine. Zander fluxed technically, but you see my point." It was Nikki who was shoveling sweets into his mouth now. "Did yours already heal up?" I pointed to where I saw his woven sink his fangs into him. He outstretched his forearm for me to examine. The fabric was moved away to reveal a bumpy collection of scabs.

"Coarse salt must be rubbed on it to prevent it from healing immediately. The venom in my body gets filtered out faster than yours, but I'm protected for a few days." My sticky fingers I held at bay from his shimmery inked skin.

I wondered, "Your tattoos. Did they require the same treatment when they attempted to heal?"

"Magic ink." He wiped his fingers on a napkin, admiring the clean black ink on the opposite side of his arm that ended on his wrist, under a collection of leather and twine bracelets. "That is my favorite engineering alchemy feat, saved me from going under the needle and salt scrubber another hundred times for touch ups."

"Do you think it can work on my back?"

Nikki pulled out the bottles gotu kola and citrus oils the healers told me to have rubbed onto my scarred tissue. "I'll assess tonight, if you'll permit me to take Zander's role as your masseuse. He is going to be out of commission for cuddles for likely days."

"You can oil my scars if I can run my hands on your tails after I've washed them."

An intentional flick of his tail brushed my knee and settled nearby. "Are you bartering my touch for yours?"

"Do you accept?"

"Yes. Hardly a decision to be made as I am a fox who craves touch to survive. Our little barter is nothing comparable to the magnitude of the blood oath you *choose* to accept." I wrapped up the roll, reboxing it for later. And... we were back to Keenan. "It was a good choice. He loves you, has great capabilities to protect and inform *and* is cognizant of the fact you had little influence in important, earth shattering decisions of your own life until now. *That*, I respect."

This cunning fox was shifting our conversation back on course, to unpack Keenan. I plopped the sucker into the pocket of my cheek. "Tell that to the Weaver. She and the Eternals are fucking with me. Ha! Quite literally."

"And you were happy. You cannot tell me or anyone who saw you and Anna in Keenan's memories, you were not elated, alive and in love. You were sheer vibrant bliss, the purest living definition of being a red blood and embodying every damn feeling. The reason many blessed envy vibrants."

"You also saw why I now have trust issues and little desire to ever fully embody those emotions again. Love is a lie. My dad was right, Anna broke me."

"Were she alive, I would have wrecked her so thoroughly for making you believe such a fucked up thing." My eyes warmed, loving the wickedness in his words. "Alas, she is gone and she set things in motion that cannot be undone. She felt you were the key to heal the world and redirect Maruc's heavy war hammer."

"Yeah? How'd that first request for aid go?"

"It wasn't the first," he reminded me. "I found this morning extensively insightful. We named our enemy and now know they crave light and life if only to destroy it. That they are going to take out the biggest threat and desire of their kind first."

I took the sucker out of my mouth. My lips pulled down into a heavy frown. "You'll die if the Elm is extinguished."

"Hundreds will die." Feeling sick, I lower the hard candy. "We will find a way to win this." He clutched the acorn seed on his necklace.

"A way that doesn't involve Zander unleashing his magic. I think if one more person demands it of him or even whispers the notion of it, he is going to throw them over the Leap where he learned to fly."

He shook his head disagreeing. "No, *you* are going to throw them over the Leap. You'll disfigure their faces and disembowel them first, but it will be you who protects our Zander. It was very endearing the way you stood up for him today, it almost seems as if you care about him and his realm. The realm you believe wouldn't go to another nation's aid."

I glared, while he rested his chin on his hands, raising a silver brow. "I do care about him. We are all friends, remember? And it pisses me off that people pressure him disregarding the emotional and psychological damage it may cause their beloved retired Overlord. I trust him to do what is best, *when* it is best. As I do you. As I hope, you'd honor for me."

His pale lashes held bits of the blue core of a candle wick, amplifying his gleaming golden eyes which slowly closed and he dipped his head in congruence. I hadn't looked in a mirror since the morning of the winter gala when Yolanda had me dressed to reflect the power I felt I held that night. A sensual goddess of vengeance. I had no need to look in a mirror and see my utterly dingy, human appearance. Standing next to Nikki and Zander on the Altar of Horns? I must have looked ridiculous. Small, fragile, drab, confused, lost. Not to mention my lash marks. I bit the inside of my cheek.

Nikki grabbed my hand and helped hoist me in the upright. He didn't let go. I turned to confront what I knew would be a serene, yet serious face.

His presence struck me differently somehow, I didn't feel the need to be reactive or sharp, against a cold world. Maybe it was his warmth that permitted me to be vulnerable and soft. "For the record, I never saw you as broken or needing fixing. You are complex. I will never tire or fail to find you intriguing."

I squeezed his fingers and liberated them from mine. "You're going to have to wait because it is time for me to learn about you. Tell me about your family."

B.B. Aspen

Chapter Seventeen

We took the scenic route to Honri's apartment complex, the beauty of the city stifled any complaints I may have had about being seen out and about after discovering I was a golden vessel.

Nikki confirmed with his perky ears that Maruc snuffed out the storm in his hands after my comment and he went quiet on the matter of me fucking his wife. Pride surged in my chest. Hell yes, I made a God choke on their words.

As we navigated each wide, round turn, Veona underwent a shift in its personality. All of the areas were lovely and unique, varying in their architecture and landscaping engineered to accommodate the population that lived among them. There was a quaintness to the inner circle we were in now, the opposite of the bustling markets run by fae and nymphs, dodging flying pixies and prankster sprites.

Nikki and I remained joined at the hip so I could easily hear all of the historical nuances of each building and sculpture we passed. Throughout our shopping spree Nikki's set of eyes became unmatched. When the milky white eyes of Zander's shone through his woven's left with transplacency I was half tempted to pry for answers, but Nikki simply showed him our intertwined hands and gold gleamed once more.

Honri lived in a community care village, where caretakers were on duty continuously should he or a neighbor fall ill or require aid. "His mind has muddled, but his heart is green with youthful passion. He loves the arts, dare I say more than the scrolls in the archives." Fedora Feign would be there at Honri's with just two of his cousins, Chaz and Rivatt, one dreamer and one Ilanthian. The rest were scattered across the west, but many were sitting in the public conclave being held tonight by Atticus and the Emperor. Thousands were in attendance, the ordeal that may last nights on end.

I was thrilled to hear Nikki kept gatherings intimate and small at Honri's. Too much stimulation wore his thinking thin. Fedora ambushed her son at the door. "Fennick! Baby!"

His posture softened. His word was a whisper of relief. "Momo."

Her brown coloring toppled into Nikki who set down his bags and opened his arms in time to receive his mother. They cried and laughed simultaneously, their necks craning around each other to twist together tightly. "My boy, you're here." She kissed Nikki's nose, who let his single tear run freely. How was he able to express his emotions so effortlessly? I envied him.

He grabbed my hand. "And you brought a new face! Welcome, darling girl. Wisteria was it? Come in, come in. Honri needs new company, he is getting restless. Picking fights over Chaz's taste in music."

"Because he doesn't respect the classics!" Hollars echoed from around the corner. "The ruckus spewing from Akelis the last hundred years is utter rubbish! Keep it in the brothels." That must have been Honri shouting from the adjacent room. I smiled. Anything was better than the fieldstomp.

Fedora clicked with her teeth at the chaos behind her, her single ruddy reddish tail wrapping around one of Nikki's. She took the bag of sweets from my grip. Fedora inserted herself. "Call me Momo. You are the second person my son has brought into the sulk. I will have no formalities over meal and warmth sharing if you are open to it."

Nikki was quick to jump in. "She may be open to warmth sharing, but she has been marked. Myself and Zander only, Momo." Nikki made sure his mother was meeting his eyes when he spoke the last statement. Her brown eyes found my neck, which it seemed she preferred more than staring at the intensity of her son's eyes.

I interjected. "Hi, Momo. Thanks for letting me in your company tonight. I've heard a lot about you."

"And I you, golden vessel." Momo's hand was warm when it cupped my cheek, her gaze drifting to the sword on my hip.

"Nikki took my anger, I promise not to swing my sword in your home."

"The elementals were present at the portal this morning and found your actions warranted. Your inner fire rivals Drommal's. I can see why my baby has brought you in. Take shelter among us, do not be swayed by hearsays. It took Nikki years to toughen up and to set his foot down when it came to setting priorities and not being offended by his status or fearing those who sought his hearts. He learned what is important and that is why he is here with family tonight, not arguing about the end of the world when there is love to spread and love to receive."

"Momo, let Wisteria inside. You have all afternoon and evening with her. Then she is sleeping with me in the Burrows come starfall." Momo clapped her hands together and grabbed the groceries Nikki abandoned on the front porch. She thought about pulling him back in, but relinquished him. He pushed by and into the front door where more happiness rang out when Honri appeared squeezing his cane in his arthritic fingers.

He shuffled into his son's arms with a staggered walk. Nikki easily carried his father's weight into the next room and tentatively lowered him onto a couch next to Rivatt who lay curled into herself in fox form.

Nikki knelt in front of his father, adjusting the pillow behind his spine which had started to curve inward and brought an ottoman under the heels of his feet. He rubbed Pa's swollen knees with fire magic spilling over onto his joints to ease the pain. "Fennick. Fennick." His son's name was a mantra on his lips. The two of them sat idolizing each other without the use of words or the many languages they spoke.

"Fennick." He tugged Nikki up and pressed their noses together. "Good, you are home Tails. The chefs don't make the cabbage nearly spicy enough and the rice doesn't stick with their vinegar wines. And somebody around here stole my acrylic paint set! I can't recreate the lilies in the night gardens of Pashtu without the right shade of blue. I want to recreate our wedding night on canvas for your mother and the thieves forbade it."

The fox on the couch leapt up and trotted in a figure eight pattern around Nikki. They both expelled fire as a manner of greeting. "Auntie Marissa visited me in the White Tower. I have boxes of her home cooked meals ready to stash in your freezer," he ensured, pointing across the room into the kitchen. The room next door was in disarray. Half painted canvases, open oil paints, broken binding of thick books, maps, ink pots and brushes.

"I prefer your cooking to your mother's," Honri whispered with a boyish snicker.

"You're in luck Pa, we have a new guest tonight. She is a master crafter, a woodlander from Numaal *and* a trained Ilanthian physician *and* Montuse fighter who has never set foot in the Land of the Gods. I was planning on whipping up something that would make her never want to leave the dinner table or sample anyone else's spice rack."

His dad patted the cushion next to him, a rust colored Rivatt sat back on the furniture awaiting for me to acknowledge her. I think. "You don't say! How did you manage to mix combat culture without leaving Numaal? Did you exchange the arts also? What do I call you?" I cozied myself down, preparing a list of answers to give him in my head. "I see Zander has protected you too, when shall we expect him? If he is eating here tonight, we ought to prepare a pork roast. Or two."

Nikki traced my jaw line with his thumb until I looked at him. "I will be in the kitchen, not cooking a pork roast." Humor etched on his smooth, shaven face. "Potato leek soup and vegetable egg noodles are on the menu". He proudly tied an apron around his waist and removed layers until he was in a sleeveless top, tattoos and teeth marks of his guardian decorated his flesh.

Chaz looked about Brock's age and build, only with two legs and blonde hair. He was none too serious as he clamored in through the kitchen smacking his cousin on the ass with a wet towel as a wicked weapon. The slap stung him across his low back, my own lashes ached. Chaz was chased around the countertop stopping only when his eyes fell to me.

"You?" I braced my inhale, not knowing how he intended to complete his thought.

Momo washed the produce that Nikki bought and I carried in from the markets, setting it on a cutting board nearest the stove. Silence stretched. "Me."

Not awkward at all.

"Not *just* you, Wisteria Woodlander, vessel of Athromancia, but you have *him*. Orion. The Temperance." His hand went up in surrender as Nikki formed a floating globe of fire in his right hand. "He's been gone for five hundred years and now he is in this residence!" He jumped up and down. "Shit, you are two-thirds of the trilogy!" My throat closed and my eyes instantly sought Nikki's for comfort.

Nikki and I hadn't talked about that yet, nor how I felt about going to the Opal Lake at all. My being a vessel was odd and unsettling. A quirky smile spilled from his lips seeing Orion start sputtering off lightning of sorts.

"I would introduce you, but he's intensely clingy—worse than Zander—Orion snapped at Maruc for even looking at him this morning." Orion lit up, his sparks beckoning my hand to the hilt as if he was demanding to be held. "You'll have to settle for an introduction with me. I'm Wisteria."

I looked at Honri and spoke slightly slower so as to not be insulting. "Honri, you can call me Wisteria. I'm Fennick's friend. Zander's too. We bumped into each other in the Southern Province and managed to all escape mostly intact after some wild adventures." His soft aged skin patted the back of my hand, he rolled it over to trace the fresh cut on my palm and examined the rest of my arm.

"Short nails, hardworking and your live within means. Some are brittle, you've not had consistent minerals or fats in your diet. Calluses, on both your palms and knuckles, a fighter and forager. That ring on your finger is stoneless, but you wear it because you are proud or you bestowed a memory into it. That ring is also not on the Numaalian's wedding finger, you are unmarried, not have you a visible Circling symbol." Honri glazed around the room, his niece and nephew were staring at him as in awe as I was.

"Your son tells me more about myself than I can often deduce myself. I see where he picked up his remarkable and occasionally maddening aptitude." Nikki's white ears peaked up and twisted in my direction. "Honri, please continue. You are doing wonderful and I'm curious to what else you can deduce about me from my appearance."

"The scars visible on your hands, arms and chin speak about a happy childhood. A carefree one that's built up assuredness. Your freckles on your nose are unhidden, you've self-confidence for you choose not to paint your face. That is a wise choice, for masks often are deceitful. Your eyes are clear, but they are filled with a shadow." He gave a tender pat on my forearm and leaned into my personal space. "Confusion is often the only way to discover what true purpose is, when you disband confusion you shine your soul. When you have clarity, a path out of confusion presents itself or you make one."

His manner of speaking reminded me of Bladetooth. *'When your kind has absolute truth, your kind has absolute certainty. A summoner must have both for then you have intent.'*

A soft pat on my knuckle beckoned me out of my pool of thoughts. "Say what you are thinking, do not filter yourself here. I often have bouts of crazy talk and my family hasn't escorted me to the beyond or to the fae forests for mind rendering." Nikki inherited his father's smile, I stared at the devious smirk briefly imagining what Nikki would like if he aged side by side with me.

Of course that would never happen. I'd be dead long, decomposing in a grave or urn while he remained untouched by time.

"The way you speak reminds me of the griffins I spoke to." I blurted out rather than announce I was dreaming about a future with his son—or lack of.

A sharp pain sliced through my right thumb. Nikki flipped on the faucet, running his hand under the stream of water in the kitchen sink and I was on his tails. All nine of them.

I grabbed his bloodied hand watching his cut mend and feeling my own pain dulled. Pain that was precisely where he had injured himself.

Our woven bond manifested.

Nikki wasn't surprised in the slightest. I leaned into his side body, not hiding the startled wide eyes. "How long have you known?" I was whispering with raw excitement in my voice.

"I suspected in Fort Fell. Confirmed suspicions in Landsfell." He washed his blood down the sink, dried off his hands as if nothing had happened and reverted to mincing red shallots. "That conversation can't happen here. Well, it can, I have no reservations, but you may if you are still eager to keep the inevitable a secret."

He was right. I would greatly mind.

He raised his chin so his voice carried around the room, "You and Zander failed to mention an encounter with griffins. How does one forget such things?"

"You'll have to forgive me, I was rather preoccupied," I snarked. "And Zander didn't see them, they wouldn't let him up into their aerie in the Howling Hills. They made a barrier with enchanted fog."

"I'm sure he reacted like a damn lunatic."

"Far worse. He threatened to detonate their nest."

His voice was low and his tone unsurprised. "The idiot."

"His dramatic, theatrical behavior is hardly shocking to me anymore."

Where there once laid a fox, stood a young girl in gauzy loungewear, charred along her sleeve evidence of her fire powers. "Griffins!" Rivatt shouted. "They are real?"

"Chaz," Honri beckoned. "Uncork a bottle, let's listen to the adventures of our new kindred."

Momo carried over a bottle of prosecco, Nikki examined the year, vintage, cork and foil. Inspecting it for tampering since his mistrust of poison ran deep. Chaz uncorked it, but Nikki poured my glass and carried it to me as he escorted me back to the couch with a brush of his hand at the lowest curve of my back. He hardly made contact with his chivalrous gesture yet the heat he radiated sunk into my skin leaving an imprint.

He must understand by now that he has this *appeal* to people. It must have been his magic trapping me in such a state. He played it safe and stepped away to finish the preparations of our meal. Honri took my free hand in his, drawing me out of a trance of surveying as Nikki tightened his apron in a manner I should not have found as alluring as I did. "My childhood history professor was the only person in my life who had seen griffins, he was of Aditi's blood line. Were they more daunting than Atticus in flight?"

Cool sweet bubbles tingled and burst on my palate. "I've never seen Atticus fly, but they are substantially more enormous than an incubus and thrice as cumbersome to converse with. Their claws are the dimension of a carriage, Stormclaw's beak could devour a stable of horses within a minute and the matron of the nest, Bladetooth, her tail whipping side to side would knock Kailynder on his overgrown ass and I would pay to see that happen." Chaz poured the remainder of the bottle until it was emptied and everyone had a beverage in their hand.

"Kai managed to make an imbecile impression within three days of your arrival?"

"Within hours of meeting him actually. He... he just sucks. So, does Judeth. Something crawled up their miserable asses and died." Chaz laughed and spilled his wine on his pants.

By the time Nikki set the table and carried over his specialty dishes on a clay warmer, I had said all there was to say about the mist, the massive truth speakers and was deeply lost in Honri's theoretical breakdown of what Stormclaw may have meant.

He had already concocted a mental letter he intended to send to the librarians of Akelis to inquire about the title and role of a summoner and this Calling. "Clearly Zander was not one. And I wasn't, *yet*. I am to come back as myself, but different." My head spun. I needed more wine.

Nikki stole my third wine glass and set it next to my place setting. Bribing me to my feet. He returned to help Honri off the couch and escort him to the table. I supported his stronger side.

Momo and Chaz opened a standing cabinet in the gathering area and began to fuss with a brass phonograph music player. I had only heard Anna speak about them, fondly I might add. They allowed her to dance without an audience to a variety of music in private.

Momo placed a disc on the wire rack. Piano and saxophone jazz played softly, Chaz embraced Momo and they danced their way to the dining room across from the clutter of unfinished artworks, maps and framed photos, stacked in a leaning tower in the corner.

Tossing his head back, Chaz extended his arm to me and gave a wily wink. A burst of fire ignited at Chaz's feet. "Alright! I won't ask her to dance! She just looks like she could use some friendly cheering up you bloody brat!" He hopped away from the flames and Nikki's hissing. "You don't need to burn holes in my socks." My woven glared at his cousin until he took a seat still grumbling about his socks.

Honri had tears welling up in his eyes as he stared at his swollen joints and his wife dancing in the background. "I want to dance with you, my love. I want to hold you and watch your smile spill over into happy tears and long nights dancing down the piers and getting lost in the Burrows."

Momo snuffed out the remaining fire and commented over my shoulder. "I've seen an incubus, on more than one occasion, lose their shit if they find another admiring a person they are also coveting or pursuing. Yet, those horned hellions cannot compare to the avaricious compulsions that coarse within our elemental spirits. Elementals give incubi and mated fae a run for their money. Best not to test him until he has had his fill of interaction with Zander. Time apart puts them on edge and proper wovens need time to warmthshare."

"Don't I know it. The coddling is excessive." I muttered under my breath. The foxes at the table turned to face me, most of them humored.

A maternal pat tapped my arm and pointed to Orion. "I will rest well knowing you will protect your males as ruthlessly as they will protect you." She promptly moved from my side to tend to her weeping husband whose continued monologue of longing pulled at my heartstrings. His wits may be about him at that current moment, but he grieved his aging body. Aging gracefully and surrounded by a loyal village was a forte of crafting communities in the Southlands. I wondered, were he not surrounded by and deeply attached to those with longer lifespans, if he would care much about the aging process and the grief of not keeping pace with them.

My chair was chivalrously pulled out awaiting for me by one of my males. I obliged.

Nikki lowered himself and took to filling my plate before I could protest the quantity or digest all the marvelous aromas of fine dining wafting about. Rivatt brought over two more bottles of prosecco, which seemed completely appropriate at four in the afternoon given the cozy atmosphere and laxed rubrics. She sat on the armrest to teach me the mysterious ways of the wooden chopsticks, laughing as I gave myself splinters.

As our delicious late lunch stretched into dinner, I became proficient enough to steal warm food off my woven's plates with the sticks. I pretended to reach for my wine glass and instead plucked a vegetable from his dish. "Still thieving?" A hot hand wrapped around my wrist, bringing the floret of broccoli clamped in the utensil to his mouth instead of mine.

His pink tongue peeked out of his lips. Never in my short absurd life did I ever think I would be enchanted by a man enough to envy the food he swallowed just to feel his lips enveloping me.

But. Alas. Here I was fucking enchanted and choking on my own words.

The chopsticks fell on the floor. "It's your fault you made it so damn delicious." I didn't bother to retrieve my utensils or thieve from him the rest of the night. I drank instead, listening to Nikki recall his sea voyage from southern Numaal to the harbor of Akelis, a journey he spent mostly vomiting over the starboard side and offering intel about the new lands to apprehensive humans. Momo and I did the dishes while

Nikki and his cousins wrapped up their conversations and tended to Honri.

Honri was bathed and outfitted for sleep when I bid him goodnight. A distinct sadness filled his eyes when he waved us off to the Burrows, his true home, as he referred to it.

Momo raced outside to send us off when Nikki and I breached the front porch. "Fennick. I dare not say this in front of your father, but the Burrows are not what you remember. Masil and Kenneth's families have already relocated into the city. They said their channels were haunted by spirits robbing them of their peace. Masil cemented off her entire section to slow the spirits' permeation of the Hallows. She told me *after* she completed such an undertaking before I could get fae to check her mentation or soul reapers to listen for leeward souls."

Smoke rose from under Nikki's shirt. "I thought Masil was losing her wits residing so close to the ruckus at the runegate, but there have been more accounts. Kenneth and his amenity woven wouldn't dare lie. But, I'm not there often enough being as Honri needs me here." Nikki rubbed his nose against her neck. "The Burrows are on edge. It may be we all sense the war coming or the monster's so near to our hallowed home."

"Did you validate Kenneth's stories? Explore his level?"

His mother nodded gravely. "It's undeniable but also infrequent. Their presence is not of this world. Discreetly, I brought soul reapers with me last year. We have yet to determine if they are worthy souls given an afterlife, barricaded and forced to return or if they are linked to the unsettled void rattling our world."

"Even if our entire community were to be evicted, we are still formidable." His head nestled under his mother's chin. His grief held at bay with his determination. "Our home, does it exist?"

"The first three levels are protected by the mother root and mirrors. Any deeper and the spirits may lead you astray. Warroh placed prayer beads to ward them off."

Beads, helpful.

"I refuse to be lost in my own home, Momo. Our home." Her eyes fell to me as her son growled into her chest. "Wisteria doesn't leave my side. She will not stray." A mandate.

Protector wovens were foreboding and bone chilling when they were threatened. Well, mine was at least. I knew of no others to compare him too.

Chapter Eighteen

From a distance, the fields surrounding the Eternal Elm danced as would a vast garden bed of autumn colored poppies caught in the current of a coastal breeze. Passed the ramparts we walked arm in arm. The closer we got to the Burrows the more buttons on my shift I had to unfasten. Nikki dried the sweat on my clavicles. The gorgeous burning plains were a stark contrast to tealing sky and sheen straining barrier, the Elm itself rivaled the sun that was slowly descending towards the horizon.

My feet stopped at the abrupt edge of the fire line. The escort at my side used his tails to cocoon and encourage me onward by barring me from the dangers the high flames posed to my fragile flesh. I was already confident that he would not let me walk into danger.

Not that I'd ever stop on my own accord.

My fingers skated along the tips of the white fur ringing around my neck. His tails and magic reflected gold off the fire beneath us. The base of my head was supported by warm pillows of his elements that moved when my body did, reacting to each movement of my arms and shoulders. Nikki synchronized his magic to me as if we were two pieces cut from the same cloth fitting together seamlessly. Unmistakably, I was the dull worn cloth and him the best silk from the merchant's dock.

Foxes were scattered around the plains, some white, some red, some brown. A female transformed into a stark naked woman with brown skin and a brown tail flicking behind her seductively as she advanced towards Nikki. She yipped a welcoming salutation and elongated her neck to entice him. She didn't glance in my direction. Who would ever think to look at the shadow of the sun?

Not one muscle on Nikki flexed in reply. Did he hear her? I glanced behind us to ensure her bark and bedroom eyes were for someone else.

Nope. Just us.

Just him.

The fiery femme stepped nearer and nine tails coiled me tighter to his side. I covertly held onto his back pocket for balance, my hands out of sight from the new and gorgeous arrival. "Missed you. All of us have." Her voice was angelic. The arch in her spine pushed up her breasts, making it quite clear what she wanted, what she had already had. "I want your kin in my womb."

Alrighty then. This moment was officially soaring its way to the top of the most indigestible conversations to unwillingly overhear. I hope Zander wasn't too focused on my sentiments at the present. He had enough to deal with than smelling my awkwardness. What would that possibly taste like to him?

"Britt. We had this conversation. The answer is the same. It will forever be no." Nikki's was no bullshit. Britt looked affronted and suddenly too fragile.

She shook her head in denial, her gorgeous hair framing her uniquely stunning face as she moved. It was her wide spread eyes that made her so foreign to me. "We are both heavily imbued with Eternal and elemental blood in our lineage. We could make more nine-tails and three-hearted." I moved my eyes to the other foxes roaming around to offer them privacy while I tried not to let something fragile in my chest break. "Impregnate me before the war. I will take shelter and treasure the gift of your seed. Preserve the sulk. Our power."

"If you desire to preserve the sulk—you stay and fight. Stay and defend. There is no present or future if the Elm dies."

Her thick brows glowered. "If I no longer allure you, there are other vixens. Most of whom you've already laid with and deemed satisfactory who are eager as I. Let us carry your potency into the light for the next generations."

Body tightened, he pulled his posture erect. His gaze cast acidic shame on her. There was no dodging his presence.

"This conversation has ended and with it all that we ever were, mere distant acquaintances, poking our paws around for mindless fun." Defeat sunk through her. "Do well to inform the others that if you or they approach me with this insult of dishonor in any manner, they will be making their grievances in the cold, alone and far from home." Britt placed her hands on her empty womb. She looked about to weep with sudden emptiness hallowing her eyes, her barren womb. "Excuse us Britt, my family and I are going to bed."

I saw the furious look on her face before she shifted into a brown fox and scurried off. I swallowed hard and touched Nikki's hand. "You alright? That was a lot."

"Thank you for inquiring. I'm great. Really and truly great actually, Wisteria." He took my hand off his back pocket and laced my fingers between his. He was chipper again now that we were alone. Alone-ish. "Over the years I've become immune to these requests, advances, imploys and arranged offspring. Because of the outrageousness and frequency of them, I chose not to permit my sexual partners to get too acquainted with me beyond corporal sex. It's a blessing Zander and I were woven. That ever present part of me that is craving a bigger family, a connection and security has been found within my woven and I have no need to place myself at risk. Zander's influence protects me from poachers seeking to steal my hearts and he extends it to my family so they are not taken hostage and abused as a bargaining token for any of my body parts, seed included."

He rolled his lip between his teeth watching me cringe. "You'd be appalled at the lengths people go to chasing elemental heirs and immortality. The royal line once had a taste, let's hope that the Faceless Fucks don't discover me for what I truely am." He circled his thumb on the back of hand.

"That's good. Not the poachers or hostage parts, but benefiting from Zander's love and growing a family with him. Although, I'm sorry you inherited his brothers too." He barked a laugh and those nearby snickered. "Don't worry, I'm here to put them in their place if you need me to."

"After today's antics, very few people would disagree with that."

Those laughing all had a singular tail which led me to my next question. "Nikki, why don't the others have nine tails or three hearts?"

"Genetic transmutation from my mother's paternal side. My great-grandfather had nine tails also, he died in the war of the Great Divide when there were no mountains to seclude the dreamers and we all mingled freely. The mountains are restrictive to our growth as a realm, we'd much like to be seen as an open nation, not a fantasy sector. Even Zander has plans to start flattening Thalren." He greeted a pair of foxes that prowled around his legs by crouching to their level and petting them among the flames. They sniffed me. I tentatively waved. "Have you left the Burrows?"

The two foxes shook their narrow muzzles. Relief fell on Nikki's shoulders. A gathering of foxes collected in our wake as we approached the tree. A tree that stood slightly shorter than Oyokos' horns, which made it over one hundred feet tall and its circumference... indeterminable.

I had so many questions. With all the ears around I said none of them. I simply gaped at the large winding branches, low and high arches in the knotty boughs of the elm. Each branch of the tree was the size of a fully grown burr oak on its own. My parents would have loved to see this.

It wasn't scorching under the fiery shadows of the Elm, but warm enough to where I worried the remainder of the fudge and cakes in Nikki's carry bag would melt. The bark held an orange hue and was smoothed and shiney from all the oil in hands touching where her wide trunk met the roots, where the entrance to the Burrows lay. Inward was our destination.

The roots aligned perfectly, forming stairs downward into the heart of the tree. Nikki hadn't stepped out of sync with me, he would not walk ahead or behind. We entered the doorless Burrow together and were greeted with a ceiling decorated with moss and mirrors. Mirrors that were angled down the countless corridors that stemmed from the large room, sending light into the tunnels under the earth.

Honri was a genius. Only a madman could conceive architecture of this extravagant magnitude.

Nikki whispered my name, directing me onward by softly rubbing the pad of his thumb in circles against me. We walked across the floors of petrified wood and into the kitchen made for dozens to gather. "Our common room for warmth sharing, meal breaking and occasional revelries. The food and beverages are safe and of superb quality. Help yourself to anything here." Pillows, couches and bowls of dried nuts and fruits were scattered around the common room along with piles of sleeping foxes and other beings thrown into snuggle sessions or more *intimate* affairs. Warmth sharing had a variety of implications. I noted his words, watching Nikki place my dessert in the ice chest. He stalled before he shut the ice chest. "Take me with you if you venture."

Nikki kissed the acorn he wore around his neck as we ducked in a hallway lined with earth and mirrors. He burned a little brighter until my feet were accustomed to the occasional trip of a root on the downward slope. His eyes stayed one step ahead scouring for danger, for haunting spirits. "You're not claustrophobic I hope," he humored, when we took yet another turn and crouched under a low root someone hand crafted into an electric chandelier.

"Apparently not." I sniffed the moss on the wall, it was dried. These tunnels were kept warm and clean, hardly any loose dirt was in sight. I sniffed an odd smaller root on the side. "Why is there ginger planted down here?"

"For cooking," he stated as if I should have known. "Garlic cloves are further back the way we came. I didn't want to plant them too close to my den. My nose is sensitive." We walked a few more feet and paused so Nikki could adjust the mirror above. Light shone into the alcove we filed into.

With a flick of his wrist he lit the candles around the den to illuminate a kempt desk, a tiled corner with a water faucet for bathing and a mattress tucked away in the corner surrounded by plush fabrics. "No ridiculous quantity of clothes in this room. I'm shocked."

"On the contrary, little vixen. My closet deserves its own alcove. I'll show you sometime and let you become infatuated with shiny fabrics." He opened a box of toiletries and gave me a toothbrush and rose water toner for my face. "I'm going to excuse myself while you get into sleep ware." He pointed to a neatly folded pile of clothes on the nightstand. "Keep your shirt off. We have medicine to apply."

"And I have ears and tails to pet!" I called after him.

Ripples of fire sputtered as he laughed his lion laugh throughout an unlit pathway. That laugh. That magically bright and healing laugh, thawed something in me that his morning's revelations had iced over. Hearing his mirth was evidence enough we were no longer separated by mountains or oceans. I was in his beloved Burrows with him. In his scared family's home.

I relayed our whereabouts to Zander who sent a gurgling wave of jealous frustration back to me. *Trapped in conclave, but I am obtaining obscene amounts of insight that it would be foolish to take exit. I may excuse myself for a few minutes of respite to tuck you two in around midnight. Although, I have an unshakable feeling it would be near impossible to return after I have you both safe in my arms. Dibs on being the big spoon!*

I exchanged my clothes, my body missing his arms wrapped around me at the mention of them. *Maruc's reaction to your vulgarness was stunned silence by the way. Ik Kygen swore he saw a hint of a grin flash at the corner of his mouth. Tell Fen, 'sweet dreams and welcome home'. Add and an 'I love you' in there for good measure. I only told him three times today and that doesn't seem like enough.*

You tell him yourself!

It's the 'L' word that makes you all antsy, isn't it? I pulled back our bond. *Oh, yes. I've struck the nerve. Good night, my flower. Good night, my fox.* He withdrew as did I, leaving pinkish adoration muddled around me.

The pajamas were a soft cherry color that reminded me of Zander's affections; only there wasn't much to them. The shorts were flimsy fabric and the sleeveless top, the same. "It gets warm sleeping with me. Or any fire fox for that matter, not that you will have an opportunity to discover that for yourself." I smirked at his declaration. "My Pa added fans, ventilation, plumbing, but it does get warm. Feel free to wake me up to absorb your heat if you feel faint." Nikki was at the threshold of the alcove, he entered fully after I laid myself down on his mattress with my back at his disposal. Orion was at my side although I don't remember placing him there.

He was shirtless, his silvery hair draped over countless black tattoos inked on his chest and shoulders. He crawled over me with the elvish medicine in his grip. "Go ahead, ask your questions. I can practically hear them without syphering."

He warmed the oils in his hands before he rubbed my low back. Questions didn't leave my lips, low moans of sanction did. Nikki worked that same area twice hearing my validation. "Do you know what feels good on my back because you also feel it on yours?"

"We aren't there yet. But, we will be shortly now that you are aware of our thread manifesting. Feeling another's physical state as if it were your own is called quintessing or body sharing, soul sharing. Useful for helping wovens know if their other half is hurt, among other needs." He worked his thumbs slowly on either side of my spine, out emerged another unmuffled gasp of gratification.

"I felt it first when you accompanied the guards of Fort Fell in retrieving the villagers of Horn's End. You *intentionally* got your head kicked in and snapped your damn ribs. I was lighting the stoves in the kitchen when my world went dark and the sharpness in my sides stole air from my lungs. Raina found me disoriented and sent me to bed. I ran to my room and waited long hours for you two to return to safety. If you remember, you lost Fauna that night and got inebriated with Brock." How could I forget the heart ache and hangover from hell? "I stayed by your side all night with Zander studying your injuries and encouraging circulation of blood flow for your healing. Our healing."

My chin lifted off the pillow as I whipped towards him. "You felt my lashes and the branding while you were riding south." A declaration, not a question. "I am *so* sorry." I swallowed the memories of him pale and pathetic looking as we fled Landsfell on horseback. His eyes were forgiving when he found mind. "I'm sorry that I hurt you!"

A forgiving sigh sounded above me. "I felt Gimly step on your hand. I felt the bruises form on your hips as you slept on the floors. I felt your body's need for hunger and sleep and warmth when you did not. The lashes were the worst. They came on so strong and suddenly, I nearly pissed myself in front of Yolanda. I vomited instead. Clearly the better of the options." His hand flew up as I opened my mouth to apologize. "Relinquish your guilt immediately. This is out of our control, it always has been. If you say you are sorry one more time I will slice my own tongue to prevent you from using yours." His lips thinned.

"Please, tell me you are not serious?"

He grabbed his griffen blooded dagger from the nightstand and licked the edge. "I'll demonstrate my dedication to my declaration instead." I wrestled it out of his grip.

I had a feeling he let go of the blade before I fully placed him in another headlock. "You made your point!"

"Good. Lay down and let me finish talking and massaging the wiggenpeel seed salve." When I laid back down, his hands graced my body again. I didn't want them to leave. They were warm, firm...safe.

"I've never been burned before. It was awful. I've never had a fever or systemic infection either. Now, I am better able to sympathize with the rest of the world when illness seizes them."

I smirked. "Wait until we get our monthly bleeding cycles, then you will become the greatest sympathizer for the hallowed bleed from hell. Zander will have to dote on us both!" The bed shook as we laughed.

"I'll tell him to bring sweets."

"On a similar note, can you feel my pleasure when I am having sex? Or solo?"

"It varies in intensity."

"So, yes?" I raised my brows in intrigue.

He applied more oils and massaged my shoulders and neck with firm pressure. They turned me into putty. "I felt your arousal and release. Not while I was at sea or when you were flying away from death on land of course, but it returned when I was in Akelis and you were in Veona."

"Can I... Does it go both ways?"

"We've already demonstrated that it can this morning. You felt my venom induced needs and reacted to them just as I felt your lusty little urges at the dinner table eyeing the tip of the chopsticks. Or was it my tongue you were fantasizing about?" My ears burned.

"The broccoli." I scoffed as if it was the most reasonable answer.

He didn't laugh at my confession. Quite the opposite, he took it in stride as a complement. "I'm flattered."

"I'm unashamed." And I was. I'd nothing to apologize for. "Does your husband know about this?"

"Obviously. He witnessed it first hand, smelt it undoubtedly, and let us carry on lusting for a few minutes. He not so secretly enjoys it and wisely he retains a healthy amount of fear regarding his nature when it comes to indulging. For now, that is." He brushed over the length of a lash, I hardly felt it, the nerve endings were numb after the medicine I received when I first arrived. This scar he touched spanned from shoulder to hip was long. "Does this hurt?"

"Not anymore."

"Does it hurt your heart to look at them? To see the double raven on your skin? To think about the mission ahead?" He created a little distance and shut his eyes. I tossed the useless fabric over my head and rolled onto my back next to him. The lights went off as his skin and fur lit up into a soft dim glow.

Stars above, he was gorgeous.

My distracted eyes were memorizing his unsystematic tattoos that sprawled across his hard abs and the scars of his chest. I told myself to breathe before I gave him an answer. Stammering over his beauty was unacceptable. "I don't know. I haven't seen my reflection since the gala."

He didn't say anything. And when he did his murderous tone made my mouth dry. "Why not?"

I pried my tongue off the roof of my mouth. "I don't want to think of Prince Torval when I am naked and gazing at my own body. I'm afraid to ask how frequently Zander is thinking of the prince when we are intimate." I swallowed the painful truth. "He haunts me enough in my dreams and beyond the runegate. The spawn took his form when they spotted me." I gave a light shrug. "Besides, it's only skin."

Needing to ease his venomous demeanor I forced a smile. "Clavey may disagree, but appearances and face glitter don't help cleanse the world of demons. But, do you know what does?"

He remained too tense to talk. He hummed through tight lips. "Silk!" I grabbed a fistful of the sheets by my feet and draped it over the pair of us.

Now, my smile was genuine. I rubbed my face in the fabric watching Nikki's stern look dissolve into a more playful one. He found a silk pillow and exchanged it for the cotton one I had been using. We laid our heads on the cushion, our long hairs spilling over and tangling together and our breath mingling.

"Touch me," he whispered in that same tone that made him a vortex I'd willingly dive into if I didn't think I'd be so easily overwhelmed by our bond. I wasn't strong enough to tear myself out if I gave into it.

His ears were down awaiting my hand to stroke them. "Touch me, Wisteria. Do not make me beg."

I smirked. "I think I'd like to see that." His body wiggled a little, softening as my fingers found their way to the straight swoop of his nose and up to his hairline that I pervaded with a single combing motion through the satin strands. I sat up so both of my hands could experience the odd texture of cooling flames and moonlit hair that manage to capture the essence of the sun's rays.

I cupped his fox ears, examining them gently. The fine hairs on them flattened with each stroke. His eyes closed as he instinctively tried to find something to bury his nose into.

It was adorable. Literally, the most endearing, cutest encounter I'd ever had.

I smiled as he found his way onto my shoulder, his scent of the forest and hearth sunk into my own flesh. Tails encircled my arms as my touch trailed down his bare side. A masculine body, unburnt by the fire pooling at my fingertip. "What constitutes me crossing the line from keeping you as my protector woven to possibly something else?" Something more? I nearly said.

He was unperturbed by my quarries. Contrary to my beliefs he welcomed them without unease. "You kissing me on my mouth. And *no* you may not kiss me elsewhere with lusty intentions or while we are feeding off each other's physical urges." He added quickly, rising slightly from my shoulder so I absorbed the seriousness of his avowal.

My fingers spun lazily in his hair. "Your hands can't grope either." He had this thought plotted out as if he had thought about it a time or two. At the comment I trailed my fingers up to his face to avoid them lingering on his unclothed navel of corded muscles.

I accepted that answer. "Then what happens?"

Mischievous wit sparkled in his eyes. "Do I have to explain the birds and the bees to a girl who mocked two Eternals and said, 'Anything is a sex toy if you are brave enough?'"

"I meant that." My diaphragm tightened as I tried not to laugh. I bet the priestesses and acolytes were losing their damn minds over that line. They would be shitting themselves if they discovered how many times Anna and I had explored that fantasy.

"Noted. I'll remind Zander of your willingness and the need for lubricants."

I ignored the latter comment, mostly so I wouldn't announce that spit worked just fine and I was plenty wet with arousal for toys to merge with intercourse.

"You told me that I would die if I had intimate relations outside of my corlimor once I found them."

"So, you believe Zander is your corlimor?" Once again I lay at his side.

"Are you implying your brother is a liar or are you doubting him and our thread?"

"Neither." He rubbed his chin on my arm, calling for more scratches down his spine. I complied after receiving permission. "I condone this level of intimacy in public, but you need to initiate it if I am any part man."

"You were mostly man when we embraced today at the altar and practically *everyone* saw that." I remember vividly placing two kisses on his sternum and wrapping my arms tightly around his neck until he swept me off the ground on which I stood. They all saw that too.

He sounded serious. "Reunions after near death experiences are different. I missed you two desperately, Wisteria. You are seen as an extension of him and therefore, my duty to protect extends to you." He examined the cut on my palm, the one that started to scab over from Keenan's vow. "He is the air that offers life and you are the salt of the earth on which I stand. He feeds my fire and you give it a reason to burn. I was sparkless and cold without you two as disbelieving as you may find it."

"Not disbelieving. I'm just surprised."

"That I missed you?"

"I didn't know you were a sappy poet. Scholarly minds are often too linear to embrace stepping out of the realm of facts and into feelings."

He snorted. "Indirectly you are calling yourself scholarly since you are emotionally paralyzed."

My hand left him to cover my frustrated face. "I retract my statement."

We both repositioned back to laying side by side with our heads on the silk pillow and Orion wedged between us. The energetic sword sharply prodded my sleeping partner. Nikki stared at the shiny steel. "Orion," I snickered, as the sword's static threatened to shock the elemental. "Orion, would you like an introduction?" The sword gleaned twice. Nikki scooted away from the pointed blade.

I held Nikki's gaze as I took his hand and placed the hilt of an eager God into it. "Orion meet my woven. One of my wovens, Fennick Feign. Nikki, this is my best friend, Orion."

One more spark emerged as Nikki closed his hand around the end of the sword. I didn't judge him as he began to spout tears of disbelief. "Orion if I die you can stay with him or my friends, Brock and Zander. They will act with justice. I would say Keenan, but I know he pisses you off." The sword vanished and reappeared on my stomach, its cool metal reflecting how toasty the den was becoming and how outright clingy he was.

"He takes time to acclimate to others, even Keenan has an impossible time tracking him down and getting him to cooperate. Probably because Keenan kept stealing him from me and they were acquainted thousands of years prior to pouring his soul into this sword." Nikki wiped his wide eyes on the sheet.

"That's Orion."

"Yes."

"*The Orion.* I felt him with the magnitude of fifty thousand mounted men preparing for battle and screaming my name as they rode to war." The lines in his face moved up as wonderment reached his bright eyes. "Do you not feel his power, his presence?" My top teeth bit into my wet lip as I thought about any circumstance that stood out.

"No."

"Fuck...I mean.... You mean to tell me, you've never been overwhelmed by *that?*" He pointed to the steel, his hand held the whisper of a tremor.

I looked at the sword laying on my body, a body as easily visible under the blush of garments. A body never overwhelmed by Orion or Anna for that matter. "I felt their absence. Their presence was consistent and when Anna died someone cut into my soul and when I staggered my way into Fort Fell without Orion it felt like I severed my own arm off."

Nikki pivoted on his side, eyes fixed on my lips and their response. "Don't think we are finished talking about the complexities of our three bonds because we aren't. You are an illuminator, you can't leave me in the dark."

"I would never dream of doing something so distastefully abhorrent. You will see the light. I believe you will become your own beacon of light and answer your own queries as our quintessing strengthens and your soulful syphering with Zander deepens. If you were truly worried about the Weaver's consequences you would not be in my bed discussing imaginary boundaries, admitting to lust or permitting my hands on you—as innocent as they are in this particular moment."

When I fed Zander for the first time in the tent months ago, I blurred the lines too. But I did it because it felt right. I'd no regrets after.

I put my hand over Nikki's two hearts and left it there. "This feels right." He just stared at me waiting to say more. "This *is* right. You know it and Zander knows it or he wouldn't have let me come down here without him."

He placed his hand atop mine. The smile on his face was a content one full of satisfaction. "And now you know it too."

"He missed you a lot, you know. Hours every day and night he would spend trying to see into that clever brain of yours, to get a glimpse of your situation and measure your safety." I said after his glow dimmed for the night. "We'd fall asleep with our hands over his chest hoping that you were able to feel us through your magic heart as we lay there missing you."

"You missed me too?"

My chest filled with nauseated butterflies. And when his plump lips twitched into a devastating smirk, those butterflies morphed into a hornets nest, leaving me just as incensed and frantic.

"What did you miss about me the most?"

"You're delusional. Don't jump to conclusions so quickly."

"Did you miss me?"

This bastard knew. He just wanted me to say it out loud. It was a decent try, I'd give him that. "It was cold where we were. Ice, snow, hail and frost on everything."

At but a touch of his hand in mine, liquid fire spread across my skin until I glowed with his magic from head to toe. I flexed my fingers under his and felt for my flaming hair. It wasn't painful. It was like floating in a hot bath. "And now? Has the cold subsided? Have you stopped missing me? Have you stopped aching for my warmth?"

"It's warmer."

"Too warm?"

I gave him a challenging grin. "Impossible."

"I'll remember those words when you are at my inferno's mercy." He retracted his magic. Sparkles abandoned my skin leaving flushed pallor in its wake.

Pushing aside the tightness in my chest I allowed my vulnerability to be stretched thinner, if only for Nikki's sake. "Yes, Fennick Feign. I missed you."

"*Nikki*. I am your *Nikki*." His quick correction cut through my confession. Just as swiftly, he remedied it. "I know you both yearned for me. I felt the longing every mile–every minute–you were away. Rest now knowing that chasm has closed and only the Weaver herself can separate us by Thalren and sea again. And if She tries... I'll find a way to kill Her."

Wordlessly, I gave my blessing for his farfetched plan to reprimand the Weaver. Separated violently and unforeseeable times was not something I could survive again.

During the span of that warm night he had whispered about his adventures atop that rocking sea coffin as he called it and how thrilled he was to be back beneath the Eternal Elm and the seeds scattered across the fire fields. He exhaled into the curve of my ear and shifted into a fox shortly after. A fox who used his nose to pry open my arms and place himself in them while he slept. I wrapped all my limbs around the large four legged fox and slept with my face buried between his ears.

Chapter Nineteen

In the pitch dark of the den there was no manner to determine time.

There were no windows, no mirrors to reflect the turning of the sky above. What I was fully aware of was the presence of an enemy. Whispers of a foul, dark language permeated the shadows in which we slept and woke me from my sleep. Orion was in my hand as I knelt on the end of the bed waiting for the voices to take form and configure themselves into something solid. Solid enough so that I may slice them down, sever their essence and rid them from this realm.

My heart beat was pounding in my ears as my blood raged with anticipation. Whatever they were moved soundlessly.

Patience was not a virtue I was familiar with. I tumbled off the bed in an attempt to strike out against the invisible darkness.

A ring of fire exploded behind me, incinerating every inanimate object in the room. Bedding, desks, decorations. All were ash.

The whispers remained. Untouched by his fire.

"They are here." He didn't need to explain further when he stole my hand and sprinted to the common room, screaming what sounded like family surnames into alcoves and hallways as we went. *Zander, does the runegate extend under the earth or only above?*

I will ask Maruc now. I sense unease. Fen's mind is too busy for transplacency. I ran to embrace him down our bond. *Talk to me.*

The Vulborg have managed to infiltrate the Burrows. Formless wraiths, whispers of demons. Momo mentioned to us yesterday a few elementals have already moved out of the Burrows. Nikki turned his room to ashes.

Did he kill them?

They have no bodies to burn. I shielded my eyes from the low light of the common room, squinting as I adapted. Morning had dawned, which meant Zander had been in conclave all night and through sunrise. Half-naked beings and foxes filed in from every direction, rubbing sand from their panicked eyes and untangling their limbs from one another.

We strode up the stairs and onto the fire plains, Nikki's hand unshakable in mine. "Zander is asking Maruc if the runegate's barrier goes below earth's crust." Eyes flickered to me. Hopefully, no one expected syphering between myself and their favorite horselord incubus.

Fluxing.

We are in the fields. Nikki emptied the tunnels.

"He is coming," I whispered, my lips against his elegant long hair. My own mane was a frizzy, wavey disaster and I still saw no need to tame it.

Zander *poofed* in from thin air. Arriving wingless with the last God, Atticus, a handful of elves, legionnaires and Keenan. The incubus knelt on the grass, his pant legs smoked as holes were burnt into them. He bowed before the Eternal Elm, many behind him followed suit, including Keenan and a wolf. When all of Atticus's sons arrived they did the same.

"Kin of the twins, I apologize for the abrupt morning greeting. Our brother," he pointed to Nikki. "had just informed me of the terrors haunting your home. We are uncertain if the rune stones deter digging. I've called upon soul reapers, alchemists, architects and Maruc to investigate the Burrows. If you have had any interactions with the spirits or heard their chatter, I will ask you to stay behind with the scribes." The foxes seemed more appreciative than aggravated when the elvish scribes removed their hoods and sat among the flames, awaiting to jot down each individual account.

"Until I can promise your safety, I ask you to refrain from returning to the Burrow and take shelter in Litlough's circle where all provisions will be provided as well as adequate space for warmth sharing for your community." I tore my eyes away from my confident, self-assured Zander onto my heartbroken Nikki who's offensive stance and perked up ears did not hide the anguish in his eyes.

I gave a gentle squeeze to the hand in mine, trying to rid that ghastly look on his face. He quickly became a shell of himself which he had shown me last night. His emotions were pulled behind armor and yet they fueled him into action.

Zander swallowed a vile of blue potion from his pocket in one go. "I cannot dictate your actions." His voice boomed over the field as that magic potion took effect and amplified his words. I stared at his assuredness and how decisively he spoke. He spoke like an Overlord. "If you choose to stay I will honor that, but I will advise against it until a plan has been arranged to ensure your lives are protected to the best of the Veil's abilities. Clavey, Warroh and Maruc, choose your companions and ask the Elm for her blessing." Clavey chose a short man with a scythe, a reaper it would appear. Warroh invited a priestess of Misotaka. Maruc waited for Masil, the fox who had her portion cemented off last year. She fumbled with her steps. I wasn't sure if she was more scared of Maruc encroaching on her space with that scowl of his or returning to the Burrow.

The group of them prostrated themselves at the roots of the Elm, it was humbling to see a God on his knees.

Anna was on her knees, but for different reasons. Reasons that involved my being naked on the edge of a bed.

Zander walked across the field, stripping as he approached. His dilated pupils not straying from my piercings poking through the flimsy fabric. Oh, lovely. I crossed my arms over my chest. The elemental nearest me backing away.

He shouted at the audience. "Whoever stared at my Wisteria's perfection, consider yourself lucky that I allowed you to leave here with your eyes. Next time, if I catch any heads turn in her direction, I will remove them." I inhaled the scent of coffee and sky on the tunic as he shimmied it over my head. "Don't call me dramatic."

"Then stop acting dramatic." He looked at mine and Nikki's interlocking hands, showing no jealousy as he had about my pajamas. "Nikki is hurting." It was stupid to tell him what he already knew, it was so painfully obvious. Nikki never held back emotions, he honored them by expressing them, something I was shit awful at. I bit my lip, as worthlessness began to creep into the vulnerable cracks in my heart. I had nothing to offer them, to comfort them.

"Fen, I will not stop you from going with them if that is where you need to be." That was all the encouragement he needed to hear. He gave my hand to Zander who took it and whispered prayers at Nikki's back as the roots of the tree swallowed him from sight.

Without Nikki at my side, my feet felt as if they were standing on hot coals. Zander wrapped my legs around his waist. He summoned his wings to cover my exposed legs and called for Alethim to send requests to the innkeepers within Litlough. We walked off the fire fields. Keenan pardoned himself from Atticus with a skewed look on his face that the pure blooded incubi interpreted quickly, leaving me to assume these two ancient creatures had long known each other. Keenan hopped on Zander's heels.

"Were there any resolutions last night?" I asked the pair of them, my mind still wondering what his look to Atticus had meant.

"Several things. One, there will be a war of worlds and what is to come across this barrier is a mere battle. Two," Zander could not stop himself from running his lips and scratchy beard along my warm cheeks. He kissed a dainty kiss on my nose. "You were right. About Anuli's heart. It was stolen from her. Maruc believes she intended to give her essence to the land itself, making Numaal the vessel of her magic and reinstate magic in the east. Even thousands of years ago there had been third or fourth parties meddling in dark arts, we are inclined to believe mortals and immortals have been working together since. I don't understand their goal if it was not for peace."

I would have given an *I told you so* smirk, but was too disgusted by what he said to boast. "Thirdly, nowhere is safe. You can run around swinging Orion at Keenan's head if it strengthens you. And by all means, get into fist fights with my brothers if it boosts your endurance. Stay strong for the darker days ahead."

I craned my neck to plant a wet kiss on his mouth, my teeth sucked in his lower lip as I pulled it into my mouth. "I know a few activities that can increase my endurance and stamina." His body vibrated with a covetous growl. His tongue pried my mouth open, slowly engaging with me, as if he was kissing me for the first time. I ached from loss when he stopped.

Our thread was covered in dull damp colors for we both worried about our woven's hearts. "I'm better off than yesterday. I'll be with my family. Go to Nikki's family. Pa doesn't know about the hauntings, Momo does. Nikki wants to keep it that way."

He called Keenan in close, his eyes were blue spheres of tension. There were too many unspoken protective threats being made as they shook hands. I gave them a well-deserved eye roll. Zander fluxed us to the patio of Horn's Keep. He vanished and reappeared a split second later with clothes in his hands. He pressed them into my chest with a stern look. I felt him screaming down our bond a single word: *Mine. Mine! Mine!*

He was mine, yes, that I agreed to. Reversing the claim, I as his, did not settle well enough. It was a half-truth. I was beginning to believe I belonged to Nikki as well.

After a much needed embrace, Keenan led me to my human companions. Brock gave me a surprised look and said, "Well, here is a first. You are sober."

I slugged his arm. "What does that mean?"

He rubbed his deltoid, his face soured at me. "Your typical manner of coping with ill news or heartache is to drown your world with an entire handle of spiced whiskey. You are stupidly violent, but that's an improvement to belligerently drunk. Or let's say insanely hopeless enough to jump off a fucking ship when you can't swim."

"I got your letters. I know you're upset." My hands were up to demonstrate I was not going to fight him further on this. "I'd make that same choice again because you are worth it."

"You are the only sister I have left and you are by far the hardest to keep alive. I warned you I'd make your life absolute hell." He dropped to his good knee, balancing himself with the sword at his side. His palm ran across the edge until a small bead of blood surfaced. "I, Brock Ironside of the Southlands, freely give Wisteria Woodlander my blood oath. My life and will are hers. I swear to be a perpetual pain in her ass if she ever fucks up this badly again." His oath was pieced together poorly, but the sentiments were there. The Ether would accept his offer.

My lips pursed. "You already are a giant pain in my ass, there is no need to swap blood or toss around fancy words."

"I have been saying these words for years."

"And you will keep saying them and abiding by them for as long as you feel that way. A blood oath to a soon to be dead girl is—"

"—what I want. You won't command anything of me anyways, you don't believe in chains and forced submission. I am doing this freely."

"You're doing this to piss me off!" Those around us laughed.

"Which is what I promised I'd do every day until we are dead because that is what big brothers do. Piss over their haughty, emotionally unregulated little sisters who are going to remake the world with their piss poor choices. You are not remaking this world without me." Orion made the choice for me and left his sheath. I sliced my hand and pulled him up off the ground by our bloody grip. He was grinning. "So, Keenan. Mister Bloodsworn Commander man. What do we do now with our High Lady Queenie?"

My jaw slacked in pure annoyance at Brock.

I turned to Yolanda who kept her hair short after her travels, Count Nicholo's sage detailed sword proudly on her hip. "He is an absolute fool, I'm sorry I left you in his presence for the last months." She was the first to open her arms.

I folded her in. It felt good to hold her. I could feel her passion to overturn Numaal was still eagerly boiling out from her chest even with an entirely different war at work here. "Good news is that his foolishness is not contagious." We were grinning while we remained hip to hip walking through the very crowded hearing chambers catching up on the highs and lows of her travels, she casually mentioned her rooming with Brock most nights including last.

When I turned to face Brock with a quip she yanked my arm and shut it down with political talk, asking me to listen for talk of Bastion among the scribes and let me know that if I chose to go to Kathra, she would navigate the courts with me.

All her chatter made me feel foreign, self-removed. That future for me seemed far out of reach and I would be lying if I didn't say I wanted to keep it that way. I kindly changed subjects. "How was the Land of the Gods?"

"Fertile. Flourishing. The White Tower is... words fail me. It's an entire city built up vertically that breaks the clouds in the sky. It overlooks a harbor, some seadrifters applied to be apprentices and were on a crabbing ship when we left yesterday."

"Is it winter there?"

"A mild one. The breezes that took our sails held an occasional flurry, Ilanthian's that welcomed us in Akelis had on petticoats and gloves. Their eye for fashion is absent, yet they were all happily bustling about their lives with simple embroidery and fitted trousers. Their architecture, however, is a vastly different story. I cannot do the museums and judicial halls justice by speaking about them. You'll have to see for yourself."

A fae with hoofs clomped by nearly knocking Yolanda into a line of folding chairs. "Morning to you too," she grumbled, baring her dull teeth as her upper lip curled.

The fae didn't so much as turn around when he tossed his hands into the air behind. Keenan buried his face under his fabric and pulled my collar over my nose and mouth. Brock and Yolanda followed suit. Angered pixies rounded on him while the red cloud of chalk he tossed disseminated throughout the massive room.

The two pixies who inhaled the brunt of the attack fell limp. The third called out, "Medic! Alchemist!" She readied her foot and kicked out the fae's knees. He stomped like a bull about to charge. "Borwall polluted the Keep!" Another fae sprinted in, this one lanky like she was made out of a limber willow tree. She used her limbs to trip him. I was choking on whatever was in the air when in rushed a water wolf to freeze Borwall into an ice statue. The third pixie hit the ground clawing at her throat.

The tree fae took up calling for a medic until Mauve and Mikleah showed themself. "It's ashwynder salts! As if we didn't have enough pandemonium rampant, now we have to fret about the hundred in this room flocking to the riverbeds or to the drinking faucets."

"What!" Yolanda screamed from under the crook of her elbow. Her wide eyes shot to Keenan demanding answers.

"The salts make you crave a swim into the depths of an ocean or have you drinking an entire river dry." Keenan gripped me under my armpit. "It's only temporary. Let's get to a balcony for air." There went my plans for today.

Fortunately, I felt fine.

Mauve had a portable cabinet of potions delivered to her. One by one she handed out miniature medicine cups of a red liquid that everyone poured down their throats like a shot of liquor. "There is no need to tell him I was in the vicinity of this silly salt cloud." I told Mauve. "I hardly inhaled it."

Keenan swiped the cup from Merna's hand and pressed it to my lower lip. "Woodlanders don't take tonics without knowing what it is." I scolded, while willing to keep my composer in check.

"Dorfhan." Mauve watched Brock take his tonic.

I knew of dorfhan. "The red seaweed dried for dermatitis flare ups?"

"One in the same." She looked a little impressed. "This is the tincture. There is no reversing the salt, but this ensures your body can handle the imbalance of fluid in case you can't stop drinking. Fae and wolves are coming to tether all of you down with ropes or ice cages so you don't run off and die somewhere." Yolanda and I shared a disturbed look. Tied down?

Warroh landed on the balcony. The banister behind him crumbled with the gruff impact. "Borwall threw ashwynder salts. The Winter Pack beta has him inside," Mauve informed without prompt and moved her cart to a group of aged pixies who hadn't stopped coughing. I tailed her and helped divvy up portions. "Their lungs are petite and easily scarred. Half doses for any pixie and nymphs." I complied and oversaw the rest of the crowd.

Warroh's heavy feet went into the Keep, taking his far-from-favorable presence with him. Yolanda muttered from the corner of her mouth. "I see forgoing sleep last night did a number on him too. Just because Eternals don't sleep, doesn't mean we all have to become insomniacs. It makes everyone cranky." She went on to tell me how she and Brock alternated snoozing on the couch and ordering coffee and hors d'oeuvres to stay involved in the conversations.

Keenan seated himself on the steps, watching different types of dreamers take to the skies. News would travel fast. Even irrelevant news such as this small stunt. "I heard the kitchen staff send for more of Havana's dark roast coffee beans. We are in for at least another twenty-four to forty-eight hours of public conclave. Possibly more if they decide to pause the discussions to interrogate Borwall."

Brock seated himself next to Keenan, massaging where his stump met his metal peg prosthetic. "He walked directly into us. How was it not intentional?"

"It was." Keenan unbuttoned his leather vest. One of the many admirers of Commander Ik Kygen happily helped him shimmy out of the garment. Stars glimmered in their eyes having briefly touched his soiled linens. Keenan dismissed the male by his first name and set his attention back to Brock.

"Although, I don't know why. As an individual he had nothing to gain other than commit an open hate crime to which no one in this nation responds kindly to. If he was working in cahoots with a new renegade an intensive interrogation can pinpoint them, but it will cost us time. It can take hours to break into his mind without shattering it. Fae glamour minds, interrogation is tricky and will require a skillful use of magic."

"Or they want to distract Zander. Keep him occupied by my 'ailment'." I joined them overlooking the morning sky of blues and raspberry pinks. I set my head on Keenan's shoulder and inhaled the stroking scent of tobacco. "Maybe Borwall is working with the Vulborg and not a rebellion party. Our theory of demons digging below the barrier into the land of the living is too close for comfort and he is seeking to delay the Veil's interaction."

"That sounds more likely." Percy perched near the rubble Warroh created.

"I dare say, is this the second time we've agreed on something in two days? That is a sure sign the world as we know it is ending."

He was careful not to let an engaging smile slip through his sulking. "Have you seen Clavey's thorny ass come this way?"

"Warroh is inside. No, sign of your rose bush brother."

"I'm sure we will all get stabbed when he scampers by. Madu is in a foul mood too; her and Namir are determined to off eachother. Avoid them." I didn't know if he was helping or duping me into a situation doomed to fail. "Your *friend* will be by this afternoon if you don't clear. You know the one that is madly in love with you?" My facial expression stayed permanently unamused. He got no rise from me.

"You're no fun today. No swords. No belittling the Makers. No drinking my apricot rum." I swallowed my saliva, gauging my thirst. I felt normal.

Keenan took the conversation. "Percy di Lucient, how long were you intending to ignore your Sivt Commander?"

"Let's see. How long ago was the First War, Ik Kygen? Some thousand years ago?" He bent at his waist to take in Keenan's demeanor. Or was it so that we could all see his lack of respect and regard for the man. I kept my head resting on Keenan's shoulder, so my glare would go noticed. "Double that amount of time and maybe I will forget my son's death that occurred while our Sivt was stationed away from where I should have been. I should have been with my Lochlin."

"Lochlin was an impeccable ranger. You choose wisely to suit him in Quat's Sivt, not a soul knew how many would lose their sons and daughters, mothers and husbands that day. The coastline—"

"The coastline is an unmarked tombstone for hundreds of Ilanthian archers. Sivt Commander Ik Kygen, you have kids now." He pointed directly at me, but his eyes held Keenan's with a disparity not known to humankind. The disparity of a lost man who has lived thousands of years with regrets and no way in which to undo his past. "A *mortal* daughter, no less. You *will* know grief. You will know eternal sorrow, you can talk to me after anguish has stolen your sanity." His finger went down. "Had she not saved your son and given hope to Moriah and your infant, you would have already known the foul, loathsome level a soul can sink. Your face, Sivt Commander Ik Kygen, makes me feel as if I am burying my wife's warm corpse all over again. I do not wish to acknowledge you."

He left. Yolanda sputtered out the air in her lungs looking caught between terrified and exhilarated, having been in Percy's emotional line of fire.

A pixie sitting at my feet, looked at me with wide round eyes. "I can see why he drinks." She tied up her greenish hair. "Speaking of drinking, I'm thirsty."

<u>Chapter Twenty</u>

The smaller built beings were of the first to start scratching their throats and looking at the sky for the likelihood of rain or precipitation. I was roughly their size. I knew the salts were building up in my system when spit no longer alleviated the dryness and I began to empathize with the frustrated whimpers of nymphs who were getting shut out from going inside bathrooms and kitchens to rummage.

A pixie wised up and took flight. Ropes of prickly roots wrapped around their legs and reeled them back to the white stone patio for their own safety. Wyatt.

The part-fae, part-incubus used his magic to tether those with wings safely to the railing using brambles. They appeared extensions of himself, unfortunately there were thorns growing on the ropes so he earned himself a decent amount of scowls for his good deeds.

Keenan surrendered his wrist and legs for binding. Wyatt's growths tore his shirts and scuffed his leather. Blood stained the fabric below. "Can't you give a man just one sip of water before you leave us to dry for hours?" I gaped at Keenan. Was he *begging*?

"The wolves will come and they may spare you an allocated drop, Commander." Wyatt didn't sound malicious, then again I was only part way listening to him. My body demanded to be heard. To be sated.

I didn't want to drink water, I wanted to bask in it. Float. Swim!

I'm sure I could convince Zander for an impromptu naked swim lesson in his fancy marble bath house. If I syphered to him, he'd have to cut Momo's visit short or not be present to support Nikki.

Meandering around the city until I found my way to Clemente Avenue was not entirely a half bad idea. Not at all. I leapt up to see it to fruition.

"Where are you going?" Wyatt sighed behind me.

I had paced over to the smashed banister and surveyed the drop, deciding I had survived worse falls then a single story jump. It would take me, what—a few hours to sprint across the city? My waist was squeezed by squiggly brambles and I was on my ass being dragged backwards. "You overgrown raspberry bush!" My palms bled as I yanked at the thorns shackling me.

"I promise you, Wisteria, I don't enjoy this either."

"You're still an asshat!"

"What happened to the marvelous raspberry bush?"

My legs were bound from knees to ankles. "You are not marvelous!" My wrists would be next. No, Zander swore no more shackles for me. I separated my arms and rolled away from him, dodging his magic.

"It's temporary. _Please_, don't make this any harder than it has to be." Crow's feet wrinkled on the corners of Wyatt's eyes, an apologetic wince.

"I'm not known to make things easy for anybody. If you want to capture me then you've got to earn it." With an utterance of Orion's name he was in my hands cutting me to freedom.

Brock's needs seemed to be aligned with mine. "There is a fountain in the back gardens!" An affected elf said eagerly, tossing his hooded cloak to the side. She was a lanky, lovely naked creature. Her limbs graceful as she started dodging Wyatt.

The howls of a pack of wolves didn't stop those of us who were untethered, but their magic did.

I cut through the wall of forming ice and rolled under the second. "Leave her to me!" A feminine voice cracked through the air. I was just happy it wasn't Judeth's. I made it down the stairs and onto the grass. The fountain within sight lifted my spirits far more than it should. I was insane and frankly I didn't give two shits. I wanted pure water falling from the heavens. "Wisteria Woodlander! Slayer of the corrupt, emancipator of the innocent, friend to a lone wolf who strayed too far from Thalren. Stop running from me!"

The wolf from Landsfell? Here?

I didn't stop running, but I did alter my destination. Her penetrating icey eyes drew me in. The water elemental and I collided. Her voice went raspy with apprehension. "I am Torvi Pimen of the Frost Pack. We are alive because we trusted each other. You need to remember that I am acting in your best interest, wild pup." My bones turned to ice and my movements slowed rigid. I couldn't take a full breath with all the frost immobilizing me. "Drop Orion and let me keep you safe. It's my element you are craving after all, is it not?" A rhetorical question.

"I'll hold you safe until your mind is clear, wildling." She seemed fearful of her own voice. Of her own demands.

Others around me were enclosed inside of spherical globes of thick ice. "Tor...Torvi." I chattered out her name. "Sit with me?" I remembered her fur being warm. I remember Nikki's room being hot comparatively.

"Sword."

It was painful to set Orion on the ground. Not because I feared another would come along and take him, he'd never allow that. But painful in the sense of moving my joints was like snapping icicles. I complied. Within a second she was at my side, whirling streams of water around until they froze into an orb encapsulating us. "Torvi. It's good..." No. "It's *great* to see you again."

To my dismay she didn't transform into a large furry wolf that used to sleep along my and Cobar's side. She stayed in this form, a two legged one, who stopped me from licking the ice with a flick on my forehead. My hands rubbed the frozen prison, somewhat sated by the element in this hard form. A bathhouse would have been better. Warmer. "I am sorry I didn't come to see you sooner."

Nikki had gone straight to his family. She must have too. "You probably hadn't seen your family in some time. You missed them."

A wolfish whining escaped her throat. A mournsome sound carried over into her speech. "I left my pack years ago. They didn't understand my need for wayfinding—of getting lost on the summits of mountains only to discover new paths to cross. It was liberating, exploring on my own, surviving on my own, meeting huntressess on the plains and learning how to live as a human and as a shieldmaiden on horseback. In a sense, I had found a people pack. As robust and trained as they were, the knights were no match. They seldom tire. My huntresses did. We fought until my skin shed," she looked down at her pale complexion.

"Months turned into years. I'd been chained and paraded around from the capital to Raj to Landsfell, where I met a young she-pup who was as much a wayfinder as I once was, only you are braver. Mortals have always been braver. You're not afraid to live your life and we are too desperate to preserve ours."

"The Frost P-Pack took you back?" She nodded. "Good." I could see my breath cloud, I touched the moisture in the air and tried to pin it in my hands, failing as if I tried to catch a wave upon the sand. My nails scratched the ice under my body, hoping to shave off a few flakes to melt on my skin. Cold or not, I did not care.

Torvi held my hands to stop my attempts, I shrieked with joy when laces of liquid water bubbled around our grip. She even let me take a single sip before turning her magic off. She cut off my groan of displeasure with a story. "My sister is the pack alpha, my twin woven. Tanya. The condition in which I arrived back at the Glacier was grievous. I required aid only the Weaver could offer. I could not shift forms without her magic reawakening mine in a blanket of security. And I dare say, I do not wish to shift back to my hunter four legged form at the moment. What the heart wishes to forget, the body often remembers. That form of myself hold too much trauma to linger in." She had been a beaten, starved entertainment slave when I spotted her. I could only imagine what damage was inflicted on her wolven body.

"I don't c-c-care what f-form you take. Can you m-make warm water?" I hope I didn't sound as longing as Keenan. But I was. I wanted to soak my skin fully.

"Only as warm as the river runs." That was a fancy way of saying no. My body shook with angry needs. "I have much to tell you to pass the day."

"Go on." She distracted me, or rather, tried to sway my depraved brain from licking the dome of ice or sucking water from her fingers. She couldn't. I snapped too often with need, so frequently that I worried this short fuse would become my personality.

While my eyelashes froze together, I listened to her stories of villages she visited, similar to Waning Star. How she was taught to throw an ax, hunt on horseback and track buffalo herds without her wolf senses. How the knights came and locked steel around her muzzle, starving her and placing her into fighting arenas for entertainment. How if she wasn't a coward she would have exploited her mind to Veona when the memorandum was filled to show how theatrically I entered Stegin's estate, belittled Prince Torval, slayed the duke and commanded the ship off the southern port.

She built me up unnecessarily. I told her as much. "You are a modest alpha of the vibrants. When you rise to queen, you'll need to work on accepting praise for factual feats."

Dull thuds echoed in our confine. An angry hammer rocked the globe. I yanked my shirt tighter to my body, pressing my knees into my chin to grasp at the fleeting heat from my blood. My jaw was too cold now to shiver. Winter had finally come to Zander's realm of eternal spring. "Torvi! Drop the ice or I will melt it and boil you inside!"

The body next to me, placed hands on my forehead. "Cool off, fox. She only just stopped drinking from my hands."

"Her. Lips. Are. Blue."

"She survived worse conditions!"

"That doesn't mean she has too. I'll take it from here."

A hard thud shook my prison. The first thing I saw when opening my eyes was a fiery fist slamming into the ice. Blazing golds splintering riveting blues as opposite elements splashed together. My surroundings melted. My body rolled around in a puddle on the stone, soaking my clothes while I enjoyed the heaviness of the water as it saturated.

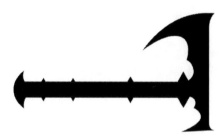

The afternoon sun was a welcomed kiss on my body. Half of us affected by the salts were freed from thorns or ice by the time I had enough control to move my limbs and roll onto my side and look to Yolanda who seemed worse for wear.

Fire cut across my vision as Nikki's tails fell across me, the most luxurious blanket I'd ever been swaddled in. "Stars above," I was gasping and groping at his fluff, savoring his element all while he stood with his back to me giving what I presumed to be a death stare to the wolf.

The snarls between them forced distance.

"Wait." My voice carried to the water elemental. "Thank you."

"You're welcome, wild pup," she tossed over her shoulder, stomping away from the ball of fire embodying a male. "The Frost Pack offers you protection, should you need it. Follow River Lissil west. My pack will gather your scent. They are looking forward to meeting your acquaintance, little alpha queen."

I grimaced at her words then splashed around foolishly in the puddle of water under Nikki's tails. Reality slowly crept into my brain as I locked onto my fox's somber features. "What's the verdict on your home?" My hushed voice hardly above a whisper.

"It's unfavorable for the Burrows to be rehabilitated. My Momo is heavy hearted. She will be spending the nights with her extended kin, grieving and waiting for the collective to give them an order of action."

"Pa?"

Nikki squatted lower. "Ignorance is bliss. His mind and heart wouldn't survive such tragic news." Our hands clasp. "Chaz will tend to him."

"I will tend to you." Through Nikki's disheartened posture he let slip a crack of a smile.

I was pulled onto my feet, magically dried and seated with my comrades at the meal table with wolves lingering to freeze people's water should they binge too liberally between bites. Nikki dried our belongings and pardoned himself to see how Wyatt's interrogation was going with the culprit at hand. Cobar found his way onto my lap and stayed on my hip after our postponed meal. Yolanda was livid that they continued to ration our water intake and we left the table, taking with us the juiciest slices of watermelon we could get our hands on. A small act of rebellion that sent us giggling

I walked around the Keep with my brother wrapped to my side, listening to the elf scribes reiterate the conversations of the prior night. They sent word to the alchemists and magic wielders to ready potions for explosives, light bombs and helfyre.

Keenan entrusted Cobar to Yolanda and I. That little tornado burnt himself out and was asleep on my shoulder within the hour that Keenan had been called away to oversee some shit with Atticus—apparently they were lifelong buddies. It was unnerving to comprehend that so many revere this simple man that helped raise me and requested he spearhead the conversations on how to best fight the demons with the eighty thousand the Veil had at the ready and the ten thousand (and growing) number of Ilanthian foot soldiers voluntarily arriving in the days, weeks ahead.

He had talked Anna off emotionally high cliffs countless times before, so leading a fancy conclave of a half dozen different weapons wielders and races came as easily as breathing to my Bloodsworn. Keenan stood at the head of the table spouting out wisdom that even Kailynder absorbed like a dry sponge. Positioned next to the elves with flawless skin Keenan didn't physically appear much older. In fact, he seemed just a year or two older than Nikki and his energy reserves were never ending.

My mind muddled as I grasped at the many truths of Kinlyra's innumerous combinations of blood and finally decided that it was Keenan's experiences that had aged him. Or perhaps, I'd only seen him fit one role in my life and he forever cemented himself into that paternal position. Never replacing my father, but standing in nicely as he had always done.

The Overlords here apparently had deep pockets. They bought physicians to have on hand from all corners of Ilanthia and to preparing buildings and tents for use as sickbays. They also purchased hundreds of tons of rice, lentils and meats from Havana and the valleys to feed their army. Horn's Keep in the days ahead would become the seat of decision making and storage for goods.

Brock was of the loyalist, most determined people I knew and the bastard kept proving that fact to me throughout the night. If he could not stand physically by my side on the battlefield for lengthy intervals, he was dead set to make himself useful in other arenas that would serve me in years to come. He hounded Veona's Left Wing until Alethim agreed to show him the ropes of running a city through written words, conclaves and public hearings.

Yolanda vouched that Brock was a fast study and with a few phrases of persuasion the elf allowed Brock to witness all it was that he was doing to keep the nation running smoothly with and without an official Overlord present.

By the tall stone fireplace engraved with grass and river rock nymphs, Yolanda and I settled down with an obscenely large bowl of popcorn and laid Cobar to rest against my sternum. When Zander and Maruc found us whispering softly about how to make ourselves useful to the outside world during wartime chatter we had already made significant damage to the snack bowl.

With seven long strides Zander was fireside and scooping me up in his arms with Cobar still in mine. I tugged at the soft brown curls atop his scalp, inhaling his sweet shampoo he'd used. On the floor Zander sat, pulling cushions off the couch near him to ease his elbows onto. "You inhaled ashwynder salts." I shushed him and demanded he speak softer to not stir Cobar.

Fangs emerged through a purse of his impatient lip. "Yes. Many of us did. And we all seem to be doing alright. It led to a lovely reunion with Torvi."

He matched my soft whisper. "Remind me to send a letter tonight thanking her for getting your ass out of Landsfell and not drowning while in my absence."

"If only we had time for those swimming lessons."

A spark of lust shot down our bond, he didn't bother to tame it. Despite my brother in my arms he made a trail of kisses from my wrists up to my neck opening his wet mouth over his bite mark. "Don't start what you can't finish," I said warningly.

I squashed the fever determined to take my body when Yolanda laughed.

His devilish chuckle stopped and he questioned seriously. "Have I ever left you wanting? Aside from yesterday's food market encounter."

"That did make me hungry." *But you don't share meals.*

I also haven't sent one I openly claimed to sleep in bed with another. Atticus feels I've betrayed our lineage and gone soft letting the one I bit lay exposed, vulnerable and out of my sight with another male at that. It matters not that he is my woven and I love him. He shudders at the notion. I find it very entertaining actually.

He doesn't trust me.

Not our concern nor is that entirely true. Atticus wasn't the only one unfavoring my being with Zander. "The reapers are removing items of value from the Elm. Maruc agreed to oversee the cementing off of the lowest living areas and tunnels of the Burrows later tonight and into the morning. Many difficult decisions lay ahead."

I tilted my head. "Nikki knows the verdict?" He pointed to his one golden eye. I waved. "I can't imagine these outcomes feel good on your spirit. Mine was heavy, aching when I realized my home was... gone." My words were for the elemental, but it was Zander's lips that sought mine out.

Are you both in there? I asked in pausing before committing to a lip lock with both of them.

The staticy reply did not elude one way or the other. *If I kiss Zander with Nikki here, does that constitute as kissing Nikki? Is this a loophole to a threesome?* Blue and gold eyes blinked anticipatingly at me.

Zander's shoulder raised in a small fit of laughter. Apparently, we had much exploring to do between our abilities of transplacency, syphering and quintessing without crossing that one boundary with Nikki.

Instead of kissing Zander, I smiled against his lips, the golden eye shone.

The echoes of the phrase *little vixen* pulled Zander's lips to his shining eyes as he secured a second laugh in his chest.

"Stop flirting and go find a room." Yolanda poured herself a glass of wine. Her judgmental brows raised at me, not on Maruc who pulled his own wine glass out of thin air. Nifty trick.

"May I rest next to you, Yolanda d'Loure?" There was a quick change in her expressions, one she didn't have time to hide. Her bewildered silence extended as she curled her feet under her to make room for the Emperor to sit next to her. "Many thanks. I hear you are invested in rebellions to the east. Tell me about them."

Yolanda cleared her throat. "I wish I could, but I've not been initiated."

B.B. Aspen

Maruc sipped the wine, rolling it on the back of his palate to dissect the emerging flavors of the beverage. "I'd very much like to understand the reasons behind your desire to join Bastion." While his attention was fully on Yolanda I told Orion off. He disappeared from his brother's line of sight, leaving my heart paining with loneliness.

I didn't need Maruc making any advancements to grab at Orion again who made it obvious he didn't wish to interact with. I'd protect him. He'd find his way back to me as he always did.

Yolanda engaged the Emperor, her composure less formal as the minutes passed on where she poured her passion out to him. They earned themselves an audience of dreamers. Wyatt rested among several wolves. All who look upon her with pointed interest. The interrogation concluded then if Wyatt was here. "Fen will disclose," he whispered to his brother.

Over came Keenan who gestured to his son. I relinquished my hold on Cobar so they could turn in for the night. A water wolf tailed them, asking Keenan a multitude of questions about the lingering effect of the salts. The other water elemental, Torvi, stayed to listen to fireside conversations, her maw resting on Yolanda's feet. *Think we can sneak away or are you waiting for the interrogation results?*

Nikki can deliver the outcome to our room. Wyatt seems fatigued, he'd given his reports several times already by the looks of it. If he were worried he would have told us instead of drinking wine from Yolanda's glass and sniffing her out.

It was settled then. Off to bed.

The weight of hundreds of dense sculpted pounds pressed me into the bed. My mouth greedily devoured his, using his horns to lock him where I needed him as he kissed me with bruising force. My hips lifted and his fingers found their way into my undergarments acknowledging my needs but not liberating me as I so clearly wanted. "You need a cock. My cock." My pants were on the floor with his.

"Get this off me." I rasped.

254

He complied, tearing open the tunic and making it unsalvageable. Between kisses I pulled his shirt overhead. He brought my hips to the edge of the bed where he knelt, my wet slit the perfect height for his thrusting. When the room filled with purple haze and wails of my climaxes did we finally settle into our exhaustion.

Zander set folded towels on the bath rack, a night shirt of his draped on the door knob for my use after. "Can you please shower with the door open? I want to keep a close eye on you for obvious reasons."

I gave him a good and teasing show. His magic of purple wispies flirted back. If they were anything tangible I would demand he fuck me with them.

When the streams of water met my body all thoughts of sensuality fled my mind and were replaced with the echoes of water wanting from the day's trials. I laid on the smooth tile floor of the shower, suds of lavender and vanilla soap frothed around me.

Warm water was heavenly. I could sleep on the steam cloud.

"Wisteria, did you know there are beds to sleep in?" It wasn't Zander's voice.

"I am fine! Are you… are you doing alright?" I meant to get up, to greet Nikki, to sit him down and talk through his somber spirit of losing his home and what I could offer to help his soul mend or soften the blow of reality. Yet, my limbs stay there splashing about as I lay horizontal, unable to convince myself to seek a towel or stand.

"I took a long cold shower while you two fucked so I didn't walk in aroused. Seemed appropriate to let a little time pass before bursting in to tell you Borwall's intention was to let Wisteria drown. He caught wind of her lack of swimming abilities and thought it best Zander not have a girlfriend given the inconclusive state of things. If they knew you were his woven, *our woven*, the rumors dissolve and strengthen our realm's resolve. It would also stop assignation attempts." I gave an eye roll. He carried on with Borwall's intel. "No fae faces are in his mind. But, he can't be working alone. Maybe they communicated with letters, blank notes or written threats."

Nikki's voice was hardened. Short. "As for how I am? I need touch. Warmth. Togetherness. I'm hurting and you two are my salve." Zander must have held him because his dump of information stopped suddenly.

"She seems too comfortable in there."

Zander murmured in agreement. "This would not be the first time she has fallen asleep in the shower. Doors have stayed open since. And with salts now controlling her, I removed the drain plug as a precaution. I wouldn't put it past our girl to find a way to meet her end in a few drops of water."

"I am not being controlled. I can hear you two!"

"Good. Then prove him wrong." Nikki was at the door frame with another's arms wrapped around his muscular shoulders and broad chest. His face was dull and streaked with sadness. Zander tucked the fox ears back under his chin while holding Nikki's back to the front of his body, he matched the sad whines that squeaked from Nikki's throat.

The pair of them wallowed while they waited for me.

It was a moot point to shield myself from their eyes. The stream of the scalding water spattering around me took care upholding my remaining modesty. "I'd actually prefer it if you just turned off the water and got out so we don't have to dissect the odds of you managing to drown in here." Nikki was not one to beg. The fatigue in his tone would not lax until I was deemed safe from a quarter inch of drizzling shower water.

Damn these protector wovens.

"Five more minutes."

"Twenty seconds. I brought the rest of the desserts from the Hallow. There are many unopened boxes that you can have for breakfast if you get out. Now."

"Four minutes. My skin is thirsty."

"I need warmth sharing." My lashes batted away to droplets to see him clearly. He looked devastatingly sad. And serious. "Nineteen. Eighteen." I scrambled to my feet, woozy with all the vasodilation. "Seventeen. See Z, she isn't controlled by the salts. Just not properly motivated. Fifteen."

"Guilt and sugar?"

"Facts and foods." He pressed his head into Zander's neck as he corrected.

"Did you bring the lollipops?" I glared, rapidly washing my body free of soap suds.

"Come find out." He continued to count backwards. His swollen eyes shut when I stepped onto the bath mat with seven seconds left, wiggling my arms into Zander's tunic and tugging the edges down towards my knees.

I was at three seconds when I tried to wrap my wet hair with a damp towel. Not that any of my efforts matter because when Nikki shot open his luminescent gaze all of the dampness was removed from my body as he took my hand and led Zander and I to his section of the living quarters, releasing us so that the incubus could draw down the black curtains. Nikki pulled dozens more pillows from his closet and threw them on the low mattress before he launched his body on them.

Wily tails burned against the night. "Centuries of my parent's and communities' hard work and engineering will be destroyed in a single night. I consented to that."

The sadness in his voice and outstretched arm beckoned us to him. I crawled to him as fast as I could, latching onto whatever flesh I contacted. "I went with Maruc only to follow behind them retrieving acorns and heirlooms. And Wisteria's sweets. There is no doubt that this is the most suitable and appropriate course of action. But it hurts. Fucking soul crushing like one of Wisteria's wounds etched invisibly on my body that is slow to mend."

Nikki's flames crept around my bare legs. He wanted me closer. Yes. He shall have me melted onto him if it takes away his sorrows for but a sparse second. His nose brushed mine to level our eyes. "Wisteria, I burnt your homeland down after it was too far lost. Mine is lost. Now, I know how you feel, my woodland creature. To my core I feel it and I am sorry for what you experienced. My home has been taken and while I agree that the best course was to obliterate it–*it hurts*."

Plump tears built in his eyes. Mine mirrored his. "My hearts, I'm surprised they haven't fallen out of my chest." He yipped as simmering tears rolled down his cheeks.

Zander arranged the nest of blankets around his stature and offered Nikki his arm to use as a pillow. "I need you two to hold them. Hold me." Nikki said no more. He transformed fully into his white and golden flamed rare bodied fox, curling into himself.

The gut wrenching whimpers brought tears out of Zander and I. The incubus didn't lift his eyes away from the trembling soul as my head found an arm to rest upon. Nikki's front paws and muzzle settled on my chest, his back formed to Zander's body. I snuggled my face in his fur, his smell of pine and smoke imprinted on me. I hope he didn't notice the closet I left open the night before last, or the scarf I had pulled out of place to just have a token of him near.

Zander's right arm wrapped around us, securing the three of us into a knot. "This is good?" My proclaimed corlimor asked into the night. My own chest perpetually ached.

"I will not be *good* until Nikki is free of anguish. Our homes have been stolen and we've been spared to witness the fall of all we hold dear. All of us have played a part unwillingly in each other's torment." The fox agreed wordlessly. Orion appeared on the nearest cushion. I knew it to be his effort to offer comfort. "If you are referring to our arrangement, the answer is yes. This feels good to offer comfort and hold each other." Zander leaned across and kissed my lips before we buried our faces in the flames.

When I woke up, I was not *good.*

Aside from the sadness swallowing me and my wovens' spirits, I was tangled with a naked man—an outrageously gorgeous one—who was not Zander. Laying on top of the stark bare male and I was a drooling horselord confining us too intimately with his arms and legs.

I hastily found pants and ran to sword practice with Keenan to sweat out the heaviness of losing the Burrows.

What an exhausting day that proved to be for Keenan and I both.

The Lies of the Eternals

Chapter Twenty-One

Sweating, bruised and ravished with hunger we sat on the rampart as rubbery pipes and hoses full of liquid cement were pumped into the miles of underground habitation. I pretended not to see Madu's pack or the group of inflight pixies or any incubi eying the decorated sivt commander dangling his feet off the edge next to mine off tower chatting about golden blooded Anna.

Amazingly enough, Keenan didn't tire of bobbing his head at those offering genuflections as they passed by. How his head had not rolled off his neck was beyond me? Why did he have to be an esteemed warrior? All the attention he brought to our private conversation was annoying. I mentioned as much. He chuckled as did the group of archers walking behind us.

"I cannot venture a guess as to how your powers will manifest, Wisteria. Not even Maruc can claim to know."

"They are not *my* powers. It is not *my* magic. It was *hers*." I wiped sweat off my neck, grimacing at the dull tenderness of a bite. "Besides, I don't know if I want to activate Athromancia's blood. I may prove to be useful in the war, but part of me just wants to keep it dormant to spite that bitch."

The tail end of Zander's scar blackening the center of his city was clearly visible at all times of day. I underestimated the size of it when I first saw it. He was powerful. I'd be more so. "Me using magic may prove to be a complete disaster." I was already a murderer, just as Zander believed himself to be.

The difference was that my kills were intentional, his were not. He retained innocence. That innocence buffered his soul to shine, even when all his saw was darkness. With the rest of my days left with him on this earth I would spend convincing him of that. Protecting it.

The Vulborg haunted me enough in the years leading up to now. Add learning the use of magic to the mix. Utter exhaustion would befall me. "What would happen to my red blood?" Malick's blood healed Zander, coincidentally Nikki. "Athromancia's blood healed the stab wound meant to kill me in the dungeon, but not any injuries after. Was it because of dormancy?"

Keenan let out an encumbered sigh. "Your body will continue to function as it does now. No fast healing, no immortality." That was a relief. Staying on this shit earth was bleak on either side of the beyond. "You will likely gain the powers to defend yourself rightly, therefore, increasing your chance of living longer if that was what you were concerned about." I ignored his suspicious brow raise and the obvious stare at my neck.

"No. You already know how much I pity you immortals." His shoulder rested against mine. "Will it hurt? What are the consequences?"

A new voice entered the conversation. "Getting molded into a weapon, manipulated for your magic, hunted by kings for your blood and perpetually second guessing every choice you've ever made are a few I can state off the top of my head." Maruc seated himself on my right side. I sheathed Orion. The crackle of sound proofing protection bubbled around us. Keenan shot up with ire realizing he was excluded from the conversation. His fist fired time and time again at the barrier until I signaled for his to stand at ease.

"Oh. So, no change?" I remarked with a loose lip, confident that the rest of the city was no longer dropping eaves. Keenan too for that matter. His eyes stared intently through the sound bubble. I gave him another reassuring glance. It didn't help. Commander Ik Kygen's teeth were bared at the God, a few passersby stopped to settle him. They scampered away from his grumbles.

I peered into Maruc's deep set hazel eyes that painfully reminded me of his sister's, his Empress's, his wife's. When his hand fell on my shoulder, I didn't shrug him off. I wasn't ready to tear myself away from those vibrant complex colors unlocking fond fucking memories in my tattered soul. "Taking you to Opal Lake will likely kill you, Wisteria."

My Bloodsworn pulled his sword at the ready and stood at my back. Maruc eyed him and continued. "Raw, awakened power funneling into a mortal vessel with its true owner *alive* to wield it one final time is dangerous enough. Athromancia is gone as is her protection from her restless magic which is capable of tearing your fragile flesh into compost before you've even had opportunities to be taken advantage of."

My eyes left him to settle on the Eternal Elm, alit with the ire and grief countless felt. "My friends would never let me fall prey to others with or without magic."

"I know that. I also know they are more than friends." His chuckle was charming and comforting.

Damn me for thinking so. "I see things that most cannot. I admire your attempts to hide such miracles from my sight, I haven't a clue why you decided to waste your efforts. All will be revealed, woodland child."

The threads of the Weaver. He knew.

Without thinking I pressed a stern finger to his lips. "Yes, yes. Alright. I'll play along if I must. You are working against a current, sometimes it is better to float and enjoy where the tides take you and not be obstinate which leaves room for a realm at war to question your motives." I massaged the wrinkles creasing in my brow.

"I relish being an obstinate rock."

Keenan pressed his face against the sound bubble with his nostrils flaring. He clearly disliked being shrouded. "You have been informed it's futile to hide her thread, right? If not, allow me to be the first."

"I know. They told me. I just *can't*. Not yet."

"It would make life much easier."

"For who?"

"Everyone. You included. Unless you get your jollies from gossip because when the world sees the three of you going about your business all chumming and cherishing they will conspire more than they have been."

Needing to change topics I carried on conversing. "What else do you believe you and I have in common?"

"Other than fucking my wife?" He slung back at me with no remorse. I felt my face wince. "Missing her. Loving humanity despite your flaws. Temperance. Being potentially great rulers of nations." My back spasmed, recollecting the Faceless Prince's wedding proposal and the brand he seared onto me.

Me, the future queen of Numaal, with my own miserable high court and subjects of demons. Maruc watched me hide my distress. I redirected as to not reveal my misery to an Eternal who refused to fight when the runegate fell.

The training fields bustled below. The sound of steel on steel uplifting enough to allow me to engage with Maruc—my anger safely barricaded with Nikki. Thank fuck for that. "Anna was such a presence it is difficult not to notice her absence and grieve the silent moments where her laugh and bickering should have filled."

Rain pattered from non-existent clouds.

The rain was gentle. It fell from the sky as languidly and tenderly as the tears leaked from the crevasse of Maruc's eyes.

"Athro, Aditi and Taite would prank the twins and bribe them into retaliation. Drommal flooded her wing of the tower with sewage and Athro fumed for weeks. It took years to replace her furniture and magic away the rancid scents that permeated her carpets. She screamed at Drommal every chance she had and finally retaliated when she trapped them into a sensory chest with four skirrats and no way to call for help. Dradion blasted the western gorge into existence to find where she had his twin." Maruc's humor was weak, but his memory fond.

Keenan and Anna would threaten each other's throats almost weekly. All too relatable. "All of your siblings are volatile."

The next laugh he gave sounded true. The sky even paused it's precipitation. "Our tears of jubilation and tribulation created the oceans and the monsters and pearls of magic deep within them. We were once entities who'd block out the stars with but a lift of a finger. With each step we took the earth trembled. With every sound made winds moved and the whispers of creatures collected within the Opal Lake. With a thought we molded attributes and breathed them into beings of water, sky and land. We found environments where these beings flourished and failed, quickly we gave them emotions to entertain themselves in our absence and insight to live and learn from consequences. Every civilization multiplied, some created and destroyed themselves many times over to bring us to where we are now. I exist, Wisteria." He was whispering now. "Before you. After you. With you. Without you. This world has all it was meant to."

"This world would not be without you. But if you don't help now and we happen to survive the clash of worlds, I promise you that all remaining and rebuilding will forget you. We will go on *without* you. I'll see to it that you are erased." Rutting hell. Where had this bout of spicy anger boiled up from?

"Barter with me then."

"What?" I blinked several times thinking it would aid me in hearing better.

"Give me an offer. One worthy enough to command myself and the Ivory Legion whenever and wherever you see fit." He crossed his ankles and rocked them over the edge.

The rain lifted.

"Okay, help and the world will remember your name and efforts."

"My name has been a curse on many lips of many worlds of recent memory. I care not about being remembered. Do better." I chewed on my lips, twisting metal in my mouth. The fate of the Veil could very well rely on my next offer. I had to make it good.

What would a God want? Need? My tongue ring tapped against my teeth.

"You can hold your brother for a while."

He shrugged and rolled his eyes at Orion. "He won't let me despite the ingrained desperation I feel to hold my woven. Try again."

"What do you want?"

"To be with my family." His shoulder leaned into mine. Hazel eyes captured mine and I grinned easily as if I obtained a revelation. "See we aren't so different after all, no need to look surprised."

"You want to die."

"You've had similar thoughts." His tone was humbly reassuring, not judgmental.

I looked now at the barrier to the beyond, trembling with iridescent beauty while it held back the sea of demons. "How do you want to die? I suspect you don't want to be mauled by Vulborg and have your soul eaten out."

"At my wovens' doing. You are not the first to have two wovens, but you are tied deeply to mine, Athro and Ori. We are three bound protector wovens onto each other." No way. I stared at him.

No rutting way. "Again, not so different, eh? We three were wovens, Wisteria. I want you to end me and send me back to the Ether. They chose you for one task. I am choosing you for another. Save their world, but end my life."

"What about your vessel?"

He shook his head. "Not important to me."

I chewed over the information I was given, swallowing our similarities as easily as gulping from a chalice of life giving waters. "I have a proposal."

"State the terms."

"Stay in Veona when the Vulborg attack. After the runegate breaks you build a stronger one—better one, deeper one, thicker one. One that will outlast time or at least buy us a sufficient amount to get our shit together as a united Kinlyra. In return, you've my promise to reunite you with your family through death after we agree upon a time."

"If I agree to this, your half of the bargain of what is owed to me remains a secret until the deed is done." I nodded. "No one can know that my death is promised to you." He shook my hand as was common after settling on an arrangement, but it was no simple crafter barter I had made. I had made a soul contract with a God. Stormy sparks ignited and fizzled away when the deal was struck.

"It will take much of my magic, but it will be a runegate unlike anything I've ever dreamt. I'll need help spelling it shut and I know just the nephew to help me." He seemed more at peace. "What you've offered is a short term solution to a bigger issue. I want you ruling the White Tower with your wovens seated as your Temperance and Emperor. I want that, but more importantly the Weaver wants that. I will not go against Her. After all I am not immune to Her will and you three are who she requires for her great tapestry she has been conspiring for eons."

My neck snapped to him. No falsities were spoken. Uncomfortable hot pain shot up my neck as more discomfort plunged into a crevasse in my gut. "The White Tower in Ilanthia? I've never even been there! That can't possibly be what the Weaver wants because I am mortal and underqualified!"

"This world has much to learn—*much to remember*." The stretched skyline of clouds parted as Maruc bestowed more clarity. "The White Tower rules all Kinlyra, not solely Ilanthia. The mountains cut the magic off from the east and over time my siblings thought it best to have overseers where Anuli, Taite and Misotaka's favorite living beings roamed to help keep the world connected without the flow of magic. A formal establishment was born to carry out the communication task, a monarchy."

I snorted. "That backfired." Our monarchy and royal line was a failure of monstrous proportions at the present. And in the past where they chose to rip out Anuli's heart. "Maruc you are speaking absurdities. I cannot... *we* cannot...there is a war! The Elm is being threatened which means all our lives are being threatened! I'm not losing my boys. Without them I will fall lost yet again and no excess of golden blood or fancy bargains will ever reverse that if it comes to pass."

I wasn't sure he was listening to my concerns. Very valid, pressing concerns. "Then I will settle for the three of you agreeing to rule within the near future on the thrones. The deal breaks if one of you can't comply fully and willingly. If you can all agree to these terms then me, my power and my Ivory Legion are yours to command. Atticus and Ik Kygen have been around since the thrones were initially constructed. You will have guidance so settle your fears." I blinked dumbly. He sounded as if he had considered this whimsical nightmare thoroughly and was at peace with it.

How would I even bring this conversation up with my two stubborn woven? They are looking at surviving the nearest future of the weeks ahead, not the years after next, much like I have been doing my entire life. "How do you plan to rescue Numaal? You've said it yourself, dreamers wouldn't rally their entire militia, risking the death of countless rare races to preserve one. Or they would have done so already, right?"

"They have their own war here. As you said, it is pressing."

"You defend them. Interesting." I pretended to watch the flight formations. Was that Zander I saw landing on the tall rut? "All of Kinlyra has fallen blind. Numaalians are not the only citizens I consider to be unwitting and downright ignorant. Too much time and not enough trust has spoilt a future of harmony. Unbalanced soup."

"Pardon. Soup?"

"Soup." He punctuated the 'p'. "We spent lifetimes perfecting ingredients meant to be blended into a palatable, exquisite soup. A concoction that should have been flawlessly balanced, even after it boiled and cooled." His shoulder dropped into mine as he whispered. "All you beautiful beings are the ingredients."

"I picked up on that. Thanks." I arched a brow. "And the boiling was the Great War?"

"Precisely. Kinlyra was always meant to thrive united and reliant on each other."

"Vulborg probably taste as atrocious as they smell. I doubt you can add strong enough flavors to cover them up or find a spoon big enough to fish them out?"

"Nope. But a new chef or three might do the trick." His laugh sent a breeze behind our shoulders. While adjusting my unruly hair I caught sight of Keenan stomping around with his eyes fixed on our chummy smiles. If he knew we were chatting about soup, he'd likely not had been so vexed.

"What issues plague Ilanthia? Can't they rule themselves?"

"The White Tower was built to oversee all of Kinlyra, not the isolated west section of Thalren. The mountains choked off the magic and restricted the Veil. The closed off world you've come to know was never meant to be quarantined nor was Ilanthia. Oyokos did stop the Great War with the seam of Thalren, but time has corrupted it into the opposite of his intent." His hand scooped up air currents and with cloud consolidation created a map of a previous Kinlyra, mountainless.

"Ilanthians, they are needing new histories for the libraries, new stories for their temples, new passion to inspire their bards and poets. They grow stale and restless. A new set of rulers is needed because a new world is coming. With an Empress who has made a bargain to save the Dreamer Realm, who went to the Opal Lake to awaken a wise magic to save what remains of Numaal from the Vulborg—a God of War at her side. And the blood kin of Dradion, Drommal and Oyokos... You are Athromancia and Orion and will have the blessing of Maruc if you play your cards right." That was six of the Eleven.

"The Opal Lake will kill me."

"Probably."

"What if I am as volatile and explosive as Anna and as uncontrolled as your nephew? I may destroy Kinlyra." I pointed to my chest. "I'm not even trusted enough to hold onto my own anger! Nikki took it."

"I always knew that fox would make a good Temperance. Balanced. He can oversee soup nicely." He was talking to himself, the stars were his audience. He must have received the reply he sought. "Keenan's training has run its course. I'll train you in magical intuition if it means getting you a decision closer to ruling at the tower."

"I'll think on it."

"Don't think on it too long because the infestation has started."

I grabbed his elbow as he stood to rise. "What if I survive and my friends don't want to be the Triology with me? Zander was manipulated to seize power by those who sought to leech from him. I will not be using the survival of his home to guilt him."

"You'd do it then? Reign a peoples who rallied against humanity?" I let him pull me to my feet. Pine, Sage, Rory, Moriah, Asher, Cooper, Culture, Rodrick, Raina. I'd people to protect, whether they knew it or not, they still had someone fighting for them. Me.

"There are innocents everywhere. Besides, I am curious who I might be if I wasn't always fighting for my life. The deal was we all agreed to it. There were no time constraints to sit on your pretty chairs. You will let me command you and yours before that time befalls if we all shake your hand." I reiterated.

He gave a loose tug on my hand. "If all three agree to it after your powers are awakened, it's a deal. I leave at dawn in three days. Be by the gate if you want to trek to Opal Lake. Unlike my sister, I will not be making choices for you."

Agreeing to the thrones would be an issue, but not *the* issue my males would be concerned about. The revival of Athromancia's dormant power within me would pose the biggest obstacle to getting them on board.

I wouldn't be telling them.

Chapter Twenty-Two

I didn't think it would be possible for anyone to rival Zander's pestering. But here Keenan stood—proving me wrong--aggravating me to no avail. In fact, it felt as if half the damn Keep decided to lurk around our bedroom door to pry and spy amid conclave. Even Maruc trailed behind me. I should have known being seen conversing with him would lead to trouble.

My teeth were worn from clenching my jaw as Keenan deposited me outside the private wing in Horn's Keep, Warroh leaned on the exact door I wanted. The door to a shower and holy silence. I stepped out of Keenan's reach and slapped his hand away. "Shh! I don't owe you answers!"

"However stealthy he was trying to keep your exchange—he biffed that cloudy bubble and I saw you shake hands. You made a deal with him. Whatever stunt you are about to pull you will include me!" I shushed him again. Members of the conclave and inquisitive dreamers to raised a brow.

"With who?" a scribe asked.

Keenan pointed an accusatory finger behind him at the innocent appearing Emperor himself. "Maruc!" Why did he have to yell? Why did everyone here have to be so damn nosey?

Brock moseyed in. "I want to be included! I am your most favorite Bloodsworn after all." Zander appeared in a swift burst of speed, stepping in front of Namir who was throwing every nearby object at Nikki's ring of fire. Vases and bejeweled items became piles of ash when they trespassed into the ten foot radius he drew around himself with scorching magic. I pinched the bridge of my nose. What chaos is this Keep instigating now?

I motioned for Warroh to move from our chamber's door. No surprise here. He didn't. He opted to make a remark about using Orion as a dildo.

I didn't get a chance to reply because Brock was breathing down my neck. "Admit it, you like me better than that old Montuse guy." The Ironside crossed his arms while I considered stealing some of Zander's voice amplifying potion and screaming at everyone to back off.

Wyatt laughed amenably and a small crowd of fae flurried in his wake. Possibly his friends or his dinner. My most recent, least favorite voice stabbed my eardrums. "Another Bloodsworn? Growing your own army of devotees are you? Maybe I underestimated your malice," Judeth snarled behind Warroh. Lovely.

"Devotees. Interesting choice in words." Warroh turned his betrayed beliefs on me. "Sacrilegious."

"Were it true. Which it is not." I sighed in Brock's direction. "Honestly, buddy? Must you always make my life difficult?"

Brock's arm hooked around my neck. I stomped on his foot with my heel, driving guttural noises out of his chest. I found myself grinning at his pain. "I vowed to do so for the rest of my days. So, what have you and Maruc been congenial about that required discretion?"

"Anna's tits. It's hard for any mortal or immortal not to obsess over them. They were fantastic." I dropped out of his touch with a twostep. Keenan steadied me with a fast hardly visible catch beneath my underarm. "And for the record we made only one bargain. The details of another are in progress, but it's a tad more complicated so I couldn't agree to the terms at that moment."

Warroh clicked his large jaw, his soul scythe and prayer beads he wore as a weapon and shield respectively. "Zander, your marked desecrates our Makers with her lack of reverence. I find her horrifying. She tainted what was to be a profound, honorific moment of sanctity by learning of her blood. Teach her to shut her mouth or rid her." Zander fluxed and reformed himself around Warroh with a death grip of an iron vice.

Maruc shook his head and whispered to himself, "Why did we give you all so much violence and so little patience?"

A sickening crunch made Brock and I lean into each other. Warroh's skull cracked. Blood smeared across the stone floor. Fist and fang flew. "Her mouth ate out a Maker's cunt and Athromancia found no desecration in that act, receiving or reciprocating. I reckon she found rutting salvation by Wisteria's talented tongue as I often do. You sound jealous." Nikki didn't step in to stop them. He gaily watched the brawl after Madu chucked her shoe in his direction. Even Judeth shook her head at the heavens to ask when these idiots would reach a point of maturity. If ever.

"I find it off-putting how shitty your judgment gets when you don't feed on a schedule. If Judeth can still tolerate you, take her as a foul fuck and leave my saint of a darling alone. Spit your poison elsewhere for it cannot tarnish what is already immaculate and *goddessly.*" Zander reared his head at Warroh's skull again; he went unconscious on impact.

Straddled across his cataleptic brother's legs, Zander looked up and cut the tension in the room. "Judeth. Whatever you are devising behind his back, end it before he awakes. The city has seen you broadening connections during my recent leave. All the way to the Ravine as I have personally observed from my feathered friends in the sky and those coiled under rocks." Zander tapped his white eye. A slit of a snake's eye peered out. Or was it a hawk's? Handling affairs indeed. "Stop luring Kai into your web of mistrust. The First Faction will be of no aid during these awful times we are facing. The Faction is a hindrance to evolution with its stagnant rubrics."

Judeth took his words in stride. Zander pressed on while he held her attention. "Kai and I spoke frankly and he is not rallying for any titles. But he is leery of sudden changes. Wisteria is a change, one myself and many welcome. You will not rid her or I will personally *rid* you–grotesquely and creatively I should like to add–and anyone who suggests that course of action will suffer a similar fate." Zander used Judeth's cloak to wipe Warroh's blood off his knuckles, his claw-like nails tearing the fabric as he did so.

"I understand why you don't place faith in newcomers, least not the women I have chosen to unapologetically love, but you fail to grasp that much of the world was kept from them, locked out of reach by rumor, magic severed by mountains and historical texts rewritten with lies. You have to allow time and grace."

Judeth snapped and took her cloak from his stained grip. "There is no time to educate or reform, let alone discern their character. I do not give strangers leverage, weapons or insight to knowledge to give to enemies. This will not end well for you. For us."

"Very few things bring people together like fighting a common enemy. If we don't rely on each other, we will all fail together in death." Cultee's words found their way from my mouth. Judeth's scowl deepened until it was cast permanently.

The last God cleared his throat. "Dreamers, hadn't Oyokos taught you to respect your differences and value each other's integrity? Is that not the foundation principle on which this realm was established?" Stillness followed, save for Zander who gave a proud nod to Maruc.

Judeth sulked. "Before you retort Judeth, why don't you hear what has to be said." Maruc crossed his arms across his chest. Namir stepped over Warroh's unconscious body. A little flock of scribes dropped their pointy ears. Wyatt was looking into each person's eyes, likely searching in their brains. Or scrambling them. "I assume Wisteria wanted to tell her friends about our deal, seeing as it was she who bought this realm more time and altered the course of the city's fate." Keenan was tight to my flank. Overbearing Bloodsworn bullshit.

I let the air escape from my lungs while the tension suffocating me released at his words. "I will mold a far better runegate than the one standing after it has been breached. I'll likely need aid, but I'll address that soon enough." My wovens stared at me, I gave an affirmative nod. "Judeth, she likely saved you and yours, stop searching for reasons to doubt her."

Keenan spoke up immediately. "What was the cost?"

"It's private. Do not press." Keenan glared at Maruc who promptly ignored him.

Zander's jaw slacked. "You made a deal for a second runegate? Is that even possible?"

"Maruc said it was." I presented. "I bought us time after a battle to end a war? Yes. I did what had to be done."

The thorny fae brother waved to the crowd. "Alright. I like her. I have no further qualms with your marked, Z." Wyatt strode away, whistling. "I'll look into the pack in question. Your report, should there be anything notable, will be under your door come morning." His small harem hustled behind him.

Maruc impatiently clapped his hands thrice. "Right. Now that we've established Kinlyra will receive a new barrier to the beyond and all souls in the world will be kept in their destination, we must merge our minds to discuss how to fight the Vulborg off when the old one drops. Long enough for me to resurrect primal magic from the stones, but not too long or the Elm dies. Or the city. Or both."

The Emperor subpoenaed the scribes with him as he detailed the time frame he would need. Zander cleared his throat. "Namir. Leave my brother in peace." Zander's tone was softer with a note of sadness. "Fennick has nothing to do with Madu or your husband, find your calamity inside yourself because that is not something I can offer you. Perhaps Dradion and Drommal will hear your pleas and see them granted?"

Namir's eyes flashed with hurt and confusion. When they stumbled on me they didn't waiver. Her anger flared as hurt contorted her beautiful face. "It's your fault."

My feet cemented in the ground. Too heavy shouldering others' blame and dodging accusations. "What is?" I tried at least to understand yet another allegation being thrown at me. Maybe Warroh was right, rid me. At least death may bring me some well-earned silence.

"Why Kashikat revisited conversations we concluded years ago about my refusal to ceasefire against Madu. I won't tolerate you filling his head with impossibilities and that is exactly what you are doing. It goes against the order of things for a marked and a woven to carry on as you and Fennick do. It's shameless and disrespectful that Zander even allows such fraternization." What on this miserable earth had I been doing that involved Kashikat's wife and woven? Had Torvi said something?

"I promise you that there is nothing shameful or unsanctioned between any of us."

"Kashikat will lose me for the last of his diminishing life if he presses *peace* between his dog and I."

Nikki's fires withered to a lesser orange glow pulsating at his feet. He muted his demeanor to appear unthreatening. He tried to damped his stunning power at least. That kind gesture went noticed. "No one here is asking that of you. You will find nothing, but empathetic ears." Some small part of me ached watching Namir run off with her crackling cry reverberating into the next room full of people plotting a war heeding her heartache no mind.

Keenan took his eyes away from Judeth's back as she too walked away, hiding her face from Atticus who stood in the shadow of a column listening. How I had missed a person of that stature was beyond me.

Keenan put an iron hand on the nape of my neck. "Are are not finished with our conversation."

"Yes, yes alright!" My arms were pinned over my head at a painful angle. There was no way out of the hold unless I slumped to my knees. There was no way I'd be doing that. I succumbed to the pin and used words. "We spoke terms of a bargain highly unlikely to come into fruition." My elbows were yanked higher. I made unpleasant choking sounds finding my breath through the gruff pull of my taut tendons. "If I decide to start fulfilling requirements of the second bargain, you will know."

"I will know *and* walk you through the trials of the arrangement of whatever you two agreed upon. Yes?" A holler made its way out of my gritted teeth. "Yes, daughter?"

"Ouch! Okay, you... you massive asshole!" He was prepared for my barrage of swift fists and precise attacks to the weak side of his torso, where his wife sutured a floating rib hundreds of my lifetimes ago. It was a dirty strike, but just as I trusted him not to snap my rotator cuff a moment ago, he knew I'd not exposed his solitary physical weakness. I slowed when his left forearm shielded lower and his stance pivoted to offense. He didn't stop advancing until I bobbed a series of Montuse lunges. "You satisfied?"

"No. An act of that magnitude of kindness from a God does not come without sacrifice. Rarely does Maruc help others outside of his siblings. You may be favored by them, but you are not one of them. Supply me a inkling to what you are promising him."

I kicked at him. "I am sworn to silence, but I can tell you it is of no harm to me."

Keenan looked physically torn as he pushed his fingers in a rough manner through his brown hair. "I don't like you keeping the secrets of the Gods. You've been doing it your whole life."

"Why stop now?"

Seeing Keenan still swinging his sword around, I moved towards Zander. "I'm done with you for the night. Brock, get your ironside ass over here," Keenan growled to Brock with a face fit to instill the look of damnation in his enemies. He was nowhere near done for the night.

He moved behind me, expecting me to shield him. "No, you are not my father. I don't have any allegiance to you, ice jungle man."

Keenan didn't put his sword away. "You are Wisteria Woodlander's Bloodsworn, you better learn to fight better than what you've been showing me on the ship. I don't give a shit if you have one leg and a crutch, you will outrun her enemies with her on your back against the winds on the Cliffs of Sound because her blood runs with yours."

"I swore to be a pain in her ass. I never said anything about sprinting as a cripple with her lanky legs dragging behind me." I stuck my tongue out at him, ignoring Nikki's full lipped grin as he latched onto Zander's side for a unrushed nuzzle.

"Then we are in worse shape than I thought." Keenan was dragging Brock in Atticus's direction by the collar. "What idiot make a blood oath to another without knowing what it fucking means? You agreed to this?" He shot over his shoulder. Talking to me—I thought. He didn't wait for my answer. The two of them were off to Dagressa's training field.

That left Nikki, Zander and I.

"Can I at least eat a meal before you two start on me?" My arms went up defensively. "Keenan is enough of a fussing mother hen to compensate for the both of you."

Zander evaporated his wings and Nikki carefully stepped aside for him to kneel at my feet.

Him on his knees was a sight that continually stalled the air in the room and rip it from my lungs. "Not a word exists to explain how I feel about you right now. I am in awe. You never cease to astound me. But tonight I need to grovel at your feet, worshiping and begging you to deem me worthy of your love." I urged him up before he made a spectacle. He didn't rise. "What you've done...I aspired to obtain I proper way to thank you. For words certainly cannot to this justice."

"You're welcome." I huffed, willing my frustration didn't make me sound ungrateful. "And you would have done the same were you given an opportunity. So, please. Just stop making this into something a 'thank you' couldn't have satisfied."

I strained my neck attempting to hoist him off the ground. He rose. His hands stayed on my body, sinking into the curves of my hips. "I will be thanking you relentlessly until I have recalibrated your scales of satisfaction with my clumsy fingers and tip of my tongue." My body screamed with excitement hearing his promise. I writhed under his touch.

"You would tell us if these deals with the Emperor come with a too risky cost. I know how wild and reckless you live your life my mortal love." Zander slithered his hands under my shirt, slowly down inching along the planes of my stomach and coaxing the need building in my core to surface.

I leaned my body into his, his hard length eager beneath the fabric of his trousers. "My tender giant," I kissed him deeply until my toes left the ground. "Is that a question, an assumption or a command?"

He cried as he kissed me. There was no manner in which he could hide his relief or falling tears with his hair freshly shaved and pulled back in braids. Internally, our bond was searing bright. His horns humbled, dropping towards me. Nikki's hand knocked into Zander's shoulder, ensuring his fingers never made it to their destination of my nipples. On behalf of my aching nipples I glared at Nikki.

"We will work out the details of my words next sunrise when conclave calls intermission, over a much anticipated serving of peaches since Fennick wants to interrupt my dinner and devotion now." I let my knees fall prey to his masculine handling of the round of my ass. My skin peppered in goosebumps when Zander brought our bond to life calling out my pent up colors to merge with his.

A belt of heat tore me off of the waistline I was determined to mount. Nikki's gritty voice cut into my lust, barring me from seeking pleasure. "Let's see what feats of fire Akelis has invented to rival my power, shall we." I shoved Nikki's hands off me, none too thrilled to be abruptly stopped by him.

"But I want more." I pouted to the pair of them.

Zander's fangs shot out, bringing me back into his embrace.

Nikki cursed the stars. Warm breath blew down the front of my shirt. I wanted that shift off, my underthings too. Envisioning his fangs latched onto my veins placed a gallop in my heart. "I sense your need. Feel it. Taste it. I want to drown in it." He pressed his excitement into me. His needs were an ocean, his raspy breathing the motivation I needed to jump into the waters.

Nikki's hot hands placed a stern thumb on each of our necks, pinching off our airways. I gasped at the unyielding fingers and deadly tone that made my stomach drop and thighs unexpectedly slick. "If you intend to swim, we will all be drowning." He released us with a cautionary look. "We are one. Use that wise blood pooling in your thighs and think before you act."

Damn it, Temperance.

Our final kiss outside the residential wing was one of pursed lip frustration.

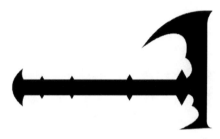

News had spread of Maruc's willingness to rebuild the gate of the beyond, less enthusiastic whispers followed containing my name. I happily noted traitor and leech weren't commonly used among them. They were; however, still used. Golden One, Harbinger of Retribution, Stray Child and Vibrant Vessel were a tad extreme. But the Wilding and Wise Crafter I could work with.

Sit on my lap, I will be discreet on the couches.

Handfuls of residents stopped by to thank me, rub their muzzles against me or on two occasions offer themselves to be my Bloodsworn. I deferred quickly. Zander recognized my weariness and uneasiness and warned the crowd forming that he would start to cast sway to keep our small corner void of a crowd if people didn't start clearing out and letting us rest in peace for conclave.

Nikki saw to it that oven baked flatbread and uncorked wine were delivered to the corner where I sat with my small frame tight against Zander's throbbing core. He held me from behind, strapping me to his impenetrable form.

The room buzzed with conversations and dozens of side parties congregated quietly.

I buzzed with carnal need pulsating between my legs. There were a myriad of people in the gathering chamber, many of which had my name on their lips. I hoped Zander would fulfill his promise to be discrete because I was in serious need of a distraction.

I piled my plate with basil, oregano and an aged sharp cheddar, washing it down with a sweet port wine and long exhales from Zander's touch slipping under the blankets. *You're too tense for a heroine, a mortal goddess.* My pants were unlaced. My stomach clenched as he stroked my slit through the damp fabric. *I don't know how else to show my appreciation for you.*

What you are currently doing will suffice. Atticus is staring.

Zander intentionally pressed his erection into my back, I rolled my ass into him. The shudders that sprung from him were ones that only I could feel. Which I'd admit, seemed like an absolute privilege.

He is watching the crowd, sniffing intentions, watching for a gaze held too long, a note passed, a spell cast. He also wants to fucking bow to you for saving his realm, my reputation and giving us a second chance to rebuild. But he doesn't have words. Let my fingers pray to you and as long as you don't bring down the walls when you curse my name with filthy prayers reserved for the peak of your pleasure... we can get away with this.

Can you cast an obscura?

I smell adrenaline fused with lust. Is it privacy that you want, love? Or do you want to try your hand at voyeurism and exhibitionism?

That does seem like something I would fancy indulging in. However; you'll be cleaning up corpses on the conclave floor after this hall hears me come.

The risk was thrilling. The mention of being caught orgasming in a room of oblivious sexual predators and prying eyes that made me twice as wet. That same thrill grew exponentially when he palmed my pussy to insert a finger inside me, working me slowly until I could accept two. I clenched around him, rocking slightly. *You are always tight for me.* He stretched his fingers inside. I savored the fullness and grounded down onto him.

He swirled the wine in his glass, looking mildly pleased at its aroma, nobody would suspect the true source of the aroma he was enjoying. My knuckles were bone white gripping the blanket, praying my hips wouldn't buck against his finger fucking without my permission.

There was one of us who was not thrilled. Not at all.

Across the wide span of the room an elemental glowered. Out elemental.

Those near him backed away from the white hot heat cascading off of him in a slow flowing stream of liquid fire. None were particularly surprised at his behaviors, foxes tended to keep to themselves and their sulk. Apparently they all wore their wide range of passionate emotions on their sleeves for the world to gawk at.

His mother was the only one he didn't scorch when she stood at his side taking the papers from his grip and recovering the charred pages of the maps, as much as one could undo what had been turned to ash.

Zander's hold on across my hip bone tightened, I must have started to writhe too much. How could I not when he did that outrageous spinning maneuver with the heel of his thumb? That alone has sent me over the edge on more than one occasion. A blinding explosion distracted my gyrating as the fireplace behind the scribes went up in flames.

Nikki cut short his conversation with Alethim and signed off on two papers Maruc and a female legionnaire in white gave him before stomping to the couch. *He is going to roast me!* Taken by Nikki's intensity I lifted my head off Zander's chest. My heart spiked as his eyes skirted across the room and fixed themselves on me.

Daring, darling flower. You know, as well as I, that I have been nothing shy of forward with you. You were warned that we'd all drown.

And you led me off the shore knowing I can't swim!

Zander offered no reply. He did glide his body against mine as a farewell. We watched Nikki drink a glass of wine. Once finished he shattered it instead of placing it on the side table, the murderous glare left Zander and befell me when I ground down into the hand between my legs.

Nikki inserted himself between Zander and me. He firmly removed his woven's glistening fingers from inside me and soothed the bunched up blankets around my waist as he pulled me into him. He hissed for the room to hear, "You two are fucking children."

Nikki was hot and solid. His arms were a sensuous, robust cage. A cage I saw no reason to escape. He held me as Zander held us both. I glared up at Zander's stupid beautiful smile cursing him and his worshiping fingers that got me into this predicament.

The bundle of nerves so cruelly neglected were aching for affection. I arched my back enough to earn a gasp from the fox alongside me who no longer was intently focused on conclave. His lips parted at the friction and his exhale stalled in the space between us.

A hot, wet mouth met the soft skin below my ear. *"Do not. Fucking. Move."* Nikki found the control he sought as his command raked over my skin. It pebbled in reply. The balance of dominance and fear that riddled his whisper robbed my words and sent quivers to my lowerlip.

The man truly did not panic. I, however, failed to recall my own name.

His lips loitered on my skin, tasting my skin perfumed of flowers and sweat. His mouth and our proximity did nothing to dull my body's desire to stroke the arm holding me in place, to shift my hips against *anything*, to roll around on the couch amid Nikki's flames and demanding Zander put his hand exactly where it had been minutes ago.

The room stole glances in our direction. It was easy to ignore them all when I was intently focused on not moving. Zander requested a bottle of spiced whiskey from a fae in passing and I remained fucking frozen when it was delivered to us. Not a muscle moved after Nikki's demand.

"I wasn't aware you knew how to follow directions." His damn mouth!

Slowly, my jaw freed from his spell. "This is a recent development for me." My own obedient actions trapped me by surprise. "Don't get accustomed to it."

"If this is temporary. I *must* take advantage of it." Moist lips feathered on my neck, while his quick fingers laced up my pants under the blanket, the intentional brush of his hot hands against my swollen apex had those strings damp. "Stand up. Pour three glasses. Don't spill."

"I will do no such thing." Heat flooded my veins.

I stubbornly pressed against him. My needs ignited further when I accidentally found a hard length throbbing down his pant leg. "*That* is reserved for good girls who listen. Are you a good girl?" My elbow launched into his gut. He pinched it hard, stopping the momentum.

It took one glance from Zander in my direction to cause him to burst into laughter. He knew my discovery of his brother's cock straining against the fabric of his pants. "My little flower is turning a shade of pink. This look on you is delightful. A blush of a rose, a hint of summer lily."

"Prick," I called him. His white and bronze speckled skin wrinkled as he laughed. Keen on avoiding more mortifying contact I rose to pour the damn whiskey like a cooperative, docile girl ought to. I glowered at Nikki when I pried off the wax seal using my teeth like a feral wildling while refusing to break eye contact.

He gingerly laid himself down, resting his head on Zander's knee. His feet kicked up onto the arm rest while Zander's hand fell across Nikki's stomach. His grin was devilishly devastating, so wicked it became painfully obvious I was in serious trouble. I was already shaking when I lifted the bottle by the handle.

The fox stroked himself. Once.

That was all it took for the bottle to fumble in my grip. Zander cast a small obscura over the couch. Nobody saw Nikki moving under the covers now.

I could though. I watched as he prepared to pump himself again. "Don't." I mouthed. There was no *good* in this girl. I would get revenge.

Murder me. He was stroking himself firmly and sinfully slow. I knew this even with my eyes smashed tightly closed. I felt him in my own swollen bud as if he and I were sharing the same body, riding the same intense wave of an edging orgasm.

"Pour the drinks." He paused long enough for me to snatch the glass bottle off the table and try this again. Whatever *this* was that I agreed to do. The faster I moved the faster I could be done making a spectacle of myself to the whole room, I was outside of the Zander's radius for the obscura.

Zander hadn't taken his glinting, humorous eyes off me. *Don't tell me you're enjoying this too.*

Then I will say nothing for I will not lie to my dripping wet corlimor. And here I thought we'd scandalize you. Not the other way around. I'm not the only woven who seeks to repay you for the barter with Maruc although I suspect he has other intentions right now.

I scoffed loud enough for him and the table over to hear my annoyance. *Fen is not toying with you, he is teaching you. I always did enjoy his lessons.* Liquor splashed on my hand when I set the first glass down, I licked it off my finger.

Heat broke through my body, pooling between my thighs. I dared not look at the culprit. "You were told not to spill."

"Fuck off," I grumbled, sloppily moving on to the next drink. And the next. The ears of select incubi and elves pricked up at my vulgarity. I stuck my tongue out at Wyatt who was sitting across from a busy bodied Yolanda skimming over a pile of books. Miserable Percy paused his fidgeting to raise a heavy brow in my direction from all the way across the massive room when he caught wind of how unrefined my mouth was.

Reprimanding came in surges of blissful indulgence. Torn between wanting to relish the sensations Nikki was giving me and walking out of the stone column gathering room full of tactical chatter I took a swig directly from the bottle. I ensured it was a decent size swallow and choked it down. "I hope that burned." I casted my anger and tension at the elemental whose hand was circling the sensitive tip of his cock.

Molten lava dripping down my inner thighs. My lids dropped when a small moan escaped. Zander gave a hardly noticeable jab at Nikki who looked as if he had found heaven and lost sight of it. Their faces were not as lusty or disillusioned as seconds ago. "I never said you could make such a erotic noise. Naughty."

The torture stopped. Stale air expelled from my lungs. He was trying to kill me by being a killjoy.

The elemental laced his fingers behind his head and gave a feline stretch while I was left remembering how to function as a human. Seconds passed where I screamed at my feet to move.

I held my head high and my thighs tight as I walked to the end of the couch where I grabbed fistfuls of decorative pillows and began swinging them with all my weight behind each aggressive punch I launched to their bodies. The obscura deepened and a soundproof bubble encompassed us.

Nikki bent his knees to shield his rock hard manhood as I toppled over him trying to smack Zander in his scruffy jaw for chortling at my expense. He surprised me by smashing a pillow to my shoulder, laughing as Nikki tightened a blanket around my arms and sealing them to my sides. "Now, this is fucking childish!" Growls escaped me, I was becoming one of these animalistic dreamers. "Orion." A sword took the place of a cotton pillowcase in my dominant hand. My grip tightened as I sought to latch onto something solid. Nikki's dominant gaze locked me in place yet again.

His knees pinched my sides to keep me immobilized, but his dominant expression already accomplished that. Obscuras blanketed the couch. Thicker privacy. Save for a magical eyed Maruc.

"Are you feeling so threatened that you summoned a God to protect you or are you simply reminding us that you have the ability to? A power move. Did you want to break free to fight as a means to expend that pent up energy in your tight cunt? Are you seeking to injure me to test if you can feel pain inflicted on you as you impale me? I assure you, pain transfers as well as pleasure. Do you had an aversion being held immobile?"

Nikki inquired and educated, leaving no time for me to answer only reel in his questions. Whatever his usual logical tactic was to calm me down and get me thinking straight. Nose to nose, his pair of suns for eyes burned into mine and yet not enough. His lips tinted with a splash of red wine ghosted with a devilish smile as he bit into them and set them a hair's breadth from my own. "Was having another control your body while you were trying to carry out mundane tasks *fun* for you?"

My struggle slowed. "Hurting you does not excite me nor exists the need to peacock around like you two raging wovens. And I don't have power moves."

Zander brushed my hair out of my face. "Says the girl who struts."

My world narrowed as I squinted. "I do not wish to hurt either of you. I hated feeling constrained and out of control." I snapped my head towards Nikki, chafing my chin on the too tight blanket around me. "You controlled my body, made me want *more*, then proceeded to physically restrain me. I panicked. It felt as if everyone could see me slipping into a fire I couldn't escape, a fire I would let consume me. It robbed me of my capacity to function and make choices."

"And I pose again, was having another control your body's urges *fun* for you?" He knelt next to me expectantly waiting. "Instead of making you pour wine, shall I ask you to negotiate for the livelihood of your race in front of one thousand beings while I stroke myself way over here? I do hope you are able to make the right decisions for the people you love with clear thoughts that don't involve running over to this couch and spilling cum across the blankets."

This was a lesson. A noxious, valuable lesson.

Zander had dealt with Nikki's lessons before and had been correct about this being a teaching moment.

My pride crumpled. "I was drowning. Like you were drowning in front of the entire conclave." I was too scared to reach for his hand in case he pulled away, rejecting me. I balled them into fists. "I'm sorry Nikki for distracting you. You were in the middle of important decisions. I was selfish." The blanket loosened. Then fell as Nikki adjusted himself in the crook of Zander's side body. "I am selfish."

"I accept your apology. Don't cry, baby. Be more aware, is all I am asking of you." Nine tails burned holes into his breeches as they made an appearance. "Momo agreed with the pursuit I chose and will see my ideas drawn up for review in the morning. No true harm done this time. Zander shoulders half the blame and for that he will suffer in ways I've yet to determine. And they will likely involve switching out his regular coffee for decaffeinated roast." A puff of purple steamed from Zander's nostril like a fire dragon.

"I understand where his need to reciprocate your kindness stems from. But, he has got to find another way of repaying you while *this between us* is so potent." The incubus opened a spot for me on the empty side of his lap. I nestled to him while obscuras slowly peeled away, layer by layer.

I stared at the outlandish, beautiful duo and resigned with a sigh of honesty. "It will happen again because celibacy isn't a lifestyle I can accept. We ought to figure out how to turn *this* off or tame my erm... *un*-celibacy better for you."

"That's not a word."

"It is now."

"No, it's not. I've read the dictionary."

"More than once by the sound of your arrogance."

"Education is not arrogant." His tongue shone through his white teeth. "Four times. And in two languages."

"Would you prefer I used the terms slut-escapades? Whoring? Tramping?"

His nose wrinkled. I saw white whiskers sprouting and instinctively reached over to stroke them. I stopped my hand before embarrassing myself further. "You are not a slut, whore or tramp. That verbiage is highly inappropriate and disconcertingly inaccurate." He scrutinized my retreating hand fidget and smiled.

"You've never seen me in a brothel bed with five other women. Perhaps the scientific terms would appeal to the scholar in you. Terms such as fornication. Coitus. Cunnilingus. Orgy. Any of those strike your fancy?"

He signaled for Zander to distribute the drinks I poured. I blushed, gripping the sloppy glass of amber liquid pressed into my palm. My tongue flicked up the cool glass, collecting stray droplets on the outside. Nikki did the same with an infuriating wicked ghost of a grin. "What strikes my fancy is you cozying up for the remainder of conclave and promising me that when we have a discussion tomorrow about *uncelibacy* you won't shy away from it or *engage* until we do so."

"I thought you said it wasn't a word."

His sharp chin dipped. "The birds, the bees and our bonds. Does that suffice?"

"You think I am going to shy away from talking about sex?"

He held up two fingers. "I said shy away from *or engage* in it. I worry more about the latter. I significantly misjudged you. And Zander too for that matter." My lips pursed. I was fairly certain he called me a floozy.

Zander's low voice rumbled. "He doesn't consider you a whore with loose morals. He enjoys your curiosity and willingness. We find it enthralling." I wanted to pinch him for giving voice to my inner workings. Zander tapped his chin looking mildly less disheveled, but still devastatingly handsome. "I too am guilty of underestimating your absolute perfection."

I put my sword away and crawled mindfully onto his knee. Once I was sure his hands were behaving per Nikki's request, I allowed myself to ease into him reaching up occasionally to toy with the long hair wrapping around his horns and pulling the silky texture through my fingers.

"She is a clever needleworker, isn't She?" Nikki whispered once he regained composure. "Now, we just have to worry about you, Z."

Zander agreed and lifted the last obscura. His family and curious onlookers eyed our informal and intimate arrangement. Or rather, I am pretty sure they had, I fell asleep nestling a fox on the retired Overlord's lap.

Chapter Twenty-Three

It was well after midnight and into the morning when we retired to bed. Intentionally, we divided into separate locations, making use of both rooms and the common space to cool the raging waters of sexual tension.

Upon waking up to a discourteous knock in the backdrop, I found a fox warming my feet and a full blown incubus face down next to the couch in the gathering room connecting their private chambers. I yawned and stretched my limbs; they were a good sort of sore from the few days of training with my world class Montuse warrior. I wondered how Brock fared with Keenan yesterday and what sort of revelations this day would bring. "Morning, boys." Orion leapt off the table and into my hand, clearly he considered himself part of the pack. I whirled him around my arms which had gotten stiffer in Keenan's absence earlier that season. Between sex with Zander and a few training sessions I remedied much of my limberness.

Lazy golden eyes appeared through an opening between layers of long silver, shimmery tails. They tracked me as I walked to the heavy door and flicked open the locks. "I hope this late morning find you well, Wisteria." Alethim pulled papers from his leather satchel dismissing Clavey and Kashikat bickering down the hall amongst a crowd of mixed beings. A beam of sun bounced off the white balcony and shone its way to my bare toes. We were all running off four hours or less of sleep, seeing as Maruc didn't call for a break until the sun merely hinted at rising.

"Hi. I'll have Fennick and Zander up shortly to review those after coffee." I leaned against the bulky door frame. "Any more news surface in the last hours?"

"Maruc, Atticus and Ik Kygen got into a verbal altercation. Probably about you, Athromancia and Zander. You lot are so loved that they fight over protecting you and your blood. It was private, so naturally everyone here knows about it." We shared a short live smile. "The Emperor alluded to his willingness to work with Zander's... *setbacks*. He proposed to train him to prevent him from demolishing the realm in the war if you or his woven get placed at risk. He spoke of making use of him to rebuild the barrier with his knowledge of the Eternal language."

My face froze. My gut rose into my throat, despising the notion of the Left Wing mentioning Zander had any *setbacks*. We were all entitled to our struggles and imperfections. "The tree is being threatened–the life of his woven is at risk–that will bring him to do unthinkable, unforeseeable things. You'll ascertain quickly how dedicated your newly acquired comrades are to each–." I shut the door on his face.

Alethim may have said more. I did not hear him through the magic barrier Zander built around the chambers. Not that I was trying to listen. I turned and smacked directly into a broad chest. *Oomph.* "Never fails to impress me how much anger builds up in your body first thing in the morning. Such volatile emotions for a gorgeous creature." Wings crossed behind me, a hug of sorts. "How have you not imploded or have been corrupted from the inside out?"

"It's productive," I reminded, wrapping my arms around his thick waist. His exhilarating scent tumbled off of his free hair.

Familiar scents, comforting scents, enveloped me when he bent to kiss me. "I vividly remember how motivational you find it. I also specifically remember telling you to wear pants when you leave this room. How many corpses of those who lust after you do I have to lay at your feet for you to understand the urgency of wearing pants?" A hand cupped the curve of my ass. Fingers kneaded the muscle and for a moment I lost myself into the rough, masculine imagery of him pleasuring me. For Nikki's sake I reeled in the anticipation that typically followed such behaviors. Behaviors I'd come to find solace and joy in.

"The threshold of the door does not constitute as 'leaving the room'. No pants were needed, oh Mighty Oppressor of Freedom."

"Uh-huh." Both hands gripped my thighs and carried me to the kitchen counter. Begrudgingly I released my knees from around him. "Let's get started on that coffee you mentioned. Fen won't budge until he smells me burning something. He doesn't trust me with stoves. Or toaster ovens. Or camping fire pits."

"I'm shocked he trusted you not to break me into six pieces."

"The day is young."

Zander intentionally fussed in the cupboard with iron skillets after he set the hot water to drip on his coffee grounds. A blur of pale white hair moved in to take the pan from Zander's hand. He swung it at him. Sluggish, given how fast I knew him to move. "See? I told you."

"You. Are. Loud." Nikki croaked. "Thundering. Deafening. Riotous."

"Yes, we know you have big words in that pretty, thick skull of yours. Unfortunately, your big brain forgot to tell you to wear pants," Zander commented, wiggling a flirty brow that he often used at the women inside Fort Fell.

Nikki adjusted his burnt boxers. "I heard it is a popular trend this morning."

I looked at my bare legs and kicked them onto the counter. "That is it."

"Get dressed before you scandalize our woman." *Our* woman. That sounded nice.

Nikki shot a fireball at Zander's feet on his way to dig up trousers. Two hanging lights were shattered by the tips of wings when he hopped onto one foot repeatedly. The fireballs on the floor skidded around chasing him until he hoisted himself onto the counter next to me, taking out yet another light fixture with his fist. The room flickered under shadows.

"Clumsy."

"You forgot coward. I will not work with the full scale of my magic even under Maruc's guidance and a million miles away." Zander kept a smile on his face, but I felt the greys and browns tarnish our bond. I patted the counter next to me. He contorted himself and his limbs until he sat. "Historically, Alethim isn't influenced by others, that makes him a wonderful Left Wing. I can sense his changing opinion and I will not be swaying it with my born powers. The Vulborg have quickened the tides, my people need action. They want to unleash Death or possibly your hibernating magic. You know where I stand on both. We are not weapons." He licked his bottom lip. "Now, if that is something you *chose* to become, then I will be the shield to your magical assault as you strike down the enemies at our door. If you've any desire to hide behind a coward that is."

"It's distasteful that you've been approached—I know you have. You've hidden it from me to protect me. I love that you feel the need to shelter me from the gossips of my own city to see my heart salvaged. I dare not dissuade any affection you show me." Rose colored adoration doused our connection. I reached for his hand to hold. Mine looked so small as it rested in his palm.

"Zander, being calculated and compassionate does not make you a coward."

His hand folded over mine. His brows pinched as he brushed off my previous statement, it was clear he'd seen himself in a different light than I, perhaps he saw himself in the shadows of the Death he wielded, it mattered not for I found all aspects of him dangerously alluring.

"Thank you for staying in the Veil despite it all. Your bravery is something I've aspired to since the first day you were brought into the dungeons, beaten, chained and on your knees. You screamed for answers, not food, not comforts, not to be put out of your misery." A pause to lift the heaviness. "I never intended to use you as a deflection for my weakness against the fear of my own peoples in wartime. But you have done just that. Then you ran off and gifted us an opening that may lead to an opportunity to stabilize a nation after bloodshed with a new runegate. I will find a permanent end to this madness. We can end the blood craft and banish Vulborg indefinitely. I know we can, we are not lacking in our appetite for peace, but we are lacking time."

"We are not lacking time. Unlike you I do not care for more of it and I have learned to make do with what I have. We are lacking means."

A mug of steaming hot coffee was offered to him along with words of encouragement. "We are three of the most tenacious people I know. We will obtain peace with whatever time is granted to us." Nikki rested his hand on Zander's knee and reached out to toy with my hair. "I assume you want yours with sugar, honey and all sorts of whipped cream toppings?"

I nearly slid off the high counter with excitement at the notion of dessert for breakfast. "Whipped cream on my coffee? I didn't know that was an option. I gladly accept." He hardly seemed awake enough to cook let alone converse, but as he stirred sugar cubes into a cup painted with lavender fields and took out boxes of sweet's from Nori's, the thought descended on me that this quiet moment may be the only serene time the three of us could privately share today. Or before I left with Maruc. Or before I died.

"The second barter with Maruc was one he actually proposed to me and I would prefer us to have that conversation before we talk about the three of us drowning in… in…threads." I tried to use my hands to better explain the intricate interconnectedness of us. Gestures didn't help. They rose brows at my pinking cheeks. "Nevermind. Can I talk about another offer he presented?"

Nikki finished up my decadent drink and leaned against the counter, slowly adding flecks of orange sprinkles on top of the fluffy cream. The triangles atop his magically lengthened hair twitched. "I'm all ears."

"There is an action you can take—all three of us have to willingly take— that secures Maruc, his magic, his armies, his council, to my will. If I ask him to rage war, help stop blood magic in Numaal, demolish wraiths, cook me waffles standing on his head, he would." The hand around mine was closing as I spoke. "How would you two feel about sitting with me on the trithrone?"

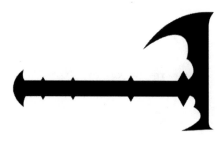

Alethim would have to wait. Perhaps all of conclave for that matter. We had little intention of leaving this room until there was some sort of agreement and understanding between us.

Zander polished off three cups and paced. His wings were intermittently expanding with his distress, a nervous tick he apparently did in private.

Nikki spoke with the intention to calm him. "Wisteria has a valid point. Agreeing to sit does not mean actually ruling as a Trilogy. It won't come to pass if Kinlyra is consumed by corpses possessed by demons. It's our best shot to preserve the homes of millions and get that lazy bastard to do *anything*."

Zander stopped pacing. His gaze locked me in place. "Wisteria, I don't question your capability to rule a nation or learn to do so. For even if you were a bride forced into marriage to that monster prince, you'd find a way to act in innocent people's best interest." He looked physically plagued just insinuating I was a bride to anyone else other than him. I was actually stunned the room wasn't smothered in violet haze or the ground beneath him fissured. "I am most concerned about your answer to the question: Do you *want* to rule?"

Me. He was looking at me.

Not Nikki who was behind me combing my hair with his fingers. "I should be asking you that same question." I licked my bowl clean of creamy yogurt. "Do you want to reclaim the title of Overlord of the Veil? You haven't even brought it up to be discussed? Do you see why I hesitated in bringing up ruling Ilanthia? Not to mention Morigan, who you made it sound like she tricked you into Overlord the first time around and groomed you to sit at the White Tower against your will. I don't want you to feel as if your hands are tied. If there is another way, we will find it without being corralled into a corner."

The male behind me tapped the back of my chair. "Answer the question he posed first. Please. It's important to us. Do you want to rule?"

"Don't get moody when I answer it."

"I welcome honesty." I dropped my skull back until it rested on his abdomen. Nikki urged me on with his sculpted chin and sharp eyes.

"It doesn't matter what I want. I'll be dead. There is this unshakable knowing in my gut that I will die in this first battle against the Vulborg. And in case you've forgotten, I ingested the Goddess of Wisdom's blood, so I'm probably *not* wrong about my impending death."

Nikki's teeth clanked when he spoke. Zander held his gaze across from me. "If you are certain death is coming to take you out from right under our noses, then why do it? Why spend the last of your days in preparation for battle, tying yourself to the thrones?"

"It's worth it because *you* matter. As does Keenan, Cobar, Brock, the d'Loure family, Pine, Rodrick, Duke Cultee. Need I go on? I'm just a catalyst for change. I'm okay with being used. Anna's manipulation really opened my eyes." My arm motioned around the room. "Besides, here is where you two will be. I will not take you away from here. Not again. This is your home, you will not lose what's left of it. It matters to you, so it matters to me. If my death can have a purpose, I want my wovens to benefit because I know you will appreciate it long after I'm gone. You would appreciate it on behalf."

I pointed up at the too serious face scowling down at me. "You better burn me."

"You don't matter?" He wouldn't react well to the reply I was about to give. I chose a retort or silence.

I didn't matter. I was just a girl caught in the middle of the Eternals emotional circus, who was loud enough to speak out, angry enough to belittle the crown publicly and dumb enough to be duped into loving Athromancia.

Fingers curled under my chin, steadying my gaze upward. His long hair obstructed my view of the hard lines on his fine face. His beautiful face heated with rile and something dark. A darkness that I was infatuated enough to provoke. "You matter."

"I told you not to get moody." His hands wrapped around my throat, tightening as he lowered his forehead on mine. Within seconds, tears pricked the corners of my eyes.

Struggling in my chair, I clawed at his warm grip which threatened my airway. He'd never strangle me, nor would he leave bruises. Yet, my heartbeat was deafening as it pounded behind my ears as I second guessed my trust in this volatile fox. Blood swarmed. Panic gripped me. "When I permit you to breathe, you will use that breath and repeat after me." Hell if I remember if I gave him an answer. His grip stayed tight until he felt my chin flex in agreement.

His chokehold lifted. Cool, eager air was sucked into my lungs. I half cried, half coughed as my ass fell back into the chair. "I matter." Nikki's words scorched my heart. "Say it. 'I matter.'"

The words I echoed back to him burned my throat and did a number on my heart for reasons I couldn't explain. "I matter."

A chipper hum signaled his improved mood. "Well, done. We will repeat this exercise if you fail to remember your importance." Satisfied with my panting he went back to toying with my hair as if this was a normal occurrence for him over morning tea. "Zander, your turn to answer her questions about the title, Morigan and the thrones."

Temperance indeed, ensuring equilibrium among his wovens.

Icy blue eyes roamed over the skin on my neck, watching my pulsing carotid and the heavy rise and fall of my chest. He didn't speak until I slowed and calmed from another one of Nikki's tactics in self-worth.

We grip our threads, I send him blues which he smelt as calm floral scents. I was safe and well.

"She glamoured me with a dusting every day, a cast so faint it went unnoticed by everyone. It built up in my system, like tasting doses of poison in micro increments daily until I was immune, until I found myself needing it, unable to survive without it. Drugged and high off her persistent persuasion. I was groomed to be industrious, fed her ambitions, worked her fields of mistrust, stepped the paths she put beneath my feet, climbed the towers she told me to conquer. She captured me from my adolescence years, before I felt any belonging or a remote sense of who I was." Sounds like the love potion Nikki ingested had nothing on decades of molding a lost, powerful half-breed since childhood. "When she died, the cloud of poison lifted and I could see my own reflection, chase my own dreams, build my own life."

"When the poison lifted, did you still want to climb your way to the White Tower?"

"I never considered it an option, powers at be delegate the trithrones. I wasn't chosen or aggressive enough to help spearhead the Ilanthian heretics in lifting that Divine rule. Short answer, no. I never wanted nor do I want those thrones."

He gave a vulnerable look to the elemental, while ghosts of his past swam rampant across his features, twisting him into an open book. "The learning curve for trusting myself was steep after I killed her. I had no idea how to feel without being told. I trusted not one of my own thoughts nor motivation for existence. You wouldn't have recognized me before Fennick brought me back to life. It took him years of undoing what had been done to me and it was an ugly process. Messy."

"But two things were certain." He held up two calloused fingers. "My loyalty bond saved me and I *wanted* to remain as Overlord. I didn't need that fae female alive to tell me how much I loved Thalren's Seam. Being seated in the White Tower is a stretch because I do not know if what I have to offer as a leader will suffice as a man of Numaal and The Veil."

I snorted. "The only one here who is qualified is Nikki."

The fingers in my hair paused and gave an abrasive yank. A strangled yelp escaped as panic choked me. "There are no prerequisites for being a Triruler, nor identifying as an Ilanthian for that matter. Not even our blood, which between the three of us is potent with Eternal lineage, dictates who is fit to sit on the thrones." I nodded dumbly in a fazed agreement. Damn his penetrating eyes. When did I give him control over me? "You said Maruc knew about our threads?"

"Yes, he hinted at it more than once. Similar threads tied him to his brother and sister, wife and husband, whatever they refer to themselves as—the

Trilogy. The Weaver bound the three of them too. Three protector wovens. I guess I can see why he is interested in us collectively. I just worry he isn't telling us all the details. It wouldn't be the first time one of the Eleven has lied to me by omission." I reached back and held Nikki's hand, twisting my fingers around his tension until he became malleable.

"My flower, you've just begun to bloom." Zander scowled as his arms were passionately flying around. "You have choices now. You've not known freedom, nor had access to knowledge and truth for much of your life and you desire to lock it away so quickly behind duty? For a nation you've never stepped foot in?"

"Not just for one nation. For the world I have yet to explore." I redirected the conversation. "Tell me why you haven't taken the title back?"

He hunched over the table, his forearm slammed into the wooden top and rattled the coffee cups. "I want you to relish life, to experience it, as much as you can while I can be at your side to watch you feel and see things for the first time. I don't want political constraints, however miniscule they may be, to take away my time of loving you."

I shook my head. "You love Veona. There will be no inconvenient restraints because it is not duty that locks you to these soils and fields of spirits. It is love."

"It will be here when you are not. And if it weren't, I wouldn't care if I got to spend my time away from it by your side doing whatever you damn well felt like doing that day. Foraging for mushrooms, picking fights, swimming in crystal caverns, wrangling kelpies, I don't care what you decide to do with your time as long as it brings you joy and I am there to witness it."

"Is he always such a nauseating romantic?" I asked Nikki who was clicking his back teeth so hard his temples pulsated. He tied my hair up and left my side to get apple slices, mechanically doing whatever mundane tasks he could to lessen the tension coiling up in his muscles.

I left my seat to wrap my arms around Zander as he paced the room, dragging me along as if I was a weightless cloth clinging behind him. New densities and shapes were intruding on our bond. Not in a good way. "Stop. Let me in. *All the way in.*" I pointed to his chest.

"You perceive something concerning?"

"Yes."

299

"Ready to color swim?" He plopped down, I on his lap in agreement.

It was hard not to feel tiny, when I sure looked like a toy doll in his arms. He opened the first layers easily and we swam directly into his inner voice, which took on the shape of a sickly spiral. A feminine essence. *Oh!* It blockaded a canary yellow linear line. "That makes sense."

Side by side Zander and I swam sound and out of his essence. My eyes fluttered opened. His were closed. I savored the stillness the present moment offered by studying the silken and scruffy texture of his lengthening beard and the dimple hiding in it. "What makes sense?" Nikki sprouted ears to hear me detail what I experienced. His foxy features twitch with intrigue. He'd never heard me describe the depths of our syphering and how we've developed it, exchanging emotions and Zanders interpreting mine with smells and tastes.

"It's Morigan."

Zander's hands were stroking my exposed legs in pensive long caresses that made me feel seen and safe. "I detached myself from her and laid to rest all accompanying memories. That's not likely."

"Sitting on the throne does not mean you are what she made you. She does not win." The horns on his head bobbed as he resolved to an agreement within himself. "The people of Kinlyra will win. She does not."

Nikki stood at our side, torn between answering another round of aggressive knocking on the door or seating himself between us to ask one of the many questions I saw ready to jump off the tip of his tongue. "These bonds. We have a lot of threads between us, manifesting in ways that would make my Pa go speechless and the scholars climax with excitement if they knew about our threads. We tried crossing our bonds before, my in Zander's mind, Wisteria tapping into him. With practice it can be effortless. I'll document our endeavors."

"You're adorable when you get off on educational fantasies."

"You'd be the first to know if I got off, wouldn't you babe?"

"Fair point."

Nikki knelt next to us with an ink pen and blank book in his grip. "Your syphering, you both learned how to turn it on and off? What is it that you perceive?"

"It's like doors. Open or closed. And ropes, tight or lax, wide or strappy. How he is feeling comes across our connection like swimming through layers of water colors, densities and emotions. I cast nets to call for him, which is throwing my energy out and waiting to be heard or felt. Smelt as it may be."

Zander explained once Nikki scribbling slowed. "Taste. I taste her on the tip of my tongue when she calls for me. And when rooted together, I smell and taste her mindset and available emotions." He spoke loudly over Alethim or whoever was determined to bust the door down. His purple swirls deepened along the walls to mute them.

"There is more, his emotions come through physically when our doors are shut or we are far away." I pointed to my left palm. "Here. I feel him here. But the knowing, the deciphering comes from here." I touched my chest. "Is that similar to how you and Zander use transplacency?"

"The net casting is a good analogy. I usually compare it to sending fireworks signals, grabbing his attention or him calling for mine if the distance is not too remote. The permission or invitation to merge is accepted or dejected. It bounces back if we are too far apart. When I was on the ship, I felt fractionated. No matter how many emergency flair signals I released, I was unseen. Stranded on that pile of floating sticks with no one to appease my elemental needs." He shivered with distaste.

Zander bit into an apple slice, debating his choice of words to vocalize his transplacency. Feet stomped on the door.

Unable to ignore it, I hopped out of his hands.

"Pants!" Two stern voices reiterated.

The three of us were put together when Zander yanked open the door, almost taking it off the frame. Nikki looked impeccably tide and composed, making Zander and I appear as slobs. I brushed my fingertips along the ends of my hair quickly to remove the frizz.

Maruc grinned. "Sorry, to interrupt your afternoon. However, I am pleased you are taking the time to thoroughly discuss the proposal Wisteria presented to you."

Alethim's stack of papers doubled since this morning. The heavy pile was not so politely dumped into Nikki's grip. "Out we go. Busy days ahead. Zander to the camps to modify offensive rotations of the sectors. Fennick to the chemistry lab. The alchemists, chemists, fae and all folk are waiting to gather and isolate fire essence. Wisteria to the sickbays. Supplies need to be organized and shuttled from the hospitals to the three temporary tents constructed last night. Ik Kygen assured me you can identify, extract and use all Ilanthian herbs properly, a feat considering you've never stepped foot where arnica, kalula, pomroy or bitterbeng grow."

I grimaced at the cluttered schedule. I wanted to sit on the floor with my wovens sipping sweet tea all day. "Not all plants. I never heard of wiggenpeel until last week."

Alethim interjected, "That is because elves keep that a well guarded secret to prevent its exploitation and from foul beings from trampling the delicate ecosystem it requires to grow." He followed with an awkward grin. "Doubtful even physician Moriah knew of its existence. There is no manner in which she could teach her pupil all she knew if she didn't know herself." He moved aside and flagged his arms to usher us from the private chambers.

It would have also required my silver family to tell me about elves...

"Out, out! With haste. Cobar Woodlander Ikgen has been pestering everyone standing in this quarter. He is looking for his sister and to keep himself busy while he waits he has taken to touching my calligraphy set with his *sticky* tiny hands. Take him and his sticky hands with you. Please." A plea, more than a command. I giggled at Alethim's desperate appeal.

Carrying around an affection seeking child was my strength exercise for the day. Add the wooden crates of antiseptics and analgesics I loaded onto a never ending train of carts, I was worn and bleary through and through.

At least I was presented an opportunity to refill my satchel with monthly teas, salves and a handful of commonly used herbs.

Cobar got a ride home on my back, Mikleah kept us company to the steps of Horn's Keep. I very much enjoyed her stories of the grueling educational regiment all physicians had to apply for. Alchemy's teaching methods seemed too dangerous for mere mortals with its realigning molecules using mental math to form bridges with time and space. Nope. Plants were just fine and dandy with me. I chewed on stevia leaves to suppress my appetite, making a plan to find food as soon as possible so Nikki didn't get the impression I hungered.

302

The conclave had expanded with its growing needs and attendees. It took up two branches of the Keep. Different nooks for each provision and growing demand. The kitchens worked overtime feeding the emerging masses. As did the inns and diners in the circles of Veona housing the influx of fighters coming to aid.

Yolanda, Cobar and I prepared a basket of food and picnicked on one of the many balconies. We chose the one that had the best view of the sunset. Torvi in her wolf form sat silently behind us and listened to us chat about Numaal. Her five hundred pound body crept closer as the meal finished, until her maw was on Cobar's lap. He rubbed her snout fondly. I did the same.

All of Yolanda's talk about Kathra, Sanctum, Landsfell and Raj inspired me to ask a scribe to send for messenger birds. News from the southern province's duke would be much welcomed, for better or for worse. I sent off a few more birds with waxy parchment paper tied to their talons. I may be a nationless rogue but, I still had things to fight for, people I sought to hear from.

I mattered. My throat ached sensing Nikki's lingering imprint on my flesh as I echoed his words internally. I mattered.

Percy looked as if he was fighting the world's most horrid hangover, spewing his stomach contents over the side rail. "Charming." Yolanda suppressed a gag under her commentary.

Percy wiped his chin on his sleeve. His hair was disheveled, his skin grey and blurry as I had seen Zander's get on occasion when he didn't consume enough energy. Percy looked awful. He sounded awful. "You know nothing about the act of charming, Yolanda d'Loure. Why, I could have you drinking my bile if I so chose to intoxicate you with lust to crave me. Sway your and Torvi's stubborn minds away from joining a far off rebellion and make you content with life here if I was feeling up for it."

He wouldn't be feeling up for anything in his state. "I would never choose a life here watching a rotten smelling, wet bat vomit after a night of binging."

"Correction—centuries of binging." He heaved over the rail.

Percy was without his overcoat, without his convenient liquor bottle. His wings shuddered with strain.

I filled my goblet with water and brought it over to him. A pointed peak of his wing nearly took my head off as he staggered upright. He looked suspiciously at the offering. Instantly, I regretted my decision to give aid and compassion.

I rolled my eyes. "I didn't poison it."

"If you were my wife, I would have poisoned it before offering it to you."

"If you were my husband, I would have drank it. Every. Last. Drop."

A smirk turned his grimace upward. Eventually, he held out his hand and accepted the offering. He trembled. He was detoxing. "If you are interested, I can contaminate it with some milk thistle, charcoal and sophrat."

He brought the goblet to his mouth. "I was informed that you can make a man impotent and kill off his lifeline with a tasteless dose of your crafting. That would end the life of an incubus. Cruel crafter." My shoulder rose in a smug shrug.

"Thanks for the insight on how to best rid Zander of his pestering brothers," I tossed. "Don't be deserving of it and you have nothing to worry about." He took the water in a slow swipe.

Under his breath his ego resigned. "Thistle and sophrat. That would... that would help?"

"Yes. They expedite the cleansing process and protect the liver. It can help with the shakes, sour stomach and migraine too." I knew now exactly where to collect the roots and tinctures I did not have.

He glowered under a strong brow. "I don't have a migraine."

"What are you, half a day sober? For humans, at least, the real fun doesn't start until days two and three. When was the last time you've gone a week or more without alcohol." His head shook as he heaved over onto the innocent bushes below him. He couldn't remember the last time he'd been sober.

Yolanda escorted Cobar away from the off kilter incubus while I brought him more water, this time with dissolvable crystals of ginger in it. He sipped it slower, swishing it around his palette. Swearing far in worse word combinations than I could have put together.

I giggled when he murmured 'knob gobbler'. The night carried on in a way I doubt the stars could have predicted. Percy distracted himself by entertaining me with profanities and I helped settle his stomach with the herbs on hand.

'Shitwhistling fuckwit' was my favorite by a long shot.

"Fuckwit? Huh? You wouldn't happen to be discussing me?" Brock strode up behind us, not the least intimidated by the slouched over winged dreamer twice as tall as I.

"Buddy, if we were talking about you, it would be a much less affectionate term."

He leaned on the banister with us, his face unamused. "Keenan is what I would call a shitstain obsessed with pain. He tried to kill me last night, Wisteria!" My shoulders shuddered. "It's not funny. He is a sadist with a sword! I would have started digging my grave if he didn't stop!"

I laughed harder, I shared his pain on many occasions. Brock stared at me as delirious belly laughs ungracefully escaped my mouth. "The first time I ever heard you laugh was in Keenan's memories. I honestly believed you didn't know how. That is sad Wisteria. Sadder than you almost pissing yourself at my expense now."

Percy straightened a bit, his elbow stretched out a cramp. "Apparently, you just weren't funny enough. You lousy cumdumpster of a fuck knuckled friend."

My sides were stitched when our boisterous profanities earned us a visit from Atticus. He was smiling under his scowl. I felt it in my withered soul. There was even a lightness to the way he thanked me before *encouraging* his son to seek privacy for the rest of the night away from the main gathering hall. He took the ginger with him. "Good night, slutmonkey!" Percy shouted through the Keep.

I lost it.

Brock had to wipe the tears leaking down my cheeks and muffle my snorts as we walked by a serious round table of nymphs dissecting their own defensive options. Keenan, along with his air of refinement, arrived back from tucking his son in bed for the night. While he caught the attention of strapping warriors and historians alike, he scared off my ironside friend. The mere sight of him invoked memories of yesterday's sadism. Brock disappeared into the dining hall, taking with him a portion of my jubilance. "My scapula got jostled blocking Dagressa's rowdy crew. I don't trust anyone else to align my joints."

"Flattered. Let's go to your room to avoid your fan club."

Now, it was Keenan who laughed. "There is an incubus here who is fond of you and I am fond of my life. So, *no* I will not be taking you behind closed doors. You can work on me by the fireplaces."

I twisted him into position and released his lower back first. Talian and Clavey decided to bring their facesucking and groping to the chair nearest us. Twice I got them to stop thrusting their tongues down each other's throats and pull away in disgust. The first time was when I pulled out Keenan's arm to place it correctly in the socket and the second time when the Bloodsworn briefly stopped breathing after I adjusted the base of his skull. "Did you snap his neck?" Clavey sounded more repulsed than impressed.

"No."

"It sounded as if you did."

Keenan inhaled, controlled and slow, before opening his eyes. "Do I look dead, Clavey Kriss di Lucient?" He rolled onto his stomach for me to finish tending to his spine. I hovered my palms above his spinal notches while my legs rested on either side of him. On his exhale I dropped my weight and set his grinding joints with a series of *pops*.

The glamorous incubi shivered, his earrings knocking and jangling as he did. "For a second there, yes Montuse, you resembled a corpse." His shimmery eyes widened as another lean and tightly wound muscular body laid down next to Keenan's. Nikki flashed his pearly white fangs at the couple reclining on the couch. "Hey pup, when you crawl back to your master make sure you tell him his pet had her knees pinned around another."

That was the moment I learned foxes could hiss. The annoyance in my gut broke free.

"Actually Clavey, he will inform him that two men were under me."

I rose to rest my knees on either side of Nikki's ribs while I explored the firm ligaments of his tails where they intertwined with his dense back structure. Nikki's hiss transitioned into a purr of pleasure and his eyes shone with pride in my defiance towards Calvey. Keenan readjusted his sword, not hiding of his intentions.

The stark and stunning whirls of clustered tattoos I traced lazily with my fingertips. "And when I see Zander later tonight, I will claim him as the third man under me."

I instructed his long inhales and subsequent exhales while Nikki told me where his neck felt strained.

He barked when I reset him with a jolt forward. An unflattering giggle escaped my throat as I coaxed him down from a startled state by rubbing the pair of furry fox ears that shot up on his head. I apologized through the laughter and sat my hindquarters down on the curve of his back. "Are you hurt or did I startle you?" Tails swept and settled.

"Neither."

"Uh-huh."

"Again."

"Gladly, just don't jump. It is hazardous."

Side to side he rotated his neck. "It's limbered."

"The stiffness?"

"Gone, little vixen."

Keenan stretched his pliant limbs and conveniently placed himself between myself and Clavey. "I intended to invite Wisteria to join us for *shenanigans* tonight, but it seems she is too rough for my liking." The petite pixie on Cavey's lap spread his wings when Clavey's hand went between his spread legs. Keenan unsubtly polished his dagger in his line of sight. "Talian has delicate wings. Your daughter fights harder than I fuck so maybe it would not constitute for a good pairing." Talian moaned as Clavey began to move rhythmically under his pants.

"She can watch while you take me. It's not like you let anyone else touch us when you invite them. You love an audience but hate the smell of other's lusting for my ass." This was too much information. Information I had no idea what to do with. Keenan got up and took me with him. Nikki hot on our heels.

B.B. Aspen

Hands tucked behind his back he walked on Keenan's left. Kailynder lurked, but didn't speak. So, much like Atticus it was uncanny. "Ik Kygen, I request your formal assessment of my stepwork and combat. I'd appreciate any and all feedback." Woah. I almost fell over. That was unmistakable respect I noted in Nikki's inquiry.

My startle remained unhidden. "You've come far from face punches."

They ignored me. "I'll pose recommendations and corrections if the days ahead provide an opening in our schedule. Now, I must be off with my boy that I've spent two long regrettable years without. He sleeps as restless as Wisteria. As you can imagine, I need to be there if he wakes up fearing darkness." Cobar. There were countless memories to haunt his blameless soul and fester on his innocence. Keenan hugged me good night and was off.

I eyed NIkki. "You don't need a formal assessment by him. I fought you. *And won*. I can tell you exactly what is wrong with your Ilanthian form."

Kailynder scoffed loudly enough to show his interest in joining the conversation. "Ik Kygen has led Sivts, armies, calvaries, and naval units during his thousands of years on this earth. You are not a Commander, you are an infant. You do not have enough experience in war or life to give advice on either."

Nikki practically spat. "And you are an ass."

I elbowed Nikki and puffed my chest out towards Kailynder. I spared my woven a look—one that translated to, independent woman. He didn't lessen the orange flames around us, but he kept his mouth shut.

"You are right. I am not a Commander. I am what was that delightful term you called me? Ah, yes. An allegientless rogue who damns this world with my presence at Zander's side. A waste of space that should leave immediately unless I can serve you and Judeth by manipulating your brother to strike down the enemy using Oyokos' power." Nikki was flaming the colors of autumn leaves. "Let me remind you this *rogue* is doing neither. Go find someone else to pester, you lowlife."

No such luck. "That was before we knew about Orion and your golden blood. Before Zander calmed my qualms, before the deal of the runegate and before I knew you to be in good standing with Ik Kygen. If your magic is even a fraction of Zander's you're needed in front of the ramparts during

308

the first waves. I changed my mind about you. Stay. Fight." How the hell could he even think to approach me with such an assumptious statement after telling me to fuck off the first night we met.

"You're a leech."

My feet stopped propelling me forward. My anger rose. "Since day one, I have offered to fight alongside your realm because it is the right thing to do and that hasn't changed. Any decent being would have agreed to accept aid especially when you so desperately need it to stop the end of the world from knocking those tiny horns from your head during the massive slaughter on the fire fields. You shot that down and with it any hopes of recruiting me. You are an idiot to refuse help, even if I am a mere mortal who befriended your baby brother and his woven. When I awaken Anna's blood, I strongly recommend you keep your selfish, opportunist ass away from me because this *rogue* will fucking hack those horns off your head and shove one in your ass and the other in your throat." His red eyes widened. Kailynder seethed. "And for the record I know exactly what critiques Keenan is going to say about Nikki. He blocks too high."

He snarled. "You're aggravating. Obstinate. I'm leaving."

"Good riddance."

Chapter Twenty-Four

Nikki showered first. He sulked around unnaturally silent given all we had to talk about. When I came out of the shower he had bowls of a cold bean salad on the counter with purple onions and cucumbers to garnish. "Did everything go okay at the chemist lab?"

"It was as good as it could be. Imitating all properties of fire is not easily done. Heat, explosiveness, brightness, unpredictability. We don't know which, if any, of the properties are most effective against Vulborg. I'm wishing we had some of those fire lancets from the Southern Isles with us. Those were brilliant and effective."

I took a bowl to the table. "Funny you should mention that. I wrote to Duke Cultee asking numerous things, one being to send spare lancets to Waning Star with haste if he on the off chance had a surplus and means. And, of course, all and any news of Numaal and the wraiths. Maybe if Count Hilderbrand wrote another letter we could have crates delivered to the continent and Zander may flux there and back with them."

This earned me a long minute of silence. "Didn't you want to run this by, say, an entire room of battle tacticians? Your wovens, maybe? Ik Kygen? You seem to be getting along with Percy now, why not bring it up to him?" He plopped down across from me, his pajama wear hung loosely. There were no sleeves on his nightshirt. It was a soft fabric, dyed a forest green that faded into white on the ends. His tattoos moved when he did. He took a few bites while I attempted to discern the pattern, if any, inked onto his body. "I will take my shirt off if you ask me too."

Yes! No?

No.

I turned my face down and shoveled the sweet vinegared beans into my face. "I don't feel my private matters are important enough to be a recorded conversation by all those busybodied scribes. I don't like the attention on me. Besides, you were off doing important things."

"By important you mean listening to you, Percy and Brock call each other stupid names and piss yourself laughing, then yes, I was doing very important things."

"I should have known you'd be stalking me. Why didn't you join?"

He stabbed his food with his fork. "I've my reasons, slutmonkey."

"Is that in the dictionary?"

"It is now." Nikki's mood improved marginally.

When Zander thundered in, the first words Nikki greeted him with shot off his tongue. "They called her a rogue." I looked between the two of them with wide eyes surely bright with confusion. "Tell me not to incinerate them." He freely spoke his mind, all that he had bottled up since we came in the room was given to Zander to do with as he saw fit.

The words that had little bearing to me weighed them down quite significantly.

Zander kicked off his muddy boots and whipped off his shirt which was equally as filthy. Twice as musky. He leaned over to kiss me. I plugged my nose and swatted him away. He was too tense to be fun anyways. "Who are we killing?"

"Kai and Jude. Then your brother approached a half hour ago wanting her on the front lines. She offered to fight with us the first night and was branded as such without trial. The fucking audacity of that fool. It needs to be rebuked so it doesn't rot into a curse." Nikki's words jumped off his tongue like wild embers.

Barefoot and shirtless, just the way I preferred him, Zander left the room. "Don't incinerate them." I shouted as the door closed. I didn't want further blood on my hands.

Nikki's right eye turned a milky white. He was off ensuring proper reprimanding happened. "I'll save Kai for you. I'm looking forward to you puncturing his bowels with his horn." Whatever Zander was doing pleased Nikki enough to leave his sight.

Nikki finished his bowl. He left to dust off his woven's boots and line them up by the door, tossing his shirt into our dirty hamper bucket by the bathroom. "You have other clothes besides the same two pairs of pants and woolen shirts from Eulid I tire of seeing you in."

"I turned away the tailors he sent to take measurements. It's a waste of resources."

He held my gaze as I washed my dish. "This better not be about money or feeling indebted."

Zander could smell my lies. Nikki wouldn't know, right? I didn't risk it. The truth found a way around by pride. "Initially, yes. It was."

It was easy to discern his discontentment after I knew how to spot it. His high pointed fox ears flattened when he was empathizing or working through mournful, concerning thoughts. "You'll accept clothes now?"

"Nothing fancy. Nothing Count Hilderbrand would wear." Pleased, his ears perked up and the corners of his eyes did the same.

He went into his chambers and flicked on the light, calling my name to summon me to his side. Boxes I'd never seen in his room were packaged and piled around his walls. All his precious wears and goods from within the Burrows. A standing dresser was between his closets. "I'm confident I got your measurements right. I've been staring at and stalking you long before you ever realized and if they don't fit your body as perfectly as I have been imagining, my seamstress will have my neck when I ask her to recreate the entire wardrobe."

"You've been staring at my body and playing imaginary dress up with it?" He tapped the cabinet with the backs of his knuckles. I suppose that was an answer. "Maybe I should ask you to remove your shirt for the sake of obtaining accurate measurements and then let my imagination run off dolling you up in pretty garments to match your pretty hair."

"Just my hair? Not my tails?" He lightly feigned an emotional wound while I reeled in my imagination. "Everything in here should fit. If it doesn't, tell me." I opened the handles and gaped at the blouses, shirts, skirts, shorts, pants, summer tops, bralettes and matching practical footwear. "In case you felt the need to step into a dress, there are several suitable for a *Countess* Hilderbrand in the bottom drawer. Loungewear is here too. I'll leave you be."

He made it five steps before I caught up and wrapped my arms around him from the back. He smelt of fresh rain water and his signature scent of cedar and pine. "Thank you."

He patted my arm gingerly and prompted me to release him. "Always my pleasure."

I chose a matching set of white silken wear to sleep in. I expected to be sleeping on the couch, yet again. Nikki had paperwork scattered across the common room. I made hot chamomile tea and tiptoed around a pile of diagrams sketched onto parchment and seated myself among books. The first titles I glanced at read, *Nicht Bvorn Bahlicht.* "War of First Light. A book of failures to learn from. History need not repeat itself." He didn't look up from the papers that stole his focus. "I'm trying to organize these historically and by relevance before he returns. That way after he bathes my full attention can be on us and addressing the fact he needs to feed before you leave in two days and our quintessing is *open*–if we are using your door analogy."

I opened the nearest book. "Then by all means, organize away so I can get laid."

Two minutes in he snatched the book from my hand, glanced at its table of contents and moved it into a different pile behind him. Zander was scolded for having his wings out on his way to wash up. "You ruffled the pile of twelfth century infused steel weaponry! Put those sails on your spine away."

"Gods forbid! At least it wasn't the eleventh century's literature of stone age advancements." Zander's voice echoed off the tiles in the shower. Not a second after, came screams of fury. "Damn critter! You boiled skin off me!"

"You deserved it!"

My smile was wide behind my tea cup when Zander emerged in a cloud of steam. A towel wrapped around his hair and another slung dangerously low on his hips. He looked to me on the couch surrounded by a neat stack of his brother's literary works. "You look indisputably edible."

"Perfect. I want to be eaten."

My words prompted a desperate growl from Zander.

The towel dropped.

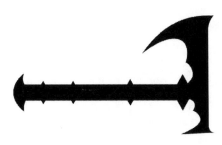

Nikki launched a wall of fire between Zander and I. Our needs inhibited. Temporarily. I reminded myself to ease the tension thrumming between my thighs.

The barricade was temporary, but stupidly effective.

The heat from his inferno made my drying strands of hair dance and my face warm. I turned to face the male who created the magical impediment. "Blunt is the only way this conversation can be had. Our quintessing is growing by the day and we have not been granted time to explore it or control it. Sexually speaking, if you come, I come."

I looked at Zander for a reaction, he was watching me with his own violet fire in his gaze. Gauging spoken and unspoken replies. Nikki continued. "You have not kissed me and I do not want you to kiss me for the sake of having your unquenchable urges met. You may kiss me when you are ready to invite me into all aspects of your life, not just the bedroom. When you are ready to have me affectionately wrapped to your side in public as a life partner and not as a friend. When you are ready for brows to raise and others to deduce our woven status."

I peered into the golden eyes of my woven. "I understand."

"My hands—my body—will not be intimately touching either of you when you and Zander commence. I need you to respect that boundary because only that kiss is keeping me restrained, civil, a friend in public, a protector and a man who can keep his hands off his best friend's... person when he isn't around. Hell. Who am I kidding? When Zander is around my urges are stronger." My boys were grinning at eachother. "Just no kissing me when enthralled."

"So, I can't kiss you when I feel like kissing you?"

"Not when it is only to have your physical needs satisfied."

There were loopholes in that request. Pointing them out was not something I was about to do. "I won't cross it until I'm ready. Until we are ready." His chest deflated as he exhaled.

"To clarify, I've been ready. In case you've wondered." He winked. "The world is ready for us too."

"Don't push it."

Zander reached a hand to Nikki. He took it, steady as always. Zander's voice lacked its normal confidence. "The dynamic has shifted. I can't pinpoint the precise moment. It was either when we damn near lost each other or when we found her, our fated, in the Southlands. Do you feel it?"

"Yes. But as I have told Wisteria, I will tell you the same. We explore one thread at a time. And being I am not your corlimor nor heartmarked, there will be caution if and when. We don't exist without her. We cannot risk killing her or continually placing her in situations where your instincts control your body despite your heart's best warning." I felt Zander's teal blue peace shroud our bond with Nikki's words, it was the fluffy texture of whipped cream. I was proud of Zander for giving voice to unrecognizable new feelings. If the fire wall's smoke wasn't a barrier I was certain they would have started kissing.

"There is also the issue of my nature. She seems thrilled that you two will come simultaneously, but I have never been in the same room with two scents. Let alone two scents that belong to me." I looked at Zander through the wall, which was thinning out slowly. "Incubi have an inability to do as you two have done and bed multiple partners at once. Wisteria is my life source." My tongue nervously tapped against the backs of my teeth.

Tap, tap, tap, the metal in my mouth went. All were aware that he smelt my lusty thoughts for his brother. He went to the extent of covering the couch with an obscura so Nikki could stroke himself, intentionally making me drench the layers of my panties. "I've been checking in with myself as your bond reveals its distinctiveness. The usual instincts are there. Possessiveness. Unaccountable coveting. Thunderous demands for castrating whoever lusts for *mine*." He looked apologetic. "I know you belong to nobody, but in my heart you are mine. Forgive the phrasing, my love."

Nikki watched me squirm uncomfortably. "What I'm attempting to say is, it is lessened, so long as it is Fennick there seems to be no issue in sharing my heartmarked. I'll rip the soul out of anyone else who yearns for your affections, who fucking looks at you with lust. But not him. You have my blessing to be with him. I love you both and if your togetherness makes you happy, it makes me happy."

My knees felt like a porous sponge. I sat back down on the couch and fidgeted with my comfort item, a tea cup. He was not only emotionally alright with me crossing boundaries with his brother, but encouraging it.

"Fennick would *never* hurt you. He will bring you pleasure, and I want that. For you. For him. It is a yes, from me. The three of us can engage, but slowly. Fen, put me on my ass if I strike out against either of you."

"And feedings? There will be two meals available, have you thought about that?"

Defeat took Zander. "To my knowledge none of my kin have ever successfully fed on more than one. Others are either ignored, maimed or murdered."

"Murdered. Well, that puts a damper on things."

"I don't know how I will react with more scents. Violent or homicidal are frequently emotions for me." He and Nikki were locked in a gaze, both had their brow furrowed. "The notion of her scent tainted makes me *unhinge* more than a little. But if it is mixed with yours, I would feel... secure."

"I will keep you both safe." The wall of fire vanished. No smoke or ash remained. The heat that filled me was from my own blood wildly thrumming from excitement and desire, not nerves. "Was this too blunt, little vixen?"

"Hardly. I have a request." Their high strung silence was my queue to continue. "Neither Nikki or I are to feel manipulated, used or consentless with our bodies. Out of respect and in an effort to maintain sovereignty, I ask that for the first time we come, Nikki and I work in tandem to get there. And when you are with me, you have to ask Nikki's permission if we are tightly linked with quintessing. I would not have my Nikki taken advantage of ever again."

Zander turned to his woven and with a silent side eye, they agreed.

With this new found consensus, I stood on the couch's armrest and had my tongue prying open Zander's mouth with desperation. He was hardening against the flat of my stomach, the tip of him slid against the silky texture of the ensemble Nikki procured for me.

Nikki leaned on a tall chair, his eyes resting on the mantle instead of us. I wondered if he was going to take off his pants when *we* came. *We.* I never saw this in my hand of dealt cards. Although, I had seen it in my fantasies. At the moment I was either too desperate or overly intoxicated with the thought of having both my boys feel and feed from me to consider the hand I was playing wasn't a good one. It seemed absolutely flawless to me.

"I'll stop you frequently, so you can keep tapping into your instincts." The grunt Zander gave was a reply enough for the elemental.

There was a knock on the door. I bit into Zander's lower lip. He slurped up the drop of blood and started to pull away. "Don't." I clamped my legs around his waist.

"It's Maruc and Honri." He opened his eyes and shot a look of bemusement above me to his most loyal.

My jaw clenched to the point it trembled. "Don't. I swear on all that the temples hold sacred, if you walk through those doors you will lose your last opportunity to fuck me as the boring human I am."

Zander savored the fabric on my curves. My skin under it sang with cruel wanting. "You are far from boring. You are that rare blend of colors at dusk that artists strive to imitate, magic can't improve perfection. Also, I promise to fuck you so thoroughly at the earliest convenience you will know desperation and yearning like no other when we stop." He licked my neck, his words softened as they were spoken against my skin. "Also, I love when you get murderous about sex."

"Correction, *lack of sex.* I shall resign to another night on the couch." I could easily guilt them into ignoring that blasted door by dropping a mention of a certain woven of theirs unlikely living beyond the awakening of Athromancia's powers and these were quite literally her last of days, hours, on earth.

I decided against confessing details. That intel they need not know.

I bitterly tied up my hair. Hopefully Zander tasted my frustration more than the undertone of sadness threatening to climb up and over the ramparts of my heart.

"Pa is here? Why would the Emperor get my dad involved when we've intentionally hid the state of the world from his fractured mind? I hate games. God games most of all." Angry Nikki rattled his brain as to why the unexpected pair was interrupting our night. More enraged that his father was brought into the conversations of war than not finishing what I leapt into Zander's arms to do. "Pants on." He suggested to Zander who then awkwardly coaxed his erection into breeches. His length strained against the fabric sending me into another wave of frustration and feeling of loss.

"If he isn't delivering a miracle in a handbasket, I will twist his limbs into one. Snapping every godly joint until he is as knotted up as a bird's nest." Yup, Zander felt thwarted in his attempts to feast. Mucky yellows sliced the puffy blues and strained lust. He forced himself to be gentle when he opened the door. Honri was seated in a rolling chair for injured persons, a content man buried under armfuls of text and loose papers.

Like father, like son.

Maruc raised a brow, giving Zander a look that essentially told him to go ahead and dare to make good on his threat to knot him into a handbasket. "Not miracles, but hard work. Honri was one of the few who I remembered in recent centuries who has memorized the contents within the sealed sector of archives. With a little bribery of the historians, he obtained what we needed."

"What is it that *we* need?"

"Out. All of you. Get to the library," he stepped back into the hallway and provided us room to leave the threshold. "If you play to your strengths you will have an eternity together and need not be pestered by me knocking on your doors. Now is not that time." He corralled us like sheep. *Play to our strengths? Eternity together?*

I eyed the God. The Opal Lake may damn well be my grave. The end of my morality, not the beginning of immortality. "I don't want an eternity." He rubbed his forehead and mumbled something to Nikki in another language. Nikki's lip curled over his teeth.

Zander looked over to me fiddling with the seam of the shift just above my midriff, my vial of replenished poppy milk swinging against my rosy skin. His lips were still wet from our kiss, I ran my hands over the silky clothes while my woven moved ahead of me. I wasn't ready to part with my pajamas for the sake of being decent. "What good will I serve?"

"When you ascend, you may find yourself speaking Eternal tongues. You ought to know what you are saying so you can make yourself useful. Spellwork is useful. Zander and I will need to memorize the chant that will build the runegate from the rubble. *Et Husset* the shield spell."

Nikki chimed in, "Direct translation is both a noun and a verb: *a haven, to shield.*"

"It would be prudent of you to listen." I swallowed, uncomfortably dry. Hearing a reference to me used in the same sentence as magic was ganache to my ears. It flustered me more than I imagined it would. "I figured *this* is an appropriate option for Zander to expel that raging magic he is miraculously keeping calm. With spellwork, I can direct it for him and he can feel good about emptying it into a structure to preserve the living. His strength will return, but it will take the magic strain off his soul for weeks to months if fortune favors him."

I had been imagining my demise, therefore I hadn't given any thought to wielding any sort of power beyond my craft and my sword. I'd zero expectations for myself. What sort of feat was Maruc planning to construct that it would suck his powers and ours too?

Maybe Keenan was correct. Acts of kindness from Eternals did come at a cost. Was there harm in emptying excess magic from a living vessel?

Nikki arranged a fleece blanket around my shoulders then proceeded to unburden his father of his paper works which proved to be a battle seeing as Honri didn't wish to part with a single one. "You are acting greedier than a goblin in a treasure trove! Let me help."

Disgruntled mumbles came from the wheelchair as Honri attempted to flee his son's extended aid. "Like you help the Burrows? No, thank you! These scripts are part of my life's work. You already cemented my most prideful accomplishment into a cemetery. I will not have you ruin these!"

Nikki froze. He effervescent color drained.

I seethed.

Zander shook. He purples have rising from the stone tiles to form protection around his woven.

Chapter Twenty-Five

Nikki's father rolled ahead of him down the hallway. He stood there, hardly breathing, not blinking at the man who sired him.

Zander barred me away from tending to Nikki's emotional wounds. Honri continued to call down the marbled corridor. "You should have told me. Does everyone think I'm some crackpot old fool?"

Hurt clung to Nikki's throat. "We did tell you." The urge to go to him intensified as his father dumped salt on his wound by disregarding him with a cold shoulder. An elf with a similar posture to Alethim slunk into sight with a hooved fae clopping along. Both scribes or scholars by the looks of it. "We've tried to have many conversations about it. It only upsets you when you cannot recollect all the details." We steadily strode behind Honri's chair until we caught up. Seeing as Nikki's hands were semi-full, Maruc took the handles of the chair and steadied the pace.

"We? Your mother is in on this absurd scheme too!" Nikki simply nodded. Honri's whetted gaze honed in on me. "And her? Who is this lady that gets the honor to learn such protected wisdom? A first year academic or lousy intern of the Morial descendants. She better be as brilliant as she is beautiful. It took me one hundred and eleven years to gain access to the knowledge she is about to snoop on."

Nikki's posed character clipped. "She is exceptionally clever and daringly inventive, you will rejoice in her company, of that I am sure."

We turned down a hall. "Don't sound so damn smugly confident about that, Tails." Nikki hardly flinched at the once precious nickname now used as a belittlement. Turmoil surged inside me. Nikki felt far out of reach but the need to protect him surged under the flesh I wore that had nothing to do with the woven's hand. What I felt for him was of my own accord.

Zander was the largest of us, the one suitable to push open the massive library doors adorned in golds with engraved feathers. "It's hard not to be inflated with confidence, seeing as you gushed over Wisteria when she had dinner with us four nights ago. I expect her to get raving reviews yet again." Now, it was Honri's turn to still like the cold wind had latched onto his crooked bones, gripping his mind in paralysis.

While he stared at me attempting to place my face I gaped at the 'library'. It was far more than a collection of books which Atticus had collected over eons and sent off to a designated room complete with winding staircases, echoing ceilings and three, possibly more, levels made to fit an incubi's height of *stories* and relics, fashioned to the quietest wing of Horn's Keep. The singular one not overrun with guests, warriors and strategists.

Lights twinkled on when I skipped into the center of the sprawling library, illuminating high up crannies and dusty tunnels. Warroh may call me blasphemous, but this was exponentially better than any temple created. This place astonished me to the point I would have removed my shoes (were I not perpetually barefooted) out of respect. "Oh my stars." Overgrown plants dropped their florals from the railings making this the coziest place I'd visited in Veona.

"That good, huh?" I startled out of my trance when Nikki spoke. "You're adorable when you get off on educational feats and fantasies." A quiet laugh shook my shoulders as he flung my words back at me with a bite.

"I'm not one for educational pursuits, but I do suspect an unholy amount of spicy romance and raunchy fairy tales to be buried in this shrine of bound books."

"If there is any woman able to unearth filthy, perilous pages, it would be you Wisteria." He kept his tone low. "Let me know if you've found one with diagrams the three of us can practice." The heat of his exhale hit a switch in my mind that completely shut off my ability to respond. Which may have been a blessing because my reply would have been non-verbal and more carnal.

Maruc summoned chairs and tables in an instant. Cool magic. But not strong enough to pull my mind away from the desire to climb the ladders standing about or find a decent romance book to submerse in.

Or re-enact with my two wovens. Yes. That would do nicely—diagrams or not.

"Woodlander." I pivot to the aged man who said my surname. Malice had left him. Clarity had found him. "The master crafter, yes. I remember you." Honri scowled at himself. His hand hid his embarrassment written in the clear crevasses of his wrinkled forehead and downturned eyes. "Wisteria, I have trouble holding onto time, onto the paintings of moments in my head. Forgive my outburst."

I softened my face hoping to ease the pain striking his. "Already done. And that was hardly classifiable as an outburst. When I get feisty, I punch people three times my size and pick fights with immortals. Nikki still hasn't given me my anger back from *days* ago."

"The heart remembers what the mind cannot. Have you got a chance to see more of the city?"

I shrugged. "Some. I was lucky enough to spend a night with your son in the Burrows before the demon whispers awoke us. Honestly, I would love to have seen all that the Veil has to offer and meet the magical beings thriving here but fate has other ideas on how to occupy my time." I paced the shiny stone floors. The smell of old pages and dusty knowledge filled my lungs as I tried not to think how I should be spending my night—interruption free. But I was here now and needed to make myself useful. Listening to spells.

Honri stuttered over my crafter name repeatedly. I helped Nikki the only way I could, rebuilding him after his father cut him down. "Hopefully, the Vulborg are thwarted in their efforts to destroy what they cannot obtain. Life, fire, warmth, feelings. Fennick's decision to vacate the tunnels was warranted as was the realm's decision to close off and impede their advancements by drenching the passageways below ground with liquid stone."

Nikki's hand was already resting on his dad's shoulder. Honri found it. He kissed his knuckles and whispered apologies. "I forgive you. Let's work out the matter at hand, why you and the Emperor brought us here—spellwork."

"*And* to find the delves my younger self had dug in the field." Nikki's luminescent eyes widened when the words finally sunk in. "When I was strapping enough to tirelessly use a shovel, I created tunnels that were unattached to the main vessels of our home." Honri's childish grin hid a little remorse. "Maruc said I ought to tell you so you can find them and see them brought down before they are acquired by the enemy."

"They may prove to be problematic, especially since I recall one of my holes leading under the ramparts into the heart of the city. The trading sector to be exact." Zander's gut sank at Honris' factually spoken statements. His flurry of tarnished rust dragged me down into the pit of foreboding horrors. Gods. If Vulborg accessed those... it'd be frightfully detrimental. "Honri agreed to locate them on the map for Fennick to investigate and seal off."

Wings sprouted from the incubus' back. The shredded remains of his navy blue shirt hung off his neck. He clawed the rest of the fabric off his arms and tossed it onto the floor. Nikki took liberties and burnt up the wad of tattered clothes. "Don't go alone. You have my blessing to dictate and give verbal orders at your discretion. You will take a diverse group with you, Atticus among them. He is probably listening and sniffing nearby, ready to offer aid." Zander's tone was sharp, but his movements precise. He spread out the maps, moving the layout of the north into the front of the stack. Nikki knelt on the floor with a red pen in hand. Meticulously, he watched where Honri's fingers traced and lingered, notating mentally and with ink blots.

Maruc didn't ask that Zander seat himself. He knew it was an impossibility. Given his fervent emotional state, neither of us could. We paced.

My left arm shook, engulfed and overpowered by Zander's strong, too tender heart. We strode around at the Last God's side waiting for him to find whatever page he sought within the bleached leather bound book. Enthusiastic arms locked me to Zander's body. He held me off the ground, leaving my legs to wrap around him. His antsy hands calmed when he brought his nose to my throat and inhaled. *You are everything to me. At this moment you are my anchor in sanity.*

When he took in every freckle, misplaced hair and rise of my chest I felt like his life source. I felt his steady damp exhale through his open mouth. *I don't like this, but I have to trust a man's weak mind and our woven's thoroughness to tie up loose ends.*

This is a delicate and difficult situation. I validated him through our bond. *Just as he and the rest of the known world are placing their trust in you and Atticus to stand resilient and Maruc to hold the second flood at bay. Trusting is taking risks. Sometimes we have no choice but to accept what is offered to us.*

There is always a choice.

His tongue escaped his four fangs long enough to taste. Whatever it was–it tasted decadent enough to purr and placed his mouth over my bruise. *What is a heartmarked?*

At the hollow of my throat he smiled. *You.* I pinched his bare skin under his arm. *I told you before we arrived that I would not be seen as just your friend, your buddy, your comrade or bed warmer. Nor will you simply be referred to as my flower. Which you undoubtedly are. You prohibited all other nouns and declarations. And you cringe when I declare my love.*

Yet, you continue to scream it from altars and over brunch alike.

You offered and honestly I was going to bite you there anyways, it just occurred before the Circling that is all.

Nikki mentioned the Circling. You intend to wed me and bind us in Ether?

That ceremony declares you my bound bride and the sole source of my food and happiness. A marriage equivalent for us hopeless romantics, where I end you begin and vice versa. A heartmarked is the chosen mate for an incubus. We choose only one per lifetime and claim them with a bite on the left side of their neck, directly above your heart where your essence flows straight into my mouth and my venom into you. Kashikat's wife has one. He gingerly pressed his lips on my mark. *Percy is the only other one who had heartmarked someone. You are seen as exponentially important, far more to then a wife or life partner. You are my survival.*

Of course he would have decided that was the best course of action. I allowed it. I asked for it. *Important friends, extended family and wovens get bitten* here. A hand wrapped around my forearm.

I accurately recall where you bit our fox. In fact, if I close my eyes, I can feel it. Shit, violent violets crept into the peripheral of our connection. Lust encroached. He needed to focus. "Learn some ancient spells then I will teach you a thing or two about speaking in tongues." I rattled my piercing on the inside of my teeth. He grunted, shifting ever so slightly to rock me on his hard side body. Two fire pellets soared at our heads.

We ducked just in time before my hairs got singed.

The fire vanished before contacting valuable papers in the room. Nikki looked up at the pair of us from under a stern silver brow. "Consider the message delivered." I stiffly unwrapped my limbs from the mountain holding me, finding my balance on my bare feet and Orion rightfully sheathed at my hip underneath the layer of blanket. I kept him hidden as I curled up on the smallest of chairs. I knew how distracting quintessing proved to be. I refused to be the culprit of igniting lusty impulses during these important hours. One time was plenty.

His scowl flipped into a sly smile. I could practically hear the next two words off his lips before he spoke them. Hearing him mutter *good girl* in his raspy, filthy, fuck-me backwards voice would either make my thigh damp or send me punching his lights out. I cut in as he inhaled. "You're welcome." I ignored his wordless taunting, but found myself blushing regardless.

The fae leaned over my shoulder to jot down the name of the book–the fragile clump of dusty, unbound papers that Maruc reverently held in his open palms. He and Zander were already conversing in the dialect that once filled the dungeons in song form. I was unacquainted with the short give and take of their discourse. The language was elegant, but after trying to isolate syllables and imitate the fluidity of their tongue my opinion quickly changed.

It was as uncomfortable as wearing a steel scratched woolen sweater in the summer. My skin wanted to shed. My brain began to rattle between my ears. My blood, Anna's blood, hammered to no avail.

For shit's sake, I was so aggravated that I chipped a tooth with the metal in my mouth. *What is it that has you on edge?*

This language.

"Some part of you recognizes the words. It wants to decipher, to discern, to engage with the dialogue." Maruc switched over to common without skipping a breath. Nosey.

I was no magic almighty being. I was a human with shit luck who wished this God would stop insinuating otherwise. "Yeah. Zander sang to Anna and I when we were dying. And to me after so I wouldn't lose what shred of sanity I had left being cuffed to her dead body." Orion warmed on my side. His way of lightening my sudden foul mood. "Let me know if I can be of service otherwise I will be found perfecting my swordsmanship by means of a dance."

There was ample space in this cavernous collection of stories. Enough to throw blades and launch myself into handsprings and roundoffs without regard of others becoming impaled or injured. The blanket on my shoulders I tossed onto the chair and roamed about the echoing abode keeping conversations within ear shot. My minimal effort to comply with Maruc's request to listen in.

Quietly and quickly, my feet scampered across the floor. Toes and ankles flexing. My muscles and mind relinquished fatigue and form to the sword dance my soul knew by heart. There was no conscious effort dictating my arms as I elegantly twisted them towards the sky, my wrist winding to showcase my honored dance partner. The song of Orion cutting through the air. A short lived *woosh* slice by my ear. My face turned up as we began.

I danced with him slowly as if becoming reacquainted with an old lover, his cold sharp edges were a longing touch on my skin. I let him have me and him, I. Holding and converging with each other however we desired. The quick restrained tempos of alternating swings and steps were a tribute to the wielder's skill.

In my early years of training, I learned that perfecting the dance had nothing to do with repetition or control. It had everything to do with surrender and intuition. Hindsight, my dance partner *was* the God of intuition. I closed my eyes and freed him from my hands. He soared, spinning twice laterally before gravity brought him back down. I caught the hilt in the hand behind my back, spinning myself thereafter in a crouched rotation on the ball of my foot.

I pulled up my sleeves of silk to better feel his indominable strength against the span of my outstretched arm. Again he flew. This time I followed under his flight stream in a sequence of acrobatic maneuvers. While upside down, I watched a scribe's face pull rightside up. His pen had stopped moving. Nikki promptly remedied his misplaced focus, his golden eyes hooked on the way Orion spun seamlessly around my wrists in the pattern of a figure eight. My feet played out the two-step Ilanthian footwork, faulting not once. Maruc and Zander's conversation became a distant murmur when I decided to see the dance through to completion.

Liberating. Exhilarating. The world and its difficulties faded away.

It was the closest thing to flying that a wingless entity could feel. Especially when I leapt and tumbled my way up to the second and third floors, following the pull of our dance as if the song of my soul was being plucked by Orion's heartbeat. Sweat caused the fabric to stick flush to my shoulder blades and bunch up on my neck line. I pushed on until the grand conclusion of spinning blades then slumped unceremoniously over a red velvet pleated bench when it was spent. Orion rested on my ribcage. The weight of him imprinted itself on the surface of my skin.

The nearness of my oldest friend settled nicely on my chaotic mind.

A sigh escaped. The type of sigh that Zander wouldn't condone others hearing. I deluded myself into believing I wouldn't have to have expended myself with Orion if he never opened the damn door in the first place and forced me to burn my body out with alternatives rather then expend my energy with him.

Any chance you can speak up? I don't have supernatural hearing.

Hearing no. But you do have two legs—two tone, flexible, sultry legs able to do the splits—that you can use to walk your ass—your spectacular perky ass—within earshot. We started spellwork a half hour ago. You've got catching up.

I propped myself up on an elbow. *Half hour?*

Fen left an hour ago, my flower. It agonized him to leave the sight of your perfection as much as it pained him to set out and complete the tasks at hand. I craned my neck every which way searching for a clock. Time had escaped me. *Honri enjoyed it. Immensely. He clapped when you used the banisters as balance beams. He is asleep now. Reasonable given the late hour.*

Spying the nearest flight of stairs, I jolted upright and spiraled down until a familiar silhouette of horns and muscle stood before me. *Time slipped.*

Easily done when losing yourself to a God. I'm a smidge jealous. The vast amounts of violet shadows leaking out of his skin spoke differently. His indolent attempt to make room for me on the chair was laughable. *Did I ever tell you how unpredictable and astounding I find you to be? As I mentioned in the Southlands, you've piqued my interest and you never cease to leave me unamazed.* I wedged myself between his thigh and the armrest, a covetous arm wrapped around my flesh, shielding me from onlookers.

There were literally four others aside from us in the room, two were obsessed with their parchments and another was snoring horizontally on the couch. The pads of his fingers brush my back like butterfly kisses, hardly there. *Your scars. We forgot the goku scar treatment after you showered.* Angered plumes of red emerged in bellows of self-disappointment.

I held his hand tightly around his knuckles. *My scars seem rather non-urgent given the how I would rather be spending my time. If not, one of my Bloodsworn can when they accompany me to Ilanthia. You will stay here and designate me a position among the lines of Ilanthian foot soldiers while you assign your legions their rotations.* The possessive plumes of tart displeasure grew until red soaked our bond.

"All existence is on the cusp of becoming insignificant to me, but your kind are pressed for precious minutes, days, weeks." The round hazel eyes of the Emperor stared at Zander from behind the outstretched pages.

Not the least bit amused.

Zander sunk into the chair, diminishing himself in the God's presence. I yanked him straight. *None of that. Do not hide.*

"Time to use collocations, not cogitations." He called us out on our syphering, his tone was short, unamused. Scribes didn't appear to notice. "We will practice the spell to convoke the awakened passive magic infused into and around the land. It will come in handy to absorb energy when you are tapped out. Or send it to another wielder to have enough power to say, reconstruct a barrier. Repeat. *Hujan dan matahari lahir.*"

We obeyed. *"Hujan dan matahari lahir."*

"*Lah-EE-r.* Not Lay-hey-ire. Repeat." I did. My pronunciation was a far cry from polished. My sounds, they were not words to me for they had no meaning, stumbled out of my mouth as if my tongue was sandpaper. "*Berbicara. Fakta dunia.*"

Yes. *Fakta* this.

Fuck this. It lulled me to sleep on the lap of the giant.

Chapter Twenty-Six

Horrors preyed upon my unconscious mind and trapped me in overpowering undercurrents of the abyss. Garbed in horned helmets and beaked raven masks they stalked me into the center of a burning edifice. The blood painting the walls in front of me was my own, the cries filling my ears were Cobar and my mother's, the wraiths that were unleashed upon me were the eighteen I had murdered.

Poppy, Dirk, Rusty, Raven, Flora, Josafin, Citrine, Rapplin, Adar'da, Maple, Serpentine, Tides, Venus, Titan, Coral, Lucinda, Evett, Fauna. I was trapped in darkness with the sole memories of their names. The murders I committed.

My chest hurt from the guilt violently racking my ribs. My throat stung from screaming just as much as limbs trembled from sprinting aimlessly through the never ending burning tower, the burning woods, the burning piles of corpses.

My joints broke. My body failed me.

I lay helplessly as the Faceless Prince descended upon me, a joyless curve on his lips. He placed a kingly crown on his black feathered head. He held a crown of black bones out for me. Vulborg bones. I smacked it away. The soulless eyes of the masked man turned the crown into a chained collar. Heavy, sturdy black metal.

I scraped my fractured limbs across the scorched floor. Yelling for Orion. I wailed when he didn't come to my aid. Yet, another Eternal abandoned me.

The collar was thrown to my feet. The Torval expected me to chain myself.

Nikki could burn through metal imprisonments. I've seen it before. Zander would never allow me in chains in the first place. But they weren't here. That didn't stop me from calling for them.

My screams went unanswered, stopping only when Duke Stegin's rusty spear head impaled my chest and twisted. The prince gave a lusty laugh. There was no golden blood to save me this time. I choked on my tears.

And let death come.

Made in his image indeed. Oyokos sure looked a lot like Zander.

Smelt like him even. Death smelt of coffee, sky and spice. Safe.

I touched his forlorn face. Scruffy. "Are you with me, love? Does darkness still have its teeth sunk into you?" My movements felt weighted. I reached for the incubus' crescent shaped horns, but gravity brought them down. "I will all too happily hunt down the demons of your mind and remove their teeth, one by one, until you are free to inflict your own damage upon them. I'm certain it would be absolutely gruesome. Your violent nature is such a delight. Erogenous to witness. And if I were to speak frankly, I'm livid another has even hypothetically sunk their teeth into you. That is my responsibility and gratifying undertaking. And mine alone. Fuck the darkness, come back to me love." He took my clammy hand and while lowering his head raised my palm up to clutch the horn. My thumb traced the chip gouged into one. The shakes stopped.

I knew this incubus. Lingering effects of night terror chafed my throat. I saw my death coming for me. "Hi."

"Hello," he whispered sympathetically, sleep and worry thick in his voice. I pressed the shell of my ear onto his chest. The slow, consistent beats of his heart might be the remedy needed to pull the rest of my sweaty, shaken self back to functional standards. Coherent and not screaming at imaginary things would be a good start.

We were still in the library. Just us. "Fen and Maruc are escorting Honri to his apartment. It's a lovely morning for a stroll. They are hoping the sight of the city may trigger more insightful moments to where else he may have moved stone with shovel. Maruc, Atticus and I decided we are all in need of proper sleep. The stress has worn on all of us and worn warriors do not win battles, no matter how wise they are or how rapidly their bodies heal."

I rubbed my face against his chest. And left it there. "That awful, huh?"

"The blame lies with the acoustics of these walls. The echoes of a page turning are amplified with this faulty structural design." His hand rubbed my back. Wrinkles on my nose scrunched. "People needed a good wake up call. I'm glad you screamed our names. If you would have screamed another's I'm not sure how I would have covered for you when my kin came barging in here."

I huffed. "You just gave a spiel on how everyone is lacking proper sleep."

His lip quirked. "My brothers deserved to be woken up. They are cumbersome shits who are wearing on my last bloody nerve. And the elementals who can hear across the city, probably weren't sleeping deeply as it stands with all the commotion." He disappeared his wings and rose with me stuck to his chest. "We are going to my home for uninterrupted sleep. I'll slacken my attachment to you when it's time for Maruc and his company to cross the portal. Your Bloodsworn are going with you to Opal Lake, I couldn't convince them otherwise. They were adamant. Fen will see himself inside my bungalow when he feels he has done his job to the best of his abilities."

I stretched and wrapped my stiff limbs around his neck. He held my weight on a single forearm, admiring the swells of my breast that were very prominent under the clingy fabric I had sweated through. I followed his gaze. "I'll help get those off."

"Don't get ahead of yourself. We have added considerations to take into account. He will be livid," I reminded.

He leaned back, I toppled into him. My arms looped around his neck. "Worry not. It's impossible to forget our 'circumstance'." He kissed my head. "Sleep beckons."

Zander slept so hard, he didn't budge when I accidentally kneed him in the ribs when his body mass shifted to smother me.

The bed was engraved with the arrangement of his heavy limbs stretched to all corners of the mattress, locking me under their weight. I tried pleading with Nikki for help in freeing myself when he stumbled in, he shook his head in his fox form. He laid himself down within reach of my free hand, knocking it twice with his wet nose until I stroked his neck and sent us both slumbering off.

I was also *highly* aware of the 'circumstance' when I woke to two pairs of legs threaded through mine. Disoriented in the tangle of bodies, I had no idea who the lean thigh between my knees belonged to only that I was doing everything in my power not to grind against it. A hand thread its fingers through mine and we rested our locked limbs dangerously close to the waistline of Zander's drawstring pants. Any lower and we'd be giving him a dual handjob. I'm not sure who would be more enticed by that, myself or Zander. I chose that moment to remember Nikki didn't always shift with his clothes on.

Heat crept up my spine and I willed myself not to lose composure this time around and run off to swing swords. I craned my neck to peer down over the arms across my body. I was in the middle of the warmth sharing pile.

My slight shift caused the two men to readjust. I was no less their prisoner, no closer to freedom.

Sleep would not return at this hour–whatever hour it was because my mind was fantasizing and dangerously close to blurring all the lines. And my body, well, my inner goddess was starved for their touch and she wouldn't be sleeping without her need met. The skydome had been blocked out with thick drawn curtains. The light in the room was dim enough to see only an outline of the furniture.

I unlatched myself from Zander and rolled off his chest shaking loose Nikki's grip. Next, I worked on freeing my legs. Softly and slowly I kicked my feet about, ridding the sheets. I jostled harder to maneuver away from the leg wedged between my knees when a stirring of pleasure roused at the apex of my thighs. Curious. I kicked a little more.

Heat enveloped my waist. I stiffened. My spine along Nikki's powerful chest turned to stone. "Must you wiggle your hips so much?" There was muffled humor behind me along with the stiff length of him pressing into my ass.

"Must you be made of steel?" My waist was released. I didn't hide my pinking cheeks. In fact, I wiggled more to fully free myself. Zander woke up when I heaved his arm off its resting place around me.

He roared like a bear cub leaving hibernation when he stretched his arms overhead, his features that of the human horselord man I met as Drift, only much more satiated. The veins on his low stomach disappeared under his loose pants. "My cock is harder than steel. Do you need a reminder?" He was rightfully overconfident, but that wasn't the statement that hung in the air to be acknowledged. "If not now, after coffee. I'm already starving at the notion of you away from me and you haven't left my lands or bed." I stopped trying to squirm off the mattress and felt for our syphering.

An accumulation of mental and emotional exhaustion were emptied at my feet, he no longer held the stress of the recent days in open boxes shuffling around. It was laid plainly for me to examine. It was so dense and heavy it was difficult not to feel a tad sympathetic seeing the extensive amount of shit he had to sort through as a notable, respected person of this realm. Of our world.

I wouldn't let him come with me to Opal Lake. Not when he was needed here. Same for Nikki. I assured them many times over I'd not be needing them, my Bloodsworn were enough. My needs in that present moment were a different story entirely.

Zander's pale eyes skimmed up my body and his hand returned to its spot across my hips. I needed him. Wanted him. Not just for what he religiously offered to my body, but also to my mending soul space.

He brushed his fingers up the grooves of my stomach, hooking the silk fabric on his pinky finger and moving it up until my ribs were exposed.

My chest rose and fell with a shudder of anticipation. The room glowed brighter as Nikki swung his feet out of bed, nine fiery tails sent shadows dancing around the room. I propped myself up on elbows. "Aren't you going to stay?" The words hastily left my mouth.

His tails wrapped around him, shielding eyes from his intimate body parts that were pressed against my body seconds ago. Yes, he had shifted naked. That didn't stop me from ogling his sculpted, tattooed body. I caught a glimpse of ink on his thighs and top of his ass. "I won't go far. Although, I am flattered you are zealous enough to desire me in bed for this *experiment*."

He was right. I found nothing shameful about the situation. With a gleaming wink, his gaze left mine and found his brother's. "If my scent so much as stiffens your spine, everyone stops. I will not let a craze or outburst befall our honied sweet cake here."

I called at his backside while he sat himself down behind the desk across the room, halfway hidden behind oddities. "I'm hardly sweet."

A wet tongue fondled my belly ring. "I beg to differ." I pulled my top off to encourage Zander's playfulness.

He moaned fondly. Gasps escaped when he sucked my breast with such lusty technique it could only be described as artistry. My head was thrown back on the pillows as I permitted the artist to decorate me as if my flesh was a blank canvas at his disposable. Sinfully slow, his mouth cut a path on my flesh, its destination my mouth. Purple fumes licked the mattress as he poured his loving essence into the kiss. The gentleness evolved into something less tamed.

I encouraged that beast. I pulled him onto me, I couldn't care less if he crushed the air from my lungs. I wanted to feel his weight heavy on my small bones and his length press against my frame and my wet entrance. When he rolled his hips into me, my hands were lost to his hair, clawing at his back.

Kissing him evoked a storm of emotions. I forbade sadness to take hold among them. This would not be our last time consuming each other in such a devastatingly doting way. I absolutely forbid it. I broke free from the darkness of tangled depressing thoughts and maneuvered my way on top of the horselord, rocking in a very sturdy saddle.

The friction was tantalizing. My knees on either side of him clenched tighter. "I almost feel like I should apologize to Nikki for how quickly and often I climax."

Hands with sharp pricks of claw tips grabbed my ass. "He can keep count for us."

Zander ripped the delicate fabric of my silk bottoms and threw them aside, earning him a scowl and a hard thump on his chest. "I was fond of those." He ignored my pounding and on his sternum and lifted his hips to take off the remaining barrier between us. His cock sprang free. I admired it as he happily inhaled the shreds of fabric in his fingers. My sweat and wetness perfumed it thoroughly and he looked as if he could come on the spot.

I undulated my hips, intentionally sliding my slit along his shaft. The size of him was astounding. I was equally awed as I was apprehensive for a raw fucking. Still livid about my new silk bottoms I hit his immovable muscle mass again.

"The more you hit me, the more irresistible I find you to be, my murderous flower." Fangs emerged. I stopped hitting and started skimming my fingertips along the length of him. He groaned through parted teeth and formed words. "Especially, when the viciousness of your passion brightens your eyes and melts them into liquid emeralds. Priceless gems. Don't even get me started on your fucking body. That damn mouth! The unforgettable things you do with it. Do you have any idea how difficult it is to tear my eyes off you when everything about you enchants me like a siren at sea?"

Me? Enchanting? I laughed, shaking my head.

It wasn't a polite modest laugh to feign acceptance of compliments. It was a subtle, dark one. Maybe he had been ensnared and deluded by Anna's blood because I felt his uncorrupted honesty. I also felt it had to have been misplaced. "One day you will come to see what I see and you will know perfection. You will call it by its name, Wisteria Woodlander." He called me out quickly.

"Not going to happen, but until then." I reverted back to exploring the coarse hair under his navel line and the sharp edges of his muscles. He sat up, lowering his chin until his scruffy mouth met mine. Our kiss rekindled. The distant fear of losing this connection spurred me to try doing what I couldn't accomplish when we were fleeing the Deadlands. Drop all my inner barriers and allow him to swim into my innermost chamber. *Follow me.*

To the end of the world and beyond. Lead me.

We leapt off our thread and dove into the airy waters between us. His colors of plum purple and summer lilacs took the shape of a stallion whose mane was braided akin to Zander's daily style. There was no clomping of hooves as we tread the water currents of my physical and mental walls. The horse swam elegantly around me, observing me insert a soul key into the damaged lock still dripping with Anna blood and smudged with dirt from the graves of the Woodlands.

It snapped open. I walked into myself with the horselord. We stepped into a watercolor image of Ferngrove. The Ferngrove of my memories. I laid myself down on the mossy river bed of my mind and tried not to weep.

You are undaunted. I've been waiting for what feels like a millennium for this moment. His lips left mine so he could start his journey downward. Inward. *Your peaceful surrender smells of fresh linen.* Lips brushed my breasts, my hips then my inner thighs. *Your soul's world smells of the terrain after it rains, of sunlight and berries, of sea and soil. What imagery do you sense?*

My fingers knotted together over my chest. *Ferngrove.*

Poetic and pure. Home is within thyself, my flower. Describe it to me.

I am lying next to Maplevine Creek. It's transitioning to summer, but the mornings are still cool and the grass gleams with dewdrops. My knees were lifted over wide shoulders. The roughness of his jaw and smoothness of his lips inched dangerously close to the piercing on the hood of my clit. My fingers unlatched from each other and busied themselves instigating pleasure.

Always so inpatient. I heard him smile through the syphering. The ripples his horse form made lead me to believe it was trotting around exploring the space I allowed him to enter. Existing here was calming. Having him between my legs was the opposite. "One day I want you to fuck me inside our minds."

"You'll have to settle for getting fucked in the tangible world. Although, I am perplexed how you think we can accomplish something that abstract." Zander nibbled the sensitive skin by my knee, keenly watching the way my middle finger circled around my vulva with well-learned knowing. I craved to be touched. I wondered if Nikki stepped closer, if my needs would change.

His forehead wrinkled as his brow raised in Nikki's direction. Despite his rising alertness, he kept his tone sincere. "Every thought transcends." He exited the Woodlands painted in my mind, the image of his stallion quickly darkened and transformed into a possessive incubus I saw in my inner and outer world.

Zander looked beyond me. His nails lengthened and pierced the fabric beneath me.Horns grew from atop his head and a single word fell on my ears. "*Mine.*" In a possessive, punishing sweep, he moved my hand away from the slit I had been fondling. A blanket was tossed across my open legs. I'd seen those same hands rip the spines from the bodies of a hundred wraiths and gently hold me the next. I knew better than to protest.

I did not know enough to be fearful. When I watched Zander stare at his woven with unfamiliarity and murder etched into his savage constitution, I applauded Keenan's awareness for opting not to piss off the one who heartmarked me by secluding ourselves.

He remained planted. Unmoving. Altogether, he ceased breathing.

Any motion from him would stir the air and scatter his smell. These virulent males were two bulls with locked horns.

Chapter Twenty-Seven

An assured voice filled the room. "I am no threat." No panicked notes carried in Nikki's hard voice.

Nikki stood tall with his tails peacocked preening proudly behind him, fully lighting up the bedroom. The room grew a few degrees warmer as icey blue eyes clashed with radiant smoldering spheres. A feral growl escaped Zander and rumbled against my legs. His body barricading me from our woven who went on, "I am not a threat to her. But I will be to you if you come at me with claws." If these two didn't bring down the ceiling with their stares I would be stunned.

"Breathe me in."

Nostrils flaring and tongue tasting the air, the male rigidly hovering over me finally decided to inhale. "Your scent. It's… " His tone raspy, ghostly. "You *want* her. Me. Us? … I recognize…" His face contorted and he repeated the action. "This aroma."

"I will always want you and her. To whatever end."

"I know your scent." The haze began to lift the incubus' eyes.

"Because I am yours. I belong to you."

"Fennick?" Two low, gruff syllables and the elemental looked relieved. "Mine."

"It's me, dumbass." A gust of clarity blew through Zander and the blanket providing me modesty was slid to the floor. Nikki's gaze didn't stray. "My pheromones will only get stronger," Nikki laced caution into his statement, his unfixing eyes outshining the sun.

Zander eased. Immensely. His weight sank back onto me. "As will hers. Do you think figs pair decently with peaches? Your scent is more decadent now." He licked the air. "Brown sugar!"

Within a second, his switch was flipped from predatory to an over excited kid in a kitchen pantry sneaking desserts. "I *really* like brown sugar."

Nikki rubbed his creased brow. Zander's desires were changing too quickly for Nikki to fully let down his guard. "You are overzealous. We are not testing consequences of fate or incubi consumption thresholds at this hour."

"I love brown sugar and peaches. Please?"

"Did you just confess to me?"

A proud four fanged grin escaped Zander. I mirrored his elation. "Yes."

"Cute. But not now." Nikki took a half step backwards earning him a scowl from the begging beast. "I intended to get us all out of here alive. No figs or brown sugar to be eaten, they are just an aromatic appeal from a safe distance."

The incubus was unable to reply because his lips were preoccupied placing a reverent kiss atop my public bone. I shivered and Nikki did the same across the room. Zander unwound himself from my slender legs and lay flush with my side body, honoring my request that Nikki and I retain sovereignty for our first time. Amongst the excitement, I found my voice. "Are you ready?"

Nikki's charming pointed grin flashed. His eyes shot down to what I presumed was a hard cock *aching* for attention. "You still have to ask? You can start."

"You can finish." Flames grew hotter and I swore even I tasted brown sugar flood the air and pour down my thigh like warm syrup.

Legs fell open. I fingered myself and pressed into my hands, making friction where I desperately craved it. Nikki's shrouded hips moving in sync with mine, his need to stroke himself was overwhelming. And sexy as absolute sin. Shortly after I started my self-pleasuring he joined. His arm flexing as he rhythmically jerked himself. His touch felt *real*. More real than my own.

I wished the damn flames and fur would vanish as I lessened my own touch and let Nikki take me to where I wanted to go. His hand worked magic on us both and cried out at the building ecstasy. My moans spilled across the room. Zander appeared elated as I surrendered to the sensations, his own hand wrapped around his girthy cock and began singing filthy praises that made me dampen the sheet beneath me.

The pair of golden eyes narrowed in on the male behind me. They combed over the sultry scene on display but honed in on each one of Zander's movements as if at any moment, he'd lose himself to covetousness. It was a high probability, but still far less than the guaranteed odds of two wovens in the house losing all resolve save for lust simultaneously.

When Nikki switched the pace I felt it and set out to shatter me—I felt it.

When his breathing quickened, mine did.

I groped my painfully needy nipples and twisted them until heat crawled up and down my body. A growl or moan or animalistic grunts of urgency pleaded across the room encouraging me to pinch harder. Electricity shot from my nipples to the ache between my legs.

He enjoyed that. Yes. Yes he did.

I groped my pebbled nipples again. Nikki groaned my name as he pumped harder, fucking his hand.

"More. *More.*" Zander simpered at my demands, fuck I wanted them both *inside* me. Zander heard my inner dialogue for he uttered *'Soon.'* against my mental walls with a devilish grin.

I roughly caressed the insides of my thigh with my nails scraping violently and watching as Nikki fought with himself to let his attention stray from the horned man pressed against my side working his own cock in his hands. "You can watch." The plea in my voice not embarrassing me in the slightest. I knew what I wanted.

His hands left his length and had the desk clutched on either side, our bodies trembled when he withdrew his touch. My hips shifted upward begging for an invisible force to break me. "Z, check in with me."

Zander didn't stop pumping himself. His reply came out as a raspy command full of yearning. "Obey her." His command stole the air in the room. "Watch her."

"That's not what I'm referring to."

Zander's lips pressed into the crown of my head. A demonstration of his control to the protector in the room. "I will not strike out at you."

"Correction, you do not *want* to. You may. Your shadows are coming out to play." Purple crawled up the walls, mingling with the elemental's light.

It was silent save for my fast paced, heavy breathing. "Stay as you were, but do not move closer. Next orgasm step near, I'll have acclimated by then." Nikki found his words to be believable. Yet, they sated his qualms only partially.

"When I say I desire little else right now than to watch Wisteria come undone, writhing with pleasure at my doing, I mean it. But Z, I know your blood and heart better than you, my brother. You won't live long if you hurt either of us out of instinct."

Zander waved him off. "I love you too. Now, drop your tails. She wants to admire *all of you*. I want to smell and feel how wet you make our woven." Their intense staring continued. Which was a blessing that let my unhinged jaw go unnoticed.

When neither spoke and no tails were removed, I filled the air with a solution. "You can have it both ways. Use transplacency. Nikki can watch Zander fuck me through his point of view and I'll make sure he feels each second of orgasmic bliss."

Zander paused his fondling to mentally sort out my phrasing. "A loophole!"

"It's a good idea."

"It's a perfect idea, since Nikki is off limits at the present. Apparently, to us both."

Burnt cedar from the wooden desk wafted in the air. "It's too brillant of an idea, as if you are determined to demasculinize me. I'll ejaculate faster than an adolescent boy discovering his penis for the first time."

"Lower your tails so I can see your penis for the first time." I pressed my thighs together, yearning for friction. "I'll behave, I won't touch you."

Metallic clanks echoed off the high ceilings. Ink pots crashed on the ground as the desk was reduced to smokeless ash in an instant. His stunned stare still on Zander. "We are sure she isn't a succubus?"

"She has denied it each time I ask."

"Gods damned. She is... she's..." Nikki stumbled through choking gasps.

When he found his footing he risked a single glance into my eyes. Only my eyes. "No, baby. I need to leave some perks and rewards for you once you cross that delicate line you are walking. Not until you are ready for all of me. At all times. For the world to speculate we are wovens." His abdominals flexed and he surely knew I was perusing his godly body, feeling the influx of lust blister through me. "Good girls get my cock. Can you be a good girl, baby, and cooperate for your males a little while longer?"

Fuck, I was doe eyed and salivating when I gave a submissive dip of my chin.

The dark smile Nikki returned reached his brilliant eyes and had his dick humming with anticipation. He was pleased. I loved feeling him so pleased and hungry for me.

"No more asking for my cock today, little vixen. I'm not sure how much longer I can hold out from tasting that tight cunt of yours and diving my dick into your slit filled with Zander's still warm seed."

What a deliciously perfect visual he painted for me.

"Right, no more asking for you. *Today.*" I understood. Truly, I did. "Alright." I unhurriedly removed my eyes from Nikki and surveyed the marbled landscape of Zander's body. Nikki stroked himself and need coiled around my swollen nerves. My greedy hands latched onto the arm nearest me, anchoring me down while my hips surged upwards coinciding with a different woven's touch. Zander provided the pressure I so desperately craved while Nikki worked me from across the room.

We were close now to seeing stars. Nikki checked in with Zander one more time before fire erupted from the corner and whimpers fell from my mouth. "Wisteria. Fucking, yes. My Wisteria." Nikki's voice was hardly there, a rough sigh of my name ghosted off his lips as we came.

My name on his ecstasy drenched mouth was right where it belonged.

I spun on my side, riding the aftershock on top of Zander's thigh. Come to find his wings were out and his nostrils were wide, rapidly inhaling. The look on his face was nothing I'd seen before. I forced my gyrating to halt while he acclimated.

It was skewed with shock, betrayal and an innocent gaze of fretfulness. A combination that left me feeling very much disheartened. Nikki didn't have to say anything, we waited for threads to break or bind us tighter.

My hips stopped rolling. The room quieted.

He locked me in place with the gaze of a predator, while every muscle in his chest shook as he closed in around me. The room vanished. Wings wrapped me in lavender dusk. *Mine.* Every shuddering exhale seemed to say. *Mine.*

I quickly tried to form a reply. *Yours. Yes. Ours. Yes.*

Fangs and lips nipped at the bruised puncture wound on the left side of my neck. "Fennick. Arm." Nikki glided across the room, incrementally offering his outstretched arm to the incubus. He sniffed his blood, then nuzzled back to my throat again to sniff mine. His grip on each of us was rough and determined. His steely eyes were a true reflection of his state. "My venom runs in both of you. No Weaver ties are broken." Zander lifted a wing to watch Nikki where his fire molding into the shape a of blade forged and ready to strike should he need to intervene.

"You didn't eat." Nikki humored behind the flaming weapon.

"Because *that* orgasm was dedicated to Fen. The next several are mine." A drawn out growl escaped his lips when we caught sight of the glistening cum decorating his brother's tattooed navel. I swore I saw something glinting beneath his shrouding tails. Something metallic. Something beautiful. Zander took his brother off guard and sniffed Nikki's cum, giving a hungry growl.

"Not the time for figs." Nikki softly rejected his brother.

"Brown sugar," Zander corrected with a defensive snap. His blue eyes penetrating Nikki's soul.

Within the next moment Zander was diving down between my legs. "Peaches. Now."

"Apparently," I exclaimed, my hands finding their comfortable spot on his horn and gripping the roots of his long hair. Strong fingers worked with Zander's tongue, he sucked and teased my swollen nub until my ache moved deeper and the evidence trickled down my flesh. Nikki's eyes preserved my modesty, I can't say mine did the same for him. What he did allow me to see, I devoured.

Zander rose to bring my ass to the edge of the elevated bed, his attention left me briefly to eye the male at the bedside holding steady on a bed post. "Consent, Fen?" The pulsing tip of Zander's cock was being swiped against my entrance, I pressed into him. Waiting was a torturous form of foreplay on its own because I needed them inside minutes ago.

The naked elemental took two steps away from the bed, his hand under a swirl of fire. "Yes. Take her." *Take us.* He let go unspoken, but we all heard it regardless.

Zander entered me inches at a time, fucking me fully brought whimpers of pain mixed with those of pleasure tearing out of my chest. Nikki struggled to remain upright when my body was being thrusted into with such savage need. He leaned against the nearest wall, focused on Zander's trembling wings. Torment and satisfaction in his starry eyes.

My hips were encircled by the giant's hands. Zander did not hold back. I'd never ask that of him. He slammed into me faster, until his name erupted from my lips. Zander crushed and contorted me to feed, drinking every last murmur of his name. He planted a kiss on my throat and released my ass. I wasn't alone in finding pleasure, the warm liquid trickling out of my pussy and the panting from the pillar of fire was evidence enough. "Keeping up alright, Nikki?" I asked.

He resigned to give me a thumbs up. "That's two."

"Collectively five," I devilishly smirked, pulling the slick penis out from inside of me and licked up the remaining cum. I paid special attention to the tip, shoving it back to my throat until he was hard again. "How about those swimming lessons?"

We arrived at a point of comfort hours into our escapades where Zander's wings retreated and I could ride him while he lay vulnerable on his back, minimal appearance of claws emerging. Progress.

When they napped in their refractory stage, I struggled to find words that matched what I the complete elation swelling in my chest. The trash bin next to Zander's desk was full of my discarded attempts to scribble not only my feelings but a farewell to my wovens in case Opal Lake was my final adventure.

The longer I spent mulling over words the more I resigned myself to the fact that Maruc wouldn't let me die. Not when he needed me to kill him as part of our first arrangement.

He was testing me.

That bastard.

I combed over the stacks of papers and books that escaped Nikki's flames. Among them I discovered a familiar penmanship scribed across the many letters, the same penmanship that the poetry book had been written in. *Zander Halfmoon Veil di Lucent.* This hopeless romantic had been unbearably forward, but also made efforts to subtly show himself to me with the poems of the Dreamer Realm and his plans for the future written on the pages behind Oyoko's journal. The flower poetry I touched myself to in his fort bedroom, that was his doing, his words. My heart warmed.

Nikki stirred in his sleepy state. His fox ears twitched and he tucked his muzzle under his back legs. He looked like a little orb of fire buried underneath the bed, warming a sleeping Zander prone on the mattress above him. I skipped sleep to watch the two of them in all their unnatural glory doze off. I wasn't at all startled when the knocks came on the door. I was dressed in trousers, armed with Orion and waiting for my escorts with a cup of tea in my grasp.

Maruc stood casually behind Keenan, Cobar and Brock. At his side, a haggard newly sober Percy. Percy shielded his eyes from the risen sun. One look said it all. The misery of migraines inflicted him.

I descended the stairs of the bungalow's porch. Cobar's hand was snug in mine when we faced Maruc. "Gather your belongings, I don't intend to return you until you've mastered the basic handling of magic or the Vulborg attack, whichever comes first." The last God had a manner of speaking that I found irksome.

I gave him the courtesy of an honest reply. "I own no belongings. All I have is my name. I am ready."

Chapter Twenty-Seven

Depositing his corlimor in the care of another—be they a God or exalted warrior who was essentially an Eternal himself, it mattered not a single damn ounce. It proved to be one of the most difficult things he'd done, which spoke volumes. Harder than keeping Oyokos' magic at bay or tempering his lust last night when he wanted to devour both his wovens.

Practically all of Veona's daytime beings gathered to send off this diverse convoy destined to Opal Lake. He smelt the nation's potent hope in the air and how it infiltrated every enclosed space. The hope rang clearer than the cynicism, both of which stemmed from Wisteria's presence. His hurt was watching her walk through the portal between Oyokos' horns without him or his elemental was the utmost painful, maddening thing that he had ever witnessed. At least he wasn't feeling all these paining, weighty sentiments alone. Fennick empathized.

They hadn't had time to commiserate over her absence yet. It wouldn't be deemed wise. Their emotional viability would distract them from preparing for a war or perhaps he may get lost in taking liberties in exploring emotions with his hands...

One thread at a time...

Regret permeated his chest like a web of ice spinning around his soul, robbing him of all ability to be committed to the present moment. He should have stopped her leaving. If he reclaimed the title Overlord, he would have found people willing to follow his order to forbid her from walking out of their secluded nation.

On second thought, if he restrained or impeded Wisteria in any shape or form, she'd run faster and further in the direction he willed her not to. Letting her go was the best thing for them. For Kinlyra.

In the span of ten minutes the number of times he thought about abandoning the conclave in the Keep to chase her down and drag her back was infinite. He didn't show an inkling of this internal turmoil as Alethim and Giathac discussed their use of elvish landmines imbued with fae spells which would entrap the demons in a mental prison, theoretically. His mind already felt like ten thousand landmines exploded and left him dazed. Wisteria was to blame.

Last night certainly had him rethinking everything he believed impossible. His self-control for one.

He had done it. Allowed another to lust after what was his and let them live to see another day. Maybe, just maybe, with two wovens at his side, he may safely unlock the cage constantly rattling in his chest.

For shit's sake, Maruc shot a sphere of deathly storms at Wisteria and she cut through it without flinching and went on to cause a storm of her own. Unharmed. The Weaver was perfect.

There may exist a way where he'd protect his people and not risk killing those he loved. He wasn't a monster. Wisteria and Orion stood a chance to survive his caged darkness.

A direct, distinct voice distracted him. Someone called to him. His Left Wing.

With a dip of his chin he agreed to the placement of landmines. A pixie approached, to whom he gave his blessing and a week's worth of provisions for him and his family who he desired to see relocated on the rough, rocky cave ridden terrain south of the city. He secured transportation out of the realm for several other families that morning and by the afternoon he had physically gone to each location of supply caches evenly distributed throughout the city. He caught sight of Wisteria's hard work organizing rows of sickbeds and lingered near the outpost to hear conversions of those who were either too dumb or brave enough to place his heartmark's name in their mouths.

His mind buzzed too loudly with all the hearsay to dive into the particulars of what he gathered. Kai making a move for the realm's seat of authority wasn't new news nor was he particularly impressed that the First Faction was demanding an audience at the Opal Lake to confirm or dispel rumors. It was, however, a terrible time to call for a caucus amongst a conclave. We were on the cusp of a war of worlds; there was no time for Zander to self-reflect.

War called for leadership. Kai possessed immeasurable amounts, but Zander's love for the realm was unmatched where his brothers were concerned. He'd hoped Kai would reconsider given that he heartmarked Athromancia's vessel and his loyalty woven descended from two other Eternals. A nymph chirped up four streets over. "Water wolf stalks her like she is pack. The tricksy fox, he knows. Not a fan of the cold, but allows Torvi scrutinize from afar. Savior she calls her. Nervous she looks."

"Wolf is cozy with the Yolanda lass. They yearn to return to vibrant lands and disband. Oh, yes. Disband with a bang! Dreamers want to accompany them. So fun, so fun! Over the mountains we go!"

The incubus turned off his ears when his palate was distracted. A memorable sweetness hit the tip of his tongue. Brown sugar.

Fennick walked past him on the opposite side of the street separating the smithing circle from the residential one. His usual light scents of concentrated magic and woodsiness were blanketed by a new flavor. One he was quickly acquiring a taste for.

Bathing never removed Wisteria's scent fully from his skin. When his corlimor began lusting for his brother, her scent stained him deeply into his skin and soul. And Fennick's drenched hers, even though his eyes never trespassed where she willed them to venture and certainly not his hands or his cock as his Wisteria wished. He was dedicated to remaining her protective woven until she was ready to accept the obvious.

Zander easily concluded Fennick was a better, meritorious male than he. Although, this morning when he found Fennick rummaging in the trash he almost teased him for succumbing to his nosey, compulsive behaviors when he held up a handwritten note from his flower—several of them.

Notes that cleaved him in half and mended him a moment later. For she wrote her sendoffs to them and signed it, 'With love, your Wisteria.'

She had felt it then. What they had. Love.

Yet, she said nothing of the sort. She simply left to embark on her next journey to awaken her deceiving lover's blood then attempt to do what Zander could not–control his magic and help people with it.

Whatever she came back as, she would forever remain his Wisteria. He could not fathom admiring her more than he already did while she was human. Scars, witty charm and all. Golden blood changed absolutely nothing. His fangs sunk into his lower lip as a broad smile emerged onto his chiseled, bearded face. He was imagining her returning to him even more violent and harder hitting. He tried not to think about his twitching pants and forced himself to look up and address the skulk of foxes behind Fen.

He crossed the street in three easy strides.

Momo gave him a kiss on his cheek then slapped it in the harsh affectionate way that his older brother's often did when they greeted one another. "Suppose you're going to lecture me. I haven't been to visit much as of late."

Rivatt shifted from her tawny brown furry form into a mostly clad young woman. She addressed him on Momo's behalf. "We much prefer dining with Wisteria. She chews with her mouth closed." Zander shook his large jaw loose, feigning a threat. Rivatt snorted. "Remain in conclave."

Rivatt left the rest of her opinions unspoken. The ones where she implied leading that damn conclave and the realm was his vocation.

Wisteria was his new vocation, his present and future. Every moment he could spare would be at her side. Not ready to tarnish the lingering scent of peaches, he passed on the embrace several foxes attempted to give him. They shifted and spun their bodies around his ankles as an alternative.

"Fen, walk with me." The southern elvish scribes stayed several yards back as they stepped up the stairs to the towers of the rampart. They leaned over the stone wall twice as thick as Landsfell's, the fields below

ablaze with the ire of wandering elementals encircling their Eternal Elm with prayers. And bombs. And landmines. "What do you feel?" He asked the male with silver hair, obstructing golden eyes and a grimace of worry.

"What I always feel. Her." He meant that in more ways than one. She was all consuming. He understood that too well.

His reply was low and heated despite there being an obscura cast. "I need to feel more of her. From the Godsdamn inside." After yesterday's intimacy, Zander knew Fennick's physical and emotional needs would soon be erupting through the patient and controlled friend Wisteria needed him to be up to this point. He'd been denying his foxy disposition and tendencies. Consequences would catch up. "I know not what mortal magic designed her perfectly to pair with us, but she does and I could not be more fucking elated. This bullshit with the Vulborg and runegate makes terrible timing for pursuing her. I don't want her to believe for a moment our consummation was rushed due to an impending war, death and regrets." The incubus risked a look upward into the elemental's molten gaze. He saw the question simmering behind them and answered before he drew breath.

"Shortly after she left I sensed a bursting, I can only assume that was the ascension. Our bond has quieted since." Their syphering had broken off after the portal swallowed her. A tattooed hand moved over the fox's hearts, over the seed and wedding rings he carried around his neck. "She is alive. Ik Kygen, Brock and Percy would have run their asses back here if things had gone differently." True.

"Why did you allow Percy to accompany them?" The peak of the vulpine nose twitched, he wrestled down the urge to bop it with his index finger or trace along his shaven jawline. He'd be requiring all his fingers to keep his corlimor satisfied upon her return, not burnt off by his best friend.

"He seems to be doing better in their company. I'd never seen him attempt to get sober, I am willing to bet Ik Kygen's presence and his paternal relationship with Wisteria is reawakening his past. The whole conversation about Lochlin may have stirred his inner soldier or perhaps

he still treasures Ik Kygen and does not want him to lose his daughter, so he unconsciously is protecting Wisteria."

"Or he is trying to reconcile before he goes into the beyond. Kora and Lochlin went into the white light when they died, he wants to make sure he earns enough merit to join them in the Ether." His hands aimlessly examined the rough stone composition. They should have been holding a feminine pair of hands which donned that scrap metal ring Wisteria was oddly fond of. The craving for his hands to hold her never lessened. Words continued to fall from his mouth. *"Besides, he is the third person in their party outside of Maruc that can vouch for events happening outside of my reach. He knows the sanctity of heartmarking. He will not sway or charm. I trust him even if he doesn't trust himself."* His older brother hardly recognized himself. But Zander saw who he was beneath the ruin and admired Percy's earnestness from a young age.

"Wisteria, gets a kick out of bantering with Percy. He got her to laugh, a real *laugh."* Mixed emotions twisted the handsome features on Fennick's face. An unhealed laceration from where jealousy struck. Similar emotions that spiked through his fuming body when he watched Athromancia and Wisteria uninhibitedly flirt, wickedly dance and embrace the love in the room without diminishing her own feelings. *"I hate that she doesn't do it more often."* The pair stiffened.

Fennick lashed. *"And I hate her separated from us. It's wrong. It's bullshit. If Maruc knows about the three of us, then he should have brought her back to the Veil to train in the mountains. Bastard wants to see us lose our sanity."* Fen pivoted and pressed his back against the stone. *"There is nothing but rubble and rock south of the city in high elevation, I should have recommended they practice there, within reach of our manifesting threads. I'd feel better; henceforth, I'd be more productive. It's logical."*

"Whatever you need to tell yourself."

The silver fox nipped at the air. *"What are you telling yourself to survive and stop the intrusive thoughts of ripping out everyone's tongue for talking and distracting you from thinking about her gyrating in the hot spring?"* Gods, half the water in the tub splashed out and spilt over the *edge once Wisteria decided to try out a new position. He'd no idea it was possible for a person's body to be so bendy, so fuckably flexible.*

"Such immoral uncelibate thoughts." Zander's arm hair was burnt off for his quip. He did not wince or scowl. He stepped closer to his fire wielder until they rested shoulder to shoulder.

"She consumes my mind. My soul. I've yet to cease thinking about her." He wasn't capable of it. Neither were. "She is out there in an unfamiliar world, embodying unfamiliar magic, to use to aid an unfamiliar nation which hasn't proven itself worthy of her. If she is strong enough to shoulder that shit, then I can do my part. Choice or duty, matters not anymore. I'm trying to keep perspective. A perspective that doesn't involve me gazing up at her from under her pierced petals." Zander elbowed the male next to him. "A perspective you could have shared were you not—"

"Were I not wise enough to retain the desire to live? To keep us alive? To prevent you from collecting more regrets? Yeah, you are welcome." The triangle ears atop his head peaked, turning against the wind. The taller of the companions dropped his composure to place a sociable kiss between the set of ears. Since no phrase of gratitude equated, that gesture sufficed.

No words were needed. They shared every heart beat for the last hundred and fifty nine years.

Warmth cupped his bicep as the hand atop it called to be touched. "The Elm will not fall. You will not leave me alone this lifetime or the one after." His palm met the backs of Fennick's knuckles and he enfolded their hands together. The incubus reached down into the tangled web of red threads and yanked on the bond. Fennick's mind jolted forward at the abrupt dominance that ushered him onto a single knee.

Submission.

Zander, for the first and only time since the Weaver interrupted their lives, called into existence the power of their loyalty bond. He did so without hesitation.

Fennick did not fight his master's will as his knee met the stone. "You are forbidden from dying. You will do everything in your power to keep Wisteria alive, as I will be doing for you both. No matter what happens to the Elm, you do not enter the beyond without Wisteria and I at your furry fucking side. That is an order, Fennick Feign."

Steam. Evidence a tear had been shed.

"Sharpest swords, cruelest spells, thickest shields, fastest wings. Best in the bloody realm, do you hear me you dense-skulled, horn-headed cloud-fucker?" The retired Overlord thumped his chest. He had already made plans to venture into the hells of the confinement. The underbelly of the beast. They were desperate enough to seek sage advice from rancorous murderers and the cleverness of the insane. "Rally your peoples Lord of Darkness and I will tend to mine. For if we cannot save this world and create peace for Wisteria to live in, to laugh in, *then I will destroy it so she can stand among the ashes and plant her fertile fields. Know this, I will pledge myself to the trithrone if gaining Maruc's legion saves any or all of us. That just leaves you to sort out your baggage because as it stands, the Ivory Legion will only protect the entrance to Akelis and Ilanthia itself."*

"I don't foresee ever submitting to that pledge."

"The Ivory Legion adds twenty thousand to our numbers, most of them full or half blessed blood. They can heal faster and their stamina is unmatched, save for the free fighting Ilanthians. We may need them on the battlefield. Actually, I'm fucking certain we need them on the battlefield."

"Or we may not. I'm not risking placing Wisteria in political chains nor seating myself on a throne when the world knows how destructive and pathetic I am." The incubus had much to sort through and for the first time since Fennick granted him immortality, he didn't have enough time to decide.

"You are not pathetic. If I hear you utter that nonsensical shit again, I will have to resort to your favorite lessons from back in the day."

He released a growl that vibrated the blacksteel ax strapped across the length of his back. "Just don't starve me and toss me into a minotaur maze."

"You emerged confident and secure of your own strengths."

"I was half dead in a desert for three months you dimwit."

"You say half dead, I say half alive. You're welcome."

Fennick was shaking with inspiration when he strode off the ramparts to the crowd awaiting him. Those few moments overlooking the fields were the last the two had together over the span of a week. For when the suspicious wolves Wyatt had pursued in the shadows began to act out— it was in the manic and aggressive form of ice shards plunged into Zander's chest.

Zander was too stunned to yell for aid as he stared down at the shards puncturing his body and the warm blood draining out of him. Luckily, the Keep snapped into action.

"Tanya missed your heart by an inch. You're fortunate," Mikleah mumbled irrelevant things to him as he lay on the library floor, Kailynder and Fennick sprinted in at the sound of the elves' warning trumpets blaring from inside the Keep. They'd been breached internally. Zander

collected the scents of everyone present and painted a target on their backs.

He would have risen to disembowel his attacker, but his loyal guardian had this managed. "Where is that ratchet, wet dog? Her twin woven won't be able to identify her corpse when I'm done." Fennick's flames were so thick they blocked out Kai's form entirely. Atticus' black mass engulfed the corner as he prepared to sway her to eat herself alive–fur, frost and all. Slowly. Starting by ingesting her skin, muscle and bone. He'd seen him sway prisoners to torment themselves. Atticus did not lack creativity. Nor did Fennick for that matter. The kill was designated for his woven now.

Alethim held the wolf down with a dagger pierced through her thigh and anchored in the floor below her. His bow was taut and arrow locked. "Did Torvi finally go mad and convince you to betray your pack and nation with a little twin woven compulsion?" Fennick was yelling. He spit. Ash flew from his mouth.

The injured horselord didn't order him to stop. For starters he couldn't catch a breath with the shock of his injury wearing off. Secondly, there was no talking sanity into a loyalty woven when their bonded was assaulted or remotely injured. The threads would not allow it.

As much as he wanted to interrogate Tayna, he knew Fennick was going to rain hellfire upon her corpse and resolve to take the heat from the council later. Alethim said his name in warning, but it went unanswered. The show began.

Snarls and screams escaped as Tayna transformed back into a female form, her mangled leg remained that of a canine's. "I am saving this nation! Our beautiful realm!" She bellowed. "Zander will unleash death upon all of us if we survive! You should be thanking me!" She stared at her executioner which took the form of a man with nine white tails running towards her with hands of bright fury. Half the room shielded their eyes from his element. Zander admired it.

The incubus bleeding under Mauve's healing hands, shuddered at the darkness of Oyokos' magic dripping from his pores when he caught Tanya's words. He had been correct all these decades to lock this magic *away. Many yet thought him a monster. Still feared and in need of repenting. Nothing he did would be enough. How was he ever to be worthy of Wisteria's love?*

Alethim suppressed a gag as the first layers of Tanya's skin were burnt off revealing the charred ligaments and structures below. Fen melted her lips together until her cries were intelligible. The Left Wing backed further away from the murder taking place when he was no longer needed. "Don't be cruel unless you are planning on getting answers," his wise old ass offered.

Fine. Her death came swift.

A severed head rolled to the elf's feet. Fennick dropped to Zander's side, slit his wrist and milked several mouthful of blood past his lips. There was no protesting or reprimanding. Hardly any talking as they lay collapsed on the floor together, one second guessing his magic and the other furiously wielding his.

Atticus would be Zander's security while he went about the rest of his day. Fennick abandoned his post to seek out Torvi and the rest of the Frost Pack to which she now held the role as their alpha.

She was a useless alpha. A broken, unravelling woven thread.

Overcome with emotion and unable to build the trust of her fellow wolves after she went wayfinding for decades and her sister tried to assassinate a citizen. Fennick watched her roll around in the icy river sick with grief. Good. An abandoned woven would either off themself or die in a way that held significance.

Wyatt was on Fennick's tails for days ensuring he didn't kill Torvi before an interrogation or devised one of his fucked up correctional lessons.

After the earth jarred one late evening, Zander and Atticus agreed to start stationing a variety of watchful eyes on the barrier with an entire family of foxes to retain alertness. A second earthquake happened two nights after the first. And entire units of archers were designated to their posts.

He inspected the runegate in the dead of night. The rune stones weren't harmed and the demons looked just as taken off guard as the living.

Somewhat of an encouraging sign. The ramparts stayed armed nonetheless.

Kashikat and Zander gave up half their purses and two hundred years of investments to a hermit in the crags. He saddled wyrms and wyvern for a living. Trained them as well as anyone might tame a dragon descendant and an earth eating, blind monster whose circular jaw constituted its entire face.

A face that could swallow Atticus into its rotting bowels with a single chomp.

Kashikat opted to fly with the sixteen leashed wyvern back to the city. Which left Zander riding atop the putrid worm. All too willingly he abandoned that filthy, spineless thing in the crystal caves with cartloads of goats and cattle bones to pick over. He paid the other half of his coin purse to the pixies who allowed him to rent out their home until after the war. The home would be unsalvageable. He paid them handsomely knowing this.

Four layers of skin he scrubbed off that night. The trousers he rode in were in the rubbish bin.

Warroh appeared to have taken a meal and not a moment too soon. Had his contemptuous, aggressive behaviors continued Atticus and Wyatt were going to lock him in the temples away from conclave until he stopped spewing religious shit about blackmailing the Gods, Athromancia needing a formal farewell and Godsdamned Judeth— Atticus had her removed from the Keep after he overheard that she and Kailynder ostracized Wisteria with a single word.

Rogue.

A rogue was a foul word. One sparingly used in the Veil. It took a true rogue years of living among the dreamers and their commitment to hate crimes to be labeled an unwanted outsider and have the kindness of society stripped from them. The fact a human who offered her comparatively weak body and few youthful years to aid strangers was isolated upon arrival sat well with none who valued their citizenship and homelands.

Atticus gave voice and presence to unity and acceptance. He saw that those virtues pervaded his home realm even if the rest of the world saw discord and segregation. For his own son to condone such a thing was disheartening more than it was preposterous. Kai got an earful about Oyoko's values and what it meant to be forged from his likeness.

Kai was lucky all he received from the nation was a cold shoulder and not earned himself the very label he bestowed onto the golden vessel. Zander could count the times on one hand his father looked at him with those charcoal eyes and the raw intensity that poured out of them when he was disappointed. He remembered the burning of vomit that erupted from him when he was first overwhelmed by the incubus' power, that was before he grew into his own horns later that day. Fuck. He didn't envy his eldest brother, but he deserved it.

The whole city looked at Kai with distaste, but they all needed him to lead his ten thousand swords and this two thousand specialized Rudins he'd been training rigorously since before Waning Star birthed its favorite spotted horselord.

Their contempt only ran so deep and forgiveness came swifter than he deserved.

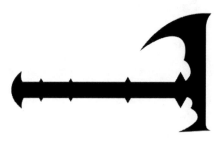

Days passed since the attack.

Torvi was in wolf form directly under the keen eyes of Wyatt, likely on the mental leash of his powerful fae brother. A disheveled Torvi leaned into Yolanda's side body. Yolanda had heard the news by now yet allowed the elemental to use her as comfort. Again, he noted they pair of them were always under Wyatt's cautious supervision.

Comradery amongst confusion. Torvi was incapable of offering any decent *company, she was hardly keeping herself alive and her mangy appearance confirmed that. By some act of what he considered psychosis she hadn't committed suicide or retaliate to the shaming cast upon her at the Keep.*

Yolanda pushed the large paw off of a heaping mail pile and began to shuffle through it. Wyatt saw what he knew to be depression and doom carved into her eyes, lingering torment no doubt. She dodged Zander's glance when he walked near them and Yolanda who busied her hands with pen and quill.

Fennick had been right to be worried. With the twin bond gone, separated woven didn't last long. Whatever damage the high courts of Numaal inflicted on her followed Torvi here. Perhaps, Yolanda's vengeance was giving her something to go out fighting for. He gave a cheery greeting regardless of his desire to imprison her in a graveyard and have Wyatt raid her mind again.

He found nothing but hollowness. Perhaps if her twin bond were intact, she'd be more pliable. She was nothing now.

"Evening, big guy." Yolanda stopped mid story to return a wave.

"Planning the demise of the Torvals?"

"And every greedy pig who supports them and their Remnants."

"Dibs on the priestess." His eye twitched when hate pummeled into his gut. To think Wisteria had caught sight of his illusion of him and Collette engaged in fuckery of any sort, sent violent tremors through his chest. Nikki said she had gotten physically ill and turned somewhat into a spiteful, ignorant bitch. Jealousy got his cock hard, knowing she was hiding behind her mislabeled emotions.

Yolanda's rounding cheeks rose. Regretfully humorous, she shook her head. "Fennick already called dibs on her. You should have heard him seething on the ship. Detailing all the ways he was going to skin her, keep her alive to heal and start the process again." Zander gave a disappointed grumph. Torvi whimpered at the mention of her sister's killer. "Havnoc is for Wisteria and Keenan. You can have the prince and the king should he be alive."

His burly arms crossed his chest. "Fine." He let out a scoff and sat next to his brother, quickly holding him to his chest and locking a fistful of his silver hair in his calloused grip. Fen mewed at the contact.

"Fine? Do you know how many people would be thrilled to have that honor?"

"Prince Torval is manipulating the love of my life into a marriage. Killing him is too fucking kind of me. His father is an idiot." The back of the couch broke when he threw his mass onto it. Wyatt was quick to reinforce it with a mound of rose bushes behind him.

"What about you? Who are you setting out to slaughter?"

She cackled. "Where do I start?"

"Gimlian Monte." He stated as if it was the obvious choice. Though he knew little of her life as a courtesan, he had experienced plenty to know how rutting awful it had to have been serving the high courts in debt, rather than as a free woman making dignified choices.

"I took my sister's sentence in the sex slave industry so she would not have to suffer the unwanted abuse of another. He fucked that up when he raped her." Her detachment and bluntness brought eyes on onlookers. "Sage will be the one to finish the job and if she doesn't want to get her hands dirty, I'll oblige." Wyatt gave a nod of approval, petite stems of greenery grew over his forearms. Zander's siblings were many things, most of them were not rapists. Clavey was the only one known to sway and charm for revenge to which there were significant repercussions.

Then there was his father, siring males of different races over the eons.

Wyatt seemed to read his mind and blew an exasperated breath from his lips. Atticus was a complex creature to sort. It hurt his cerebellum to embark on that mental expedition further. He had tried to tackle the enigma that was Atticus di Lucient since his childhood and succeeded only in muddling up his father's perception and their familial communication. He was surreptitious about his inner workings, lucky one of Zander's brothers had been born of a succubus and offered what insight he could about their elusive predisposition to crave influence and be seen as competent.

His sensitive gouge on his left horn ached from where Kailynder tried to diminish his power when he was but a young buck. When Wisteria touched that little spot with her healer hands, pain never seeped in. Even when she gripped them firmly while she rode his face, agony was the furthest thing from his mind.

His gaze floated around the bustling room while his mind replayed Atticus's reaction to Wisteria grabbing his horns to draw him into a lip lock with zero awareness of his public surrender to her. He snickered at her idea of walking around oblivious and carefree with his bite on her neck. Wife wasn't even an appropriate term for what he had declared her.

The Weaver would tend to the rest in due time.

Touching an incubi's horns was essentially a death wish. In the primitive days of civilization they were. His father had many sentenced to lifetimes in the Squandering Seas for even asking to behold his horns, the source of on incubi's power. He nearly lost his shit when he saw his youngest son forfeit his entire being and might to a human girl who had just finished breaking Ik Kygen's face and wrapping her arms around Fennick.

He'd surrender himself and grovel at her feet to all but hear her say his bloody name. Not pathetic. Love was anything but. He often wondered if Atticus had ever truly loved any of his child bearers.

The sound of dull thunder echoed faintly from the mountains. His gaze was cast out one of the many windows as the room tensed.

"That's not thunder." Yolanda placed a hand on Wyatt and another on Torvi to steady herself as the Keep held its breath waiting for the ground to rumble. This was a smaller earthquake, hardly anything to notice this time around outside of a few swaying lights. "It's like the ground we live on is grieving all the innocent blood that has saturated it." Yolanda pulled her arms back and felt for the sturdy sword Fennick had gifted her in Landsfell.

"Are all humans this optimistic?" Wyatt's flat tone spurred a fist to form from the woman at his side. "Before you launch that at me, try to see my words for what they were. A compliment. Or go on, strike me and find your knuckles ridden with splinters." Her scowl stayed. Her fist lowered.

"Let us hope the earth is merely grieving." Thinking about demons inhabiting the ground under them caused Zander's skin to prickle up his scalp. "Little Moon, whistle for your nephew's falcon. I saw it flying around hours ago. It refuses to land."

Sharp tones piped through the air in a series of short inflections. His calling cut through conversations time and time again before a shrill returned. His milky eye took on the wide pupil of a bird and he smiled as he saw the worlds through the familiar falcon's point of view as he had learned to do with receptive animals across the three nations.

Crescent glided gracefully from the rafters, perching on Zander's outstretched arm with sharpened pinpoint claws. His fingers were a bit relentless until he untied the waxy parchment on the bird's talon. No sooner was it removed did the bird take flight. Zander combed over the words, torn between elation and shock. "Wyatt, prepare your mind for more optimism. Humans, two hundred strong will be arriving in Veona any day now."

The room quieted, but Zander didn't notice because he was too busy watching Yolanda's reaction as he handed her the letter.

A letter written by Bastion. The leader of her rebellion.

He was coming.

Chapter Twenty-Eight

A purple firework captured his attention in the corner of his intellect, distracting him from stalking the Frost Pack any further. The last flair Z had sent him to accept their transplacency was after Tanya stabbed him. That bitch.

The fox curled into himself and disappeared from sight under a glacial patch of snow. The wolves in the area knew he had been sniffing around but they didn't see him as a threat. Just a messenger for his woven, a male they respected. Mostly.

He killed their alpha—it was within his rights to stalk about as threatening as he saw fit. And if it weren't, he'd do it regardless. Woven liberties and the soul contract allowed him to be as overbearing as he needed to be to satiated his tendencies. And without Wisteria here, he may have considered himself a tad fussy.

An attempted assignation had been wrought on all of their lives. That sky shifter at least was consistent in attracting death assuring Fennick that all the precautions in place for his wovens were in fact not over the top, but necessary. Wisteria and Z didn't even know the half of what he does to ensure their lives run smoothly. He excelled at keeping them alive. He latched onto the mind flair, Zander instantly anchored him in his perception.

Zander opened a paper. He showed him a letter which he devoured and promptly took off sprinting down the river bed of the north facing mountain. This was not the letter he'd been expecting. There was no Monte emblem on it. He checked in with the owlery twice a day to try and intercept any letters from the Southlands returning to Wisteria, so he and Zander could handle the reply and possible repercussions for her undermining, should accusations arise.

In his fox form he sprinted down the snowy incline and sent a fireball to scare off the eagles perched by the elf in charge of the mail exchange. They shat on his boots and he chased them down and out of the vicinity.

Fennick took the opportunity to shuffle through two leather bound bags of mail. He stole the one with the name Wisteria Woodlander inked on it and leapt out the east facing window with the parchment in his maw.

He was not exactly sure what to anticipate from Bastion and his gang of rebels and purchased arms, but it certainly wasn't manners. He was stunned into quiet surprise watching the unkempt and exhausted men and women pause respectfully over a warm meal awaiting their hosts to break bread first. They were disheveled and clearly in awe of this Dreamer Realm, but humble.

They arrived worn and thin, Veona ensured that they were fed before their parties exchanged intel. The more he evaluated the room, the more Fennick came to uncover the layers that constitute the enigma of the man known as Bastion.

He would have to have been well learnt in manners and have a great familiarity with the courts to move about as he did with finesse and stealth. Count Hilderbrand had heard several of his most triumphant feats including sabotaging trade routes and spreading that food and wealth among rural towns, killing the queen's knight in the Pits and seeding educational reforms in the poorer areas. He gained the majority of the general public's favor. Unfortunately, the wealthiest top ten percent of the Kathra's populace made all the financial decisions and allocation resources for the masses.

Bastion's grimy hair and skull tattoo on his throat did nothing to inspire confidence, yet Yolanda hadn't not stopped ogling him for the brilliant bastard he was. And he was boldly, yet modestly a mastermind. She waited with baited breath at Zander's side, eager to pounce on introductions. Going as far as to elbow Zander's side to speed things along. Wyatt's shade of green envy sprout foliage around his collarbones.

The expansive marble room of hundreds seated themselves and started on a delayed afternoon lunch. Honestly, it was a welcomed feast for new peaceful friends after how hard the realm had been working days on end prior. It was a pause in the dread. And thanks to Wisteria's arrival, new incomers from the east did not correlate with trouble. They actually inspired more hope, vigor and curiosity. Their arrival reinforced to the dreamers that far more was at stake then we understood.

"I know you, horselord." Bastion washed his first bite down with water and set his goblet to the side. "You were Cultee's enthusiastic first hand, Drift. I had eyes on you since the moment you showed up in the Southlands. I didn't know if you were dangerous or possibly up for recruitment when I saw you trying to weasel and enchant your way into the inner circles."

"Flattered." His woven gave one of his personable smiles, he must have smelt decent intentions or he wouldn't have offered that much. "And what have you concluded? Am I trouble?"

"No. But you would have been in deep shit if the woodlander didn't rescue you from the trap you ensnared yourself in while schmoozing up to Remnants. Was it bones that fell to the floor? She has some gusto, ey?" The table laughed. Gusto? Is that what they were calling her unpredictability and recklessness?

"That she does."

"Speaking of the woodlander, when will she be back?" He looked expectantly around the room. When Zander didn't reply he looked to another. Him. "Count Nicholo Hilderbrand, correct? My sources among us confirmed that you were the man to purchase that silken white robe our stunning savior wore to the winter gala. You seem to be close,

maybe you can provide answers. Have you an inkling when she will return?"

Our savior? Our? No.

Not his. Not theirs.

The elemental's hand pressed into Zander's back, absorbing the anger that was causing his jaw to lock and knuckles whiten all while he felt the same violent irritation strangling each breath and beat of his hearts. Possessiveness. His magic drank emotions in and burnt them away in a downpour of fire under his feet.

The dreamers and Numaalians around the city had not hidden the recent developments regarding Wisteria's blood or the Vulborg at the gate. Wisteria's underfed corlimor was less than thrilled to hear another lay claim to the woman that would be his wife. The one to draw a circle around the trio and bind them together.

The fire curled around his toes and he let flames unfurl at his fingertips for show. "There is no South Isle count present. I am called Fennick. Ilanthian, fire elemental and friend to Wisteria who you seem to think has personal business with you."

Bastion raised a calm brow. "Apparently, you are not close with your friend if you believe she does not have business with me. Maybe she doesn't know who she had been in cahoots with since each time we met each other, we used aliases." There were multiple occasions where Wisteria had been working with this sullied, backwards genius?

The moisture in his mouth was burnt out. The air around him tasted of volcanic soot and cinders that his greedy lungs welcomed. The napkin on his lap was crisped in seconds. "I came here looking for the one person who can save Numaal from itself and found a nation on the brink of war to the same plague assaulting us. I found those here are selfishly hiding her away when she belongs to everyone. And now, I hear she has Athromancia's magic and Orion's blessing... the east needs her. Your scribes confirmed there was mention of blood crafting, she needs to pummel the capital before it is too late."

"Woah, woah. We are not hiding her," Wyatt approached behind Zander trying to prevent what happened next. *"Take it easy with your assumptions. My brother has made it clear she is a lady who makes her own decisions. She had her own agenda to fulfill with the Eternals and is off with the Emperor and by no means intentionally avoiding a return to her unsalvageable homelands."*

Fennick did nothing when Zander erupted in a vicious display of wings, horns and fangs. Snickering, he added golden fire essence to merge with his violet extension coiling around the table like a serpent analyzing his prey. He hoped Bastion would choke on his damn words and think twice about his unlawful declarations. Atticus looked pleased while the ragged looking fighters at Bastion's side gave a warning snarl after they finished gawking at the transformed horselord. For once the incubi brothers at the table kept their damn mouths shut. That was seven less arguments to be had.

A human girl shoved by Wyatt, unperturbed by the thorns nicking her arm. "Cut it out, Zander. You made your point, you love her. We all see that, but stop picking fights with our allies. The enemy of our enemy is our friend, right?" Yolanda reached across the table with her hand outstretched. "Yolanda d'Loure at your service. I've been trying to contact you for years, but with the false ploys and murders of courtesans and our buyers—I couldn't risk it." Bastion took her hand and blinked several times as if his eyes deceived him. As her name clicked into place, he allowed the fond smile on his face to grow. I could practically hear his gears working on how to best use her magnificent strengths of political knowledge and lethal secrets to his advantage.

"Yolanda? Landsfell's diamond?" She offered a characteristically snarky nod paired with a well-practiced alluring grin. "You'd shot down my two attempts to meet your acquaintance, so I pushed on gathering intel the difficult way. By paying off shadows and getting my hands bitten by deceitful snakes. I'd no idea you were interested in the uprising. How did Madam Marmancient ever let you go or did you flee in the chaos of battle as did most indebted?" He released her hand, but kept her engaged. Wyatt hissed at Bastion's lingering interest.

"Myself, Fennick and Brock Ironside lit the pyres that warned the city. I was leagues south by the time the wraiths attacked."

A pregnant minute passed. "You were a free woman prior to the gala." It was neither a question or statement. Bastion's wheels turned. Yolanda ran her fingers through her short, feathery hair. "The price of your debt wouldn't happen to have been seven hundred thousand and forty-three hundred in pastels, would it?"

Yolanda and Fennick glanced at each other, unsettled. "How could you possibly know that?"

Bastion drank from his goblet. "You have a good friend in Wisteria. And that is putting it lightly."

Yolanda was shouting what she felt entitled to know. "How did she earn it?" Bastion's eyes met Zander's. There was a smugness to them that questioned his love of Wisteria. Of who we came to know as Wisteria.

No wise soul at the table vocalized their look of surprise that innocent, unaware Wisteria had been dealing with the rebellion conductor right under their noses. For better or for worse by the looks of it.

They comprehended her better than she could fathom herself, this asshat was just working his way under their skin. As infuriating as he found him, he was not stupid enough to turn away the potential extra help. Zander was not Kailynder. He gave a temper smile at Bastion. "You should ask her. It's an inspiring tale that led to a chain of events. I'll even go so far as to say she is the reason Drift got promoted and taken into the tight circle of the Torval's family as a knight just days before the winter gala. She threw her spare change at me to hire mercenaries to protect the hospitals and orphanages in Landsfell the night leading up to the wraiths. She has got a big heart, but unfortunately a death wish and limited means."

Yolanda's face was full of bread and her hands were flourishing around as she tried to make sense of things. "Zander got promoted because the queen's knight was slayed in the Pits." The rough suited man who reeked of tobacco, stale shit and traveled adjacent to Bastion chortled. That fucker knew something too.

The night he'd been playing chess and drinking spirits with Brock— Wisteria stayed absent. She didn't arrive till later the following morning smelling of blood, death and sweat. "She fought in the Pits." Fennick spotted the twinkle of confirmation in their company's faces.

Fucker leaned over his brimming plate and laughed loudly. "There wasn't much fighting. She executed her opponents straight out the gate. Few had time to pose a challenge, the rest were too busy underestimating her. Or him. She was dressed as a male and went by the name Keenan. She was the most beautiful star sent affirmation that the uprising had been praying for all these years."

Bastion's hand went up. Fucker went silent. "That's enough, Pete. I'm sure they know how skilled she is when properly motivated." Fucker had a name. Pete. Bastion's brown eyes softened when they relocated to Yolanda. "She made it out unscathed and I did as she requested when she came back a week later and threw a bag of coins at my face."

Yolanda looked lifeless for a long minute. "She killed for my freedom?"

"She triumphed as morally as anyone could leaving the Pits. No remorse clung to her as I sent her out of the slums. Perks of being the prison Warden, I provided the criminal records of those who she faced with a master and she rid foul convicts, serial killers and perverts."

Pete carried on. "The whole crowd fell in love once she started demonstrating showmanship. I was sad to see her run off with her earnings." He bit his lip and made a noise typically heard over a slice of pie. Wisteria was not a pie he'd ever get a slice of. "Soaked in blood and bids, she ran off with my heart."

Fennick retracted Pete's name from his memory. Fucker. His name would remain Fucker.

Fucker snapped at Fennick who had unintentionally melted his utensils. "Stop orchestrating my death in that fiery skull of yours. I kept her from being hunted by shadows when she left and froze her ass off on the roofs until sunup. She made it almost the entire night without any trace of her Ilanthian's training being detectable, only the contortionist circus act imprinted on the audience. Until the last two fights, her backsteps were a wee bit too quick and she was pegged for a silver. I made sure no royal or high lord's assassins found her or turned her in for a pretty penny while you slept."

He had not been sleeping. He was drunk and conceding to Brock in a chess tournament.

Fine. His name was Pete. Only because he saved Wisteria's life.

"That idiot! She could have gotten herself killed." Yolanda seethed. Her tears as stubborn as her resolve refused to fall.

"She should have been killed when she spat in the face of the royal family and shouted their secrets to the room of thousands who were duped, but instead she walked out with an Ilanthian child and a marriage proposal." Bastion was blunt. "She told me to go west if I survived the bloodshed at Landsfell. Judging by the looks on everyone's faces, I take it Wisteria probably threw that comment out there on a whim. Alas, here I am. Alive. Westward. Ready to take on Kathra with Athromancia and Orion's love child at my side if she will consider it. And you too, Yolanda d'Loure. For Wisteria lacks the grace required to scheme subtly. She is more of a go for the heart kind of woman, surviving off of anger and adrenaline. Together, you balance each other out. Two queens in Kathra is better than any quarter of a king."

"Wisteria lacks nothing." Fennick and his woven growled in unison. Damn if that moment didn't give away their equal devotion and claim they had on the simple crafter in which princes, Eternals and rebel leaders all sought after.

Zander's cutlery twisted into a metallic ball in his hand. One wrong word and he would be ripping tongues out and grilling them for dinner. His predatory stillness blanketed the room with morphing magical tension that rippled up the sides of the white stone pillars. It was Fennick who spread his fire around the parameters of the room, burning up excessive murderous intentions and breaking the high strung silence. "Wisteria Woodlander, makes her own choices. Whatever she chooses, wherever she journeys, she does so on her own accord." He emphasized the final statement tearing from in between his canines. "But she does not go alone."

Alethim raised his chin and motioned to the rippling barrier stretched into the skyline. "There will be no where in Kinlyra to journey should our efforts here fail." The elf drew the humans' attention.

"Sounds like you need extra blades, some bows and some red blooded grit."

"Are you offering?"

Bastion grinned. "Depends. It sounds as if it is the correct and only action to take, if what you are saying about the Vulborg are true. My final decision will be made after I speak with the woodlander."

Kailynder raised his hand. Waiting for his brother and father to grant him permission to open his treacherous mouth. Zander was too preoccupied holding back his claws which led Atticus to approve his eldest's request. "How do we know you aren't a Remnant or a spy of those who've resurrected demons? What proof have you to give to assure us that you are not working with the blood crafters or without mind control at the present?"

Bastion appreciated the hesitation and turned his dirt cover face towards Yolanda. "Have her interrogate me with details of the Landfell's underbelly and beast of its courts alike if you've questions about my identity and mission. I'll happily subject my body for inspection of bone shards or wraith bites, but none have been placed with my knowledge. As for my mind, well, don't you have magic to break into it? Potions perhaps? Alchemy? I heard rumors of some fanciful feats from the mix-blooded brokers we've had dealings with "

Wyatt found Zander's eyes, offering the service of his fae specialty. Hardly seemed necessary given how willing Bastion was. A waste of Wyatt's time and magic when he had weapons to enchant. But, taking a risk this late in the game? No. They'd be thorough. Especially when it relates to Wisteria.

Zander would have him investigated if this man was to be in close proximity to their woven. "Yes. The fae have enchanted means. We can also make them unpleasant should deceit be detected. My brother Wyatt will be intruding on your thoughts before you step a foot in Wisteria's direction. Yolanda will be at his side to confirm details." The pair of them agreed wordlessly and Wyatt's attention trailed up and down the long tables, sniffing and sensing the newcomers.

"Do what you must." Bastion easily yielded and went on to finish his braised meats. Conversations picked up over the duration of the meal. Humans once again impressed the elemental how they adapted. Where he expected disgust, they saw intrigue. Where fear may have shaken those educated by the courts, these free peoples met the unknown with more questions, especially where pixies and fae were concerned, but rarely any unease.

Zander surrendered his seat to Yolanda who jumped directly into details of how she had imagined reforming Numaal, starting with basic rights to true education, food, shelter and occupational training. As for the dukes, royal family and courts—they were to be dismantled. Violently.

The girl had vision, Fennick would give her that. Democracy was in Numaal's future if she had anything to say about it. And she had a lot to say.

She had lived on both sides of the nation's wide set margins and if anyone knew how to close that gap, it was her. Now, Fennick and his dreamers had to ensure enough of the realm and its beings remained standing to give her the best shot to fix her homeland. That was, before the runegate had an opportunity to fall a second time.

Fennick dropped his fork. Threw it was more accurate. It landed at the heels of a rebel.

He couldn't eat when his mind and stomach were in shambles. Worrying sick about Wisteria's absence and then Zander had to go and get himself stabbed in the chest, the elemental hardly rested or had time for snuggles. His back hurt from shoving himself into narrow tunnels with buckets of wet cement that made even him feel claustrophobic.

Wisteria would make it better. All it took was her roaming hand stroking the fur down his spine as he curled into her. He'd much prefer she held him in his man form, but that would require him to embody more self control and find a better location for his raging hard on than inside her.

At least in his fox form he could crawl up on her toned body and nestle his face under her chin to inhale the pheromones which were most potent right behind her ears and in the perfect shadow between her thighs. Wisteria had no reserves holding him in his creature form. So until her red, tantalizing lips met his–that was his fate. Four legged.

He came this far without stepping out of line by making advancements towards her. Over the last weeks he developed a habit of mindlessly touching the parchments in the breast pocket of his button up. He knew Wisteria was close to deciphering her feelings and their bond. He prayed in every language he knew that she would act on them. And soon.

Bastion's dedication to his cause gave him fervent dedication to Wisteria. And it was not blind. She had unknowingly proven herself to be the biggest player in Numaal's political game. As he thought when he first caught sight of the headdress on the floor of her apartment in Landsfell, she was a contender in a game she didn't know she was playing.

Her, Yolanda and Cultee together in the east? A force of change for all vibrants. And with Bastion's resources and knowledge behind them. Numaal will see brighter days and hopefully accept help from dreamers and the blessed until Thalren in flattened and rumors are dispelled.

The tall doors opened and in walked Maruc, Ik Kygen, Cobar and Brock. Percy and Wisteria were notably missing. He felt himself grimace and stare at the emptiness where she should have been standing.

The scribes paused their writing, blotching their well of ink on parchment. "More vibrants! What a joy!" Maruc grinned an earnest grin, disregarding the humans falling to their knees at the tableside. Fennick felt his own chin dipping as if the back of his head was pushed down by an invisible hand to give respect.

Warroh rose from a deep prostration and offered the Emperor his seat at the table to which he differed. He introduced himself, signaling for those who lowered themselves to rise. "We have returned for a brief stay, a night or two so Wisteria can sleep. She doesn't sleep well separated from her dreamer comrades as evidenced by the earthquakes and drawing blades at anyone who startles her."

"She is responsible for the shaking earth?" Brock's limp had lessened significantly since his strength training. He went to Yolanda's chair and patted her shoulder. She wasted not a breath in spewing out her excitement over the new company.

Zander closed the distance. "Where is Wisteria?"

Maruc accepted a chalice of wine. "Delivering a set of acrylic paints to someone in the city." He massaged the wrinkle in his forehead. "I told her to grab anything she wanted from my sibling's rooms in the White Tower, thinking she would have grabbed Morial's armor as we are heading into a nasty war. She walked about with Aditi's hand blended paint set." Behind his beverage his face was both baffled and amused.

Fennick's fire slingshotted back onto himself, illuminating his flesh bright enough most believed he to be descended from the stars themselves. Just when he thought his attraction to that wild human peeked, she became all the more alluring and found a way to enrapture his hearts.

"We've returned earlier than expected. We've learned the hard way her nightmares collapse mountains. And when she is feeling homesick she creates portals to the Deadlands."

"Portals that wraiths throw themselves into." Brock looked abashed for interrupting the Emperor. He was easily forgiven. "I think Percy finally realized how truly nasty the demon infestation is."

The room buzzed. A mortal who could move mountains? Create tears in the space warp? The fear and awestruck excitement was contagious. This human was powerful enough to move Thalren itself.

This human was his.

"Ours." Zander corrected as if he heard his thoughts.

"Z. To Pa's." Of all the Eternal's possible belongings Wisteria had access to, she had chosen to replace his father's misplaced acrylic paint. Above all else. This woman.

For fuck's sake, if she didn't recognize that as an act of love, she truely had no sense of self.

Fennick's voice was strained. "Zander. Fucking now. I need her."

It took all but an instant to flux to his father's care complex and twice as long to reorient himself. Zander set his woven upright, leaving almost immediately for the Keep after he watched Fennick sprinting towards the front door. Percy didn't bother to stop him as he leapt over the porch he sat beside with a water canteen.

His enthusiasm was pulled back only enough so he didn't rip the oak door off its hinges. Fennick stopped entirely (hearts, body and soul) when the sight of Wisteria and his father waltzing around the living room covered in paint burned into his soul.

Chapter Twenty-Nine

Honri's hand trembled markedly causing his brush strokes to translate onto the canvas with turbulence. He was dead set on painting star lilies and tipped over two containers of muddled water in his frustration. After a fortnight of striving and struggling to access Anna's magic, I knew a thing or two about frustration.

"Here." I wedged myself in front of him, slipping the wooden brush from his arthritic grip and into mine. "I've no artistic abilities, but you can guide my hand." He hummed delightedly, encompassing my grip in his. Together we busied ourselves working on the smallest of green and brown shrubs. He flicked his wrists gently, forming the most miniscule of leaves sprouting off the foliage. If I only had that amount of delicate precision over my influx and outpour of magic then the past half turn of the moon may have gone a little differently.

Not causing landslides and opening doors into night terrors would be a good start point.

"Now, for the star lilies." He swirled whites, blues, violets and greens incrementally onto a palette with a spatula, adjusting the shade of blues by the slightest of hues each time. Unsatisfied with the blend he created, Honri pulled out a fresh hard palette and began the process again. "Not right. Not at all. My dull memory stole this vital detail from me." His excitement soon faded. More frustration surfaced. "What say you? Is this the proper color of a star lily covered with dew and kiss by moonlight?"

I looked at the lovely blue held in front of my nose. "It is a catching color, but I'm afraid I've never seen a star lily nor heard of the night gardens of Pashtu. I was sheltered and my immortal family didn't tell me nearly as much as they should have." I had yelled quite a bit at Keenan this week about his failure to inform me on anything outside of combat only to learn

Anna gave him a gag order to keep his mouth shut about the wonders of the rest of the world. She didn't want me to run off in search of something or someone greater. Or run off and get myself killed on an adventure. I cursed her selfish name again as magic swelled in my chest washing over me like a tide pulled by the moon, receding slowly with a few calming breaths.

"But you've magic. Can't you flux us there or conjure the memory for me?" His grey eyebrow peaked and his aged, eager eyes pleaded with mine.

Again, I was useless.

I swallowed my failure. "Magic is new to me." That was the best way to announce my abilities were *lacking* and I was exhausted from the times it did manifest, because when the gates opened. They swung *wide open.* "It escapes from me when I am sleeping, but when I concentrate–seldom anything happens." I held out my empty paint speckled hands.

"Ah-ha. The subconscious mind knows best."

"Maruc said something similar, *'That my limit is my imagination because magic is formless. Magic is instinctual'*. Maybe for dreamer beings who grew up in this fantastical realm and Ilanthians accustomed to accurate histories and magical feats. Not for me. I once thought I was creative, but apparently not imaginative enough for Anna's magic. It's like water. Sometimes, it's in a sealed bucket and won't come out. While other times I'm drowning in it as if it were an ocean. Rivers escape me left and right, but I can't take a damn sip. I sense it though." I pointed to my chest. "Watery tides, pulling and pushing."

Honri wore a goofy side grin. He grabbed a scarf off the closet hook and proceeded to cover my eyes. "You're overthinking." The base of a paint brush wiggled its way between my fingers.

"We've established that I am no artist."

"Shush!" I pursed my lips tight.

"Well, point me in the direction of where you want me to ruin." My tired sarcasm bit at him.

The back of my hand stung as he slapped it. "Shush. Paint the lily." I protested. He was quick to interject, "I care not if you've never seen one nor can you see currently. Create from here." A firm finger jabbed at my sternum. I felt a bruise form.

I pitied the arduous academic lessons Nikki sat through as a child. Now, I understand why Zander drank during lectures.

Nondominant fingers fumbled their way to the edge of the taut bleached leather frame. I swirled the brush where I remembered globs of paint to be and in my mind's eye envisioned the twilight blue horizon from above the clouds, the sight that confirmed my love for flying in Zander's arms. The brush met the canvas, destroying all the efforts we made on the foliage with ungraceful accents of blue. "Stunning."

"You beautiful liar."

"Keep going. Add texture and shadow."

"How? I have zero awareness."

Another slap. "Trust yourself." It was hard to do that after my nightmares had caused the faces of mountains to crumple. I was lucky no villages or valleys were inhabited near the Opal Lake. And I was exhausted from my Bloodsworns prodding me awake each time they thought I appeared restless. I almost gutted Percy when he tried kicking me awake when the fire went out.

Sleep was the reason for our return.

"Yes. Delicate work, excellent work." His praises, however unwarranted, allowed me to explore the canvas with less self consciousness. Cool water sensations pooled at my fingertips as I relaxed with his dictation, his heartening guidance.

I tapped the excess water off the brush and spun it around on the earthy palette to the right with a little guidance from Honri. There ought to be different types of flora surrounding the lilies. He said Poshtu was a proper, full garden after all. Every green space needed ferns to brighten the world and soften the steps beneath one's feet under the canopy of the forest. They also needed lilacs. Anna ensured every farm bed had at least one tree of lilacs. "Is there a light lavender tinted paint?"

Honri took my brush and replaced it with another. Lilacs were so very intricate with the hundreds of baby blossoms clinging to the stem. I focused as much as I could through the blindfold.

Maybe too much. I took a deep inhale. "I must have let the imagery consume me for I am catching wafts of lilacs in the air. Or Anna's magic is alive. I often pretended I smelt them after her murder."

"Not Anna's magic. Your magic." The scarf that I had ripped off my face I let fall. Green berm sprawled out from where I stood. Infant ferns curled around my toes and young lilac shoots spun around the base of the easel like fingers reaching up from the earth. The liquid sensation on my finger pads were bursting with life.

I gawked and gaped.

I had formed something from nothing.

The paint brush in my fingers dropped with a faint *clink.* "I did this." The cumbersome sleep I had been fighting for days suddenly disappeared with the explosion of joy thrumming through me.

"*You* did this." Honri motioned to the tiny patch on which I stood. "You cast magic."

"I cast magic! And you didn't feel the ground shake?" He denied the latter. My magic had manifested on a small scale. A controlled scale, for the first time since I emerged from the waters of the lake. "Sweet fuck. I did it! You unlocked something in me." I skipped into his arms, weeping tears of relief. Shortly after clobbering into him I apologized for knocking him sideways. My words were swept aside by his pats of appreciation.

He didn't release me. He ushered me into the kitchen where he insisted we open a buttery oak barreled white wine and celebrate with his most cherished jazz record he received when he was abroad with one of his classmates. All of this sounded amazing. Far better than walking into rooms full of stressed out scribes and combatants raving about their feats.

I didn't protest the cloying wine and after the second glass I cared not that he blindfolded me, yet again, and taught me to move synced with him and classical music. "I've never danced to music without drums or a lyre before. I'm going to crush your feet."

"Nonsense." He set his cane aside to take my arms and share in my stability.

"The blindfold is necessary. It prevents your mind from creating limits and believing that they exist just because you see them. Feel the music as you felt the magic."

"Don't blame me if I break your toes."

"Shush! Now, step to your right and then back. A basic box step. And one, two, three..."

Two songs into our 'dancing', roughly around the time Honri fatigued with joint discomfort and I managed to stop tripping over myself, my dance partners switched.

Golden blood did not give me any awe inspiring physical attributes as I had secretly wished for. No super senses or strength. Grass and ground breaking? I had you covered. I didn't hear another enter the vicinity. But holy stars above did I sense him like a wild fire consuming me and burning through every cell of my body when he brushed up against me.

Worn, crumpled hands were replaced by strong assured ones which threatened my heart to combust by his inferno.

The hand that held mine pressed a subtle squeeze, a greeting. While the left rested at the curve of my back to all but lifted me off the ground in a sweeping motion. Gods had I missed him. My time away from him only confirmed what I was beginning to understand.

Nikki gave no time for second guessing my movements as the music seamlessly spilled into the next song and my body was locked into place following his lead. "I love what you've done with the place. Who knew moss made such a great dance floor?"

Muckross moss was what had been growing by the oaky smell of it. "It also makes a decent meal in a pinch." I retracted my hand from his to pull the fabric off my eyes.

Heat broke through my chest as mine collided with his. My body sunk into his touch, wanting more of the comfort and fervor that his warmth offered. Nikki obstructed my attempt to tear the fabric away then proceeded to send my feet awry. "Leave it." Scents of cedar infiltrated the floral perfumes while we breathed in each other's air. "I don't want you baffled and bumbling about when you realize I shifted naked."

Bumbled I did. Until long seconds passed where I felt for the fabric of a fitted shirt with my hand stationed on his shoulder. I punched him. "Prick." Unphased and likely smiling, he redirected me back into rhythm with faster steps this go around.

"Easy, vixen. I'll happily tie those feisty fists behind your back."

"You wouldn't dare."

"I would. Protecting you from yourself, of course, as I promised to do." His honest curtness led me to step on his shoes. Accidentally, of course. "And you will revel in every heated moment of it. Beg for it even."

"I would not revel in being shackled. I've been in chains and cuffs before or have all the fumes you inhale while cooking gone to your forgetful head?"

He said nothing. That bastard let my imagination roam.

Our dancing took us around the room, the clank of Honri's wine glass oriented me to where the kitchen would be. I sent lilies his way and felt the well of magic in my soul mercifully get emptied. Even ciphering off small increments seemed to help lessen the feeling of overwhelm. How Zander kept this unruly sensation imprisoned was beyond me.

Maruc reinforced how necessary it was to continue to drain the magic so it didn't overflow and cause problems. Problems like earthquakes. I breathed slightly easier without the weight of power burdening my being. Honri gave a delighted cheer from the kitchen. I couldn't help but share in his joy. "Why did you bring him paints?"

"I thought he'd enjoy them."

"That's it?"

"Do I need a lengthy reply for such a simple answer?" His shoulder rose in a shrug. "I stumbled across some untouched art supplies and thought it was a shame for them to sit around collecting dust when they could easily make someone happy."

"Thief."

"I did not steal them."

"Of course you didn't."

The hand on the low arch of my spine pressed with enough force to remove any space between our chests. I struggled to keep my thoughts decent. "Honri's smile was as bright as your skin's gleam when I arrived. And they've made me happy. Your Pa was the first person to help me tap into my powers in the awake state. You don't know how monumental this moment is for me."

He readjusted my feet by tapping them into the proper stance with the toe of his shoes. "Tell me then. Tell me about the trials you've faced and why the moss is monumental."

While our hearts beat against one another's, I divulged all that was required of the ascension. A quick skinny dipping adventure into the gem filled water in a lush, green valley. It was all very scenic. The process was painless, but as the magic piled higher and higher and I failed to express it, it wore on me. Mentally and physically. Disappointment and pressure of Anna's seemingly endless power was crushing, but not life threatening.

Maruc was not at all surprised when I emerged from the lake unscathed. Neither was I for I'd been right about his deceit.

I told Nikki and Honri about the earthquakes, portals, wraiths and rockslides. And the reason why Percy, Keenan and Maruc dragged me back to Veona was for a short respite. "The only time I haven't had a nightmare was when I slept near you both. I think Orion and Anna conditioned me that way, to require two people present. Two people with a profound presence. Please, warmth share with me and Zander."

Nikki's chin rested atop my head. "That is all I've been dreaming of doing."

"Good. Because the citizens and visitors here don't need to worry about Thalren falling on them in the days ahead."

"You're quite right. They've much else to worry about, like building a temple to the first human vessel."

I pinched him. "Shut up." He was quick to bend our outstretched arms behind my back and pinning it there as he pressed me against a wall. My free hand dove into his hair and anchored him to me. My hips bucked against the hard cuts of his statue. I gave a gasp as his fingers solidified into a brace around mine, preventing me from grinding against him in front of his father.

He sniffed behind my ears and tightened his hold around my wrist. Maybe, just maybe, I'd enjoy it if he tied me up.

He spun us around in a grand twirl as the music crescendoed and my blindfold slid off.

My body was freed from his steel arms. But before the song had come to completion, his fox form was weaving in and out between my legs, rubbing his face and side bodies on my thigh. My stomach dropped in disappointment, I was looking forward to hearing what he had been up to. "I guess we are done conversing. And dancing."

And not a moment too soon. Anger rippled off Percy as he stood outside the window glaring in as if he had caught the two of us in a trap. "If I have to smell any more of your pheromones I'm going to snap both your heads from your sacks of flesh and deliver your unfaithful corpses to my baby brother."

"You're mean when you don't take the blend of supplements I give you." Percy shook the water canteen unclasped. Empty.

Percy's roar shook the glass. I've seen him fight wraiths, he could demolish that wall between him and I in a swipe of his hands. My glare was a dare in and of itself.

Nikki snaked around my legs, turning his backside towards the seething spectator. A middle finger. "Don't let Atticus or Clavey catch a whiff of your arousal, they will hunt you down—for different reasons. Either way, you will be exposed for what you are. Fucking dishonorable cumquat shitbags." I felt my eyes warm with pinpricks of hot tears—not from shame or the guilt Percy thought I should be feeling. But from how far he was from the truth.

During the brief nights in Ilanthia I had come to see Percy as someone on the same plateau as Brock. We'd stay awake talking about the nuances of life, love and loss. I'd thought he began to see me as someone to trust, not just his personal hangover healer or his brother's consort.

The fact he was revolted by me, hurt. Revolted failed to describe the manner in which he glowered at me. At us. He was horror struck. And I was certain he was going to throw up from repulsion. Infuriatingly sensitive incubi noses.

Honri hovelled his way to untie the curtains. Percy didn't stop. "Clever fox, shifting into another form. I bet you would have fully betrayed your woven had you continued your little dance in a bedroom." Nikki kept his eyes pressed tightly shut. "His *heartmarked*, Fennick. Do you have any respect for what that entails? He is her sole source of life. His future." He swallowed his spit from protruding canines while I looked at Nikki in a brighter honorable light, assuming if what Percy said was true about his shifting forms.

"You couldn't find any other pretty face to flirt with? Look, you made her cry." Slowly, Honri managed to draw the curtains.

"I'm crying because you're a nosey, clueless idiot. Do not shame us, you oversize rotisserie chicken!"

"Shit on a stick." The window went still after Percy exhaled his conclusion. "He knows, doesn't he? He marks you both because he is hiding your triss. You are all hiding *this*. Whatever *this* is." I was immobilized with resentment for his accusations, not regret from my actions.

Hells, we hadn't done anything intimate *yet* and I didn't know he was aroused currently because we weren't quintessing. Just flirting. And well, maybe I enjoy him pressed against me too much as we danced.

Honri tapped the end of his cane on the wall. "Then you are wise enough to retrieve Zander now before Wisteria gets to the Keep."

"Fine. But, I'm returning with my brother. And he will give answers." There was a swoop as Percy took to the sky. I finally exhaled when he vanished from my sight.

Honri turned a knowing eye towards me. "More humans wandered their way in, we are all tickled with the influx. They arrived not but a day ago from Numaal, many from the south. They are asking for you."

My stomach twisted, attempting to fall from my diaphragm. "The Torvals." My breath shuddered. "Have they sent knights after me? Did the wraiths follow me here?" My knees hit the floor, the moss slightly cushioning my descent. Nikki was quick to fill my arms. The shake of his muzzle, a curt answer to my concerns. Not my enemies then. Soothing.

"Pine? Rodrick? Oh, Cultee?" My upwards inflection was met with more shaking of his head. I wiped my wet nose and rubbed my disgruntled face hard against the heels of my palms. Maybe curious horselord friends of Zander? *Oof.* Nikki dropped onto my lap. It was futile for me to readjust under the two hundred pound fox. He pinned my back to the wall with his weight and buried me under nine silver flamed appendages. "You know this would be easier if you could talk. I have questions."

A long exaggerated exhale blew across my neck. I pulled strands of my paint decorated hair off his pristine fur. It was a sin to taint his loveliness with my messy existence.

Honri raised his glass and excused himself into his cluttered, forest floored art studio. "Years ago Fennick and the Overlord spoke to me privately about hypothetical theories regarding... well... what I now realize to be you. You can't hide from Her magnificence, you will fail and create discord. But, I am comforted knowing you don't shy away from it." He observed his son obstinately snuggling on my lap. "Either of you."

Chapter Thirty

Zander's horns impaled the wall behind me and he lurched himself forward to squeeze me into his arms. Nikki protested the strength of the hug with two short yips being as he remained squished between us. Shuddering with rejoice, my mouth was open by the time his sought mine out.

Whatever fire Nikki started, Zander stoked it.

Together they calmed the turbulent waters of my magic. I drank him in as if I had spent a year in the desert, not ten days in a lush valley. I pouted when he pulled away. "My world ceased to have color whilst you were out of reach. My eyes must be deceiving me for here I find my love spattered head to toe in blue resting among a bed of vivid greens. The loveliest flower in the forest."

"Always the poet. I should have known that the whimsical composition of poems and picturesque recollections you brought to Fort Fell belonged to you."

His smile widened when he stepped closer. "Took you long enough."

"Who's at the Keep?"

"Patience." I wanted to bite the finger he raised. "First things first. Fennick comes with me to get marked, while you tidy up the kitchen so Pa doesn't hurt himself doing dishes." Nikki hopped off my legs. "Percy will land shortly. Sort out your feelings regarding how much you want him to know."

"How much do you think he's put together?"

"He isn't expecting *Her* involvement, but possibly that we've all gone off and completed the Circling. Which confounds him because you are currently a mortal and there are three of us in this *entanglement*." His manner of talking was confident. He'd already thought about this ceremony.

"Can three people do the Circling?"

"Yes."

"Do you trust him?"

Zander rubbed Nikki's neck and coaxed him the rest of the way off me. "I do. More so now that he is sober. I've wanted him as my Right Wing since he found me young, dumb and intercepting dangerous slave trade routes while I was attempting to keep distance between Fen and I. Percy is maddening, but his reasons for going to war are far better than most. He is a depressed sap, but he cares. A lot. The death of his heartmarked and son torment him, that is why he numbs himself. Until now. Until witnessing you, Cobar and Keenan preparing to go to war." Nikki strode into the first room on the left. A flash of fire and his lean male form leaned against the doorframe. He rolled up his left sleeve.

"Do you know what else is maddening? You not telling me which Numaalians arrived." He lifted me to my feet and flicked my nose.

"Do you want a clue?"

My arms barred across my chest. "I thought the guessing game stopped after I called your name from the roof."

He stepped back towards the bedroom. That handsome, devilish dimple dented in his scruffy face. "Nuri the nymph said you were good at riddles so how is this: 'He met a mask who lacked any copper, dead were all who tried to stop her. He took a chance and it paid, for the coins she earned she made a trade. His skull tattoo no one would have guessed, she left him to remove a headdress. They met again, another name, she paid him, mercenaries came."

The corners of my tired eyes wrinkled. "Warden Rhett. He survived? That's great news. He's a little rough around the edges, but he followed through with his word. I'd like to think we helped some families survive that night." I walked into the kitchen, my toes savoring the sensation of being barefooted on the moss.

Zander rolled his neck counter clockwise. He and Nikki shared a relieved look followed by a sarcastic laugh. "If you think we are not going to discuss you fighting in the Pits you are sorely mistaken, young love."

Disbelieving. I shook my head. "No. You don't get to be overbearing. There is nothing to discuss, old poet. Go bite your husband while I wash up and water the lilacs."

The pestering incubi countered. *"Our husband."*

There it was. An open outright implication that I belonged to them, them to I. I wavered, begging my thoughts to realign and provide clarity, provide direction. He winked, but I saw the bright colors of hope and promise fade slightly when I failed to speak up fast enough. "Too forward?"

My weight shifted, but my heart settled. "No." The shimmer returned to our internal thread at my concession.

"Wisteria." Zander turned on the music before he walked to Nikki's side. My name was profound against the non-lyrical notes filling the air. "Do as I say, just once. Don't come in." I felt my neck sweat and agreed regardless of the urge to disobey.

The door shut behind them.

I ran the water faucet to drown out the needy, lusty grunts of Nikki and the clamor that came with the physical struggle to restrain him. Honri was humming merrily in the adjacent room, I held onto those light tunes as I peered upon the growth covered floor boards and felt for the well of power within myself. The vegetation shouldn't stay. Uneven grounds would pose a risk for tripping and the cane was useless for stabilizing on slick, bermy foundations.

I imagined myself bathing in the cold, shallow waters of Opal Lake. The raw, uncontaminated power that was held in each individual drop and gem. Recognizing that the same water flowed in me, I began to spill magic out through my hands, coating the floor with my desire to remove what I had summoned.

"No. No, no, no!" I rummaged in the drawers until I found towels. All I had managed to do was summon the actual water. Nifty, but I saturated the apartment in puddles. My pants were drenched as I crawled around mopping up the flood before the wood warped.

Grey scuffed boots stomped on my towel. "Make yourself useful and fetch towels from the bathroom."

Percy hunched over, wings bonking frames on walls, attempting to make himself smaller as he grumbled out of annoyance. He threw large towels at his feet and began to sop up the mess leaking towards the front door with heavy strides. "What exactly were you trying to accomplish? Growing mildew and molds too?"

At least he acknowledged the fact I did something with my magic.

"Fungus actually, jerk. The fun mushrooms that paralyze people who piss me off."

"Jerk? Generic. I taught you better than that, fucktrumpet." I was sour at myself for laughing. "Flowers and floods are preferable to ancient mountain ranges crashing down next to my sleeping cot or having you swinging Orion in my face. Or say, cheating on my brother. Are you scheming to obtain Fennick's immortality? Because if you are, fuck you. That isn't something stolen. It has to be given, greedy bitch."

Immortality? Definitely, not. Although I admit I was particularly bitchy thanks to his unwarranted comments. Him being bent at the waist with heavy wings draping behind him helped tip the odds in my favor. I'd take this mouthy prick down. With what traction my toes found, I launched myself at his knees.

I underestimated his mass. He gripped me between his elbow and knee, clamping me with his immense strength as we fell backwards. My sides were bruising and my angry blood was rushing. He spewed crude profanities and landed on the boney webbing on his wings. I tucked my arms up to prevent his right arm from successfully placing me into a headlock. "Boys, get out here before I stab him!"

Zander's dark obscura visibly fell over the apartment, guarding us from eyes and ears from the street. He stepped out of the room with blood dripping from his chin and half his tunic melted away. His bellow was thunderous as he growled at Percy. It was cute to see him all worked up, Percy didn't agree. He swung his body mass around the purple obscurities trying to wrestle them down.

Percy and I released our holds on each other and crawled away, relatively unscathed. I did kick his shin as I scurried off, priding myself on the deep grunt that followed.

Atticus' offspring stood nose to nose in the cramped hallway. "You finally see me, Percy. There is lucidity in your eyes, but not your brain. Refer to my heartmarked as a greedy bitch or a whore again and I will give you a reason to drink yourself into the grave." Zander stepped over a leeward pool of water to get to his brother and coincidently placed himself between the two of us.

I rung out my shirt sleeves and several towels in the sink, the tenderness in my torso fresh.

"Apologies, I know better than to insult a heartmarked. And for the record little brother, I've always seen you, it was just that there were occasionally duplicate copies of you flying around." Percy spun his index finger in the air before he got serious. "I see you, yet I fail to understand you. Protecting Fen from Clavey and marking Wisteria as your own are understandable. But what I saw, *what I smelt between them,* was enticement towards each other. Compatible, yes. This was more. The same compatibility scent I caught drafts of when she arrived from Wanning Star with you. Her appeal should not smell of the same devotion that I can smell now from her now towards you and what I caught minutes ago. It's traitorous."

Zander peered at me from over his shoulder. Unfluctuating hues of cobalt blue and teal embraced me, holding me tightly in a safe net. I explored them and caressed his mental walls with affirmative kisses. "Permission to divulge, my flower?"

"Wait for Nikki. Hopefully, Percy didn't bruise him too."

"And how would I have accomplished that?"

Nikki straightened his disheveled ponytail and blouse. It was untucked enough that my eyes stole traitorous glances as his bare waistline. "Our quintessing is graciously unaccessed at the moment." He tucked his shirt into his pants, which were wrinkled and undrawn. "I have salve for your injuries. I'll tend to you in private."

"Body mirroring?" Percy's face froze into a vacant expression. "You two are wovens."

Zander put his hand on Percy's arm to guide him into the living space with moderately higher ceilings. "It gets better. Wisteria and my bond manifested as syphering. We are all wovens." Wings rearranged behind him as he sat on the armchair. Zander pointed to Nikki and I. "Their threads aren't fully explored so brace yourself for a variety of scents—from all of us."

Percy chortled a disbelieving laugh and rubbed his chin. "This explains everything—*changes* everything. Holy shit, you need to tell the conclave before one of the rumors take root. They believe you are planning to use her as a weapon or she is using demon bones to overpower you. Not to mention Morigan left a bad taste in the realm's mouth when it comes to the women you court and there is the whole, chosen by the Eternals thing that is luring Gods and demons alike to her presence. They can't decide if she is a curse or blessing."

"I've heard them all." His face looked as if he swallowed a pile of salty rocks. "I'll need you to disband them, especially the ones regarding manipulation and Fen's lineage. Diffuse tensions subtly while we work on establishing our bonds. They are all false, you can reason why."

With a touch on my tunic, Nikki's magic had my attire dried. The floorboards were next. He burnt a path in the moss and gestured that I sit across from Percy on the footstool. "A corlimor bond?"

"So Zander claims." That remark earned me an eyeroll. "I saw that."

Percy stared at Zander. "I doubt you are corlimors. You wouldn't have let her dive into the Opal Lake given the risks." My throat constricted as if an icy serpent coiled around my airway. It was too late to give a silencing gesture to Percy, three pairs of eyes already stared at me trying to disappear behind my hair. "You didn't tell them?"

"Tell us what?"

"Fuck you, Percy." My left arm shook with Zander's rage, my right scalded with Nikki's. "There was nothing to tell. I knew Maruc was lying because his sister was deceitful too. It's genetic. Eternals are flawed."

Flames encircled my seat. Screaming, I leapt onto the stool. I'll admit I was panicked when the cylinder of fire grew as tall as I, stealing all the oxygen from around me. "What were the risks?"

They were whatever word described an emotion stronger than furious. Relentless fury swept through our bonds on a magnitude I had I'd never known existed.

I wished I was not on the receiving end. "Obviously there were none!" I shouted through the roaring flames. A fist punched across the barrier and grabbed a fistful of my tunic. A yelp tore through me. "Maruc said the ascension might kill me! *It didn't,* so cool off." Zander's nails lengthened, tearing the fabric on my collar.

I screamed, trying to make a run for the door. His shadow magic beat me there. It was rutting futile. I got nowhere. Not a damn inch. "You are angry with me and have every right to be. I put all our lives on the line. But you wouldn't have let me go if I said anything and if I don't see this bargain through, Kinlyra will perish." The flames thinned slightly.

Zander lifted me off the stool with a single hand. "I don't care about anyone else's life on this earth more than yours. My own and Fen's included." Finger nails retracted and his flesh gave way to a darker grey hue, the bronze sun kissed coloring was seeped in ink. "In what terms do you need this spelt out for you?"

I looked up at his piercing blue eyes rimmed in violet. "You don't have to. I hear you."

"Do you?"

"Yes, but—"

Blackness took the room, awe took my heart. Flames vanished under the dense air. "No 'buts'. For there are no exceptions. Your understanding of the depths that our souls are bound is inept as is your communication, if you feel the need to agree then immediately counter your statement with a 'but'."

Tears formed from frustration. "Feel for our bond! Breathe in my essence!"

"I want to consume your essence, how dare you give up on life and abandon true joy with us."

"You are unbearable! How can you not see I was doing the opposite of abandoning life? I'm preserving lives!"

His voice raised and caused the hairs on my arms to stand. "By forfeiting yours? Fuck the rest of the world!"

"You don't mean that."

Percy interjected. "Yes, he does."

My focus was solely on Zander, not on his irritating brother. "You love Kinlyra, humans, dreamers and blessed all the same. I do too! Even with all their flaws. You'd never want darkness to fall over them. And I connected the dots hours before I left and figured Maruc needs me alive to carry out the deal we agreed upon. He was testing me. Dying at the lake was never going to happen and you never had anything to worry about. I didn't need to add more weight on your shoulders."

A scrunched, furrowed brow was not a look I'd seen on Nikki. Not when it was paired with pain. Out of his front pocket he pulled a wad of folded papers. He opened them. I stared at the familiar words, cringing internally. "These were meant to be your goodbyes." I nodded.

Nikki traced the ink tenderly with his thumb. "But I discarded them because I knew I'd survive the ascension and perhaps become brave enough to speak them outloud. Intuition told me I'd return." Wordlessly, I summoned Orion into my grip. God of intuition, assuredness and swift action.

My males seethed. "Intuition led me up the dock to greet Anna. It led me to blurt out to Rhett to head west. It led Orion into my hands. It was the same knowing that told me to dive in the lake and the same knowing that tells me I will die in this war when the runegate falls. I trust this feeling in my gut."

"You should trust your two wovens. Trust us when we say, we will not let you die in this war of worlds despite what your gut and dreams tell you." Zander's surge of emotions were still causing my arm to shake. It was a struggle for him but he released my tunic and lowered me onto my own feet. "I should have tethered myself to you after the griffin incident."

I flinched. Harsh bitterness filled my gut as I stared at Zander. "If you so much as tie one strand of fabric to me or shackle me, you will have lost me forever. I will not be tamed because you fail to grasp my actions."

He grumbled so low it sounded like distant thunder. "Fail?" Zander's chest puffed. "That isn't something I do."

"You. Are. Failing." Contrary to his bitter face his movements were slow, soft and composed as he laced his slacked fingers in mine.

"Since I've known you, your life has been about survival, sacrifice and revenge. You are of the few crafters who managed to live through the last decade of blight and stubborn enough to march back into the infestation to deliver retribution. You agreed to take me with you." His nose flared.

"There was no danger."

"Bull shit."

"You are failing again, Zander. It is not about endangering myself—which I did not." I bit my lip until I tasted blood. How did I convey the storm in my chest? Why couldn't he feel them and stop his assault of concerns? "I don't write poems or sing ancient vespers. I cannot fly above horizons to show you beautiful things for the first time." Nikki held my free hand, fire awoke in my center. "I can't splurge on silks and chocolates, nor can I give you books you've never read or surprise you with dinner and farfetched, enchanting history lessons. I have nothing to offer either of you."

I swallowed the hot air. I had nothing. Or I would, if I ever lost them.

Feeling empty despite the waves of magic and turmoil crashing inside me, I willed them to understand. "The people I love have died or been violently taken from me. Fighting ruthlessly for what I cherish with blood, sacrifice and risk is the only way I know how to exist and express myself. Clearly the letters were shit." I eyed the parchment in Nikki's pocket, moving my gaze anywhere but their sets of eyes. "Let me protect what you love. Is it so difficult to see that this is how I show affection?"

My jaw clenched. Sky and cedar clouded my already muddled, infuriated thoughts. Zander called my name, sighed it was more accurate for it sounded slightly breathy with equal parts apologetic and angered. "I love you too," he declared in the same husky simper.

"I did not say that." I let him kiss my forehead before pushing his bulky biceps away when bashfulness crept up my neck in the form of flushed skin. Nikki gave a courteous dip at the waist, his mind working ceaselessly behind the golden stones set in his strikingly handsome face.

Amidst the argument Honri had joined Percy sitting on the couch. Concerned, enlightened and amused, they observed. Percy sniffed the air. I was quick to stop admiring Nikki. "Stop grinning, Percy. You ruined the afternoon with your stupid mouth."

All too satisfied, he stretched his arms behind his neck. "Oh, please. I prompted your confession. You meant to thank me and my brilliant sense of smell."

"I will break your crooked, grisly nose if you refer to this argument as a confession, of any sorts, ever again." My eyelids narrowed.

Percy leaned over his knees. "Now, all those late night conversations with Brock and I around the firepit make so much more sense." Fuck. The conversations where I ask them about love proclamations and how Brock's sisters spoke of their experiences within relationships. The conversations where I tried to sort out my feelings towards my wovens.

"I'll bust your mouth too for good measure. Maybe rip out your tongue and feed it to a hungry falcon."

He looked to Nikki who had moved into the kitchen, scrubbing his forearm with salt. Better he do that awful ritual of bite preservation before our quintessing opened. "Is she always like this?" Percy was stifling another laugh.

"Yes," Nikki replied with the edges of his mouth curling up. He gave Zander a tight squeeze around his shoulders and let his firm, fiery hands linger until Zander had visibly unwound and the violet flames following my wake subsided.

"Am I always like what?" I asked the room.

The males ignored me. My wovens released each other after the elemental burned away their anger. Nikki tended to the paint drops drying on his Pa's clothes and Zander saw to answering his brother's short list of questions. "She will need a fresh bite before going back to the Keep. I'll scrounge up a wheelchair for Honri and meet you there." Percy raised a brow at Nikki. "Do you stay for this or are you coming with us?"

I jumped in when the fluttering in my chest grew too heavy. "He stays." We couldn't risk our quintessing snapping into place and him breaking out into orgasmic fevers in public, right?

"Damn. Alright. You're good with this arrangement, Zander?"

"It's damn near flawless."

"I don't know if I should be gravely concerned or jealous. Be careful, if you kill either of them..."

Zander looked haunted. "I know."

Nikki massaged his father's joints. Alleviating his pain by lifting him up right from his underarms. "Percy, out front."

Zander had me on the counter the moment Percy wheeled Honri away from the apartments. Obscuras draped over the room.

"I'm not sorry." I pressed my lips onto his. He parted immediately and his tongue swarmed my mouth. Blood. Nikki's blood. It was nothing like Anna's. Not coppery or harsh, but smooth and warming. I swallow it greedily.

He laid me on the granite counter top I had cleared, yanking my trousers off. My bare legs looped around him and brought his hips to mine, where I rolled against his arousal. "You seldom are apologetic. It's infuriating."

"It's impressive."

His hands stoked the length of my legs, slowly tracing the round of my ass. "I wish we could make this encounter an all evening affair, but conclave calls."

Nikki entered and spoke curtly. "Should our quintessing rip over, you both have my consent." He escorted himself directly into an adjacent room. I frowned at the closed door. After our experiments less than two weeks ago it felt wrong not to include him or have his warm attentive presence at our sides. *I feel the incompletion too. But, we have to respect his distance. He is retaining his sanity.* His fangs nipped closer towards the shadow between my thighs.

I want him. I ventured. *You want him.*

The nips stopped and a firm, wet tongue entered me. The edge of the counter I found and anchored myself onto the surface so I could roll my hips on Zander's face. "He is a man of his word. He will not engage until you cross that line with him. Being around you, the insatiable and willing vixen you are, makes it hard for him to keep his composure and restraint."

In entered a finger. My pussy drenched his knuckle. I moaned as he worked me wet. Zander looked at the closed door. "You coming will be a cruel sound for our woven, but he wants to hear you be satisfied even if he isn't the one to be fucking you. Yet. Don't stifle your pleasure, my love."

Zander's pants were at his ankles and the head of him glided over my slit. I waited too long to be fucked. I sat up, grabbed his hips and pulled him inside me. To hell with slow acclimation. No. I wanted the fullness and burn to consume me. He read my need and pounded me so hard my ass would bare bruises of his hand's outline that I would proudly flaunt. I tore myself out of my remaining clothes, Zander lifted me off the counter with his cock still inside and took me to the door that Nikki stayed behind.

He fucked me on that now half shattered door frame until we were seconds from tasting the bliss of falling stars. I readied my neck for him.

As prepared as I mentally made myself for his venom, I was as disbelieving and shaken as I had been the first time. "When you come, say his name." He commanded. The hot sting of his bite flooded my veins and pooled in my clit. My nerves were swollen and needy. My chest rose and fell fast. My hands mindlessly stroked any inch of his flesh within reach. "Scream for him. Let him hear how badly you want him."

I did want him. "I do want him. You're okay with this?"

"Yes, love."

My panting mouth licked up the blood, my blood, dribbling down his face. "If you don't finish me soon, I'll die."

"You are not going to die. You need to breathe so you don't faint when we come." I stared at him in disbelief. "Now, inhale so I can fill your tight, throbbing pussy and feel it spasm around my dick." That didn't help me breathe. I rocked on the cock inside me thinking how this pleasure might one day soon translate for Nikki. Zander growled and let me take what was within reach.

His woven's name easily tore from my lips and the door charred with flames. "Nikki, I am going to come. Don't stop. Keeping fucking me, Nikki! Oh, fuck Nikki."

Cursing, Zander joined me in screaming out Fennick's name. His hips hammered into mine stopping after his blood tinged fangs engulfed my mouth, taking in every last ounce of sexual energy I offered.

We freshened up, while the venom in my body faded to a dull simmering ache before we tapped on the door. A yip replied. I turned the handle and out walked a foxy Nikki, who rightfully glared daggers at Zander. His clothes were a charred pile of ash behind him.

Regardless of annoyance, he leapt into the incubus' arms as I attached myself to their side.

Chapter Thirty-One

"Rhett?" Baffled and bemused, I stood amid a conclave that was overrun by voyaging folks from the Southlands whom trekked a decent amount of mud tracked across the floor.

I signaled for him after spotting the familiar ink stained throat across the hall. He strode towards me, closing the distance. I tossed him the final silver I owed him and he cracked a grin.

He pocketed the change with a smirk heavy on the humored side. "I went west."

I crossed my arms and made room for Brock to stand next to me. "Appears so! You and quite a few mercenaries made the trek and I have to confess I am happy to see you all. Last I remember, you were running to sabotage the royal carriages aimed for Kathra. How did that go?"

He clicked his tongue. "Too protected. Unfortunately, most of the capital carriages made it out of the city. They took Gimlian Monte with them, he was screaming profanities to your name as the priestess ordered the knights to stuff him into restraints and gags. He was in a world of pain. What did you do to that bastard?"

I gave a wicked grin. "Nothing he didn't deserve. Slashed his skin with a drop of igmu snail secretions, that's all." The pad of my thumb traced the ring on my finger.

The prison grunt next to Rhett shook out his dreaded hair. "Snail *what* now?"

Keenan found his way to my side, straight backed with his hand on his sword. "Igmu snail secretions will melt the flesh off of anything living. The more water you try to soothe the burn with, the faster it spreads. Within minutes it's excruciating, within a day it will eat away at layers of muscle and the bones will be visible. Until that dissolves too." I turned to Keenan, who gave me a proud grin. "He deserves a long drawn out death, inflicted with as much misery as he inflicted upon others. Which seems to be an infinite amount from what little I have gathered." He gave me a proud fatherly nod.

The grunt shook his head at me. "You are bloody as horrifying as you are honorable."

"I am as spiteful as I am smart and deadly as I am determined."

Rhett gave a fulsome, praising look as he gestured to his bannerless company. "Many amongst us watched you in the Pit. You won't find one whom disagrees. They saw you storming around naked with daggers in the gala, they won't be stupid enough to be deserving of your craft, Master Woodlander." He gave a stern side eye to those around him. "It's time for honesty." Brock and Keenan were too comfortable for his disclosure. Not exactly the sign of comfort I sought.

"Honestly. There is always time for that."

"Rhett is not my name." My toes tapped impatiently while I held my pattering heart at bay with false confidence and a quiet twitch of my lips. "I am Bastion Basitill, founder of the rebellion." How perfect! I drew fresh air into my chest.

I gave his outstretched hand a firm shake. Yolanda would be beside herself. I glanced around the conclave, searching for her rosy upturned cheeks. "I have a friend who has done nothing but run her mouth and devise plans to converge interests and join your cause. I hope you have room in your ranks for a wildly ambitious woman to see to the high court's demise."

Our hands retracted. "Yolanda d' Loure. Yes, we've met and she is off with my sharpest minds revealing court intel and private affairs of lords and ladies that will be invaluable when the time comes, of that I am certain."

"Wonderful."

"Truly. Now, let's talk about why I followed you west."

"Followed me?"

"I assume when you told me to go west, you'd be trekking that way as well. Initially, I didn't intend to come this way in search of you with any of your names Keenan, Ivy or Wisteria until I heard of the arrangement with the Faceless Prince. I knew we needed Ilanthia's cooperation."

"There is no *arrangement* with the royal family. He is threatening to kill people I love if I don't marry him." I corrected, my fingers brushing Orion. "He spent years experimenting on my brother and likely countless others. His does not make ideal threats, he is coercing me into marriage."

"Why did he choose you?"

"My best guess is the wraiths' reaction to my blood. That or my crafting and physician knowledge would benefit his experimentation on Ilanthians or aid his father's failing health. The only people living who knew about my blood would have been my family." I knew Keenan never would betray me or his Goddess, but they had his wife and her children. Who knew what admittance they tortured from her. My brow arched. I rubbed the wrinkles in my forehead. "Keenan, would Moriah have said something under persecution?"

He looked ill. His olive skin was pasty at the mention of the notion. "Perhaps. But even if the Faceless Prince knew about your blood, that doesn't explain why he chose you or let you go."

Bastion agreed. "It does not. But he wants you back. He seems to think you've reason to return to him."

"I assisted Moriah's labor with Rory. I was there when Athromancia cut her umbilical cord and I was the first person to carry that babe to her mother's breast. I have always intended to liberate them and if they are in Kathra, then that is my destination after this eminent battle with the beyond. Bastion, do you prefer me to walk into his clutches?"

"Not without a plan."

"Not without my new friends either."

He did a double take at Keenan's stiffening posture, Nikki's blazing tails and Zander's tall horns. "You have magic now. Magic that his demented mind should never be permitted to access. I want us to formulate an approach to invade his inner circle of demons and dukes to overthrow the Torvals after you wed them in name so by law you are reigning sovereign–the queen." The Weaver thread anchored in my chest shuddered. Revolting.

I choked. "I am nobody's queen."

Zander's words rustled the back of my hair. "You are mine."

I elbowed his gut. Wyatt and Kashikat exchanged money. "I will not sit as queen."

Bastion posed to the still room as calmly as a breezeless morning. "Details and titles can be sorted later."

"Later? As in the afterlife? The palace won't be graced by my rage if their demon minions conquer Veona and eat their way to a soul sucking triumph in darkness."

Bastion gave away no details of his inner thoughts. He stood observing me like a clock on a mantle. "He has Ik Kygen's daughter and wife. Others too, I'd imagine. He has been hunting for decades now. You have a chance to weasel in and stop this madness."

"So does everybody else–so *did* everybody else–they are just too cowardice." I saw Keenan's face fall and tighten with emotions that were too tangible. "There will be no weaseling. He will be expecting me and my personally branded back crawling on his doorstep the day before the dark of winter descends. He will anticipate tricks and, to be frank, he has the upper hand with his blood crafting, bones, Vulborg army, demons, Remnants and secrets. The amount of fucking secrets that even Yolanda's best investigating couldn't uncover."

"Perhaps beings here have means to expose treachery?" Yes. Yes they did. But would they volunteer to help? "We will write out a proper plan, one that includes Ilanthians and dreamers in the mix–the palace will not be expecting unity when we come to usurp it."

"As I said they won't be expecting *anything* if we are all dead and feasted upon, Bastion. This conversation is a moot point until after the runegate is rebuilt and if we are both alive." The crowd behind him grew restless. My thumb traced my lip as I walked around Brock to observe the large crowd of humans, well trained, by the look of their bulk, build and weaponry. "Tell you what. Let's make a bargain."

"I was hoping you'd say that." Of course he was.

The gleam in his eyes made it evident he had been waiting for me to see his cards and offer a bargain so we both may both benefit. He and I were survivalists. "You and your able soldiers fight on the side of the living when the Vulborg sweep across the fields side by side with Ilanthians and dreamers. If we all survive, I will work with you as much as I am comfortable. I will return to Numaal in one fashion or another to see the Torvals removed from power and the nation's morality renewed." His facade cracked. A glimmer of joy escaped. "Bear in mind that equipping me to your cause also comes with my Bloodsworns, two dreamer friends and hordes of wraiths that follow the scent of my blood." I pointed at the fox spitting fire and towering beast behind me muttering prayer to me as I stood.

Bastion pardoned himself and turned to his crowd. "Rebels, what say you?"

Two stomps of semi-coordinated approval echoed around the Keep, save for a handful of rebels who requested to see the mark on my back prior to committing to the bargain. Brock made a gagging sound as he pivoted around to face the opposite side of the hall, he loathed seeing me remotely naked now that our relationship had peeked as siblings.

I dared not look at Zander's face or any of his kin when I untucked my top. His voice boomed. "If anyone thinks about touching her, I will cut their hands off. I smell intentions. Best you keep your cocks and cunts in check." Zander was riled up too much to sypher. I wasn't stupid enough to remind him that he was being dramatic.

Alethim stepped quickly to Zander's side. Atticus aimed his horns down as I passed. His eyes pursed shut. Torvi and what appeared to be her pack watched from the corner, the pixies from above.

Down the line I walked unbuttoning my shirt enough to hoist it over my head and display the double headed raven seared onto my right shoulder. *'Damn. Collette maimed her.' 'I thought my scars were ugly.' 'At least she can fight. Take revenge for her stolen beauty.'* I blocked out the commentary that followed and kept the same swagger in my step that had been there when I wore the silky white robe and red lingerie. Torvi grimaced and turned into her pack's shoulder, evading memories or guilt.

Nikki summoned a shield of fire while I made myself decent. Took all but two seconds to drop my shirt, but he used that time to fasten himself to my side and run his body against my legs. He was under my heels when I walked to the head of the rebel party, his tails wrapped around my thighs with his agile steps not once colliding with mine.

"I do not know what the future holds for Kinlyra, but I know this much to be true. You are a woman of your word and virtue and I, Bastion Basitill, hereby accept your bargain." His cracked calloused hand gripped mine in a solid shake. A wet nose knocked into my wrist. Nikki sniffed the linked hands. He bared teeth ready to break a wrist should it come to that.

Atticus approached, several humans dropped to their knees taking in the sight of his towering form encroaching on their party, Bastion considered doing the same by the widening whites of his eyes and paling of his skin. I guess the male was comparatively monumentally massive.

With a hand below and a hand atop, Atticus enclosed my and Bastion's handshake within his large palms. "My soul sings in ways that cannot be translated into adequate declarations." Dark grey eyes held mine long enough to witness his sincerity and moved to Bastion's. "Nothing I say or do seems sufficient as a token of gratitude. I say to you, my home is your home, now and always." Atticus straightened and addressed the newcomers. "This goes for all of you. Our arts, education, goods and magic wares are open for you and your families to explore and immerse in regardless of if we survive the wars ahead. You are most welcome to stay."

Nobody was brave enough to mumble a word of appreciation, but heads nodded. He was well acclimated to their lagging reactions. Talking hid a miniscule wrinkle of joy in his face, the dimple he shared with his son. "The elves will see you off to comfortable bunking accommodations but not before you've been educated regarding the abilities and nature of the beings that reside here. You may find us outlandish and our appearances peculiar, but in order to fight safely side by side with a fae that fights with mind control or a river kelpie slinging potions you must learn their strengths and weaknesses. And they yours. We've not much time to amalgamate; Bastion, get your fighters out front and your political minds to the east hall for immersive learning with alchemists. Have you children or ill in your caravan?"

The reverence in Bastion's head shake spurred an apology from Atticus. "I'm sorry for your loss. We can celebrate their lives by preserving their mission. If you have customs, you can request what you need to see them escorted into the beyond. The Veil as Numaalians call it."

Atticus removed his hands from ours. I looked up at the purebred dreamer, my skull tipped as far back as I could bend it comfortably. "Maruc stated the ascension was successful, but you are in need of deep sleep. Take rest. Recuperate." That's it? Maruc didn't mention my magic was noncompliant or I too inept to use it?

"You're not going to pester me about my magic?"

"Would you like me too?"

I snorted. "Gods, no. I'm fucking exhausted and the magic gets heavier when my mind is weary."

"Take my son and his woven, I do not wish the mountains to come toppling down in the wrong direction."

I eyed Keenan who quickly turned to Cobar and offered him affectionate squirmy tickles. "That happened one time."

"Twice!" Percy shouted over the moving crowds. I was going to break his nose, mouth and tear his eavesdropping ears off his head.

"Once. The other two times were stampedes of wraiths coming from a portal." Handfuls of wraiths ran at us, which our small party had to quickly come together to slaughter. Maruc did more watching than fighting, but he did behead a few when he wasn't admiring Orion slicing through body parts.

"All the same. I prefer those without wings not to be buried under the land on which they walk."

I reached behind me, feeling blindly for Zander. "I couldn't agree more."

"Wisteria." Atticus spoke my name with unrushed wonderment. "As I have told my son, I will tell you. What you've done already is enough." Zander's bewilderment and comfort came through our bond in steady streams of blue. "You need more time to manifest your magic with your will, Maruc mentioned as much. I cannot guarantee you will have the days after tomorrow to grow confident, but I will try to hold the ramparts if it gives you a minute more. Please, remember that if you cannot, or choose not, you've already done enough." He backed away quickly, my guess is he didn't want to see me cry.

Scruffy beard itched the side of my face. "He has his moments." Zander kissed my cheek. "You need to eat and bathe, who knows when you'll get luxuries again once the war starts."

"Where will you be?"

"I'm finalizing the security details for the three safehouse locations tonight and starting to move people in. I will not be far behind. Cobar decided he feels plenty safe with Yolanda and she has agreed to stay by his side in the glacier."

"Keenan will be at his side."

A rough hand was on my shoulder. "I will be at yours." Cobar hung off Keenan's hip, making scrunchy goofy faces at me. I stuck my tongue out at him. "You are my sovereign."

"He is your child."

"You are my child."

I stuck my tongue at Keenan now. "I am not a child and I am not yours. Not fully."

"Alester's blood runs in me as mine did him." Finality must be in the air. It was making all the men in my life irrational and emotional. "There is no difference between Cobar's blood and yours. I will not lose either of you to this madness, nor will you fight me on this issue."

"I spent years worrying sick, wondering if my brother was dead or alive. You have to stay with him, Keenan. I can't do that again. I won't."

"Is that an order? You know my blood craves your commands now that I am your Bloodsworn."

Sarcasm. An acquired trait in the family. "No, it's not an order. It is a suggestion you will comply with."

"Sissy, I'll be okay. Yolanda has a sword and she has good stories. There are other kids going into the glacier too." Cobar pulled his dad's leather straps and fraying gold stitches on his backpack, slowly making his way into my arms for a hug. I crouched down, memorizing his small hands in mine. They've grown ever so slightly since we were taken from Ferngrove. I kissed each finger while he stayed silent, trying not to cry. "You'll come for me, right?"

He collapsed against me. "Always. I will always come for you." Cobar ran back to Keenan, for fear had introduced himself once more to the young boy. He was scared of seclusion, of being left to live when his family left to die, of unspeakable anguish. It was remarkable to think he had suffered so much at the hands of humans, yet chose them to protect him when a war pounded on the gates. Yolanda had worked magic of her own to soothe his soul.

I sniffed away tears and looked to Keenan. "Don't you want to take him to Ilanthia? Have you not missed your lands?"

A punch perfectly placed on my deltoid left me staring, dumbly at Yolanda. Nikki switched forms, his bones breaking and straightening, his inked flesh quilted together over a lean body of fire.

The shift looked utterly painful. Nikki didn't show any ounce of discomfort as he shielded me from Yolanda's raised fists with a bare, broad chest. He was in her face growling as I tried pushing him aside to get to her.

"What the f—"

"What the fuck was that for?" She finished my thoughts. I nodded, still tense. "You fought in the Pits."

"Yeah, it was fun."

Nikki caught her arm before her second fist made contact with me. "You fought in the Pits for money. For me."

I stood on my tiptoes to look over Nikki's shoulder. "Would you rather I have slept with Count Hilderbrand? If I am remembering correctly, you'd have killed me if you thought I was whoring for money. Killing was a better option than groveling or asking for money." Nikki released her. Her face wasn't any kinder.

"You could have been killed!"

"But I wasn't."

"You could have been."

"Yes. I could have been just as I could have been by the restless or the knights in the years leading up to then. You could have been at any point in your escapades with dangerous buyers. This is a stupid thing to be fighting over."

"It was a stupid thing you did."

I practically clawed my face off trying to explain myself to her. Which I didn't need to be doing! "I can't change what is done. What do you want from me? To yell? Hit? Go ahead, add another bruise to my collection of disfigured flesh." I dropped my hands and turned my face within clear striking distance.

Nikki's chest pushed against mine until I was forced to backstep. His outstretched arms boxed me out of Yolanda's reach. Our skin sweltered at the minimal friction. The tingles creeping up my arm signaled the arrival of our quintessing. Lovely.

Was there ever an opportune time for the bond to snap into place? I could only be grateful the venom was out of our systems.

Yolanda's fury became a distant, irrelevant hazard for in that second I was battling Nikki's demons. The very adamant ones that were desperate for pleasure and begging to be held. It was a struggle not to enfold the man nearest me into my arms. So much so it hurt. He physically hurt from being untouched. Such needy males the Weaver gifted me. And I had been right about his aching back. He needed an adjustment in his lower lumbar.

Too stiff and shocked to separate myself from his chest, Zander nonchalantly stepped between us, an arm over each shoulder. "Yolanda, darling delicate desert cactus." His charming name calling redirected her annoyance at him. "If you are done picking fights with your friend, may I suggest a civil discussion to be held as you escort her to bed for the night? You need to hurry off shortly and collect belongings before the glacier is sealed off."

"Fine." She didn't make eye contact when she agreed. "You'll never understand, Zander. You've never had a master."

She was right. Zander could not relate to the feeling of having nothing but a name or the weight of a debt unpaid. I knew Yolanda was grateful. I knew her pride. I knew she had been cultivating a renewed sense of self the moment she asked me to shave her head. I also understood that, like me, she hated the feeling of being indebted. She has been paying debts off her entire adult life.

"I threw myself into the Pit for selfish reasons, Yolanda. For starters, I needed to practice my swordsmanship, I was getting rusty. Of course, my ego needed to be stroked by disemboweling and decapitating a few notorious monsters and their haughty high masters. Not to mention I didn't have any living female friends so by freeing you, I'd hope you'd break up the monotony of these testosterone driven buffoons. And delivering you to your sister? Can you imagine how selfishly thrilled that reunion would make me?"

She calmed, but her eye roll was theatrical enough that the pixies on the balconies spotted it. "Let me guess, since you never had money of your own you wanted to know what the ruckus was all about?"

"Exactly. What better way than earning a million moneys drenched in blood?"

"*Pastels*, Wisteria. Those *moneys* are called pastels." Arms crossed she began to take strides towards the sleep chambers. "We still aren't even. I'm still upset that you put me in debt again."

"I offered, you agreed. How is that debt?" She and Nikki moved ahead of me. I stood frozen amidst a windstorm of heat wrapping itself way up and down my limbs wondering how the hell Nikki had been functioning this entire time feeling so needy... and aroused. "If you want to balance the scales you will keep Cobar alive. I want him entertained with the best gypsy stories that have ever graced your ears. I want him brimming with joy and laughter when Keenan and I come for him."

"Then we are even?"

Unable to do anything physical, including walk, I replied with a single syllable. "Yes."

"Good, because you're the biggest pain in the ass friend I have ever had."

"Me?" My finger thrusted into my own sternum. "Not Brock's whining, Zander's loud chewing or Nikki's inflated intelligence?" The males shouted, growled and snapped at me accordingly.

"No. Because now that I actually consider you my friend, I hate agreeing with the Rebellion to send you back to the devil himself." We stared unblinking at each other, a tender moment. Or so I thought. "Why aren't your feet moving?"

Because my body was high on heat. Delicious heat.

411

Nikki dropped back to stand at my side. A glowing specimen of hybrid perfection. It was a strain on my eyes not to fix them on him knowing the rest of the room had theirs fixed on me, definitely the nosey nymphs and annoying incubi. "Do you need to be bribed with food?"

"Yes, actually. Chocolate." He extended his arm in the direction we were destined, gallingly diligent keeping with my stride. Zander kept me moving onward with gentle urges on the low of my back. He'd been smelling Nikki's needs for how long?

"You'll never guess who showed interest in joining Bastion?"

"Who?"

"Torvi. She was adamant just last month about never going back to Numaal, but after her sister stabbed Zander and Fennick killed her woven I think I was able to talk her into taking her own revenge."

"I'm sorry. Shit. Wait. What?" My head shook hoping I heard all that wrong. With my finger held up to silence Yolanda I shot a fatal stare up at Zander. "Did you just forget to mention the or were you waiting for me to beat answers out of you, princess?"

He lifted his shirt to show zero evidence of damage. My imagination conjured up gruesome details of what his injury would have looked like. "I planned to tell you tonight during our discussion about the reply letter from Duke Cultee you received but if you are adamant—"

"Which I am!"

"—then short answers will have to suffice." My lips were in a tight line. I smacked Nikki's hand away. I didn't want my anger taken from me, Zander deserved my wrath.

"Fen and I took the honors of opening your letter. Cultee would fight with us, but it's not plausible to make it here in time with the ice, lacking food and knight blockages. He would likely lose his life and his guard's on the way. The wraiths have traveled north, congregating closer to Kathra. They are using them to defend the capital walls against attacks from its own people which tells us Torval has ownership or influence of the demon armies and that Numaal has started to see the atrocities of royal courts for what they are. The cloud of ignorance is lifting. Oh, he sends well wishes to us and Cobar!" He looked so damn cute avoiding the information I needed.

I cracked my knuckles. "Get to the part where you almost died. Or are you two allowed to have deadly adventures and secret?"

"Tanya stabbed me with an ice spear announcing that I would be the one to destroy this nation should we survive the war. Old news, I'm afraid. Fennick decapitated her before we could get answers. Torvi isn't talking much and her mind is useless. I don't trust her. I gave her a choice, to kill herself on the front lines fighting the Vulborg or go to the prison and kill herself there." He looked at Yolanda. "You shouldn't trust her. She is unhinged and will choose to enter the beyond at any unannounced moment. Just because I swayed her into submission, doesn't make her any less raving."

Zander looked paranoid. And inspired. He whistled for Alethim. Told him to look into the Frost Pack's census and current whereabouts of every single member and sent him off. His colors dimmed when he got lost in his thoughts of keeping tabs on every moving piece. Rust exhaustion filtered in. "Nikki, did she suffer before your mercy?"

"Yes." No amount of suffering was enough for an attempt to assassinate my woven and further harm him with her false words. His self-doubt and sorrow was the last thing he needed going forward.

"Good."

"But not enough."

"It would never have been enough."

I replied to Yolanda's excitement once her disgust in my announcement subsided. "You hardly speak of other topics outside of returning to Landsfell to turn the world on its head. Maybe you brainwashed Torvi in her vulnerable mentation."

She scoffed when Brock snickered. "Dreamers and humans get along just fine. It's just us red bloods have a lot to learn and are disadvantages for just about everything, but their company is refreshing. It's nice even when all she does is cry and coat my clothes in tears of frost. We all want the same things in life. Except Torvi looks ready to die. I can give her a cause. Revenge."

To imagine if Tanya triumphed in stealing my Zander away from me...*misery*. I'd be inconsolable were I alive. "None of us are that different it seems."

Brock glanced behind himself, eyeing my wovens. "Except for those two."

"Shit, don't I know it. Try having to stand next to them all the time."

"Rather you than me."

Zander cut in. "What are you two implying?"

"Seriously? Do you not look in mirrors?" Yolanda was walking backwards to stay involved in the conversation.

"How else do you imagine I get so impeccably dressed in the mornings?" Nikki emitted a hint of his Hilderbrand persona, accent and all. "Not like Wisteria who hasn't caught much of her own reflection since the day of the Gala when you bejeweled her."

"She outshined the sun that day. But every other day, she is the moon reflecting your shine." Her hands went up when Nikki's fire sputtered. "Take it easy, I'm not insulting my friend! Madam Marmacient would have had her pulling in more pastels than me if she had a more docile personality. But I am trying to say that you and Zander are still, well, *you* and *Zander*."

Nikki's feet stopped moving. "Wisteria, translate that for me with your expansive vocabulary."

A childish smirk escaped. "You are pretty. *Really pretty.*" He clicked his tongue in disgust. "Everyone who stands near you looks mundane and probably feels inadequate being they are not mutants from the Eternal's lineages."

His face fell. "Do you feel inadequate next to us?"

I evaluated his wicked disposition and choose my words wisely. "I am not everyone."

"Indeed you are not." His pale, colorless ponytail flowed down the center of his back as he turned left down the hallway where the torches reflected off the white stone floors. I followed the black swirls around his scapula and down to the dimples above his butt. "Do you feel you appear mundane or lackluster?"

Yolanda and I both tore our eyes off his ass to stare at the holes Zander's nails cut in my shirt along with my broken braid of brown hair. I certainly had drab bags under my eyes from avoiding sleep and was too thin. I shrugged. "I mean even with Orion and the wardrobe you got me—which Zander proceeded to botch—I'm within the limits of ordinary."

"Do you feel you belong among us?" Obviously, I did but I wasn't going to call out threads here.

"I am branded like cattle. I perhaps belong in a herd." I was afraid to look at Nikki when I replied. I took to admiring Zander instead.

Zander examined his handy work on my neck as I spoke. His smug smile was absolutely tantalizing. I popped up on my toes and stole a kiss there in the hallway. Brock trekked on refusing to witness his sovereign swap spit.

"And without a botched blue blouse, do you feel adequate?" Nikki demanded my attention from the threshold of our room.

Like a dog with a bone he would *not* let it go. I wasn't about to get bit. "You have ears. You heard what the room said about my scars." I pointed behind us. "Hell, I even heard it. But seeing their diverted pity painted a clear enough image for me I don't need to look at my scars. Besides, you've seen more than I have. You tell me the answer to your own question and stop aggravating me."

His flames sputtered across the ground. Brock's commentary about lacking a foot to fry helped me ignore what was clearly an upset fox prowling towards me. "Say goodnight to our comrades, Master Woodlander." Oh, no. Not *this* tone.

Refusing to engage, I obstinately backed away. Landing directly onto Zander's hard body. Chipper farewells left his mouth as he bent over to kiss me one last time. I trapped his lips in mine and pleaded, "Don't leave me alone with him."

"I'll be back after I see Yolanda and Cobar to the safehouse and get Brock fit for a balanced boot."

"What happened to sleeping without night terrors? I'm exhausted."

"Nikki has to reform your infuriating self-assumptions first. I'll be back and under the sheets with you two before you miss me."

"I don't need reforming! What have I done to offend him?"

Zander gave a gingerly peck on my cheek and then waved Brock to his side. They were to help carry Yolanda's few personal belongings from their shared room to the Glacier. "His methods are deviant but historically proven successful the few times I've seen him work on stubborn behaviors. Mine included. I'm sure you will tell me all about it along with how he has since erased the words 'grotesque flesh' and 'cattle herd' from your word bank of self-descriptive identifiers."

"You've got to be kidding me." I shouted at Zander. Those offhand remarks are what prompted his personality change? Stupid.

"The people in the hall use far harsher adjectives." I was speaking to no one. And everyone. Yolanda shed her frustration enough to let other emotions surface. I embraced her hug, whispering a loving threat of what would come if she or Cobar weren't alive when Keenan and I came for them. Brock half hugged me and was quick to exit with Yolanda.

Zander turned on his heel. "Fen, glorify our goddess."

That left me with Nikki. His tails were rigid. "In."

"No."

"Why? Do you find me scary?" That didn't deserve a reply. "This is nothing, baby. In."

I tiptoed around him. "Just so we are clear, I am inside because I am exhausted and you implied there'd be food." My hair stood on end from the static of his stare. The door shut behind us.

Chapter Thirty-Two

Wordlessly, he moved pumpernickel bread to the table with cinnamon butter spread. Chilled tomato bisque followed. He didn't eat, he sulked off to his room where I heard the groaning of heavy furniture being moved. Waiting to see my punishment was causing my anxiety to race and mind to swim in dreadful possibilities.

I eyed my escape. His voice echoed into the kitchen. "I'd catch you. Don't bother." He had worked up a sweat exerting himself. I watched his dewy skin gleam as he leaned against the door to his room. I took my dishes to the sink and attempted to escape his watchfulness by hustling towards the washroom. "Strip, but don't step in the showers. I'll be needing your clothes off for what I have planned."

I gave a longing glance at the exit before the ability to speak returned to my shocked senses. "Is this necessary?"

"You've seen what happens when you fail to listen or make me repeat myself."

I unlaced the waist of my cotton trousers. He was wrong. I *felt* what happened when I failed to pour the drinks without spilling. My shirt was tossed onto the floor with my bottoms.

He surveyed my progress. He was pleased. Though not pleased enough. "Do you need help with the clasps of the bralette?" I shook my head. "Kindly request that Orion give us some alone time. He must learn to trust you with me, no better time than the present." I set down my steel friend on the side table and worked towards the rest of his request.

My breasts hung heavy. I lifted the strap of my thong. *"That* stays." The need pulsing through our bodies tempted me with the unruly idea to remove it. The muscles of my groin tightened. I looked at the bulging culprit in Nikki's pants, pressing my thighs together.

"Are you certain about that? Feels a lot like you want me to step out of my panties."

"Ignore it."

"I can't."

Nikki signaled me closer. He unbound the rest of my braid only to twist it in a tight knot at the top my head. "Find a way." His warm breath swept across my newly exposed neck line. My toes flexed with unseen delight; although, I anticipated what was to come would not be making my toes curl.

"How do you ignore it?"

"Practice."

"Care to divulge the secrets of your success?"

"Time."

I scoffed. "Of course the immortal answers with unobtainable solutions for the human. Well done. Great job illuminating. Helpful."

He held both of my shoulders and brought his nose to mine. "Are you done being satirical?"

"Depends. Are you going to answer with a better, more applicable answer?"

"There is no answer. The urges are here and difficult to ignore. But I do it because I respect you."

It was painful to ignore. "Maybe you should disrespect me." I sighed into his chest, which rose and fell in his normal unbreakable rhythm. I wanted to press myself onto his warm flesh, coax my fingers down that tantalizing V dipping into his pants. "I should have kept all my clothes on."

"No. I need you as you are. I need to interpret what it is you see and instill in you what I see with a little help from the Eternals." He held out a hand

and I took it. It calmed our needs before they erupted. His thumb clamped down on my fingers. There was no escaping the inferno. Only facing it.

He led me into his room which was rearranged with many mirrors standing and facing each other in a circle. I didn't need his prodding and sultry voice in my ear to tell me the obvious next steps. "Are you coming with me?"

"Do you need me too?" Unable to willingly let go of his hand, I nodded. "You first. Then the lights come on."

I wedged myself between the tall pieces of glass, feeling more exposed despite being surrounded by furniture. More nervous than I anticipated I'd be, I took Nikki's second hand and faced him, waiting for his flames to brighten my reflection. He let me fidget. My tapping toes and shifting weight teetered me into him. My palm sweated.

A ring of fire unleashed from Nikki's will and coiled around the parameter of mirrors.

My image was unavoidable.

When I caught sight of my back in the mirrors over Nikki's shoulder it wasn't rage or disgust that surged within me. Disbelief. I squinted to get a clear view at the damage that had been done for it was far more infeasible than I had been picturing in my mind's eye all this time.

The flesh looked as if it had been shredded with a field plowing machine, the ones Conrad had barters for years ago. It was barely fused together over the bones. My tattoo was unrecognizable with the ribbons of scars placed every which direction and angle over the canvas of my back. Many healed an angry red coloring, looking as if they were placed days ago. But, the double headed raven was distinct with its clear raised edges.

Dread came.

Without closing my eyes, I saw him. Stark, midnight feathers consumed my vision. My racing heart blurred my peripheral. I blinked the panic off my face.

I could see nothing other than Prince Torval's black beaked mask peering down at me while I lay in my own blood and bile, fighting futilely against the white hot branding. Spurred by my reflection this dream haunted my awake hours now. My palms sweat and my heart raced as if any moment he would rob me of that organ as well.

Such sickening ownership in the manner he *allowed* me to leave as if he knew I'd one day choose to accept his offer. All good feelings fled me, arousal included. My gut sank as if it was made of stone and iron eroding on the ocean floor.

Spilling my blood and inscribing my body with his emblem wasn't enough. He further sought possession by adorning me in his garments. Shivers racked me, recalling the perfumed scent of his clothes wrapping around me. I left the haven of Nikki's safe arms. I was so close to the mirror now my breath fogged up the glass surface.

It was dreadful. Yet, I couldn't turn my thoughts away from the Faceless Prince. As long as that symbol stained me I would think of him. And it would always be on me. At least until it serves its purpose, evidence that I was the unfortunate soul damned to be wed to the royal wraith. Nikki would jump at the opportunity to melt that chunk of flesh off my body when I asked it of him.

Warm, steady knuckles brushed mine. "What do you see?

"Prince Torval."

"I feared this was the case when you first mentioned to me you've not laid eyes on your back nor glanced at your reflection." A sigh left me. "The cattle comment? That is bullshit. Shut it down now."

I gave a grimace with my next sigh. "I can't let you remove his emblem. Not yet. And even if you could, he will never leave me. His wounds are deeper than what you can see. My rage keeps his crimes alive. My rage never eases, therefore he is ever present."

"He will leave you. I'll see to it myself." Patient and displeased. "Give me details, the particulars, of what you are looking at."

"Everything that I can possibly recollect about him. His aged voice, his arrogant demeanor, his ghastly perfume, the texture of his overcoat. That eerie raven's mask, I see it hovering next to me in each one of these blasted mirrors. I feel him staring at my body. Touching my body." I spun to look at Nikki, but only caught my reflection in ten other directions. The prince looming in all of them.

He vibrated with anger as if all fibers of his being were thrumming with winds of a hurricane. All the excitement we felt walking into the room was buried under his pissy mood and my self-loathing. "He *touched* you?"

"What did you expect?"

His hands knotted together behind his back as he tightened his posture. "Where?"

"He put a finger first to my lips." Nikki stared at my moving mouth. "Then he brushed my hair away from my back, along my chin."

Nikki moved in and held me tightly as if we were in his father's family room dancing. A hand on my back and the other he brushed the side of my neck, soothing the stubborn strands of hair that refused to be pinned atop my head. His wet lips roamed up and down both sides of my neck. Firm, but never parting. Light lingered where his lips journeyed. "Where else?" He was breathing deeply in the pocket of my neck and chest waiting for my reply.

"His boot crushed my hand when I reached for a weapon."

Lips met my knuckles and grazed their way to the tip of each finger and onto my palm. "Where else?" I was memorized by the light holding tight to my skin. Purging memories of trauma in it's aftermath.

I pointed to my jawline where the prince pinched as he inspected me, rubbing my blood between his thumb and forefinger after his priestess spilled it. My mind momentarily went blank while his closed mouth stroked the column of my extended neck and swirled around my chin. "Eyes open." I complied, watching him nuzzle into my temple. The raven faces stared at us from the mirrors. They seemed jealous. "Where else?"

I could lie to him. Tell him my intimate bits were tarnished, knowing his mouth would follow there. "My back. He put slathered petroleum on before the layers of clothes." The truth came forward much to my body's disappointment.

Out came a lone chair. "Straddle it."

I spread my thighs and sat pressing my breasts over the high back of the chair. "Perfect," he purred. Nikki locked onto my eyes in the mirror. "When that monster of a man disappears from your sight, I will stop. Not, a moment sooner. Alright?"

I whipped my head around to meet his physical form. "What am I agreeing to exactly?"

Nikki stepped around the chair intentionally dropping to his knees in front of me. His bright flaming eyes drew me in as if I was a moth drawn to the light. "When that twisted fuckall of a man ceases to exist when you look at yourself in the mirror, I will stop. Not, a moment sooner. Alright?"

"What happened to sleep?"

His arms jerked out and gripped the chair. Reflexively, I latched onto the high back. He tipped me forwards on two of the legs to better view the molten intensity set in his face. The same intensity that pervaded each one of his muscles. His physic bulged. "The first thoughts that grace your mind when you are naked are those of another man. An abuser. A demon lord. A blood crafter. A killer." His lips pressed into my forehead and resistance left me. "Unacceptable."

Fatigue aside, I caved into his vortex of madness. "Alright, fix me."

"Nothing is broken. This is a purging. I have some Eternal gifts of light and am learnt in purification ceremonies. I've adapted this one for you."

On his knees he shuffled directly behind me. While he summoned Drommal and Dradion I saw my own apprehension in the mirrors. The manner in which he stared so unobstructed at my scars and my ass in such a close proximity was spellbinding. Adoration and lust. He didn't bother to hide his smile. Nor the wickedness seeping through when deep seeded hate emerged and darkness brushed the surface of his twisted mind. "You are safe with me." Nikki's raspy tone signaled the end of his prayers that drew down two of the Eleven's power. He was close enough to their bloodline for the summoning to work.

"I know."

"You will watch every second of my worship. If you turn away, I'll start from the beginning. Which is approximately... right... here." Lips came crashing down on my spine.

I straightened feeling his smile. His amusement came out in bursts of hot air brushing against my flesh. "Wisteria, you are absolutely divine. Sinful and sacred. Wild and wise. Infuriating and infatuating." I swallowed the complements. "You damn me with your presence. If denouncing the Eternals and kneeling before you solidifies my afterlife in a world of repentance, I'd happily go to die in the darkness of the beyond." His gaze was no longer on my shocked expression, but on each minuscule detail of my scars' webbing, rolled edges and pursed texture.

His hands started on my hips but soon joined his mouth caressing my defects with the utmost devotion. And the manner he held me, touched me, looked at me, *was* devotion. Did all protector wovens carry traits of amity bonds?

Nikki traced the scars long and short, deep and superficial, until he and I were certain each one had been blessed by his touch and trail of light. But, he was nowhere near complete. The stone hard chest and abdominals of my woven pressed firmly against my back. "You like me on my knees."

I did.

"I do."

My resolve was melting. My ass on the edge of the chair shifted into Nikki, I swayed into him as if that was answer enough. His cock shifted under the taut fabric of his pants as I ground down. "I'm starting to envy that chair. I should have made you sit on my face. There will be a puddle under you when we are finished and this wasn't even the intent for the evening."

He locked gazes with mine. "If you turn away my blushing vixen, we start all over again."

I smirked. "Maybe that's what I want."

He touched the outer edges of the circular symbol on my right shoulder. His mouth followed, this time with his tongue unbridled. My arm reached over my shoulder. I buried my fingers in his hair while heat broke through me in blissful waves. "Nikki." Fuck. That touch was what I wanted. But the amount available to me was not nearly enough.

More. I needed him more than I needed water on ashwynder salts.

"After I banish haunting evils, you will tell me what you want. Precisely and explicitly." A whimper dislodged from my throat. "Look in the mirror at your cheeks pinking up. Aren't you the most beautiful woman?" I obeyed because I had too.

I took in the sight of my partially open mouth gasping from his fiery, minimal contact and my freckles falling in awe as he worked over the burn on my shoulder. Painless fire coated me. "Do you see what I see?"

"What is that exactly?"

"If you have to ask, then you do not." He spoke in my ear and pushed himself slightly away to better take in the state of my spine in its alit entirety. I rested my chin on the heel of my hand watching him get lost in the butcher's design on my back. Happily lost, I might add, as if he was reading the scars like one of his most favorite historical texts.

"You are exquisite. I'd always seen you as such, down to your core. In fact, your soul speaks to me more than your flesh, more than your words. Written and unspoken. Although, the call of your body to mine is undeniable. You are, as you phrased it, 'You are pretty. Really pretty."

The whispers of touches paired with his muttering of constant praise heated my cheeks more. Disparity sent a whining noise through my chest. I leaned into his hands, demanding more of his touch. I rolled deeper into his crotch. His hands ensnared my hips, dragging me into his hot embrace and against his stone hard bulge in his pants.

He kept a slow burning grind of friction between us that had me moaning more than once. He kept that tantalizing pace as his lesson in self-love persisted. "Your scars are the star's way of displaying your soul. They scream *strength, survival*. They rally *purpose*. They attribute *confidence*. They tell of the lengths you go for love." He paused to gauge my smile. And I was smiling because he was right.

I tried reaching behind me to caress his tattooed flank. His response was the swift removal of his belt, which he proceeded to use to bind my wrists to the top of the chair. I blinked, unsure if I wanted to protest or continue on with his lesson. He moved his lips out of reach from mine. "You cannot have me now. Not while you are lusting." He gave a gentle reminder and bit down into my shoulder. Well, a not so gentle reminder that I was encroaching on the line. "When you cross that boundary, I need you clear headed for that choice."

I tore my eyes away from the leather binds and onto his cold, white smirk. "But what if I don't want my soul flaunted to the world? What if I want to keep it protected?"

His grip on me lessened when I didn't fight. "Then taking off your shirt in front of conclave and when you fought Ik Kygen on Taite's temple was probably not the best idea. Zander wasn't the only one wanting to go around ripping eyes from sockets and cutting off tongues." I cast a glare at him in one of the mirrors. "Purpose struck me when I first saw your scars in the Deadlands. As it does every time after."

"My scars give you purpose?"

He sucked in cool air behind my ear, my spine twisted. "Yes, baby. Ask me all the ways I have planned to hunt down and torture Collette?" His eyes smoldered now. Steam rose from them when his voice went dark. "I've forged enough weapons with the heat of my own hands to strike her stupid for at least seven years and never repeat a whip or iron prod. I can't wait to divulge what Zander and I have planned for the monster who hurt you and offered our woman a fucking marriage proposal within the span of the same breath."

Nikki watched the delicate bob in my neck as I swallowed. "Will it be savage?" I began to turn towards him, the leather binds preventing me from chasing down his mouth with mine. I stiffened when I managed to regain control over my body. He was absolutely correct in restraining me from crossing a lusty line.

"Yes, carving out his organs in a savage act of passion while Zander bends his mind and brands him with his stallion medallion. Blood on the walls, screams down the halls, wails across the nations."

"I want in on in it."

Between his restrained cock thrusting against me and the rhythmic teasing way he moved I went weightless in his arms. That was until a gritty tone met my ear. "Of course you do, my crafty bloodthirsty vixen. I will happily oblige." He set me up right and shifted out of the line of sight to the full span of my back which had golden lines of fire every which way. My skin glistened with his magic. I felt more stunning as if kissed by the stars themselves.

"I do look beautiful."

A howl of joy erupted from Nikki. I couldn't help but crack a grin. "Tell me that Prince Torval is gone and I'll provide you the opportunity to start describing those explicit desires you want fulfilled."

"Would you fulfill them or do you simply enjoy torturing me with what I can't have yet?" I fixed my gaze on the binds he placed.

His smile was sinister. My heart dove into my gut and flipped, tossing butterflies every which direction. "Wisteria, I've hardly begun to torture you. Besides, I never said I wasn't going to indulge your filthy fantasies. At least a little."

I matched his raised brow and contented grin. "No, you are coyly avoiding telling me *when* you will. *If* you will."

He was on his knees resting gloriously in front of me with the whirling outline of his tattoo blazing shadows against his golden skin. I combed over him with my eyes, triumphantly giving a faint grin when I discerned the image inked on him. He muttered Drommal's name and the strains of twinkling lights on my back ceased to shine, leaving the same gouges in my skin that were there when we started.

I dared a deeper glance. The double beaked crow mask snarled over my shoulder. My tunnel vision went to its charcoal black beady eyes. "He is still here." The defeat in my confession only sparked inspiration in my woven.

With a loud scrape that echoed, he dragged the chair I was strapped on over to the nearest mirror and pivoted us so I could see the red steel dagger dancing around his knuckles. He had skill with a blade, who would have thought that turned me on as much as it did when I watched the griffin heirloom twist around his knuckles. He pressed his sternum to the back of the chair. My hands caught awkwardly between us. The blade of his heirloom dagger pricked along the edges of the longest transverse scar. "If I cannot carve him out, I will carve myself in." My head nodded in agreement.

It was fucked up, but charmingly and poetically so.

"Yes." My reply was quick.

He paused and gave space for a retreat. A retreat that I would never take. "Nikki, I want to see you when I see my scars. I want to recall visions of you on your knees when I catch my naked reflection."

The response was the sharp edge of his dagger splitting my skin. My nails bit into my palm. "Eyes open," he ordered. I sagged my chin against his collarbone and let my gaze fall to the small rivers of scarlet trickling slowly down my back.

"I feel each cut, each dragging pull, each piercing edge. Now, we share this pain. This burden is not yours to keep to yourself any longer. Tattoo them on me if we must." I winced as he took to slicing a half dozen marks on the cushion of my hip. Our quintessing let him feel each sharp sensation. I was not alone.

He whispered his name and reiterated how lovely he found me each time he drew blood, pouring himself into each open cut as my own blood poured out. An exchange of essence.

His furrowed brow held a bead of sweat when we neared completion. Our pain and determination glinted on pale lashes. Fatigue and loss of precious fluid pushed me to slump over the chair, the belt held all my weight. "My vision grows bleary." I announced before my eyes shut. I physically could not afford for him to restart this process when my eyes closed the world off.

He retracted his dagger and moved his long silver hair matting in blood off of his heaving chest. He had been so invested in carving himself into me it seemed a miracle he was able to bring himself out of his intensely captivating work. My blood decorated his hands, wrists and large sections of his silky hair. "Tell me what you see," he panted.

I set my focus on my fresh wounds. Tunnel vision dissipated. "I see a strong girl with her pretty woven. A crow flies behind them."

His lips pressed to my forehead in a sigh of relief. "Progress." With five tugs on the belt my wrists dropped free. I flexed them working out the soreness. I peeled myself out of the chair, blood pulled beneath my thighs as I rose. "I want you to drink my blood before we shower."

"We?" My heart skipped along stupidly until the request in his statement sank in. "I have an aversion to drinking Ilanthian blood."

"I am offering it to you willingly to heal *us*. There is no deception at play other than my wish to mend you, prevent pain and fainting." Balancing me with strong arms he drew me near, admiring his handy work as I nestled close. "And, in full disclosure, I selfishly desire to feel your lips pressed against my skin. This is the most decent thing I can think of at the present moment that involves your mouth and my body." He held out his left wrist pointing just below Zander's mark.

I bared my dull teeth. He flashed his sharpened ones, solving the problem I spotted. "Say it. That you agree."

"I'll drink your blood." Nikki spun me until my lacerations were against his chest, I growled at the outrageous sting of open flesh and bucked away in painful protest.

Teeth dove into his wrist and punctured the vessels beneath his skin bringing it to my mouth a half second later. I lapped up a leeward drop with the flick of my tongue before sealing my lips around the two holes gushing with blessed blood. "That's my good girl." Nikki groaned in my ear. The kind of noise that urged me to pull his blood harder.

Iron and a tangy taste of sunshine splashed against my palette. I swallowed three mouthfuls of sunlight, feeling his puncture wounds shrink each time my tongue passed over them. My throbbing cuts on my back dulled. When his blood stopped flowing my back closed into an array of scars.

He was pleased with himself as I reluctantly released his wrist. We exited his bedroom and he led me to the showers which were already running warm. Steam clung to Zander's naked body as he stood there with lathered sponges in each hand sudsing his chest hair—waiting for us.

Nikki relinquished me to Zander who rolled down my blood stained thong and kicked it aside on the tile floor of the shower. The glass door was left open. Nikki made himself at home on the counter by the sink watching scarlet evidence of the lesson spill down the drain.

Papers poked out of Nikki's pocket. I pointed to them. "You're still carrying those around?"

"Did you mean what you wrote?"

I found courage inside myself to get a single syllable out. "Yes." And what a loaded syllable that was. In typical illusive Nikki manner, he said nothing further. Not letting his mask slip to give me a glimpse into how my disclosure was received. Other than his raging stiff cock.

Zander; however, doused me in reciprocated loving hues that were strong enough that I'd have felt them on the opposite side of the world. *I love you too.* His breathing faltered behind me. I'm certain he was near tears. Standing under the water faucet I waited for Nikki to say something.

"Then I'll cherish them." He intended on letting me initiate everything. Awkward conversations included.

The waters around me ran crimson as my body was scrubbed clean and hair conditioned. Nikki yipped twice when Zander's fingers slipped between my legs, the connection between us was already electrified since he allowed himself to watch me in the shower and his erection had been begging for attention for hours.

I toyed with the idea of enticing Zander's hard on, but the gaze from Nikki deterred me and steered me towards choosing the option that would let me leave there with my life. "Wait for us in bed." Nikki wrapped me in a towel when I emerged from the waters. He stripped and offered me his backside as he stepped in front of Zander who took to washing Nikki's hair and dried blood off his body.

I perched myself on the counter to watch the two of them rinse each other and exchange words in low tones. Gods, they were sexy. Nikki closed the glass door with a warning, "Bed. Before I pull you in here."

"I *want* to be pulled in there."

Zander was jumping up and down with jubilation which made my heart lighten. I heard a rough smack of a wet towel on skin shortly after that told me I better get my ass to bed.

Nikki said nothing about wearing clothes to bed.

Turning off the lights behind me, I slid into the large bed. This mattress was ten times more preferable to sleeping on a cot in the same filthy outfit for days on end or bringing wraiths to the valley. I banished those thoughts along with the woes of my magic, to give myself the best opportunity I had to rest at peace.

Zander found his way back to me first, laughing delightedly at what he found. He pulled me to his side, carefully stroking my spine and not mentioning a word about Nikki's messy methods. The tidal waters of my magic ocean receded. I dozed off waiting for Nikki, but proudly smirked when I heard him mumble under his breath. "She is a fucking menace."

"The best kind," Zander agreed. "A menace that loves us."

After a cart load of curse words, there was a *poof* as Nikki changed forms and a heavy white and warm fox climbed onto my chest, wedging himself between Zander and I. I repositioned my arms to hold them both tightly.

I dared Death to take them from me.

Chapter Thirty-Three

I woke up to Zander massaging my shoulder and scrutinizing my back with kind eyes. "Let's let Fen sleep in. His nocturnal rhythms are skewed." I agreed, placing a kiss on the wet, whiskered nose before we got dressed in silence.

"No mischievous magic escaped from me last night?"

"Only mischief. No magic," he winked and cupped the round of my ass before I pulled up my pants.

Zander's brothers, their partners, woven and niece gathered around the breakfast table with Maruc, some Ivory Legionnaires, my Bloodsworns and Alethim. Keenan placed a walnut muffin in my grip, I felt his urgency and began to eat. Crumbs fell down my blouse when I questioned the energy in the room.

"My best guess says the runegate will fall before sunup in three days. Four if fate favors us. Two if She wants to fuck with us." Maruc informed. That explains why the halls of the Keep were emptying quickly. They went off to be stationed at their assigned posts. "My Ivory Legion will be summoned to encompass the Altar of Horns, but they will not be sent into battle. They will protect the entrance to Ilanthia. I will leave the sidelines *once* and that is to rebuild the runegate. Unless you and yours have decided on an answer that would convince me otherwise." He arched his well groomed brow at me.

"I'm in. All willing." I shot my hand out for a shake.

Zander grunted, knocking my arm away. "I'm not."

I pushed his chest. He didn't move. "What are you doing?"

"I want you to live *free*."

"Well, this deal *drastically* helps our chances to remain alive. I'll pledge myself now."

He shook his head, his bearded jaw flexing. "Not unless it is absolutely necessary. It is a standing bargain and we know where to find him cowering away from the frontlines should we need to seal our fate."

"Suit yourself, vessel of Oyokos." Maruc handed me water. "Fill your stores, Wisteria. Our training begins in three minutes. I don't intend to go easy on you if the war is on the horizon. We've not much time to get your magic sorted out." My stomach protested. I wanted to spend all morning with a plate stacked of flat cakes not in combat against the sword he aimed at me.

Percy made comments of me chomping nuts as hungry as a squirrel tending to his nut sack. I crumpled the wrapper and chucked it at his face. He unsheathed his sword enough to threaten me and I escaped by crawling under the table. Kashikat, Nyx and Warroh laughed, Clavey's slender legs tried to kick me. I punched his knee cap. He jerked upright. "Ass," I muttered fully knowing he heard me.

"Do you like it down there? Did Zander train his new pup how to please him on her knees?"

The table erupted above me. Curses and cutlery flew. Zander–assumably– put his fist through Clavey's face. There was way too much laughter and not enough punching. I watched nimble elf feet hop away from the chaos and I scurried towards freedom, towards the fireplace. Maruc's shiny boots closed in on me. Yet, it was Keenan who scooped me off the ground. "Thirty seconds," Maruc hummed playfully.

My gut twisted. "It is never a good sign when Eternals are feeling playful." I grasped Orion. "Swords or magic?"

"Both."

Maybe I could plant some slick moss under his feet to offset his balance. Maybe a night lily would distract him. I resigned to my embarrassing fate while the sons of Atticus let their diversions die down. My time was up. I had not a second to spare to tap into the sensation of my magic well or direct it with my intentions. I blocked a series of strikes and tried my luck kicking off the nearest stone pillar to gain the upper hand.

Too easy. I sliced right through Maruc which meant that he had magicked illusions of himself. Whipping around I caught sight of two more Emperors, identical in every manner. I took my chances.

I chose wrong.

The true Maruc's open palm smashed me square in the sternum and sent me flying. My words were drowned out by my gasping noises as I greedily attempted to suck air into my lungs. A contusion had already formed on my chest. The brutal landing left a mark smarting on my ass cheek. Zander was growling from across the room. Maruc held him at bay with a whispered spell. Gold and blue eyes pierced through the crowd and fixed on me.

He looked down at me sorting out myself on the floor. "I'm sure the fox didn't appreciate that." I found the painful truth in his words. "Do better. For both your sakes. Because you care too little about your life, maybe the right motivation is to threaten those you love."

I imagined Nikki binding me up last night and rocking his length against my ass. I would have kissed him ten times had he not stoked my damn fire so much and left me at a loss of words. I looked to Zander. *Tell Nikki I am sorry. I'll wise up while he works on cutting off the quintessing bond.* Zander agreed, although his mood was now rotten.

Of all the profanities on the tip of my tongue I chose to reply with earnest. "I will."

"You know, if you had been wearing Morial's suit of armor, the blows of magic *and* might would be more tolerable." For you both—he let the latter go unsaid.

I steadied myself on my feet, refusing Keenan's aid. "Is it still up for grabs?" I muttered regrettably.

He pointed to the clock on the wall. "Sure. I will be striking at you next when the long hand reaches the twelve. That gives you sixty seconds to suit up. Starting... now."

I'd no super speed to dart there and back, even with the city's portal. I hadn't managed to successfully summon inanimate objects despite Maruc spending two full days teaching me how. I closed my eyes and easily found the waters of my power rippling over the surface of my soul. I ran my fingers across the glassy surface that sent the magic beneath roaring.

A portal. I could do those.

Not well. Frequently it was anchored to the noxious Deadlands, but for Nikki's sake I'd try. My arm outstretched and cool, raw magic glided over my skin into the outer world. I felt relief when the bubbling magic left me. Which meant... "You've lost seventeen seconds." The last God declared. I stared at the oval doorway suspended in the middle of the breakfast hall.

I'd done it. Percy, Brock and Keenan had their swords at the ready. Last time I cast a portal, wraiths sprinted out. Oops.

Keenan grabbed my collar with his free hand, yanking my foot out of the misty portal. "You cannot just fling yourself into unknown doors!"

I twisted out of his grip, his eyes fixed on the terror that may spill out. "Then come with me you boring old man. Live a little!" I pulled him with me and together we tumbled into the elaborate dressing room of Morial. There was no time to *ohh* or *ahh* at the Goddessness of her wardrobe. I knocked over the life-size wooden mannequin holding the gleaming majestic pieces of her armor. "Hurry, help me, I have no idea how to wear this!"

Keenan was at my side tugging breast plates over my head and fastening the left shoulder scales. It fit as if it was designed for me. A second skin. A tougher skin. "Ivory is not your color." He lifted the pure fabric flowing behind me and cut it off with his dagger.

"Neither is gold." I pointed to his current Bloodsworn ensemble. The color debate would wait. I pressed gauntlets, a mantel and thin sheets of chainmail into his burly arms as we took off leaping through the portal that led us here. The landing was little improved, I was bulkier and clumsier with the added weight of the metal formed to my muscles. Not a drastic difference, but it'd take time to adjust.

Zander's amethyst colors of lust bit at my heels when he saw my tumble in. I spared him a glance and realized Morial must have infused her beauty into this gear for several sets of eyes tailed me. If they didn't remove them soon, my woven would see them plucked.

Five seconds to spare I grinned at Maruc. Which was quickly wiped off my face when he began to summon magic into his blade. His steel darkened and the weather outside hummed with a wayward current visible from one of the many balconies.

Eternal's personal protection or not, I was not risking Nikki's life getting struck by *that*. My magic ceased pouring out as I closed the entrance to the private chambers in the White Tower and I drew it into the pool in the center of my being. "Block me," he demanded. A gust of wind knocked Orion from my grip.

My friend shot lightning at his brother's head from across the hall in bitter protest. Maruc's weapon was raring to strike amid the tantrum Orion was lashing out. There was no time to pull off a Montuse dodge or an Ilanthian two-step. I pressed my hands into the floor and pulled the crust of the earth over my head as a shield.

My work shattered on impact. Stones the size of my skull crumpled round me, burying me under the rubble.

"Wisteria!" Angered reds and anxious slates swarmed my bond with Zander.

I wormed and kicked my way out. "I'm alright!" I rubbed dust from my eyes. "More than alright, actually." I whistled for Orion and he flew back into my dominant hand.

Stepping around the gaping hole I dug up, I flexed my body in the new protective layer. Testing its range of motion and my ability to successfully land handsprings. I fussed with the shoulder guard. "Don't even think about removing any piece of that." Zander grumbled from his perch on top of the kitchen table. His brothers had all gathered around openly making bets on my fate. Asshats.

"It's compromising my–." Yes, fine. Nikki. I'd make it work.

Maruc centered himself to me. "At the top of the minute we go again."

My speed lagged; and therefore my predictability was lusterless. I couldn't fix speed without months more of physical training, but with my magic I may have a way out of this yet. Now, only if I could get it to obey me.

"Shutting your eyes is foolish on the battlefield. I don't recommend that, especially when your enemy just multiplied."

I swatted his words away and beckoned my magic forwards to be accessed. I opened and closed my palm, feeling the tides of my power come and go.

The chilliness of it invigorating. The magnitude of its depths, terrifying. All oceans had bottoms, right?

There were three of him. I'd take out one at a time. A second before the minute hand struck vertical I started my sprint, not at him but at the wall. I cast a portal, another right after, and ran through them consecutively until I popped out behind Maruc with Orion ready. He blocked me, but I was off into another portal in the corner of the room before he countered.

I emerged on the left of one of his images and crouched to stab him in the flank. An arm appeared from the portal. It grabbed the blade before it met his Godly flesh, blood oozed from his hand. "You forgot to close the passages behind you."

I was flung into a portal and skidded out by the fireplace where two Emperors came at me. I dodged on defense, drawing in the magic I cast.

I poured magic beneath our feet and together Maruc and I fell into the floor. We dropped from the ceiling.

Frantically, I grasped at a beam fifty feet above the kitchen table while Maruc crash landed on his back far below me, splintering the marble floor every which way beneath him.

Percy, Kailynder and Zander collected money from Kashikat and Clavey. *As if I'd ever bet against you my vicious love.*

Flattered. I blew him a kiss. I spared a raised brow to Kailynder who had put his coin on the triumph of a rogue and high tailed it across the narrow wooden beam until I found some stability against the wall. I closed the portals while I tried to formulate a way down.

Maruc merged duplicates. The playfulness in his laugh was consumed by mischievousness. "Now, this is more like it." He rose off the ground entirely unharmed to soothe the damage he and I both caused on Atticus's flooring.

"Let me guess. At the top of the minute you are going to try and knock me down from here?"

"Not try. I *will* knock you off the rafters." He swirled his arm and gathered an orb of wind. "It's up to you how not to die. Portals. Rising earths. Soft landings. Montuse acrobatics. Figure it out." Zander was the first on his feet, pacing below where I stood. His beautiful black and white wings came to two points above his broad shoulders. All too soon, a gust slapped me across the face. Gravity claimed me.

Unable to orient myself to create a portal, I tried the next best thing. I grit down on an awful scream as leathery wings ripped through my back and through the straps of fitted armor. I opened them timely enough to lessen the momentum, but still crashed into the coffee table with my elbows and knees. A chair flipping on top of me was icing on the cake. I was surprised Clavey wasn't stitched with laughter. Kashikat was. Nyx too.

The chorus of painful gasps and cheers rallied around me. "Looks like she really is one of us. Welcomed to the wing club, little sis'!" Warroh whooped. Warroh of all the brothers. I made a gagging noise.

"Speak for yourselves," Wyatt cut in with his thorny attitude.

"She isn't anywhere near ready for the flight division. Let's throw the little bat off the Leap!" I wiped blood from my forearms, glaring at Kashikat. Somehow his aging skin youthened when he was grinning like an idiot.

Zander crouched beside me, admiring the webbing projecting from my spine and the slits in my tunic. I latched onto him as a shudder rang through me when the pads of his fingers caressed the spines of the wings. Pleasure of the carnal kind prompted me to ask him to touch me there again via syphering. I scowled when he denied me. *Let's add it to our list of foreplay and fuckery. I'll kill whoever watches you shiver like that. Family or not.*

I ran my fingers through his three silky braids as an apology. He lifted me to my feet where I promptly fell back on my ass again. A laugh I once found irksome reverberated around the entirety of Horn's Keep. Now, it was a beautiful noise.

My woven was happy, even with war so near. "Little love, those wings weigh more than you." He wiped a tear from his bright blue eye, while the gold one simmered with mirth. "Try pixie wings next time if you want to fly instead of faceplant." I'd never examined a pixie's up close. I likely wouldn't have pulled it off on such a short notice.

"Carry me while I figure out how to make these bat wings... go away." I latched myself onto his side where he lifted me up and secured me to his hip. Percy made a bird call that Atticus silenced with a single look. Percy's hand reflexively went to his pocket to whip out a canteen. When he rummaged around and came up with a tea bag, the faintest of fatigued smiles tugged at his lips.

I spun my will around the wings on my back where muscles I didn't know existed burned, after a long breath the weight of them lifted and my magic retreated into its container. Which was still full. Too full. Maruc informed me our practice was far from over. "Brock!" Maruc called across the room. "You are off the hook."

Brocked whooped and shimmied his shoulder in my direction. "Oh, sweet salvation. You have no idea how happy I am to hear that." He filled me in before I inquired. "If you didn't start using an ounce of magic to defend yourself, I agreed to let him start swinging at me because we are almost certain you would pull it off to protect someone else."

"You're both incredibly maddening."

"Yes, but it would have worked."

It did. Maruc had to go and bring up my body sharing woven. I fought for him. "You're right. I would have." My glare deepened at Maruc who went on chatting insouciantly with his legionnaire in ivory.

I didn't release Zander's side. I locked my thighs around him and kissed his jawline as he pointed it towards his father. "After we eat, who is up for a friendly game of Pitfall?" The incubi thundered with approval, Nyx launched herself at Atticus who stuffed the tiny pixie in the crook of his elbow. Nyx was contently cozied by his arms and playing with the long beads of berries and gems Atticus wore. He frowned when she chewed them, but didn't reprimand her. Hopefully, they weren't of the poisonous sorts.

"What's Pitfall?" I asked, watching Maruc repair the ceiling beam with magic.

"Two teams chase exploding leather balls around the field. We try to score in without losing a limb," Percy offered and began to divide the room into teams.

"Sounds barbaric."

"It's brilliant. It will help us bond and relax before this place goes to hell and back."

Wyatt's hand clasped Zander's shoulders. "Where is Fennick? You'll need a fireback to counter Madu's watershield. Unless the Woodlander here starts learning how to pellet diamonds with accuracy."

"She's not playing." A new voice cut in. My drowsy fox's. "Dagressa will want in on the team opposing Kai. Make sure she gets an invitation or we will never hear the end of it." The elemental emerged from the hallway with a blanket wrapped around his head. His eyes barely conscious slivers of gold. He grumpily walked across the hall and buried himself into Zander's opposite side. The world was too loud, too awake for him.

Wyatt flicked Nikki's ear. "Does that mean you're in?"

Nikki lashed out with a flame directed at his head. "Foxy, this could be the last Pitfall game of your lifetime."

"Fine." Nikki fell asleep standing up. His face squished against Zander's chest in the most adorable way.

After Nikki yielded, Namir and Madu fought about who'd be tending to Nyx on the sidelines. "She is *my* daughter. Mine and my husband's blood. You're irrelevant to her."

The water wolf bared her teeth. "Your husband is my woven. Protecting him, includes protecting his bloodline and who he loves, including you, ungrateful bitch. The Weaver of Fate's bond is stronger than your marriage because there is no second guessing."

"Until you ruined our marriage there was never any second guessing. He heartmarked me long before you were born. Besides you will outlive us both, you can tend to our kids then you selfish mut." Kashikat moved in quickly to separate the two. His wife and woven shoved him away just as fast.

"Scary." My wovens agreed.

Percy sipped his tea and cleared his meal. "I've got a solution." They glared at his audacity. "Damn, you women of the Keep are terrifying." He cleared his throat. "Kashikat watches Nyx and you two settle your shit on the pitch. Pulverize eachother or learn to work together for the children's sake."

They agreed instantly to be on opposite teams. Atticus bit back a grin and deposited Nyx into his son's arms. "Match starts at midday. I'll ask around for more players and refs."

B.B. Aspen

"We got Alethim to referee the ground level last time." Clavey swung his arm around the Left Wing's astute, narrow shoulders. He looked none too pleased at the suggestion.

The testosterone in the room erupted and they all stomped their feet in a slow call to action. Alethim took his hood off and shoved Percy. "Fine! I'll do it again under the condition kelpies are not permitted to use their feces as ammunition." The room lightened at the elf's expense. "Do you know how many potion's I had to use to remove that stench?"

"At least it's not wyrm excrement." Zander made a gagging sound. "I'd seen enough of their massive shits to last me a lifetime. Step in it enough too."

Wyatt cackled with brilliance. "We should have collected it and found a way to utilize it as a weapon. 'Fecal launcher vs. Vulborg'."

"It's in the caves under a twelve ton blind beast if you are feeling motivated, twinkle toes." Wyatt declined the dare. Which got me wondering what exactly was a wyrm and why was a creature so revolting living under Veona?

Maruc strode to me, my vigilant Keenan matching his stride as if he would interject himself at a moment's notice. "A noon Pitfall game leaves plenty of time for Atticus and Zander to discuss the reclamation of the title Overlord." I expected Zander to grumble in protest, instead he agreed.

His words prompted Nikki and I to stared at him. I held Zander tighter hoping he smelt my admiration and felt Nikki's arms tighten around his waist. "Amid a war is not a time to have two leaders with opposing orders. Nor is it time for Kai to suggest a caucus and rally. People will die, my people, and I will not have that." Atticus raised his horns hearing his son's greedy tone.

I felt a pissing contest coming on. The room quieted.

"Unless there are objections, I hereby accept the role and responsibility of the Overlord of the Veil until peace is reestablished in the immediate wake." His eyes were not locked on Atticus, but on Kailynder.

Zander released me to the floor where Nikki held me up right in his absence without skipping a beat. Our incubus bound across the room in a leap. Zander snarled in his brother's face, claws and violet smoke screen on full display. Kailynder didn't lock eyes as Atticus had when I first arrived in Veona, instead he dropped his wings and enfolded his brother, his

440

Overlord, into his arms. Clavey was a bundle of nerves when he approached the pair. He was quickly pulled into their arms before he could faint.

One by one, all seven became a thicket of wings and horns. And thorns. Alethim looked as if he was crying. He declared loudly, "Scribes! Document this sentimental, sappy moment so I can't hold it above all their spiky heads as collateral." The gang of them shifted with a somber chuckle.

Zander's voice emerged. "Seeing as my role is temporary and contingent on peace, I would like to assign a temporary Right Wing. Percy, as long as you remain sober, will you command the nation, should I not be present, and hold the realm's fate and wellbeing above your own?"

Percy's brown head of hair shot up right. "Pardon-the-fuck-out-of-me? The last war I fought—"

"Your family isn't leaving you this time. I'll be with you each step of the way until the last demon is ash in the winds beneath our wings." Kailynder's deep sincerity left me choking on my own tears.

"Alright. I, Percy di Lucient, accept the role and responsibilities of Right Wing of the Veil under the current standing Overlord." Warroh placed a hand on their shoulders and recited a long list of prayers. Not one of his kin mocked him now as he interceded for their protection, strength and a family reunion after the war of worlds.

The Overlord's first order, happenstance, the Right Wing's first command, was to divide Veona among themselves to profligate the spread of news. Of an emanate war. They were to inform every street circle of the timeframe and notify families that their loved ones were to be expected home for a meal any time before then as long as the gate holds out. The rest of the brothers volunteered to dissipate the schedule of duty rotations to each branch of their militia: flight, potions, healers, glamourers, swords, archery, elementals, supply, rebels, and watchers. Because time with loved ones was not only limited, but it would remind all of them what exactly they were fighting for. An epic morale boost. And also, the most compassionate thing to do. The brothers all agreed to start conquering the city that morning as to not delay their game come noon.

Keenan knelt before me to fasten gauntlets over my shins. It was done in such a humble manner that made love for him swell up in my chest. "Fennick?" he called to the bundle of standing blankets. Nikki looked down at the warrior tending to my feet. "After evaluating your form, I've a few suggestions to improve your performance."

Hastily, Nikki dropped the blanket off his head. "Certainly, Ik Kygen." To think this man actually punched his idol when they first met—on my behalf—was comical. I spent many fond memories of my childhood aiming to punch him and make him bleed in the woods and quarries.

Keenan rose to fasten a pliable mantle around my neck. "For starters, you block too high." Kailynder tossed a bag of coins to Warroh. I plastered a huge smile on my face and made no effort to shield my smirk from Kailynder who was forced to eat his mockery of me. Keenan tapped my shoulder. "Wisteria, show him the flaws of blocking with your shoulders raised."

"Now? Wearing this?" I gestured to the getup.

Keenan glared. "How else are you going to get comfortable in armor if not fighting in it? Yes now. In that."

Nikki unwrapped himself and wiped sleep from his eyes. "No swords. No Montuse or magic. Clean Ilanthian." We were instructed.

The shin straps didn't interfere with my jumping as I thought they would, nor were they restrictive around my joints. I bobbed around waiting for Nikki to instigate the spar. When he did come at me, my intent was to demonstrate the benefits of mid blocking and not get us injured. Our footwork fell in sync with one another like we had been fighting side by side for years, he ebbed where I flowed. Another dance of sorts, not a waltz nor a political one. But one I was good at.

Once we fell into the more complex steps I added full punches and jabs. It took one duck under his arms and upward elbow thrust into his sternum for us to stop the spar session. He grunted with the impact. Sucking in air, I held my ribs. Damn, I landed a hard hit.

Nikki mended fast and the pain dulled before Keenan got to our side to reposition Nikki's elbows. "You have two hearts in there. Two eternities she could have ended if she used a dagger instead of body weight. Stagger your forearms. Biceps tight to your flank." Nikki adjusted and Keenan praised.

We sparred again, simply to demonstrate the effectiveness of staggered forearms. Wanting to feel his warmth, I leaned into his side body. He gave a distant friendly pat, which left me cold and scrambled because I was able to admit that I wanted more of this man.

I wanted all of him.

I loved him with all of his precarious lessons, emotional perception and stalking behaviors. I love him just as much as I loved Zander's fondness for forwardness, his strength in his softness and his zest for life.

Holy. Shit. I love them beyond friendship, fucking and fondness.

I was *in love* with them both.

He smiled at my blush as if he knew the epiphany I'd uncovered. I jabbed his ribs in a lame attempt to play it cool while my heart somersaulted into my bowels and sunk like concrete.

Percy and Brock gave me a mocking look that made me want to shove nails in their eyes. "Don't tell me that after all of our campfire chitchats, you haven't told them. Is it because of the audience?" Magic splashed around in my gut and I removed the ground under Brock out of pure annoyance.

Of course it was because of the damn audience. I rushed to the deep hole I carved into the ground, not to help him out but to glare at him. Nyx and Warroh scuttled to the edge of the small cliff. "I don't need to tell them. They *know*."

"What do I know?" Nikki murmured calmly and curiously as he stood behind me. My chest froze. I couldn't even turn around to look at him. There were too many heavy emotions saturating the air that the massive Keep suddenly felt too small even for a tiny human like me.

Wyatt, Kashikat and Kailynder were linked arm and arm as they approached the ten foot trap Brock struggled in. "What do we *not* know?" I rolled my eyes at them. "We've our suspicions, but Percy assured us none are correct that you are not a spy, abusing their magic stores or stealing from archives." Kashikat's finger waved at me. "Which is absolute bullshit, by the way that he gets in on this secret."

Percy shrugged. "Technically, it's not a secret. Six people know."

"Blessings above. Not cool, Zander," Warroh tagged on.

"With the incubus flair for dramatics this conversation got misconstrued and messy. I'm out." I threw my hands up, middle fingers high, and walked straight through the many halls and out the doors overlooking the balcony. Zander convinced everyone that wasn't Keenan or Maruc to let me go. *Everyone in here was feeling the finality in the atmosphere. I'm sorry about my family.*

You don't own fault in this, Overlord *Zander.* Golden joy kissed me. *What does my pride in you smell like?*

Palm trees.

Interesting. *Temporary or not, I am proud of you.*

As I am you, my magic crafter.

I make holes.

In dirt and *in the time-space plane. Do you know how phenomenal it was to watch Maruc shatter his spine when he fell on his ass?* Hardly. He was upright within seconds.

Almost as cool as me falling on my face from the ceiling with useless wings I imagine? I made wings. I reminded myself. A human. It was a feat that I was able to tap into my well at all.

Lust curled up my arm and coiled around my waist. *You were a vision with those wings. And you make Morial's armor look so good that I want to tear it off you after I fuck you in it so people stop gawking.*

No one is gawking.

Because they know I'll kill them. They are definitely stealing glances at your ass. It looks great under that corseted waist plate.

I snorted. Keenan stood at my side puffing his rolled cigarillo until the end burned cherry red. He offered me an inhale. I took a smoke and smiled finding a bit of Conrad's dried hemp laced in the tobacco. "He always had the best hand with herbs."

"I had enough sense to take his supply before burning Ferngrove. Now, what do you say you, me and Maruc here go for a little stroll with a silencing bubble and you can rid whatever is festering at your heart. Eh?" I linked my elbow through his.

Have a good walk. Stop by the pitch when you can escape those two for a bit.

Chapter Thirty-Four

Holes. I shaped them. Formed them. Fractured them.

Repeated.

I conceived doorways on one part of the training field that led to the other. And dug up Dagressa's field only to lay the turf flat shortly after to cover my tracks. Maruc reiterated we were aiming for proficiency in opening and closing my will to the magic now that I had a grasp on what it felt like flowing through me.

I guess the term 'vessel' was chosen for hosts of Eternal powers for sensible reasons.

Keenan ceased his tidings of merriment to bring me an orange fruit from the south called mango (which was rapidly becoming my favorite fruit) and sweet rice. Ever since I mentioned the woven situation he had been beside himself with joy. Thankfully, speechless. Still, he acted like a buffoon who drank the ambrosia of the Gods.

I scraped the bottom of the basket and dropped my voice. "Keenan, you really need to stop. You're drawing attention and making a mountain out of a molehill."

"A mountain has nothing on this *phenomenon*. It's a mountain range! Everyone can already see it, they just are dumbfounded into thinking it's an impossibility. Because it should be. I'd no idea about Anna, Maruc and Orion threads either!"

"Shh." I popped soft goat cheese into my mouth. "Speaking of molehills, best I get dirty digging." Maruc was chatting with Bastion on the sideline, Orion and I interrupted. "Hey Emperor, how much longer before we practice something else?"

He leaned against the cabinet of shields with the rebels, shooting the breeze like old friends. "Have you mastered the summoning objects from thought without me knowing?" I shook my head. "We will be at this well into Pitfall's first quarter."

"I've an idea that still involves me continuing this repetition, but on a bigger scale and that holds importance to me."

"Alright. What do you have in mind?" He agreed. There was no backing down.

A winged shade shifted across the field. I squinted upward at the midday sun.

"Percy!" He caught the next breeze down. Adjusting the metal set of wings pinned on his lapel so it caught the sun and blared light in my eyes. The small token somehow made his position more legitimate.

"Slutmonkey, I am on official Right Wing business for the next half hour. I'm trying to make a reputation for myself here."

"Want to be known as my favorite incubus brother?"

He tucked his hair behind his thin and twisty horns. "That sounds way more fun than being Right Wing. What do you have in mind?"

"I need you to distract my males until this afternoon."

"Tell me why and I may be more agreeable." My arms barred across my breastplate while I searched for nondescript words.

"I want to do something special."

"Uh-huh." He tapped the two swords on his hip. He saw right through me. I knew he heard my heart gallop faster, spotted my blush crawling out of the mantle around my neck and watched my dry swallow sticking in my throat. "I can buy you an hour after the game if you can find more of those ginger crystals for my water to last me a fortnight. And those anxiety herbs? The flowery tincture?"

"The valerian, kava and ashwaganda blend. Yes. I should know it, I made it."

"I'm out. I will need twice that much if I'm going to make it another month sober amid a war reliving the worst days of my life." I approved the arrangement. "Zander will be livid after he catches on that I'm diverting him from seeking you out, but I expect you to make it up to my little brother for the rest of your lifetime." I turned away from his smirk. "This might be your last chance to avoid the burden of regrets. Make the most of it. Don't chicken out."

I chucked a water canteen at his knees when he took off baucking like a feathery hen. *Cluck, cluck.*

There was no denying my emotions and physical needs nor the fact that my woven were collectively the ones capable to see them met. Being as today was the day the Overlord declared to warriors and residents alike that spending precious time with loved ones and their families at home was priority, I ought to get working on our new home.

A cozy spot to hopefully fill the wound in Nikki's chest and bring Zander closest to his lineage. I had just the place.

Maruc wasn't as unbearable with Brock and Bastion constantly rattling off questions to him and his white bloused Ivory Legionnaire, Adul, who Keenan told me he had trained when he first left the Ice Jungle after a warm century melted the lands into semi frozen marsh. He told me about it as he insisted on coming with me to run a few errands before I portaled us out of the Veil.

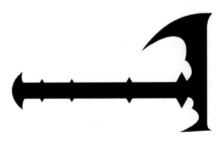

Extra flannels, satin blankets and an odd assortment of clothes finished getting stuffed into a travel bag. Brock slung it over his shoulder, readying to follow Keenan into the portal I opened to Waning Star. I grabbed his arm. "Hey, buddy. I know you and Yolanda have gotten close since leaving the southern port. It mustn't have been easy for you to watch her get relocated to the Glacier."

He looked like I punched him in the gut. "It was a hell of a lot easier watching her get led to a safe house than watching her and Wyatt flirt incessantly with their repartee." My grip softened into little strokes of comfort on his elbow. "They are a good match, if they can work past the blatant issues of her escaping the sex slave industry and him needing to fuck to survive. They could make an impact where it matter." He wouldn't appreciate details of all the manners in which energy is transferred. I kept quiet. "So, if you are going to tell me to stay behind or offer to portal me to her tonight–don't."

Brock let his vulnerability stay exposed as he slumped into my side. I welcomed him.

"I yearn for more than what this world is offering me. I don't give two shits if I am selfish. To hell with its teasing of hope and dangled carrots of contentment. My soul is being called away from here and when you dragged me back from death I latched onto your fury and let it take me this far. I have more yet to travel and your own journey is far from complete, we're not done my sovereign, my friend."

He was right, given I didn't die in the war ahead. I wanted to live a few more good years with my wovens to whatever end that entailed. "I was never satisfied working the quarries, nor did I feel peace staying in the White Tower, nor here in this whimsical land. Whatever I am reaching for it is far above me. I'm going after the stars, for myself."

He was a beautiful soul and absolutely worth every decision I had made to keep him safe. "If I can be of any assistance with my digging and unquenchable rage, you will tell me. You are most deserving and brave. You will walk on the stars and I want to help you do so."

He sighed, which almost sounded like he was shaking off residual doubts. "This might sound witless, but I think there is someone out there searching for me too. Or at least, I'd want to believe that."

"They are." I tapped his chest. "But I for one am glad I found you, Brock. I wouldn't have made it out of the darkness of my own grave had you not been at my side. The fucking thorn that you are."

He prepared himself to step across the glossy oval suspended in front of us. "Until our red blood stains our spiffy new armor, I am the dutiful pain in your ass." I pushed him the rest of the way into Waning Star, his chortle abruptly went silent as I closed the way after him.

Clavey and Wyatt held Kailynder in a headlock while Percy pelted worn leather balls at his backside leaving welts on the thighs. Gods was I glad not to quintess with him. His flesh blistered instantly. Zander was stuck in Wyatt's vines. They were a tense mess of spontaneous energy which apparently did not get expended in the game.

The whole lot of them were rowdy. Nikki was bickering with Alethim about a bad call on the pitch. That penalty against the ground runner cost them the game. Apparently.

 Warroh used Kashikat as a living shield against the incoming bolts of ice from Madu. Eventually, she slicked the floor in frost and took out the unexpecting winged roughens. The elves gracefully steered their way off the slippery surface and the pixies hovered, the humming sound of their insect wings filled the air beneath the grunts of the seven sons of Atticus.

Speaking of Atticus, his mud strewn clothes and dusty wings diminished the otherwise dark ethereal appearance he had going for him. I tipped two fingers in his direction to acknowledge the giant as I tiptoed into the most debatably dangerous zone in the Keep. Zander's sharp nails sliced through the ropes around his legs. He kicked himself upright and stomped his brooding and beautiful self over to me. "And where were you? You missed the perfect opportunity to admire my athleticism."

His physique was all hard, sculpted angles as he leaned over me. I made it painfully clear to everyone I was admiring him now.

I pressed up onto my toes to give me height. "I am grieving from such a loss. I'm sure all your egos colliding on a pile of dirt was as glorious as your claim." His mouth fell to mine, knocking any reasonable thought out my ears. His kiss was placed not to silence my retort but as a distraction to steal the satchels of herbs from my pocket. Zander whipped it above my head, out of reach.

I found Nikki's gaze as he hustled away from Alethim scowling and loudly shouting in a foreign language. They were definitely curses in elvish. I laughed at him relishing his feathers getting ruffled for once. Scowl still set, he gritted at me. "What?" He bit down so hard his jaw flexed under the displaced strains of white hair.

"I like you like this." His glare deepened. "Disheveled. Uncomposed. Moody."

I made a swipe for the satchel in Zander's possession while Nikki pulled his hair back into a tight pony leaving cute ears peeking out from his head. "Who is the thief now?"

Zander juggled it from hand to hand, the satchel itself disappeared behind the closing fingers. "What do we have here?" He sniffed it. Excitement fell from his face. "Welp, your contraband lacks luster. Plant roots."

Percy choked out from under another's wing. "It's ginger and other medicinal herbs you dimwitted dumpster. And it's mine."

Zander tossed the goods across the room with expected accuracy. "Why are you keen on helping Percy?"

A roguish grin escaped. "He is unexpectedly useful and cheap to bribe. Judging by the disastrous state of this room he kept his deal up and busied you two for the last few hours." His face mocked betrayal when he heard me thank his Right Wing. I grabbed his arm before it dramatically was thrown across his chest. I was spun into Nikki's and stayed there. "I have a surprise. Well, two actually. The first will be walking in shortly."

Nikki's teeth tapped. "I'm not fond of surprises." I grabbed his hand and laced my fingers between his under the room's attention. The curious pads of his fingers locked around mine firmly returning the hold.

Keenan stepped aside as Brock and Bastion ushered in Duke Cultee and a few familiar faces. Zander didn't wait for the duke to introduce himself to the parties present before he had him suffocated under a bicep. My gentle giant was teary eyed underneath the knot of long hair shrouding his face. "Capt!"

Cultee showed no hesitation in embracing Drift's altered physique. "You put yourself on the line for me, mine and ours. It would be my honor to return the favor for a true friend." Now, it was I who teared up.

Nikki took hasty steps forward dragging me alongside him seeing as he refused to let me go. He snatched Asher and Copper by the shoulders. "We are long overdue for proper introductions. I am Fennick. You know me as the coalminer in Fort Fell and Count Hilderbrand in Landsfell. Damn, are we glad to have you here."

The youthful Numaalian guards no longer wore their red capes or crests of the royal family. Instead, they sported practical leathers and extra pounds of muscle which were visible when they lifted their arms to welcome Nikki. They gawked at the tails preening behind him and Drift's changed characteristics. When their eyes drank in the variety of dreamers scattered around the room they widened more.

Disbelief was kept out of their tone when they managed a reply. "Wisteria can be quite convincing about the end of the world when she totes along an Eternal to back her story up. And the whole portal walking thing I wasn't going to pass up on." Asher eyed Maruc who was slowly making his way towards Atticus. "Keenan did his best to fill in the holes about Vulborg, an entire nation of magic beings and that the Southland's last woodlander is now wielding Athromancia's magic and Orion's will."

"I would hardly call it magic."

"You made a door between nations and walked through it. What precisely would you call that?" Copper shaved his red hair down to the length of a knuckle, but his freckles remained prominent making him distinguishable with a sprinkle of innocence.

"I'm not sure. I'm getting acclimated to associating myself with magic." The magic under my skin swelled as if to prove me wrong. It liked being used and dispersed today, not draining me terribly much, which Maruc mentioned would come after I ungracefully hit the bottom of the well.

Cultee fought his way out of Zander's arms and into Nikki's. I released him. "Thank you, Fennick for keeping Fort Fell warm and for seeing our civilians to safety on their trek to Sanctum. You made sure we were never without heat, warm meals and means. I will do my best to protect the source of your fire because you are a light this world cannot live without." Zander kissed Cultee's cheeks and dove in for another hug on Nikki's behalf. The duke wiped off his slobbery affections.

Bastion and Pete carried in crates of fire lancets, the spare that Count Hilderbrand shipped in for the battle of Landsfell. The curious pixies and fae mosied closer to the curiosities for examination.

"I would have brought more guards with us, but Maruc insisted if word spread Landsfell was left defenseless and leaderless, chaos might take advantage. My sister was among the handful who witnessed the portal appear in the middle of the great hall and the meeting that took place after. Calabress will hold the city stable for as long as I am needed here. And if I never return she will disseminate knowledge about the Vulborg and the Dreamer Realm I'd died in." Cultee knocked Zander's shoulder, forcing space between them. "Enough fondling Drift. I've got to review the strategies conjured against our enemies and see where my blade would best be of service."

Bastion took to explaining the explosive devices to an alchemist fae with a pig's snout. I tapped Keenan's shoulder, his signal to lead the three newcomers towards Horn's Keep's owner, Atticus for introductions. "The Left and Right Wings can manage our friends from here. I have got another surprise that cannot wait."

"I am inclined to adjust my outlook where your surprises are concerned," Nikki whispered and rested his chin atop my head.

I cast a portal in front of us. "No wraiths are lurking behind there, are they?" Zander pointed to the reflectionless door.

"I've been there for the better part of the morning and haven't seen any."

Nikki fingers scattered warmth up my wrist. "Where is *there*?"

My cheeks rose to my eyes. "You'll see."

"What if we are needed here?"

"Maruc and I sorted out the finer details of communication. Stop overthinking."

Cultee chuckled. "Drift, reinforcements are here. Go with Lady Wisteria before she concocts an outlandish idea as your retribution."

Clavey uncrossed his arms and stood next to the simply clad duke. "You speak as if she has an unhinged mind."

Cultee gave a modest laugh. "When I asked for her opinion on how to draw the previous duke's attention to the wraith's infestation she politely told me to mail my brother the corpse of a wraith with a letter written in blood and nailed into its skull." The dagger strapped on my thigh I emphasized when I gave Clavey a devious wink. Tailon dropped into his arms for comfort. Zander's uncomfortable brothers were a lovely departing sight. I pulled my wovens into the portal with me.

It didn't take long for their concerns to fade and questions to fizzle out once the cold winds rolling off the Plains of the Horselord swept up their mostly bare torsos. Nikki's tails climbed up mine and Zander's legs as we walked to the Halfmoon home, emitting warmth against the frosty weather.

Euclid was measuring a shieldmaiden for a horse in the corral on the nearest part of the village, the rest of the village was sipping warm wines on porches of the community tavern with ferocious looking ax wielders.

"Can you use your magic to shield your residence for silence?" I asked when I led us to the threshold of his wooden archway.

"If it gets you talking about what this visit is all about then absolutely, my flower." The door shut behind us and a familiar shimmer went up all the walls. Nikki was unusually quiet as he prowled and padded a step ahead of me, eyeing the new decorations I added among the living space.

He didn't make it very far. He stopped abruptly in front of the first frame.

It was the first hand drawn map his father had sketched of the Burrows after they were first constructed, the same one that was tattooed on his body.

A few mirrors salvaged from the tunnels, I took the liberty to borrow them for this moment. Nikki's almond eyes were glistening already and I hadn't started yet.

"What is all this?" Zander examined the added frames, pointing excitedly when he caught sight of the oil painting I had added here for him. A painting of a black and white stallion that Atticus had kept all these years. His mother's prized stallion.

"This," I gestured to the cozy living space, trying to keep the tremble of excitement from my voice. "This is my '*I love you*' to you both."

B.B. Aspen

Chapter Thirty-Five

Zander's eyes were both crystalline blue as he reached to hold Nikki's arm to prevent him from wavering. Nikki didn't notice the incubus latching on him nor did that prevent him from moving next to me. His next step placed us toe to toe and I happily inhaled his pine and cedar scent.

I took a steadying breath and grasped both their hands once more, weaving the three of us together. I felt for my connection to each of them while they let silence build my resolve. "Zander gave an order today. For those at risk of losing family and friends to return home and be in the company of those they love. I don't have much of a family. I don't have a home and I may never claim any structure, in any nation or realm as my home ever again. But, I have something better. I have Fennick Feign and Zander Halfmoon Veil di Lucient and when I am with you two I feel as if I belong. I am sheltered and strong because your arms are the only four walls I will ever need. I love you Zander and I love you Nikki because you make me want to live, not just survive."

I saw myself reflected in Nikki's eyes becoming confident because the truth in my words I no longer feared. "When I am with you both I know I am safer than in any palace, tower or cabin. When I am with you there is more warmth and light in my soul than in some great stone hearth of a family room. When I am with you my soul is fed and my curiosity is nourished more than a fully staffed kitchen. I accept that the threads that bind are not tethers. You keep me free, even if it goes against every tactical and overly protective bone in your bodies and for that I couldn't be more grateful."

Zander's rose colors were about to swarm me. I held them at bay for a moment longer so as to not lose myself in them. "I choose to run to you, to return to you–threads or none. I love you and I want my home to be wherever you two are. You are my family now. And this–" I pointed once more to the photos on the wall and the curtains I placed over the tunnel my magic dug out. "This can serve as a temporary solution. Nikki's home is gone, but Honri helped me design a small alcove for us that would accommodate things nicely under those beautiful aspen trees outside." I pulled back the velvet black fabric on the rod to reveal an entrance underground.

Nikki remained unnervingly quiet. I guided him over to the point on the floors where I needed him and angled the standing mirror just so. "Okay. Light us up." His body was consumed in a lively white flame that bounced off the three standing mirrors between us and the bedroom below. Nikki froze in place. His penetrating gaze locked me in like a passing deer caught by a hunter.

Zander kissed my cheek whispering devotions that had my toes curling. He frolicked ahead of us down the short path beneath the roots of the aspens whistling impressed tones. He must have found all the linens Maruc permitted me to take from the White Tower.

Amongst the other things.

The elemental blinked at the map above the entrance and the illuminated tunnel. "I thought he misplaced that parchment decades ago. When it was lost, I presumed he lost the majority of his architectural gifts alongside his memory." I took the strong, fiery hand he outstretched to me and happily let myself be pulled into his chest. I melted into him. "How you've come into possession of this particular piece of parchment is beyond me, but speaking frankly, I don't care how you found it. I'm just relieved it was found. Although, I am interested in *why*."

My fingers clutched the hem of his sullied tunic. On my tippy toes I managed to pull his shirt over his head. Shamelessly, I stripped him. "I've started to memorize all these swirls and lines inked over your flesh." My free hand pressed onto his sternum where two hearts wildly pumped beneath his ribcage. I'd never imagine he'd have a reason for a racing heart. Or two.

I skated the pads of my fingers across his clavicle and down his solid stone abs. His throat bobbed when I tugged at his waistline. Fuck. I loved being the reason for his immortal hearts skipping beats. "During our mirror encounter I realized these were roots and passageways. A map." His stomach muscle clenched when my touch teased just above the buckle of his breeches. "I'd seen something similar in your Pa's office sticking out from between an old canvas and stacks of encyclopedias. He was more than happy to give it to me as a gift to you in our new home." The tears that fell from his eyes were of the purest form. Sunlight reincarnate. "He wrote a few words on the back. Said they were meant for his grandkids and grandpups should they ever seek the wisdom of a departed man or wonder who loved them long before their conception."

His eyes darted to my womb. When he said nothing I knocked his ribs to force an exhale from him. "Birthing pups with tails or wings is not in our *near* future."

"But it is in *our* future, nonetheless?"

I shrugged coyly forgoing any commentary about Death seeking me out first.

"Did I hear the mention of wings on our pups?" Zander was at my back, a singular arm wrapped around Nikki's waist dragging us all in tight.

"I thought your hearing was excellent, Overlord. I'm not repeating myself."

A kiss was placed on the back of my skull. "It is infallible. I just want to hear you say it again to restart my heart which is stuttering irregularly since I heard you imply my being a father of your kids the first time."

My fingers sprawl across Nikki's stunning scars. "Do you know what is also infallible?" I paused a beat before answering. "Us. The three of us together." My hand tucked under Nikki's hair, grabbing the nape of his neck to tilt his lips down to where mine were. We breathed in each other's essence for a moment before I pulled his soft lips onto mine. Time stopped.

We were not an immortal and a mortal embarking on an intimate journey of exploration, for neither of those exist without time and when his tongue broke through my lips time ceased to be a concept.

And when an incubus' mouth latched onto the sensitive spot he had marked on my neck the world stopped spinning all together and began to revolve around the three of us.

Hands roamed through my hair and moans escaped on the cusp of each breath as I savored every punishing kiss. "Look at me." Nikki's guttural command brought my lashes open. Zander slowed the stoking on the curve of my ass and my vision flitted to Nikki's staring at me like the uncaged, feral animal I wanted him to take me as.

I swallowed my lust. "I see you. I want to feel you." I ground against the erection hitting my hips. Quinetessing was in full bloom. I blossomed immediately for them.

His teeth and tongue nipped at my jawline, heat from his mouth slowly inched back towards my lips. He captured my jaw in his firm fingers, directing my gaze into his soul. It fell to his wet gently swelling lower lip. "I love you, Wisteria Woodlander. I love you deeply, darkly and with every part of my being. Even the parts of my soul which belong to Zander are too claimed by you." The devious growl from the chest behind me encouraged and approved of Nikki's confession.

"When I first caught sight of you in the dungeon all I understood of this world tore at the seams and was slow to come together as yours rapidly fell apart. No amount of thread, even those as robust as the Weaver's, could salvage what became of your life after the knight attack. My presence would not bring clarity, stop wraiths or be the salve you needed for at the moment I didn't know what ailments you had or how deep you had been cut.

"I let you run away from our safe house the nights after I invaded Stegin's dungeon. I refused to let Zander haul you back. I sent him away to pass intel and make a name for himself while I stalked you to the caves between the Cliffs of Sound and the quarry. There I camped out for days on end, waiting for you although you seldom left that stone nest. You never spoke, only cries of heartbreak came from the cave."

The lines around his lips creased. "The frantic, cloaked Keenan would forage for your food, I heard him go without just to offer you the full supply of his endeavors. Two times I saw you emerge, once to see the stars and the other to see the sun, I'd been hoping you'd *see* me and this bond we had would beckon you to my side. Alas, I was a petite fox, white as the whitest snow and your eyes of emerald stumbled across the landscape unaware."

"Why didn't you come to the cave?"

"Just as it went against every fiber of my being to leave you in an unknown male's hands and in such a turbulent state, interfering abruptly was not the solution. I trusted Her to complete our tapestry on Her own accord while I sought for other means to familiarize myself with you. Do you remember our first interaction when you spotted me as a coalminer?"

I'd been by the kiln, sent to work on the pathetic medicine closet of Fort Fell. "I waved."

He tipped his head in accord. I moved several satin strains of moonlight away from his face, his golden complexion a flawless texture under my touch. "And you asked if I had insulated gloves for my line of work. I heard it in your tone—the willingness, the determination—they were sharp below the surface of the tame Ivy you wanted to portray to the fort. You asked my needs knowing full well you had no means or manner to get ahold of them if I had gestured I was lacking. I ran off before you decided things for yourself. The second time you bumped into me, you left me bread in the stables." He smirked. "Thank you for that, by the way, I just realized I'd never thanked you properly for tending to me as unnecessary as it was."

"You're welcome. Although, the food you found for me was markedly better."

"Don't do that." His voice was sharp when he cut in.

"Do what?"

"That. Diminish gratitude given from an act of kindness you'd done. You gave food when you had been starving for years. You are a decent person. Own that. Say you're welcome and shut your perfectly plump lips before I find something to gag you with."

I scoffed. "You are welcome and shut your per–." A finger was pressed to my lips. I stopped there.

"It wasn't our bond that forced your hand to regard me kindly in any way, that was abundantly clear after you stole a horse and tried to fight me off."

"Not just any horse. My horse, Rosie." I looked upward and Zander peering down with delight. I rolled my eyes hoping he'd seek corrective actions later. He bit the air and I knew he had every intention to reprimand me.

Nikki interlocked his legs with mine, pressing me against Zander. Shifting my hips slowly, I rode his leg. Our urges doubled... tripled exponentially.

"You were kind to everybody deserving you encountered inside the premises of Fort Fell and those skirted around the Southlands. I found your soul and body stunningly addictive long before the gala, but it wasn't until Landsfell did I begin to narrow down my list of suspected woven bonds. When we arrived here it became all the more obvious you matched my needs in every way imaginable. And I've had time to do lot of imagining."

I licked his chin and sucked his lower lip between my teeth. "I know. Now, fuck me because I am tired of waiting and fucking a corpse doesn't sound enjoyable for either of you." Fingers enclosed my throat. Tears pricked at my eyes after a long second of gasping.

"Not. Remotely. Humorous."

I pried his fingers off my neck and finally inhaled fully. "Nikki, I love you."

He toyed with my hair, aggressively pulled the roots of my braid this way and that before deciding to unbridle it completely. His smirk was pressed against my mouth, while his eyes found Zander's. "You are comfortable risking your life fucking me with Zander so damn confident you two are corlimors?"

I shamelessly groped his chest and danced my fingers down to his ardent cock, pushing against it through the fabric. His manly groans encouraged me to stroke it slower. I bit his ear lobe, uttering, "I am having you both."

Nikki unbuttoned my shirt while Zander worked on ridding me of those pesty pants. "Your confidence is alluring. Now, tell me why you can have us both?" His tongue traced my lips before darting into my mouth, fondling the metal bar rubbing against his eagerness.

"I deserve you both."

"You do. You deserve us in any manner you want us because you are a *good fucking girl* right now," he agreed and brought his hands up to cup my breast. I startled when his thumb and forefinger pinched my erect nipple on the breast he firmly kneaded. I shot him a glare and he captured my attention. "You want to risk our lives, end our eternities, for a threesome?"

Damn that blush that painted my face with heat. "I'm not risking anything."

"You are not? Then are we, the ones you love, going to be left to pay the price of your un-celibacy?"

I gave an unsettled laugh as he and Zander simultaneously sucked the sides of my neck, their hands teasing me with touches that weren't nearly firm enough. Nor low enough. Nor deep enough.

Zander steadied me when my chest rattled with desperate breaths and the impact of Nikki's radiating heat wrapping around our bodies. "It's not a risk. You are both my corlimors."

It was as if those words released the lever on the floodgate that held them at bay. The dam broke. "There it is."

The two of them rained their all-encompassing power down. Gold flecks of fire infiltrated deep hues indigo upon me and I didn't care about swimming, I drank in their intensities and embraced the lack of caution we used as the pair of them carried me down the tunnel to the sanctuary I created as a new haven for us.

Nikki's kiss lightened as his gaze lifted. My name fell from his lips.

He spun on his heels taking in the three heavily adorned dressers I had moved in from Aditi's living quarters, Morial's armor standing on a display mannequin, Misotaka's premonition mirror and a fully stocked wine cart of oak barrel aged wines and rums from Taite's personal stash. Nikki ran his hand over the gold plate engraved with the God's name. Again, my name graced his lips in disbelief. "There is more."

I sat on the edge of the black silk bed made to accommodate the size of a half dozen humans, perfect for myself and my corlimors. From the side table I pulled out a speckled teal gem the size of my palm and pressed it into Zander's. "That belonged to Oyokos. Maruc referred to it as his brother's 'peace pebble' because he would always hold it before making any decisions or when he was too empathetic about the souls on the fields crossing over too soon."

While Zander admired the smooth crystal, I handed Nikki a kite and what Numaalians called a firecracker. These were children's toys, no explanation was needed for the prankster twins. He set them aside and joined me on the bed.

The bed sank as Zander followed him. "And what did you *borrow* from Athromancia?"

"Nothing. Yet." He tucked my hair behind my ear and planted kisses on my freckles.

"I can smell your unease when I mentioned her name, my flower."

"Can you two be there when I go into her rooms for the first time?"

Nikki sat on my other side, slowly lowering me down until I was laid on my back with them on either side. "Yes. We are yours to do with as you please." Zander fiddled with the vial on my navel.

"As I am yours."

He emitted an incomprehensible grumble. "I'm ruined." Zander collapsed onto me. "Say it again, Wisteria."

"I am yours Zander. I belong to you as you belong to me." He kissed the corner of my mouth and repeated the gesture as his loyal brother inched towards my parting lips. Watching his possessive approach mesmerize me like a snake charmer. "Which is as much as I belong to Nikki and him to I."

With the anticipation building, I forgot to breathe. Nikki savored the static erupting between the three of us by working his way intentionally slow to join the kiss. Two tongues swept into my mouth and summoned the stars out of the heavens. I chased them down with my own.

The slickness and heat of them enraptured me into a state of sheer bliss, where I didn't know what sensation would strike me next, nor did I particularly care as long as they never stopped touching me nor stopped loving me. Their hungry arousal fueled me to rock against the ardent cocks pressing into either side of me while our tongues danced in an intricate and messy kiss.

As they claimed my mouth, their hands explored the peaks of my breasts and the valley nearest my thighs. I writhed under the blanket of fire that caressed a few choice erogenous zones. The firm touches below my navel and the harsh, biting heat around my right nipple were of the two most delightful places I could dream of being groped by fire magic. He knew exactly what drove me to the brink of an orgasm. Our quintessing gave him power that I willingly fell prey to.

That knowledge was power and it went in two directions.

When I sat up, I made a point to keep them laying down so I could admire what belonged to me. My palms pressed into their sternum with all my weight behind the action. They watched me strip them of their pants and gape at each erection with avidity. Nikki had something I desperately wanted to try tasting and riding. A cock piercing. I was impressed and equally dazed about how exactly I was to take them both and walk out of here onto a battlefield without a limp.

I placed a knee in between each of their legs and moved my fingers up and down their shafts. Zander lifted his chin and cast his gaze next to him. "Fen, when did you get that done exactly?" He pointed to the glint of curved metal poking through the tip of his penis.

"Since I discovered Wisteria had one." He shuddered when my grip tightened. "That and I had been sexually frustrated and bored as hell jerking off alone while waiting for the Weaver's cards to finish being dealt." I knocked the bar in my tongue against the metal in his tip. *Clink, clink.*

With a quick swipe of my tongue I licked the bead of precum off. That was all the warning given before I swallowed as much of his length as I could fit into my mouth. He sunk into the mattress and Zander's side trying to keep himself from ejaculating. My own arousal poured down my legs with each suck and hollow of my cheeks.

His hips bucked as he slammed the back of the throat, I twisted my fists around him and worked my way back to the head and removed myself from him before we came. "Goddess bless, that reckless mouth of yours."

Zander turned to Nikki, his left hand exploring the elegant tattooed column of his neck. "Fen. I love you more than any brother should love his woven." Zander moved slowly, giving Nikki time to back away from his kiss should he desire to. Fen leaned into Zander's lips with his own pursed. The pair of them slowed their breath as they investigated the changing relationship between them. Watching two exquisite men express their love while I held their cocks in my hands was purely exquisite.

My thighs trembled while Nikki and I coaxed ourselves down from the brink of an orgasm. "Just, wow." That clipped, dazed phrase was all I had to say about that as they separated and fixed their attention on me. The pad of Zander's thumb wiped saliva off my chin then he knotted his fingers in my hair.

He brought me to his lips, sniffing the air as I moved in. "Kiss me so I can familiarize myself with his taste." It was odd to see Zander studious and serious about a kiss. I complied under Nikki's astute gaze.

His fangs were on the cusp of emerging, but stayed retracted as he drank in Nikki's flavors via my mouth. The kiss deepened until we were panting. When the grip in my hair eased, Nikki relaxed and fell into a rhythm of stroking himself. I shuddered with delight gyrating against the air to the rhythm he conducted. I was his Gods' damn puppet. And absolutely fine with that.

I brushed my breasts over the hard plains of Zander's stomach and crotch as I brought myself down to suck his cock. "You take him so good. Look at how great you are making him feel, Wisteria. Only you, our insatiable Goddess, hold influence over a creature as mighty as he." Nikki's words encouraged me to work our woven harder and left Zander staring at his brother with a new level of appreciation.

"Deeper. That's a good girl, stroking such a beautiful shaft. Can you suck two cocks with your sultry little lips?"

Not bothering to wipe the spit off my face, I nodded readily and grabbed the base of him. Midway through my second pump I was forced to stop by the pleasure simmering between my legs. Purple haze clouded my vision. "What is wrong, little flower? Quintessing got your cunt?"

I popped the tip of his cock into my mouth and bounced back to the one with the piercing. "Yes, actually." I alternated sucking them off until I heard Nikki question how Zander was fairing and if witnessing him plunge his cock into me would send him into a violent rampage.

"How do you want to approach this? In turns or together?" Then I paused to hear the answer, my chest rising and falling.

Zander took a long moment to weigh his options which he used to lust after me. Time well spent. "If we claim her together you will need to use your blood to heal her after. But I need you to take her first. You've been patient far too long and I want to watch you shatter. Up close." His words were friendly, yet horns prodded upwards. "No feedings until I make you both cum, which I will." A promise.

A smirking Nikki found a pillow for Zander to lean against. "I give you my consent now and forever, brother. I'll show you how fun sharing can be when you have the both of us as life partners." The room came to life with golden flames and a marvelous naked man stood amid the circle wielding them. Unharmed, he reached over the flames and snatched my waist. "I love you." His confession was lost to the moans of pleasure that dripped off my lips when he dove into the wet opening between my legs.

He abused the dainty nub under the pierced hood until I was certain he couldn't last longer. I locked his head in my knees and laughed as I trapped him there. "Get underneath me," I commanded, not caring in the slightest how desperately I sounded to have him inside me.

"No," he challenged, rising to his knees. I did love him on his knees. Especially when the lower half of his face was glistening with the excitement of edging me.

My lips pursed. "No?"

"I'll repeat since you are busy ogling instead of listening. No." His tattooed arms crisscrossed over his inked artwork.

I leapt to my feet. He tore the blanket out from under me and sent me on my ass. "Oh, I love a little game of cat and mouse." The light dimmed quickly. I blinked frantically trying to orient myself. My feet found the floor. He found me a step later.

One arm slung around my hips while the other moved up my chest and wrapped around my neck. "The problem is I am fed up with waiting and all of my good manners have fizzled out."

"Then lay down and let me fuck you." I fought him off as he reached for me. "Why won't you submit?"

His mirthful lion laugh echoed around the room. I squirmed as he carried me back to bed. I was not some weak hearted woman to be mounted when I did my best work on top. I thrashed to prove my point. Light returned and Nikki captured my mouth in his pressing my body against a hard asymmetric form. Zander. "You heard your corlimor. He wanted an intimate view of our first union." He looked just above me and gave a devilish smirk. "Consider this revenge for fucking her against the door frame I was standing behind, you prick."

Zander chuckled while Nikki bent my knees and ran the head of his cock against my slit. "You loved it when she screamed your name."

"I loved it a little too much and ruined my pants before I had them at my ankles."

He smacked his piercing against mine. "Let's not disappoint him." He smiled tauntingly and thrust himself into me, the piercing on his cock shattered my expectation of pleasure as it slammed into my cervix. We were screaming each other's names and hardly holding back an orgasm before a half minute passed.

Every nerve ending inside and outside of my body was electrified with the all-consuming current between us, my nipples were erect and the walls of my vagina were already clenched. He slid in and out of me, jostling me against Zander's chest. Zander's erection pushed into my back which only made me more lusty and wet.

Nikki eyed Zander's trembling arms and gave him something to do with his restless hands. "Hold her open for me. I want you to feel her quake each time I fuck our woman. I want you to soak in her pleasure as I take her."

The hand of the horselord hooked under my leg and lifted it, allowing Nikki to fuck me so deep and hard tears pricked in my eyes. He knocked against the glorious spot aching for release inside me.

Need, carnal fucking need, spiked my heart and brought pleas from my throat. "*Please.*" He had me begging. "Please, Nikki. Take it." I didn't have time to despise myself for groveling because I was too busy pleading with my corlimor to ride me until I felt his cum filling me.

I sought his eyes behind his pale fiery lashes and sweat dampened brow, they briefly settled on Zander's before they bore into me. They shone like diamonds among coal. Demanding my soul burn with them. We were safe. More than safe and if I didn't come in the following three seconds I was going to slam him beneath me and take what I'd been craving.

My name shot off the tip of his tongue before his teeth caged it in. The only reply I had was shrieking in ecstasy as gratification cleaved me in two. He emptied himself into me with my pulsating waves holding him in place. And of course the vines my magic called upon were taut around the three of us.

When we calmed, I laughed picking a sunflower I had grown next to the bed and tucked it behind Nikki's ears.

His weight dropped while taking in the garden bed surrounding us. His chest against mine made his thrumming hearts pound against my own and echo in my soul as if I was a drum.

I tossed my head back on Zander. Realizing his heart was synced with Nikki's fast rhythm I made myself attune with them. It was like being caught between two storms. Oh, how these two have stolen the wind from my sails and blown me off course. I'd let them take me anywhere and everywhere.

Nikki kissed my nose and reached behind me to twirl a strand of Zander's black hair. "Satisfactory reviews or shall I make her come again and scream *your* name this go about?".

"I can make her pray to me without your help. I'll demonstrate." Zander hadn't released my thigh, nor had Nikki removed his dick from inside me. A dick which was still hard as had been a quarter hour before. Holy shit.

I rocked my ass against Zander's hard on. The two pairs of hands on my hips pushed and pulled me until our friction tantalized us into action. Nikki buried his mouth in my cleavage, his length pumping inside me still. Zander whispered endearing nicknames softly in my ear. Then he lifted me up with Nikki's help.

His erection was between my legs and his woven's pelvis, Nikki intentionally shifted his weight into it when he thrusted. I heard Zander's breath hitch as his cock was massaged and well tended to. We all wade in uncharted incubus territory. "Their will be two prayers offered to you, my Overlord. Don't disappoint."

"I never intend to." Nikki removed himself, his cum flowed out and onto Zander. He was smiling while keeping a watchful eye on Zander's movements after he finished sniffing the air. The male beneath me stroked his girth and slapped it against the wetness of my petals, shimmering with my and his loyal's cum.

When the head pressed in, I gasped and pivoted my hips to take more of him. I needed to feel his fullness after Nikki lubricated our fuckery. I nearly exploded on the spot. "Amazing," Zander praised. I bounced harder onto him, Nikki licked his lips with sheer savageness as he was mesmerized by my tits he finally gave himself permission to admire.

"Feed from me."

"As you wish, my nectar giving flower." His pace quickened. Nikki cast fire magic around our bodies, but that wasn't what took us off guard. "What–!" Nikki's mouth dropped to my pussy which was currently being stuffed by another. As if we needed any more fuel added to our fire he lapped up the blend of cum leaking from me.

My nails bite into a body. Tongue and teeth grazed my clit as intimately as they did his brother's shaft. He taunted me with his sucking and stimulation and when his mouth wasn't on me the groans of panic from Zander's told me exactly where Nikki's attention had drifted to. Nikki gave me a subtle wink of triumph when Zander didn't swat him away.

Nikki stroked our thighs with a demanding firmness. "She is ready." Nikki told Zander whose fangs broke free. "Take us, brother."

I twisted to offer him the meal that would escape my soul shortly. Nikki gyrated against the pair of us, his hot cock driving onto my clit while Zander pumped himself in me. Wide hands gripped my jaw and he drank in my cries as I unfurled them. Drizzles of warm, pearly cum decorated my pubic hair and once Zander had his fill of peaches he joined us in ecstasy.

They fell onto the bedding, me locked contently between arms and legs. We were perfect together, where one ended the other began. Seamless horizons merging with boundaries nonexistent. And all of our existence was the embodiment of love for one another, of the purest kind. The kind I never thought I'd get to experience again let alone be promised to for the end of my days.

In every capacity.

To whatever end.

There was no inkling of sadness, betrayal or loneliness in any crevasse of my heart, for they explored that as thoroughly as they had my body. They found the completion, joy and love that I had.

"We will clean you up."

"Not anytime soon." I still had filthy fantasies to bring to fruition. "Get the blindfold. I've been wanting to tie you up for a while now, Nikki."

Chapter Thirty-Six

We stayed isolated in bliss for the entirety of that night and most of the following morning. We hardly spoke about war strategies until the artifact Eternals communicated with seared red. We were summoned to the ramparts and not a moment too soon according to Keenan who carried Morial's helmet in his grip as he followed my sprint behind Zander's steps.

Kashikat intercepted our walk towards Atticus, Adul and Percy and pointed to the flight division readying themselves to launch off of the peaked rampart west of where we stood. "Your fellow wings are waiting for you before I give my orders for air assembly." Kashikat's voice was slightly raised to be heard above the roar of the fire fields which were wild with wicked flames below the stone structure

"I'll be there," the Overlord promised with honorable amounts of esteem.

Kashikat's woven found him on his assent and wrapped him in an embrace that resonated too familiar inside me. Nikki wrapped his arms around me, his lips pervading my hairline as we watched Madu plead with him, *beg him*, to command her to stay at his side. Even when tears fell, Kashikat did not give the order. "Don't you dare die on me."

The aging pixie with incubi attributes snorted his salty tears away and finally gave in and folded her into his arms. "Not even death can part us, Madu." Madu's bones bent and broke. Her skin thickened and darkened until she stood as a large wolf at Kashikat's side, sending him off with a howl.

Percy ignored Zander's request for updates and weaseled to my side. "Congratulations. The three of you are officially a *thing* now. Did they convince you to run off and complete the Circling with them?"

"I hardly need convincing."

Nikki felt the need to kiss me as our space was encroached on by more curious armored peoples and the Right Wing. His hot tongue skated around my mouth destroying whatever words were considering leaving it. He gave Percy a reply while I collected myself. "No. We will have plenty of time for that after the war."

"I want an invitation to the ceremony."

"Are you any fun sober at revels?"

"We can find out. Ain't that right, slutmonkey?"

My gorgeous armor clinked when I slugged his shoulder. And it was gorgeous, I had time over the last day to admire it both on the mannequin and on me as my males had their fun fucking me with various pieces of steal on.

Keenan and I settled on a forest green for my cloak and the attire of my two Bloodsworns. Keenan happily ditched his golden threads for the bright green of Ferngrove—of life. Brock was just happy to have new clothes without gaping holes in them and a decent cloak. They both bounced on my heels.

Up the stairs rose step by step another pair of wings. My corlimors and I were quickly scrutinized by his dark gaze. Kailynder detached from the woman who'd been latched onto his arm with an awkward two words of gratitude. She obviously fed him recently to replenish his stores enough to make his body double in size. "How does it work between the three of you?" He adjusted against the stone wall. Incubus hearing was just a delight. "Better yet, *why* does it work? It shouldn't."

Against better judgment I gave him a response. "But it does. Extremely well. And for that I am elated because I love them both. Unapologetically and wholly." Kashikat stumbled a little on his way up the ladder upon hearing my words. His fault for dropping eaves with his abilities. "I don't need to elaborate further to appease your curiosity. How is the barrier holding?"

"It's not. It's paper thin and tearing at the base." Kailynder moved aside, pointing to the stones where there were clear striations ripping with the tension from the demons pooling behind it. Not a moment too soon indeed. "We've hours at most."

Nikki's quick gaze scoured the fields leading up to the Eternal Elm on the barrier's eastside. And the rows and rows of swords, spears, magic casters and what I thought looked like small baby dragons. "Wyverns. Winged lizards. Nasty little shits with steely scales. Be glad you aren't going head to head against them." My gaze widened a bit more catching sight of Bastion's lackeys merrily saddled atop them. Asher and Copper too. "Zander paid for the wyverns off the black market and the only ones brave enough to mount them were Numaalians. Go figure."

Zander stripped his tunic and unfurled his massive wings. Straightening into his full formidable form. I smiled at the claws and nails breaking through flesh that were sharper than the teeth of wraiths and far more efficient than the weapons of steel he carried. "No surprise there. Us humans are notoriously valiant." I admired his chiseled physique one last time before he looped leather, an ax and a sword to his back.

One by one, Kailynder meticulously ran his fingers over the heavy iron straps of his chest plate which hardly covered his stone muscles. He ensured nothing was out of place nor too restrictive for the maroon wings protruding from his spine. "Their enthusiasm was terrifying, but welcomed. Just as you are welcomed in the Veil, sister. I apologize for outcasting you as a rogue. I've no excuse for my poor judgment."

"Redeem yourself by not getting killed. You'd be much more problematic and—believe it or not—far less tolerable if your dead body was inhabited by Vulborg."

Brock clapped the Overlord on the back. "Copper and I were wondering what the winner gets for securing the most kills."

"A kiss from me is no longer an option."

"Figured." His brows rose. "And don't say whiskey or bragging rights. That's boring and you are a violent, emotional drunk who I refuse to deal with."

I stuck my tongue out at the pair of them. "You have no choice but to deal with me Brock. Your will is bound to mine."

Copper tossed a crooked grin over his shoulder. "You could steal something from the White Tower."

"Don't let Warroh hear you spew that blasphemy, he will choke on his prayer beads and shit them out." Brock and I looked up at Kai's towering form in unison with disbelief painted on our faces.

Kai's black hair pulled away from the sharp obsidian horns protruding from his scalp. Brock elbowed my side. "Did you know he was capable of sarcasm?" He muttered between half parted lips. "Good thing someone took the stick out of his ass before the—"

"I can hear you, underhill." Kai adjusted the sheath on his hip that happened to be in Brock's direct line of sight.

Nikki stepped aside as Zander finished arming himself. The Overlord of the Veil dropped to his knees and I wasted no time buried myself in his chest. Nikki folded us in from behind once Kashikat's orders to the flight division were given and my corlimor was summoned to battle with his people. For his people. "I'll be keeping a close eye on the Elm from the skies. Get the fuck off the fields and behind the rampart if you get injured or exhausted. We live together. We love together. We die together. Use our connections to our advantage so we can avoid an adventure into the beyond." To which of us he spoke to was irrelevant.

I tasted his tears when he kissed me. Tears that were wiped away on Nikki's shoulder before he let out a startling laugh. A laugh turned into a wolfish battle cry.

His fancy, terrifying ax in one hand and a sword in the other he struck them together as he prowled his way across the wide stone ramparts and up the tower summoning bellows of wrath from the masses. Their clamor summoned a rhythm from the lines of shields which was joined by stomps and howls of Veona's fierce defenders.

The ground was shaking and not by my doing. My hair stood on end as the thunderous shouts pervaded what had to be all of Kinlyra.

The intensity of nearly a hundred thousand strong sent Nikki stumbling into my side when the crowds parted for us. Emotions glistened in his eyes when we found our stations in the third line furthest from the Eternal Elm next to his cousins and mother, who all flaunted the seedlings around their neck proudly.

Even those in fox forms were seen with acorns tight around their legs or ankles. "One for you vixen." A smile played on his lips as he took an acorn from Momo's outstretched hand and slid it into my back pocket. The heat from his hand flirted in a caress against my ass.

"Who am I to deny the mementos of past Eternals? Pissing off the twins while Kinlyra is on the brink of obliteration is not a fate I care to tempt." As if pulled by marionette strings my chin tipped upwards and mouth parted for his.

Hot honey poured across my tongue. I drank until full. "Maybe you should put another in the second pocket strictly for balance."

He ran his right palm over my steely corset and settled it next to his left on the top curves of my bottom. He locked me tight to his body. I did the opposite of resist. Among the battle cries, there was a finality humming through the air as if bleakness laced in the winds blowing from the peaks of Thalren. "I just got you. I can't lose you."

His hardened jaw was pressed against my hairline which he had reverently brushed and tied back in a sleek pony when we woke up in Waning Star. My helmet, Morial's helmet, Nikki took from Keenan's grasp and secured it over my head. It was a simple headdress that seemed more like a decorative crown to protect my skull. "You won't." The golden pair of eyes staring at me disclosed the recent revelations my soul had proclaimed a day ago. I was so deeply in love with Fennick Feign I couldn't untangle my existence from his. Not that I would ever want to. I was his and he was mine. I would die beside him defending his flame of life for his sake, my sake and our Overlord's, a man we both loved.

Let's hope our Zander understood why Nikki and I had already taken Maruc's hand in our own and pledged ourselves to the trithrones of our free will. Unbeknownst to him, as it were, Zander was all that remained between binding the Emperor to my command.

Under the tall burning branches of The Eternal Elm we announced our love in hushed tones, between stolen kisses. Zander's rosy affection and red currents of jealousy coated our syphering. I let him in and Nikki did the same with transplacency.

I love you. I sent to the elemental now possessing one white iris. Two voices sounded in my skull returning the sentiment. Nikki gave a small hop a satisfaction and subtly thrust his fist into the air.

"This is unimaginably incredible."

What would be incredible is your quintessing turned off. Zander's nervous humor slicked the inside of my left palm. *I am all tingly, which is not how an Overlord should be feeling next to armored pixies and avians staring down the jaws of darkness.*

Tingly, huh? Nikki assessed his own transmitting physicalities. *Not the first word for a hard prick I would have chosen, but then again you have never been known to pay attention to the scholars.*

Bookbitch.

Nikki was no longer looking at me, his gaze narrowed on the far, far side of the ramparts onto a flight tower I couldn't see. *Bookbitch? A whore of knowledge is better than a sky slut.*

You are too scared of heights to enjoy the thrill of falling from the heavens and being cradled by clouds. You nearly killed us with a panic attack the two times we tried to fly tandem.

I elbowed Nikki. *So, you do panic?*

Zander was booted out of Nikki's head midway through his snarky reply. "You can't stand there and honestly say to me that you fancy plummeting to a spinning earth leagues below?"

"I do now."

"More than a cozy cuddle in the forest?"

"As much as a cozy cuddle." He looked disbelieving. "But neither are better than spools of silk draped around me." He snorted a laugh while detaching from me. His nine tails cocooning us both before he shifted entirely into his fire fox form. We took our stance next to the others, a Bloodsworn in the line in front of me and behind. Orion stood at the ready with a gorgeous silvery fox at my side. Momo licked her son's ear before crouching down into the tall grass of the fields to watch the inky black Vulborg throw themselves at the barrier, precisely where the seam was the most fragile.

The minutes dragged on.

I fought with myself internally as I was certain countless were. Resisting the easy urge to succumb to the thick volatile emotion of fear clinging to each exhale or prod oneself forward to rally hope.

I would not lose my corlimors, my friends, my family or my world—despite the disastrous state of Kinlyra. It was mine. It was *ours* and no void demons leaching life and thrills could ever feel the determination raging through me. I gave a gritty growl at a particularly wretched scaly form beyond the runegate who was taunting a group of foxes by instilling dread.

The Vulborg morphed. The two headed raven mask on Prince Torval's shoulders pointed to me. Nikki barked bitterly when he caught its marking gaze transfixed on me. He had worked so hard to remove this image precise from my memory and here it stood there mocking him.

Spit formed in the corners of my mouth while I growled the second time. The tip of Orion I directed at the image. "I fear nothing!" The ground shook. "Nothing." I pulled my magic inside, locking it under my flesh and Morial's armor. I was warned not to wield it until we learned the Vulborg's weaknesses. I could not allow them to track me down and possess me.

For a second, I deluded myself into believing I scared off the demon piece of shit with my declaration, but when the entire mass of darkness at bay stilled and redirected their beady gaze upwards, Orion slacked in my grip.

A rip-roaring, resurrected dragon carcass slammed into the barrier from the ceiling of the beyond and the runegate fell.

Chapter Thirty-Seven

Amorphous demons sprinted across an invisible line that once separated the living souls from the destinations of the dead. Loud bangs erupted. The first of many fae landmines were detonated by those rushing to the Elm. "Good news, these fuckers bleed and burn." Keenan widened his stance while shouting play by plays over his shoulder for me to hear. "Bad news, they don't seem to care about their lives or the spawn next to them. Makes for a gruesome battlefield."

Black clouds of demons clashed with the first of the many defensive lines encircling the Elm and protecting the massive stone ramparts. Hot, molten glass shards impaled the limbs and core of the demons. The ones nearest the mines went down. The many behind them flocked onward changing ghastly shapes to frighten swordsmen and women. A tactic that worked by the screams of horror flitting around the front lines.

Vulburg were void of life and emotions, not intellect. They manipulated.

When steel rang out, the acid in my gut soothed as I relaxed. Killing things. I could do that. And well.

I would not be adding these scummy nameless filth to my list. Intel trickled back from the first wave. "Decapitation! Decapitation, send them to their end." Lovely.

Lobbing off heads was the proven method to their demise. Morial's armor wasn't going to retain that shine for long out here. At least, they could be stopped in this murky semi-physical form. Keenan sneered in a sadistic way that gave me goosebumps. I'd seen him with such a look only once. The night the ship departed from the south port. He looked every bit regal and able to lead an army as he did now.

Brock left his post to stand at my side. He used me as a crutch to better view the collision of spawn and fire magic outstretched for a long mile where the Veil to the beyond once stood erect. My attention wasn't on the massive blot of darkness beginning to pour across the land screaming with high pitched horror, it was on the beast of wings and rattling bones soaring eastward untouched by the arrows on the ramparts or by the flight division who leapt off the towers and were hovering defensively over Veona. I wasn't sure Kashikat nor Zander knew how to take down an undead dragon. Nor Atticus for that matter. All assigned and available avians, pixies and blended breads with wings protected the skies above their white stone city and its people gawking below.

I hope Maruc got a visual of what we were up against. A rutting undead dragon! Maybe he'd think twice about offering his Ivory Legion instead of ordering them to surround the Temple of Horns and Akelis.

"And they have a dragon. A *draaa-gon.*" I emphasize the obvious to Keenan who gave no inclination he heard me. He was analyzing our nearest enemy roughly three hundred feet away using their fallen corpses to put on the fire under their feet and inch their way closer to the Elm. A tad revolting, but they were managing to create a bridge across the embers with their putrid bodies. Shit. A bridge of corpses.

Brock posed to the line. "Are they leading with their greatest weapon or is the dragon a distraction technique?"

"Either way it is as impressive as it is horrifying. I can see why the griffins sought to destroy them, my soul feels swallowed by dread just spending a minute in its presence." The dragon flew far away until it was a speck in the midday sky, leaving tacticians and warriors speechless with confusion in its wake. It wasn't attacking. Yet. "How in the seven sons of shit do we prepare for the return of that *thing*?"

Nikki half transformed and was in my ear stifling a laugh. Graciously it was unbridled enough to usher in warmth to my spirits. Warmth I didn't know I needed. He was my mate, my corlimor. Seeing, smelling, observing, feeling everything about me to learn me better than I understood myself. "*Seven sons of shit.* I'll be sure to use that at the next brunch the Keep hosts and stay to see how well that goes over."

"Please, do. Report back to me if anyone loses a limb or gets their mouth sewn shut. If you can still talk through the wires in your jaw." I let my heart lighten one last time before Orion sparked with anticipation in my fingers.

"I'll report nothing, golden goddess. You will be at my side witnessing Atticus's blood curl or hack a lung from laughing." Finite. I would stand with him.

"I will be at your side. He will be at our side."

"To whatever end."

A long exhale left through parted lips. "To whatever end." Our tender moment was intruded on by a thunderous bellow. Kailynder inched forward alongside the impenetrable wall of interlacing shields and long swords he had trained arduously during his eons of incubi existence. The manner in which his legion uniformly stacked their rectangular shields atop each other reminded me of fish scales.

Ranks of elves ran by us to stand behind Kailynder's unit armed with flaming crossbows. What an inspiring sight. Their unison and precision was immaculate. "Release!" A command was given every three seconds followed by a wail of pain and anger from the Vulborg. "Release!" The battlefield worked tightly in unison to keep a straight, unbroken line. Maruc would need a defined clearing to draw up the new runegate and the Veil would fight like hell to make that happen.

The combined tactics injured and incinerated hundreds to which fae sprinters and pixie flyers darted across the steel line beheading the fallen on the parameters of the fire field as time drew on. My breath hitched witnessing the demons take on the form of wraiths only larger and ghostly. They gathered the fears of the humans present and embodied their hauntings on the offside Copper repositioned himself on the wyvern's saddle. That poor beast was choking on its own terror.

When pixies were struck down with willowy, blade-like limbs and Ilanthians fell and were feasted upon, my magic itched at my fingertips as I thought about parting the earth and burying them alive in a mass grave. "Easy, my vexing vixen. Save your fury. Don't paint a target on your back." As requested, I conserved most of my magic to donate to the runegate's rebuilding or at least to give us an element of surprise if the Vulborg got too complacent. I would not conserve my physical exertion.

Bloodshed crept deeper into the Veil as lifeless bodies of our army squashed the flames of the fields with their corpses falling next to demon filth. More filth stomped over them leaping and lunging at Kailynder's first line, nearly breaking his shield wall with the ceaseless impact. The volleys of arrows increased until fire streamed by in a blur of a comet's tail. Guarded supply runners zoomed by refilling the elvish arrows and burners.

Brock sputtered off vulgarities as two men retreating with wet pants set off landmines nearby disrupting the careful line formations. He took it upon himself to pivot and better guard my flank. "This blood oath is powerful. I don't think I meant to do that." Uncomforting.

It was difficult to hear one another over the encroaching battle. The elemental's sensitive ears must be aching with all the deafening commotion. "Our friendship is powerful." I shouted back, fully knowing his blood oath means he'd lay down his life for mine unless I ordered him otherwise.

I ignored his grumbles and watched as the shadows merged, digesting each other's essence until they were a towering spider with too many hairy legs and three heads with snapping jaws. I caught its foul breath in a down breeze. Decay and rot. It was tall enough to peer down at the purebred incubi who was using his wings to shelter an injured soldier beside him.

Kailynder's units reformed with an abrupt whistle. The swords nearest the spindren encompassed as many archers as they could obtain and moved into an impenetrable half sphere deflecting the stabbing legs and sharp pincers crunching the through bones and metal alike. Each time the dome was punctured, the unit reformed their shields, overlapping them tightly.

More monsters congealed together. One took the mouth of a king cobra snake and struck at the ankles of warriors while the spindren shot darkness like webbing and slicked the ground with rot.

Smoke rose from the dousing fire and the burning of flesh. Each shrill of triumph from the demon led to a cry from an elemental. War was no time to warmth share or grieve. We were hours into war and all shaking with adrenaline. The notably absent dragon was cause enough for anxiety to fester.

Much footing still had to be gained before the Elm was within corruption's reach, thankfully I knew Veona had many more tricks up their sleeves which was good because as dusk approached the gruesome spilt blood took on a nauseating sheen as it inked closer to my feet.

"Hold!" My line was cautioned, although I was eager to fight since Keenan darted into battle hours before me. Nikki was pouncing paw to paw barking with pain and a familiar emotion of rage when the elves began to move backward. For respite not retreat, the commander of the archers insisted on passing. If Keenan hadn't shot us our second warning to stand down, I would have sprinted all the way to the landmines to start expending the energy building inside me.

With the first line morphing into a defensive arrangement and Kailynder unwilling to unleash the risk of unorganized fighting, the flight division tore through the air above, casting fast moving shadows against the descending sun. They soared overhead dropping vials of scorching gasses directly into the never ending stream of demons, gasses meant to burn the lungs and cause blindness. Who knew if Vulborg needed air or had sight.

It pissed them off good and well though.

I'd no inclination if it was successful or effective, but watching the scene unfold reminded me of disrupting a beehive in Marybeth's honey garden. Chaos spread from where the vials exploded and the damaged demons sprinted in a frenzy; clawing, climbing and slithering every which way, taking down friend and foe alike.

Kashikat and Zander each led a swarm, one took to the high towers in the city and on to the fields. Zander's team grounded and unsheathed their weapons, purchasing precious time for elves and the shields to fall back and regroup. I followed suit and parted for the first wave's withdrawal to safe grounds where there would be offered food, rest and aid to the injured.

Zander was brilliant to watch. Only he could rip off skulls and kick through the ribcages of demons with his boots and still make me want to fuck him in our enemies blood. *Peaches.* He managed to make eye contact with me after landing his ax in a panther shaped Vulborg's head. *Think that is sexy? Watch this!* He disappeared his wings and rammed his horns into the bowels of a beast. He removed the carcass and stood up with drizzles of death running down his braids. My head was shaking with revolt.

Percy rounded to Zander's side fending off a handful of demons while Zander stared proudly in my direction. *Stick with tearing spines and axing assholes. That was a mood killer.* He frowned. "Blasted lunatic!" Percy interjected with his wings slamming into his brother's side. "Stop flirting and start fighting, Moonbeam!"

The sight of a gash above Percy's brow triggered Zander's instincts and he spearheaded his grounded flyers into the center of their army. Keenan's line moved forward to end stragglers that broke through. Zander called off the pixies, but kept winged fae and avians on the ground protecting those taking flight. Luminescent pixie wings elevated out of the chaos. It was difficult not to notice how few of them there were comparatively to an hour ago when they descended. Some feathered, injured avians bolted from the tangle of demons spawn as well.

I borrowed Zander's anguish and anger searing down my forearm and stepped up into Keenan's line. Brock and Nikki followed. "Wisteria." I hated the warning in his tone. I felt for Zander. He was unharmed and unafraid.

"Father dearest."

I was rather shocked he heard me give the absolute intensity of the volume approaching. "Affection terms won't sway me into letting you break formation." I leaned into his shoulder with more angst than intended. "Recycling defensive and offensive divisions help replenish our military stores. I'll not have you tuckered out before the Alchemists and Numaalians arrive. If we don't keep our lines, pandemonium sweeps in and it will be near impossible to corral them backwards. If we can't hold them or push them back to the rune stones a new runegate cannot rise. So stand down."

He kissed the center of my helmet. "Too soon you will be out there and when the order is given to fall back and recuperate, you will comply."

I didn't reply. We damn well knew I wasn't going to get off that field unless I was dragged or unconscious. Brock groaned. I bet he was rethinking his blood oath right about then. Maybe Keenan too.

The Vulborg were encroaching. A few more feet of precious fire field was stolen and distinguished. Zander's war cry boomed from someplace in the pitch dark in front of us, he ordered oil to be spilled. Down descended Numaalians on the backs of wyverns. Lights exploded as fire lancets went off outlining the battle scene to be seen from the ramparts and miles around the isolation nation of the Veil. The flight divisions hustled away from the flames, many were lost to them. Zander's formation took to the sky, while my woven followed the tug of the bond and sprinted to me. To us.

Nikki and I fed him our energy, letting him take as much as he needed. He remained spry, he only absorbed a minute of affection before I demanded a lip lock. His hands locked around my head as his kiss deepened and threatened to consume me. I'd let him. A curdling cry called our attention as the spawn figure regrouped tattered and torn pieces of themselves into several horrendous beasts imitating the shape of a wyvern trying to take flight. Bastion brought it down before air caught under its wings.

One timely glance behind me showed Maruc standing garbed in immaculate unsoiled white linens gazing down at the unfolding scene. "Is it time to make our bargain?" Jaws snapped in my ear.

"We are but tens of thousands to their countless, but we have something worth fighting for. Never underestimate a well-motivated militia, my love. Maruc can wait there until he sees an opening fit to do his work." Zander kissed Nikki's ears and shot Keenan a glance that was clearly a warning, more accurately a threat. I punched his shoulder and sent him away on wings.

"I can see to my own survival. He has no right to walk around with his chest all puffed and pointing fingers." Keenan's chuckles settled me.

"It's his nature. You are lucky he didn't lock you in the Glacier and that he left you alone on the line." Keenan pointed to the long line of elementals and skilled foot soldiers behind him. My assigned line.

My hands were thrown in the air when I walked back. "He didn't! I'm with his loyalty woven!" Now, NIkki chuckled, he sent heat up my breast plate. Literally warming my heart.

By the time magicked combustions slowed and came to an abrupt stop, Keenan's line was already engaged with the Vulborg, the men and women who had been idolizing the ground this man had been walking on all month, or lifetimes, were now fighting side by side with the object of their veneration. Keenan did his best to learn all their names and I knew he would do his best not to let any of them fall because he was too damn honorable.

In the amber light which the fields offered, I saw blades and black beasts strike out with equal ferocity and lethality. The skirt of conflict was stark now that night blanketed the world. But there would be no rest tonight.

Not for many long, long nights.

Stay safe, my flower. Zander's presence in my head alerted me to my approaching defensive duty. He couldn't remain in my thoughts, he would serve as a distraction and I was already going to be fighting conservatively because of Nikki's quintessing open and placing us both at risk. I booted him from my mind as a trumpet blasted, signaling my footing onward. Orion sang out as he met shadows of fleshy carnage. I dove the tip of him into the boney bodies of gaunt Vulborg.

My head was ringing with the sounds of their shrill deaths when I arrived at Keenan's flank in time to guard him from a strike of a bear clawed demon. Dawn came. When his line was called back for respite, he stayed and encouraged each strike I took that sent filth back to the bowels of hell. "Atta girl! Alester would be so fucking proud of our daughter!" My face heated under the helm. My Ilanthian footwork danced me around Keenan and out of the way of sprinting elementals.

One hundred foxes did more damage collaterally than the fire lancets due to the precise control of the wielder. They were the essence of fire given embodiment. An unstoppable wildfire bit the heels of our enemy whose eyes widened with envy, fear and greed. It became abundantly clear how much more potent the Feign's family magic had been when Momo, Nikki and Riveret shot embers in the shape of daggers into the inky masses where they were swallowed after hitting their mark. My nine tailed woven quickly became the desire for nearby Vulborg, the crowd of them staggered around a fixed demon in the middle of the swarm.

That shadowy figure extended a lengthened straight finger at Nikki and those around him obeyed wordlessly. "Keenan! Brock! I spot our next victim!"

"There are more demon dictators distributed down to the western rune stone. Tell him," Keenan commanded. I pulled the bond once and it came to life instantly. *There are certain Vulborg who control the demons in their vicinity. Nikki caught one's affection.*

Take it down. I'll observe the behaviors and pass on your intel. Left, right, left. Duck, dodge. Hilt to the gut, blade through its neck. Repeat. Repeat. I made a few feet of progress when a snake coiled around my legs. Keenan cut me free. More spun around my waist and neck. I bit through them and spat out the necrotic ooze.

"Not a snake. Tentacles!" Brock speared one its wiggly arms and sliced until the grip around my waist slacked. I heaved up a bit of the blood I swallowed. "If you swallowed a chunk of it, does that still make you vegetarian?" I bared my bloody teeth at him and pushed my way into the thickest of crowds, crowds that mobbed me on their way to get to Nikki.

Elbow to an airway, Orion in its gut. I tripped as many as I could to make it easier for my Bloodsworn to decapitate or stun them behind me.

The dictator stood in the form of a bulky man, the silhouette of a wide blade sword loosely set in his palm. "That's a Numaalain made sword he's got there. Well, the outline of one." He caught sight of the scrutiny and sent another two dozen demons in our direction with a dip of his chin. Sweat dripped down my back as I worked with my friends to avoid another close encounter with death. The ground beneath us trembled. I had no time to digest what that meant for the fate of the city.

"How do we get to him?" I asked Keenan between swings of steel and screams of terrifying restless clawing at my throat.

"From a distance." Daggers. Arrows. Vials of potions. "My dagger is in the skull of some sick fuck being scorched alive. We will have to come back with better equipment."

"Magic."

Keenan didn't bother to wipe the scowl or soot from his bearded cheek when he pivoted to me. I ended the demon crawling on all fours towards me with a blade in its back. "Then you will be the target. They cannot claim you." Nikki's fire scorched the earth behind me, I felt no fatigue or pain from him but he was expending a lot in a short time. While at the Opal Lake, Maruc told me magical fatigue had physical consequences. I hope neither he nor I encounter that while quintessing. Nor ever.

"Only if I get caught."

"Wild Wisteria."

"I'll be subtle." Hopefully.

The Vulborg coming at Brock had its severed head dangling from a tendon. Blood globed down its body. After he killed it he spent a good three seconds staring at the mangle mess deciphering what it was he was looking at. After another, and another, and another demon horde sent to us my guardian agreed to my magic use. "Which type of hole will you be digging?" The sun was rising now, it seemed as good a time as any.

"The kind that buries that spawn beneath Zander's boot."

Incoming. Demon via portal! I reimagined myself in Honri's apartment and how soft my magic translated from my mind to the tangible world. Magic leaked from my soul and pooled subtly beneath the commander's feet.

Confirmation arrived. *Ready.* I opened the portal beneath its feet and in they fell along with another nearby monster. *You shipped two!* Hastily, I withdrew my magic. It cooled under my skin.

Keeping you on your toes, my love. In my distraction Keenan had tugged me away from a leeward flame that sputtered out when a demon tore the responsible fox into two halves and discarded them behind it. I let Keenan shelter me a tad longer as I looked over my shoulder to ensure *my* fox was not ripped into clean halves. "We must relocate. We cannot appear conspicuous." He was shouldering Brock who had already managed to tear his new green cape. "Protect our backs." I did as he asked.

It was discernible, the moment the commander was ridden. Like the world around us paused to expel an exhale. The closest few hundred Vulborgs staggered as if they were bobbing in and out of a trance yet still drawn to the light. Myself and several observant elementals took full advantage of the lapse in their judgment and pummeled our way through the mindless Vulborg in tandem.

It felt great to unleash the pent up exhilaration that had been gnawing on my nerves since the bloody damn dragon shattered the gate. We reclaimed the few precious inches we lost earlier.

Foxes were grinning as wide as I under my helm and when the time came for the wolves to hold the advancements we gained, they skipped and scurried away. After getting a small taste of the icy winds engulfing me in frozen armor, I managed to thank Keenan when he pulled me back to the fire fields and into a tent.

My helm was off. Hastily, Zander saw to the rest of my armor. I knew he was inspecting the flesh beneath for injury. All he'd find were bruises. He started on my shin guards. "The demon you sent me could talk. Wyatt and Bastion tortured some information out of it before it swallowed its tongue and extinguished himself. By extinguish I mean dropped himself on a blade."

Bastion threw open the flaps of the tent. "Not just a demon. But Duvet–the Queen's Knight. You know the one you killed in the Pits?"

Water was pressed in my hand. I drank mouthfuls at a time and set my sights on the basket of bread passed around the benches. "The tin can? Yeah, I remember. Not much of an opponent." My words were muffled under sourdough.

"He was a Remnant. One of the poor chosen fools given venom and thereby accepting a Vulborg soul into their bodies. Not your average Vulborg either, an Amir, a princely clever piece of shit. He's got some influence over his subjects."

Keenan wiped the blood from his sword onto his equally filthy breeches. "Death didn't sever them?"

"Apparently, it goes both ways, their souls stay bound in the Ether and Duvet retained an awareness of himself. If we can get our hands on another one, I'm sure Wyatt can get more information from them. Find a weakness, discern their plans with that blasted dragon flying about."

"They may be susceptible to sway. Even charm." Atticus entered on his knees so his stature didn't collapse the tether of the tent. A humbling sight. "I want to try it on an Amir before blasting the battlefield and potentially swaying our own army to walk off the face of the earth."

"Wise, the last thing we need is a giant orgy." Brock snorted in my ear.

"I don't think that is how it works."

Clavey flicked his tongue out of his mouth and licked his top fangs. "That is exactly how it works. I am impressed Zander never let you catch a whiff of his charm."

"I never had to use it on her." Zander found more food for me to devour. "I'll inform the others of the plan to target these Amirs, killing or capturing them will be a second priority after holding the line. If we have a consistent agenda they can't weed or single one of us out and may be keen on defending themselves rather than gunning full speed at the Elm." Or Nikki. They wanted his tails plucked off. I'm sure Zander witnessed their change in swiftness after our woven shone too brightly.

"You've got seven hours to rest." Zander ran his hand down Nikki's spine and let it rest on his haunches. "At full peak sun Kai's unit is back out with Dagressa this go around. It will be interesting to see them working together rather than trying to pulverize each other. You won't need to be stationed until then."

I poked his bare chest. "What about you? When do you rest?"

"When this war is done." I rolled my eyes and signaled Keenan to take exit with me. He gathered Morial's battle suit. "Where are you going?"

"To help. I felt rumbling under the rock and soil. I assume you'd like me to collapse those tunnels with my magic before those night crawlers emerge on the other side of the rampart, right?"

Atticus' swearing I interpreted to mean yes. I was naively wishful in hoping Nikki and Brock would stay behind with Bastion and the others to rest. At least Zander carried Nikki's heavy fox form easily in his arms while Brock had no such luck limping along in my wake. We got to the grass ground directly in front of the rampart. That is where I choose to let my magic out to investigate my earthy element. It traveled through the ground, over rocks, cements, roots and clay until it encountered void. "I found them. Two tunnels intersecting under our catapults." I pointed to the opposite side of the pitch from the Elm.

"Can you crush them and prevent them from spilling out in the city?"

"I'm tempted to say yes." Wow, Wisteria. Way to inspire confidence. I mended quickly, "But the surface may fissure and the uneven footing may be disadvantageous. They may spill out *here*."

"Benefits outweigh the risks, my love."

Keenan dropped his tone. "What is the plan to distract them from catching on to her magic?"

Zander's handsome face paled with revolt. "There is a wyrm who ought to be hungry enough for a decent sized meal." He was disgusted at his own realization he'd be mounting that rancid wyrm. He straightened and withdrew his ax. "Archers at the ready! Calvary saddle up! Take the catapults back to the rampart's iron gate." His orders were heeded and countless swarmed into action leaving my head spinning.

"I'll block off their exits that are the market circle, it doesn't feel like they've made it that far as of yet. I can do that from anywhere. I won't touch the intersection until your arrival."

Zander's wings were gone. "Oh, it will be an arrival you won't forget and one I wish I could." He gagged. "I'll be scrubbing the scent off my flesh for decades." Zander vanished in a puff of purple magic. Now, it was up to me.

I moved out of our enemies line of sight and sent ribbons of magic into the crevasses surrounding the silent and slow moving Vulborg, softly stampeding under our feet. With my eyes closed and senses awakened, I discovered the opening and pulled the minerals and metals out of the soil until they created a makeshift metal wall. I curled my fingers around the air in front of me visualizing the narrow walls of the tunnels falling in.

They did. Nikki was curled on my lap, I gave him a successful nod.

The rumors of this nasty wyrm Zander kept going on about did the invertebrate justice. I smelt it shortly after I caught sight of its pale wrinkled flesh peaking up from under the ground it broke through. It was more rancid than dead rodents swimming in clogged sewage pipes.

I buried my nose into Nikki's fur to take a cedar infused inhale before I set my magic back into the earth's crust. The wyrm ripped through the surface as I shattered the ground below, choking the air from our fiendish enemy's lungs.

The ground quaked as it obeyed the will of my magic. Rivers of power flowed out of me to comply and once the tunnels had been cut off the demons sprung from the field like daisies. I kept my magic pulsing upward to the beyond and buried the entrance from their end. I was quick to open my eyes and take back my magic after it got a single taste of the vast nothingness of the beyond and the infinite number of Vulborg standing at the ready. *There are so many of them.*

The mouth of the wyrm could swallow Atticus whole with its rows of razor sharp jagged teeth. Zander directed it to make pass after pass under the ground and through the heart of their tunnels and when the wyrm bucked him off its back to go its own way, Zander wasted not a second in rushing to my side on the ramparts.

"Release!" Arrows flew at the countless Vulborg arising.

The wolves panicked now that their enemies were surrounding them on both fronts. Mounted riders galloped across the field, thousands of them, to protect the elemental's back and remove the threat with ease.

I was helped off the ground from my under arm and my face was studied. "Their numbers felt as infinite as the number of stars in the sky and grains of sand in the seas. As if every soul that had ever departed found their way back as a Vulborg." Zander's forehead wrinkled as he stared at my mouth contemplating the words that dripped from my lips while I watched swift retribution befall the tunnel dwellers who'd likely been the course of the haunting in the Burrows.

He looked on the verge of tears. I opened my mouth to apologize and he stopped it with a kiss. "We have to get that wall up." His neck snapped towards Warroh. "How many units do you think are ready to pursue these fuckers together? Maybe we can overwhelm them with the extra four thousand mounts still in the stables and all capable sword wielders. That's nearly fifty thousand bodies."

"We can't all fit in *that* allotment of space. We are lucky it is a narrow opening because it funnels the enemy to us. What happened to isolating an Amir or two? If we can sway them they may in turn be able to retract their numbers. It seems less likely to end in bloodshed and extend our resources given we've lost precious lives already."

The Overlord punched the stone steps of the rampart gouging out a crater with his knuckles. "Damn it. Fine! Stay the course." I attempted to latch onto our syphering but his mind was so busy and buzzing I let go of the rope to stabilize my own thoughts. We needed something big to hold the line while Maruc worked.

I hustled up the steps two at a time, a fox nipped at my heels with every step. I spun to address him with a kiss on his nose. "Nikki, I promise to rest. I just want to run a possibility by Maruc." Nikki lit the path on the bustling ramparts until Maruc's white robes and aura was evident.

"I told you to reserve your magic. The war is young." He wasn't looking at me when I arrived at his side. Adul stepped aside for me.

"You're doing enough reserving of magic for the both of us." Why bother hiding my annoyance now? Adul stood in perfect whites while the rest of us were dirtied in blood and filth. And to be frank, the legionnaire looked embarrassed by it.

Good. As he should be.

"Would moving the rune stones each up fifty yards allow you enough space to work?"

"They can't be moved. Nor can you throw up a giant stone wall tall enough that they will not climb over or dig a hole deep enough that they won't crawl out of." He finally tore his eyes off the fields and onto me.

"You cannot move the rune stones with magic nor use the earth around them to bring them off the edge of Ether. I would have done that myself were it an option. I'll give you credit for using your imagination." I didn't care about good credit in the perception of a God, *this* God in particular. My nails bit into my palm as my hands closed into tight fists humming with potent annoyance. "Clear the space around the stones that way Zander and I are free to spell weave, while units protect us long enough to get a barrier erected."

I knew the plan. I wasn't asking him to reiterate it for me. We've gone over it so many times that I was sick of hearing about it because after knowing what I know now about the untiring innumerable Vulborg, we were in trouble. If not today, then tomorrow or the weeks ahead if fatigue didn't see to our demise first. I knocked into Keenan's shoulder hustling back down to the tent. "Don't cop an attitude with me. I could have told you Maruc was a lousy, selfish God of War if you asked it of me."

"Sorry. It's loud. I cannot think." I pointed toward the loud horse whines, wolves howls and demon screams erupted from. "I have vigor left. I should not be sent to take a nap. You fought for two consecutive lines—a half day! I can do that!"

"You unfortunately will likely have to. Which is why I want you to pick a cot and sit your ass in it. I don't care if you sleep, but you will rest your body and gain awareness of how your magic refills and how fast so you don't hit a dry, deadly bottom." Those around us pivoted to hear our conversation, which was getting louder each passing second. I guess I wasn't the only one on edge. "You may have magic but you are a mortal and will not heal as fast as an Ilanthian nor consume energy like an incubus. You have limits! Honor them or face consequences."

"Limits? You mean flaws?" I glared. Keenan's posture stiffened as he stepped chest to chest with me. Brock whistled away from the conversation. He laid himself on a cot near Pete who helped Brock remove the metal peg stump. He winced at the bloody scabs chafing off.

Keenan whipped off his gloves and snatched my chin. I'd not choice but to look into his brown eyes. They were youthful, unaged. It must have been his wisdom and experience that aged him into a paternal figure for me. *"Limitations are not flaws.* I have a vastly different set of limits that constrain me as does every being in Kinlyra." Frustration made his voice come out lowly and fast, no louder than a murmur. But it hit me hard enough.

I lowered my forehead, to kiss twice between my brow. Once for him, another for Alester.

Nikki pawed a cot furthest from the rowdy battlefield and away from the torches that illuminated the early morning. I closed my arms around him when he plopped onto my stomach and inched a nuzzling nose under my chin. "I'll sleep, but I'm not happy about it."

I heard Brock quip to Keenan. "Told you this 'rotating troops by the thousands' was going to pose a problem to our queen. You're lucky she didn't disguise herself and sneak off already."

"Don't give her ideas!"

"She's already done it! Used your name too in case Bastion never told you."

Yes, I did. I thought proudly. And I'd do it again.

Chapter Thirty-Eight

Fingers wiped away the sweat on my brow. Pink notes of love merged with yellow joy as Zander coaxed me out of a dreamless sleep. Warm, skilled fingers massaged my skull and brow with little flickers of flame lingering like an afterglow. I wiped my drool off Nikki's chest which Zander found charming enough to smile at. "I wanted you to have time to eat again before your line stands at the ready. Kashikat's sky patrol landed just now. It's late in the day."

"Keenan's already out there?" He nodded while diving in to kiss me. "Did you need to eat?" Another subtle nod. I kissed back and stopped when I discovered the room was packed with panting water wolves who just came in from a hazardous bloody battle. They'd be needing our cot by the amount of gore present and back legs that looked chewed on. I ran my hand through Nikki's unbound silver hair that rivaled Zander's in length, massaging his scalp slowly until golden slivers shone.

"You're the sexist warrior in existence, baby." His long warm fingers brushed over my lips parting them with the pad of his thumb. "I wanted to fuck you on that field. And now we share the tent with hundreds of nosey dreamers and I can't request that you sit on my face." His attention turned to glance around the room. All wolf ears were perked, save those already sleeping. "I wanted to tell you sooner, but you know–fox form." He sat up, carrying me with him, my knees pinned to his sides.

"There are obscuras for that. I'm game if you two are." I kissed the corner of his sultry grin. Not giving a shit about being perceived as a whore.

"How are we holding?" His eye found Zander's.

"Give and take of life and land. No worse than last night, certainly no better this morning despite what Kai would like to claim. At least he captured two Amirs." Afternoon's dispersed sun shone through the threads of the tent. A meal sounded good. Nikki finished his hair and took to braiding my own in a single thick braid down my back.

He sniffed the spot behind my ear and kissed me there. I was beginning to think that was his favorite spot to give me affection. I certainly loved receiving it there. The closeness I felt inhaling his exhales was comforting as if we were sharing one body. I let him hold me while Zander met with his Right and Left Wings.

I was on my feet following Alethim while he explained how one of the Amir had killed themself before they were able to extract coherent words. But Atticus had successfully been holding the second demon at bay from this man's soul with his sway–hibernation he referred to it as. Our pace quickened hearing the urgency.

The tactic tents felt small with the crowd gathered around the Amir. Clavey and Percy wielded torches to keep the inky statue cornered. Atticus's eyes were locked on his prisoner with a triumphant snarl buried under his fangs. "Who were you?"

The voice of the being fluctuated between panic and relief. "I can't recall my name... I lived where dessert blossoms stretch to the horizon..." The being cocked its head and stepped near Atticus with his beady eyes gleaming, more curious than threatening. "Who are you?"

"Atticus, the incubus."

The form shrunk away from Percy's torch. "Dreamer Realm?" Atticus nodded. "It has not fallen to the Dark King yet. In time, it shall..." A breathy pause. "The Dark King is good at... stealing time."

Stealing time?

The body stilled. "I'll share what I can remember, if you kill us...me..." Its voice was airy, neither male nor female. "There is no peace... not with it...leeching..." The one controlling the sway agreed to the terms. "The Dark Lord is his father, himself and his son... His name changes but never his pursuit."

"What is the pursuit?"

It shrugged. "Longevity... perhaps vengeance... to feel like an Eternal with his creations... to retaliate against wrongs. He invited the darklings... but Vulborg need hosts. Experiments. Shipments of silver children... immortal hosts to groom... the red guards turned out *wrong... wraiths...* Bones to control the Dark Amirs and the gate..." The soul twisted in torment. Its words changing into a dark language that sounded as if they burned with each violent syllable. The Vulborg fought for reclamation.

Atticus' voice deepened, those in the room fell silent as his sway robbed the room of their speech. Nikki and I were graciously unaffected. Bite perks. "Vengeance against whom?"

"Amir has teeth in me... End me. Send them back..." The soul convulsed on its back.

The interrogation did not ease. "Who or what is your Dark Lord pursuing?"

"An antidote to a broken heart. To cause more pain... helps him..." It clawed its throat and began to shred its mouth, dropping flesh on the floor.

"Who is he? Where is the dragon?"

"Release me..." Torment stretched on for minutes with no answer to be granted. Atticus gave mercy. The head fell with a thud. Nikki incinerated the remains. The darkling was purged by light and was shadowless. Gone.

The conclave had much to discuss in our absence.

We fluxed to Zander's home off Clemente Avenue and wasted no time in accomplishing both a bath and meal simultaneously as I fucked and fed my males in the bathhouse in ways I'd never had dreamt of being taken. The fluctuating fates of all of us made us desperate. We fucked so savagely Nikki had to supply me with a few drops of blood before I was comfortable to walk straight in my armor. When we arrived at the stone threshold of the ramparts I was still frazzled, heated and half put together. That changed the moment my cohort stepped into action with hundreds more people missing then last time we fought.

I fought as hard as I had fucked. Yet, it took me an hour to find Keenan who bore a gash across his bicep. 'A scratch' he called it. His scratch hadn't healed which meant he needed sutures to aid the process. "Where is the underhill?"

A Vulborg stole a sword off a corpse and swiped it at me. I rolled backwards while the Ilanthian next to me buried her blade in its gut. Then hacked at the spawn's head. "He is assigned decapitation duty."

His free hand roamed up my armor, the solid metal reassurance enough that I was sound and mostly uninjured. "The foot soldiers alongside me made progress and left plenty of undead that need to be tended to. Brock will be busy."

"He will be miserable."

"That too." Without verbal direction, I moved to his injured side to protect his back should his range of motion or speed be impacted by the gash. The day dragged on and it became clear in his grimace and the way he swung his body to drive momentum his left arm was compromised. He needed a window out and with the Vulborg only getting more monstrous, he wouldn't leave me willingly.

I pulled myself off of the grimy rotten ground where I had been tackled by a gangly shape and narrowly avoided colliding with ten others. "Dagressa's berserkers have started flinging themselves towards the next Amir, you need to start falling back." Keenan looked in the direction of my gaze and as fate would have it we witnessed one of her headstrong fighters blow herself up as close to the commanding Vulborg as she could.

I shielded my eyes from the incoming downpour of sludge and gangrenous body parts. Wetness crept under my armor, I cringed at the odor and texture of the thick blood. My helm was thrown down as I vomited. An Ilanthian offered me a kerchief to wipe the bile dribbling down my chin and neck. *What's wrong?*

Queasy.

Nikki's voice entered. *She got blasted with Vulborg innards.* I scowled at the humor in his inflection. *It is rather revolting. I'm second hand nauseous smelling it.*

I'll take another bath if you two join me. Violet blossomed quickly until red and grey severed Zander's rising lust. Anger, fatigue and frustration seeped heavy into his bones.

Wyatt just informed me that water nymphs found a sleeping draft in the canteens in Horn's Keep. Alethim and his assistants are looking into the culprits and for any drowsy victims. This petty, backhanded shit is the last thing Kinlyra needs. I tripped over my helm dodging a vicious demon troll's maze. An orc smashed into its chest and headbutted the Vulborg.

The orc's size and bulky statue matched that of the spawn, I was a mouse in comparison. Offering a returned favor of saving a life I crouched down and sliced through the ankle tendons of the demon, the orc finished the job with his bare hands. "Thanks Golden Girl!" He hollered above the screams of battle.

I smiled. "I'm just happy you spotted me before I ended up stuck to the bottom of your shoe!"

"That bastard was designed for me." He cleaned his green fists on the rags around his neck. "It smelt my distrust of mountain trolls the moment I stepped out here and it thought that would stop me from protecting my caves! Ha!" He was screaming at the unmoving Vulborg. "Stupid bastards!"

"They are stupid." These things fail to grasp fear fuels many and when you have something worth protecting. Of course that thought spiral was immediately disrupted by the remembrance of the Faceless Prince. That summoned not one but *three* Vulborg to shift their forms and prowl towards me.

All six raven heads cawed.

The orc stayed by my side, narrowing his stance at one of the incoming figures. "This wouldn't have to do with that Torval bastard would it?"

"It has everything to do with him." Around the hilt of Orion my fingers curled.

"Show him just how little control he has, Goldie."

I charged. Two figures struck out against Orion with their own black swords, I two stepped my way between them searching for a vulnerability. My hair whipped wildly around me without Morial's helmet taming it. The Vulborg smiled while I locked my eyes on the details of their attire. They had every minute button and tassel exactly as I recollected, down to the damn shoe laces. I slammed my heel into one of their toes and launched an elbow back into their vacant expression.

What if these Vulborg had his face? He'd no longer be faceless. No longer be terrifying without an identity. "Orc friend! Change in plans. Kill two, unmask the third!"

"Yzell! My name is Yzell!"

"Pleasure to meet your acquaintance, Yzell."

"Yeah, yeah. Let's get to slaughtering and unwrapping these presents!" We laughed a sadistic laugh and together marked two for death. The third tiptoed around us. "I don't exactly want to hug it or tackle it. What now?"

Magic. Subtle magic.

I molded the earth around his feet, ankles and upwards until stone encrusted over his waistline. Yzell rushed in front of me to hold his hands down while I reached forward shakily and tore his mask from the bridge of his nose. His skin was patched together like a quilt of flesh. His lips were thin and scarred, his nose hallowed. Angered black eyes dualled with mine while he screamed for freedom.

The tip of Orion dug out his eye slowly. He oozed and writhed. Yzell didn't let go while I did the other. Keenan called my name. I didn't turn to his stern voice because I didn't want to miss a moment of taking my power back from this bastard as metaphorical as it was. I pressed Orion through its skull, twisting as I plunged. Its inhuman screams ended when I lobbed its head off. "Sorry about the extra spatters of blood on you, Yzell."

He watched my magic crush the rest of its corpse and level the ground under his feet. "It goes nicely with my complexion, don't you think?"

"Green is my favorite color." I pointed to the cape clipped to my chest and back. Another suicidal berserker blew themselves up and managed to kill the Amir with his sacrifice. The crowd of Vulborg fell dazed and despite the sticky coating of my skin and the growing burn of my muscles under the armor, I stayed by Yzell's side to finish off as many as we could until more Amirs arrived and quickly reformed their minions.

Our enemies quickly adapted to our strategy, opting to mimic Kailynder's shield wall technique with the use of their own bodies to protect the Amirs as they filed out. It was effective. The minds of the conclave were furious and resorted to sending multiple units out, but never of the same specialty to keep them guessing.

Keenan cursed the entire Ivory Legion, some of whom had left their post at Altar of Horns to stand at Maruc's side on the ramparts. "They weep because they know they sacrificed their lives and donated their will to a coward." I'd never seen him snarl. Never *heard* him snarl. Shivers crept over my skin as he grumbled Montuse vulgarities.

As I was called back from the front, I watched hundreds of our fallen friends being carted off. Four tireless days from that alarming moment, half the fire field had been taken and the number of dead bodies being recovered from the bloody war rose into the thousands.

We were on the losing side.

Zander's colors grew more hostile by the hours, the sun in the cage rattled each time I dove into his essence to ensure he hadn't succumbed to the frailty of the situation. Watching Nikki's power diminish in increment by increment was more painful than *feeling* his power weaken and body tire as I had been.

We considered ourselves fortunate that neither of us took a life threatening blow. I welcomed small fractures, burning muscles and ugly contusions over the alternative. Besides, sharing damage was how we discerned if each other were alive when we'd lose sight of one another for hours and days at a time while fighting.

Kashikat had been rendered incapacitated, his wife and children were tending to him privately which left Zander leading the flight division heading into the seventh night. When they weren't dropping oil and flame, they were scavenging the scene for bodies to burn and bury. Wyverns were placed in metal spikes and sent riderless through the demon horde, only half of them returned. Bastion grieved loudly, but not as loud as the wolves howling their sorrows and outrage all hours of the night. They took a massive loss when the Vulborg had begun to make use of the rock, soil and weapons they stole from us.

When they constructed their own imitation of catapults and launched heads and dismembered body parts of Kinlyrans as ammunition, I stormed back into battle with magic rolling off my screams. No one stopped me.

Yzell and Momo got me close enough to their stone and bent metal contraptions for me to shatter the earth below and swallow their devices. And a decent amount of Vulborg for good measure. Not that it mattered. Their numbers continued to pour out of the gaping hole between life and death, while ours were dwindling by the hour. Even silver bloods were not recuperating fast enough to hold the line for another night, let alone another week.

Partially hidden by the fabric of Keenan's cloak I grappled and fought my way back to Nikki's side. I stumbled twice. "Loose gravel." I ensured Yzell. He swung his arms and cleared a marginally wider path for us to scrapple through. Momo's expressive eyes told me I hadn't been covering my wear and exhaustion. "Nothing a coffee can't cure." Momo's teeth nipped the air around my ankles until we arrived at the sealed entrance to the Burrow.

Nikki shifted into a man, a naked one, long enough to fold me into his arms and pressed our bodies and lips together. Zander would be joining us shortly, the Vulborg were too close to the Eternal Elm for either of us to consider leaving our woven's side. The dark masses chewed through the roots, risking burning to death to cut off the life sources to the heart of the Elm.

My stamina dipped. Or was it Nikki's? Either way we were relieved when Zander completed us.

I was kissed hard on the mouth and not a moment later Nikki was fighting off the same fate, narrowly dodging Zander's desperate affections. Our overbearing incubus wasn't satisfied until Nikki allowed himself to be held against Zander's strapping chest and surrendered to the embrace. "We can hold them off another day or two if we condense all our resources *here* but that would leave the ramparts as the only sturdy structure between *them* and the city." Nikki's tattooed arms ran along Zander's side body.

There was no choice to be made, not where the Weaver of Fates was concerned. "I am to choose between life and light when we need both. *I need both.* I've made my choice to stand here, the realm knows what I will choose, what order I will give. I don't expect everyone to comply."

Violet magic and fiery threads pulled me to their sides. I slid vines of wisteria around them. Home. Zander Halfmoon Veil de Lucent. My sword and shield. My hopeless romantic of a dreamer. My possessive and playful corlimor. Fennick Feign. My guardian in the shadow and wielder of light. My inner voice and reason. My dominating corlimor of compassion. And I, Wisteria Woodlander, child born of red, lover of silver, infused with golden, was a woman who would not let Kinlyra crumble. If that meant flooding Veona with every last drop of my magic, sitting on trithrone or even suffering through a marriage proposal—I would see it done because I deserved a beautiful life with my wovens just as each living being deserves a life of joy and goodness.

I was not Wisteria Woodlander. No, I was so much more than a crafter of the Southlands.

Beneath me the ground was shaking as I brimmed with Athromancia's fully awakened power. It coursed through me as I had once believed Anna's blood to have and in her honor I grew a lilac tree.

Not by me, but at Maruc's feet.

His Athromancia never wanted a war of any kind. My Anna certainly did not. If he wouldn't send his Bloodsworns to stop it. I would send his sister's.

"I can feel Oyokos' magic. He slips through the cage you created for him. You're expending more energy locking him away than if you were expelling it. Not all of it, Maruc needs you for the gate, but some would help put you at ease and possibly aid Nikki."

There was the briefest flashing of betrayal in his eyes. "I can't."

He let me kiss him amid his bemused stare. "I know. I'm not asking you to." Zander would do it. Unleash the Eternal's magic to save Nikki. He has said it many times over he would watch the world crumple and light the match that burns away everything but the three of us. But it would inflict a deep wound on his soul to do such an act. I couldn't let him. I pulled back and spoke into his mouth. "*Hujan dan matahari lahir. Berbicara. Fakta dunia.*"

"The transfer of essence spell." He and Nikki looked at eachother like glossy eyed lovers.

"It's worth a try. Oh, don't be mad. I also shook hands with Maruc. My part of the agreement is completed. So is Nikki's. We agreed to his terms. Do what you must to keep our husband alive until I return." Their grips around my waist and neck lifted me off the ground. I pulled them away with a snap of the vines. My shouts carried across the death on the stale winds to their ears. "There is no time to explain! I know you hate being separated. It's a shared sentiment. I feel like I am dying without you two, but you need to trust me!"

"I do."

"With my life."

I wedged distance between them and I. "I don't have much time to pull this off and come back to hold my two reasons for living." They slacked their hold on me. "I love you."

They replied in unison. "To whatever end."

"To whatever end."

Kailynder landed on the outskirts of the smoldering tall grass and ran towards us with his great dual handed sword still raised high. "If you break my little brother's heart, I will seek you out and eat yours."

"I have no heart to consume. I relinquished ownership over it when I fell in love with those two." I pointed over my shoulder. "Now, if you will excuse me. I have to demonstrate how beneficial it is to have a rogue fighting on your side *saving your hideous fat ass and inflated ego.*" Percy's chortle was audible to even my ears. Zander's brothers arrived at his side without him having ever given an order.

I was grinning on the outside, wailing on the inside each step I placed between my corlimors and I. I didn't let any sorrow or worry into my heart when I created a portal and rushed into the Howling Hills with Brock and Keenan clutched in either of my hands.

Chapter Thirty-Nine

The scent of ambrosia dissipated.

He no longer tasted the bitterness of her anger, the limestone flavor of her stubborn resolve or the sweet water of her love. Their syphering snapped closed. His soul was left frigid.

"Wisteria left the realm." He was all too aware of the longing in his voice. And the many ears that heard it.

"She did not leave us, Z. She left for *us. There is a difference." Fen was the only person on the face of the earth that could pull him out of spiraling emotions to act with assuredness. He had done it before. Every day for decades, Fen set Zander straight with his absurd methods until he was able to trust his own inner guiding compass.*

He trusted Fen's voice more than his own.

The elemental lay enclosed in his arms, shifted as mostly male. Zander hadn't released his oldest and truest friend, nor did he have any inclination to. He'd been watching Fen's flames soften in hue over the days and the accuracy of his element had been off since the last time he hit the frontlines.

His magic casting was never off. Not ever. That bastard prided himself on perfection.

"She completes us. Her absence hurts more than wings ripping from my spine and the emptiness I feel is infinitely worse than living my life without ever flying into another horizon on the winds of spring." The Overlord cared not if the world saw how much they needed each other, desired each other, loved each other.

"Wisteria is brilliant and clever and too stubborn to know when to quit. She is coming back. Now, if you are done with the sappy dramatics, can you usher life back into the Elm with spellwork? Unless you wanted more than one absence to grieve." Nikki was panting heavily against Zander's chest and held no reserve in dropping all of his weight onto his brother to hold.

If the most powerful descendent of the twins was this exhausted the rest of his kin had to have been depleted beyond functional capacity. But, here they all stood. Fighting.

The last stand.

Kai, Dag and Clavey acknowledged Zander with a dip of their horns as they strode by. Kashikat would have been there with them, were he alive. Zander had no time to grieve the loss of his older brother, not when he needed to stop the death of the Eternal Elm.

Six of the Sons of Atticus were going to attempt to sway the putrid filth piling up and flowing across the Fire Fields. Shit. His father too had joined the westward end of the conflict which was twenty feet shy of the rampart and was starting to sway the Vulborg to turn around. Elves and Ilanthians were firing arrows at will.

Claws scratched his waist. "Start speaking spells or you will be shaking hands with Maruc momentarily. I know you've been looking forward to that moment."

Zander made a noise that sounded like a pissed off bobcat, but started talking in a cadence that made him sound as if he was singing. Fen rested his ear against the scar on Zander's sternum savoring the vibrations and heartbeat strumming through the both of them.

Siphoning magic from his warriors was off limits. And outside of the Elm, there was little else other than death he could sense once the spell illuminated life forces. Of the people and natural formations within a half mile, the pixie crystal caves east of the city and the garden beds within Veona shone the brightest and their energies were the most willing. There was no soul but a sentience to them. They readily gave him what he sought.

The spell was repeated again and again, each time with deeper intentions of placing vibrancy into the Eternal Elm. The daffodils and crystals selflessly gave and allowed Zander to serve as the conduit for the transfer of life force. The funneling sensation was unlike anything he'd ever experienced

503

which said a lot coming from a male who survived off of drinking energy. He used his magic to guide the energy to its destination. Wisteria was right, the tension of his own power softened as it was used passively.

With its roots being devoured by demons, the Elm accepted the transfer of life. Fen still looked like utter shit with his imperfect ponytail, translucent under eye skin and body canvas painted with bruises and welts over his ink. He cringed knowing their corlimor felt each twinge and she said absolutely nothing other than yelling at Keenan not to stop her when she threw half of Morial's armor on and dashed onto the field next to every race and breed of beings in existence and fought like the God of War himself trained her for decades. The truth of her training wasn't too far off, it was just so damn breathtaking to watch. Just how many injuries did his wovens hide from him? He should have stripped all their clothes off yesterday in the stables, not just the lower half for easy access. He damned himself.

"The Elm burns steady. Whatever you are doing is working."

"It's not without consequences; however, the earth is willingly donating. I hope the little flowers and gems keep some sparkle for themselves." Little flower... Be safe.

The howling intensified. "The wolves have come."

Torvi, looking mangy and thin, led the remaining members of the Frost Pack in front of the ramparts as the Amirs sprung forward commanding their spindren and serpents and wraiths to topple the massive stone barricade. Ursula led the Twilight Pack. Donnie the Winter Star Pack. Yennyfer the Abyss Pack. All packs were accounted for, their members unfortunately significantly less than last week.

Nikki was no more revived and yet he transfigured himself fully fox and rallied his kin. There were hardly four hundred fire elementals left. All of which stood side by side, encircling their Elm. Even if they survived, they'd already lost so much of their magic, their lives.

The ramparts were breached with stolen catapults. Fighters, well and wounded, were called into battle when the sound of gongs and the crumbling stones of the walls fell. The sick bays and healer's tents were emptied, as his realm's finest warriors, along with Ilanthian and Numaalian allies, used their bodies to seal the breach and press our enemy back to the depths of hell.

Hurry Wisteria! *His heart screamed for her.* Hurry. Fennick is almost out of time. *The more that harrowing realization dawned, the more burst of violence spat out from him. His control was slipping.* "Hujan dan matahari lahir. Berbicara. Fakta dunia." *He channeled all his intentions into keeping that Elm alive, his loyal woven alive.*

Momo limped back towards the twisted trunk, her brown fur matted in her own blood. Momo was the closest woman he had to a mother, she accepted the burden of raising him too when he had shown up drawn to their Burrows covered in red Weaver threads. Zander scooped her into his lap and placed pressure on the wound. The darkness inside him permeated his chest as Oyokos' magic swelled.

His magic was reaching for the key to the cage he kept it in. If the icy winds of the wolves hadn't shot a barrage of ice needles in his back he would have handed it over.

He snarled at the pack behind him as their sloppy magic whizzed by in another attack of icicles aimed at an Amir. His calf burned with bitter cold as he yanked out a splinter of ice from it. A wolf pup, hardly double digits, apologized with a yelp as he followed his black furry family into the heat of battle. A wraith struck him down effortlessly. How many children had died? How many orphans had been made or grieving parents left to sorrow?

Zander stopped breathing as his failure to protect his people became evident. The wolf who led the charge stared numbly at the small corpse and in doing so made himself vulnerable to an attack. A fucking child and father just died in the five seconds he sat there and did nothing.

Zander's screams brought Percy to his side in a frenzy.

One look and his Right Wing knew. "We do not fear you. We never have. We fear a world without you, Little Moon." *Percy threw down a heavy shield that was too small to be of use to him, he must have taken it off a body.* "And I hate to admit it, but I fear our enemy and I think if you let go of the control you've been obsessing over our enemies will fear you. They look a little too cocky and deserving of fear, don't they?" *Zander stared through Percy as if he was a ghost.* "I cannot lose another brother in this war. Neither can you."

He caught sight of nine tails saturated in blood bobbing and weaving under the feet, hooves and scales of the Vulborg. Their minds merged. Zander pulled Nikki into his head and showed him the powers of death congregating in his hands. Just a half second glimpse was all he needed to see to know he had mere moments to get to his woven's side before his Overlord made it an order.

Nikki shifted and worked his bare arms around Zander's wings to embrace him from the back. The solidarity of Nikki's strong arms and his warmth stabilized Zander enough so that the power weighing down his hands didn't bring him to his knees.

Men, women and children were dying before him. More would die because the magic that plagued him did not seem to differentiate between friend and foe. "I don't want to do this!" Even now, at the end of the life as they knew it, Zander was a coward. Afraid to unleash this monster lurking inside him dreading it may consume him and all he loves. He didn't want to become anyone nor anything else. He had all he wanted and needed. And his life partners loved him how he was.

Could they love a monster? Could he love himself?

Wyatt took a timely glimpse at the Elm and spotted his brother's growing aura. Nikki had a matching white one. The aura was odd, but that wasn't what concerned him. The luminescent orb in his hands did. He was quick to collect a young pixie and snatch a fae around the waste and move them out of Zander's line of fire or at least draw their attention to it. Awareness spread amongst the Veil's army as dawn crept in from the east.

Maruc turned a silent and watchful eye on the pair of glowing wovens. He damn well heard Zander cry out again. "I don't want to do this! It will break me. You both deserve better than the shambles of what will remain."

Maruc did nothing.

He also heard Fennick's reply. "You don't have to. Wisteria has arrived. I can feel her renewed hope."

Atticus dropped his swords and choked on his next words. "... with griffins.

"

Chapter Forty

Griffins. Godsdamn griffins.

So fucking unpredictable, but so fucking perfect.

Fennick yanked Zander's braids to angle his face towards the majestic sight of nine ferociously beautiful beasts soaring overhead. Their screeches were powerful sound waves that blasted the Vulborg, sending them back to the hell they crawled out of or splicing them clean in half.

Zander was stunned into silence, yet his orb remained ablaze. "You are safe, your people are safe, I am safe. Put your hands down brother."

Zander shook like an autumn leaf preparing to drop for the cold season. Fennick held tighter, pressing his face between the shaky leather wings. His own strength had all but been depleted, but he would not fail his duty in life to be of service to the most honorable man he had ever met.

He scrounged up his empty reserves to talk Zander off the ledge and retain his hold on him as he rattled his bones with primal power. "There is no need for your magic here. Drop your hands."

The elemental prayed to the dying vessel of Drommal and Dradion that his Overlord would sense and smell the reinvigorated realm and lower the sphere consolidated in his hands. "Where is she?"

Griffins cleared the filth by the thousands with the songs of the sky.

One male creature, of greater size than Horns Keep, descended onto what was left of the fields of fire. Brock gave a gallivant scream from atop its back as he prompted the griffin to release a squawk that frazzled everyone within earshot—the entire realm was called to witness the pushback of the Vulborg. Brock and the griffin he rode, had just given Maruc the chance he needed to do his rebuilding.

Zander's magic reabsorbed and his arms fell limp. Fennick collapsed into them. Cradled in Zander's arms, he dazed dreamily up at the morning sky and the mythical beasts soaring through the gold glinting clouds.

Hopefully, his Pa was staring out his courtyard window at this unbelievable view. He'd be beside himself with joy. He shivered as the winds from above swept ash across the trampled grass. "You're cold." The Elm's glow simmered to a dull flame. His gut cinched. "Fennick!"

Cold? No.

Well, maybe? What did cold feel like? "Tired. Keeping your company this long has been an exhausting job." He feigned a smile although Zander's worry only deepened when he looked at the fire fading from his irises, as if his eyes had already closed. Another wind gust sent him curling into Zander's lap. When the wings enwrapped him, their shared aura became noticeably brighter. "It has also been an honor, my brother." And it had been.

"Don't you dare!" The scream ripping from Zander's throat was drowned out by the sound of splitting stones. From the southern Thalren to the ground beneath their feet—the world rumbled. Then yawned opened.

Wisteria's ferocious war cry emerged as she bolted out from the ground with gold garbed Bloodsworns at her back. A Godsdamn sight that robbed everyone with eyes of their breath. Even if the white aura hadn't been there, it was painfully obvious that this woman was a queen. No. The Queen, The Empress and the embodiment of life that all nations would willingly fight beside and protect. Mine, he thought.

Athromancia's legion rallied and made a clean cut through the demonic darkness in a singular sweep. Atticus roared with what had to have been a bellow of relief and proudly followed his son's corlimor with his blade and horns high. Wisteria led the assault of her deceased lover's Bloodsworn. She discarded all armor but she still stood out among the butchery and carnage with her attitude of invincibility and blade skill to back up her wicked mouth.

She launched diamond shards into the air and with a whistle, the griffin Brock rode had them hailing down on the Vulborg, incapacitating their enemies before they grasped what had happened. Stormclaw.

The Amirs changed their orders. They chased Wisteria as she led them away from the tree, which by then had lost all its luster and the elementals remaining sought out each other for warmth. Keep him warm. I'm almost there! I need to steer them away from the roots and the trunk! *Nikki heard her echo in Zander's heart and head, while he struggled to keep his eyes open.*

In a flash a portal appeared and Wisteria threw herself out of it. Maruc behind her. "Nikki!" *Her wails spurred tears from a nearby Momo. Nikki felt her lips hastily grazing up the column of his neck and the backs of her hands anxiously pressing against the cold sweat on his forehead.* "Not now."

Not ever, he wished to reply but his mouth opened and out fell an apology. "Sorry. I'm so sorry." *Wisteria silenced him with her lips which tasted like paradise and salvation. And blood.*

Maruc stood by watching as Wisteria pulled Nikki into her arms with the same tenderness she would have shown an injured bird. Her disbelieving eyes refused to settle and her panic ran through her like a storm off the sea. Her lips, hands and breath flitted over the tight cord of his muscles, searching for any ailment she could cure to restore her lover. Nikki's tightened grip in her hair as he took in the dried blood she had tried to wipe off her face, but it still trickled from her nose.

"You were warned, Wisteria, about expelling too much magic when we do not know the depth of your power. You may fight like an immortal, but you cannot withstand as they can. If you continue to use magic, you will have forfeited your life."

She ignored the Emperor altogether and collapsed into Fennick's chest with the hard realization of what was happening to him knocking her heart from her chest.

Without removing his eyes off his wovens, Zander rose because he must. He must spellwork the new barrier while the griffins and Bloodsworn held the plague at bay. He let his heartmarked and Kinlyra carry the battle this far, it was time to step up in a manner in which didn't cost infinite lives lost.

"I'll see the world can live, after we die." Zander crouched to kiss Fennick's cold lips. "To whatever end. I love you." The elemental felt the fire in his words even though he failed to summon his voice to tell him one final time what he meant to him. Wisteria hurriedly kissed them both.

Maruc requested a portal. The golden vessel complied. Then it was the two of them amid the chaos and the dyeing Elm.

Wisteria and Fennick lay amid the scattering ash. Silence befell their world when their gazes held. They had done it. Wisteria had done it. But it didn't matter now that his magic was leaving him a husk of a male who wouldn't live long once the last lit leaf of the Elm fell on the destruction below.

Ritualistically, his hand clutched the acorn and rings strung on the metal chain at heart. Wisteria's warm hand quickly squeezed and intertwined his grip.

A kiss befell each of his knuckles followed by hot salty tears on his flesh. Her tears and blood mixed and smeared across his naked torso. Momo padded nearer, Wisteria welcomed her. Unforgettable emerald eyes traced his tattoos, he understood her to be drinking every detail of him in as if it was their last moments together.

Which it damn well was. The Elm would not recover.

She choked back sobs when a rush of Ivory Legionnaires burst forth from the gap in the ramparts and reinforced what Athromancia's Bloodsworn had accomplished.

Her grief stricken gaze stopped at his chest. He let her shake his hand free of the keepsake, not that he had strength to fight off the gesture. He was hardly able to keep his eyelids open or swallow his own spit. The acorn sprouted roots and stretched towards the drops of her blood as if drinking them in.

She sputtered off filthy proclamations while choking on tears. Percy was beckoned and soon Fennick found a cloak draped over him and his mother. Inspiration reared Wisteria into throwing her body upright, she dug a hole and buried his necklace, rings and all.

Fennick's eyes drooped close, but he felt Orion's sharp edges cut into her wrists. He didn't wince, he was too preoccupied with gripping onto the tail ends of his threads. The threads to his wovens were the only things anchoring him on this plane. To life itself.

More time passed. More curses came from Wisteria's mouth that he was currently reminiscing about the moments she used it to fulfill his fantasies. And then some. "Not the time, Nikki!" He'd happily die with an erection. Maybe Wisteria could make use of him one more time after he died. As if she heard his thoughts she smacked his shoulder. "I'm almost starting to feel bad for the times I slung my morbid humor at you." Nikki's lips twitch. "Almost."

Then she went silent and got to slicing more of her wrists and arms. He vaguely felt the pain of her self-inflicted injuries. He was cold. Numb.

Percy was uttering some odd sorts of insults, which Fennick knew was his form of encouragement. Wisteria clawed at the dirt, ash and grass at his heels. "Easy, sister. Zander will lose you both if you are not careful."

Wisteria was panting. "Percy, blindfold me!"

"What?"

"Do it! It helps me not think!" Fennick did not register being jostled, he wasn't entirely sure if he was tethered to his body anymore or just a whisper of a thought left behind to wait for his wovens to join him in their new adventure beyond.

He heard the wolves howl before the victory hymns of the griffins saturated the air. The runegate was up.

Wisteria should be cheering, but she wasn't. Her screams were so loud he felt them thaw his mind and melt the ice trapping his stiff body. Warmth was returning to his bones. His quivering lips attempted to call for her, to settle her soul. But he couldn't.

Ik Kygen's fatherly voice was cracking with worry. He must be near too because he scolded her in an outburst of brash words that prompted Kai to intervene on Wisteria's behalf. Kai of all people. His love certainly turned their world upside.

She gave no quick witted replies nor continued her tangent of screams because she hit the ground next to Fennick and soaked the soil with her warm blood.

Chapter Forty-One

Without opening my eyes, it knew it was there. The aura. Our aura. The cackling sparked my skin to life. My corlimors each had a hand on my body to keep the Weaver's threads out of sight.

It cackled and sparked against my skin, irritating the fresh cuts, contusions and fractures from the first Vulborg war, but I didn't mind because it meant I was alive. And by some stupid act of grace, my males too. I spun lazy circles over any amount of their flesh exposed until the Weaver snapped the visible strains and strands from sight.

This glaring halo remained as we tumbled into slumber again.

The amount of healers, hands, salves and prayers uttered over us was excessive. I didn't swat them away, not even Warroh or his clerks when they came bedside in the healer's tent offering purifying water or when two pointy eared elves wrapped my lacerations. Besides, Zander wouldn't let me refuse care even though he had every person who approached us trembling under his snarls, scrutiny and threats to make their contact with my skin brief.

The thought did cross my mind to kick out Keenan when he factually stated that our aura was suspiciously similar to what Maruc, Athromancia and Orion once had. The fact Athromancia legionnaires agreed to his statement easily made my gut sour. "Pissed off," I garbled then proceeded to vomit whatever it was Mauve was slipping down my throat. Cobar gagged in disgust and went on to pester Mauve on what she was giving his sissy to make her ill. I thought it was adorable he puffed his woodlander pride about and brewed me some gentle tea.

I retained an iron stomach until he left, then spilt my guts again. Zander was asking for more food—different food—to be brought before I even finished emptying my stomach. The fussing was intolerable, but Nikki and I were in no state to decline it.

The tent was brimming with both injured and those offering aid, I'm certain the lovely sound of my wrenching was therapeutic. "Very healing ambiance," Brock teased. I was surprised Zander allowed him to bring the lanky, luminescent shifted form of Stormclaw near the bed's edge without a dead stare or pissing competition given his height and stature in man form rivaled Atticus'.

Turns out griffins were air elementals who can only be summoned by mortals. And Brock quickly discovered what a woven was the second his and Stormclaw's fell into place. The first air elemental woven since before the creation of Thalren. "I knew there was someone waiting for me far beyond my reach, just like I knew following you would eventually lead me to them. I didn't expect it to be a man bird." I bite back a broad smile. "Definitely, did not anticipate strangers leaving gifts at my feet to congratulate me on my new feathery friendship. Super odd."

"Super." Zander's arm tightened as I agreed.

Stormclaw wrapped a protective taloned hand across Brock's shoulders as if he were a lion claiming his pride. "Let our Queen rest. You have her legion to tend to." Stormclaw chattered his sharp teeth as if he would have done in a part eagle-lion form. "Adious sends his well wishes. How fortunate he was of Athromancia's Bloodsworn and spent the last few months watching you dig yourself and the Southlands out of the grave. A testimony he gave. The Legion you have earned, Summoner."

The last time I saw the chatty scholar was on the carriage to Landsfell where he told me his journey would continue to lead him westward. To Athromancia's stationed legionnaires he went and when I arrived—via portal—with Keenan and alongside griffins *only* able to speak the truth to her army, Adious was of the first to step forward with his cane and aged smile to offer support and encourage they act now to save the continent we knew as Kinlyra.

"Fate, as twisted or unfair as it has seemed, aligned your destiny just so friends and foes fall in and out of your life only to collide later when you have become who you are and yet to be. Oh yes, now you are more you, Wisteria." Brock elbowed his long winded woven to get him to comply to silence.

"Let's go, Stormy."

Zander snapped at the air elemental when he came to hold my hand. Brock pulled him back and left the tent with Stormclaw. "Happy to be summoned. Come, my Brock. Fly, fly with me!" Stormclaw was such a jabber bird.

Momo eased my head back down onto the pillow, looking as if she had more to say than reassuring words of a safe world. For now, anyways. The road ahead was an ugly one.

Warroh volunteered to get more of his blessed water, while I chose to hide myself under the two sets of arms and legs locking around me from behind. Fennick was asleep in the middle, his limbs thrown over me in the manner in which Zander's were thrown over the pair of us. Nikki was warm again. That notion alone sent me off to a peaceful sleep.

What was likely the following day, I awoke to an inferno raking down my body. Zander and I both leapt out of bed before we were burned by a fully ablaze nine tailed fox. A territorial growl made the entire tent ignore my presence as Zander yanked a sheet of the nearest bed to drape across my shoulders. "Mine. Both mine! Keep your head's down or I will remove them." I spotted Yolanda who was next to Wyatt and Bastion, all three quickly dropped their gaze. Zander, claw lengthened on display, moved my knots of hair aside to view what remained of his bite mark. His canines were out. I reached to kiss him but my knees buckled and Zander scooped me up, pulling me into his chest.

"Our woman is in no condition to engage." Nikki gave a lazy yawn. "Not after she moved mountains and created an entire forest of Elms." His mouth moved to me ear. "You really do love me."

Zander predicted my needs and sat me on the bed so I could launch myself at our elemental. "I do. I love you, Nikki." It was an ugly cry, but I wasn't the only one with tears rolling down my cheeks. Zander stroked Nikki's tails and accepted three bowls of savory grits from a food cart. I mixed the melted butter and braved a bite. Grits were better than holy water. "A forest? I only intended to grow the one."

"Whether by your blood, earth squirrel magic or sheer will—all the seeds that fell in the last century's fire dance took root. An entire *grove* of Eternal Elms lay between the imbued barrier and rampart." Nikki was scraping the bottom of his bowl and eagerly accepted Zander's.

"And the remaining elementals?" I swallowed my second bite. It needed honey.

"Alive. Warm. Thanks to you." I turned to press my dried lips to cheek, not willing to tarnish his glowing golden perfection with how filthy and disastrous I was. "None of that, baby. You're exquisite." My jaw was pinched between his thumb and forefinger and he claimed my mouth as a means of displaying his relentless love for me. Within seconds he had me wanting.

I groaned, missing how thoroughly he left me roughly wet and ravaged. Zander sniffed the air and tightened the sheet around me going as far as blocking mine and Nikki's bodies from the incoming visitors.

Atticus, Maruc and a decent dozen peoples from conclave walked and flew in the cramped chambers of the tent. Brock's presence made me relax. I found myself grinning as Duke Cultee proudly stood at their sides. The other several hundred beings laying on the rows of cots pivoted towards the commotion. "Is now a good time for post-war updates? To discuss city rebuilding, what came of the sleep tonic found in the Keep and funeral arrangements or do you require another two days of napping, my Overlord?" Alethim half grinned as he took out his parchment and quill. "Or we can chat about this rather sudden onset of aura, if that tickles your fancy."

My words practically jumped off my tongue in a hiss. "It's not sudden. And no, we are not talking about it." Nikki quirked a manicured brow at his brother. I stood on the bedding to make myself taller than Zander's seated self and peered over his form. "What did happen with the whole sleeping potion situation?"

Atticus and Maruc shared a seen glance. "A thief happened. The bone shard is missing."

Zander stiffened. "Any leads?"

"Torvi went missing after the barrier went up. Her singular track was picked up trailing east."

Wyatt sucked on his teeth. "She didn't kill herself after losing her twin. Which means whatever claws are sunk in her skull are making her an obedient mutt to her Dark Master. And it is rutting powerful. And we are facing a new caliber of trouble if those bones get into the hands of someone with blood crafting knowledge."

Percy wore golden sheen bangles on his forearms, which I had seen before on Kashikat. He kept them on display. Proudly. "Worry not, Little Moon, your trusted Right Wing sent mounts after her." Yolanda looked forlorn and disappointed, as if she should have seen this act of betrayal coming. She'd been warned. But, what was she to have done locked away in a safe house of ice while the wolf ran?

Zander was too tense to reply. I ventured into the conversation. "How many lost lives are we preparing a burial service for?"

Alethim ignored my males and spoke to me. He's dealt with their behaviors enough over the last century to know how to survive their possessive shit. "Forty-three thousand. Another seven thousand are being tended to in the tents and hospitals across the city, Ilanthian physicians arrived by the hundreds at the start of the war. With their care, hopefully we will not lose many more, Wisteria." Half the initial forces... dead. Zander smelt my emotions and gentle fingers sought to give comfort.

"What of the damage done to Veona when the Rampart fell?"

"A decade of rebuilding, likely less than a day if you stay and use your earth carving magic. Or build it with diamonds, that would be magnificent. Minimal lives were lost in the inner circles thanks to several leeward Ivory Legionnaires who worked very hard to seal the breach from the back."

At the mention of my magic I instinctively reached a hand into the well of my waters. Dry. I was dry save for the very few drops at the bottom. I had more spit in my mouth than magic in my soul.

Nikki set aside his second empty bowl. "Ivory? No shit. Really?" Nikki grabbed a canteen of water. "Glad to hear Maruc finally decided to help. It was starting to look like a massacre out there." I pursed my lips at the Emperor. "I guess you do still care about your creations." When the Elm was dying Nikki must not have seen the rush of white capes sprinting alongside the gold of Athromancia's legion.

"I didn't give such orders." Maruc's voice was calm, but his eyes were wild enough to make Zander act. I was pulled down by my knees and hidden completely behind Zander's broad back. Sharp points of wings were prodding under his skin. He once told me it was not as painful as it looked. The discomfort stopped after his fourth decade of shifting frequently. Still, it looked agonizing to say the least.

"Several of my finest abandoned the Ivory Legion willingly and without proper acquittal choosing to fight as free agents or dawn green in hopes Wisteria will one day accept their swords or oaths. Step outside this sheltered tent Woodlander and you will find many have exchanged their ivory cloaks for those of green. Those of gold have done the same. Violet and red too."

"Getting the green scarfs off Asher and Copper will be difficult. They have taken to decorating their pet wyvern with a woolen sweater." Cultee laughed. "No surprise that this particular wyvern is the loudest and brawniest in the bunch. It earned itself the name Drift."

"I have a namesake? Fantastic! Rightfully so I might add." The duke gave a snort at Zander's hoots. "Almost as awesome as my woodland flower unknowingly swaying warriors away from their allegiance to a God. That feat I'm particularly impressed by."

Thankfully, Zander and Nikki towered in front of me so the party of wise, ancient beings didn't see the slap of being dumb stricken invisibly sting across my face.

The rest of the tent and those dwelling on cots had though. It was an effort not to cover my face with the nearest pillow when Yzell popped his thick skull up and lowered his chin with a respectful dip. The best I could do was offer the orc a modest grin.

Zander rumbled with a childish laugh. "Hey Fen, do you think I'd look good in forest green?"

It was wonderful to feel Nikki radiate heat again after he all but died in my arms—cold and grey. A vision that would haunt me for the rest of my life. "We'll have to get one tailored to fit your bulky butt, but I suspect that green would look flattering on everyone."

Their banter allowed me a moment to internally recover from the shock of my *own* legion of trained and untrained warriors and scholars roaming about outside. I crawled out from between my males. Nikki purred as I stretched my legs over his and whispered for the whole tent to hear, "Your new garb I had cut from a bolt of silk from the Crescent Isle, I had requested them the moment I arrived in Veona. Because you were already my Queen, my Goddess, my object of worship. I am more excited to take them off you than I am to see you in them."

That makes two of us. Yolanda wasted no time in gesturing at my rosy cheeks. Her prior profession as a courtesan gave her the uncanny ability to know my thoughts without having to be in my head.

Three of us, actually. At my reply, Zander decided the sheet around me was not opaque enough and stole one from the adjacent bedroll to tie around me.

"The runegate is holding, but we cannot let whatever forces we have left here to venture far in case it should shatter unexpectedly."

Maruc turned his head to Alethim. "It won't fall."

"It has before."

"Not this one." The confidence building in his wide, hazel eyes was enough to convince a sane person the sky was down and the grass was up. The last God stood every bit Godly. "And as long as they do not have another resurrected dragon to impale it from the beyond it will stand long enough for Kinlyra to stop the Remnants and send the Vulborg back to their void—their ultimate death. We spelled it strong, Zander and I." Maruc risked a glance of Zander who was still to be found observing myself and Nikki for any signs of immodesty.

Alethim swung his satchel across his body to place his hands on his hips. "Ah, yes. I am glad you brought up the matter of the dragon. Another reason to keep our defenses alerted. If this Dark King controls a dragon that is more reason to keep reinforcement here to bring it down prior to it shattering this runegate."

Cultee helped Wyatt rise up from the corner without tearing the leather with the thorns in his spine. "That dragon is destined for Kathra, flying to The Dark King with Torvi. Who knows the torment it is bringing to every village and town along the path back to its master. Every day that passes more wraiths emerge from the death of innocents and the deeper demons' claws sink into Kinlyra, darkening hearts and stealing lives. The gate won't protect you from what already festers here, eating its way through nations and yes, even the glorious Dreamer Realm will fall. We need to move east."

I mustered up a pinch of my diminished arrogance in hopes to sound confident. "The injured stay here to recover. The strong and willing will rebuild what has fallen. The dead we shall honor immediately. The brave will return to their families and celebrate life on behalf of those who sacrificed themselves." Keenan was already shaking his head, with Cobar looking expectantly at me. "The bulk of warriors will stay at the ready here until we call for them after having assessed the situation in Kathra and the capital cities."

Cultee's nose flared as he snuffed back strong sentiments of appreciativeness. "We will not be leaving all of Numaal defenseless and vulnerable against a tyrant, demon lord who is using the shells of the living and blood of the undying to house Vulborg spawn's souls. They will comb across Kinlyra, the Southern Isles and across the seas if we do not stop them at their doorstep."

A harsh squawk erupted from Brock's woven. I rammed my index finger into my ears and Nikki dove into my chest covering his fox ears. "Dragon! Currupter!" *Squaaak!* "I want to slay a dragon. Yes, yes. My Queen, summon us to do so?" Stormclaw stomped his bare feet. His head rotated unnaturally, toppling his straw yellow curls out of their tie.

Atticus blinked at the odd griffin shifter standing a few inches under his height and made room for him to continue prancing his feet. Brock welcomed his spontaneous, affectionate touches leading me to wonder what type of wovens they were.

"Griffins defeated the dragons the first go around, I see no other beings better and equipped to do the job. *After* we establish a rough sketch of what the fuck we are actually doing."

"Come, my Brock. To the Aerie to awaken the nest! Finally, we are summoned by humans. Took too long for Kinlyra to remember our purpose to protect and now my sisters have fallen asleep." Stormclaw jabbered off.

"Buddy," I called at his back. "Be safe."

One stone cold warning look from Zander and Brock rethought approaching me for a hug. He settled for an affectionate flip of the middle finger and was off.

If Cobar wasn't on Keenan's lap, Zander wouldn't have allowed him closer. But he was a sucker for kids. Keenan inched in, stopping when a thunderous growl echoed in a warning. Keenan and Cobar ceased advancing in their proximity.

One glance at the guilt racked expression on Keenan's face I knew the turmoil grinding against his soul before he even said anything. Nikki stopped him. "She won't go alone, Ik Kygen." Keenan held Nikki's gaze, I swear I watched a layer of fear frosted on his heart melt away. "I know at the present, the three of us look worse for wear, fragile and unthreatening."

"Unthreatening? You three look like a shit storm rained down and drowned you in a sea of sewage where you lost your clothes and briefly your will to live."

Steam rose from Nikki's collar, but he managed to keep a civil composure. "But I promise no one will love your daughter as we do nor be as willing to risk their life and destination of their souls in the afterlife with the actions we are ready and willing to commit if it means protecting your daughter."

Keenan chewed his lower lip so hard it bled in the corner. "Her love for you nearly cost her life."

"Her love for me saved my life and the fire elemental race. Her love for Zander brought a flock of griffins to the battlefront so he'd not have to battle his own grief and resentment. Her love of Kinlyra earned her the respect of Numaalians, Dreamers and Ilanthians. If you think for one moment, I would allow a love this pure and bright to be hidden amid the darkest time, you are a far cry from delusionally wrong.

"She is what this world needs and while it goes against every fiber of my soul to keep her sheltered, protected and away from danger I'd never asked her to choose an easier path because her heart points to the truth. And the truth is never easy." Zander's arm tightened around Nikki's hips while he kept jabbing his blunt words into Keenan. "Her world was kept small. It was both beautiful and tragic. Her world has grown, with it mine also. And while together, we have stumbled across atrocities that have shook the known world, she still finds people to love and reasons to keep fighting. We will not be leaving her side, but I will ask you to not stop her from demonstrating her love for others. You included. If she wants to free your wife and child, you will let her."

"Are you going to allow her to marry Torval trash to see that bargain to fruition?"

Zander's growl cut the static building. "Wisteria will never belong to him."

The incubus unclenched his jaw. It looked painful for him to set his face straight although every muscle movement screamed 'Mine. Mine. Mine!' to anybody who wasn't blind or pulseless. "Ik Kygen you are not being asked to stop loving her. You will never be asked that." He huffed through his nose to collect himself, his hands sought out Nikki's flames and he buried his knuckles in the fiery fur.

"You are scared to lose her as you have lost your wife, infant, woodlander family and even the Goddess you've served since you were formed from clay. If she never took a risk and followed that wild rhythm she dances too, Cobar would never be in your arms. There would be no promise of hope to obtain Moriah and Rory. The Remnants would be just another mysterious high society. Numaal would have never learned the truth of the royal's corruption. Griffins would not have taken flight again. Cultee would not be duke or with means to protect crafters like those families you fell in love with all those years ago when you came to the Southlands... and..." Zander shook his mane, pressing the heel of his palm to his forehead. "And... wait..."

In a whisper of smoke and concern, Nikki inquired on our woven's loss of concentration. "Something the matter, Z?"

Zander looked as if he had more to say but passion tied his tongue. "Just tired and helplessly in love."

I cut his misery and monologue short. "Are you done, Zander?"

"For the time being, I suppose I can stop." Serious sentiment swam over our bond. "Under the condition you complete the Circling with Fen and I, so we never have to mention you legally wed to any other person for the rest of my life–then I can be done smothering you." His brothers laughed while scribes found nearby chairs to rest on to continue their documenting.

Maruc bit back his own chortle. "Overlord Zander, we both know that it isn't possible for her to be with anyone else regardless of ceremonies and titles." I gave a warning look to The Emperor as he tiptoed around our little secret. Percy chewed his cheek and dawdled by the cutout windows in the thick textile.

"Right. Because they will be dead." He whipped his neck behind us. "Speaking of which, if I catch one more rotten scent of lust for either one of *mine* wafting downstream I will sniff you out and add you to the pyres to be lit tonight!" Nikki smacked him with a flame. Zander didn't flinch as he grumbled, "You both need to put clothes on before I skin the skinny fae wearing fish scales in the back left corner to keep you modest." His comment shut up the snickers from the back. "And you two with the lilac hair, I will scalp you if you look at them again."

Atticus glared at his sons for their childish gestures prodding Zander. "If it gets you to stop acting like an outright, dramatic idiot I guess there is no harm in having the ceremony sooner. Besides we need something to celebrate after the next few days of burials. I'm sure Honri would love to officiate the ceremony. Wouldn't you think?" Nikki mawed me in his male form crushing me into Zanders chest. "Is this a yes?"

Colors and kisses made it vibrantly clear I was engaged.

Alethim threw his notebook at Zander to get him away from the left side of my neck, which he was inches away from clamping down on. "We've not finished settling arrangements. We have to delegate and map out destinations for holding points if you spread the armies."

Zander grabbed the notebook that thwacked his face. "First, I'll need some time and privacy to prepare a eulogy for the brave Kinlyrans traveling beyond. Percy, Cultee, Keenan and Kai can start listing their top holding grounds for armies that can easily access Veona and run east when the time is right. Athromancia's Legion stayed hidden in Thalren, I bet they know places to take respite while spying. Do chat with them."

The conclave fidgeted a bit and slowly dissipated. I called over the Left Wing. "I should also like to request lots of paper and an ink jar."

"Define lots of paper."

"Let's start with forty-three thousand. Hopefully, I will not be asking you for more."

Alethim paused the hand that was digging around in his side satchel. "Wisteria, you can't possibly accomplish grievance letters to each of the kin."

"Why not?"

Pity flashed. "It will take you too long. A month of your short life—"

"A few weeks of our lives *well spent*. And she won't be doing it alone." Nikki nuzzled into my chest, glaring at Alethim for reminding him of my short, mortal life. I kissed the spot between his ears, running my fingers up his back as I did. He dropped his tone. "Thank you for making significance of the lives lost."

Percy loitered. "Even if the apology and mention of my son's bravery came seven hundred years too late on the talons of an aged pigeon, it would have mattered. Greatly, mattered. Even if you only manage to mail out a few hundred names off that too long list, you'd have made a difference to someone. I'll get you the addresses and more papers if you need them." He stopped at the tent's flaps and took a long inhale.

He spun quickly back around to find wings bursting through Zander's skin and blood dripping down his back. "I'm going to find pants and you will follow me. If you three stay here Zander is going to keep his word and start fileting some fae for admiring the two of you."

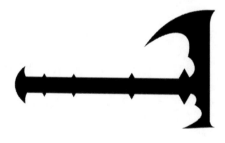

I walked like a newborn foul, Nikki was not much better. But we succeeded in getting upright. Zander didn't fuss when I refused to be carried out of the tent. However, he did knot the string of the elastic of my pants so rutting tight I feared not being able to remove them to pee in an emergency situation.

Thankfully, I was dehydrated.

Zander fashioned the shreds of sheets into a shirt and grumbled at Nikki when he refused to cover up with a blanket insisting they would burn if they touched him because all the Elms I grew made him too hot and formidable.

From behind the ramparts I discerned a few dozen Elms stretching into the midday sky. They were massive and downright magical. "I think Nikki was right, a shirt would burn off his back."

"The spoiled pup just wants to watch me fuss over him without a bite mark activated."

Nikki used Zander's elbow to steady himself as he took step by step. "This lively fox just wants a damn bath and a decent button up that doesn't smell of demon piss. But feel free to dote over me, darling. I do love it when your fangs spout drool on my hair."

The rattle of teeth clanked. "I'll wash your hair as soon as we find a water nymph hole to bathe you in. How long do you think you can hold your breath?"

A lion laugh. It was beautiful. "Look at you cracking cynical jokes. Took you long enough."

"Not nearly as long as you were willing to spend with Imuik. How many mud puppies do you think you would have conceived by now? Hundreds?"

Against the stone stairs leaned relaxing archers and a swarm of defenders green cloaks and scarfs. They bowed to us from atop the stone wall. I dipped as low as I could while not falling on my face, which screamed in silent disbelief. There were more than a few banners and bracelets of forest green tied to tents and wrists. Emeralds on earrings and jewelry pieces. The more we walked the more we came to realize the dedication of all nations in preserving each other.

Life itself was uniting. About damn time.

Behind the rows of recuperating warriors the new violet barrier to the beyond stood as tall as the atmosphere extended. Zander's magic looked stunning infused into such an eternal feat. He hardly glanced at it, he was too preoccupied shielding me from passersby and fellow fighters running up the gravel path behind us and fending off cuddly fire kin from swarming our legs.

Remorse hung heavy in the air as the lengthy parade of dead and dismembered bodies being carted off by the thousands on the backs of shields. My face dampened. My stomach threatened to empty the two bites of grits Zander forced in it. Percy casually pressed a handkerchief into the hand that wasn't holding Orion. I didn't remember ever picking him up. Or being parted from him for that matter.

Percy smoothed back his brown curls and resigned to offering me his thoughts. "Only the dead have seen the end of war. For that reason alone, I find myself envying them. They do not ask for our pity, only remembrance and commitment to ending crimes such as those enfolding." Zander eyed his hand nearing my shoulder. His attempt to offer comfort was revoked. "It is also acceptable to be sad. And mad. And confused. Just so long as you never lose sight of what you love you can move through the harder emotions and step into brighter days. Best not to hit the bottle too hard if you are feeling overwhelmed. You've seen first hand how glamorous that life is, ey?"

His weary eyes lingering on the death procession. His brother was among those being carted off. "Percy. I am sorry about Kashikat."

Zander's hand fell heavy on my shoulder. We had many matters of the heart to discuss. "Thank you, sister. I would accept the hug you want to give me, but Little Moon will have me skewered for touching you. I look forward to receiving your letter of grievance."

Pyres were being built outside of Veona, between where the reapers harvest and where the slopes of Thalren begin to spike higher. We didn't walk that far. Physically, I couldn't. We were ushered into an inn along the outer ring of the trading circle which was offering its rooms and kitchens to the cause. Zander pressed the two small beds together to make one decent sized mattress. Nikki stalked around the outside of the establishment inspecting the solidary of the structure before coming into the bedroom and immediately shutting the curtains.

With a promise to return with clothes and parchment, Percy left.

Obscuras were cast. Waters were run. Bodies were scrubbed raw. Food was brought in and once my wovens were certain I was not going to upheave the collard greens and lentils, they spoon fed me morsel by morsel in bed until Percy arrived with clothes. Zander didn't open the door more than a crack and shut it immediately once he retrieved the attire.

Dressed in casual battle-black pants and crisp green tunics we welcomed the Right and Left Wings into the room. At nightfall, the first of the pyres would be lit. We had enough dead among us for the pyres to stay ablaze for a fortnight without going cold. My face fell into my hands, my heart sunk to the floorboards.

So many dead.

Nikki and I were on the brink of becoming two of the casualties. For the following hours, I considered myself lucky and even shrugged off my recurrent dreams of death claiming me during this war. My terrors had not come to pass.

That was until my syphering with Zander went slack.

My callings unanswered.

Our bright, lively bond fell colorblind.

Chapter Forty-Two

The familiar feeling of severed syphering jolted me up right in bed.

I knew those bone wielding bastards had their chains around my corlimor's mind somehow. If Tanya's declaration was right, Zander would be the demise of the Veil. Not by his own doing or desire, but by the Dark and Damned King. I had to stop him before another similar minded to Tayna took action and stole my mate from me.

His name was a desperate prayer on the tip of my tongue. I called him over and over to no avail. A name so deeply carved into my soul that when he looked at me with vacant eyes I felt myself reverting to the untrusting Ivy, caged, confused and chained to a dead lover.

Zander pushed me aside as if I was weightless, disregarding me and all my attempts to strap him down with vines of magic. Nikki shifted forms, his endeavors to halt Zander earned him a full scale incubus bellow that not only shattered the windows but sent a still mending Nikki on his ass. We both took damage we could not afford.

Fingernails dug into the wooden door frame as if Zander's body retaliated to the orders being spoken in his head and just for a moment I thought he would turn around, that he would break the hold on his mind. Tears were hot on my face as the seconds dragged on daring to ignite hope in my worried heart.

Zander's mental door rattled as I sent him vows of my undying love and promised to free him. And yet, he prowled away.

Together, Nikki and I watched Zander walk from the inn without so much as an utterance of affection or farewell. Nikki screamed profanities that made me recoil. Still, he did not get a rise from his brother.

And then he fluxed out of our sight.

Just vanished.

We did not call up and down the streets for him because we knew he could not answer even if he wanted to. Crying was of no use. So, I stopped. I tapped into a familiar emotion.

Rage.

My Bloodsworn felt the call of my blood. "The Remnants have him!" I blurted to Keenan who ran down the stairs with Cobar in his arms. "And this time they know *exactly* who they have."

The horn at his hip was brought to his lips. It sounded up and down the streets nearest the rampart. "Veil! Get to safety!" The peoples who had hardly found peace were sprinting down back allies half-clad to get to the rampart and find weapons, while civilians were making their way to safe houses.

Percy dropped in from a roof with Wyatt. "What is all this about?" Kailynder's form a stark silhouette in the evening sky, loomed above. Listening.

"The bone shard! Zander!" I screamed a tearful declaration at everyone within earshot, wrangling a stray horse that was startled and trotting down the cobblestone. Nikki leapt up in the saddle pulling me behind him. One arm wrapped around his waist the other had Orion thrust into the air. "Keenan, take Cobar and return to Akelis."

"No."

My mouth became coated in thick sorrows. I never planned on using the power of our blood oath for I always believed taking away another's free will was abhorrent. But this. *This* was different. Or at least I told myself to silence the guilt. "Keenan, as your Bloodsworn sovereign, I am giving you your first and only order."

Keenan's hand wrapped around my ankle and tore me from the saddle. The stones below caught me abruptly. I ached. In more ways than one did I ache. The pain in my chest was unbearable.

He hovered above me. "Don't you dare!" Spit was flying as he pointed a shaking finger at me. I pushed myself off of the ground and yanked on our blood bond.

He could not lie now. Not to me. "Do you trust me?"

"I trust no other living person more than you, not even myself." Good. That confirmed what I was about to do was the correct course of action.

That didn't mean I would be any less excruciating to cut him out of my life.

"I, Wisteria Woodlander, command you to take Cobar to Ilanthia as soon as possible. You will take him to safety and stay with him there." He was screaming his profound love at the top of his lungs, but I didn't stop giving my order in which he would be forced to obey. "I command you to live out the rest of your days filling Cobar's soul with joy and memories of a happy childhood. You will forget about your blood oath allegiance until I see you again. It is my will that you be happy."

He was on his knees now. Begging.

The renowned Montuse warrior, creator of the Ilanthian sword dance, commander to most and conqueror of many was *begging* any bystanders to intervene. Scribes of the conclave and dreamer beings rushed into the ruckus and stopped when they saw Ik Kygen prostrating.

Percy stood there, lost in his own memories and unable to move. The next words cut my throat as I spoke them with the assurance of a woman worthy of such a mighty Bloodsworn kind enough to love her. "You will not miss me. You will not come for me. You will not return to my side or engage in combat on my behalf. You will not be compelled to keep me safe. If Cobar mentions me you may reflect as if I were a fond memory. Nothing more. You will not grieve Moriah and Rory because you put your hope in the right woman. Be happy, love your son, live long."

My commands were already sinking into his soul. Panic and disarray abandoned him. His demeanor calmed and he looked... he looked... happy.

I fucking envied him.

As if unsure of his own movements, he backed away. I rose and saddled up behind Nikki who pulled me flush to him, his unspoken way of demanding this burden be shared. Clarity panged through Keenan's once furrowed gaze as he looked to me. "You will continue to be a fantastic father to

Cobar as you were to me. And with that, my most beloved Ilanthian father, I bid you goodbye. I'd love you forever if I could. And thank you."

I banished tears that were collecting in plump dew drops on my lashes and welcomed the wind in my face as we thundered onto the fire fields, galloping east to where our woven beckoned our souls. Many on the ramparts didn't heed the order to vacate the realm nor did Zander's remaining kin nor the surviving forty thousand among the stubborn and proud. They were a force in our wake and I would not dare stop them.

A menagerie of broken winged beings, potion brewers, elementals and several hundred loyal strangers garbed in glints of green and violet stormed after Nikki and I. We slowed on a hilltop where the eastern plains led up to Veona where we caught sight of two angelic slivers of moon reflecting atop Zander's head.

Zander's back was towards us as we approached. He didn't turn around. He didn't offer a witty greeting. He was motionless, numb to our existence. His wings were glorious in the setting sun, purple hues glimmered beneath the black and white patches on the webbing. My eyes left his magnificence as a double headed raven mask emerged from Zander's shadow. At his feet a dead wolf. Torvi.

Nikki swore in another language.

I couldn't form a thought. It was a damn miracle my body functioned. I dismounted and sprinted towards my corlimor with no other need than to hold him, to have him see me.

Weak fire lashed me. I broke through it easily enough, but the message was clear. I stopped. "He is lost. The risk of getting captured, or worse *manipulated*, is far too great."

"He is not lost! We got him back before!"

Nikki kicked his leg over the mount and did a damn great job of masking his limp. "Temporarily, he is lost. We will never permit him to exist or suffer in the hands of another forever. We will find a way and bring him back to us, where he rightfully belongs and keep him for ourselves, baby. I know we are hurting. I know he is hurting. He cannot lose us, for then he will lose himself and hope entirely. For him we stay safe. Alive or in death together."

My teeth clenched down hard on the fabric of my shirt as anguish stuck me to my knees. Nikki's body softened my descent. "Focus on being useful to him. Look for the staff or another shape long enough for the femur."

I tried to make myself less useless. Really, I did. But The Dark King opened his rutting mouth and shot his soulless eyes to me. "How fortunate I am to reunite with my betrothed nine months before our wedding day!" The bastard spoke as if he was on a podium, his arm raised as if giving thanks to the stars. His sharp peaks pivoted to Zander. "What luck, she brought the fox!"

"I come on my own accord." How did he keep his tone so even keeled?

"You will die then by such a foolish choice. Although, having Zander obliterate you does seem like poetic justice for all that he has taken from me." His hatred ran deep and it had been running for a long time.

This was no Faceless Prince. This was the Dark King.

Nikki's upper lip curled in a snarl. "Who are you?"

"A man that has been in need of a new fox skin overcoat for a century now. Yours to be precise." I stepped in front of Nikki, placing a hand on his griffin dagger. His slight nod told me all I needed. I would stab him before I let his hearts fall into the enemy's hands. "I almost had it. My darling Morigan was so close to bringing your waterlogged corpse to me. Together, she and I, were meant to achieve the impossible." He turned to regard Zander with a loathsome scowl. "Zander ended that dream for me, so I created a new one that has gotten infinitely more intricate as the decades tally on."

Winds whipped as Atticus landed in front of us. "Who are you?"

"You may call me as my many subjects do, the Dark King." The gold and red tassels on his coat jingled as he chortled. He moved his hand to his mask and started to unbuckle it. "You wouldn't recognize me if I showed you my face. But I will do you the honors, Atticus di Lucient. If only to haunt your nightmares as the face of the man that stole your son, demolished three nations and claimed two worlds for his own. In the name of love, of course, because that makes every wrong–right. Does it not?" Nikki held me around my wrists, his fingers resting against my thready bounding pulse. "At least, that was what your realm declared after Zander murdered Morigan and how many others? Out of love for the fox, the others died justly."

My chest throbbed. Young Zander knew not the depths of love as he does now, nor was murdering Morigan an act of love for Nikki, it was an act of hate against his abuser.

The heavy bird mask was thrown at Zander's feet and the patchwork of skin with raven eyes sneered in Zander's face. "Familiar, puppet?"

"Vaguely." The man paraded his marred skin, pacing back and forth in Zander's line of sight, waiting for a name to click. "Jeorge. King Jeorge."

I heard that name once. The renegade fae of Morigan's family were in cahoots with him and the slave trade industry. A man that should be dead. I recalled the Amir's words, *He is his father, himself and his son.* "You're the Faceless Prince, King Torval and your predecessors." This charade had been going on for over a century too long.

The leech clapped jubilantly as his guise was deciphered. The rumble in the crowd went eerily quiet. Atticus walked to the top of the hill to better view the monstrosity. "I'm not sure which is more of a grievance: blood crafting with stolen gold and red blood, accepting demon promises and allowing your nation to be slaughtered, ingesting silver blood to prolong the inevitable or damning all souls that have passed in the beyond! You are foolish Jeorge! All for what? A conniving whore?" Fury rippled off Atticus as he spoke on behalf of everyone present, tongue tied Zander included.

"*Whore?*" He snorted and looked at Atticus again. "That is a little rich coming from *you*, is it not?" Jeorge walked tight circles around Zander, stepping over Torvi's disregarded corpse. I noticed Torvi held a knife in her hand, the tip of which was still stuck in her throat. Suicide.

"Conniving, yes. My Morigan had the most deliciously cunning mind. I'm sure Zander recalls how wicked she was in the bedroom. She'd make love to me as we talked about our future ruling Kinlyra together, douse herself in scent concealing potions, and then go tolerate the likes of the naive boy incubus. And bed him hours after having her fill of a true king." He ran his gloved fingers across Zander biceps and gave them a mocking squeeze. "She was cunning enough to convince a young Overlord that he was worthy of love, when he was too aimless and uninspiring."

He wrapped his fingers around Zander's neck and lowered him onto his knee. "You were useless then and after what my Amirs told me about the battle, you remain useless to your realm. Pity. I was hoping for more of a challenge after all these decades of plotting. But you are still pathetic, falling in love with women that don't belong to you." The three drops of magic in my well felt like a tsunami as they tried to break free and drown this demon in the ocean of my loathing.

"Did you not see my branding on her?" He opened his hands seeking a reply.

"Yes."

"And what did you think?"

Zander's sense of self was shaking with ire while he prepared a statement. "She is perfection, with or without it. Whenever I see Wisteria I am consumed by love and am only able to think of the depths of what we share. And when by chance my eyes befall a pair of dim witted birds, I imagine all the ways I plan to torture and break you slowly. It will be Wisteria who end's your wretched life. Then we will fuck in your blood." There he was. My protective incubus was given a chance to speak and found slack in his leash. "You will never have her! Mine. Mine. Mine!"

Yours! Yours! Yours! My bleeding heart replied. Zander's gut wrenching cries of his claim were heard across the valley. He screamed until he was backhanded and given a single word order. "Silence."

Every trace of him vanished as he was forced to swallow his sentiments. My arm shook, but it wasn't me trembling.

Nikki was panicking. My shadow fox was losing his collected composure.

Zander didn't blink after the fifth slap. He was so far gone not even the sting of flesh could bring him forward unless he was summoned by Jeorge's authority. The Vulborg's remains. "Not only did you murder Morigan, you had to go and shut down the trade routes we worked hard to construct. Just know, hundreds more slaves died rebuilding those routes and we made sure each one knew your name and of the uncontrolled monsters of myth that lurked in these mountains. For a century I instilled fear and laced lies in gypsy caravans and scholars. Monsters far worse than the high lords and ladies of the courts. Those children's blood are on your hands, Zander."

Atticus pushed the tip of his sword into the grass. "You are a fool. Why chase the unobtainable, tip the scales?"

"It wasn't unobtainable. I am proof of that." He dusted his gold trimmed jacket. "It is you who are foolish, Atticus. To insult the man who holds the fate of this world *and* the next in his hands. Not to mention your son, my new favorite toy that is mindlessly mine to wind up and punish as I see fit. I don't know if I want him as a weapon or a dancing buffoon yet to entertain my Remnants in our court. Want to see something neat?" His wide eyes were locked on Atticus. I looked for the damn staff or any new object of the correct dimension and found none. Nothing nearby was calling to me the way that femur bone had.

"No." Atticus's reply was ignored.

"Spread your wings, Zander." Zander obeyed. Jeorge held out a dagger. "Take it."

"No. No!"

Taking him away from the stars would be burying him six feet under. His hand was outstretched, his callous fingers reached toward the black steel blade. There was no hesitancy as he swiped it from King Jeorge's grip. "Incapacitate yourself so you can not take flight. Return my blade when you've done it thoroughly. Don't even think about killing yourself or me."

Atticus drove his boots in the soft ground and launched himself at his son's back. Amid their brawl the dagger landed on the hillside between us.

Leaving Nikki's side was a dumb thing to do. Especially, since I knew the shackles that bound his mind were absolute and unbreakable commands given from a jealous sociopath. I got to the dagger first. Zander wrestled it from my grip in two quick maneuvers and held it far out of my reach. Nikki drew me away from the chaos, dragging me limply towards the horse and the winged kin.

Growls tore through the hillside as Atticus bound Zander's legs with his arms and brought him down to eat a face full of dirt. Zander kicked backwards to free himself and carry out the barbaric self-mutilating task ordered of him. "My boy, listen to me! *Listen to your heart,* not the whims of a demented king and corrupted bones." Atticus was flattened beneath Zander who clung to the dagger and sliced into the webbing of his wings without so much as batting an eyelash or grimacing as he stabbed his bloody appendages a second and third time.

From my place on the ground, I knelt shrieking at the horrific sight, choking back the bloodcurdling scream building with each panting breath I took.

This could not be happening. We fought off the first wave of Vulborg and scraped by without lives only to have all hope stripped from our hearts while the graves were still fresh and upturned? No. This was wrong. All wrong.

Stone faced, Zander took to shredding his second wing. The gagging and weeping from his brothers nearby confirmed the hell we entered was our new reality. If Jeorge could get Zander to do this... Kinlyra was in trouble. We had no future. Maruc and Adul dismounted their steeds and watched the Veil's Overlord mutilate himself.

If Zander could have stopped himself, he would have done so.

Nikki's tears glided down his porcelain skin, leaving streaks of liquid light rolling down his jaw. Fuck. There was too much hurt buried into their souls and nothing I did would help either of them. I couldn't survive in a world where I had to feel agony for my lovers every minute of every day. How was I to stop *this*?

Blood spattered on Atticus' clothes. He was shaking his son's legs, pleading for any amount of himself to emerge from the spellbind. "My son, hear me! Give me guidance. Where is the power of the bone channeled from? How can I help you?"

All was silent except for the final few wet gashes Zander hacked into his leathery extremities. A sound and sight so sickening and agonizing it felt as if he had butchered my heart. Once complete, he tossed the gory, crimson coated dagger at Jeorge's feet.

A vile sneer graced my enemy's debauched face as he lifted the blade to his mouth. He laughed while he sucked my corlimor's blood off the sharp edges with his filthy tongue. The delight that sprung to his eyes when the taste of his blood hit Jeorge's palate sent my soul shaking. "Anuli gave my ancestors her heart. They ate it. Your dirty blood, little pet, is an acquired taste. But I guess I'm not one to talk when I myself am also tainted with traces of gold."

"I have no doubt your savage lineage ate my sister's heart. But, do not insult her claiming it was *given* to your ancestors when her compassion and naivety were preyed upon then manipulated by Underling Fae. There were witnesses that sinful night when the Eleven became ten. Taite was many things, but a liar he was never."

Jeorge slipped the dagger into his belt loop. "Perhaps, he was too drunk or high to recall the event properly." Maruc stopped breathing. The winds reacted to his rage, carrying clouds across the dimming sky. "Anuli's final contribution to her vibrants was her magic to the royal family. We were chosen by the Goddess so that we could protect the lives that the mighty, magnificent Eternals created." False exuberance slicked his sarcasm. "She didn't specify which lives exactly. That was her fault. Her love made her blind."

"Power made you stupid."

The man who called himself the Dark King countered quickly. "Anuli was stupid. Our beloved mother Goddess taught mortals blood crafting long ago at the time of the Great Divide." A whistle of wind blew over the valley where we all stood with disbelieving ears. "Until my reign started a century and a half ago not one person in my family had the courage to sacrifice themselves to the practice of blood craft. Anuli's magic is distant and dilute in my blood, but Morigan saw something great in me."

He cocked his head at Maruc. "Did you know your daft, darling Anuli carried around an eclectic case of tokens and souvenirs from previous worlds, monsters and beings you've all conjured? With a little fae persuasion and a promise of hope to help those worlds, she told us everything we needed to know to draw the Vulborg here. They handed my ancestors the bone of the their fallen leader, Duhathr."

Jeorge stopped his story abruptly and looked dead in Maruc's eyes. "He sends his best by the way. He'll be able to tell you himself shortly." Lightening cracked above our heads. Maruc's hands curled into firsts, while Jeorge brushed his wrinkled fingers through the silky length of Zander's hair. A low tone growl rumbled through Nikki's open teeth. "My new pet will make a sturdy vessel for Duhathr if he can do what the last several hundreds have failed to do—survive the liberation and consumption as he enters your body."

My lips moved and my whispered spells carried on Maruc's storm. "*Hujan dan matahari lahir. Berbicara. Fakta dunia.*" Lively essence from the wheat fields, tangerine groves and red clay underneath agreed to join the three drops of magic hammering with ire in my bloodstream. When the spell illuminated Maruc's energy stores, I found them dull, depleted. More so than Zanders, but not as critically low as mine.

I slammed my eyes closed and repeated the spell, locking out that Monster King's tainted touch on my corlimor's face and mangled wings. My magic was as dry as a dessert dune. That didn't stop me from staggering to my feet. "Release him."

Jeorge rose a scarred half brow to me and strode two steps closer. The whites of his eyes gleaned black as he and the demon inside him sniffed my scent on the wind. "I'll admit this much, Woodlander; you make the darkness in me stir with excitement beyond my comprehension. But, now that I have the man who murdered the woman I loved and stole my future with her..."

He didn't know.

He didn't know about Anna's blood.

Torvi may have returned the bone to him, but she'd not aided him further than she had too. This could be advantageous if I have a scrap more magic in my watery well.

Heat pressed against the back of my legs. Relief and sickness punched my gut. "The marriage proposal is off? What happens to my silver family then?"

The corrupted expression of an eroded grin on his face was terrifying. "Zander, protect me." Bloodied bits of leather flopped behind Zander as he guarded Jeorge's back from Maruc's aggressive winds. "Summon Oyokos' power and kill anyone who poses a threat." Instantly, Zander's hands were encapsulated in purple, flurrying with a different sort of storm. Death.

"This can go one of two ways, Wisteria Woodlander. In a matter of minutes, Zander is going to destroy everything and everyone he has ever loved. I think it is romantically poetic that he kills you, another woman he claims to have loved, as a penance for murdering the previous one we shared. You can stand against him and die in the carnage or you can live another day, as will that silver blooded bitch and her baby you are keen on protecting by leaving with me after he releases his magic upon Veona." My teeth bit into my lip until blood ran with my tears down my chin. "Zander will kill them personally if you do not accompany us."

Five sons of Atticus and Atticus himself were in chaotic discord. Percy tackled Wyatt before his thorns reached Jeorge's throat, getting an earful about not losing another brother over a mad king. When the elementals and elves reiterated Jeorge's words to the thousands draped behind us in the valley. Maruc had the stars hidden under his magic.

I didn't give him an answer. How could I? No matter what path I walked, I'd fail and innocents die. "What use have you for me? You said you've no need for me, now that you've gotten what you've ultimately wanted."

"If you agree to help dissect and reconfigure a few dirty bloods we'd been experimenting with at my palace, I'll permit you to join the harem of whores that will feed Zander so he and Duhathr can grow strong together." Bile shot from my mouth. I heaved and heaved until my head was buzzing. Him with anyone that wasn't me or Nikki... he'd kill us both.

I dry heaved again as Zander blasted a stream of magic at one of Kailynder's sword wielders who launched himself at Jeorge. There wasn't a corpse left to fall after the magic struck him. Zander turned his focus to his master once more.

The blood crafter clapped gleefully and stared enviously at the plum purple emanate from my corlimor's fingers and forearms. He was half invested in our conversation and half invested in wounding my mate. "Don't worry. Our marriage will be delightful. Zander can officiate the ceremony then watch us consummate and watch me take you anytime I damn well please." There would be no consent for that. Not that it mattered, if our threads were dishonored, the Weaver ensured consequences. "I also think letting Zander watch me degrade his whore would be a creative form of torture should he start becoming uncompliant."

Using his sleeve, Nikki wiped the acid from my cheek. Devastation and destitution wrecked his composure and refined beauty. "There is always a choice." He sounded so fucking broken, he *felt* so fucking broken for I shared his pain too. In our hearts, we were one, but not for much longer. If he had found the strength to speak those words, I could listen to the implication in them and scrap up any amount of composure to give an answer.

My spine straightened just enough so the world stopped spinning and I saw the sewn together face of a monster I was speaking to. "I'll stay." He could not have me. If he learnt of my being Athromancia's vessel, the damage I'd bring to Kinlyra... I understood now why Zander held a healthy notion of fear when he regarded himself. We were weapons.

"Disappointing. You understand sacrifice, you thrive on hate and refuse to acknowledge limits. Were it not for your impossible, insufferable morality you could have done it. You would have made an exceptional queen embodying all of the vibrant's best qualities. A true red blooded specimen for Numaal and Vulborg to revere for her zest." The rings on his fingers glinted off of Zander's magic as he reached for my face. He squeezed my chin until I was forced to stare into his eyes and see the horrible truth behind his next words. "Everyday I will remind Zander that you abandoned him. That he was unworthy of you. That you chose the convenience of death over a life with him."

We are woven. There will never be peace for us.

"He will become the very thing he hates, the person he fears. He will become unrecognizable. So much so, your souls won't identify each other if I ever permit him to die or if Duhathr hasn't consumed him entirely." With a brisk flick of his arm, I was thrown on the grass. Wyatt's rope of thorns lifted me back onto my toes. Percy and Nikki stabilized me. I was lost to my tears.

I sobbed listening to that undead, Dark King give my gentle Overlord the mandate to exert himself and cast a surge of death over Veona. He was to retain just enough magic to flux the two of them back to Kathra.

In the dips of the hills, people were either scampering for their lives or kneeling in acceptance of their fate.

There was always a choice.

Zander would be haunted by this massacre. It would fester in his mind and kill off his spirit slowly. If he had any chance to fight off the consumption of a Vulborg demon and his bitch king, he would need a reason to keep fighting. Veona always inspired him and I'd try to see it always did. I had to protect it.

Jeorge hurried behind Zander as violent outbursts of magic shot from his hands to deflect Maruc's pointed arrows of lightning striking at him from the sky. Maruc was aiming for the pair of them. And he was not holding back. If by some miracle I made it out of this alive and were to keep my bargain with Maruc, I was going to make his death fucking painful and slow for daring to harm my woven.

"Et Husset aihi satund." The shield and haven spell. I'd protect Zander from Maruc, as I'd protect Veona from its Overlord. *"Et Husset aihi satund. Et Husset aihi satund."*

Flat disks shone in front of my palms as the spell strengthened. Red. The same deep, dimensional red as Anna's hair. Goddess. Why was I thinking of her at a time such as this?

Stiff and shaking, I managed to pivot myself between Zander's growing orb and the citizens, when Orion caught on to what I was doing–making a barrier from whatever magic lingered in me yet. Orion flew out of his sheath on my hip and into my hand, not for me to wield, but for me to drain from. "If I die Orion, know that I'm happy to die side by side with my best friend." His song thrummed in my veins in a reply that sounded an awful lot like a goodbye.

"Et Husset aihi satund."

With each utterance Orion's magic flowed into my core and our magic united in the form of brilliant crimson discs merging and widening together. Nikki embraced me from behind. "To whatever end."

"He would want this."

"Undoubtedly. We do this together, my love. Don't allow the Dark King to see you wield magic."

His lips graced the nape of my neck as he continued to hold me upright to wield the magnitude of the wall forming. Jeorge glanced around Zander's sphere consolidating in his open arms, then again at my weak attempt at a wall. Nikki adorned the haven spell with licks of flames on the rims of the red glow. We needed to hold off Jeorge's suspicions for a moment longer.

"Et Husset aihi satund."

Red loops of liquid magic poured from my hands and clung together stretching above my head and wide enough to surpass the wingspan Zander bragged about. I stared at my corlimor through the wall. "I love you, Zander! Now and forever, to whatever end!" His arms drew overhead and his magic slammed into the shield I held, knocking Nikki and I backwards several feet.

The powerful strike of Zander's hand was a relentless stream of might that drilled continuously at my attempt of spell work. It wasn't going to hold much longer. Myself, Nikki and the Veil would be obliterated. *"Et Husset aihi satund! Et Husset aihi satund!"* Orion burned bright in my grip and he emptied the last of his essence into my well. Temperance's farewell kiss to me was a whisper against the walls of my intuition. There was no time to mourn despite the fissure in my heart.

The longer I held the shield wall, the less damage would be inflicted. It cost Zander effort to keep casting this magic at me, effort that could have torn through homes and hearts. *"Et Husset aihi satund!"* Zander's magic narrowed with intensity, my shield shook almost as violently as my body. The unyielding warm, strong muscles around me tightened.

Storms in the sky stopped. Maruc grabbed Orion off the ground next to us. When his brother didn't retaliate to his touch, the Emperor belted a sobbing scream and joined me in chanting.

I knew he didn't have any monumental magic reserved to blast Zander or Jeorge off the face of the continent, but with him spouting out the ancient words with me I felt confident that this was a cause worthy of my life. Zander was sweat drenched as he approached me with death aimed right at the center of my shield. At my heart.

Zander looked as if he was nearing the end of his power. Stars above, I hoped he was. Because my end was inevitable. My dreams told me that much.

Seconds ticked by like hours. I held Zander's gaze throughout each tortuous moment, never once seeing a monster looking back at me. Only the man I loved.

His magic punched through Maruc's reinforcement and sent him barreling sideways. Now, the intensity of his magic came crashing down upon me heavier than all the iron ore in the Thalren mountains combined.

My spell weaving stopped. It was impossible to chant with no air.

Breath was crushed from my lungs. My heart on the brink of combustion beat with fierce love for my wovens, even then. Blood wept from my eyes, nose, ears. I'm sure every pore on my skin deteriorated as magic burned through me.

The bottom of the well. Not only had I found it, I collided with it. Hard.

Pitch black button eyes emerged in Jeorge's skull. A serpent's voice rattled in his throat as the demon within angered. "End this! We leave at once!"

Blood smeared down my face as I cleared my vision in time to witness the spearhead of his impact shatter the remainder of the flimsy shield. The final push of his magic wasn't enough to demolish the realm. It was more than enough to strike through my heart and demolish me.

Zander's magic laid me limp in his brother's arm and he and the Damned King fluxed from sight. Blood pumped and poured from the cavity in my chest. "I couldn't have asked the Weaver for more perfect corlimors." Shock robbed me of further physical functioning.

There was a silence around me. A silence that was so very comforting. "To whatever end..." As my heart stopped beating, I thanked the stars that it belonged to Zander and Nikki.

Death attempted to usher me to my end but... the end never came for the Weaver was clever. For better or for worse She was fantastically, fucking brilliant.

She had her threads precisely layout and diligently constructed over decades. There was no foreseeable way Nikki would permit me to leave this earth alone or at all. Certainly, not while Zander existed in chains against his will believing he had murdered his corlimor and betrayed his realm.

Nikki's blood, tears and cries graced my lips, forcing me to swallow his essence by the mouthfuls while my soul balanced between two afterlives, skirting a fine line.

A drum pounded in my skull.

Disoriented and bitterly, I returned to my writhing body and broken soul. There was a beating in my ribcage. A rhythm I recognized, but that was not my own.

An immortal heart pulsed and pounded in my chest.

Fennick Feign, what have you done to me?

B.B. Aspen

The Weaver is hard at work, while souls, stitched and shattered, fall into despair.
Her tapestry completes in

Book Three of the Realm Weaver Trilogy

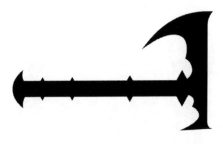

B.B. Aspen

ABOUT THE AUTHOR

B.B. ASPEN

Bethany has been immersed in fantasy realms since childhood and now see to it that her three daughters talk to fairies and run barefooted. When she isn't writing or dreaming about far off fictional worlds she is traveling the one she lives on, gathering magic, lore and inspiration from the many beautiful countries she has crossed off her bucket list. She plans to live in the woods practicing earth magic under the moon with a community of self-loving women who want to change the world. And have a garden. A big one. With crystals, books and oversized coffee cups on every surface.

Bethany rocks many roles in this realm including a full time registered nurse, mother of three wildlings, indie author and wifey to the man who holds down their chaotic home and lets her live out the adventures inside her head and hop on planes.

@B.B.Aspen_Author

Stay wild.

B.B. Aspen

Scan below to stay up to date on B.B. Aspen's magic.

Including book release dates, new fantasy series, leave reviews, follow her indie author journey & add to your TBR piles with ease.